WHEN LEGENDS LIVED

VOLUME TWO
JERICHO D. MCCAIN
TEXAS RANGER

R.C. MORRIS

HELLGATE PRESS   ASHLAND, OREGON

WHEN LEGENDS LIVED
©2023 R.C. Morris

Published by Hellgate Press
(An imprint of L&R Publishing, LLC)

All rights reserved. No part of this publication may be reproduced or used in any form or by any means, graphic, electronic or mechanical, including photocopying, recording, taping, or information and retrieval systems without written permission of the publisher. This is a work of fiction. Names, characters, and incidents either are the product of the author's imagination or are used fictitiously. Any resemblance to real persons, living or dead, is purely coincidental.

Hellgate Press
72 Dewey St.
Ashland, OR 97520
email: sales@hellgatepress.com

Cover and Interior Design: L. Redding

ISBN: 978-1-954163-60-7

Printed and bound in the United States of America
First edition 10 9 8 7 6 5 4 3 2 1

Other Books Written by R.C. Morris:

The Ether Zone: U.S. Army Special Forces Detachment B-52, Project Delta

Don't Make the Blackbirds Cry: A Novel

Tender Prey: A Novel

*Gone to Texas:
Vol. One: Jericho D. McCain, Texas Ranger*

What Others Are Saying About *Gone to Texas* – Volume One in the *Jericho D. McCain, Texas Ranger* series

"*Gone to Texas* by Raymond Morris is a remarkable work of fiction that harkens back to the 'lawless west,' in early Texas, a period that marks the first stage of what will be known in coming decades as the 'Wild West.' The hero's journey begins when Jericho McCain, who has lost his parents and sisters, sets out to find his brother Taylor, a member of the Ranger unit in Texas, but the coming-of-age tale of a young Jericho is more than that. It's a history of men called to use violence to remedy the acts of violent men. Jericho's journey to manhood takes place as Texas and Zachary Taylor's army are fighting the forces of Santa Ana. At the same time gangs of lawless men and Indian tribes ravage the countryside. Because the army of the Union is engaged in war and local law officials are inept, only an elite group of Rangers offer hope of interceding in the violence wrought by evil men.

Morris, a retired Army officer familiar with combat, captures the varied conflicting elements through often spare and stark scenes of violent battles that depict both courage and cowardice. Ultimately, as is the tradition in classic Westerns, Jericho's story is a tale of honor. His is also a story that celebrates our deeper humanity as depicted in the honorable actions men perform in battle, as well as in the humor they express and the heartfelt emotions they mask in tragic moments. In the end, Jericho is a stronger and more poised man, and a humble hero as well who echoes the noble virtues embraced in traditional Western fiction, values that seem to have taken a hiatus in 21st Century America."

—H. Lee Barnes, author of *The Lucky*,
a Spur Award Finalist

"If you liked the *Lonesome Dove* trilogy, you will love *GTT!*"

—Aaron Gritzmaker, U.S. Army Special Forces,
Texan and an avid Western reader

R.C. Morris

"In reading *Gone to Texas* it became quickly apparent that the author was writing about times, places, and people he identified with and wanted to portray well! I read the entire book, word by word, story by story, in less than two days. Each time I placed a bookmark between pages to take a break, I found myself being pulled back, almost needing to see where Ray was taking me next! His rich descriptions and well woven events are magic to those of us that love westerns! This book is already a hit for me and reminded me too why I have admired and had deep affection for its author for almost forty years!"

—Major Jerry R. Bailey, U.S. Army Special Forces (Ret)

"Powerful, gripping, suspenseful! This heart-warming and inspiring tale of a young man's survival and success through hardships on the pre-Civil War frontier is a fast-paced, satisfying read. I've been a fan of the late Ray Morris's writing for many years, be it crime novels or military non-fiction. *Gone To Texas* is perhaps his best yet, and will garner him many more fans!"

—Hank Cramer, retired soldier and singing cowboy, Winthrop, WA

When Legends Lived

Prologue

IT'D BEEN JUST PAST noon on their second day out when the searchers found the drover's body. The thing they talked about for years afterward was how it'd been left in exactly the same place as the last one — almost six years earlier. Normally, they would've stopped sooner, it being the hottest part of the day. But they'd wanted to reach the King Tree first, because it was the only substantial shade within twenty-five miles. The King Tree was a giant old oak, the kind usually found a lot farther north. As far back as any of them could recall, it'd marked the four major trails intersecting the region, and provided weary travelers a brief respite during the hot siesta hours.

As they topped the ridge, the rare old tree dominated the parched landscape for as far as the eye could see; its prominence and grandeur unmatched amid the low-growing brush and dwarfed trees. A hard day's ride in any direction would not find another of its kind. Like a majestic ruler, it resided over the arid kingdom, woody arms spread widely as if basking in adoration from lesser, bowing wind-whipped subjects.

Local lore speculated on its origin; perhaps one of the infrequent strong winds out of the Panhandle had carried it there when but a twig or seedling. The constantly shifting grainy soil had probably covered it over during an uncommonly wet season, allowing it to take root despite the intense heat and drought-like conditions that might've killed it altogether. There had been conjecture that an underground stream or spring lay near the surface in that particular spot, allowing a particularly deep tap-

When Legends Lived

root to suck life-giving moisture from the crusty earth for more than two hundred years. Disease and termites had taken their toll in recent years and limbs now littered the ground under the once magnificent tree. Black cancerous areas of decay on many of the remaining appendages indicated that more discards would soon follow. Weakened though it was, the old tree was still strong enough to hold the heavy weight that swayed gently in the slight breeze on one of its lower limbs.

From where the horsemen paused on the distant ridge, the swaying object appeared smaller than it actually was; perhaps it was a flag of some sort – or maybe a shirt hung out to air. As the riders slowly approached and the object became more vivid, the impression was that game had recently been dressed-out and hung, out of reach of small animals, to cure. Once closer, what it was suddenly became sickeningly clear.

It was a man. Or once had been.

Hanging up-side down by one foot tied to the low limb, the area of his genitals left an ugly wound were they'd been savagely removed. Nearly all of the body's skin had been peeled away, muscles and sinew left exposed to the elements. Angry clouds of black flies swarmed the quickly crusting blood. A gentle breeze caused the butchered remains to slowly turn, twisting the rope taunt, and then reaching its limit, reversing, to slowly unwind. As the corpse turned, empty eye sockets searched the surrounding landscape for rescuers who would arrive too late.

Reaching the tree, the riders formed a semicircle beneath the gruesome sight, sitting in uncomfortably embarrassed silence, each trying to avoid looking into the empty accusing eye-sockets. What couldn't be ignored was the jagged wound slashed along the entire right side of the dead man's face from eye to chin. It had been almost six years to the day since the last body had been found with that mark. Only two of the older riders had ever seen it, but the others had heard stories through the years. Several riders shifted uncomfortably in their saddles, gazing anxiously at the surrounding landscape and nervously fingering the triggers of their Winchesters.

Foreboding hung heavily in the air and each of them read it in the other's faces. To a man, they all knew who'd done this terrible thing, and they knew with certainty why he'd placed the mutilated body in the old tree where the four trails came together.

He was back – and he'd wanted it found!

Additionally, he liked the way the Captain always called him, "Mr. Penny." He'd been a virtual shadow of McCain for the past ten years.

The never-complaining Moses loyally followed McCain into the hot afternoon sun once again. "Cap'n, do you think it's ever gonna rain again?"

"I don't know, Mr. Penny," declared McCain, "but if it does, we'll have that dam ready to catch some water for the next dry spell."

"I think it'll rain pretty soon, Capt'n. I feel it in my bones."

"I sure hope you're right."

Unaccustomed to such hard manual labor, especially when combined with the long ride just a few days previous, McCain grunted with discomfort as he stooped to retrieve the battered pick he'd discarded earlier. "If Roosevelt could find it in his heart to lend a hand, we'd probably already have this damned thing done." He wasn't feeling any too charitable toward Poe right at the moment.

"Rosie says his back's 'acting up' again," Moses said, looking downright sympathetic. Then he swung the heavy pick over his head and sank it into the hard rocky earth in the creek bed. "He thinks a little whiskey might help. 'If whiskey don't cure it, there ain't no cure.' That's what Rosie says."

McCain snorted in disgust. "His back always acts up when there's work to be done," he retorted, grunting with the effort of a hard swing of his pick. "If whiskey could cure laziness, he'd be a well man today!"

Moses Penny chuckled softly as he labored and McCain glanced up to see sweat dripping off the huge man's face, glistening against his coal black skin as it ran down the heavy muscles of his arms and chest. Standing over six-foot-four inches tall, he was a giant for the days—powerfully built and without a doubt, the strongest men McCain had ever known. He'd often said Moses could out-work any man alive, without even half-trying.

The sun was slowly sinking behind a crimson horizon when the two men finished work on the dam and gathered up their tools. As they trudged wearily toward the lighted ranch house, Matt Jennings and Pete Yates, two of the ranch's three hands, rode up and dismounted near the corral. Jennings was a steady, knowledgeable hand whom McCain depended on to keep the other two in line when they were out of his sight. He walked up and squatted in the dust near the porch step where his boss sat.

"Lots of Injun sign out there, Captain."

McCain watched as his foreman slowly poured tobacco from a cloth bag onto a thin cigarette paper and adeptly rolled it into a perfect cigarette. The foreman struck a match on the seat of his pants with the first try, and lit up. He allowed Jennings a deep drag on the cigarette before acknowledging the remark.

"What kind? War party?"

Jennings frowned and appeared to think about it for a moment. "Don't really know, Captain. Mixed bunch maybe – some breeds surely. Renegade mostly, I'd guess from the looks of their camp-site. Filthy bastards. Ate – crapped – slept – everything in the same place. Looked like about ten of 'em. Could be real trouble though."

McCain possessed a keen insight into human nature and had an acute ability to read those around him, a fact that had kept him alive long after many of his contemporaries perished in the line of duty. Right then, he knew there was a lot more troubling his top hand.

When Legends Lived

"What else?"

Jennings gazed at him for a moment, taking a deep breath. "We ran into Luke Kincade yesterday morning," he remarked. "He's the new foreman for Mr. Thompson over at the Circle-T. He had ten drovers with him, all armed to the teeth. Claimed one of their Mexican wranglers was found two days ago hanging in a tree; looked naked as a jay-bird from a distance. When they got close, they could see he was almost completely skinned."

Jennings scowled with distaste, but continued. "Lived most of the time it was being done to 'em, too, was their guess. Then someone castrated him and burned his eyes out. Real professional job."

McCain waited patiently, knowing Jennings would get to the real issue sooner or later.

Jennings stubbed out his butt in the dust, spit and looked up. "Face-cut," he said suddenly. "From here-to-here." He made a motion against the side of his face with his thumb.

McCain grew very still, barely breathing as he waited. Finally he spoke in almost a whisper. "You think it was Scar." It wasn't a question.

Jennings stirred uneasily. "That's what several of the Thompson crew said when they was telling the story."

Although McCain's face showed little change in expression, Jennings sensed he'd hit a raw nerve. He sat quietly, rolling another cigarette as he avoided his employer's eyes. Jennings had known the Captain for almost two years and had found him to be fair, although sometimes pretty demanding. He'd heard something of McCain and Poe's history with the Rangers, while working over in New Mexico where he'd worked before coming to Texas. Since starting work for the Rocking-R, he'd personally had the occasion to observe J.D. McCain during two of his famous outrages. Even though he was a full three inches taller than his boss and out-weighed him by fifty pounds, after witnessing those events Jennings was convinced that he wanted no part of the Captain when he was in one of those foul moods.

While he was sure both Poe and McCain could be dangerous adversaries, most of the things he'd heard had come from Poe, and as with most of Poe's stories, seemed too far-fetched to be believable. He'd also heard a few tales from Moses, but figured the black man was so awed by McCain that he probably added to the yarns just to make McCain seem much more imposing. What Jennings *had* heard in New Mexico though, was the story of a half-breed named Scar and the two old Ranger's relentless pursuit of him for more than a decade throughout the southwest territories. Almost catching up with him on numerous occasions, wiping out his band on several, he'd always seemed to be just one step ahead of them.

During those years, the outlaw Scar had left the remains of butchered men, women, and children, as he slaughtered and raped a path across three states. Each time they'd chased him until his small band had either been killed off by the Rangers, or becoming weary of the chase, had finally fled into Mexico or the territories to hide out. Then, after a few quiet years, Scar would resurface to continue his destructive path. It'd been almost six years since he was last heard of in Texas.

Jennings had also heard the story of one of their encounters with the outlaw six years earlier. McCain and Poe had tracked Scar, four of his renegades, and the woman and two children they had stolen, to a remote canyon just across the river into Mexico. There, they cornered the band, killed the four renegades and shot Scar nearly to pieces; only to find when they eventually entered the camp, that the hostage's throats had been cut and Scar had disappeared again. They tracked his blood-trail for three days, winding deeper and deeper into Mexico until at last the trail simply dried up. Twice they were almost caught by the Mexican Ruralis and finally had to give up and return to Texas.

McCain sat and pondered the latest troubling development long after Jennings had gone inside. *We were damn fools,* he thought, staring out toward the mountain range to the southwest. They'd convinced themselves their old enemy had surely perished of his wounds in the dry Sierras. Now, McCain knew they'd only kidded themselves. Scar was back. It was going to start all over again and there was nothing he could do about it. Hell, he wasn't even an active Ranger anymore.

It might be worth a ride out to the campsite and take a look though.

Just the thought of even a short ride like that, made him grimace, and his hand instinctively went to a tender spot in the middle of his back. McCain was still stiff and sore from the previous long ride from which they'd just returned, not to mention the latest physical labor of building the dam out back. Still, he thought. That last ride had been necessary.

* * *

Several days earlier Quint "Fish" Fishburn, had returned from personal business in El Paso. McCain, Poe and Moses Penny had been sitting on the front porch as the evening sun dropped, enjoying the meager breeze that periodically blew in their direction. Poe had seen him first, from about a mile away, "Coming like a bat out of hell."

As soon as he'd come into view, Fish had began shouting and waving his arms, but based on the distance and his propensity to stutter when excited, none of the men could remotely make out a thing he was yelling. The tall, lanky Fishburn abruptly brought his horse to a sliding halt in front of the group covering them with a fog of dust and debris, and was instantly out of the saddle like a circus trick-rider, running right up on the porch. He was completely covered with a thick coat of dust. Pointing in the direction he'd come, he'd finally placed his hands on his knees and gulped for air, then stuttered to beat the band as he'd tried to tell McCain what he was so excited about.

"C…Captain, we got t…trouble. Som' bitches are s…stealing our hors…hors…livestock!"

After they'd gotten him calmed down enough to talk, they'd found out that on his way back from El Paso, he'd happened to travel by way of Fort Stockton and rode in from the southeast. That's when he'd first spotted a large herd of horses headed toward the Mexican border. Even from a distance he'd been able to recognize the "Widder-maker."

Fish had also taken the rare opportunity to return one of the many digs he usually suffered at the hands of Poe. "That big black som' bitch that p…pret near…et o' Rosie up last Spring, hee-hee."

Poe had scowled real hard at Fish for the slight, but maintained his silence – for once.

"There w..were 'bout a dozen of 'em, Captain," Fishburn finally stated, more calmly. "Had almost f…fifty of our horses w…with them. Looked like they were headed straight for Vila Ahumada."

Poe had caught McCain's eye, who said what both of them

were thinking. "Old man Martinez and his vaqueros again Roosevelt. We should've hanged that old horse thief years ago."

"Yeah," said Rosie Poe, with a twinkle in his eye. "Imagine that old thief coming all the way up here to steal back the horses we stole from him in the first place."

It'd been common practice for years for Texas ranchers to run into Mexico and bring back cattle and horses from Mexican ranchers, and few considered it stealing. They rationalized that the Mexicans had probably stolen them from hard working Texans in the first place. In many cases, they were probably right.

McCain had noticed Poe's sarcasm and stared at him for a moment. "I suppose you just want to let him have fifty head of our livestock, without even an argument from us?" He waited for Poe's answer, and none came. "If you don't want to come, just stay here and look out for the place until we get back."

"Don't figure you boys could git along without me fer that long," Poe had answered smugly, spitting at a fly on the step.

McCain just snorted in return, saying, "The cemeteries are filled with men who thought the world couldn't get along without them."

"Aye God, jist fer that remark, I ought ta' let you go alone and git yerself into a bunch o' misery." Then, without looking at his partner, Poe slowly got to his feet and said warily, "Oh, I guess not. It has been just a tad boring around here since little Flora left with that gambler." He placed his hands in the middle of his spine, stretching backward, looking at the others. "All right girls, what are you waiting for? Let's get saddled up 'fore old Jericho busts a gut or something."

Poe had walked off towards the corral, chuckling to himself.

The four men had rode and slept in the saddle for the next several days, and eventually caught up with the Martinez family about twenty miles inside Mexico. Moses easily found their tracks and had flawlessly predicted the route they'd take back to the Martinez Rancho. When the Mexican raiders crossed the Chonchos River with their herd of stolen horses, they'd found McCain, Poe, Fish, and Moses Penny waiting for them on the other side. The Texans had quietly remained on their horses and waited until half of the riders crossed the river, then rode out of the tall bushes lining the ridge that overlooked the river valley.

The young vaquero riding point had seen them first, shouting, "*Los Tejanos Diablos.*" He'd then turned his horse in terror and spurred to the rear.

Several of the others had attempted to flee as well, but old Martinez and eight of his vaqueros decided to stand and fight. It was the type of fighting the early Rangers had built their reputation on. Poe had led off and the others followed, whooping and spurring their horses straight into the opposing force. Instantly, they were among them, shooting with both hands, emptying their deadly pistols at close range into the disorganized bunch of men. It was over almost before it'd started.

As the echoes faded away, Poe had circled around and quickly checked the bodies. "Looks like old man Martinez escaped again, Jericho," he declared, spitting into the running water as he went about his grisly task. "Ain't so sorry that he did though, cause pretty soon all our enemies'll be gone. It'll be plumb lonely around here after that. 'Sides, I kind of admire the old bastard's gall."

"All right, let's get 'em rounded up and headed north!" McCain had yelled. "That old man will gather up some of his boys and be hot on us if we dally."

McCain had pushed them hard without rest, until well back inside the United States. Still, Moses Penny rode cover to the rear nearly all the way back to Bluebonnet. They'd recovered all but five of the fifty horses Fish had estimated the raiders drove off, and arrived back at the ranch tired, but in high spirits.

Now, having just received more bad news, McCain rubbed his stiff shoulders once more as he thought about the recent raid into Mexico. *It was a good thing Fish spied them when he did though, otherwise, losing that herd would've been a heavy blow to the ranch. Well, better let Rosie know about the Face-Cutter when he gets back, and plan for the worse.*

Two

"John Wesley Hardin was the most worthless skunk that ever lived. Not only was he a cold-blooded killer, he was a lawyer as well."
– "Peg" Lewis, 1900

BLUEBONNET, UNDOUBTEDLY NAMED FOR the endless acres of the little blue flowers that had grown wild in the area before the drought, was actually nothing more than half a dozen dwellings providing shelter for the town's few inhabitants. A livery stable, stage office, general store, four small houses – which were nothing more than shacks – and Paco's Saloon, the only two-story building, made up the town of Bluebonnet.

In addition to being the only saloon in the area, Paco's business was also the only 'sporting house' within a hundred-mile radius. That probably explained why most of the cowboys within a day's ride usually showed up with some regularity at least once a month. It might also have explained the occasional bad element that drifted through. The town had no elected sheriff and folks were generally left to settle their own disputes as they saw fit. In spite of that, Bluebonnet had experienced only two shootings, a hanging, and a minor knifing in which "only a Mexican" was killed, since it came into existence.

One of the shootings happened when a surly gent by the name of Higgins tried to enter the saloon while wearing his six-shooter. Everyone just naturally wore their guns all the time in and around Bluebonnet, with the exception of a few cowboys who'd occasionally discard them while performing with one of the ladies of the evening in Paco's upstairs parlors. However, after countless complaints from his working ladies, Paco finally posted signs in each of the upstairs rooms that read, *"Hats and Boots Must be Removed."* It appeared guns were an essential item of the wardrobe and as such, were allowed.

Ben Higgins, being a nice enough gent when sober, turned mouthy and a little nasty after a few drinks. Two weeks earlier he'd picked a fight with Molly over her choice of gentlemen for the evening and it had nearly turned violent when Higgins started waving his six-shooter around, cussing everybody in sight. That was when Paco, having finally had his fill of the man, shoved the short double-barreled Greener under his nose and invited him to vacate the premises, pronto. Paco also requested Mr. Higgins never enter the establishment again while armed. Being at a sudden loss for words, Higgins hastily did as requested.

One evening two weeks later, he arrived at Paco's with three other cowhands, and it was apparent the men had been celebrating since early morning. As Higgins entered the saloon, Paco laid the double-barreled bouncer on the bar as he continued to wash bar glasses.

"Mr. Higgins, I hope you aren't thinking of coming in here with that sidearm," he stated quietly but firmly.

Though Higgins was always loud and boisterous when drinking, there was just something about the empty holes of a doubled-barreled Greener looking at you that had a settling effect on most people. Being the kind of guy he was, Higgins however, just naturally had to make some small attempt to salvage his pride and impress his riding buddies.

"Can I come in with my gun if I unload it first?" he said.

After contemplating his answer for a moment, Paco nodded that it would be fine with him. Higgins then pulled his pistol, aimed it at the ceiling, and calmly emptied it through the roof of the two-story building. The problem with that was that it was payday, and all four of Paco's whores were carrying on business in the upstairs parlors.

Three ladies of the evening came screaming down the stairs, followed by wild-eyed cowboys in various stages of undress, some clutching pistols, all swearing to the top of their lungs. As things quieted down, it was soon discovered that Les Parmington, the town's blacksmith, had been shot through the buttocks with the bullet exiting through his thigh, striking his companion Lucy in the left eye. Lucy, of course, was as dead as the bluebonnets that used to grow around the town prior to the drought. Les, himself, was in a great deal of pain – not to mention having to put up with endless questions of how it was possible for the two of them to sustain such wounds in the first place – him through the buttocks and her through the left eye.

Paco, in addition to being the unofficial mayor, also acted as the town judge when circumstances required. He held a speedy trial and hung Mr. Higgins from the livery stable rafter, all within thirty minutes of the shooting. It seemed Miss Lucy had been the local clientele's favorite sporting lady and figured to be missed considerably.

The second shooting happened when John Wesley Hardin stopped in Paco's for a drink, and encountered another fellow who could have offended him in some real or imagined way in the past. Or, maybe he just didn't like the man's looks. A person's looks often tended to offend Hardin more than they did most folks.

When Legends Lived

It seemed as though that particular hombre and he had a disagreement about a card game over in Gullytown a few months previously. Gullytown was a small outlaw hole about fifty miles away in some pretty rugged country. John Wesley Hardin, a sick-looking, extremely filthy specimen with scabs all over his face, shouldn't have had a legitimate complaint about anybody's looks. So most folks figured the fellow just happened to catch the gunman in one of his notoriously bad moods. In any event, it turned out to be the stranger's unlucky day, because Hardin shot him full of holes, then calmly mounted up and rode out in the direction of Gullytown. No one offered to try and hang John Wesley Hardin.

Through the years, famous lawmen and outlaws drifted in and out of Paco's. Most minded their own business and eventually moved on. Toward the end of the town's existence, Butch Cassidy and the Sundance Kid even stopped there once on their way to San Antonio, where they hoped to spend time visiting Fanny Porter's Sporting House, then on to meet their destiny in a small South American village. Most of the gunmen and outlaws drifting through weren't a problem, and some were even made to feel welcome. However, cold-blooded John Wesley Hardin was one man most folks around Bluebonnet would just as soon never return.

* * *

The Wells Fargo Company built the stage office primarily because its location was about midpoint between El Paso and Fort Worth, give or take fifty miles or so. Another reason was for the proximity of a small, walled-in spring well and a flowing creek that ran through the area where the town stood, with a wooden bridge right at the city limits sign. The well still held cool water, but the once flowing creek had long since dried up. The bridge still stood though, as if hoping to be of some use when future rains returned.

Hector "Peg" Lewis was given the job of running the stage office when he retired from Wells Fargo after twenty years as a shotgun guard and driver for the stage-line that ran between El Paso and Amarillo. Hector wore a wooden peg since losing his right leg after being kicked by a company horse. He swore for years that he'd actually been kicked in the other leg, and a drunken doctor had taken off the wrong one.

In his words, "If your time ain't come, not even a doctor can kill you." In spite of the wooden leg, he was as still spry as when McCain and Poe had first met him over twenty years before. As they recalled, he was old even back then.

After the Wells Fargo office was built, next came the saloon, followed by other small businesses and living quarters. The town was barely kept alive by the stage coach stops and weekend visits by cowboys who came to drink and visit with the whores at Paco's. One of the largest nearby ranches was the Thompson's Circle-T spread, several days ride to the East. There were a few Mexican regulars and once in a while a stranger would pass through looking for work or obviously running from his past.

The working ladies at Paco's came and went so frequently that no one seemed to get to know any of them well, except for Roosevelt Poe. He called all of them by name, preceded always by "Mizz," and much to McCain's disdain, treated each and every one like a lady; a concept completely lost on the straight-and-narrow J.D. McCain.

"Whores ain't the only people that sell themselves for money,"

Poe had once told him. "They're jist the only ones that're honest about it."

Poe had that rare gift absent in most opinioned people, which allowed him to get away with comments that would've caused serious offense from others. It went without saying, that among those who knew him well, Rosie Poe had very few enemies.

As shadows filled the small room, Poe sat on the side of the bed in an upstairs room at Paco's, completely undressed except for his large felt hat. He watched the sun drop below the horizon. Then slowly standing, he grimaced with pain as he rubbed the small of his back, stretched, and gingerly reached for his pants. He pulled them on. Damned if he didn't still feel naked without the ever-present long-johns he habitually wore in both winter and summer.

Be glad when this infernal hot spell is over, he thought, so I can commence to dressing like a man again.

As he sat back down on the side of the bed to pull on his boots, and felt Rita stir beneath the covers of the bed. She sat up, stretched widely, and looked at him through sleepy eyes. She was a dark pretty woman—and would've been beautiful except for a large dark birthmark on the right side of her face. Rita looked at him disappointed.

"Leaving, Rosie?"

"Yep. Gotta git back to the ranch, Miss Rita. They can't git along without me fer long," he chuckled.

"When will ya be back, Honey?"

Rosie caught a whiff of her soap-scented body and was tempted to return to the rumpled bed. Then he reluctantly stood and buckled on his gun belt.

He thought about the folded scrap of paper in his shirt pocket.

"Don't know. Maybe three-four days. Might have 'ta go to Amarillo with Jericho. Now don't you fret," he said as he opened the door to leave. "Maybe I'll bring you something nice from Amarillo."

Rita instantly brightened up and flashed him a wide, beautiful grin that made one instantly forget about the birthmark. "What?"

Poe winked at her, as he closed the door. "A surprise."

There were several regulars lined up at the bar, as he came down the stairs. They gave him the usual crude remarks and whistles reserved for someone well-liked, as he walked through the bar and out the front door scowling at them.

Arriving at the ranch just as full-darkness set in, he encountered Matt Jennings leaving the porch steps.

"Howdy, Matt," he said cheerfully.

Matt grinned at him as a greeting. "Better be careful, Rosie. Sabi's got a burr under his saddle tonight."

Poe gave him a knowing look and without comment, entered the door.

McCain, hearing their remarks, tilted back in his chair, sipped a cup of black coffee and watched Poe enter. He and the cook, Sabi Carlos, were the only ones remaining in the kitchen. Poe shot a quick glance at the rope where his jug of sour mash was hanging in the spring, licked his lips once, and headed toward the table in the center of the large room.

"Supper's done," Carlos said, sourly.

Poe ignored him as he poured himself a cup of the strong brew and sat down. "Just as well if ya ask me. I don't much take to hog swill anyway." Often enjoying his own humor more than those around him, he chuckled at the comment.

In the middle of the table on a tin plate were three flour tor-

When Legends Lived

tillas, rolled around something that looked a little like smashed black beans. He reached for the plate, as Carlos moved rapidly to grab it.

"That's my supper!" the cook bellowed.

"Lord hate a hog!" Poe laughed, as he held the plate of food just out of Sabi's reach with one hand, and stuffed a whole tortilla into his mouth with the other. Quickly picking up another one, he pushed the remaining tortilla on the plate back to the center of the table.

"That's your supper," he mumbled with his mouth full of tortilla. "Next time, make more. Hee, hee."

Carlos stomped to the wood box, picked up a hatchet and glared at Poe who was slowly munching his food, and staring back, apparently amused. Fuming and spitting out epithets in several languages, Carlos stormed out the back door toward the wood pile while McCain calmly observed the whole drama.

"Someday he's gonna cut your throat while you sleep," he stated noncommittally.

Poe snorted, spraying crumbs, and said, "I sure liked him a lot better when he was a thief stealing goats from his neighbors. At least then he was in Mexico. Now he's moved north of the border and become respectable. Even calls himself a cook!" He snorted again. "Horse-apples! Likely poison us all with his greaser grub. Most everything he cooks tastes like my underwear smells after a hard winter," Poe chuckled even louder, pleased with his remark.

McCain continued observing him without retort. There wasn't a glimmer of good humor on his face. He figured he never would understand his long-time partner. Most of the things Poe said didn't make a lick of sense to him. Both of them knew the ranch was fortunate to have Carlos for a cook, and it was primarily because of the good food that they were able to keep steady ranch-hands while other spreads suffered heavy turnover.

"You know one of your biggest problems, Jericho?" Poe said around the last of a dry tortilla.

McCain didn't answer, sure he was going to hear about it anyway. He did.

"You never laugh. Hell, you never even smile. You just plain don't know how to enjoy life!" Swallowing hard, Poe chased the tortilla with the last of his coffee, and went on. "You always have that pained look on your face, like you have'ta break wind, or something."

McCain scowled, but remained silent, hoping his partner would eventually run out of steam so he could get on with the business at hand; at the same time, knowing Rosie Poe usually had more steam than most folks. He was right this time, too.

"Ya ought to try it once in a while, old hoss," Poe said. "Just raise a leg and let one fly. Makes ya feel a whole bunch better. Hell, babies do it all the time. That's what folks say makes them smile so much, hee, hee. If you can't do that, at least make a little noise once in a while. Offer an opinion on things."

"Noise proves nothing," McCain said stiffly, still not amused.

Poe smacked his lips a few times, looking hungrily at the rope hanging down into the spring. Then seeing his partner wasn't going to offer, he finally said, "How 'bout a little snort just to wet the whistle before we turn in?"

"Drinking makes fools of some people, and since most are big enough fools to begin…" McCain started.

"Aye God! I find fewer things harder to stomach than someone trying to set a good example, Jericho."

When Legends Lived

Mumbling to himself, Poe strode to the walled spring, cautiously peered inside, and apparently satisfied there were no scorpions or rattlers lurking down there, pulled on the short rope anchored to a wooden peg. Retrieving a squat brown crock jug, he pulled the cork out with his teeth, braced the jug on the crook of his arm, and smacked his lips again as he raised it to his mouth. Catching McCain's disapproving glare over the top of the jug, he winked broadly.

"God deliver us from any man who can eat without drinking," he said quickly and swallowed some of the fiery brew.

Just then McCain said softly, "Scar may be back."

Poe choked, spewing the hard liquor across the room. He finished his coughing fit, and McCain watched as he wiped a wet chin. Then he told him about his earlier conversation with Jennings.

"Think I'll take a ride out there and look at the signs the Circle-T man told Matt Jennings about. Maybe take Moses along. How's your back? Up for the ride?"

"I wouldn't miss it fer nothin'," Poe said, when he could breath again. Watching McCain leave, he shouted to his back, "Tarnation, Jericho. Ya damned near strangled me."

* * *

It was still an hour until sunup when the three men rode away from the ranch. All wore revolvers and carried Winchester rifles. Additionally, Moses Penny carried his always present Sharps rifle. The men rode quietly and were all business as they arrived at the flat area called Halfway Rock. Nobody seemed to be able to recall just what it was "half-way" to, but it had been called that for as long as anyone around there could remember. Without speaking, Moses slipped off to the right and Poe drifted to the left as they entered the area where they suspected the abandoned camp was located. Convincing themselves the camp was still deserted, they met in the center.

"Whee," said Poe, "I smelt this place an hour before we ever got here."

"How long do you figure they were here, Mr. Penny?" McCain said.

"About a week," interrupted Poe, giving another of his often uninvited opinions.

McCain still looked at Moses, who looked around for a few more moments, then finally answered his Captain's question. "Three days."

Poe stared at the black man, mouth agape. "Now, how the heck do you know that fer certain, Moses? Jericho? He's making it up!" Poe slapped his hat against his leg in frustration.

Moses Penny was unquestionably one of the best trackers either man had ever known. Still, Poe and many others, considered Roosevelt Poe to be a "right smart" tracker himself. He took some amount of pride in that fact and wasn't one to simply accept second fiddle to anyone. Not even the formidable Moses Penny.

"Moses, be so kind to explain to me how you know it was only three days, and not a week like I said? You been acting like you know so danged much more about reading sign than anybody else ever since I know'd ya. I still say it was a week. What-da-ya think about them apples?" he said.

"The dung," Moses replied.

"The...what?"

"The dung," Moses said again.

When Legends Lived

Poe, who was beginning to suspect that he might've overreacted a little, said, "Well, what about the danged dung?" He conceded that, as a tracker, Moses was a pretty close second to himself, therefore, deserving of some consideration.

Moses went on in his deep rich voice. "Tracks show there were nine horses tied here. Nine horses mean nine men. Count the dung piles. Horses drop twice a day, man drops once a day. Count the piles. Three days worth of dung." Moses smiled softly to himself as he turned his head so Poe couldn't see it.

Poe, still not quite ready to concede defeat, followed Moses complaining, "Well jist how the hell do ya know one of the men or some of the horses wasn't all bound up from eating this loco weed around here?" he said sarcastically, then smiled smugly.

"Check the dung," Moses said as he mounted his horse. "None of it's firm."

He and McCain rode away chuckling to themselves, leaving Poe to catch up, feeling as if he'd just somehow been fleeced.

When they were about an hour from the ranch, McCain broke the silence again. "Mr. Penny, ride over to the Circle-T and see if you can take a look at the wrangler's body. Might be able to find out something."

Moses knew his captain was thinking about Scar. "Right, Capt'n."

Poe drew even with McCain and Moses, still smarting from the suspicion the two men had somehow made a fool of him. That was hard to do, especially since Rosie Poe was usually the instigator of almost anything that ever happened to those around him. Reaching into his shirt pocket, he handed McCain the folded piece of paper he'd carried since picking it up at the Wells Fargo office the evening before.

"You might find this interesting," he said.

McCain unfolded the opened letter, not commenting or thinking it strange that Poe had already opened and apparently read it.

> *Dear Captain McCain,*
>
> *The Southern Pacific Railroad is offering you a very lucrative opportunity. I request you meet with my representative in Amarillo. He is registered at the Cattlemen's Hotel under the name of James Packard and will be there for the next two weeks. I think you will find our offer to be quite generous.*
>
> *Your Servant,*
> *Frank Chase, President*
> *Southwest Area, Southern Pacific Railroad*

"You going?" Poe said. "Money's what makes the mare go."

When McCain didn't answer right away, he continued, "This man, Chase, said it could be very 'luc-ra-tive'…even generous… and hell, we sure could use luc-ra-tive and generous these days."

"Don't want anything to do with the railroad," McCain stated. "I never trusted them and they've ruined the country."

"Aye God, Jericho! If that ain't just like you," Poe said softly. "They'll pay you! They have money! You remember money don't you? It comes in green paper and sometimes it's heavy and gold-colored. That's what *luc-ra-tive* means, Jericho. Money… and Lord knows we do need luc-ra-tive money!"

McCain just looked at his partner like he'd quite suddenly lost his mind.

"These men are rich, Jericho," Poe implored him. "They're educated men of property, and they are asking *us* to work for *them*."

There was the obligatory snort from his friend, who then retorted, "Some of the biggest fools I ever met were educated men."

Poe, seeing McCain was in one of his stubborn moods, made a disgusted sound, slapped his horse, and rode on ahead. McCain stared after his longtime friend thoughtfully. He was still mildly irritated that Poe, fed up with the drought, now spent most of his time playing cards and drinking at Paco's – or, as McCain would occasionally remark sourly, "sniffing after" one of the three whores currently employed at the sporting house. Come to think about it, that was nothing new. Poe had been like that for nearly all of the years McCain had known him. Not being one to frivolously waste his time with things like that, he had to admit none-the-less, that the whores did dearly love Rosie Poe.

Hell, most of the time he don't even pay for it. Just as well though, with the ranch doing so poorly and all.

Although he hadn't mentioned it to his partner, lately McCain had began to think of some other line of work. Maybe do some marshaling. He'd heard of an opening over in Del Rio. He still had a little money left over from his Rangering days, but the real problem was finding a buyer for the ranch. Nobody was buying land. And now, with Scar acting up again, that wasn't likely to change. It was now just a waiting game since the ranch was paid for. The drought would eventually pass and things pick up, or the drought would linger and somebody eventually buy them out – or they'd just eventually ride off and leave it. Either way, it all came back to the drought.

Being frugal was his nature and in the Rangers he'd spent little except to replenish his ammo, or replace a saddle every ten years or so. When he and Poe first joined, they'd had to furnish their own horses, side arms, ammo and clothes, all for about thirty dollars a month. In later years, the Rangers provided them with horses and when he retired, even gave him the big bay stallion he called "Grasshopper." He'd taken his savings, and along with Poe, bought the Rocking-R just outside of Bluebonnet. Lately, most of the local folks had even taken to calling the ranch "Bluebonnet" as well.

Things had gone pretty well for them for the first few years as he and his partner provided good horse flesh, first to the Army, and then to the stage lines. That was until the railroad began to force out the scattered Wells Fargo stage offices. Then the drought killed off a good part of their livestock.

His conjecture put him into an even worse mood then before. *Seems it all comes back to the drought – and the god damned railroad.*

Three

"There are those that say the railroad is the vessel through which this nation's life blood flows. I say, it is the wound through which it ebbs."

– Texas rancher, 1878

THE LETTER IN MCCAIN'S pocket had been written two weeks earlier by Frank Chase's assistant, Jack Cranwell. Chase had been president of the Southwest Area, Southern Pacific Railroad for the past five years. Before that, he was one of the visionaries who supervised the building of the Union Pacific. He'd always been a railroad man and would be one until he died. At that particular moment, Frank Chase was a very troubled and unhappy man. The Southwest Area had been operating in the red for the past three years. It made the stockholders unhappy, Southern Pacific's president unhappy, and that made Frank Chase unhappy. There was an old saying, "When powerful men get unhappy, less powerful men had better start to worry." Frank Chase was worried.

Sitting at the desk in his finely furnished office, Chase finally shouted through the open door. "Cranwell, get in here! *Now, dammit!*"

Jack Cranwell had worked for Frank Chase going on twenty-five years, and during that time, he'd seen many people come and go. Chase was often ruthless when it came to cutting his losses, especially if he thought someone could no longer do him any good. Jack Cranwell, had entered, looking calm and unworried. He was Southwest's ace trouble shooter whom Chase always called upon when he had a serious problem. Putting on his most serious face, he seated himself primly on a luxurious leather chair.

"Yes, sir?"

"Cranwell, we've got a problem," his boss had started out.

Chase had talked for fifteen minutes telling Jack about several bands of outlaws that were robbing one out of every five trains passing through the Southwest Area, and killing off the railroad's construction and repair crews. The worst part of it was, they didn't just rob the trains but murdered all the passengers and train crews as well. This had the sobering effect of causing the number of passengers traveling to El Paso and beyond to dwindle each and every day. Likewise, freight companies and ranchers preferred the safer alternative of hauling their freight by wagon and driving their cattle to market, instead of shipping by rail. As Frank Chase described his troubles, he'd observed Cranwell's face. The little man appeared smug, almost as though he'd already hit upon a solution. Chase had finished and waited for Cranwell to reply.

"Give me a while to work on it, sir. This is going to be a tough situation to rectify," Cranwell said, politically positioning himself, for he'd already sent a letter off to J.D. McCain.

* * *

Two days later, Jack Cranwell was seated once again, in Frank Chase's lush office. He'd asked Southern Pacific Chief of Security, Thomas Randle and Randle's new son-in-law, James Packard, to join them. Randle had served ten years as a Texas Ranger and came to work for the railroad after getting married twenty years earlier. Cranwell knew him by his reputation, a capable man, adept at handling difficult situations. Randle's son-in-law, James Packard, had recently graduated from Harvard Law School where he'd met and married Randle's daughter, Hattie, against the wishes of her father. That had been six months before.

"Well, what have you got?" Chase said abruptly.

Cranwell stood and quickly walked to a large map covering nearly an entire wall of Chase's office. Texas and a large portion of New Mexico and Oklahoma were outlined with a thick red line, showing the S.P.'s Southwest Area. Cranwell pointed to a quadrangle between Fort Worth, Amarillo, San Antonio, and El Paso.

"This is the most serious problem area," he said confidently. "There are only four hundred Army troops to cover that entire area, one company of Texas Rangers who have to handle other criminal activities as well, and the local sheriffs who only tend to worry about things that happen within their town limits. The general feeling is that this is a railroad problem and they just don't have the time or resources to go off chasing a couple of outlaw bands across Texas, and most of Oklahoma and New Mexico. Besides, sir, Mr. Randle tells me they don't like us very much out there anyway."

"So, what're you telling me, Cranwell? That there's nothing we can do?" Chase demanded gruffly.

"No, no, that's not what I'm saying at all," Cranwell responded hastily. "What I'm saying is that we'll have to handle it ourselves."

"How?"

"Mr. Randle used to be a Texas Ranger before coming to work for the S. P. We believe the solution is to hire our own people to track these outlaws down and eliminate them. Mr. Randle thinks he just might know of someone capable of handling it for us."

Cranwell had his superior's attention now, so he hurried on.

"Mr. Randle served with someone just before the war, Captain Jericho McCain. He retired from the Rangers in 1880."

"Before the war? Why that would make him close to fifty years old now!"

"Fifty-two actually, but please bear with me, sir," Cranwell said. "Captain McCain was one of the best they had—tough, resourceful and stubborn. He just doesn't give up until the job is finished. He didn't retire due to health problems or loss of ability."

Cranwell leafed through several sheets of paper and found the one he was seeking.

"Official reports state that during the last year, just before he retired, he tracked down Desert Wolf and four of his men and killed them in Mexico, two hundred miles south of the border. They say that when J.D. McCain gets on your trail, he never quits. The good thing about McCain is, you hardly ever have to worry about a trial when he's through. If he doesn't have to shoot them, he hangs them. I think it's worth a shot."

"What makes you think he would want to do it?" Chase brought one hand to rest under his chin, giving his full attention to Cranwell.

"He started a small horse ranch over near El Paso with another old Ranger and the drought has just about wiped them out; along with all the other small ranchers in the area. I think he might be ready to try something else, especially if you could talk the Governor into maybe 're-activating' him as a Texas Ranger.

Of course, we'll need to finance a small force to work with him, but the comparable cost will be minimal."

Chase walked to the window over-looking the vast manicured garden below. He stood quietly with his hands behind his back and gazed out, then after a moment turned around. "Okay. McCain—if you can get him—and five men. I want one of our security people to go along. This is railroad business and I want it to remain railroad business. When it's over, I want everyone in the territories to know it was the railroad that took care of them and protected them from these outlaws. Who do we have that we can send along, Randle?"

"I don't know of anyone available that could withstand the rigors of such an operation, sir," Randle said. "Most of our people were hired to investigate railroad type crime, not go riding off in pursuit of outlaws and bandits for months at a time."

Chase pointed at Jim Packard. "What about this young man? He certainly looks fit enough to me."

Randle turned and gazed with amusement at the stricken look on his son-in-law's face, then slowly smiled. "I think that's a fine idea, sir. A very fine idea. He can leave tomorrow."

Four

"You'll hush, and close your eyes now! The dark man with the scar will get you if you don't go to sleep!"
– Unidentified west Texas mother, 1873

THE DROUGHT OF THE early '80's rolled across west Texas and southern Oklahoma like something alive. It seemed to hungrily devour every living thing in its path, leaving only dry cracked ground and dead vegetation in its wake. Ranchers of the era claimed there were sand bogs large enough to swallow entire wagons with a full team of horses. The bloated bodies of horses and bleached bones of stray cattle were a common sight along the many trails connecting the few scattered towns throughout the region. No one knew just how many head of stock, or for that matter, human life was lost during the years the drought continued. Small ranchers, barely surviving as it was, were wiped out entirely. Even the larger ranchers, like King, Goodnight, Shanghai Pierce, and Thompson's Circle-T, suffered heavy losses.

Religious folk said it was the Lord's way of punishing the region for its evil ways. Even some of the "tame Indians" viewed it as something sent from an evil spirit. Only the tough, still unconquered Mescalero Apaches to the west of the Pecos River initially accepted it as a natural event and went about their daily lives, seemingly unconcerned. But soon, the drought affected even them too, as the absence of antelope and deer forced them to move many times in order to survive.

When Legends Lived

Looking out over the dry landscape, one could see thick heat waves rising in the afternoon stillness, and an occasional horned toad or sidewinder slither from mesquite to mescal cactus, across the hot sand. Giant turkey buzzards dotted the afternoon sky, patiently waiting for what they instinctively knew was going to eventually happen—somehow, someway. What few people would've seen was the unmoving figure which squatted, partially obscured in the shadow of a large rock. Despite the fact that the sun had been beating down relentlessly since daybreak, the lone figure remained squatting without moving for several hours, gazing out over the flat area to the east. Like the turkey buzzards, he was also patiently waiting.

As the sun moved past the rim of the giant rocks to his left, it revealed the face of a dark-skinned male, which appeared to have been chiseled from the piles of surrounding granite. Except for the jagged scar that ran from the right side of his eye across and down the bridge of his nose, ending at the upper lip, there was nothing particularly remarkable about the face. He was between thirty-five and forty years old, and had never known his father, even doubting if his mother did. He was part Mescalero, part German and part of many other unknown strains; but the Apache blood dominated his genes. Except for the eyes.

To an observer from a slight distance, he appeared to be a full-blooded Apache. The way he stood, the loose cotton garments he wore, and the easy, almost arrogant manner in which he moved, all said Apache. Except for the eyes – they were sky blue.

Few people knew what he looked like, except for the scar, and those who did see him were usually dead within moments. At least, the lucky ones were. Mothers used his name to frighten their children into taking a nap, or being good. The Rangers, as good as they were, couldn't kill him, and the few army troops scattered around the area were ineffectual. He came and went as he pleased. It was his land and everything in it was his prey.

Now, as Scar sat and waited in the hot Texas sun, he remembered the good feeling it had given him all those years ago to stick his knife into the Colonel's soft belly and then slowly drag it across his face. So many years ago. His first kill, there had been many others since. His only regret was that he hadn't also marked the Colonel's pretty blond wife. He'd killed many white women since then and had found he enjoyed sticking his knife into their pale bodies – even more than killing their men. But first he would play with them—so he could smell their fear.

Reluctantly, his thoughts returned to the business at hand. Two-Noses, he knew, would already be at Adobe Springs with the fresh horses. That was good, just in case there were Rangers in the area when he finished his business. His business at the moment was Samuel H. Thompson, owner of one of the largest ranches in the region—perhaps just behind the King's Ranch over by Houston, Colonel Goodnight's spread and maybe Shanghai Pierce's. Two-Noses' sister had learned from an old Apache cleaning woman at the Thompson's, that the rancher was taking the Wells Fargo stage line from Odessa to the rail-stop at Abilene. There, he would pick up a wagon for the last leg of the journey back to his ranch. Traveling with him was his young son. Two-Noses had been sure to quickly let Scar know, telling him too, that the rancher would then meet his daughter at the rail-stop who would join the Thompson males on the trip back to the Circle-T.

Of more importance to Scar, Thompson would be carrying

the payment from his latest stock sell to the Army – enough gold for Scar to arm at least fifteen, maybe twenty more men. With that many well-armed men, he could stop every train and stagecoach running through the territory, and kill every man, woman and child riding on them. He could literally wipe out the small ranchers and nesters that dotted the territory west of the Brazos River.

So, he sat nursing his hatred and like the giant Turkey Buzzard, waited. Patiently.

Five

SAMUEL THOMPSON HAD COME west five years before the Civil War started. In just over twenty-five years he'd built one of the largest ranches in the territory. In the process, he'd married, brought his young wife to Texas, and fathered two daughters and three sons. Theresa, his seventeen-year-old daughter, was just returning from a finishing school in Pennsylvania and would meet him at Abilene. His twelve-year-old son, Todd, had taken the stage to Odessa so he could help his father teamster the wagon to Abilene and then back to the ranch. Both father and son loved those trips when they could be together. It was now especially nice because Theresa would be traveling with them. Dixie, his nineteen-year-old, was helping his eldest son, Nathaniel, "Nate," look after things, back at the ranch. Dixie was dark and beautiful like her mother was at that age. Theresa was fair and favored his side of the family.

Sam Thompson had made Nate foreman of the Circle-T the previous year when he was only twenty, not because Nate was his son, but because he was simply the best darn cowhand Sam had ever seen. Nate was also good with the other cowhands, and Sam could see they respected him for his abilities, not the fact he was a Thompson and the owner's son. At six-two, two hundred and twenty-five pounds, Nate could out-rope, out-ride, and out-fight just about any of the other men on the Circle-T. And the fact that Nate could whip out his long barreled Colt

When Legends Lived

and hit a Jackrabbit on the run, didn't hurt either. If anything happened to Sam, Nate could carry on at the ranch just fine.

Brady, his second son born two years before Theresa, was a cripple—a word that made Sam inwardly cringe. Brady's pony had fallen on him when he was just five. Since that day, Brady spent his days hobbling around on a cane or crutch, and reading the books he kept sending off for, from some publishing company back east.

Samuel had blamed himself for Brady's condition, because on the boy's fifth birthday, he'd finally given in to his pleadings and bought his son a pinto pony. Brady had sneaked out of the ranch house early one morning, somehow saddled the pony, and ridden off alone. The pony spooked about a mile from the house and threw Brady into a rocky ravine. Juanita, their cook, found the pony standing at the watering trough when she went to get water for breakfast. Ranch hands quickly spread out and found the boy. Brady's leg was caught between two large rocks, broken in several places and, more critically, the leg was pulled from his hipbone, destroying many of the large muscles in the upper leg and hip. He'd hovered between life and death for three days and the local doctor—actually the local horse doctor—used whatever skills he possessed to save the boy's life. Brady eventually recovered, but despite numerous trips back east to see top medical specialists, they couldn't repair the damaged leg muscles. He would remain a cripple for the rest of his life, leaving Sam feeling guilty—and Brady suffering in silent rage.

As they jerked along, Sam glanced at his daughter sitting beside him on the wagon seat. Once again, he marveled at her transformation during the two years she'd been away to school. He'd hardly known her when she stepped off the train in Abilene. In just two short years she'd transformed from a skinny awkward girl into a beautiful young woman. Swearing under his breath, Thompson allowed he'd kill the first man that came calling on her.

    He cast another glance at the sophisticated young lady riding on the wagon seat beside him, remembering his pride as they'd walked arm-in-arm to the buckboard. Todd, happy to be started, had settled into the back of the wagon with his hat pulled low over his face. In a short time he was snoring softly. An hour out of Abilene, the sun was just past midpoint in the sky, assuring Thompson that he had plenty of time to reach the overnight Way Station at the cross roads between Odessa and the Circle T. Traveling slowly, the wagon's wheels still kicked up small puffs of dust on the dry surface and trailed lazily behind them.

* * *

    The dark man with the scar sat and watched the faint puffs of dust to the east, and knew his wait was over. He raised his right hand briefly and two shadows nearby moved silently down the ridge. He watched the distant trail dust for a few minutes longer, picked up his rifle, and silently slipped down the hill.

Six

*"I don't trust the railroad...or Republicans either,
for that matter. They've ruined the country."*

– J.D. McCain, Captain, Texas Rangers, 1882

MCCAIN AND POE HAD both signed on with the Texas Rangers within a few months of each other, about the time the Mexican War ended. They'd cut their teeth on actions against Mexican raiders and later, Iron Shirt, the famous Comanche war chief. When Governor Runnels finally got fed up with the Army's inability to handle the situation in Texas, he authorized the Rangers to expand to battalion strength, and appointed John S. (Rip) Ford as Commander with supreme authority to, "go after Iron Shirt and don't come back until you've got him."

By that time, Poe and McCain had already achieved reputations for being savvy and fearless, and McCain, despite his youth, was promoted to captain and given his own company. Poe eventually made captain as well—in fact, several times—but because of his loose interpretation of the rules tended not to keep it for very long. Unlike McCain, who remained a commissioned captain until his retirement, Poe went up through the ranks from sergeant to captain and back down, with some regularity.

They'd been with Ford when he crossed the Red River in 1858, killing Iron Shirt along with 300 of his warriors. They chased the Mexican bandit and self-proclaimed revolutionist, Cheno Cortinas (the Red Fox) from Texas after a battle on the Rio Grande River in which a hundred Rangers faced more than six hundred of Cortinas' vaquero troops. Sixteen Rangers died that day, but several hundred of Cortinas' men were killed and many more were wounded. Cortinas never again entered the state of Texas. Once again, Poe and McCain distinguished themselves in such a manner that Ford praised them as his most capable and trusted officers.

After the Civil War ended, they returned to the Rangers, first serving in different companies then eventually together again, working the roughest towns and wildest areas of west Texas. Although not officially sanctioned, they even ranged into Mexico and the Oklahoma Territory in pursuit of their quarry.

Once, the two men chased three Mexican outlaws who'd held up a small bank in Waco where they'd ruthlessly shot the teller and three customers before fleeing. Their trail nearly led all the way to Flagstaff, Arizona.

When Poe and McCain caught up, the three outlaws had joined up with three others along the way. McCain and Poe indiscriminately shot four and then hanged the other two. They didn't "cull them too close" as Rosie Poe explained later to their battalion commander.

Together and separately, they enforced the laws of Texas during its wildest and most lawless days. In doing so, they became closer than brothers for more then twenty-five years—at least well enough for McCain to know that Poe, who thought work to be the "curse of the drinking man," was usually hard to find when there was work to do.

Although the thought never quite formed in McCain's mind, Roosevelt Poe was probably the only person he felt he could always count on, if ever needed.

When Legends Lived

Those that knew the Captain just naturally understood he tended to react somewhat violently when others failed to see his point of view, or stood in his way of completing some mission he had set for himself, or for somebody else. Poe was the *only* person who wasn't intimidated by his temper. He was also one of the few people that could get away with calling J. D. McCain by all of his three names together; Jericho Duane McCain. Still, Poe's whoring and drinking never did set real well with the straight and narrow McCain's sense of *right* and *wrong*.

* * *

It was beginning to grow dark and as usual, McCain sat alone on the ranch house porch trying to take advantage of any cool evening breeze that might blow across the shadowy landscape. Periodically one would, and he'd catch a whiff of the coral; a smell he'd always found rich and satisfying in some odd way. A single oil lamp cast a glow through the only window in the front of the small house. He also smelled the tantalizing odor of strong coffee as it brewed away on the dying embers of the cook stove fire, and was tempted to go back inside to refill his empty cup. Instead, reaching inside his shirt and producing a cloth tobacco pouch, began to fashion a smoke.

The other two hands had returned earlier and he could hear the good humor of the group gathered around the kitchen table, swapping stories and kidding each other, as they usually did following the evening meal. He listened as the ranch hands laughed loudly at Poe's relentless goading of Fish.

"When you gonna have nerve enough to climb back on that broken down old nag, Tadpole, and take another crack at gentling him?"

R.C. Morris

Poe's question sounded innocent enough, but McCain knew from experience that his needling sometimes bordered on meanness. There were several soft snickers from around the room.

Fish Fishburn had bought Tadpole, a large, fine-looking black animal, from a slick horse trader the last time he'd gone to El Paso on "personal business." Poe told the others, in a tone that implied he knew all about it, that *personal business* was only an excuse for Fish to visit the expensive whores at the new hotel there anyway. Of course Fishburn protested that, but like as not, he would come back flat-busted, with a sheepish grin on his face. Only the last time he went to El Paso—he came back with Tadpole.

Fishburn, basking in the glow of the other ranch hands' envy and filled with his own self-importance, repeatedly told the others how he'd completely suckered an unsuspecting old man out of the stallion for half of what it was worth. As the old man reluctantly let the horse go, "due to health reasons," he'd told Fish it only needed a "little gentling" and it would be the finest piece of horse flesh west of New Orleans.

After a little prodding by the other men, Fishburn had saddled the stallion, and to their obvious amusement, had to nimbly jump out of range of its clicking teeth several times in the process. Then as the others watched, he'd swung lightly aboard. It lasted no longer than it took for his bony buttocks to hit the saddle, for he went flying a good fifteen feet in the air and landed on his face in the dust. Not only that, but if he hadn't been alert, old Tadpole might've finished him right there and then. The enraged stallion flew at him with the fury of the devil for which he was *originally* named, back before his name was changed to one less intimidating; Tadpole.

When Legends Lived

Even before Fish had hit the ground, the wild-eyed stallion was after him, attempting to stomp, bite, and kick him to death. In the ensuing confusion and the billowing dust, the horse was screaming, Fishburn was screaming, and the watching men were calling hardy encouragement as he, crawling frantically and screaming loudly, was finally able to roll under the fence to safety. As it was, he'd been bitten numerous times on the leg and shoulder, two of them requiring several weeks to completely heal.

Fish had quietly lain in the grime of the dust and dirt, blood seeping through the shoulder of his ripped shirt, and sweat and tears making tracks as they ran down his face, as he attempted to gulp air into his tortured lungs. Suddenly, he seemed to notice the silence, and looked up to find Poe and the others peering down at him.

"Next time, ya ought to try to sit into the saddle for a while," Poe told him helpfully. "They tell me that it's the continuous weight of a rider on a horse's back that gets him used to carrying a person."

"Yeah," Moses Penny offered solemnly. "They just don't respect ya none when they see ya sobbing and crawling around in the dirt like that."

With saucer-like eyes, Fish had stared at the enraged animal that had just tried to kill him, as it stood in the middle of the corral, quietly glaring back at him, nostrils flaring and eyes burning with hate. He'd wiped the tears from his eyes, and after several stammering attempts, finally allowed that he would never try to mount that *man-killer* again. In fact, he just might take a gun to it before it sired anymore of its ilk. The incident had resulted in endless hours of prodding by the other hands and been a major source of discomfort for the simple Fish.

* * *

Quint Fishburn was a tall lanky man, with big hands and large feet, and prominent ears that stuck out from the side of his head like, as Poe put it, "the doors of an outhouse." His small round head set upon a long neck that included a large Adam's apple, which tended to jump up and down rather rapidly when he was excited. As the men in the ranch house now kidded him about his purchase of the horse, that Adam's apple was jumping wildly in his throat and he was beginning to stutter just a bit.

"I a...ain't n...ever gonna g...get on that m...man-killer again," he said.

"Oh, come on, Fish," Poe prodded. "That dumb old man you stole him from said he needed a little *gentling*. Hee, hee."

Fish looked at him annoyed, Adam's apple jumping in his throat.

"Yeah, Fish, just take some of them roofing tacks Moses has and nail yore britches to the saddle, then we'll sneak you on board when he ain't looking, and maybe you can stay in the saddle long enough to git his attention," one of the other hands interjected.

"Guess you could always sell him back to the old gentleman who sold him to you," Moses said innocently. "He might give you a good deal, seeing as how he is so fond of old Tadpole."

Fish's Adam's apple jumped some more at that. "I'll s...shoot it f...first," he stammered, then jumping to his feet. "I don't w...want to discuss I...it any f...further," and walked out.

He paused momentarily on the porch steps beside McCain. "Those f...fellows can sure g...git annoying, Captain," he said shaking his head as he walked toward the bunk house. McCain

When Legends Lived

could hear him still mumbling to himself as he disappeared into the evening darkness.

The talk went on for another fifteen minutes before it broke up and the hands slowly made their way back to the bunkhouse, each pausing to pay their respects to McCain as they passed. As the last of them departed, McCain stood and walked into the kitchen, where he found Poe alone. He retrieved the large coffee pot from the stove-top and poured some of the thick tepid liquid into a used cup on the table. Taking a chair at the table, the two men sat without talking for a long time. Then, as if their earlier conversation had never been interrupted, Rosie Poe started up again.

"What harm would it do to jist go and talk to them?" Poe said to his partner for the tenth time that day. He jumped up and began pacing the kitchen floor, back and forth, waving both arms to emphasize his points. "You don't have to agree to a thing. I'll go with you jist like always to keep you out of trouble."

McCain took another swallow of coffee and snorted. "You? Keep me out of trouble?" he said. "That's a laugh."

"Look, Jericho, they could be trying to buy the ranch. Hell, we don't even know what they want," Poe pleaded.

"The railroad…" McCain began,

"…has ruined the country," Poe finished.

"Them…and the Republicans. Glad to know you agree with me."

"I don't agree with you!" Poe shouted. "For cat's sake, Jericho, if you ain't the most pig-headedest man I've ever met. I just can't see what one little meeting would…"

"Okay."

"…do to ruin the…"

"Okay."

"…country. What?"

"I said, okay," McCain stated for the third time.

"You'll go?"

"Said I would, didn't I? You going deaf in your old age?"

Rosie Poe let the dig go unchallenged, but a self-satisfied little smile indicated he was pleased to have won his point. "Well, that's more like it," he said. "When do we leave?"

McCain sighed deeply. "Might as well get it over with. We'll leave in the morning. Early, if that bad back of yours don't keep you from getting out of bed."

Ignoring the last remark as well, Poe suddenly got a sly look on his face. "You reckon to stop by Big Springs and see Kate on the way?"

McCain sat looking at his boots, not answering.

Poe studied the other man's face for a moment and pushed. "It's practically on the way."

McCain still didn't look up, but said, "Its practically fifty miles out of the way. Besides, I want to get this over with and get back. We need to run another roundup to see how many head we still have. Like as not no work will get done while we're gone, anyway. I won't tolerate slacking."

"You know she'd be glad to see you," Poe persisted.

McCain's mouth grew tight, before he answered. "She wouldn't give a hill of beans if I never came around her another day."

Poe straightened up in his chair and blurted, "Now that jist ain't so and you know it, Jericho. You and Kate were real close once."

McCain snorted. "Yeah, real close. That's why she married that rancher…Shaw…or whatever his name is."

When Legends Lived

"Duncan Shaw. And that ain't fair, Jericho," Poe said. "You know that if you'd asked her, she would've married you." Poe warmed to his subject, now. "Besides, you went riding off and for fifteen years, never so much as sent a letter to her. What was she supposed to think?"

Poe sat there for a long time and finally reached the conclusion that his partner wasn't going to respond. "Now-a-days a woman won't wait over five…ten years for a man to make up his mind, ya know. I'm surprised that Kate, being as headstrong as she is, waited as long as she did for you to ask her."

"You get something on your mind and you just keep gnawing on it don't you?" McCain responded. "And I don't know any such thing either. Anyway, how was I supposed to marry someone? I didn't have a pot to piss in or a window to throw it out of. I made less than twenty dollars a month and had to buy my own ammo. You just can't ask a woman to marry you and not be able to provide for her. What if I'd been bushwhacked or something? Then what? She was much better off married to the rancher. At least he could take care of her."

Poe stared at him with his mouth half open. "Danged if that ain't the most words I ever heard you string together at one time," he said whistling softly. "You must've really had a soft spot for Katie."

McCain sat with his head down for a moment without speaking, then slowly got out of his chair and walked out of the room without another word.

Poe stayed at the table for a long time after McCain had gone. He felt his own pangs as he thought about Kate Shaw. He'd last seen Kate four years before, when he'd gone up north to buy horses for the ranch. Though nearing forty years of age, she was still as beautiful as she was back when he first saw her. On that trip, he took a detour after selling some horses up in the Panhandle area, stopping at the Shaw ranch to say hello. He didn't stay long because old Duncan Shaw acted like he, as Rosie Poe put it, 'had a poker up his arse' all the time he was around. Poe departed after first promising he would return in the near future, then ignoring the glares of Duncan, hugged Kate and rode off, singing all the way back to Bluebonnet.

Kate was one of the smartest women he'd ever known. Tough, too. Proof was, he liked to say, in her not marrying him like he'd asked her to do so many times. Not that he hadn't spent a considerable amount of time courting her on the sly and trying to get her to accept his proposals. But Rosie Poe could see right from the start, Kate and Jericho McCain were attracted to one another from the first time they met. The funny thing was, Jericho couldn't see it. Although Poe had tried to convince him of it countless times, his friend had stubbornly refused to discuss even the possibility.

Kate's father died suddenly about two years after they arrived at Mineral Wells and, not much more than a child herself, Kate began running the store and looking after her younger sister Bethena and brother Thomas. He and J.D. McCain took to hanging out at the store and soon the three of them could be seen almost any Sunday that the two Rangers weren't out chasing bandits, picnicking on one of the many streams running off the Brazos River. He and Kate, joking and talking, J.D., sitting quietly and occasionally answering when Kate tried to draw him into the conversation. Rosie suspected he was being used by Katie to bring her and J.D. together, but his love for her was so great, he didn't care, if it meant he could be with her as well.

When Legends Lived

He used to think, *Who knows? Maybe she'll find out just how boring Jericho is and start to like me better.*

Her kid brother Thomas, was enraptured with the handsome young Ranger, J.D. McCain, and followed him everyplace he went. Even started to walk and talk like him. When Thomas was seventeen, he joined the Texas Rangers and was assigned to the San Antonio Company. Three months later, word was received that Tom had perished along with fourteen other Rangers in an ambush by Comancheros. Only one Ranger survived the massacre. The next morning, most of the small unit at Mineral Wells, to include Poe and McCain, saddled up and rode toward the Edwards Plateau, south of Brownwood. They were gone three months and word finally filtered back that the Rangers had found and annihilated the band of Comancheros responsible. When the detachment did finally return to Mineral Wells, J.D. and Rosie weren't with them. They'd been left, along with several others, to replenish the Ranger garrison at San Antonio.

Somehow, McCain blamed himself for the boy's joining the Rangers, and consequently, for his death. All of Rosie's talking couldn't change his mind and he was convinced Kate blamed him, as well. They were stationed at San Antonio, sometimes operating far into Mexico, for the next three years. It was during the third year, that they'd received news from a new replacement, Kate Hopkins was now, Mrs. Duncan Shaw. He'd said her husband owned a ranch over around Big Springs, and she'd sold the store and moved with her sister, to live there. Poe remembered how J.D. had just sat and stared straight ahead when he'd broke the news to him. Then, he'd quietly gotten up from his seat and walked out, just as he'd done earlier this night.

R.C. Morris

* * *

Light was just beginning to show in the sky to the east of Bluebonnet, when the two friends rode out the next morning. For the first time since buying the ranch, they felt a freedom they'd almost forgotten. As it was, the long journey to Amarillo was almost a pleasure, rather than the task it should've been; though the hard ground felt a little less forgiving than in past years, and sore joints didn't limber up until several hours into the next day's ride. They set a leisurely pace for themselves, and throughout the journey talked about old friends—most long departed—and times and places far away. Of course, Roosevelt Poe did most of the talking; none-the-less, both men arrived in Amarillo more at ease with themselves than they had been in years, despite the rigors of the journey.

Although Poe didn't complain, McCain saw him easing himself into the saddle each morning and favoring one side and then the other throughout the ride. He rightly assumed his partner's bad back was acting up again. Arriving just past noon on the sixth day, they went straight to the Cattlemen's Hotel and found a suite of rooms reserved in the name of Captain J.D. McCain, Texas Ranger. In spite of themselves, the two men were pleased. Within minutes, they were soaking in tubs of hot soapy water, while drinking a pitcher of cold beer.

"We've got plenty of time before we meet with that railroad man, if you want to see Doc Burnsides concerning your back," McCain told his friend.

Poe squinted at him clearly annoyed, and retorted hotly, "My back's doing nicely, thank ye very much. Besides, I don't remember inviting you to discuss any parts of my body in this conversation. For your information, I don't care how much time we got, I ain't gonna see that old horse doctor."

"Well, why not? You've been bellyach'n for a month about your back hurting and all about how you can't do any work because of it." It was clear that McCain was going to keep the pressure on. "Why don't ya just go and get it looked at?"

"I don't do any work, J.D., because somebody's got to use his brains in this business," Poe shot back.

"Well, I don't know about the second part of that, but I picked up on the part about you not doing any work," McCain said, not backing down.

"I'm not going and that's final!"

McCain stood up in the tub and reached for a towel. "If you don't beat all. I just don't see why—"

"Sawbones," Poe interrupted.

"...you don't just go and....What?"

"*Sawbones*, I said!" Poe sounded peeved, taking a deep drink from his whisky bottle. "If ya must know, I hate being around them damned sawbones." He'd lowered his voice and was almost pleading now. "You remember how it was in the war, Jericho. One day, I got me a little nick in the arm. Just a itty bitty scratch, it was. Didn't even hurt none. But the Major sent me back to get it tended to anyway. Well, there they was, jist a'sawing arm bones and leg bones off with a hack-saw lickety-split, and tossing 'em in a wagon. Aye God, Jericho! They must'a had 'bout a cord of them limbs ready to be toted off by the time I seen 'em."

McCain knew there wasn't any reasoning with him when he was like that, so he waited patiently until Poe finished blowing off steam.

Having plenty of steam left, Poe was clearly getting agitated again as he flung his arms around, sending soapsuds flying in every direction. "Ya go in there with jist a little something wrong with ya and before ya know it, you're scooting around on your butt in the middle of the floor for the rest of your life. Ya know why? 'Cause they done cut off all your arms and legs, *that's* why!"

McCain just stared, perplexed. Seeing his partner's sudden bewilderment, Roosevelt attempted to compose himself somewhat.

"Old Doc Burnsides is always a coming at me, a poke'n and a prod'n me in the back with one of them little pointee gadgets. Well, he ain't fooling me. I know what he's thinking, and I'm having no part of it. I'll jist keep all the limbs I was born with, thank-ee kindly," he said, nodding his head with finality.

McCain still stared at Poe with his mouth agape. He started to say something twice and stopped each time, as if at a loss for words. Finally, he got it out. "Tragic," he said, as if totally amazed. "If you ain't just *tragic*. Christ, Roosevelt, you've been shot full'o holes more times than I can even count, stabbed twice that I remember, stomped by your horse, fell off a cliff and had the hell beat out of you at least a dozen times over the…"

"Not that many times."

"…past twenty years. Now you tell me you're afraid of a little poke'n and prod'n? Tragic, just plumb…tragic."

"Well *that's* the way it is, and *that's* the way it's gonna stay," Poe told him stiffly as he turned around in the tub facing the wall, and spit tobacco juice at cockroaches until his friend had left the room.

By the time they'd finished cleansing themselves, the black suit McCain had sent out earlier to be cleaned was back and the two men dressed and went to find "The biggest steak in Texas."

When Legends Lived

It was just after dusk when they returned to the hotel. As they entered the lobby, a tall handsome young man in a stylishly cut suit stood up and approached them. He spoke in a cultured Eastern voice.

"Captain McCain?"

"I'm McCain. You James Packard?"

"Please, my friends call me Jim," said the well-dressed man.

McCain squinted at him for an instant. "Then I'll call you Mr. Packard until I determine if we're gonna be friends or not," he said without rancor.

Smoothly, Packard laughed. "That'll be just fine. Shall we have a drink first or get right to business?"

"Both," said Poe, a little annoyed at having been ignored up to that point.

Turning to face him, Packard said, "Will you be discussing business for Captain McCain?"

"Nope."

"Then will you be waiting in the lobby?"

"Nope."

"This is Roosevelt Poe, my business partner. We don't have any secrets," McCain said.

"I see. Will you both follow me then please?" Packard said easily, as he headed toward the stairs.

Packard's suite was equally as comfortable as the one he'd reserved for McCain and Poe. On the table sat a full bottle of a fine Kentucky bourbon and a half dozen Cuban cigars.

"Well look-ee here, Jericho. Working for the railroad appears to be lu-cra-tive, and have *some* benefits,"

McCain gave his friend a stern look of disapproval. Undeterred, and unasked, Poe sat down, lit one of the cigars and rocked back in his chair, pouring a healthy portion of the fine bourbon into one of the glasses. As Packard set about pouring McCain and himself a full shot, he used the opportunity to observe the old Ranger more closely.

Seven

"There's some kind of new wire called barbed-wire. And there are some pretty smart people working hard to invent a smaller version of the steam engine to pull a wagon. I believe we'll all live long enough to see it."

– Jim Packard, 1883

ALTHOUGH HE HID IT well, there was a sick feeling in the pit of Jim Packard's stomach. He was convinced that Randle had made a terrible mistake in his selection. *My God, he's an old man, small too.* Packard had expected someone with whom he could at least look level at in the eyes. *In fact, they're both just worn out old men.*

He forced himself to take a deep breath, determined to proceed and get back to his old job. *Well, it's not my problem, anyway. Randle selected him, so all I have to do is set up the deal and stay with him a while until he peters out. Shouldn't take too long. Then, I can go home...maybe eventually get Randle's job. The main thing, is that I have to get McCain to agree to the deal and sign on the dotted line, or I haven't fulfilled my part of the mission.*

He'd married Thomas Randle's daughter just six months earlier and had known from the beginning that it was without her father's approval. At the time, it'd seemed like a good career move because he planned to be Chief of Security by the time he was thirty, and eventually, the youngest Vice President Southern Pacific ever had. His young wife, Hattie, had proven right away to be spoiled, self-centered and just a little mean. Packard was already wondering if he'd made such a smart move after all. Still, if he successfully wrapped up this little piece of business for the railroad, he'd be back on track with his ambitious plans.

When Packard had first heard his father-in-law outline the operation, it'd sounded as if it actually had a chance of succeeding. Although he'd been Randle's son-in-law for only a short time, he'd known the older man for much longer and knew him to be cool under pressure, exercise good judgement, and had never known him to stretch the truth. Tom Randle simply didn't lie. Before committing railroad resources, Frank Chase had wanted to know the nature of the people who would, in essence, have the reputation of the railroad in their hands.

Randle had explained that the Texas Rangers, originally a militia force of battalion size, were actually formed to protect Texan's lives by assisting the Army in their fight against the Indians and marauding Mexicans. Perceived by the military to be undisciplined rogues, they'd greatly out-performed the Army in this task and gained vast respect among the state's citizens.

Once the Indians had finally been all but wiped out as a major fighting force, Governor Cook gave Major John B. Jones six additional companies of Rangers. Those companies, called the Frontier Battalion, were used to suppress lawlessness and crime throughout Texas. Attesting to his competence as a lawman, Major Jones personally gave J.D. McCain command of one of the companies and over the next decade, the battalion was stationed in some of Texas' most lawless and chaotic regions. Within a six year period, the Texas Rangers had just about closed the wild frontier.

When Legends Lived

Oh, Randle went on, that is not to say they entirely put a stop to all aspects of western attitudes about law with a gun, for that heritage of violence is so deeply implanted that it will take years before it can be changed. However, before the implementation of the Frontier Battalion the local climate was total anarchy, where every man depended solely upon himself and his ability with his Colt for protection; the six-gun was judge, jury, and in many cases, executioner. The coming of the Rangers had changed it into a climate that is now only extremely violent, but one over which the laws of an organized society can at least rule.

Randle had pointed out that because the Rangers were almost always out-numbered, a single Ranger sometimes had to subdue an entire town; or, two or three Rangers had to find and deliver – or kill – a whole band of marauders. They lived and existed in a tough segment of society, through which moved thousands of killers and thieves. The Rangers, widely spread, outnumbered, underpaid and with little gratitude from the State, were able to survive and accomplish an impossible mission due to a mystique, their growing legend, and unsurpassed skill with a gun.

Randle had also pointed out that Rangers are a ruthless breed – plain and simple; that most of them are killers and they have to be in order to survive. Killing, he explained, is an almost casual occurrence, especially in the western regions of Texas. What sets them apart from the lawless killers is that it was their code to always give fair warning to the criminal elements, then strike without mercy, never giving an order twice. He went on to say that they are given vast latitude in the way they carry out their duties and are subject to little accountability for their actions while upholding Texas law.

Additionally, they don't seem to worry much about prisoners because jails and legitimate courts are usually miles away. Often a lone Ranger capturing a fleeing outlaw in a hostile area, will like as not, simply shoot or hang him on the spot, rather than risk escorting him back through dangerous miles of unfriendly territory for trial. Since their existence, Randle explained, there had not been a single instance of corruption or dishonesty by a Ranger.

He'd told them the Rangers exercise an economy of efforts, meaning they tended to hate the deviousness of the law that allowed known killers and thieves to go free. In their early days, after they spent long periods of time tracking down and capturing notorious gunmen and outlaws, such as King Fisher, they'd had to stand by helplessly and watch as the outlaws went free due to corruption or technicalities. When local politics, and sometimes the law itself, hampered their work in cleaning up a criminal element, they soon found that a bullet cut a much straighter line than the law system. Randle said that when Major Jones died, most of the principal captains, including Captain McCain, resigned. Randle remarked that McCain and some of his Ranger friends ended up buying a horse ranch over near Odessa. Packard remembered that his father-in-law also told them the drought had come and nearly wiped out their ranch.

Now, attempting to hide his disappointment by putting on his best smile, Packard said, "Captain, the railroad wants to hire your services. We've been having a lot of trouble lately with a few outlaws who are destroying railroad property and killing our employees. Naturally, we want to protect them, along with the rest of the citizens of Texas."

McCain looked at him with hard button-like eyes, making no response. Poe was busy studying the ash at the tip of his cigar.

Bravely, Packard continued. "I've been authorized to pay you your expenses, and one thousand dollars each, for putting an end to this illegal activity by the two groups I'll identify to you. Plus, we'll pay one hundred dollars for any additional enemy of the railroad you bring in, or terminate. Dead *or* alive, no questions will be asked. Your actions will be fully backed by the Federal Government, and your methods won't be scrutinized. I have with me a letter from the Governor of Texas, authorizing Captain J.D. McCain and five men to be named later, to act as Special Agents of the Southern Pacific Railroad in the interests of the United States of America. All local and Federal officers are instructed to cooperate with you and lend their support in your effort."

Packard paused. Still, McCain made no response and Poe was now studying the bottom of his whiskey glass. No longer as sure of himself as he'd been initially, Packard took a deep breath.

"The two groups identified, number between ten and twenty men each at any given time. One of them is led by a brut named William Reid. His men call him Bloody Bill. Let me assure you, he is. I have the names of some of the killers that usually ride with him. Some are white, as he is, the rest are Mexicans, Indians and half-breeds. My list may not be complete."

Plunging on, he said, "The second group is somewhat less definitive. We don't know the name of the group's leader. All we know is that more than likely, he's a half-breed—with blue eyes. This report was received from a Pinkerton detective we hired to guard one of the railroad's payrolls. There were twelve heavily armed men on the three car train that was derailed just outside of Mineral Wells. All of them were butchered—some partially skinned. Most of them had a cut running down across their faces."

He saw them stiffen slightly and for the first time, Packard sensed he'd somehow gotten their attention, and hurried on. "The Pinkerton guard was dying when he was discovered and pretty much out of his head," he hastily went on. "Before he died, he was able to tell our people that the outlaw's leader appeared to have the same distinguishable scar running down the right side of his face, across the bridge of his nose, ending at the corner of his mouth. It was cut into the faces of all the victims."

Poe and McCain were now sitting straight up in their chairs, unmoving, staring intently at Packard.

Ah, something I said?

"That's about all we know," Packard concluded. "Do we have a deal?"

McCain and Poe looked at one another for a moment without speaking. Then McCain said, "I'll give it some consideration. You run on back to St. Louie…or wherever you come from… and tell Mr. Chase I'll let him know in a spell."

"I'm afraid I can't do that, sir. I must get your answer before I leave here."

McCain stood, leaving his untouched glass of bourbon on the table. "Then wait here 'til I make up my mind. I'll send you a letter from Bluebonnet."

He walked out followed by Rosie Poe, who downed McCain's drink and pocketed the remaining cigars before departing.

* * *

Arriving at their room, Poe whistled low and said, "That was surely a piss pot full-o-money, Jericho."

When McCain didn't answer, he went on. "Quite a nice looking young man, wasn't he? You could tell he was educated, too."

"An educated fool is even more dangerous than an ignorant one."

Poe squinted in his direction and McCain knew he was about to be the target of one of Poe's caustic remarks.

"Why is it that anyone you ever met, who is clean, wears nice clothes, and appears to have plenty of money, is plainly a fool? Makes a man wonder just how all them damned fools ever got to be so well off, don't it?"

McCain didn't answer, so Poe immediately changed subjects, satisfied he'd made his point. "Guess it's to be pretty dangerous work anyway, huh?"

McCain sensed what was really on his mind, saying, "It's the face-cutter—Scar."

"Yeah, I know. I sure as hell do," Poe said. "That's a bit of business that I wouldn't mind clearing up before traveling to the other side."

After continuing to discuss it for another hour, they reached no conclusions, and finally went to bed.

* * *

Saddled up and headed out of Amarillo as the sun was just coming up, Poe took up the subject once again, as though they'd only recently dropped it. McClain did his best to ignore Poe's persistence. Less than a mile out of town they heard a horse trotting up behind them, and were surprised to see the young railroad man gallop up.

"Going somewhere?" McCain said.

"With you," replied Packard grinning.

McCain snorted and said, "Like hell."

Determined not to let this scruffy old man intimidate him,

Packard drew himself up straighter in the saddle. "Look, if you won't let me ride with you, I'll just have to follow you."

"And I'll just shoot you out of your saddle," said McCain dryly.

Suddenly tired of the way this man looked at him like he was something he'd just scraped off the bottom of his boots, Packard leaned forward on his saddle-horn and stared at McCain for a few seconds, then calmly replied, "You do what you have to do, Captain. I'll do what I have to. Right now, I can't leave without your answer."

Taken aback by the young man's sudden display of backbone, McCain replied tartly, "Just stay out of my way." He turned his mount and rode off, and as Packard and Poe followed, Poe winked at the young railroad man.

"This may turn out to be a very interesting little trip."

His remark was followed by a little laugh Packard was beginning to find somewhat annoying.

For most of the first day, the trio rode without talking much, Jim Packard writing in a small, black leather book he kept bound in oilskin. By the second day of the return trip, young Packard and Rosie Poe were talking like old friends, much to McCain's disgust. He rode mile after silent mile, clearly a man in a foul mood.

Having none of that, Poe attempted to draw McCain into their conversations. "Jericho, maybe we ought to git out of the horse business. Mr. Packard thinks horses are going to become obsolete in a couple of years."

"And git into what?" McCain said sarcastically. "A general store?"

"Cattle! We ought to git into the cattle business. People are always going to eat cows!" Poe sounded excited.

When Legends Lived

"And just what do you suppose those same people are going to ride to git them cows to market, Roosevelt?" McCain said, followed by his famous snort.

Poe looked to Packard for help.

"There may be a lot of truth to what Mr. Poe's saying, Captain," Jim interjected. "Back east they've invented something they call a windmill. It pumps water from deep-wells. No more worry about droughts, it seems. Some people think this might open up dry areas like western Texas for farmers and such."

McCain spit in disgust.

Seems like he has the same feelings for farmers as he does for the railroad, Packard thought.

Undeterred, Packard went on. "Also, there's some kind of new wire called barbed-wire. It's supposed to keep stock in—or out of—certain areas."

Noting the shock of the two old Rangers, he continued. "There are some pretty smart people working hard to invent a smaller version of the same type engine trains now use, too. If they can do it, many folks think they can build a small wagon that doesn't even need horses to pull it along."

McCain snorted, louder this time. "That's ridiculous."

"Well anyway, that's probably a long time away," Packard said. "But I believe we will all live long enough to see it."

"God forbid," said McCain.

Jim Packard and Poe dropped back and talked without pause for the rest of the day. McCain, feeling as though he was carrying a heavy burden, rode ahead and silently brooded. His discussion with Poe the evening before they departed the ranch, was still fresh in his mind. It'd been years since he'd even seen Kate. Then why did the mere mention of her name cause him such anguish? Did she still hate him for the loss of her young brother? Did Bethena? Probably "yes" on both counts.

Anyhow, he reminded himself almost angrily, Kate Shaw was a married woman. He would not dishonor her, or himself, by thinking of her in these terms. *He – would – not!*

Still, her face swam before him as the endless miles wore on.

Periodically, the talking would abate and Jim Packard would cease writing in his leather-bound book to marvel at the greatness of the country they were riding through. He'd heard comments about the severity of the current drought and wondered how the landscape would look if all the creeks they passed were flowing, the dead vegetation was green and the ground covered with the famous blue flowers he'd heard so much about.

"How do people live in this heat and dust?" he said suddenly.

"Hot enough to make cactus sweat, ain't it?" Poe chuckled softly. "It's a hard land boy, but uncommon to be *this* dry. Some years it's not unheard of to even have people washed away in flash floods."

Packard gawked at him in disbelief.

The older man chuckled again. "It's gospel. Several times a year some poor cowboy will hunker down in a dry-wash to find shelter from the wind. Then comes a frog-strangling rain someplace miles away, and suddenly he looks up to find twenty feet of muddy water hurling down on him. Few survive something like that."

Poe warmed to his tale now. "Two years ago, the entire Hogan family was crossing one of them washes over near Odessa. Five of 'em in a wagon. Damn gully was dry as a cornbread fart and not a cloud in the sky either. Quicker'n you can say scat—they was gone. Wagon, family, team of oxen, the whole caboodle.

When Legends Lived

Never found hide nor hair of 'em. Probably floated 'em all the way to the gulf."

Young Packard looked horrified, which was exactly what Poe had intended.

Stopping for camp that evening, Poe got a good look at the new Colt .45 Jim Packard wore in a buttoned down flap-type holster, high under his left armpit.

"Can you use that thing?"

"I am a crack shot, sir," replied the young man, without modesty.

"Show me."

With that, Jim pointed to a small limb sticking out about ten inches, nearly thirty feet away. Poe watched as Packard unsnapped the flap and slipped the Colt from his holster. Shifting his feet about shoulder width apart, he slowly raised the weapon, carefully sighted along the barrel, and gently squeezed the trigger. At the loud report, the limb snapped and fell to the ground. Packard turned back to Poe proudly.

"How's that?"

Poe took time to spit, before he turned away. "Even a blind pig can find an acorn once in a while," he muttered over his shoulder.

"What?"

"A fine shot!" Poe said, louder this time. "Just the kind of hit-miss target-shooting that's sure to git ya killed the first time ya have to use that damned thing."

He chuckled dryly as he turned back toward the camp site.

"Just hold on. Wait a minute. What do you mean by that?" Jim half-shouted.

"Just what I said. Out here you git it out real fast and put it away real slow. All that dammed pointing, breathing deep and such, is just likely to make that young wife of yor'n a widow."

"How do you do it then…?" Jim blurted out. He'd been forced to check himself, almost saying "old man," for Poe's caustic remarks had turned his cheeks red with embarrassment.

Without answering, Poe bent down and picked up a rock the size of a small potato. Walking a few steps in front of Packard, he suddenly flung it hard and straight, as one might throw a baseball. Before the rock had traveled twenty feet, the evenings stillness was broken by the loud report of Poe's heavy Walker Colt, and the rock literally disintegrated in mid-flight. Poe stared at the spot where the stone disappeared for just a second, then nodded his head, smacked his lips, and walked back toward the area the horses were tethered.

Packard stood frozen where he was standing, his mouth agape, stunned at what he just witnessed. McCain, who'd also witnessed the shooting exhibition, and knew Poe had always been a fine hand with a pistol, smiled thinly to himself, pleased that his partner's shooting skills remained sharp.

"Will you show me how to do that?" Packard shouted, running after Poe.

For the next hour, the two men discussed the fine points of shooting throughout their meager meal, right up to bedtime. Then preparing to settle in for the night, McCain and Poe laid out their bedrolls on the ground near the fire. Though it was still relatively warm, the seasoned veterans knew that when the sun finally did set, the night would become bitterly cold. They looked at one another in amusement as the young railroad man picked a level spot some distance from the fire and spread a single blanket out on the ground, laid down upon it, placed the second blanket beneath his head, and began to write.

As Poe unrolled his blankets, a small gift-wrapped package fell out. Although he quickly tried to cover it, it was already too late.

"What's that?"

"Why, Jericho...that's uh...a present for Miss Rita at Paco's. It's a genuine mother-of-pearl toilet-kit," Poe answered proudly.

Jericho gawked at his partner in amazement. "I just don't understand you, Roosevelt. You bought a present for a *whore?*" he said incredulously.

"And, why not?" Poe sounded amazed. "You gotta reward people for doing a good job."

"Roosevelt...not a *whore*," Jericho said pointedly, still dumbfounded that anyone would spend hard earned money to buy a present for one of Paco's soiled ladies of the evening. "A whore don't do a *good* job. They don't do a *bad* job. They just do whatever it is you want them to do, then you pay them and you *leave*. Period."

"Jericho, I never really noticed before, but you got a very narrow way of looking at things." Poe was looking at McCain like he was from another world.

"I've got a narrow way of looking at things? I've got...?" McCain stopped and just stared some more at Poe, clearly exasperated.

Seemingly unaffected by his partner's disdain, Poe continued making his bed for the night, laid down on it, and gazed up at his partner. Finally, he said, "Jericho, if Sabi or one of the other hands worked real hard rounding up our horses and driving them to market, would you give them a bonus?"

"Of course, I would. But what bearing could that possibly have on this conversation?" McCain fired back.

"That's what I mean about your narrow vision, Jericho. These ladies are dealing the only product they have to bargain with, and when they do it well, they need to be rewarded. That's all I'm saying. Jist give them a little bonus for providing a good product." Poe looked satisfied, like he'd made an important point.

McCain often took to wondering how he'd ever put up with the antics of his old friend for so many years. As far as he was concerned, they didn't have the least thing in common.

This was closer to the truth than even he realized. Although they were roughly the same age and stature, Poe actually being about two inches taller than McCain and several pounds heavier, the two men were about as opposite as any two people could possibly be. McCain was a quiet, serious, no nonsense type with an explosive temper.

Ever the philosopher, Moses Penny would often comment, "still water runs deep." It was a comment the black man liked to make about the man he admired most in the world; Captain J.D. McCain.

As far as McCain was concerned, the less a person said, the better. The best way to bring his anger to bear was to sit around "shooting off your mouth" all the time. Often when Poe commenced one of his lengthy discussions, McCain would simply get up and without comment, walk away, leaving his old friend talking.

"The Captain," as most people called McCain, wasn't above having a little snort of liquor once in a while, but unlike his partner Rosie Poe, no one could remember ever seeing him drunk. That in itself was remarkable, in an age when men were just expected to periodically get falling down, crawling home, puking on the floor drunk, at least once or twice a month.

When Legends Lived

McCain's idea of conversation was the less said, the better. Poe on the other hand, loved to talk.

"That Rosie Poe," according to Moses Penny, "shore do love to palaver."

Additionally, Poe was slow to anger, considered laziness a virtue, and had never met a stranger. He was even friendly to the Mexicans. It wasn't that McCain mistreated them, but rather, that he treated them in the same curt, business-like manner that he treated everybody else he knew—which was to say, in a way, that the easy-going, agreeable Mexican population couldn't quite comprehend.

While Captain McCain was a short spoken, no-nonsense type, Roosevelt Poe had an opinion on just about everything and everybody. He liked to read and generally knew a little something about almost any subject that happened to come up. Most of the time, his knowledge about the subject was just enough to stir-up some controversy, or at the least, completely confuse his audience. To make matters worse, he had a tendency to fill in the blanks of what he was unable to remember about a particular subject, which he probably never knew in the first place, with some very imaginative facts he was convinced could become true, if given half a chance.

Often the points he tried to make were elusive to begin with, and like as not, even his subject would change in mid-sentence. At that time, he would likely throw in a few long words he had learned somewhere along the line – or just made up on the spot – to further impress his audience.

Poe's opinions and questions came so fast and were sometimes so interwoven, that those around him could only grunt and nod, unable to think fast enough to keep up. With all the grunting and nodding going on, most folks who met him, were convinced Roosevelt Poe was a great thinker. The truth was that Rosie was really just putting them on. He loved to tell a story, and when there was no one to tell the story to, he often took to talking to his horse, and occasionally, even to himself.

"All it takes to be a good liar, is a good memory," he was often heard to remark.

Now, still shaking his head in wonder, McCain turned his back to Poe and pretended to sleep.

Taking the opportunity of the lull in the conversation, Jim Packard, for the next hour, asked question after question of Poe about how to improve his shooting ability. "What's that old pistol you carry?"

Poe slid it from its holster beneath his head and passed it over. "It's an original Walker Colt, young man. A Ranger by the name of John Walker went back east almost forty years ago and conflabbed with Samual Colt. Together, they came up with this piece. It's the finest shooting instrument ever made."

"Cap and ball, aren't they?"

Poe laughed. "Even worse than that—nipples. But Jericho and me had 'em modified a few years ago. Sent 'em back to Saint Joe, Missouri where we heard a German feller had a young gunsmith working for him—a wizard with such things. He re-chambered 'em, fitted 'em for cartridges, and fine-tuned 'em to beat the band. Don't really know all the modifications he made, but when we got 'em back, they practically fired themselves. Best side-arm I ever handled."

After a while, the conversation turned to Jim Packard and his leather bound book. "What's that book you're always writing in?" Poe finally said.

"It's an official account of what we're doing here," Jim answered. "Someday, it might be important to somebody."

Poe said with a small chuckle, "Well, just be sure you spell my name right and if you're gonna tell any lies about me and old Jericho there, make sure they're whoppers, hee, hee."

He quickly dropped off to sleep, leaving the young railroad man to wonder at all the sounds of life going on in the darkness surrounding him, punctured at regular intervals by the loud snores of Poe and McCain. At last, Packard also drifted off into a fitful and uncomfortable sleep.

* * *

Taking up where he'd left off the previous night, Packard's tutoring continued throughout the next three days, as Poe instructed the young railroad man on the finer points of off-hand shooting. Their route was peppered throughout the days and evenings by the report of Packard's Colt.

By the end of the third day Poe drew abreast and told McCain quietly, "That feller is gitting to be a fair hand with a gun. He may not be Ranger good yet, but he's certainly better than your average run-of-the-mill cowhand."

McCain nodded, squinting at the sun-baked trail that stretched ahead of them. "Keep working with him Rosie. We may need his gun before this is over."

At first, Samuel Thompson wasn't sure of where he was or what had happened to him. His hearing was gradually returning and he had a metallic taste deep in his throat, but he couldn't feel his legs. He vaguely recalled that he'd just told his daughter about old man Patton stepping into a bucket of milk and the three of them were laughing, just like they used to before Teresa left for back East. The force of the heavy round had lifted Thompson out of the wagon seat, propelling him onto the rocks along side the trail. He never heard the report of the rifle and must've blacked out for just a short time.

From where he was lying, he could see his son struggling with someone much larger, but he couldn't move to help him. It was almost like everything was happening in a dream, as he watched the larger figure almost casually lift a wood hatchet and split his son's skull. From a far-off place, he could now hear someone screaming.

It was a woman. He felt he should know her and fought to remember.

High-topped rawhide boots moved into his line of vision. Rough hands grasped his shirt and hoisted him into a sitting position against a large boulder. His body felt lifeless and although he couldn't move, he felt no pain. *Only tired. Very tired.* As he opened his eyes, he was looking into the bluest eyes he'd ever seen. Otherwise, the man squatting in front of him appeared to be an Apache. He had a hideous scar running across the entire length of his face and Thompson's mind shivered as he realized who he was looking at.

"Hello, Mr. Thompson. How are we feeling today?" the man with the scar said pleasantly. "What did you do with the gold from the sale?"

Thompson could clearly see the sprawled body of his son lying beneath the overturned wagon, and knew by the way he was laying, that Todd was dead. The screaming had stopped and he could hear his daughter whimpering somewhere behind the squatting figure, but he was still unable to move even slightly in order to see around the man.

After several attempts, he painfully answered through his teeth, "You ignorant heathen, haven't you ever heard of *banks*? It's in a *bank* in Abilene."

"Now, now, Mr. Thompson. There's no reason for name calling. It's just a business deal, that's all," Scar said amicably. "By the way, we met your daughter. Nice lady. I hope you don't mind if we invite her to our little party—do you?"

Scar slowly rose and moved out of Thompson's line of vision. He could see one of the men was on top of her making humping motions as five others crowed around, watching. Two, appeared to be white, the others Apache. Thompson watched in horror as Scar slipped an evil-looking knife from his belt and slowly sharpened a small tree limb, smiling at him all the while. Then he walked to where Teresa was lying and, kicking the man off the top of her, stuck it's point deeply into her soft belly.

That was when Sam Thompson began to also scream.

Eight

JENNY WAS ALONE AT the school, finishing up correcting test papers she'd collected earlier. As she went through the routine motions, she began to lament about how unhappy she was—*in this stinking town.* Jenny loved life and felt as though her present environment was slowly strangling her to death. As she pondered her predicament, Jenny thought about the circumstances which had brought her to this point in her life. Her father, Reverend Person, had strict and unbending beliefs; he'd made Jenny's life unbearable and she'd been determined to get away from him as quickly as she possibly could.

Two years ago she'd sneaked out of her bedroom window and met a young cowboy at their secret place down by the river. It wasn't long before she'd achieved what she'd set out to accomplish—she was pregnant. Her plan had been to get with child, force him to marry her, and take her away from El Paso. *Anywhere* away from there. Maybe even San Francisco or some place like that.

But that's when things began to fall apart and before she knew it, the young cowboy was off for parts unknown, leaving her alone with a child on the way, and no one to pin it on. However, being resourceful was one of Jenny's long-suits, and having noticing the new deputy had eyes for her, quickly began to cultivate his attention. In a short time, they began to meet in that same secret location—and things just naturally happened.

Deputy Rosco Bookbinder had acted pleased when she'd told

him she was going to have his baby, and naively insisted they get married right away. She'd "reluctantly" given in and the hurried ceremony concluded with little fan-fare or publicity. At first, it'd been sort of exciting being married to the Deputy Sheriff of El Paso. Especially after Rosco killed those two Hacket brothers. Just about everybody had come up to her to talk after that, and Jenny dearly loved the popularity and attention. But it gradually wore off and people's attention turned to other things. When it did, Jenny sought attention from some of the local cowboys from the surrounding ranches and while many were tempted, the fact that she'd married the fast-handed Rosco Bookbinder—who'd laid the Hacketts low in a tenth of a second—had a sobering effect on their passion for her.

When the baby had just begun to show, Jenny secretly went to the old Negro woman who lived on the south edge of the town. She'd saved the required fifteen dollars by shaving a few dollars here and there from her household food money, and knocked on the old woman's door just after dark, in her third month of pregnancy. The old woman had taken her money, given her a foul smelling concoction, and told her to drink it just before going to bed. Jenny did as instructed, and had become violently sick for two days, then the baby had aborted, to a vast outpouring of sympathy by the town folks and local ranchers. Ah, attention. It was like a tonic. That had been short lived, too, and now, once again, Jenny was bored and sick to death of El Paso.

* * *

Roosevelt Poe, who'd always had the sharpest vision of the two, saw the buzzards first. The mid-day sun had become unendurable and the three men were thinking about finding shelter from its intense heat, until the hottest part of the day had passed. Then McCain noticed him looking at a spot on the horizon and following his line of sight, spied the lazy circling patterns the huge scavengers made in the sky. The partners silently looked at one another and with no other form of communication altered their course, traveling as fast as it was possible to travel in the intense heat, toward that graceful dance of death being performed in the distant sky.

Topping a small rise, an overturned wagon came into their view first. Grasshopper snorted and fought the bit as McCain pulled his rifle from its scabbard. Packard watched in amazement, as without a word being spoken, the two men split, Poe gliding to the right and McCain to the left. He couldn't believe these two professional man-hunters were the same bickering old men he'd listened to for the past three days discussing the ridiculous point of whether to give a whore a gift, or not. Jim Packard stuck with Poe as he silently moved around the flank. Guns ready, Poe and McCain entered the area from opposite directions and found three bodies; a large man and the nude bodies of two mutilated children.

Packard instantly felt the gorge rise in his throat as he fought down the urge to flee the scene. Images flooded his mind of the time when he was a boy, and his father took him to Chicago on business. The business had taken them to the vast Chicago stock pens, and they had visited the adjacent slaughter houses. It'd upset him so badly that he'd had nightmares for a week afterward.

My God, his mind screamed as he looked frantically around. *My God, no! It's like a slaughterhouse.*

With his finger, Poe made a circle in the air which Packard

supposed meant he'd check the area, and was suddenly gone. McCain quickly knelt and checked the boy and then the girl for signs of life, with the demeanor of a man who already knew the answer. There was dried blood everywhere, and the giant turkey buzzards had been at work for some time. The overpowering stench of decaying flesh assaulted his sense of smell, and still fighting the urge to be sick, Packard nervously scanned the bushes around them. McCain continued to squat quietly, meticulously inspecting the horror of the scene. The constant buzzing of huge green flies seemed to grow louder and louder in the late afternoon sun, drowning out all other sounds—and Jim Packard desperately fought for self-control.

He hadn't heard nor seen Poe since he'd slipped into the sagebrush and cactus plants on foot. It seemed like an awfully long time ago, but he knew it had only been a moment. The sorrel mare stood where Poe had left it, reins dragging the ground, nervously stomping the dust at its feet. Packard had the uncanny feeling that Crazy Horse and the whole Sioux nation could come charging out of the bushes at any time. He also had the notion that if something like that happened, that damn horse would probably stand right there and wait until Poe returned.

Apparently unconcerned about Poe's safety, McCain spoke softly from somewhere behind him. "Bring me some blankets from the animals."

Grateful to be away from the horrific sight, Packard moved to the horses where he finally gave in to his urge to purge. Over and over the heaving sounds came, gradually becoming drier and drier, until finally, they faded away entirely. After a few minutes Packard returned with the blankets, looking pale and shaken.

"Stand watch," McCain ordered as he swiftly moved to where

the old man was propped up against a rock. Complying, Packard gratefully turned his back on the scene once more, and tried to think of other things.

"This one's alive," he heard McCain say quietly. "Sam? Sam Thompson, can you hear me?"

Samuel Thompson slowly opened his eyes and blinked.

"Bring me a canteen!" McCain said in a voice that sounded like he was used to giving orders.

When Packard returned with the canteen, McCain was busy examining Thompson's injuries. He held Thompson's head and allowed him to swallow a few drops of the water.

Thompson coughed and whispered, "Don't…worry about… me Captain. I know the score."

"Who was it, Sam?" McCain said.

"The face-cutter…Scar…ambushed us. Never did see…him," Sam croaked. "Back's broke…couldn't move. Made…me watch what…they did to Teresa."

A dry cough — another cough. Blood with bubbles in it was running from the corner of Thompson's mouth. "Took… hours…then…they killed her. Can hear her… screaming even now. Be glad when…I'm dead. No more…screaming."

Another fit of coughing, followed by more gushing blood from Thompson's mouth and nose.

McCain didn't look up but heard Poe silently coming up behind him. He turned to Packard. "Give him a few more drops of water. Be careful not to give him too much." He walked over to where Poe waited, and though they talked in low tones, Jim Packard could still make out most of what was said.

"Looks like six horses, Jericho. Maybe four—five hours ago."

"Thompson said it was Scar," McCain replied softly.

"Can't prove it by me. One of the mounts had a small half-moon shaped dent in the right front hoof," Poe told him. "If I see it again, I'll know it. They moved off to the northwest, Jericho. Toward Big Springs."

The two men looked at one another for a few moments sharing their fears—Kate.

"Thompson's back was broken by the round. Big slug—probably a .50 caliber," said McCain. "No way we can move him. He's got maybe a couple of hours left. Might even last through the night. I'll stay with him, then take the bodies to his ranch. You go warn Kate and the ranches around Big Springs."

"McCain!" Thompson yelled.

They went to the man and knelt beside him.

"McCain, I want...you to take my kids...home," cough, weaker this time. "Promise me you...will...get...that animal," Thompson whispered. "Give me...a gun. Leave. You don't...have enough... horses...for...all. Send someone...back...for me."

McCain looked into the dying man's pleading eyes, then went to his saddle bags and withdrew an old Navy Colt. He returned and placed it in Thompson's right hand. As realization sunk in, Packard watched in horror as McCain positioned the hand on the rock, the large pistol muzzle only inches from the injured man's face.

"Thanks, J.D. Now *git*...take my kids...*home*."

They prepared the bodies for transport by first wrapping them in the blankets and tying each with a rope. Then they placed the bodies over the saddle-horns of McCain's and Packard's mounts. Poe would be spared the added burden because he'd be traveling hard in the opposite direction.

"The Colorado's about three hours ride west of here," McCain informed them, thinking about the safety of numbers. "We can stay together until then. Should be able to get there by dark. We can hold up there tonight, then you can light a shuck for Big Springs in the morning and me and Jim will take the children's bodies to the Thompson spread."

Poe nodded his agreement and they started off, Poe riding far ahead of the other two men, his eyes slowly scanning the landscape, holding his rifle lying across the pommel of his saddle. Fifteen minutes into the ride McCain spotted Poe riding toward them, leading one of the horses from Thompson's wagon. As they hastily loaded the two bodies onto the spare horse, they were startled by the faint report of a firearm from the direction in which they had just come. No one said anything as they were left with their own thoughts about Thompson and his final moments alone.

They arrived at their destination on the Colorado River just before dusk, nearly the entire journey made without talking. The once mighty river was shallow, and they could see they would have no difficulty finding a fording place the following morning. No one felt like talking as Poe set about gathering dry wood for a fire that would produce little smoke. McCain unsaddled the horses, watered, and then rubbed them down as Packard put on the coffee pot and covered the bodies with a canvas tarp, carried for such emergencies. Then, fully clothed, they took turns jumping into one of the few remaining water holes left in the river, happy to clean the layers of dust from themselves. In the hot dry evening air, their garments were dry within a matter of minutes.

As they settled in for the evening McCain spoke to Packard for the first time since they'd found the bodies. "You got the names of those hombres riding with Scar?"

The question took the young man by surprise. He fumbled

When Legends Lived

with his oil-skinned packet, then from his shirt pocket retrieved a small slip of paper on which he wrote the outlaw's names and passed them over to McCain.

The next hour was spent planning what Poe and McCain knew would be a long and dangerous expedition.

"The railroad will let us have four more men, not counting you and me," Poe said. "Moses Penny is in. He wouldn't let you get out of spitting distance of him, if he knowed you was about to git into a ruckus. That's leaves three more. I heard Stump Henry went to work for Kate about two years ago. Maybe he's still there. I could feel him out about joining up with us, for the duration of the run."

They both remembered the times Stump had been on previous runs with them after Scar and other outlaws, during the old days. He'd said many times during those chases, "I'd give ten years of my life to git that bastard lined up in my sights, just one time," tenderly patting the stock of his old Sharps rifle. Maybe he still felt that way.

"One of the Clayborne boys returned from El Paso last month. Said Jake Kellog was dealing blackjack at one of the saloons there," McCain told them.

Jake had also ridden with them in the Texas Rangers. He was several years younger than Poe and McCain and both men remembered McCain saying, "Jake walks a fine line between being a Ranger and being one of the men Rangers hang." A few years before, Kellog had gotten into some trouble with the Ranger brass and had just up and quit. He stopped by Bluebonnet once, full of ideas about how to get rich without having to work too hard for it. After that, he'd dropped out of sight until the news from the Clayborne kid.

"Jake's a good man to have with you in case of trouble," Poe said. "Where we're going, there's sure to be plenty of that."

Packard sat listening, without speaking. While he was pleased Captain McCain was likely to accept the railroad's offer, he was disturbed at the casual manner in which the two old Rangers had placed the gun in the dying man's hand and just rode off, seemingly unconcerned, leaving him to blow his own brains out.

What manner of men are these people? he thought. *I've got to get out of this country, back to civilization.* Which also meant, back to Hattie, he reflected. *That's a problem I've still got to face.*

They rapidly went through several more names and after a short discussion, discarded each, leaving the decision on the final name until a future time. Poe and McCain agreed to meet at their ranch as soon as Poe could get to Kate's ranch and return to Bluebonnet. They decided that McCain would take the bodies to Thompson's ranch, swing by the ranch and pick up Poe and Moses Penny, then head to El Paso where they hoped to find Jake Kellog. They figured McCain's trip would take the longest to accomplish, for like as not, he'd have to stay for the burying. An hour before dawn, the men were in the saddle.

"Take care," McCain told his old friend, looking into his eyes.

"You, as well," Poe answered, not blinking.

He rode off, followed by Packard who now had his own horse back, thanks to Poe's finding the wagon-horse on which to transport the bodies. McCain, leading the horse loaded with the bodies of Todd and Teresa Thompson, started off on the lonely journey to the Circle-T and the thankless task of returning the remains of two children to their mother. Neither man looked back.

Nine

> *"The things a man does, don't count for that much. It's the reason he believes he done them, that's important."*
> – Roosevelt Poe, 1882

EL PASO WAS STILL a rowdy cow town, struggling to become respectful. The large cattle herds that literally exploded after the Civil War had begun to dry up, and the Salt Wars had been over for several years. The timely arrival of the new railroad turned the town into a shipping center for all of the ranches in the area, and had given the town just the shot in the arm it needed to maintain its growth for the next decade

With the railroad came the card sharks, riffraff, and gunmen that always seemed to follow the rails. To off-set that unsavory crowd of folks, came the lawmen. With the lawmen came wives, sweethearts, teachers, store owners, and churches. A church was usually viewed by certain elements as the beginning of the end, and when one was built in many a town in the west, old timers could be heard to say, "Time to move on. It's getting too civilized around here."

That wasn't to say there wasn't the usual monthly shootout on one of the main streets running through the town. Or that someone wasn't occasionally fished out of the watering trough where he'd been pushed after being robbed and having his throat cut. But, all in all, things were slowing down, as the schools and shops went up in ever increasing numbers. At least things weren't nearly as bad as they were just a few short years before Dallas Stoudenmire became the City Marshall.

Stoudenmire had been well respected by the community and given a wide berth by the unscrupulous element of El Paso. When Doc Manning and his two brothers killed Stoudenmire over a long-running feud, the town council brought in a tough and violent lawman by the name of John Brockman. Hardly anyone ever called him anything except "Silent John."

Silent John had been in the war and served as sheriff of several Colorado mining towns. Later he worked as a deputy for the Earps in Tombstone, Arizona. There were some that said he was too rough on El Paso's citizens. Still others maintained, what was a few split scalps as opposed to being shot full of holes? Silent John always carried the short "Billy-Club" given to him by a constable from Chicago. He kept it in plain sight, hanging from his wrist by a leather string. The locals referred to the appendage as "Silent John's piss-Elm club."

Shortly after taking over as Sheriff of El Paso, Silent John Brockman hired two young deputies whom had previously worked as his deputies in the mining camp at Cripple Creek, Colorado. One of those deputies was Rosco Bookbinder. He was a tall slender young man, always dressed neatly in a snow white shirt, black broadcloth vest, a matching black hat, and two of the new Colt .45 six-shooters that were becoming so popular. Those that saw the shootout between the young deputy and the two Hacket brothers shortly after he became Silent John's deputy, talked about it for years afterward.

Local lore said the Hackets entered El Paso, having passed the sign at the edge of town telling travelers to check their side arms straight away at the sheriff's office. Instead, they proceeded directly to the saloon and began drinking and trying to pick fights with other patrons, none of whom wore guns. Silent John was away on business, leaving Bookbinder to run things while he was gone. Jimmy Guntherson, the son of old "Gunny" Guntherson who owned the livery stable, burst into the barbershop where the young deputy was getting his weekly haircut.

"The Hackets are in the Blue Garter drinking! They're wearing their guns and starting trouble, Rosco!" he cried.

From beneath a wet towel, Rosco muttered, "Thanks Jimmy. Tell Pop Martin at the general store to give you a sweet water, on me." Then closed his eyes and finished getting his trim.

A short time later the brothers decided to head across the railroad tracks to the "Stables," a sporting house on the Mexican side of town. It was just as they were leaving the Blue Garter that Rosco encountered them.

"In town for a little fun, boys?"

The Hacket clan had shown up around El Paso in the years immediately following the Civil War. The war's end had brought a lot of their kind to Texas. They were known to be a tough bunch and mostly folks just steered clear of them, if at all possible. There was the old man, Gus; his four sons, Pat, Hank, Clinton, and Jass. There were also two cousins, but they mainly didn't come to town. The two Hackets in town that day were Hank and Clinton, both known to have mean streaks and quick to reach for their firearms.

Unnoticed by the two brothers, Rosco had slowly positioned himself so that the late afternoon sun was in the eyes of the two men. The brothers, being large rough men raised on whiskey and fighting, clearly didn't think much of the neatly dressed, slightly built youth standing before them.

"As a matter of fact, we are," the one called Hank, replied belligerently. "What's it to ya?"

"I'm Deputy Bookbinder. It seems to me that you've forgotten to check in your guns, amigos." The young deputy seemed unafraid, patiently explaining in a manner one might address school children.

"I don't give up my guns to every horse-shit town sheriff that wants them," replied the ill-tempered Hank, slightly turning his body to the side to present a smaller target. Still silent, Clint moved a few steps further away, making the situation even more difficult.

On that particular day, it was just their bad luck that Silent John wasn't in town. Aware of his reputation, the Hackets would most likely have surrendered their guns without incident, whereby Silent John would've simply collected them up, quickly busted their heads with his club and carted them off to his jail. They'd likely have received somewhat more once he had them securely behind bars—but even that would've been better than what followed.

"Then we haven't anything else to talk about," said the deputy. "Pull 'em and start shooting."

The Hackets, prepared to do a little more talking before they backed this young deputy down, or at least before things got serious, were taken aback.

"Wh-what?" the talkative Hank was suddenly having difficulty with words.

"I said to start shooting. I just can't see any other way out of this." Rosco's voice never changed.

"I'm going to kill you, boy!" Hank cursed.

According to the story, the deputy smiled softly, and infuriated,

When Legends Lived

the brothers' hands flashed for their guns. The old-timers said Rosco Bookbinder never moved until both men's firearms cleared their hostlers, then in a space of time too short to even blink, the deputy shot both of them. His shots were the only ones fired that day, for the two Hackets lay on the ground, both shot squarely between the eyes. The story rapidly spread and grew with each telling, and El Paso suddenly seemed to be a good place to stay away from, especially if you were an aspiring young gunfighter and wanted to live to be an *old* gunfighter. There were those who said that if he hadn't just up and vanished one day, Rosco Bookbinder would've been even better than Wild Bill.

Silent John's second deputy was a young killer by the name of Donny Pence. Pence's name was well known throughout Missouri, Kansas, and most of the Oklahoma Territory. Word had it that when Pence was seventeen, he had out-shot Hickock at a turkey-shoot in Hayes City; though others said Hickock had been drunk that day. Since then, he'd also planted his share of men, and the citizens of El Paso walked lightly whenever he was around. So far, he hadn't needed to kill anyone in El Paso, but he'd proven himself to be nearly as ruthless as Silent John by viciously beating several townsmen half to death over trivial incidents.

Now, as he went about his duties as deputy sheriff, Rosco spent little time reflecting on the gunfight with the Hackets three months earlier. In fact, in recent days, all he thought about was his new bride, Jenny. She was on his mind at the moment as he hurried about his assigned tasks, filled with anticipation at seeing her again. The afternoon sun had moved just past midpoint in the sky when Bookbinder finished serving the jail's only occupant his noon meal, and went to lunch.

As he ate, he again thought of his young wife, daughter of the Reverend Person, or as some folks called him, "Parson Person." At the moment, she was probably at the small one room school house a mile out past the town limits, grading papers where she taught fifteen students in grades one through eight. Jenny was good with kids. She'd make a fine mother. He day dreamed about his young wife constantly during the long days and nights he was on duty as a deputy. He realized she was acting peculiar lately and knew it was likely due to her losing the baby. The miscarriage was difficult on both of them, but especially Jenny. Well, he would just have to make it all up to her. God, he dearly loved that girl. He would do anything to make her happy.

* * *

Immersed in her work and dreams of eventually leaving El Paso behind, Jenny heard the sound of several horses come to a halt in front of the school house. Remaining seated, she watched the front door, listening as heavy footsteps approached. Soon an extremely large, heavily bearded and somewhat soiled man wearing two pistols, entered and looked slowly around. Apprehensive, she remained still until he looked directly at her.

"Can I help you?" she said softly.

"Well now, I'm sure you can," the giant said, looking her over. "I'm just really sure you can."

He walked to the rear of the desk where she was seated and peered out the small window. "Anyone else around?"

She considered lying to him but discarded the notion because she was pretty sure he wasn't the kind of man who would just walk into a place without first knowing everything about it. "No, I'm alone," she replied.

When Legends Lived

The large man's movements reminded Jenny of a huge cat, as he glided over and placed his hairy hands on each side of the desk. Leaning forward, he stared deeply into her eyes. Jenny's heart pounded loudly in her throat, but strangely enough, it was more from excitement than the fear she probably should've felt. She looked back at the rugged face of the stranger and forced a shaky smile.

"Who *are* you?" she said weakly.

"I'm William Reid. Call me Bill."

In that instant, she knew who he was. Many times she'd heard Rosco and Silent John talk about the outlaw William Reid and his many atrocities. It was Bill Reid. *Bloody Bill.* She stiffened slightly and it wasn't missed by the big man.

"Scared, girl?" he said softly, showing his large white teeth.

"No."

"Liar." He continued to smile. "No reason to be scared, though, if you do as I say."

"And what will that be?"

He didn't answer, but still looked at her hungrily.

"Are you going to...to rape me?" she inquired, now with her first small shiver of fear.

His smile grew larger.

"Then what'll happen? Will you turn me over to the others?" she continued, her voice trembling slightly more now. "Listen, you don't have to do that. I'm not stupid. I want to live. I'll do whatever you say and cooperate, if you don't turn me over to them later."

Bloody Bill straightened up and stared down at her for a long time. "Kind of spunky for such a little thing, ain't you?" he said. "Let's see how spunky you really are." He took off his two gun-belts and hung them on the back of a chair. Walking over to her, he placed his hands on her shoulders and looked into her eyes. "You have eyes like I ain't ever seen," he said. "What color do you call that?"

While not filthy as most of his kind tended to be, the large man had obviously been on the trail for many days, and Jenny caught his musky smell when he drew near. "Some folks say they're violet," she answered quietly, as she fought down the terror threatening to burst forth.

"Violet," he said testing the word, letting it roll gently off his tongue. "Looks like lilacs to me. I ain't ever had a woman with violet eyes."

Bill slowly slid his hands down her back, watching her face for any reaction as he did so. Jenny shivered slightly, fighting down an urge to resist. Jenny, who'd often secretly thought Rosco a bit too prissy about his appearance, was surprised to discover she didn't find Bill's muskiness at all unpleasant. *In fact,* she thought, *he at least smells like a man.* It was really kind of exciting in a way. She felt his hands grip her buttocks tightly, as he crushed her against him. Jenny caught her breath as she felt Bill's obvious excitement. Slowly she slid her arms around his neck and raised her mouth to meet his.

"Don't hurt me, please," she muttered hungrily against his mouth.

Bill crushed her almost savagely against his hardness and grinned down wolfishly into her face. Jenny shivered again. That time with total excitement.

* * *

As McCain rode south leading the horse with its sad burden, he thought of Poe headed in the other direction and felt envious of his old friend's destination. He wondered how Kate looked these days. Did she still have her incredible beauty, possess her grand manner? Had she grown old like the rest of them, or merely blossomed with age? According to Poe who'd been the last to see her, it was the latter. Upon returning from last year's horse buying trip up north, Poe had told him that she was even more beautiful than ever before. Of course, Poe almost always tended to stretch the truth about everything. Why did it have to be Poe that went to see her every time? Why not himself? Why couldn't he just...drop in?

'Cause Poe's safe, that's why, you old jackass. Kate's a married lady.

Okay, fair enough. He didn't have to go see her to know she was alright. He only had to send Poe around once in a while to check things out. Besides, if Rosie Poe knew how he really felt about Kate, the damned man would rag him to death about it.

Then there was this other business, and that took priority over everyone's lives. Getting Scar was no small matter. It'd take a miracle to track the face-cutter down—and even more of one to kill him. But kill him was what McCain meant to do this time. He'd seen the destruction and death the man had visited upon the region in the past and felt a terrible foreboding in his soul—and for the future of them all.

At the mere thought of Scar, he felt such a deep burning hatred that it nearly over-came him—a hatred so biting he could literally taste it. Now, all the frustrations of his failures and the vivid memories of past attempts to corner the renegade rushed forth, causing him to subconsciously grip the worn handle of his ancient pistol. It'd been his job to protect the people from that madman and he'd failed miserably. This time, he vowed, he wouldn't stop until one of them was dead.

Oh how he longed to rip the very heart from that devil's living body! To finally know he was dead. How many ghosts would find peace if only he could do that? Each night he lay back and thought of Kate, then slept—and dreamed of Scar.

McCain arrived at the Thompson ranch in the afternoon of the second day of traveling, with the bodies of the two Thompson children. Although he'd wrapped them in every blanket he and Poe could find at the ambush site and covered them with the small canvas he always carried with him for such emergencies, the smell was almost over-powering by the time he sighted the boundaries of the Thompson ranch.

The first person he encountered was Nate Thompson. He was still approximately five miles from the main ranch house when Nate and three of the ranch hands suddenly came riding out of a thicket about fifty yards from the trail. McCain had already seen them and wondered as to what their intent might be, staying hidden that way. Nate and the Circle-T hands rode to a point ten feet in front of him and lined up across the trail, as if to bar his passing.

Without preamble, Nate said, "Where you headed?"

"Well, hello to you, too," McCain stated sarcastically.

Aware of how he looked, no bath in recent days and with several layers of trail dust covering his clothes and person, he probably didn't look like a real upstanding citizen. Still, it rankled him that he hadn't been shown the usual courtesy accorded to most strangers who were traveling through and apparently minding their own business. Besides, he was tired, hungry and anxious to be on his way to link up with Rosie.

Nate Thompson's face flushed dark red at McCain's remark and he appeared to be studying the dusty newcomer intently.

The eyes which looked from beneath the wide hat brim said to the cowhands, *"Don't push too hard."* Close scrutiny of the stranger, revealed a well-worn holster that partially concealed an old Walker Colt. The Colt looked to be clean and well-oiled, despite the dusty and unkept appearance of the old man. The steady gaze of the man suggested he wasn't in the least bit intimidated by the fact he was outnumbered four to one.

"You got a name?" Nate said.

He didn't get an answer right away. Just a silent steady gaze from a man who seemed overly relaxed, in spite of the ominous situation which had developed. Then the dusty, silver haired stranger answered softly.

"I'm older than you, boy. If for no other reason than that, you best show me a little respect."

He paused for just a moment, keeping his gaze steady, then went on. "I don't hold with youngsters showing disrespect toward their elders...and betters. I won't tolerate it. So, sir, will be just fine for now."

Not lost on his audience as he talked, was the manner in which he slowly used his knees to guide the big bay around until it was standing across the trail, and the stranger was sitting sideways to them. His hand hung limply at his side.

"If you can't put a civil tongue in your head, I'm going to ride around you and go about my business," he told them bluntly. "If any of you are stupid enough to try to stop me, I reckon I'll have several more bodies on my pack—instead of just the two."

Taken aback, Nate sensed his men nervously shifting weight in their saddles, concerned that this relatively minor encounter with a stranger had suddenly escalated into a possible deadly confrontation.

"I...I'm sorry, mister," Thompson suddenly blurted out. "A lot has been happening around here lately. I'd like to start over, if you'll allow me. I'm Nate Thompson. My father owns this property and he's been missing for a few days. We're all a little jumpy."

"I'm Captain J.D. McCain, Texas Ranger," he said, and saw the impact on this group that his name usually had on people of the region. "Kind of thought you might be Sam's son. Look a lot like he used to when he was about your age," McCain said. "Not as hospitable as Sam was though."

Nate squirmed. "Captain McCain, my god! We heard you were dead. What're you doing around these parts, sir?"

"Afraid I got some mighty bad news about your daddy, son," McCain informed him. He climbed stiffly off his horse and said, "Reckon we better sit a spell, this ain't going to go down very well with you."

He squatted on his heels and rolled a wet twisted cigarette. By the time he'd finished smoking it, young Nate Thompson was aware his life was changed forever more. Pale and shaken, he said, "Better let me ride on in first, sir. I need to break the news to Mom, and my brother and sister."

"Of course," said McCain, standing and walking to where his horses stood.

Looking at the canvas covered bundle on the pack horse, Nate Thompson seemed aware for the first time of the smell coming from that direction. Turning a little green, he said, "That them?"

"That's your brother and sister," McCain answered.

Ten

IT WAS MUCH LATER when he was lying beside her on the bare school room floor, that Reid first considered taking her with him — at least for a time. *That's a crazy idea*, he thought. *Just slow me down and cause trouble among the men.*

But...she was some woman. Bloody Bill Reid had been with women who were willing partners and he'd taken many others by force, killing most of them along the trail later. Most of the willing ones had been either prostitutes or Mexicans and smelled nearly as bad as he did. The unwilling ones usually smelled right good, but of course, he had to force them and later cut their throats. But the girl next to him, she'd been willing, even eager, and Lordy, did she smell good. When she looked at him with her large "violet" eyes, well, Reid couldn't recollect ever having been with a woman as pretty, was so willing, or had smelt so good, all at once. He felt himself start to react once more.

"Maybe I'll just force you to go with me," he said in his low, deep voice as he gazed down into her face, stroking her breast softly.

"Maybe you wouldn't have to force me," she replied.

Startled, he looked into her eyes for a long time, thinking. *This is some woman, and I'll be damned if I'm going to kill her or turn her over to the gang.* He certainly wasn't going to just ride off and leave her there.

"Who would there be that cares if you go with me?" he said.

"Probably just my husband," she said. "His name is Rosco Bookbinder. Maybe you've heard of him. He's the Deputy Sheriff for El Paso. He may kill you. He's killed others."

Bloody Bill reared back his huge head and roared with laughter. "Kill me? Kill me?" he bellowed. "Lady I've killed more deputy sheriffs than your man has ever seen. Let him come, 'cause I'm gonna take his woman with the 'violet' eyes, and he can go to hell. You do want to come, don't you?"

"Yes. I want to come," she said, reaching out again to grasp him in her soft hand. She was once more beginning to feel the over-powering heat of excitement, spreading through her. It was a full hour later that Jenny and Bloody Bill exited the front door of the small school house and Bill ordered his men to mount up.

Unmoving, twelve-year-old Andrew Pullman stood in the tree line and watched the huge bearded man, the nine mean-looking men in his group, and Andrew's school teacher, Mrs. Bookbinder, ride swiftly toward the tall mountains to the east of El Paso. Then he turned and ran as hard as he could toward town to tell Sheriff Brockman.

* * *

From the time McCain reached the ranch, and throughout the following day, everyone seemed to go out of their way to make up to him for his initial encounter with young Nate. Especially Nate. They'd buried the Thompson children early that morning, not daring to wait longer. Mrs. Thompson was composed and fully in charge throughout, but McCain, with his uncanny ability to read people, saw that she was dying inside as she went about the business of burying her children. Nate identified three of his vaqueros to take a wagon to the ambush site and return the body of Sam Thompson to his family. He asked McCain if he would consider showing them the location, and though he was in a hurry to meet up with Poe, he had little choice but to agree. Once the burying was over, Nate and the remaining ranch hands quietly went about collecting their guns, packing and otherwise preparing to chase Scar down and hang him.

Catching Nate alone, McCain said, "Nate, I'm not one to meddle in someone else's business, but I recommend you don't go chasing off after Scar. Your mother don't need to lose another one of her kids and I know you wouldn't want to get some of your friends killed."

Nate stared at him for a moment. "You're right, Captain," he said. "It ain't your business. We all appreciate what you've done for the Thompson family and want you to know you'll always be welcome here. However, this is family business now and we'll take care of it from here on in."

"I can see there's probably nothing I can say that will change your mind, Nate, but I know Scar about as well as any one person can know another. I've chased him, shot him, even been shot by him — and he's still here."

Not used to talking so much, McCain paused, as if wanting to choose his words well. "He's not like an ordinary man, son. He's the most uncanny bastard you can imagine and once he discovers he's being chased, he won't run. He'll work it around until he's the hunter and you're the prey. Then he'll kill you off, one by one."

"He'll be the one that gets killed this time, Captain," Nate said with certainty, walking away.

He stared after young Nate for a long time after he'd broken off, at first, unaware of Nate's younger brother standing at the corner of the barn, listening to them talk. Brady limped up beside McCain, startling him, for he'd been deep in thought.

"Bout gave me a heart attack, there, son."

Young Brady leaned against the fence and looked up at the famous Texas Ranger. "Sir, I know about everything you ever did in the Rangers."

"I hope not everything," McCain answered, embarrassed.

"I could never do any of those things, being a cripple like I am, but I've read every newspaper story ever written about you and Roosevelt Poe, sir," the boy went on. "About Captain McNelly too. My dad thought it was all a waste of time. To read so much, I mean."

Brady Thompson stood silent for a moment and then continued. "My dad and I never got along too well, you know. He never did anything, except raise cows and boss people. He always had someone to do the hard things for him."

McCain was growing uncomfortable at the turn the boy's talk had taken.

"If he'd been a little more like you and Roosevelt Poe, he wouldn't have let Todd and Teresa die."

"Whoa now, boy! You hold on there! Your dad came out here when this land was nothing more than a wilderness. He fought Comanches, Kickapoo, Kiowas and Mexicans to build and hold onto this ranch for you kids."

He looked down at the boy now, and said more gently, "Son, I knew him when he was a young man, before you kids came along. Kids have a way of making a man want to be more careful with his life. That's so he can stay around and enjoy them for as long as he can."

Brady had grown quiet at the Ranger's words, and McCain continued. "Don't look upon what I did as being all that great a thing. What people like your daddy did out here, long before most of the people that now live here arrived, was much harder and more important then anything me and Poe and McNelly ever did. It took way more guts to raise a family and take care of them during those hard times. I couldn't have done it, that's for sure."

He paused, then finally said, "Your daddy was a brave man, son. Don't you ever forget that. What he done here will live long after I'm gone, and remember, he built it for you and your brothers and sister."

Brady's eyes focused on the dirt in front of him for a while, then he turned without saying anything, and walked away.

Hell, thought J.D., *I'm turning into a bigger old windbag than Roosevelt Poe.* Catching a movement out of the corner of his eye, he saw Dixie, Sam's other daughter standing a few feet away. His first thought was that she was a beautiful young woman.

"Does this whole family sneak up on everybody they meet?"

"It keeps them on their toes, Captain McCain," Dixie said, with a small laugh. "I wasn't trying to eavesdrop on you, I just happened to be out looking for Brady and saw the two of you talking."

He saw that her eyes were red, as if she'd been crying. She avoided his eyes and stared over the grass land. "I come out here in the evenings. Sometimes when the wind is just right, you can smell the river." Turning to look at him, she continued. "Guess you'll be going now that the burying is over. Will you be going back to your ranch, over by Bluebonnet?"

Knowing she was just trying to make conversation, he told her about his and Poe's small horse ranch, and what the country was like around there. She told him about what a great life she had on the Circle-T. As they talked, he could see the intense hurt the young girl was going through and thought, just one more thing to answer for when I catch you, you heathen bastard.

After a few more moments, Dixie unexpectedly stepped close and hugged him. "When you catch him, please kill him for my family," she said, then ran off toward the ranch house.

He stood looking after her, and thought, *Now how did she know that I was going to kill that son-of-a-bitch?*

Being around the Thompsons made McCain acutely aware of his own sparse life – his lack of family ties, home, a desire to pass the McCain name along. If he and Kate had married back then, he'd have grown-up children now, maybe grandchildren. He snorted to himself, then looked around to see if anyone had heard. What a bunch of rot! He needed a bunch of snot-nosed kids running around like he needed an other nose in the middle of his face. What he really wanted, was to get on the trail of that heathen before he killed anymore of the productive citizens of Texas. If he could just do that, he could die happy.

* * *

The sun, looking like a giant orange ball of fire, was just beginning to peek over the gentle rise to the east of the ranch when McCain saddled Grasshopper the next morning. About a dozen cow ponies swished their tails at persistent flies as they nibbled at the short dry grass on the forward slope of the ridge. *Looks like another hellishly hot day*, he thought, aware that it was as cool as it would likely be until the sun finally set that evening. He and the three vaqueros munched biscuits and hard bacon as they back-tracked his earlier trail toward the ambush site.

When Legends Lived

It'd been a full hour before daybreak and he'd still been in his bunk, when he heard Nate ride out, leading his men in search of the killer, Scar. The old Ranger shook his head sadly as he thought about that green bunch going up against someone like his old enemy.

The round trip to the site of the Thompson massacre was slightly more than four days, during which the vaqueros conversed in Spanish among themselves, unaware that McCain understood everything that was said. He didn't speak more than a dozen words throughout the entire trip, content to just listen, and to formulate a plan for what he knew he had to do once the body was recovered. Arriving at the location on the second day, they found that vultures and animals had been at the body of Sam Thompson, and it was scattered over a large area. The vaqueros were able to find most of the remains, which they wrapped in blankets and canvas and placed in the back of the wagon brought for the purpose of transporting Thompson's remains.

The trip back was as silent as the trip out had been. As the recovery group arrived back at the ranch, Mrs. Thompson met them and immediately started making preparations for the funeral of her husband. She was short and rotund, with an inner-toughness that made her seem like a sister to most of the women he'd known throughout the region. They often seemed stronger than their mates when it came to doing the important things, like the dirty business of taking care of the dead.

In a hurry to join up with Poe again and finally get the "run" organized, he departed for Bluebonnet the following morning after saying a hasty goodbye to the Thompson family. Young Brady was no where to be seen.

Just south of Odessa, he came upon what was left of Nate Thompson's party — huddled in a shallow draw along side of the main trail. He recognized Nate first, in spite of the bandages hiding most of his face. There were now six left of the original fifteen man force that had ridden out to seek revenge on Scar and his group of renegades. McCain spent some time with them, using his considerable skills at removing bullets and caring for the wounded. One died in the process and was wrapped in burlap and buried, rocks piled on the grave to mark it, as well as protect it from roving animals.

McCain cooked food for the demoralized group and as he handed Nate a cup of the strong coffee he brewed, said, "What happened?"

McCain listened intently as Nate explained how he and his men had gone to the small Kiowa village over near the Pecos River to obtain information about Scar's whereabouts. Nate conceded that the Kiowas, likely as not, had warned Scar about Nate's group, because not long afterward they'd found two of his scouts hanging in a tree with their genitals stuffed in their mouths. Each had been marked with the face-cut.

"It seemed like after that, one or two of my men was getting picked-off, one way or another every time we turned around," Nate said. "Finally we gave up the chase and turned around to come home." He spoke in a soft monotone, his voice lifeless, devoid of emotion. "It was just like you said it would be, Captain. Almost like he didn't want us to leave. It was even worse when we was trying to run than it was when we were chasing the bastard."

The horror he'd witnessed during the last few days seemed to wash over the distraught man finally, as he described the carnage to McCain. Finished at last, he raised his head and said, "Captain, he didn't just kill. When we would lose a man, we would find him later when we rounded a bend in the trail, hung up-side-down...gutted...or his privates removed."

Nate looked drained, as if he were about to cry. "We woke up one morning and find Charley Bates with his throat cut when we went to wake him."

Nate dropped his head again and his shoulders shook silently for several minutes, as McCain waited for him to compose himself. When he finally looked up once more, the dust on his face was lined with the tracks of salty tears. "These were my friends, Captain McCain," he said in anguish. "I've known some of them most of my life...and we ran. When we found their bodies, we ran and left them there. Didn't even stop to bury them."

"You did what you had to do," McCain told him.

"Maybe," Thompson said, still looking down. Then he raised his eyes to find the older man's eyes on him. "He was like smoke, a puff of wind. How do you fight something like that, Captain?"

McCain, remembering his own failures with catching the elusive half-breed, could only share the young man's grief in silence.

The following morning, he helped the beaten group get started for the Thompson ranch and as he stood looking up at the mounted Nate, the young man said, "I don't know if you can do it, Captain. Hell, I don't know if there is a white man alive that can do it, but if you mean to try it, then kill that animal. Kill him and gut him for all of us,"

Nate's heels kicked savagely against his horse's flanks and he rode off in the direction of the ranch, his small party trailing behind.

Eleven

"P ULL!"

Stump Henry grunted and strained as he grasped the foal's front feet and struggled to free it from its mother's body.

"Pull harder!" Kate Shaw demanded.

She was kneeling on the stable floor, arms buried up to her elbows in the slimy mess that was the difficult birthing of a male colt. She had turned the foal and it had seemed at first, as if the hardest part was behind them. But the mother had been weakened by the ordeal and she now lacked the strength to extract the baby animal from her body. It was up to the two humans to accomplish what nature was unable to do.

"Here it comes!" Kate said exuberantly. "Almost there now."

In what seemed almost anti climatic, the small animal slipped out and let out a pitiful bleat.

"Hey! What we got there, a goat?" Stump Henry chuckled.

"Oh, he's a beauty," Kate said happily.

The young colt was struggling, already attempting to stand.

"I think his mother is going to be all right, too." She wiped the sweat from her eyes with the soiled sleeve of her denim man's shirt. "I wish Duncan could've lived to see him," remembering this mare was her late husband's favorite mount.

Kate knew that Stump watched her appreciatively from the corner of his eye. He'd never married, and Kate knew he had

When Legends Lived

"feelings" for her. As for Stump Henry, he'd always allowed that he'd marry Kate Shaw in a minute, if she'd only say the word. At nearly forty, Kate appeared ten years younger, and to Henry, was still as achingly beautiful as she'd always been. That was when he was still with the Rangers — and with Rosie Poe and Captain McCain always present whenever he'd a chance to talk with her. When he'd heard Duncan Shaw had been stomped to death while trying to break a half-wild mustang, he'd immediately headed to the Shaw ranch and obtained employment from the newly widowed, Kate Shaw.

Kate vaguely remembered him as a friend of Rosie and Jericho and was relieved to have the extra help at such a time. It'd been plain how he felt about her right from the start, but he'd been with the ranch for almost a year and had never gotten up the courage to make his feelings known — for which Kate was thankful.

Kate was happy as things stood. She'd always been smarter and more competent at running the ranch than her husband, and decided right after the death of Duncan that she could get along just fine without the cumbersome attachments of having a man around. Her younger sister, Bethena, tended to feel the same way. As beautiful as Kate, Beth was fair whereas Kate was dark. They both had the same fine features, slim bodies, and fair skin of their long dead Scandinavian mother. Kate, however, had inherited her father's strong will and determination as well. The two sister's beauty was widely known and Kate had sent more than one randy cowboy packing at the sight of the new Winchester rifle her late husband bought for her just prior to his death. It was that knowledge primarily that probably kept Stump Henry from stating his case.

"Someone's coming," Stump said.

Kate wiped her hands on a piece of the old sheet she'd torn

up to use in the birth of the foal. Walking to the barn door, she squinted into the bright sunlight, trying to see who it was.

"Sounds like more than one," she said. Then she let out a loud whoop and ran out of the barn wildly waving her arms and shouting.

Rosie Poe brought his horse to a halt in a cloud of flying debris, and dismounted almost before it came to a stop.

"Whoa lady," he chuckled. "What's the matter? Your barn on fire?"

Screaming and laughing, Kate smothered Rosie's dusty face with wet kisses.

"All right. All right, settle down," he said pulling his head back, clearly pleased. "Too much of that sweetness might not be good for a feller."

Kate stepped back, smiling up at him. "You look wonderful, Roosevelt," she said, breathless.

"Yeah, I do, don't I? You don't look too bad your own self. Maybe a little long in the tooth but other than that, still a mighty healthy filly," he chuckled again, and hugged her close one more time before reluctantly releasing her.

He looked around and said, "Where's that jealous husband of yours."

Kate got a serious look on her face, and said, "Duncan's been dead for almost a year now, Roosevelt."

"Darn, I'm sorry Kate. I didn't know."

He saw Kate looking at Packard, who was still mounted and said, "Kate, I'd like you to meet Jim Packard. He's with the railroad. Jim, Kate Shaw."

"With the railroad, huh?" she said. "Well, hop down anyway, Mr. Packard. If you're with Roosevelt, I guess you're okay."

Her glare gave Packard the distinct impression she didn't think too highly of the railroad.

Stump remained silently watching from inside the dark barn as chattering, Kate and Rosie walked arm-in-arm back toward the ranch house, Packard following silently. He heard Poe say, "We got a lot of catching up to do, Kate. There are a lot of things happening that you have to know about."

Kate answered, "Beth and Billy will be back tomorrow. Then the girls return the following day. I hope you plan to wait around to see them. They'll be so disappointed if you don't."

"We'll talk about it," Poe said as they disappeared from view.

Stump remained looking at their retreat for several moments, then went back to attend the colt.

* * *

More than a little embarrassed at forgetting that the two men were friends, Kate later invited Stump to the ranch house for supper. It was only the second time he'd been inside the house during the year he worked for Kate. The meal was the best any of the three men had experienced in a number of months. As Rosie Poe worked on his third piece of apple pie, Stump and Packard shoved back from the table, nursed their coffee, and lit cigars that Packard provided from his saddle-bags.

Kate studied Poe, then said, "Much as I would like to believe it Roosevelt, I don't think you just happened to come all this way to see me."

Poe finished the last bite of his pie with as much relish as the first bite, sighed, and said, "Kate, did you ever meet Sam Thompson, his youngest boy or his daughter, Teresa? They have a ranch over by Odessa."

Kate nodded her head. Of course she'd heard about the Circle-T, the largest ranch west of Houston. She'd met Sam Thompson and his family at an auction near Odessa, about ten years earlier. Although she couldn't remember the son, she smiled as she recalled the flaxen-haired little Teresa, screaming with laughter as she chased butterflies around the yard of the large ranch house.

"Two days ago, Jericho and I found Sam and the two kids about ten miles east of the Colorado. The kids were dead when we found them. You don't want to know any more about it than that. Sam was dying when we arrived." Poe saw Packard glance at him out of the corner of his eye, but ignored him, continuing. "He told us it was Scar."

At the name, both Kate and Stump Henry bolted upright in their chairs.

"It was an awful scene, Kate." Poe hesitated. "Jericho took the bodies to the Circle-T."

He carefully left out the part about leaving Thompson behind. "That's where Mr. Packard comes in. The railroad has hired me and Jericho to track down Scar and kill him, and we mean to do just that."

"Jericho? Working for the railroad?" Kate gasped. "Now *that's* a laugh." Then she suddenly sobered, and bluntly told him, "Roosevelt, the whole thing's ridiculous. Look at the two of you. You're both way too old for such nonsense as that, now. You chased Scar all over the state of Texas and most of Mexico for more than fifteen years and never got close enough to smell his horse droppings. What makes you think you can do it now?"

Kate was getting louder and Roosevelt, amused, was beginning to see some of the fiery temper she would occasionally put on display when they were all younger.

"She's right, Rosie," Stump Henry said. "We all chased him and we were young, tough and full of piss…excuse me, Miz Shaw…and vinegar, in those days. We were damned good, but still never got close to him."

"He'll kill you both, Roosevelt," Kate said. "Give it up. I don't want to lose my friends."

"Well, thank ye both kindly for your vote of confidence," Roosevelt Poe stated sarcastically. "You certainly have impressed my employer, Mr. Packard here. He probably feels real good about hiring us right about now."

Packard squirmed uncomfortably in his seat, trying to study the color of the room's ceiling.

"I was hoping you'd throw in with us, Stump," declared Poe. "Or don't you still hate Scar the way you used to say you did? You always was a good talker."

"Now, you look-ee here, Rosie," said Stump Henry, starting to get red in the face. "I still hate the heathen, but as a man gets older his priorities start to change."

"Yeah? And what might *your* priorities be, Stump?" Poe pointedly glanced at Kate as he asked the question.

Henry's face grew even redder. Stump Henry was a tough man. He'd seen his share of gunfights in the Rangers and wasn't known to back down from many men. But tough as he was, Henry had known Roosevelt Poe for twenty years and knew Poe was more than a match for him in any kind of fight they might get into. That knowledge cooled his temper and turned him into a somewhat more agreeable man.

"Hell, Rosie, no need to go getting your milk in an uproar. I'd like to go with you," he remarked. "Guess I even envy you and J.D. some, for going yourselves. But I got plans and I want more out of life than an old horse and a rusty gun when I die. Like a family and roots, some place I can call home."

Thoughtfully, Poe studied his old ranger buddy. "Then I truly hope you get whatever it is you want, Stump. A man should have his dream. Just be advised that Scar was headed this way when we lost his trail. He won't care about your dreams or that you have other plans or not, if you happen upon him. He'll gut you the way he did those Thompson kids," he said bluntly and Packard cringed.

Poe abruptly shifted his attention back to Kate. "Kate, how many men you got working the place?"

"Seven — counting Stump," she answered.

"I'd recommend you keep half of them at the ranch at all times and pair the rest up to get the work done. This is one bad hombre. He don't just kill — he butchers," Poe told them. "I got to leave in the morning for El Paso to meet Jericho. We need to round up some good men to help us." He looked pointedly at Stump Henry, who avoided his eyes.

"Then you intend to go after Scar, anyway?" Kate said.

"We don't have any choice. I seen those kids he slaughtered, Kate. I know what they did to that little girl before they butchered her. I don't want the same thing happening to you or Beth, or your girls. Yeah, I'll go. I'd go if I knew I was going to die tomorrow. That's how bad it was," said her old friend.

Kate sat quietly with her head bowed down. At last, she raised her head and looked into Poe's eyes, her own eyes moist. "You know I didn't mean those things I just said, Rosie. I know you got to do what you say. Nobody will be safe until Scar's dead." Small tears now formed at the corners of Kate's lovely green eyes, making all three men's hearts ache. "I just don't want to lose anyone else I love," she said softly.

When Legends Lived

"Even an old man like me?" Rosie joked, trying to lighten the mood.

They all laughed.

"*Especially* a man like you," Kate smiled, carefully skipping the "old" that time around.

They continued talking for several hours, seemingly reluctant to end what each felt might be the last time they would be together like this. At last Rosie and Packard stood to say goodnight.

"Roosevelt," Kate said, "please stay one more day. Beth and Billy D. will be coming back tomorrow. Beth would buggy whip me if I let you get away without her seeing you."

"Well, I *would* like to see her and young Billy," Poe said as he walked away. "Maybe we will hang around."

Stump hung back till after the others had gone. When he was sure they were out of hearing, he said, "Kate, do you ever think you will get married again?"

Shocked, Kate looked at him for a long time. "Stump, are you asking me to marry you?"

"Well, yes. I guess I am," he said. "I don't have much, but I would treat you like a queen for the rest of your life."

Kate placed her hand on his arm and smiled into Stump's eyes. "I'm honored that you ask, Stump. We've been friends for a long time and I value no one's friendship over yours. But, I'm not ready for marriage again. I don't want to give out any false hopes, so I must tell you that I honestly don't know if I will ever be again."

Stump Henry sadly looked at Kate, with great love in his eyes and finally said, "Well, I had to ask. Take care, Kate." He walked away without looking back.

Kate remained for a long time, staring after him, then went inside and closed the door softly behind her.

As Stump walked into the bunk house, Poe and Packard were getting into bed.

"Turned ya down, huh?" Rosie said without tact.

Henry glared at him for a second then slowly smiled and said, "Yeah. Guess she's smarter than I figured. That job still open?"

The next morning, Poe was just finishing shaving when he heard the wagon and knew Bethena and Billy had arrived. Placing his hat on his head, he strolled out of the bunkhouse door just in time to catch a bundle of flying golden hair in his arms. It was Beth.

"Rosie. Rosie. Rosie," she said as she hugged and planted kisses on his face.

"Seems like I been through this before," he chuckled. "Not that I couldn't get used to it."

"It's so good to see you, Rosie," she said. "How's that worthless old partner of yours?"

"Now, don't you be too hard on old Jericho," he said. "He's hard enough on his own self."

They all laughed as they made their way to the house to meet Kate's son, sixteen year old Billy. He marveled at how Beth and Kate stayed so beautiful all these years; still as straight and slim and full of energy as the day he had met them in Mineral Springs before the war. And Billy had the same fine features and underlying sense of strength the rest of the family possessed. Even their father had it, Poe reluctantly recalled. He hadn't seen Tina and Rachel, Kate's two daughters, in over two years, but remembered the five and seven-year-old girl's blonde braids and cornflower blue eyes, and how they had always called him Mr. Rosie; cuter than bug's ears.

When Legends Lived

The visit with the two sisters and Billy was almost painful for Poe, as he considered that, but for the luck of the draw, that could've been his son, daughters and wife. He had a few minutes alone with Kate at the end of the joyous day, and mentioned his thoughts to her.

"Roosevelt, if you and I had married, things would've been no different. Oh, you would've stayed for a while and we would've been happy for that time. Lord knows, no one can make me laugh like you can."

Kate looked out over the grassland and frowned. "Then Jericho McCain would've called, and off you'd go with him."

Poe made as if to argue, but raising a hand slightly, Kate cut him off. "You know it's true what I say, Roosevelt. I believe you do love me in your own way, but you love him more. Always have, always will." Turning to face him, she continued, "I love you, too, Roosevelt, but what I feel for you is more like what I feel for Beth, or Billy and the girls. It's much different than the feelings I would have for the man I want."

"Then you must've loved that Duncan feller a good deal," he said.

She was silent for a moment, then said, "No, not Duncan. At least not in that way."

Looking back across the valley, she leaned her elbows on the top of the fence. "Oh, don't get me wrong. I cared for Duncan, but I didn't love him in that way either."

She was silent for a few moments again, then continued. "I didn't deceive Duncan, you know. It's important to me, Roosevelt, that you believe that. I told him how I felt and he still wanted me to marry him."

Kate climbed up on the top rail of the fence and hooked her

feet through the second rail. "I don't regret it. He gave me Billy and the girls, and he treated me better than anyone ever has in my life."

She stared at the horizon for a minute with a sadness that made Poe want to take her in his arms and protect her from any further hurt. "Jericho McCain. It was always Jericho, Roosevelt. I would've run away with him in a minute, left my family and everything else behind, if only he'd asked." Kate sighed. "He never did, though. Probably just as well, anyway. He would've been no better than you about running off whenever the whim took him."

"You haven't seen him for a long time, Kate. How do you know you still feel that way about him?"

"I don't. I don't know Jericho McCain at all any more. Possibly, never did. Sometimes, I think I was in love all those years with the memory of what I thought someone was, and that person never really existed at all. When I'd hear stories of the men he killed…oh…I know, I know," she said, holding up her hand once more to cut off Rosie's protests. "Every one of them were bad men. But men just the same Roosevelt. I would wonder how that kind gentle person I loved so much could kill so many people — so easily."

Kate, looked down at Poe from her seat on the fence. "At the same time, I know what you and Jericho have done for the people around here. Without the two of you, Texas would still be as lawless and as unbearable a place to raise up a family, as it was when my father brought us out here. And…" she paused, then went on, "…that's why I know you and Jericho have got to get that creature, Scar. Help me down please, Roosevelt." She held her arms out to him.

When Legends Lived

He gently lifted her down to the ground, holding her just a moment longer than was necessary, then stepped back.

"You deserved more happiness in life, Kate. You always gave more than you received."

"Where do you want to be buried, Roosevelt?" Kate suddenly said.

Taken aback, Poe hesitated, then said, "Well, I guess I never really thought about it too much."

"Everyone should have a place to be buried. It should be near those that loved you while you were still living." Pointing to a clump of trees on a small round hill, about a quarter of a mile from the ranch house, she continued. "That's where we buried Duncan and Beth's husband, Howard. We buried Beth's only child there too. It was stillborn. The doctor said she could never have another." Kate stood and gazed at the hill for a few minutes with a deep sadness in her eyes, then said, "My firstborn is also buried there. He was two when he got the fever. Died within the week."

He heard her sniff and gave her some time. After a while, she went on. "I plan to be put to rest there, as well." Turning, Kate took a few steps back toward the house and stopped. "I guess my whole family will finally be put to rest on that little hill. I hope so. I think it will help make eternity go by a lot faster if I'm with my loved ones, don't you, Roosevelt?"

"I'm sure it will, Kate," he answered sincerely.

"What I'm saying to you is that I would like it very much if you would consider being buried here with us, when it's your time."

All at once, Poe was overwhelmed. He turned away, as a large lump formed in his throat and his eyes began to sting. He faced away from her for a long time, saying nothing, then cleared his throat. "I would consider it the greatest honor of my life to be buried here with your family," was all he could get out.

"It's your family, too, Roosevelt. Just do what you have to do, and then come back when it's over. Remember, you will always be family here," she said as she left him staring after her.

The three men were saddled and ready to ride at dawn the next morning. Kate and Beth had risen an hour earlier than the men and fixed them a large ranch-style breakfast, to see them on their way. As they prepared to depart, the group was filled with a dark, hollow sadness that seemed to invade their very souls. There seemed to be an unspoken feeling that they might never meet again and find things exactly the same as they were at that moment. Bethena hugged Rosie and a small tear rolled down her face, then without a word, she turned and ran into the ranch house. Billy held out his hand and with a strong grip told Rosie that if he needed help he was available. Kate was last. She kissed him tenderly and again told him to come back. She would insure that her daughters were there the next time. It wasn't until they'd been on the trail for some time, that Poe realized she hadn't mentioned him bringing Jericho along.

Twelve

BETHENA LEFT THE RANCH about an hour after the three men's departure, heading in the opposite direction toward the Parker household. Kate's daughters had gone to visit with Liam and Cinda Parker's young daughter and had been there for the past four days. Wanting to get away from the ranch for a while after the emotional goodbye to Rosie and Stump Henry, she volunteered to make the trip to get her young nieces. The slow, more comfortable ride of the wagon, made the round trip long enough so that she would reach the Parker place by noon and still be back at the ranch by dark. She looked forward to seeing her nieces whom she looked upon as surrogate daughters.

Bethena rode along deep in thought, thinking about Rosie's visit and the handsome young Jim Packard who was with him. *Jim. I like that name*, she thought. *I wonder if Rosie will bring him along when he comes back*. Beth had seen the young railroad man stare at her throughout dinner the night before and knew he was attracted to her.

Almost at once, as her mind usually did when she thought about some man, her thoughts switched to her deceased husband, Howard Beck. The raw cutting hurt she experienced initially after learning of his death had long since been replaced by the dull ache she now routinely experienced each and every time something evoked his memory. After all the years, she still felt tears burn her eyes as she recalled a certain event or an act of gentleness Howard had shown her.

Just look at yourself, girl. You've got to put Howard's death behind you and go on with your life, she told herself for a thousandth time.

They'd had so little time together, and on top of that, had lost their baby at birth. So much sadness — and so much happiness — in such a short time together. Howard had been her life's love, and until now, she'd never even considered another man. Maybe there was someone out there for her. Once more, she forced herself to think about young Packard.

Beth was still seeing Jim Packard's face in her mind as she rounded a bend and saw the man standing in the middle of the road. He remained motionless and, as she came closer, she began to become somewhat alarmed. Beth startled as she heard a slight sound behind her, felt the wagon jar, and as she turned around to see what caused it, was just able to make out the features of the man standing in the road. He had a large scar running down his cheek and across his face.

Then, everything went black.

* * *

Jenny Bookbinder stretched and gazed into the sleeping face of the man beside her. Then she looked around the cabin where she and Bloody Bill had spent the previous night. As she remembered the frenzied flight of the night before, all of the details came suddenly back to her in their shocking entirety. Stunned, she lay quietly for a while trying to sort out her feelings. They'd traveled all day after Bill had kidnapped her — *no that's not the word* — she'd told him she would go willingly. But did she really have a choice, anyway? Would he have killed her if she'd refused? *Maybe. Probably. If not him, then his men.* Jenny was convinced Bill would've given her to that gang of cutthroats without a moment's hesitation if she'd refused his invitation to go with him.

When Legends Lived

As she remembered her encounter with Bill in the small schoolhouse, Jenny's face burned. *He sure had been anxious*, she thought, and then giggled softly.

Jenny was satisfied she knew how to handle a man like Bill and besides, he was giving her what she wanted most — a way out of El Paso. *All that killing though*, she thought with a shudder, when she remembered what had followed. *But it's not my fault, I didn't kill anyone. I didn't even have a gun.*

She remembered how Bill had wanted her to take one of his pistols and shoot that old man. Frightened, Jenny tried to do as Bill had ordered, but the truth of the matter was her hand was just too small for the large butt of the .44 caliber pistols Bill carried. Finally, in apparent disgust, Bill had taken the pistol from her hand and almost casually shot the defiant old man to death. She remembered how the large slug suddenly lifted the frail old man's body in the air and propelled him into the railing of the cabin's porch. Hanging there for just an instant, he slowly folded without a sound as if he had suddenly grown very tired.

Jenny also recalled, although she was frightened to death the whole time, how all those men fighting and shooting also made her more excited than she could ever remember being. *And afterward.*

Yes, afterward, Bill was an uncontrollable animal. Jenny stretched again, remembering the way Bill had ravaged her over and over the night before. *And I didn't give a hang if he did*, she thought, smiling.

Of course the events of the previous day had been unsettling for her, even terrifying. But thinking back now, she remembered she'd also felt an uncontrollable excitement. They'd been almost to the mountains, riding hard, when they ran upon a small Army resupply convoy of four wagons. Manned only by the four drivers, a corporal and one officer, the soldiers never had a chance. In addition to regular monthly supplies for the small detachment at El Paso, the wagons were also transporting several wives of the officers who served at the garrison.

The carnage was complete. Two of the women who remained alive after the first fusillade of fire from the outlaw group's pistols, subsequently paid a much dearer price than their sisters who'd been killed outright. The surviving women were taken with them as they continued their flight into the highlands. They rode hard without rest, then about dusk the bunch came across a small homestead occupied by an elderly man and his wife. The old man's wife was bedridden and unaware of any problem, right up to the moment she died. The farmer had been feeding the livestock, and was surprised and quickly overcome by Bill's scouts. When Bill and Jenny rode up, the old man was standing in front of the one room cabin, battered but still defiant, his hands tied behind his back. Bill pulled his pistol from its holster and had offered it to Jenny.

"You want to do it?" he'd said, grinning wolfishly.

Jenny had shuddered and looked away as Bill shot the old man through the head then told his men, "Get rid of the old woman. I'll use the house tonight."

Long after she and Bill went to bed, Jenny could hear the screams of the surviving soldiers' wives and the grunts of rutting men from their camp a short distance away. It had gone on for hours, until at last, there was only silence. Now, it all seemed like a dream, as Jenny slipped from beneath the covers, being careful not to disturb the huge shape beside her on the bed. Quietly, she bathed herself and looked through the old couple's wardrobe, finding what was surely the old woman's best Sunday dress. Jenny slipped it over her head and fixed her hair to look nice for Bill when he awoke. Jenny was smart and knew Bill liked her because she looked good — and smelled good. She must never forget that or she could end up like those other women had the night before.

Jenny wondered if, upon waking, Reid would simply decide to kill her anyway. He'd certainly demonstrated he was capable of it. Finally ready, Jenny gathered her courage and climbed gently onto the bed. Slowly, she began to stroke Bill's face and run her soft fingers through his hair until he slowly opened his eyes and stared up at her. Then he slowly grinned a wolf's grin and she relaxed. *I'll just have to wait for another day to wear this pretty dress*, she thought as he pulled it over her head and tossed it in a crumpled heap onto the floor.

* * *

On the day Beth was taken by Scar, Billy Shaw paced between the corral and the ranch house, searching the road for any sign of her and his sisters.

"Ma," young Billy finally called. "It's getting late and Aunt Bethena and the girls ain't back yet!"

Kate, suddenly aware of the time, anxiously went to the window and gazed up the road, toward the Parker homestead. "Let's give them another half-hour or so, then if they're not here by then, we'll ride out and fetch them. Probably broke an axle, or something."

The time painfully passed with both Billy and his mother growing more and more nervous as the minutes ticked by. Picking up her Winchester, Kate told Billy, "Go get your rifle and meet me down by the corral."

Within minutes, they were saddled and riding swiftly toward the Parker home. Billy saw it first, reining his horse in sharply.

"Ma, that looks like Aunt Bethena's wagon, by the side of the road yonder," he said, pointing. "You better wait here. I'll check it out."

Kate pulled her rifle from its scabbard and sat with it pointed generally in the direction of the overturned wagon. "Okay, check it out, but go slowly," she said, "We don't know what happened here, yet."

Billy slowly rode to the overturned wagon and dismounted. After a few minutes, he waved to his mother to join him. "Someone shot the horse, Ma — a whole bunch of times. It looks like a lot of horses was here and they took off in that direction." He pointed west toward the mountains. "I think they took her with them," he said in a shocked voice.

Kate's body grew icy cold as the realization of what must've happened began to set in. She gripped the saddle-horn with both hands to keep from falling from her horse. Billy was speaking to her, but she couldn't make out what he was trying to tell her. Instead, her mind was absorbed by what Rosie had told her about the Thompson children, and their father.

My God. Beth. They took my baby sister!

Thirteen

"I saw Earp in Tombstone once, practicing with that long-barreled pistol of his...and if everything I heard about Hickok is true, he was a consequential shootist as well. Roosevelt Poe could'a killed 'em both."

– J.D. McCain, about the gunfighter Poe

Martin Gates was sore — he was tired — and he was dirty. He'd left St. Louis over three weeks before and since then had ridden a steamboat, horseback, several trains, and now a stagecoach. By far, the worse ride he'd experienced was this damnable stagecoach, he thought, painfully trying to stretch his cramped legs as he blew the caked dust from his nostrils.

If someone had told me just how uncomfortable these damn things are, I'd have gladly walked from Fort Worth.

Gates was rotund, thirty years of age. He sported a dark, neatly trimmed goatee of the times and wore a stylish suit of light gray wool. On his head, set a gray derby hat.

Martin Gates was a newspaper man. He worked for the *Chicago Dispatch* and was well known in the eastern states for his widely read stories of happenings west of the Mississippi River. He knew eastern folks dearly loved stories about the rugged cowboys and frontiersmen and women, which helped them escape from their otherwise unbearable jobs and the prisons of their dreary lives. *The things I don't do for my readers,* he thought, *and of course, the money.*

When Frank Chase contacted him several weeks earlier with information about a possible story on some Texas Rangers chasing down outlaws for the railroad, Gates jumped at the opportunity to do the story. As it was, most of his material was starting to get a little stale and redundant, and his boss had expressed some concern about declining customer interest in his stories. He was well aware that Frank Chase's interest in providing him the information was to further expose the Southern Pacific Railroad's involvement in the two ranger's attempts to wipe out outlaw activity in the Territories and West Texas. He'd readily agreed to slant his stories toward putting the railroad in a favorable light whenever possible.

Now, Gates wondered if his jumping at this chance had been a mistake. Well, he would know for sure if there was a story, or not, once he got to Bluebonnet and talked to this Captain McCain.

Bluebonnet. Now that's a pretty name for a town.

He could hardly wait to get to the place he pictured as a small town, nestled between rolling hills, surrounded by miles and miles of the famous blue flowers he'd heard so much about.

* * *

Beth came to, realizing she was riding face down over a horse and was tied securely. Her head hurt and it was hard to remember exactly what had happened. Then gradually, she remembered the man with the scared face. Scar, that's what Roosevelt had said his name was. She suddenly recalled what he'd said had happened to the Thompsons and wanted to scream, knowing if she did, that she'd die immediately.

Her head throbbed savagely as she bumped along, and she could see nothing but the ground passing beneath the feet of the horse she was tied to. After a while, she was able to determine there were six of them besides Scar. Beth heard Scar cuss all of them enough to know most of their names and was able to associate the names with certain types of footwear the men were wearing. The high top moccasins was Dog-Soldier and the low moccasins belonged to Choctaw, the rawhide leggings were Devil-Man, the high-top boots with beads around them was Kiowa Jack, and the one with the low-cut town boots was called Johns. The one Scar called Three Finger Ned left sometime on the first day and hadn't returned. He'd been the only one to touch her — so far — patting her rear as he headed off for an unknown destination.

Beth heard Scar tell Johns to ride on ahead and find a campsite.

Johns whined, "You ain't gonna let the rest of the boys have any of that little lady while I'm gone, are you, Scar?"

Without saying a word, Scar rode close to Johns and kicked him hard enough to unseat him from his saddle. Under her horse's belly, she could see Johns as he glared up at Scar from his seat on the ground.

"Ride ahead," Scar said again in a flat tone.

With that, Johns mounted and rode on ahead.

Thirty minutes later, after more traveling through thicket and trees, Scar held his hand up and the men dismounted. A moment later, the rope holding her on the horse was cut, and she immediately slipped to the rocky ground where she lay, unmoving. Someone kicked her in the side. Hard. She groaned and struggled to regain her breath. Scar turned her over with his foot. He coldly stared down at her for a minute and then viciously kicked her again. This time she involuntarily screamed. At the sound of her scream the other men turned to watch, excited, sensing it was near their time to be with her.

"Get off the ground *puta*, and make your worthless ass useful. Build a fire. Get supper started.

Scar walked away and lay down on the ground, resting his back against a large pine. Watching her with flat, dead eyes.

Painfully, Bethena dragged herself to her feet and began to search for twigs and sticks for a fire.

"If you want to run, go ahead, bitch. When I catch you, I'll have Dog-Soldier take a twig, sharpen it, and poke a little hole in your bottom lip." Scar smiled evilly. "Then we'll loop a piece of catgut through it and tie it to a tree limb with some rawhide — after that, we'll see how far you run."

Beth kept her eyes averted as she cooked and served each man his meal and as she did, endured countless indignities and insults by the filthy group.

"Bring me some more coffee, *puta*," said Kiowa Jack.

As she bent to pour the half-breed's coffee, Johns, sitting nearby, slipped his hand under her long dress as far up as he could reach. Turning, she flung the pot of scalding coffee onto his face and he fell screaming to the ground. The other men ignored him as he moaned and thrashed around on the ground. They were now staring intently at Bethena.

"Looks like she's flirting. Maybe it's time somebody tamed her down a bit. Who wants a little taste? What am I bid?" Scar said.

"I got a dollar," Dog-Soldier said, not removing his eyes from the terrified woman.

"Let's see it."

Pulling the dollar out of his pocket, Dog-Soldier shoved it over to Scar, who put it in his pocket.

"She's all yours, who's next?"

The other men scrambled to find anything of value to trade to Scar for the privilege of sharing the white woman.

Johns continued to moan and twist on the ground as he screamed, over and over, "My eyes! My eyes, I can't see! The bitch has made me blind!"

Approaching the injured man, Scar stood over him for a moment and looked down un-pityingly. Ugly blisters had quickly formed on the eyelids and swollen face of the scalded man. Scar savagely kicked him in the side.

"Shut up, you piece of dung — before I skin you like the dog you are," he said coldly, then turned to watch the other four men take their pleasure with the white woman. "A worthless piece of trash," he said to no one in particular. "Take your turns, but don't damage her. Maybe I can trade her to some Kiowas over on the Pecos for a good horse — or maybe I'll just cut her throat."

Scar watched the scene before him without emotion or feeling. He smelled the woman's fear and relished it, just as he often smelled the fear of the men who served him. That was his pleasure. He didn't need women. His life was such that he lived for the day alone, having little reason to remember all the yesterdays — or think about any tomorrow.

He would've had to think hard to remember his real name, for he'd been called Scar since he was a youth. That was a name that had shamed him when he was young. At first he'd hated that name, but through the years he'd eventually come to embrace it as he realized that it could summon immense fear. It was the fear that the name produced, that he relished the most. One of those smart eastern doctors probably would've said he enjoyed instilling fear into others because it fascinated him. The real truth was that he simply didn't understand that particular nature of people, because he'd never felt fear himself.

Even as a very small child, before his acquirement of the scar, when he was beaten nearly every day by the old women of the village, he didn't feel fear. He knew they'd beat him because of his white man's eyes, but he'd never tried to escape or cower. Sometimes even the village men would hit him, usually after they'd consumed a healthy amount of mescaline or some of the stolen white man's whiskey.

But the worst treatment he suffered was at the hands of the other children. Many times he was beaten so badly he was unable to walk and had crawled back to the lice infested lodge he shared with his mother and whatever male was available. Often his mother's current man would kick him out as well. When he was older, around seven or eight, his mother took up with a Russian whiskey trader and they left the village, moving into the white man's town of Tucson. There, he was despised even more because he looked like a *damn Injun*. The fact that he had blue eyes, somehow only made it worse. He soon learned to stay away from home for longer and longer periods until, eventually, he'd left for good.

The old Russian had treated him okay except for when he was drunk; even showing him how to shoot a pistol. It was because of the target practice that he'd received his scar. It was an event that was to produce one of the most infamous names of the times. A name so hated, it would strike fear into the hearts of those living in the southwest United States and a large part of northern Mexico for nearly two decades — *Scar* — a name to make the blood run cold.

Before that eventful day, he'd been known by several Apache names, which, when ran together, meant, "the boy with white man's eyes." In the white man's town, the locals called him

When Legends Lived

"Conches," which was as close as they could come to pronouncing one of his Apache names; or more frequently, he was simply called, "the Injun boy."

On the eventful morning of his marking, he'd waited until the old trader drank his whiskey and fell asleep on the woodpile. Then he took the old man's rusty cap and ball pistol and went to find a rabbit or something else to eat. A mile out of town he spotted a gopher sitting on a small knoll having lunch, about twenty feet from the main trail. He silently moved to get a better sight at it, leveled the pistol, and squeezed off his shot just as the old man had taught him.

Unfortunately for him, it was about that time that a prominent rancher known as Colonel Nathaniel Billingsly chose to ride by with several of his cowhands. The "Colonel," as Billingsly wanted to be called, was somewhat of a dandy and always carried the silver and gold decorated sword he claimed was given to him by an English Duke, during the War of 1812. The thunderous report of the ancient Russian-made pistol spooked the horses and Colonel Billingsly landed in the dust at their feet, soiling his fine broadcloth suit and smudging his highly shined boots. He'd just managed to remount as the young boy exited the tree line proudly carrying the dead gopher and the smoking pistol. In a rage, the Colonel drew his beautiful silver and gold sword and slashed it down across the youth's face.

"Damn Injun!"

The Colonel hastily rode away as his stunned ranch hands stared for a moment at the bleeding boy laying on the trail, then followed.

Two years later, the Colonel was discovered lying in his bed, his throat cut from ear to ear, a jagged scar carved from one side of his face to the other. his pretty, young wife, sleeping beside him, didn't hear a sound, nor awaken until the next morning when she discovered his body beside her. No one ever saw Scar around there again, as he traveled east, first into New Mexico then on into Oklahoma and eventually western Texas. He was fourteen years old.

In the years that followed, his name began to be spoken more frequently by the various ranch hands and towns folks in the area....*A small Apache raid over near the Saddle Horn wiped out a family of five...three children, the youngest was five...all had been hideously tortured and left with a jagged wound cut deeply across their faces...two cowhands were butchered while searching for strays...their faces also cut.* It became known throughout the area as Scar's trademark: "the face-cut."

A muffled scream drew his attention back to the activity before him, and he watched silently as one-by-one they mounted the struggling woman — her screams growing weaker and weaker — until finally, the only sounds coming from her were an occasional whimper, much like those made by a small hurt animal.

When all that could be heard was the grunts and an occasional curse coming from the sweating men, Scar finally rose and moved toward them. "That's all you paid for. If you got more money, maybe I'll give you another taste tomorrow."

Kiowa Jack was just beginning his second turn and looked up resentfully. Seeing the empty stare in Scar's cold, blue eyes, he quickly rose to his feet and hurried away, pulling clothing over the exposed source of his discomfort.

By the second day, Bethena emitted no sounds of protest as she'd made on the first day of her ordeal. Throughout the day, one of the men would occasionally drop down on top of her but she only lay and stared at a place far away and made no sound, even when they beat her to get her to respond. Her stoic behavior didn't set well with the men and because of it, most of them were rapidly growing tired of her. Scar knew that soon all of them would want to start cutting on her. That is, all except for Dog-Soldier, who begged Scar to give him the female to be his own woman.

The three men rode silently for most of the trip into the small town of Big Springs; Poe and Stump because their minds were occupied with the beautiful Kate Shaw, and Packard out of respect for their silence. Poe now regretted he hadn't been more insistent with Kate that she give him due consideration as a possible mate. She needed a man around there to help her run things; not to mention raising a boy and two young girls. Despite his sadness at being rejected, he nearly chuckled aloud at the thought of Kate needing any man.

Hell, what's Kate want with an ornery man hanging around all the time? Let alone the likes of me. She's done just fine so far. All I'd likely do, is up and ride off with old Jericho first time he beckoned.

Still, Poe continued to brood, wondering if he and Jericho's friendship could survive such a turn of events, if Kate should ever chose either of them.

They'd come into town because Poe had wanted to get Packard a reliable holster to replace the flap-top holster he was wearing. He was sure that before this adventure was over, he and Jericho would have need of Packard's gun. The general store at Big Springs was small but well stocked with most of the necessities they'd need to sustain them for the two week trip to El Paso. Poe decided Stump would leave them at Big Springs and go directly to Bluebonnet to pick up Moses Penny. He and Moses would wait until McCain arrived, or contacted them and instructed them differently. Poe went to the telegraph office and sent McCain a message of their intentions, then he and Jim Packard rode with Stump to a crossroads outside of Big Springs for final handshakes before the men parted ways.

On the trail once more and hungry for material for his diary, Jim attempted to draw out the unusually pensive Poe.

"What kind of man is the Captain? He seems kind of short tempered; I can't see why he was selected to run this operation…say over you. I mean. I've seen you shoot and I can't believe he could possibly be any better."

"Ummp!"

Undeterred, Jim plunged on. "Well, are you faster than the Captain?"

"Considerably."

"Are you a better shot?"

Poe cocked an eyebrow and glanced at the young man for the first time. "Marginally so, if you're talking pistols — but I wouldn't want to have to live with the difference. Rifles? Well, that's something else entirely. J.D. McCain comes from the Blue Ridge Mountains. He learned to shoot a squirrel-gun before he could walk. He may just be the best rifle shot alive. Certainly among the top three. I'm not talking about trick-shooting and such. I mean real life-or-death shooting — distance, accuracy, with someone shooting back."

He squirted tobacco juice at a rock as he rode past. "But what makes old Jericho the best, is that he has the Injun sign on ya before you even start."

Noting Jim's puzzled look, he explained. "I seen plenty of shootists with fast hands go against him. They're all dead now.

Just as I would likely be if I tried it. Call it bull-headedness, stubbornness, or jist cussed meanness, he has the edge the Injun sign. He jist plain don't ever quit! Once he gets something in his head, he never gives up on it. I swear you could kill him and he'd keep coming until he finished you off 'fore he up and died too."

The conversation subsequently turned to fast horses, whisky and then to women. Jim offhandedly brought up the subject of the Shaw family and when the conversation turned to Bethena, he said, "Beth married?"

"I thought *you* was married," Poe said pointedly. Seeing the look on young Jim's face, he quickly went on. "Things not going too well, huh? Well, there are some good marriages, but few happy ones."

Jim heard the chuckle that, after only a few days together, had already began to get on his nerves.

"You know what the man said, 'the most dangerous food a man can eat is wedding cake,'" Poe said, followed again by that awful chuckle again.

Embarrassed, Packard admitted, "Guess she was too young and I was too ambitious, and it was just sort of doomed from the start. Now, I don't know what to do about it."

Riding a spell longer, Poe finally said, "Beth was married to a feller named Howard Beck, a procurement agent for the Army. From what I hear, he was a good man. Treated Beth and the rest of the family real good. They were married for ten years. No children. I think it was Beth that couldn't have any."

Rosie rolled something around in his mouth and spit again. "He was on the overland stage coming back from one of his trips to Missouri, when one of those freak Northerners rolled through," he said. "None of the passengers were dressed for it. It was so bad the driver couldn't see the trail any more and they got lost in the storm. Soon as it cleared up enough, the stage line sent people out to look for them. When they finally pieced the story together, it looked like the stage got off the trail, broke an axle and got stranded. The party must have lived for several days, burning most of the stage to keep warm. Five people, including the horses, all dead."

Poe stared out over the vast landscape, then looked back at his traveling companion. "Beth took it real hard," he said. "She said she was never going to care that much for another man. Guess she meant it. A few years ago, she took up with a gambling feller and they was together for a couple of years, but try as he would, she refused to marry him. One day he up and took off with one of the young things that worked with him and Beth moved back to Kate's ranch. That was four years ago."

Poe spit a foul looking object onto the ground, and continued. "Two pretty women living there without husbands sure sparked a mite of interest. Wasn't long before most of the young hard-legs in the county started coming by, just to see if they needed anything," Rosie chuckled again. "Soon as Kate explained it to them with that Winchester rifle of hers, they quit dropping by."

The two men continued to ride without conversation until Packard said, "You think their minds are made up to be old maids, then?"

"Son, I think that if the right man comes along, and is smart enough to know he is the right man, any woman will get hitched," Poe said, thinking of J.D. McCain. "But with these two, it will damn sure have to be the right man."

They rode in silence for a long time, then more for companionship than any burning desire for information, Packard said, "Those things hit very often around here? The blizzards, I mean?"

"Every few years," Poe answered. "The problem is you never know when they're gonna blow up. It can be nice 'n sunny like now, one minute — then here she comes!"

Poe took a dirty looking mess that was his "plug o'chaw" from his shirt pocket, bit off a piece, and offered it to Packard. He declined, failing to completely hide his disgust. Undeterred, Poe gnawed off a large piece, and the rest disappeared back into his pocket.

"Been through several, myself. You can live through one of 'em if you know what to do. Wouldn't recommend it for the greenhorn though."

"What kind of things?"

"Well, I knowed a feller who gutted a cow and crawled inside to wait one out," Poe said, watching Packard from the corner of his eye, as if trying to determine how much of this he was buying. "But it was just having to go about your everyday business, that was hardest on folks. It gets so cold spit freezes in your mouth. A person's lips split wide open as soon as they're licked. Hard to get through the day and not lick your lips, even once. You know how hard that can be, young feller?"

Packard nodded his head tentatively.

Poe smiled smugly to himself, satisfied he now had Packard hooked. "We had some pretty bad winters back in Iowa when I was a boy, too. We learned a few tricks to help us get through the bad ones."

"Like what?" Jim said eagerly.

"Like how to keep from licking your lips while you were out working in one of them bitter cold days, for one thing."

Poe observed the younger man leaning slightly toward him watchfully, and fought to keep from chuckling.

"How did you do that, Mr. Poe?"

"Well, we had this old mule, and every morning my daddy would make me kiss that mule's arse," he said with a straight face.

Packard's jaw dropped and he stared at him in disbelief.

Poe squinted his eye at the young man, spit in the direction of a small bush, and said in all seriousness, "Take it from me boy. You kiss a mule's ass? You won't lick your lips the rest of the day! Hee, hee, hee!"

He was still chuckling ten minutes later.

* * *

It was on the second day that Poe spotted the tracks. At first, they held mainly to rocky surfaces and the sign was difficult for him to read. After several hours however, the riders seemed to have decided that secrecy was no longer important and the trail became easier to read.

When they finally came to the foothills and began to encounter more and more trees, the tracks crossed a small stream. As Packard watched the mounts to insure they didn't take too much water, Poe, more curious than anything else, walked to the far bank and knelt down. Instantly the hair rose on the back of his neck and he let out a soft whistle to alert Packard. Slipping his heavy pistol from its holster, he followed the tracks up the bank and into the far tree line. Packard, his own gun at the ready, though he didn't understand exactly way, followed a distance. Soon, Poe returned.

"You remember that little half-moon gouge in the front shoe

When Legends Lived

of one of those mounts at the Thompson ambush? Take a look here," he said, as he pointed to a location in the still wet dirt.

At first, Packard could see nothing. Then as he was about to give up, he saw what Poe meant. Fear griped his bowels and he jerked his head up to survey the tree line closer.

"Don't worry, I've already checked it out. They're gone," Poe assured him.

"What are we going to do?" Packard asked. "Follow them?"

"Boy, the *next* thing you learn, will be the *first* thing you know," Poe answered. "That would be the best way I know of to git ourselves killed."

Packard supposed Poe's folksy comment meant he didn't know a thing, and instantly felt just a little insulted.

Poe, seeing he'd hurt the young man's feelings, then remarked more gently, "We'll have to wait until we git more fire power."

Suddenly, Poe stopped dead still, staring back down the trail in the direction they'd just come. He cocked his head and listened. Jim, beginning to respect the old ranger's uncanny abilities, suddenly felt the hair rise on his neck once more.

"Someone's coming. Git behind that big rock and I'll git over near the bend in the creek. That way, we'll have them in a crossfire."

Packard was not all that happy about splitting up, but managed to do as he was told without opening his mouth, which he was sure would have been a big mistake at that particular moment.

As the rider came into view, they saw it was young Billy Shaw. He was riding with a rifle across his saddle horn and it was apparent he was reading the trail they found. Poe softly called out from behind his cover before standing up. "Billy. Billy Shaw. It's me. Roosevelt Poe."

As it was, Billy almost shot anyway. Poe, moving carefully, went to where Billy sat on his mount. From the pale haggard look on Billy's face, both men could tell something was terribly wrong. Instantly, Poe's heart turned over as he thought of Kate.

"What 'ya doing way out here, Billy?" Poe said softly.

"Those murdering bastards stole Aunt Bethena," nearly choking as he cried it out.

"Git off your horse, Billy. You need to tell me all you know about it, then we'll decide how to handle it," Poe said.

Dismounting, Billy told them about he and Kate riding out to meet his aunt because she hadn't shown up at the ranch before dark as she had always on previous trips to the Parker's place. He relayed how he and his mother found the over-turned wagon and the horse shot full of holes on the side of the road. After an argument, the two had decided Kate would ride back to the ranch and get the ranch hands. Billy would follow the trail, being careful not to be seen, leaving signs along the way that Kate and the ranch hands could easily follow. Both men could see the boy was nearly exhausted and on the verge of tears most of the time during the telling of the story.

"Billy, I want you to listen to me and do exactly as I say," Poe told him. "Do you understand?"

Billy nodded his head.

"Do you trust me?"

Billy remembered all the stories he'd heard from his mother and Aunt Bethena about the two Rangers, Roosevelt Poe and J.D. McCain. Slowly, he nodded his head again.

"I want you to get back to your mother as fast as you can. She's in danger and you have to be there to help protect her," he said. "These are real bad men, Billy. The worst. Your mother and her men wouldn't have a chance without knowing what they're up against. Git to her and tell her it was Scar. Tell her to protect herself and I'll bring Beth back. That's all."

He glanced at Packard, who was staring back at him in disbelief and appeared ready to interject something. "That's all," Poe said again. "I'll bring her back home."

As Billy headed back down the ridge line, Packard harshly said, "Are you trying to get us killed? You said yourself we needed more men to go after them."

"That was back when we didn't *need* to go after them. Thing's have changed considerably. Now we need to," Poe said grimly and spit a stream of juice onto a nearby rock. "Besides, a group that size wouldn't get within pissing distance of Scar. Just the two of us might have a chance though."

"Well I think it's crazy and we should wait for Kate and her men," Packard said.

"You're welcome to your opinion," Poe said, sounding as though he wasn't. "I just ain't interested in it." He walked toward the horses and said over his shoulder, "Git mounted, and if you decide to turn back or delay me, or hinder our effort in any manner, I'll shoot you out of your saddle without so much as a warning."

He paused with one foot in the stirrup for just an instant and gazed at the young man, as though to ensure he was making an impact on Packard. "I mean what I say, Jim. Much as I like you, I'll put you away. That's family out there. That's Beth. I've known her since she was this big, and I know what that little gal's going through right now. If she's not dead already, she's not going to have to endure it for any longer than it takes for me to find her."

He mounted his horse. "Then I'm going to put a bunch of holes in each of those murdering mother's sons that took her."

Spurring his horse, he moved up toward the tree line between them and the high peaks to their west.

It was nearly dark when Poe finally stopped and carefully moved his horse into a thicket beside the trail. They'd been climbing steadily for the past three hours and the mountain air was beginning to have a nip in it. Dismounting, he placed his forefinger to his lips as a warning for Packard to be quiet, then led the horse away from the trail for what seemed like a long distance. At last, he once again moved higher up the ridge line. They traveled for another thirty minutes before Poe tied his horse to a branch and sat down with his back to a tree, facing the direction from they had just come.

"Do we sleep here tonight?" Jim said.

"No. We wait here until it gets full dark, then I go down and take Beth back," he said.

Packard was clearly taken aback. "You know where she's at?" he said incredulously.

"I smelled smoke back where we left the trail. We were real close then. I'll know exactly where they're at when I get down there."

Clearly worried, Packard said to Poe, "How do you plan to do it?"

"I'm just going to ride down there and kill them all," he said simply.

"Sounds like an excellent plan," Jim said, sourly.

"I don't need you," Poe said. "Just stay out of it until it's over. If I ain't back within thirty minutes after the shooting stops, you light a shuck back to Kate's ranch and tell her…" he paused, "…tell her I tried and Beth's not suffering any more."

"The hell with you! I didn't ride all this way to sit hiding in the woods while you act like a damn hero alone!" Packard stated angrily.

When Legends Lived

"You'll do as I say."

"The hell I will! What are you going to do if I don't? Shoot me?" Jim said hotly. "One shot will bring all of Scar's men down on us."

There was a profound silence between the two men for several minutes.

"There are no heroes in this kind of business, son," Poe told him, tiredly. "After a while, you lose all your kindness, your ability to feel, and any shred of decency you might have had. You do things to other men that civilized folks would find repugnant. You wonder if you have given up any chance of ever going to heaven."

"Why do you do it then?"

"For Bethena," Poe said simply. "For all the scared, hurt little Beth's that can't do it for themselves. The look on one of those frightened faces after you've come to get them out answers all the questions about why you do it."

"Well, I'll be there with you when you do it this time," Packard said stubbornly.

That abruptly ended the conversation for the next two hours. Suddenly, Poe rose to his feet so silently, that if Packard had been slightly dozing at the time, he would've failed to hear him. Quickly, he followed, but not nearly so quietly. Poe's hard eyes bored through him, annoyed at the slight sounds. Ignoring Poe, Jim followed him back down the trail they'd made into the thicket earlier. Both men led their horses.

Poe held out his hand and they halted, then Poe placed his hand over his mare's nose to keep her quiet. Packard did the same to his horse. Just across a small stream to their front, he could now see the glow of a small fire and the shapes of several men sitting or lying on the ground nearby. Near the fire, they could make out the shape of Bethena laying on the ground, naked except for what remained of her dirty tattered dress, which she merely pulled over herself to keep warm. They were so close now that Jim Packard could hear some of the conversation between the men.

"Let's hang her on a tree and pull some skin off of her," one of the men said, taking a long drink from a crock jug.

"In the morning. First, I want to tap it one more time, and I'm so sore right now that I won't be able to until then," said the half-breed with the leggings, as he slowly rubbed his crotch. Three of the men snickered.

"I say we cut her throat now and follow Scar," said Kiowa Jack as he jerked the whisky jug from the other man's hands. He too, took a deep swallow of the fiery liquid and set it on the ground within easy reach.

"Boys, give me a drink of that whiskey. I hurt awful."

The plea came from a man lying near the outer edge of the circle of light, being cast by the small fire. He appeared to be injured.

"Shut up Johns, 'fore we let this hell cat come over there and scratch those blisters on yore face," said the outlaw with the beaded hat. The others laughed loudly and "Johns" didn't retort.

Packard watched as Poe silently slipped into the saddle and pulled his long-barreled Walker from its holster. Packard climbed onto his mount, as well, and imitating Poe, drew his own pistol.

"You try skinning her and I'll skin you!" Dog-Soldier said, his voice pitched. "I bought her and Scar said I could have her as my woman!"

"You stupid dung-eating dog. What are…"

Without a word, Poe suddenly spurred his horse straight at the camp and was among the outlaws before they were aware

When Legends Lived

of him. He shot Dog-Soldier first and Kiowa Jack next. So fast were the shots that both reports seemed almost as one. Devil-Man screamed and scrambled up the small bank toward the place where the horses were tied. Savagely yanking the reins in his left hand, Poe pivoted his horse in a tight circle as he shot him between the shoulder-blades. Then without waiting to watch him fall, quickly turned his gun on Choctaw who seemed to pause in mid-motion of raising his own pistol. In that split second, the outlaw realized he was dead — then he was.

Leaping from his horse, Poe ran to where Beth huddled on the ground, yelling at Packard. "Check 'em for life! Scar's not here! Be alert!"

Packard, shocked at the short amount of time it had taken to kill four men, suddenly realized he hadn't fired a shot. Dazed, he dismounted and did as Poe instructed. Three of the men were clearly dead and the fourth moaning slightly, was near death. The last, lying nearby on a blanket, blisters and scabs almost completely covering his face, hadn't been shot. The man squinted at him painfully, cowering in fear as Packard pointed his pistol at him.

"One of them is still alive but about dead. This one's alive," he told Poe.

Poe, gently cradling Bethena to his chest and speaking softly to her as she lay unmoving, staring straight ahead, didn't look up. "Then kill him."

"I can't just shoot him in cold blood!" Jim shouted, keeping his pistol aimed at Johns.

"Give him a gun first — and then shoot him. Makes no difference to me. Either way, he's gonna be buzzard food before we leave here, and that's a fact," Poe told him as he tenderly wiped Beth's dirty face with his handkerchief. "After you do it, bring my canteen."

Instead of shooting Johns, Packard slowly backed to the sorrel and retrieved Rosie's canteen, his pistol never wavering. Keeping his eye on the blistered man, he started to hand the canteen to Poe who ignored it.

"Give her a just a sip," Poe said. "We don't want her sick."

He made room for Jim to take his place beside the injured woman and stood. Beth made her first sounds of protest which Poe instantly took as a positive sign. "This is Jim Packard, Darlin'," he said gently. "You remember Jim. He's gonna look after you for just a minute and then I'll be back. I promise."

Replacing the cartridges in his pistol as he walked, Poe moved to where Johns lay silently staring at them, and squatted down. He shook his head slowly and said, "If you ain't a pitiful sight."

Johns remained quiet while trying to avert eyes that were half-swollen shut.

"Where did Scar go and who was with him?" his antagonist said quietly.

"You're Poe, ain't you?" Johns croaked.

"I'll ask the questions," Poe replied. "We don't have much time here, you see. You ain't got much time left and I want to keep this as painless for you as you'll let me."

"Why do you think I would want to tell you anything, if you're gonna kill me anyhow?" the man said weakly as he squinted at Poe through watery eyes.

"Because there's dying — and then there's dying," Poe said softly and spit. He slowly slid a long thin blade knife from the top of his right boot. "There's the quick, bullet-between-the-eyes kind of dying, and there's the long-drawn-out-strip-of-skin, by strip-of-skin kind of dying. You tell me which kind you're interested in and we'll git started."

The look in Poe's hard eyes convinced the doomed man he had but one alternative. He and Poe talked quietly for a few moments, then Poe suddenly stood, and in one fluid motion, pulled his pistol from its holster and shot Johns between the eyes. The report was loud and seemed to echo and reverberate through the canyons and ridges for a long time. Without looking at Johns's body again, he approached Kiowa Jack, still somewhat alive, near the fire. His sleeve was starting to smoke. As Poe raised the heavy pistol, the renegade smiled a nasty smile and started to say something. Again, the loud report rang out. In turn, he walked to each of the unmoving men and put a single round through their heads. Pausing briefly to reload, he placed the pistol back into its holster and walked over to his sorrel, where he removed a shirt and a pair of trousers from his saddle-bag. Then he briskly moved to where Bethena and Jim waited.

Poe ignored the pale, accusing look on the young man's face as he said, "Murdering trash like these have a tendency to come back to life, if you don't make dead sure. I know. Scar done it to me and Jericho about eight years ago."

He knelt beside Bethena and gently told her, "I've come to take you home, girl. First I want you to put these pretty clothes on."

Tears formed at the corner of her eyes as she slowly shook her head from side to side, and moaned softly.

"Now don't you worry," Poe said softly. "Everything's gonna be just fine. Kate and the girls don't care what happened out here. They love you and just want you back home. I'm gonna be right here with you, all the way."

That seemed to calm her somewhat; however, her gaze soon returned to a place on the distant horizon that she could see but no one else could.

Fourteen

A Smith and Wesson beats four aces every time."
– A Western gambler

JAKE KELLOG DEALT THE battered cards to four other men sitting around the table, much as he'd been doing for the past three hours. There was little talk among them and in the silence each card made a small audible click as it landed on the bare table. As Kellog studied his cards, he also studied the poker players at the table. "Digger," the undertaker, was about even for the evening, and young Callahan had just about lost his months pay and would be dropping out of the game soon. The next player looked like he could be a soldier, but wasn't in uniform at the time. Probably a deserter, or maybe just recently discharged.

The man in the black suit, however, looked like trouble. *A professional gambler no doubt,* Kellog thought. The gambler had the mean eyes of a person who had seen and done things he hoped other people wouldn't find out about. The game wasn't going well for him, hadn't been for quite a while. For most of the past three hours he'd been losing steadily and growing increasingly agitated after each hand he was dealt. After the last losing hand, he threw his useless cards toward the middle of the table accompanied by loud profane curses, which caused others in the room to turn and stare.

Jake, finished the deal and set the cards aside. Digger bet low and the table called around to Jake, who studied his cards once more, then raised. The man in the black suit glared at him with undisguised hostility. Jake smiled back "Your raise and one better," Digger said, shoving a small stack of chips to the middle of the table.

Callahan threw his cards into the discard pile, and with soft a curse, rose to leave. The "soldier" called, as did the gambler, and Jake raised once more. Again, the man in the black suit looked hard at him. Again, Jake smiled.

"I don't know what you're so proud of," Digger said, eyeing Jake's exposed cards. "Call!" he finally said, shoving more chips to the center.

Everyone else also called around the table. Jake laid down his three Kings and two Jacks, without saying anything.

"You're just a little too slick with that dealing," Black Suit said.

Jake stopped in the middle of raking in his winnings, looked mildly amused at the man, and said, "Meaning?"

He looked relaxed, like he'd been here before.

"I mean, every time you deal, you win." The man's eyes looked like buttons.

Jake had encountered more than his share of trouble in the past and could easily recognize it when he saw it coming. He saw no reason to let it get out of hand if he could help it. "That's it, gents. I'm out of the game," Jake stated as he started to rise.

"You're not out of anything," the gambler said roughly. "Not until I get a chance to get my money back."

The place grew completely quiet and everybody was watching the by-play of the two men.

"Mister, you've pushed this about as far as I'm going to allow you to go with me," Jake said quietly. "I'm done."

"You're done, all right, you bottom-dealing, cheating bastard!" Black Suit yelled as he stood and flashed a hidden sleeve gun to his palm with a slight flick of his wrist.

Jake Kellog had seen it many times, and was even expecting it. His shot hurdled the man backward and sent him crashing into adjoining card tables as he fell to the floor. The gambler gurgled once but didn't move. Harvy Cummings, the bartender, ran out of the saloon door as fast as his fat little legs would carry him toward the sheriff's office. As suddenly as it had started, it was over and the saloon returned to its normal activity, the old piano banging away off-key.

Within a few minutes, Silent John and his two deputies entered the door. Jake had placed his pistol on the table and was standing at the bar, twenty feet away. The two deputies spread out and stood on either side of the room with their hands resting on gun-butts. Silent John walked over and stared down at the man in the black suit and white ruffled shirt, marked with a conspicuous red stain on its front.

"He have a gun?"

"On the bar, Sheriff," Digger volunteered.

"Since I doubt he shot himself, where is the other gun?"

"Over there on the table, Sheriff." Jake Kellog pointed across the room.

"Your gun?" Silent John was still staring at the dead man.

"Yes."

"Self-defense?" he said, looking around the room as each person who had witnessed the killing nodded their heads.

Walking up to Jake, he smiled. "Well, it looks like a clear case of self-defense to me."

Then, without warning, he slammed his "piss-elm club" into

the side of Jake Kellog's head, dropping him instantly to the polished floor. Jake lay as if dead. Silent John clenched his jaws tightly, causing features to appear chiseled from stone, as he stood over Jake for a moment looking down at him. Then he kicked him viciously. Again he kicked Jake, as the patrons in the saloon grimaced with each sickening blow. For several minutes the sheriff savagely kicked the unconscious form of Jake Kellog with the full force of his pointed brown shoes, grunting with the effort each time. Breathing deeply, he finally turned to Donny Pence, mopping his brow.

"I don't like guns in my town. Lock him up. We'll give him a trial when the judge gets back — then we'll hang the son-of-a-bitch."

* * *

They rode down the mountain the way they had come up, Jim Packard a little ahead and Poe riding behind cradling Beth's unmoving form tenderly against his chest. He led the mount he'd taken from the outlaws, in hopes that Bethena would be able to ride later. Packard knew Roosevelt Poe was suffering with severe pain in his back by the way he grimaced each time he shifted his body to accommodate the extra weight of Beth on his horse. Despite Packard's offers to spell him, Poe continued to carry the injured woman on his mount as they descended mile after mile through the rough country.

When they reached the stream where they'd first seen the tracks and met Billy Shaw, Poe told Jim, "Find a spot up the ridge where you can see this crossing. Take your Winchester and give us some cover while I make Beth more presentable for her family."

When Legends Lived

As Jim settled into the position, he took out his black book and a pencil, then paused, as he saw Poe carry Bethena to the water and sat her down on a flat rock. From where he was crouched on the rock, he could hear Poe's soft murmurs as he pampered the unresponsive woman. As he watched, Poe took the bandana from around his neck and soaked it in the stream, then he removed the shirt and men's trousers he'd put on her earlier. Lifting her gently by the shoulders, Poe eased her into the cool water, while she stared at the horizon. He appeared unmindful of the cold water as he wrung out the bandana and used it to clean the grime from her face.

Jim noticed Poe kept his eyes averted modestly whenever possible throughout the bathing. Watching from a distance, Jim wondered at the makeup of a man who could calmly kill five other human beings, seemingly without any noticeable remorse, and then display such gentleness and tenderness toward this helpless tormented girl.

Recalling the night he'd first met Beth at Kate's ranch, Packard remembered how he'd been drawn to her from the first. Now, seeing her like this, stirred feelings in him he'd never have thought possible just a short time before.

Poe watched for any signs of recognition as he went about tending to Beth. So far, there hadn't been any. The toilet-kit Poe had bought in Amarillo for Rita, the working lady at Paco's, was complete with soap, a Mother-of-pearl brush, and a comb and brush set. He chuckled softly as he remembered the way Jericho had almost thrown a duck-fit over him buying a whore a gift. Poe took the scented soap from the packet and thoroughly washed Beth's long blond hair and dirt-caked body, with it. Then he gently scooped handfuls of the clear, cool water over her battered and bruised limbs. Finally, he fully clothed her in his clean shirt and pants once more, and sat her down again on the flat rock. He continued to talk softly to her as he gently combed her hair, then brushed it over and over until at last, it was dry and shiny once again.

Packard faintly heard Poe speak as stepped back and admired his work. "There you are, darl'n. Pretty as a picture."

Bethena slightly turned her head and looked directly at Poe, but remained silent.

"Don't you feel much better now?" he said.

After waiting a while for an answer and failing to get the response he had hoped for, Poe continued. "I thought so. Now, how about a little bite to eat? I make about the best sourdough crawl-fish bread you ever 'et in your life." He chuckled.

With that, he helped Bethena to her feet and started her back up the hill toward the spot they had selected as their campsite earlier. He didn't comment on the fact that she was walking on her own. Poe's back pain had eased somewhat, too, now that the riding-double part of the day was over.

That night Bethena remained attached to Roosevelt Poe as though another appendage, clinging to his arm. Although Jim made several attempts to share in Poe's caring of the woman, all he received for his efforts was a low moan of protest every time he tried to dislodge her from Roosevelt's side. Soon, he gave up and just took care of the camp duties for the group. By noon the next day, they were well into the foothills and able to move more rapidly toward the Shaw ranch; however, it was late the following day before they arrived.

As they neared the ranch house, Kate, Billy and the girls ran to meet them. Kate's forced smile couldn't hide her deep concern and from behind Beth's head, Poe made a precautionary sign that all wasn't well.

As Poe reined in his burdened mount in front of the small group, he said, "See there darl'n. I told you your family was waiting for ya."

Kate lifted her arms for the injured woman and Poe gently eased her down into the waiting arms, then watched as Kate tenderly hugged her sister and brushed the hair from her eyes. She tenderly wrapped her arms around Bethena's shoulders and cast a worried look at Poe as she led the dazed woman up the steps.

"Girls, go turn down your Aunt Beth's covers, she's real tired and will want to lay down," she said. Obediently, her daughters ran to do as they were told.

Forgotten for the moment, Poe and Jim took care of their horses, cleaned themselves up a bit, then returned to the ranch house. Kate met them at the door and placing her finger over her lips, whispered, "She's sleeping soundly."

She led them into the kitchen, where they could talk without disturbing the sleeping girl. "God bless you both," she said, tears seeping from the corners of her eyes. "I'll never be able to repay you for what you've done."

Embarrassed, both men averted their eyes and shifted their weight from foot to foot.

Poe said, "She sort of latched onto me a mite after we found her. When she wakes up and finds I'm not here, it could get a little dicey. Better keep someone with her at all times."

"How bad was it for her, Roosevelt?" Kate said.

He hesitated, then said, "As bad as it can get, Katie."

"Did you kill him?"

"I killed five of them," he stated matter-of-factly. "Scar had left before we arrived but it won't be for long. Me and Jericho plan to stay on him like ugly on a pig this time until he's deader'n dirt."

"When do you and Jim have to leave, Roosevelt?"

"We better be going and git this little chore over with, so I can git back here for some more of your apple pie."

"You're absolutely indestructible, Roosevelt Poe," she smiled. Then more seriously, "When it's over, ask Jericho to come back with you next time."

"He'll come. One way or the other, I promise I'll bring Jericho here, if I have to hog-tie him and drag him with a rope every last mile between here and Bluebonnet!"

Walking over to Jim Packard, Kate hugged him and said, "Consider yourself family around here as well, Jim. You'll never need a home as long as I own this ranch."

A lump formed in the young man's throat and perhaps for the first time in his life, the smooth, sophisticated Jim Packard was totally without words. From close behind he heard Rosie Poe's soft knowing chuckle.

Upon awaking from a death-like sleep the next morning, they found that Doc Blanchard had arrived sometime during the night. Despite their plans to leave the following morning, Blanchard convinced Poe that his not being present when Bethena awoke might send her into hysterics; or worse, a deep coma from which she might never recover.

"I guess there's just no alternative," Poe told Jim the following morning. "I got to stay a spell. I'll tell you the route and you've got to git to Bluebonnet and let Jericho know what's going on before that heathen's trail gits too cold to follow. I'll meet up with you somewhere along the way."

When Legends Lived

"I think I know a way for you to find us when it's okay for you to leave here," Jim told Poe. "The railroad has a telegraph method of communicating with the executives of the company when they travel around the country. They send out an 'all stations' message and that message can be picked up at any railroad or telegraph station in the country. When I get to Bluebonnet, I'll set it up."

He paused. "That is, if I can even find Bluebonnet," he said grimly.

By early afternoon Jim Packard had saddled his horse and looked, for the tenth time, at the map Poe had drawn for him, then started on his uncertain journey with a single wave of his hand.

"Give your back a rest," he said, in parting. "I could tell it was hurting you on the trail."

Poe nodded glumly as he watched the young man ride away, feeling just a bit left out of things. He sighed deeply, turned and went inside.

* * *

Rosco Bookbinder had been alone for nearly two weeks now on the trail of Bloody Bill and his outlaw band that had stolen Jenny. At first, there'd been thirty others with him. After they'd discovered the army resupply wagons and a day later, the old couple's homestead, most of the men decided they'd left important business back in El Paso. For the few that remained, it was the discovery of the captured wives' bodies that ended the posse's existence. The outlaw band had taken the women along with them, for another three days beyond the old people's cabin.

The pursuers had smelled them first. When they got closer

the sight was enough to drive a civilized person to madness. Body parts were everywhere; a head here, a leg there, a hand farther along. A complete torso over there! The posse retreated back down the trail with handkerchiefs covering their faces.

"Looks like they might've drunk themselves into a frenzy and got carried away," said Hank Torme, who'd scouted for Tatum in the early days of Texas. "Thought I'd see'd everything, once or twice. I never see'd nothin' like that!"

That discovery marked the unraveling of any collective bravado they'd initially mustered, and the remaining members of the posse turned around and headed back towards El Paso. All except for Rosco. That was Jenny out there. She'd expect him to come and get her. Probably scared to death and no telling what's happening to her. *Well, no matter,* he told himself. He could overlook *anything* for Jenny. Jenny was his family.

In fact, Jenny was the only family he'd ever really known — Rosco Bookbinder was an orphan. He didn't remember his father, and his mother had died on the trail out from Kentucky when he was ten. An old German gunsmith named Haike had finally taken him in, more for the free labor he could provide than for a desire to do good. There, he learned about guns and how to shoot. In the six years he was with the immigrant, he couldn't remember a single word the old man had spoken to him that wasn't either an order, or a curse.

For years at night, he'd often sit on a keg in front of the gun shop and watch well-dressed men and women walking with their families, laughing and talking as they hustled by. How he'd admired their fine clothing — and envied them their families. Sometimes, he'd pick out certain ones and pretend they were his family. After a while, he could recognize almost every family

When Legends Lived

in the town of St. Joseph, Missouri. The good folks of St. Joe, never gave an indication they even knew he existed.

When he was fifteen, he told the old man he wouldn't work simply for food, and a blanket in the old tool shed out back, anymore. They'd argued and he'd prepared to leave, but the old German's eyes had deteriorated rapidly during those last two years and he couldn't see to work on the guns brought in for repair, or to the make the new ones already ordered. Through the years, he'd grown increasingly dependant upon Rosco's nimble hands and fine eyesight, and he'd received countless compliments on Rosco's superb craftsmanship.

In the end, he'd relented and Rosco worked for him another year at decent wages, which he saved. With that money, he bought the fine clothes and horse he'd envied for so long. On his last day, he'd simply packed the black suit and white shirts into a saddle bag and saddled the tall horse, took the two fine pistols he'd spent over a year making for himself, and quietly rode away. He never said goodbye, and he looked back.

He'd drifted north to Colorado, where he'd been offered the job of deputy by Silent John, after the town marshal had seen him out-shoot all comers in a local shooting contest. He'd used his earnings to buy even better clothes, and a finer horse, but he'd kept the pistols. They were the best brace of handguns he'd ever seen.

When Silent John was offered the job of Sheriff of El Paso, he'd asked Rosco to come with him. That was where he'd first seen Jenny, and he'd loved her from the very first moment he laid eyes on her. When he'd bravely mustered his courage and finally asked her to marry him, and she'd agreed, he'd been the happiest man in the world. At last, he had a family. Losing the baby had hurt a great deal — but they'd have more kids. But first, he had to rescue Jenny and take her back home with him. There wasn't a force on God's green earth that could keep him from doing that.

After the others had left him on the trail, he'd followed the outlaw band across the Sacramento mountain range through a pass lying to the northeast of El Paso, and was now well into the hot dry flatlands. Back where the foothills had ended, it appeared as if three sets of tracks had left the main group and were headed due south, towards Odessa. Surmising that the outlaw leader might somehow have known he was being chased and decided to split with the main group, taking the hostage with him, Rosco followed the smaller group south.

It'd now been more than three hours since he'd picked up the trail. Never once had the tracks converged with any of the main trails in the area, which were becoming more numerous the further south they traveled. He carefully followed the three sets of hoof-prints into a deep ravine and had traveled only a few hundred feet when he rounded a bend and suddenly came face-to-face with the three people he was following. All were men.

Upon catching sight of him, the three outlaws went for their guns without a word. Rosco instantly shot the nearest one through the heart and then turned his gun on the second man as that one leveled his pistol at the deputy. Rosco also killed him with one shot and swung toward the remaining outlaw. The third man was good. He fired an instant before Rosco and the lawman felt the heavy .44 slug smash his right thigh, just above the knee. Rosco squeezed off a shot as the other man fired his second round, and briefly saw the bullet hit the last man in the face. Simultaneously, he felt something hard slam into him causing his entire chest to go numb. Dream-like, he felt himself slip from his horse, slowly floating through the air into the vast black void beneath him.

* * *

The three Thompson ranch vaqueros had returned to the ambush site earlier and repaired the wagon Sam Thompson had been driving the day he died. Afterward, they had sat in the meager shade it provided and ate their cold bean wrapped tortillas. They were just struggling to turn it upright when they heard the distant shots. Chico, the old man of the group at twenty-four, decided they should check it out. Within minutes, they were looking down into the deep ravine at four unmoving bodies. Leaving the others to stand guard with their rifles, Chico carefully climbed down the steep embankment to investigate. With gun in hand, he first checked the three bodies clustered together. Then he walked the short distance to where Rosco lay. Quickly searching he found a faint heartbeat — and the deputy sheriff badge.

"This hombre's alive — I think. Bring the wagon! *Darse prisa! Darse prisa!*"

As the others rushed to obey, Chico carefully removed the young deputy's shirt and used it to slow down the bleeding. When the wagon arrived, they hoisted Rosco's unconscious form to the lip of the ravine, loaded it onto the rickety wagon, and immediately started for the Thompson ranch. Although the vaqueros traveled day and night, it still took two full days to reach their destination. At first, the tall stranger in the wagon lay as though already dead. Then, sometime during that first night, the fever hit. After that, the delirious man alternately cursed at Bill, and then called tenderly for someone named of Jenny.

By the morning of the second day, the exhausted ranch hands were convinced their cargo was as good as dead and all their efforts to save him were futile. By then, the sounds coming from the back of the wagon had been reduced to mere muttering, and the man had the look of death about him. The superstitious, younger men wanted to leave Rosco by the side of the trail and finish their mission. They cast worried looks toward the wagon and crossed themselves repeatedly, muttering prayers long idle. Chico berated them with insults, until convinced their very manhood was at stake, they silently, but reluctantly continued the slow journey.

The party finally arrived at the Thompson spread, with Rosco barely clinging to life. Slipping in and out of consciousness, he hovered for another three days, but on the fourth day, he opened his eyes to see Dixie Thompson bending over him.

"Are you an angel?" he whispered weakly.

"No."

"You sure look like an angel," Rosco insisted.

"Well, I'm not an angel. And you're not likely to see one any time soon."

"Where am I?"

"You're at the Thompson ranch. I'm Dixie Thompson. Three of our men brought you in near dead, three days ago. From the looks of the mess where they found you, you shot it out with three tough-looking fellows and came out on top, but just barely," she said. "Now don't talk anymore. You're not out of the woods, yet."

Rosco tiredly closed his eyes and slipped back into the welcome void. He didn't open them again for the next two days. When he did, he lay dazed, his mind foggy, not knowing where he was or how he'd gotten there. Then, it all came back to him in a rush. Jenny. The shootout in the ravine. Wildly, he thought, I've got to get going, pick up the trail of the main group before it becomes lost forever. He saw something move at the edge of his vision and turning his head made out the features of the young woman he had talked to before. She was sewing.

"I've got to get up," he said, "I've lost time."

"Sure, go ahead," Dixie said, looking up.

She watched with a disapproving frown while Rosco attempted, several times, to drag himself from the bed, and then weakly fell back on his pillow, groaning.

"Well, dammit! Help me."

"Oh, no," Dixie responded. "All of you tough men are always ready to do just what you want to, no matter if everybody else says it may kill you the very next minute. I will not help you kill yourself after I've spent a whole week trying to nurse you back to life."

Bounding to her feet, she glared at him. "If you want to kill yourself, I'll just have someone bring your gun and you can shoot yourself!" She angrily marched out of the room.

* * *

Two more weeks passed before Rosco was strong enough to move to the front porch and sit for any length of time. During those two weeks, Dixie was nearly always present, leaving only when Rosco had to use the small chamber kept beneath his bed. That chore was left to Juanita, the Thompson's housekeeper and cook for over twenty years. Juanita weighed well over two hundred pounds and was as strong as any man Rosco had ever known. She had little difficulty lifting his weakened body out of the bed for that purpose or to change his sheets. The thing that embarrassed him most was when Dixie or the fat Juanita came to empty the chamber. He solemnly vowed to himself that if he didn't die outright the next time he got shot, he would take his gun and blow his own head off.

His slow progress improving, a few days after being moved to the large chair on the front porch, Chico, presented him with a pair of handmade crutches. For the next few days Rosco tripped and stumbled as he awkwardly attempted to master them and he was always surprised when Dixie seemed to come out of nowhere to rescue him, especially when he seemed to be on the verge of a bad spill. In fact, he found himself relying upon pretty young Dixie Thompson more and more as the days flew by. On those days when she was away on errands, he would find himself impatiently watching up the road for her return and experience a sense of extreme happiness when finally he did see her. Under Dixie's watchful eye, Rosco progressed. Finally, he was able to get around reasonably well with the cane she brought back from Odessa for him. He saw little of her brothers or the Circle-T hands. The few times he saw Brady, the boy appeared sullen and hastily limped away without speaking. Rosco wondered at the tragedy that had befallen one so young which resulted in him having to go through life hobbling around on such a bent and twisted limb — and so angry at the world.

Rosco's nights were still filled of dreams of Jenny and a faceless man named Bloody Bill. Sometimes she would suddenly become Dixie Thompson — then, both women at once. Even when he was awake, they would become jumbled in his thoughts, sometimes Jenny, sometimes Dixie, and each a distinct part of his

When Legends Lived

family. He made up his mind he had to leave soon or he might never go.

One evening as he and Dixie Thompson were taking their usual walk around the large pond to the back of the barn area, she remarked, "You don't seem to be using the cane as much as you did yesterday."

"No, I feel pretty good. I think I could ride a horse now," he replied.

"Then I guess I'm about ready to lose my patient," Dixie said brightly, averting her eyes.

A deafening silence lasted for several minutes. Then Rosco said, "You know we've never talked about how I came to be lying at the bottom of that ravine, all shot to pieces. And, you never asked."

Dixie looked slightly amused for a moment. "Deputy Rosco Bookbinder of El Paso, Texas. Bloody Bill Reid stole your wife after one of his raids into New Mexico, and killed a bunch of other people near El Paso too — Army folk. You took in after him with a posse but they all lost their nerve and turned back after they found the Army's convoy ambushed. You continued on and was ambushed by the three men we found you lying near in the ravine."

Dixie paused, "Sheriff Silent John says you are the fastest thing with a gun he has seen in a month of Sundays. Did I leave anything out?"

Stunned for an instant, Rosco just looked at her.

"Well," she said, "we couldn't be expected to just take some wounded stranger into our home and let him stay without at least finding out something about him."

Rosco threw back his head and laughed. It was the first time he'd laughed in months, and it felt good. Soon Dixie was laughing too.

After a while Dixie said, "When will you leave?"

"Soon."

"Don't just up and ride out one night, Rosco. At least come and tell me."

"I will." After a while, he said, "Dixie, I have to go. She's my wife."

"I know you do, but if things don't work out the way you hope, just know that…well, that you have friends here and… just come see us sometimes," she said, trailing off at the end. "And try not to get yourself all shot up any more."

Reaching into one of the deep pockets of her riding skirt, she handed him a small rawhide pouch. She forced a small smile and said, " Here, you might need this. It was a gift from Daddy, I think he'd approve."

Taking the pouch, Rosco removed a small tubular item. He'd never seen one, but he knew instantly what it was. Without encouragement, he pulled on each end and the overlapping sections of the small tube extended to a ten-inch length. The telescope was exquisitely crafted, encased in soft gray leather and trimmed with fine silver. Raising it to his eye, Rosco scanned the countryside. Finally, he lowered it and softly whistled.

"I've heard of these things but I've never looked through one," he said in amazement. Then sighing deeply, "Miss Dixie, you've already done too much for me. I'll always be in your debt. But… I can't accept this fine gift. Your father gave it to you and I know how precious it must be to you, now that he's gone. I'm sorry, but I just can't."

"Then take it as a loan. That way, I know you'll have to come back…to return it. Please. I really want you to."

Looking into her face, Rosco was overcome with the urge to

take her into his arms and kiss her. *What the hell am I thinking about?* Then he sadly thought, *I'm a married man*; and the moment was gone. Shaken, he silently nodded his head and stepped back.

Dixie stood unmoving for an instant longer, then as she turned to leave said, "Word is that Bloody Bill Reid and his bunch are raiding farms and small ranches south of here. The Odessa sheriff told my brother Nate they derailed a train down near Fort Stockton on the Stockton Plateau."

Then she was gone.

* * *

Several days later, nearly two full months since the vaqueros first brought the deputy to the ranch, Dixie walked into the barn to find the deputy sorting his gear and making preparations to leave.

"Tonight?" was all she said.

"I was going to come right up to the ranch and tell you," Rosco said shamefaced. "I really was going…"

Dixie started to turn away, then turned back. "I'll miss you something terrible," she cried and tears suddenly filling her eyes, ran from the barn.

Rosco looked after her long after she'd disappeared. "And I, you," he said softly, suddenly feeling as if he'd just lost his best friend.

He left before dawn the next morning, riding south toward the Stockton Plateau without speaking with Dixie Thompson again.

Fifteen

A Texas Ranger ain't nothing but a paid killer. The whole bunch are just low-lifes and riff-raff who spend their time drinking, cussing, fighting, and whoring around. I ain't met one yet that has an ounce of military bearing in him. They ride like the wind, shoot like the devil, and ain't scared of anything that walks on the face of this green earth. They ain't fit for nothing but what I'm using 'em for ...and lord, I wish I had another thousand."

– General Zachary Taylor (1864)

STUMP HENRY HAD ARRIVED at Bluebonnet two weeks earlier. Within several days, "that railroad man" came riding in, looking tired, hungry and filthy — or as Moses Penny said, "looking like something the cat drug in."

Lordy, is that young man ever starved, Moses thought, chuckling softly. Between mouthfuls of food, Packard relived for them the story about Beth's abduction and how he and Poe chased the outlaw bunch into the mountains where Poe had killed them. To his credit, Packard didn't try to spare himself when it came to telling about the rescue. Still, Moses thought the boy showed some sand by just riding along with Roosevelt after he'd already seen some of their earlier handiwork. *Yes sir, a considerable amount of sand.*

Only four days earlier, Stump had seemed determined they should all ride toward the Thompson ranch to try to find McCain, but Moses was adamant. The Captain had said to stay there and wait for him, and that's just what he was going to do.

When Legends Lived

He told Stump, "I ain't gonna git the Captain's temper up by disobeying him. He won't tolerate disobeying. If you want to risk it, there's the road. Be sure and tell us how it turns out."

Explained to him like that, Stump allowed that he could wait a spell longer.

As a Black man, Moses Penny was never afforded the opportunity to wear the badge of a Texas Ranger, nor, knowing the climate of the times, had ever aspired to wear one. Being minus the badge, however, didn't subtract from the capabilities or skills possessed by the man, for it was well known by the other Rangers that Moses Penny could shoot someone's eyes out with the old Sharps rifle he always carried, faster than one could blink. He could ride with the best, brawl with the best, was a topnotch tracker, and one of the finest stock-handlers around. A mutual respect had developed between Moses and the tough Texas Rangers during those days, and he was just considered by them to be another "Ranger."

Moses Penny's description of McCain was always, "The Captain's a man of respect."

* * *

Within three days of their conversation about the Captain's intolerance for disobedience, first Poe and then McCain rode in. Stump Henry just looked at Moses several times and rolled his eyes, as if to say, "I owe you, Moses."

Moses nodded his head and kept a straight face.

McCain told the others about Nate's disastrous expedition against Scar, and Poe related how Beth had finally begun to respond to the doctor's attention, on the third day after Jim left. The doctor's prognosis was, that it'd take time and understanding but he expected her to fully recover.

After dinner, McCain immediately began briefing the group concerning his plan to run down the half-breed Scar and hang him. There was never any discussion about anybody else having a say in orchestrating the plan, and the other men wouldn't have dreamed of questioning the Captain's sole right to construct it. Like Moses said, he wouldn't tolerate it.

"We'll head for El Paso in the morning. I've been told Jake Kellog is working there and I mean to have him with us when we go up against Scar's bunch."

Again, there was no room for discussing the possibility that Jake Kellog wouldn't want to go with them, or perhaps couldn't go with them for some reason. They just assumed that if the Captain wanted Jake Kellog, the Captain would get Jake Kellog. After all the years they'd known McCain, no other alternatives seemed possible.

"After we latch onto Jake, we'll head south, toward Eagle Pass. Scar has a lot of friends down there in the Comanche villages. If we have to, we'll grab one and let Moses talk to him for a spell. We'll get our information, one way or the other," McCain said.

"Once we cut his trail, we'll stay on him hard, never giving him a chance to rest. We'll stay with him for as long as it takes, wherever he goes. Oklahoma, Arizona, Mexico, hell, I don't care if he goes all the way to South America. We'll be right with him…and this time, we'll be there until it ends."

He paused. "It's going to be a long run, and its going to be a hard one. Some of us probably won't be coming back. Those of us that do," he said, looking straight at Jim Packard, "will not be the same men as we are now."

"How long do you figure we'll actually be gone, Captain?" Jim said.

When Legends Lived

Walking over to pour himself some more coffee, then passing the pot to Stump Henry, McCain looked annoyed. "We will actually be gone until the bastard's dead. That's how long we will actually be gone. I thought I made that clear. That's another thing you might as well know about me. I don't like repeating myself and I don't believe in democracy when it comes to 'captaining' a run such as this. There will be total obedience to Captain Poe and me. I won't tolerate disobedience, or shirking."

At that, Moses looked pointedly at Stump, who rolled his eyes again.

No one thought it strange that McCain had suddenly elevated Poe to the rank of Captain again, one he'd held for brief periods of time in the Rangers.

"How's the back, Roosevelt?" McCain inquired. "Been acting up?"

"For your information, my back's fine, Jericho," Poe stated tartly, seeming a little peeved that McCain would bring it up in front of the others.

"Because this is going to be one of the most difficult runs we've ever been on, I will give each of you — this don't pertain to you, Roosevelt — a chance to reconsider your decision to join up for the run." He said it in a voice that told the group that as far as he was concerned, the decision had already been made.

McCain stared at his cup in silence so long that some of those in the room started to squirm, then he said softly, "Our time is almost done. There won't be any more runs like this one. Soon, progress is gonna overtake us and law enforcement will change accordingly. There are only a few real bad ones left anyway. Scar's the worst. Billy Reid's a close second. Ben Thompson ain't no angel, either, but they tell me he's gone straight now. Even took up being a lawman over in Austin in '81'. Guess he's still there."

Again, he paused. "We killed Sam Bass and his gang…that was '78 wasn't it, Stump? That Comanche, Lone Wolf…the day we killed him I almost felt sad. John Wesley Hardin, a worthless lowlife turd if there ever was one, is locked away in Huntsville for life, I hope — no, there ain't many left that are worthy of sending a bunch of hard men like us out for. I'm afraid this will be it for us, boys," McCain said, looking sad, then he abruptly stood up. "Those of you still here in the morning will be considered government agents and reconstituted as Texas Rangers, officially signed on for the run. You will be in it till it's over. No withdrawals, no re-considerations. Of those remaining tomorrow morning who attempt to leave before I disband you, I will impersonally shoot. Good night."

The men got up and filed out, leaving Poe and McCain alone in the kitchen. Poe whistled softly.

"Aye God, Jericho, I do believe you're gitting better and better at that little speech of your'n," Poe said.

McCain just stared at him and Poe went on.

"Do you really believe there won't be any more runs after badmen?"

"Not like this one, Roosevelt," he said, sadly. "Not for us anyway."

As he left the house, Stump stopped and started to roll a smoke at the edge of the porch.

"Does he really believe he can get away with shooting someone just because they may want to drop out of this chase later?" Packard said to him.

When Legends Lived

Stump squinted up at the taller man and spit on the ground. "You drop out after tomorrow? He'll plug you right between the eyes mister, and there won't be any discussion about it either. The Captain won't tolerate it."

Stump walked away leaving Packard to stare after him in wonder.

The next morning, Quint Fishburn was waiting on the front porch when McCain walked to the outhouse.

"Morning Captain," he said, as McCain passed. He looked as though he wanted to say more.

On the way back, McCain paused on the steps and casually remarked, "Anything the matter, Mr. Fishburn?"

"How come you never asked me to go on this run with you, Captain? I been on a lot of runs with you, and far as I knowed, done a good job. Least you never told me you was displeased."

"I'm not displeased. I just didn't think you'd want to go, Mr. Fishburn," McCain told him. "I seem to remember how you said when you retired you'd never chase another human being again for as long as you lived."

"He ain't no human being. Not after what he done to Miss Beth," Fish said.

"No, I reckon he ain't at that," McCain said softly. Then, more sharply, "We leave in an hour, Mr. Fishburn. Be ready if you want to ride along. We won't wait."

"I'm ready to go right now, Captain. I already packed — last night." He looked immensely pleased with himself.

* * *

As the days passed on the trail to El Paso, McCain began to sense he'd made the right decision in allowing Fish to go with them. Just like in the "old days," he still seemed to be the best medicine for lagging spirits after a hard days ride. At night he generally sat off to himself and planned the pursuit, worried about their ranch, and like as not, the face of a young Kate Shaw would invade his thoughts.

Earlier in the evening, Poe had joined him. As they smoked, Poe said, "Jericho, just thought you might be interested — old Duncan is dead. Got stomped by a mustang, and up 'n died three days later. Kate's a widder woman, now."

The news had stunned McCain, who silently stared off into space, trying to digest it. After a while, Poe became disgusted with him.

"Well, gol-durn-it, ain't ya got nothing to say?"

"What do you want me to say? I didn't know the man, so I can't say he'll be missed."

"Don't ya find it just a bit interesting that Kate ain't married any more, Jericho?"

"Why should I?"

Poe turned beet red in the face, then said, "Cause...she wants you to come visit her, that's why!"

McCain jerked his head up and stared at Poe. "She say that?"

Poe hesitated, then said, "Sure she did — though for the life of me, I don't know why."

McCain snorted loudly, causing Poe to jump to his feet and stomp away, muttering under his breath.

Sometime later, his belly full of Fish's inventive cooking and enjoying a custom rolled smoke, McCain sat slightly off to himself once again, thinking about what Poe had told him and listening to the good natured give and take of the others.

"Fish, you gonna introduce us to all those young ladies at that new hotel when we git there?" Stump Henry said. "You're prob-

When Legends Lived

ably the only one that knows each and every one of 'em by name."

Stump looked at Roosevelt Poe from under his hat, and gave him a conspiratorial wink.

"Probably knows all their birth marks too," Poe threw in. "I can hardly wait to git there. My old tallywhacker is harder than woodpecker lips!"

"Don't kn...know any of the ladies in El Paso. Only go there for b...business," Fish said, his face reddening. "When I do g...go to the hotel, it's only to b...buy a glass of Sarsaparilla."

The others hooted and laughed at that, with everyone expressing various degrees of disbelief. When things looked as though they'd finally settle down for the evening, Moses spoke up. "Ya should've brought that big black horse with you, Fish. Maybe you could've sold it back to that old gentleman who sold it to you."

"That old c...crook better stay c...clear of me. I just might s...shoot him on sight," Fish told them, his Adam's apple jumping wildly.

The laughing started up once more.

The trail between Bluebonnet and El Paso was a long and difficult journey, but the group of experienced trail riders, thanks to the thick skin of Quint Fishburn, made excellent time, and though dusty and tired, arrived in high spirits.

"Moses, you, Fish and Stump circulate around town," McCain instructed. "Without asking too many questions, see if you can find out about Jake. We'll meet you at the saloon when you find out something." He nudged Grasshopper down the street toward the El Paso Palace Hotel & Saloon, sign. Poe and Packard followed.

The Palace was one of the finest and most sophisticated hotels and saloons west of St. Louis. The builder and owner, Diamond

Jim Walcott, brought in the teak, marble, and crystal chandeliers all the way from New York City. The hotel was six stories of luxurious suites and rooms fit for royalty. Two sets of large double doors gave entry from the hotel lobby into the Palace Saloon, which housed a richly glossed mahogany bar. It ran from one end of the room to the other — over a hundred feet in length. The entire wall behind the bar was covered with one large mirror decorated with murals of half-clad reclining ladies, in fashionable wear. Velvet pictures and oil paintings covered the other walls, and everywhere one looked, it was clean and shiny. Men in dark suits and women in tasteful dresses sat talking or playing cards at the green cloth-covered tables. Even the relatively few cowboys present appeared clean and unusually neat. There wasn't a gun in sight.

"Whoopee!" Poe slapped his dusty hat against his leg as he stepped into the saloon. "Jericho, ain't this the prettiest whorehouse you ever did see?"

Two expensively dressed and fashionable looking young ladies of the evening were sitting at a table just inside the door — an obvious advantage point that would allow them to grab the more likely looking prospects, long before the other girls had a chance to reach them. At the sight of the dusty trio, they raised their noses a full two inches in disdain and looked down them in apparent disgust. Overlooking their haughty contempt, Poe smiled broadly and tipped his hat to them as the group passed. Marching up to the bar, he slapped his hand on it.

"Bartender! Bring whiskey for me and my friends!"

Two mustached bow-tied bartenders were wiping bar glasses at the far end of the long bar. The stocky bald-headed one said something about "God-damned cowboys " in a low voice, which elicited chuckles from his tall skinny companion and the two well-dressed businessmen seated at the far end of the bar. The stocky bartender hurried toward them holding up both hands.

"Please be quiet, sir," he hissed. "You're disturbing the other customers. I'm afraid we don't serve cowboys off the trail dressed the way you are. First, you must discard your guns, then the hotel will provide baths and a barber. After that, we'll be glad to serve you and your friends."

Packard watched Poe spit on the polished floor and without a word, slam the bartender's head on the bar so hard it sounded like a pistol shot. Using his left hand to hold the head in place, Poe placed his Walker Colt on the bar just inches from the man's eyes.

"Listen, you little pissant," he said, snarling at the man. "We're Texas Rangers. This here is Captain Jericho McCain and I'm Roosevelt Poe. We demand respect and a drink, in that order. Now, when I let you up, barkeep, you will quickly and quietly bring me and my friends some whiskey and serve it up with a due amount of respect — or I'm gonna shoot your nose off."

He let the man loose and the bartender hastily jumped back out of Rosie's reach, staring at him in shocked disbelief, while rubbing the side of his bruised head. Poe again spit on the polished floor and looked pointedly at the man's nose. Convinced, the bartender nearly ran to the other end of the bar and whispered urgently to his co-worker, who hastily departed through the double-doors leading into the Palace Hotel lobby and disappeared.

Poe, McCain, and Packard were on their second whiskey when Silent John entered the saloon. Without looking at another person in the room, the lawman, flanked by two young men wearing deputy sheriff badges, walked to within ten feet of the group. There, he stopped and smiling slightly, stood without speaking for a full two minutes. The two Rangers simply ignored them until Packard began to feel uncomfortable.

"Howdy, gents," said the sheriff, finally. "Are you enjoying your stay in our little town?" His lips were smiling, but his eyes remained cold.

"Ain't had so much fun since my little brother got et up by the hogs," Poe said sourly, not looking up. The words were clearly belied, by his tone of voice.

"You old boys must've missed my sign at the edge of town," Silent John said, still smiling. "You know, the one about checking your firearms?"

"We seen it," said McCain, not looking up as he sipped his whiskey.

"I'm the sheriff of El Paso."

"We know who you are, Silent John," said McCain, still studying his half empty glass.

"Then you know that I get real unhappy when people carry firearms in my town," Silent John said. Letting his hand brush the heavy Elm club, he smiled as though relishing what was to come.

McCain slowly turned, apparently looking at him for the first time. He made a slight motion towards the side-arms the deputies had strapped to their hips. "Your boys are carrying guns."

"Well, that's right," Silent John said, laughing. "But you see, we're law officers."

McCain snorted. "There are a few folks around that would probably dispute that remark," Poe said sourly and again spit something brownish onto the shiny floor.

"Well, I try not to use a gun myself, if I can avoid it," the

When Legends Lived

sheriff said. He was still smiling but his ruddy face had taken on a deeper glow.

"Yeah, we heard how you just usually have your hired guns here cover you until you can cuff the poor gent, and then you beat him half to death with that billy-club you're carrying on your arm there," Poe said.

All present could feel the tension in the room rising and watched as Silent John's face grew bright red. "Don't push," the sheriff said softly.

Poe grinned at him wolfishly. Something about it unsettled the sheriff a little.

At that, Donny Pence shifted his weight slightly so he was standing nearly sideways to the dusty trio. McCain turned his head, stared at him for a time, then said gently, "Now you just go right ahead, sonny, any time you're ready."

There wasn't another sound in the room, as the few spectators held their breaths and watched the tension mount between the sheriff's group and the three dusty strangers.

"Hold it, Donny! I'll run things here," Silent John quickly said, holding out his hand. He turned back toward McCain and Poe. "This is my deputy, Donny Pence. The other one's Jessie Oats. Maybe you've heard of them."

Silent John said each name as though he was expecting some sort of reaction from the two Rangers. If he was, he was disappointed, for the two older men only stood without expression, staring at El Paso's sheriff and his two deputies.

"Just another pair'o low-lifes, as far as I can see," Poe finally said nastily, and spit again, this time aiming for the spot he'd made earlier. He was looking at the young deputy in a manner much like a wolf might watch a rabbit, just prior to ripping it apart. Clearly not intimidated, Pence glared back at Poe.

McCain stepped forward and pulled a slip of paper from his pocket. "Send your pup away, before he ends up getting his ass rubbed with a cob and turpentine poured on it. Here, read this." He handed the wrinkled slip of paper to the sheriff. "These gentlemen and three others in town with us are government agents, hired by the railroad to track-down and hang Scar and Bloody Bill Reid. We're Texas Rangers."

"J.D. McCain and Roosevelt Poe, huh?" Silent John mused as he read the paper. "Texas Rangers, it says here. I heard you two boys retired several years ago," he said with a smile that didn't quite reach his eyes.

"This little piece of paper gives us the right to reinstitute ourselves for this mission," McCain informed him tartly. "It says so right there, backed by the Governor and the President of the United States. Federal agencies and other lawmen are supposed to support us. If you can't do that, stay out of our way."

"Besides, once a Texas Ranger, always a Texas Ranger," Poe threw in.

"You McCain?" the sheriff said, addressing Poe.

"I'm Captain Poe. You wouldn't find J.D. McCain palavering this much. He's Captain McCain. He requires respect and he gits tired of useless talk real fast," Poe said pointedly, as he continued to stare at Donny Pence.

"I've heard of you boys," Silent John said. "I thought you were dead by now."

"I'm getting just a little tired of people telling me that," said McCain.

"Well, it seems like this is all in order," Silent John said. "I hope you'll finish your business and leave as soon as it's over. What did you say your business was while you're in El Paso?"

"Our business is our business," Poe informed him.

"Well, just don't start any trouble while you're in El Paso, gents," the sheriff said smoothly and nodded at his deputies to depart. They heard Poe chuckle softly behind them as they walked stiffly away.

Outside, Donny Pence beat his hat against the side of his neatly pressed trousers, stating angrily to his boss. "You should have let me blow them out of their socks, Silent John!"

"Donny, outside of Rosco Bookbinder, you're probably the best shot with a pistol that I've ever seen. And fast, too. Too bad Rosco took off after that no-account wife of his. In speed, you and Rosco would be about even. That's a hell of a pair of guns, and I sure could've used him back there," Silent John admitted. He stopped and stared at his deputy so Pence would know he was deadly serious. "But the truth is, if you go up against those two old men, they'll kill you. Straight and simple. I have a feeling we came out of that real lucky not to have ended up at Digger O'Brien's for a fitting."

Seeing the doubtful look Pence still had on his face, Silent John continued. "McCain and Poe were well known around here once. You ask some of the old timers still around and they'll confirm what I'm telling you. Take my word for it, Donny, those two are killers. Don't even think about going up against them unless the odds are well-stacked in your favor. Not if you want to live to be sheriff someday."

With that, Silent John walked back toward the jail.

* * *

Moses, Fish, and Stump entered the Palace looking for Poe and McCain. Without any greeting, Moses said, "They got Jake locked up in the jail, Cap'n. They're gonna hang him tomorrow for shooting some gambler feller."

Thoughtfully, McCain rubbed his chin as he considered this new development. "Was it a fair fight?"

Stump broke in. "We talked to some of the witnesses that seen it. The other man had been ragg'n Jake all night. Pulled down on him when he tried to leave the game. Probably didn't know who Jake was, but…yeah…other than his being just plain stupid for going up against someone like Jake Kellog — I'd say it was a fair fight."

"Then we'll go over and have the sheriff release him," said McCain as he walked toward the door. Nobody but Jim Packard acted like it was unusual that the Captain could simply accomplish this task, in spite of their near fatal brush with the town sheriff earlier.

As they passed the table where the high-priced young ladies were still seated, Poe again tipped his hat and said, "Good afternoon ladies. Ain't you just prettier than a picture?"

This time both women made eyes at Poe and fluttered their thick lashes. Rosie winked broadly and the ladies giggled behind their hands.

"My, my," he said. "Wouldn't old Roosevelt look good on that?"

"Put it back in your holster, " McCain said dryly, as he walked through the saloon door and out into the street. "We got work to do."

Looking disappointedly over his shoulder at the two smiling women, Poe reluctantly followed. "I surely don't know what you

When Legends Lived

got against a little relaxation and enjoyment, Jericho," he said. "Just because you deplore the whores is little reason for the rest of us to have to give up our natural needs. Very few things are harder to put up with than the annoyance of someone trying to do the right thing all the time."

"Some day that peeder of yours is gonna get you killed," McCain said, marching briskly and not looking back. He seriously hoped Roosevelt wouldn't choose that particular time to buck him on the matter. He was relieved to hear Poe chuckle softly behind him.

"Well, I certainly hope so. Can't think of a better or more fitting end — nor for that matter, anything worse than sitting around waiting to die of old age."

"Hold it a minute, Captain McCain," said Jim Packard, hurrying after them.

"The sheriff has Jake Kellog in jail for murder. They're going to hang him tomorrow morning, and you saw those hired killers he calls deputies. He's not going to just let us walk in there and leave with their prisoner."

McCain slowed his pace a little.

Feeling he'd made a point, Jim hurried on. "Silent John doesn't strike me as being one to back down too often. He didn't let things get out of hand in the saloon earlier because it wasn't in his best interests to do so. But this'll be different."

"Maybe you're right," McCain told the young railroad man. "Stump, take your rifle and get across the street someplace where you can see the jail. Moses, Fish, find yourselves a good spot to cover in a crossfire. Come on, Roosevelt." He started walking briskly toward the El Paso Jail.

Stunned at how his remarks had backfired, Packard watched

as the two men walked away, then hurried after them. Without being told, Poe stopped just outside the jailhouse door and leaned against the wall. Jim rightly figured that he was looking out for the other young deputy who might be roaming around out there someplace. McCain, followed closely by Jim Packard, entered and stood before the sheriff, who was seated at his desk. Donny Pence sat at a second desk, also facing the sheriff. McCain got right to the point.

"You got one of my officers in here, Silent John. His name is Jake Kellog. We came to get him out."

"Afraid I can't allow that, McCain," said Silent John, smiling broadly and rising to his feet.

Pence also rose from his chair, an evil smile playing at the corner of his mouth. Apparently they'd been talking and now had their courage up, McCain realized in disgust. "Jake Kellog is a Texas Ranger and I'm not letting one of our own hang, just for killing a low-life in a fair fight," McCain allowed.

"Ex Texas Ranger," Silent John smirked.

"Once a Ranger, always a Ranger," McCain retorted. "I'll tell you something, Silent John, Jake Kellog was catching and hanging hard cases like you and that deputy of your'n for over fifteen years. Jake personally shot and killed J.W. Coates in a stand-up fight, and he was in on the run where we tracked down and killed Sam Bass and his whole gang."

As he talked, McCain watched Pence out of the corner of his eye. "You don't hang a man like that. Least ways, not when I need him as much as I do right now. I'm deputizing Jake Kellog as a special agent of the government, to assist me in tracking down certain specified outlaw gangs and hanging them," McCain told the sheriff. "Don't oppose me on this, Silent John. I won't tolerate it. I ain't got the time."

When Legends Lived

Packard watched with rising apprehension showing in his face, as Silent John, grasping his famous piss-elm club, walked around the desk and stood towering over the comparatively frail-looking older man.

He said, "I am well aware of your reputation when you was a Texas Ranger, McCain. But those days are long gone and I seriously doubt that you're anywhere near as good as you were back then." Bending down, Silent John pushed his face close to McCain's, sneering, "You're a paper tiger, old man and I'm real tired of your horse-shit. Now, you take those other old saddle-tramps and get your asses out of my town."

Later, Packard was unable to follow exactly what had happened next. It seemed as though Captain McCain's hand blurred as he slapped Silent John along side of his face, then swiftly turned and did the same to his young deputy. It happened so fast, Packard was frozen in place. Pence instantly dropped to the floor motionless, but the sheriff remained standing — wobbly for sure, but still standing. It was only after McCain turned back to the sheriff and took the club from Silent John's limp hand, that he holstered his large Walker Colt and Jim became suddenly aware that it was actually his pistol and not his palm with which he'd struck the two lawmen.

Without a word, McCain grabbed Silent John's shirt and mercilessly clubbed him in the head and upper body with the sheriff's own piss-elm club. To Packard, the sound of the club slamming into the big man's body, and the grunts of both men, seemed to go on forever. The old Ranger viciously slammed the billy club into the sheriff's body over and over, keeping him on his feet by holding the much larger man upright, with abnormal strength. Packard realized McCain was out of control when he released the sheriff and allowed him to slide limply to the floor. Then he saw McCain calmly reach down and grasp Donny Pence by his collar, pull the groaning deputy to his feet, and with a vacant stare, commence to beat him in the same manner.

Packard ran to the door and yelled outside. "Come in here, quick! He's killing 'em! He's killing 'em!"

Hurrying in, Poe quickly assessed the situation and said calmly to Moses Penny, "You git his left arm I'll take the right. Ready? Now!"

He grabbed McCain's arm just as he raised the club to strike the deputy again. McCain looked as if he didn't know who Poe was and might even strike him, then Penny took hold of his other arm.

"It's me, Jericho. Roosevelt! That's enough, now!"

McCain stopped swinging the club but his eyes remained vacant, as if he still didn't know who was talking to him or what he'd just done. Then he turned back toward the unconscious deputy, whom he was still holding upright, and made a motion as though to lift the club once more.

"Jericho, damnit, now I said that's enough!"

Poe flipped his Colt around to grasp it by the barrel. "Don't make me have to whop you one!"

Almost at once, it seemed as though McCain's eyes were clear again and he was back in full control of his actions. Breathing heavily, he said, "All right! Let me go, it's over. Let me go!"

Poe still looking a bit dubious, nodded at Moses and the two of them slowly released McCain's arms and stepped back.

Taking deep breaths, McCain stared down at the two wrecked men. "Life is hard enough without being stupid," he gasped. "Perhaps they'll learn by this for the future, and not interfere in

When Legends Lived

the business of the law." His breathing was slowly returning to normal.

"Oh, yes, Jericho, they should learn from this," Poe chuckled. "Aye God, they should certainly learn from this." He picked up the jail keys and walked to the back of the jail where the cells were located.

On a cot in the last cell, arms folded beneath the back of his head, lay a severely battered Jake Kellog. His face was several shades of green and blue, and dried blood coated the dirty bandana loosely tied around his forehead. Other then that, he seemed unbowed.

"Howdy, Jake," Poe said, politely. "What'd ya do this time?"

"Hello yourself, Rosie," answered Jake, still not moving. "You know what they say. 'Never do card tricks for the boys you play poker with.'"

He smiled slightly. "That the Captain I hear out there?"

Leaning against the wall, seemingly in no hurry, Poe nodded, slowly rolling a smoke. "How long ya planning to stay in this here hotel, Jake?"

"Oh, I don't know, Rosie. They feed you twice a day and you get a lot of sleep. Why? You got a better offer?"

Poe struck a match and placed it to the end of his cigarette. "Might," he said. "Gonna take a little vacation myself. Ride along with Jericho and some of the old gang down south. Get a little sun, go fishing and maybe set a hook into Scar."

Jake sat up and reached for his hat. "I might as well. The hotel manager is getting a little too friendly lately. Comes in almost every day and brings that little stick of his. I'm starting to get tender in a few places."

Poe unlocked the cell and the men grasped hands strongly.

"Figured I'd about run my string out, Rosie. How did you manage to spring me?" Jake said.

"Jericho paid your bail," Poe said with a chuckle. "Where's your gear?"

"Silent John put it in a cabinet in the outer office," Jake replied.

"Good. Moses chased ya up a horse and it's out front. Let's git to gitting," Poe said looking around. "You may not have a nice comfortable bed like this one for a few months, Jake."

* * *

Tired, dusty and sore in places he hadn't even known existed, Martin Gates arrived in El Paso after having missed Captain McCain and his little band of Rangers at Bluebonnet. Bluebonnet, Gates thought with disgust, what a name for such a stinking, scorpion infested piss-hole. Some madman must've thought up the name for that place. Probably the demented old Rangers he was trying to catch up with. As he left the stage office and started toward the Palace Hotel, he became aware of shouting coming from the small building displaying a sign, indicating it was the El Paso Jail. Even with the thick layer of dust coating it, Martin Gate's newspaperman's nose started to itch, and he immediately veered towards the commotion.

Getting nearer he grabbed a young boy by the arm and said, "I'm Martin Gates of the *Chicago Dispatch*. What happened here, boy?"

"Two Texas Rangers broke Jake Kellog out of jail. Thrashed Sheriff Silent John and his deputy within an inch of their lives. Really laid it on 'em. Silent John might not make it. Donnie Pence is all crippled up, too and just sits and shakes," the young boy answered, pulling away.

"Where are these two Rangers now?"

"Rode out about an hour ago headed toward the mountains!" the boy shouted excitedly over his shoulder as he ran up the street.

The newspaper man from Chicago slowly walked to the hotel, disappointed that he'd once more missed an interview with McCain and Poe, but starting to get excited now, for the first time.

Sixteen

"...there's courts, jails, judges, and executioners. But when it comes to dealing with renegades like we got out here? Shoot...it just ain't no contest. Jericho McCain is the Grim Reaper, Saint Gabriel and the wrath of God, all rolled into one...and he's a damned sight quicker and less expensive, too."

— The gunfighter, Roosevelt Poe

KATE LEANED AGAINST THE corral fence and gazed out over the vast parcel of land that was her K/D Ranch. A slight breeze had picked up, and she could smell the river. Despite the drought, things were going well for the spread, due mostly to the fact that much of her acreage fell adjacent to tributaries of the Colorado River. Kate was popular with ranchers and the few homesteaders throughout the valley. Unlike many ranchers of the era who feared insufficient water more than any other catastrophe, Kate was willing to share her abundance with the others.

When she and Duncan had first arrived in the valley, there were only three other ranches within a hundred-mile radius. One was Thompson's Circle-T, near Odessa. Now, several other small ranches and homesteads dotted the area. In the early days, real wars were fought over land and water — but primarily water. As a general rule, however, cattlemen recognized each other's range and water rights. What many of the ranchers failed to distinguish, was the relationship between an unbranded calf and its branded mother. An unbranded calf was considered to be public property by many, and most cattlemen rounded up as many as they could find and rarely considered themselves to be thieves for doing so.

At least they didn't have to worry about squatters and homesteaders like the other ranchers to the east of them. The K/D was located west of the 100 meridian, so the Homestead Act of 1862 wasn't a problem. Kate and her fellow ranchers considered the Act to be a disastrous law to begin with, but the truth of it was there were simply no federal public lands for farmers and homesteaders to claim in the first place. The few that were able to acquire small sections of land from the local ranchers were usually starved out or killed off by Indians or renegades within a year or two and the ranchers promptly moved back in to claim it again. Those that weren't, just eventually gave up in favor of a less hostile environment.

At a time when there were no more than a hundred men within a thousand square miles, each man was a law unto himself. Fair play was the unspoken code and under that code, no man could bushwhack another, shoot an unarmed man, shoot someone in the back or molest a woman. Those offenses called for rapid justice, usually at the hands of whomever had the most resources — namely the ranchers. Those principles, however, applied only to Anglo-Saxons and were completely overlooked by the Comanche, Mescaleros, and Kiowa who'd lived in the region long before the white men came. Likewise, to the few roving bands of renegades, outlaws, and comancheros, any law simply had no meaning for them.

Our mistake, thought Kate, *was thinking things are more civilized than they really are. We should've given Roosevelt's warning about Scar more weight. Maybe then Beth wouldn't have been hurt.*

She hadn't heard from Poe since he'd brought her sister home, but one of K/D's hands traveled to El Paso a couple of months earlier had brought back word of McCain and Poe's release of Jake Kellog from the El Paso jail. Silent John had since retired and wasn't able to get around very well, due to his being crippled-up by Jericho's beating. Donny Pence had left for parts unknown, also none the better for his injuries from the beating. From what the ranch hand told her, the two injured "lawmen" weren't much better than the criminals they were supposed to protect El Paso from, anyhow. The returning K/D hand said McCain's group had headed south, toward Fort Clark. Word was, they hung some of the Bloody Bill gang somewhere down there and were since seen down in Mexico, looking for Scar. Maybe it was all rumors, but that was all she had to go by until she heard from Poe again.

Kate hadn't heard from, nor seen Jericho McCain in over ten years, and didn't expect to. Still, every time she heard his name or thought of him, she felt the familiar thrill and then the subsequent pain it nearly always brought. Grow-up, she angrily told herself for the thousandth time, that's behind you. Her self-recriminations had never worked before and they didn't work for the present. *How could someone whom you haven't seen in over ten years still have such a hold over you?*

When Duncan had asked her to marry him, at first she'd said, no. She told him no exactly six more times over the next five years. Then one day, after thinking about Jericho all day and feeling a deep, almost fatalistic depression over his not attempting to contact her in all those years, she finally told Duncan, yes.

Although her decision to marry Duncan was a mistake, the marriage was not, for her years with Duncan were good years.

When Legends Lived

From the union, she had her son Billy, and her daughters, Tina and Rachel. She'd sorely grieved at Duncan's passing. Although she'd never loved him in the way she always felt a woman should love the man she married, Kate, nevertheless, felt love for him. His death had left such a void in her life that she felt a loneliness far deeper than any she'd ever known before. After Bethena's husband, Howard Beck died and Beth came to live with her and the children, it became more bearable. But Beth's recent depression caused by her abduction made any conversation with her difficult.

Her thoughts now on her sister, she felt concern that Beth wouldn't ever fully recover from the ordeal. She'd often heard Beth scream in her sleep and saw her sitting and staring out of her window with unseeing eyes enough times to know she was suffering severe emotional trauma. *Still,* she told herself, *lately I've seen some improvement.*

Hearing voices, she turned and saw Bethena and the girls holding hands as they walked around the large pond to the north of the ranch house. Once full to the brim, water barely covered its bottom now. Still, it remained one of the girls' favorite places.

They were laughing as Kate's youngest, Tina, pulled her Aunt Bethena toward the water. Eight year old Rachel, who'd just had a birthday, acted as though she were trying to push Beth into the pond, as the three laughed again. The sight temporarily interrupted Kate's brooding. At the moment they looked so happy that Kate was tempted to join them. Then they saw her and shouted, waving. Kate waved back and smiled sadly.

The girls deserve better than this, Kate thought bitterly, and Billy, too. She remembered how her son had followed Roosevelt Poe around the few days he was at her ranch. He'd taken young

Billy down by the river and let the boy target practice with his pistol. She recalled how Billy came in all excited about how Roosevelt could hit rocks in the air, or some such thing. It was clear Billy was starved for a man's influence in his life □ a father. Maybe she would give consideration to the proposals she'd been getting lately from one of her neighboring ranchers. Nothing to do with love, it'd been purely a business proposition. But wasn't that best? At least she'd have help raising the children — and maybe it'd help her to finally put these day dreams about J.D. McCain, to bed once and for all.

Where are you, Roosevelt? Where is J.D.? You said you'd come back and bring him with you. You promised!

* * *

Having released Jake Kellog from the El Paso jail, McCain's group of Rangers headed southeast across the Sacramento mountain range, emerging at the Pecos River. From there they headed south toward Fort Clark. Moses still had a few contacts with the Mescaleros who migrated along Devils River, and McCain felt confident they could obtain information about Scar from them. They'd broken camp an hour earlier and were nearly to the river when they ran into a posse led by the sheriff of Del Rio — Cotton Underwood. For a moment it looked as if the posse would commence shooting.

"Captain McCain and Poe, Texas Rangers!" McCain shouted.

Cautiously, the posse moved forward and Jake suddenly shouted, "Cotton! Cotton Underwood! It's Jake Kellog!"

At that, Cotton recognized his old friend and became convinced that McCain's bunch were who they claimed to be. "Howdy, Jake," said Cotton, pulling up.

When Legends Lived

Jake leaned over and shook hands with the Del Rio Sheriff. "Good to see you again, Cotton. I want you to meet some of my friends." Jake introduced the men around and Cotton did the same. "What's the problem?"

Cotton Underwood had been the sheriff of Del Rio for three years and had the reputation as a dedicated and capable officer of the law. "Bloody Bill Reid killed a homesteader and his family over near Del Rio about two weeks ago," he said. "Right after that they derailed a Southern Pacific train and killed the entire crew — that is except for one man who was shot through the head. He was able to walk to the stage trail, where some cowboys picked him up and brought him into town. The doc thinks he's going to be all right."

"Shot through the head," Poe marveled. "Imagine that."

The men dismounted and shared their chews and smoke "makings."

"Reid and his bunch were over at Eagles Pass 'bout a month ago, visiting with one of Reid's old rustling pals, King Fisher," Cotten said. "I don't figure Fisher to be noth'n but a notch above Bloody Bill and his bunch, anyway. We've been chasing them lowlife ever since they killed the homesteader's family. Three children, the smallest one five. Placed the bodies in the house and burned it. We been in the saddle for two weeks and are plum tuckered out."

"Where do you think they're holed up?" McCain said.

"Do you know this country, Captain?"

"Roosevelt and I chased Lone Wolf back-and-forth through here several times a few years back," he answered.

"Well, about a half-day's ride back that way," Cotton made a motion with his thumb over his shoulder, "there's a fork in the trail. One crosses the river. That's where Reid's bunch split. Some went south toward Eagle Pass and the rest headed this way. I don't know how much longer me and the boys will be able to stay with them, but since you're headed toward Eagle Pass anyway, I'd be obliged if you would kind'a keep an eye out for that other group."

"Be happy to, Sheriff. If we run into them, you won't be having any more trouble with 'em around here," said Poe.

The two groups ate and talked some more, then shook hands and parted ways. The sun was high in the sky several hours later, when Moses, riding ahead as usual, spotted the outlaw's tracks Sheriff Underwood had alerted them about. Galloping back to meet them, he shouted, "Six of 'em, Captain. One of the horses is lame and the rider's leading it!"

McCain spoke to Poe. "With one being lame, can't see them going far today. How 'bout it, Roosevelt? Want to tag along?"

"Let's dance. Too dry to plow," Poe said, and kneed his mount in that direction.

Within the hour they rounded a bend in the trail, finding once again, Moses sitting on his horse, grinning at them.

"Well?" McCain growled impatiently.

"About a quarter of a mile ahead, Captain. No guards out. All of 'em are sleeping like babies," Moses said, his white teeth gleaming. "Looks like the poor lil' things are jist plain tuckered out from killing and burning innocent folks."

Following Moses lead, McCain's group quietly walked their horses right into the outlaw camp. Remaining in their saddles with weapons drawn and pointed at the six men, Roosevelt Poe loudly broke-wind. When nobody stirred, he shouted, "Reveille, girls, rise-n-shine! Turn loose of yer cocks and grab yer socks!

When Legends Lived

C'mon, now, I mean it! Crawl out of them fart-sacks, 'fore we start ventilating them!"

Appearing bewildered and looking sleepy-eyed into the big bores of the ranger's pistols, none of the outlaws even thought about trying to fight it out. To do so, would be to die instantly in a hail of gunfire. Soon, tied with rope and standing in a row, McCain inspected them. Four of the men were scruffy looking hard-cases, of the variety the Rangers were accustomed to dealing with. One with a patch over his right eye, spit at McCain and he stepped back to avoid its trajectory. A large man with a beard who, according to Fish, acted "a little touched in the head," glared at him, growled like an animal and showed his teeth. A well-dressed young Spanish male flashed a dazzling grin as he passed. Two others stood quietly with eyes cast downward, as though by not looking at him, might themselves be overlooked. The sixth outlaw was a boy, no more than sixteen or seventeen years old. McCain hesitated in front of him.

"You're the Blacksmith Parmington's boy, ain't you?"

"Yes, sir, I'm Jimmy Parmington."

"How long you been with this bunch, son?"

"About a month, sir," the frightened boy said, looking around at the group of armed men who were watching the conversation.

"You with them when they burned that homesteader's place?"

Jimmy nodded his head. "But I didn't kill anyone." Tears formed at the corners of his eyes.

"What about the train? You with them there, too?"

Again, Jimmy nodded his head. McCain turned away and walked to where Poe and the others were standing. "Get some ropes," he told Moses, who moved to obey.

Packard looked at Fish, stunned. "What's he doing? You can't just hang these men without a fair trial.

Fish stared back sorrowfully.

"That one's only a boy," Packard went on.

"Yes, sir," Fish said, nodding his head sadly. "He surely is, but you put a gun in his hand and he becomes a man. Old enough to know right from wrong, and a lot older than those children back at that farm they burned."

Fishburn gave him one last sad look then walked to his horse and untied his rope.

Packard sensed someone looking at him and turning around, found McCain's eyes on him.

"They get the same kind of trial as that homestead family got," McCain told him grimly.

"Dammit, one of them is just a boy," Packard insisted.

By that time, McCain was helping Moses and Fish fashion hangman nooses from the six ropes Moses had produced. Finished, Stump threw them over a stout limb of an ancient oak tree nearby and tied them off at the trunk.

Moses and Stump Henry grabbed each man by the arm and placed them one-by-one in their saddles. The man who'd stood with downcast eyes kept falling off his horse. After several times, Moses finally tied the noose around his neck first, and then placed him on his horse. He then stepped back and looked as if to say, 'Now, fall off.' The well-dressed Spaniard asked to write a short letter, giving it to McCain to mail at the first town they came to with a stage line.

There was no fear in his eyes as he looked at McCain and said, "You should let the boy go, hombre. He wasn't really one of us. Probably didn't even fire his gun."

"No, but then maybe you didn't fire your gun on your first ride either," McCain replied.

When Legends Lived

The Spaniard stared down at him for a moment, then flashed his brilliant smile again. "You make a point, hombre. I'll be waiting for you in hell." Then, kicking his horse in the ribs, caused it to bolt forward, unseating himself and breaking his neck cleanly.

The commotion of the Spaniard's horse bolting caused the horse of the man who kept falling off his horse, to bolt as well. He kicked feebly several times as he struggled to breathe, then ceased moving altogether — leaving four condemned men left to hang. Jimmy Parmington was crying softly and the bearded one was cursing McCain, the other Rangers, and all of their ancestors.

"Anybody else want me to write a letter or carry word to a loved one?" McCain offered.

"Sir?"

It was young Parmington.

Walking out in front of the boy so he could be seen, McCain gently said, "What do you want me to do, Jimmy?"

Sniffing quietly, the boy blinked rapidly several times while Jericho waited patiently for him to continue. "You know my father, Captain McCain. Do I have to hang? I didn't hurt anybody," the boy said.

"Jimmy, you had a chance to leave after they murdered that homestead family, but you stayed. People can't step on the law of the land. When they do, they have to pay for it."

Swallowing hard, Jimmy forced himself to stop the crying sounds and said, "Sir, will you tell my father I didn't hurt anyone? And tell him I didn't beg." Tears flowing, he softly whispered again, "Tell him I didn't beg."

McCain stepped back and looked at Moses. Then he nodded,

and the big Negro fired his Sharps into the air, the sudden report causing all the horses to bolt at once. The lawmen stood silently and listened to the sound of the rifle shot reverberate through the hills, then silence, except for the eerie sound of six bodies swinging back-and-forth on the tree limb. Packard, pale and shaken, glared his hatred at McCain.

"He hurts the good that spares the bad," McCain told him unflinchingly.

Fishburn just stood there, looking sad.

"Get a shovel, we'll bury the Parmington boy. Leave the others where they are, just in case their friends come back looking for them. I want them to worry," McCain said. "We got a long ways to go, so let's bend to the task."

Jake and Stump buried the Parmington boy and Moses looked over the outlaw's horses, selecting two mules and the Spaniard's sleek roan for their own use, then turned the rest loose.

"Nary a keeper in any of the others," he informed McCain.

Since they were fairly sure the trail they were on went to Eagle Pass, McCain decided to stay on it and take the chance that it did. By noon the next day, the two men began to see some familiar terrain features and knew they'd chosen correctly. From a distance Moses saw a lone rider coming in their direction, and returned to let them know. They watched him for almost an hour as he wound his way up the trail, until at last he rounded a bend in the trail and came face-to-face with them. Stopping abruptly, the stranger slowly turned his horse sideways so he was sitting with his side toward them. Other than that, he didn't appear apprehensive. The actions of a gunfighter for sure, thought McCain, studying the man.

"Howdy, Pilgrim," Poe greeted him. Keeping his hand close

to his holster, he introduced himself and his companions. Visibly, the young man relaxed.

"I'm Rosco Bookbinder, Deputy Sheriff of El Paso. I'm looking for six riders I've been trailing for two days. They may be part of Bloody Bill Reid's bunch." The deputy's tired eyes slowly slid over the group.

"One of 'em have a patch over his eye? Another a Spaniard looking feller?" McCain said.

"That's them. Where did you see them?"

"Oh, they was hanging around, up the trail apiece," Poe said, chuckling to himself, pleased with his own joke. Packard still looked a little "green around the gills" as Poe had remarked earlier, and none of the others looked even close to laughing.

McCain bluntly said, "We hung 'em this morning. About four, five hours on up the trail. You can't miss it."

"You seem to be a right smart piece from El Paso, Deputy Bookbinder. A tad outside of your jurisdiction," Poe remarked.

"I'm not exactly on official business. Reid's gang stole my wife several months ago and I've been after them, ever since."

Rosco went on to tell them how he'd started out with a posse and finally ended up alone after the discovery of the army convoy massacre. He told them about the gunfight with the three outlaws in the ravine, and how he was badly wounded and finally recovered at the Thompson ranch. He'd heard about the train robbery and the killing of the crew that was associated with the Reid gang. He was told there was a white woman with Reid at the time, and had picked up their trail about two weeks ago when the gang had broken down into several small groups.

"And that's why I'm following this bunch," he finished.

"We ran into Cotton Underwood, the sheriff over in Del Rio.

Had a large posse with him. He was chasing Reid, too," said McCain. "They was pretty near beat, having been on the trail for several weeks and all. But, if you hightail it, you might be able to catch them before they give it up. Sheriff Underwood said he was going to check out a place over on the Devil's River before he quit. Me and Roosevelt think he stands a good chance of striking pay-dirt there."

"How do I find this place?" Rosco said.

"If you ain't never been there, you probably won't," McCain answered. "Stump, do you remember the place with the narrow entrance where we almost got ambushed by the Comanches, back when we were chasing Lone Wolf?"

"Sure do, Captain," Stump said.

"Would you be agreeable to showing Deputy Bookbinder the way? Maybe meet up with us in Langtry, in about a week or so?"

"Be glad to do anything I can to help git your wife back from that trash," Stump told him.

The two men departed without formalities as McCain and the remainder of his group watched Stump and the young deputy ride back up the trail from the direction they had just come. Without a word, Moses led the group down the mountain trail once more, toward Eagle Pass.

Seventeen

*"The Rangers arrest me in Maverick County?
Hell! I own Maverick County."*

– King Fisher, 1876

HUNGRY AND TIRED, FIVE dusty riders first spotted the town of Eagle Pass, an hour before they arrived. Once a hideout for cattle rustlers and outlaws, it hadn't changed much with its new found, and highly disputable, respectability. As McCain remembered from his visit years before, only a half-dozen tumbledown buildings consisting of a saloon, dry-goods store, blacksmith and stables, stage office, and a five-room hotel, made up the town Eagle Pass, Texas. Several large tents and other temporary structures dotted the perimeter of the town.

Determined to get a warm bath and a hot meal that day, they pushed on without stopping. It was four o'clock in the afternoon when they pulled up in front of the saloon. Trooping inside, they headed straight for the bar. Poe slammed his hand on the wood planks of the bar and, smacking his lips loudly in his usual manner, ordered.

"Whiskey! Whiskey for me and my friends! Don't need any of those little sissy glasses, just bring the bottle! No, make that two bottles!"

The bartender, a large man with greasy black hair and dead looking eyes, continued to wipe the bar with a dirty rag. Finally, he looked up and said without rancor, "We don't serve Niggers in here. There's a tent set up across town for 'em."

McCain moved up to the bar until he stood directly in front of the cheeky bartender. His voice was soft — but dangerous. "Mister, we've been riding a long time. We're tired, dirty and thirsty. *All* of us are thirsty. Now you just get that bottle and set it on the bar. We'll pour our own — and keep your name calling to yourself."

"You must be hard of hearing, cowboy, 'cause I said we don't serve Niggers in here and that's just what I meant," said the man with greasy hair as he moved closer to the bar and stood with his hands out of sight.

"Roosevelt," McCain addressed his partner, who was standing at the corner of the rough wood bar. "I speculate this slick hombre has a scatter-gun stuck under the bar where he's standing. I wouldn't put it past him to shoot me with it either, right through the bar." He paused and looked at the man with dead eyes, then said softly, "If he does, would you please kill him for me?"

"Love to, Jericho," Poe said cheerfully.

"Hold on there!"

The words boomed out in the quiet room. Turning, McCain and his men saw a large bearded man, dressed in a black suit, standing at the open doorway near the back of the saloon.

"What in Hell's name is going on? I'm the owner here. I'm King Fisher," the large man said.

The bartender immediately sounded apologetic, "Sorry, sir. I was just discussing your policy about serving Niggers in here."

"Well, Pete, seeing as who our guests are, it'll be okay today," said King Fisher. "This is the famous Captain J.D. McCain, of the Texas Rangers. Hello, J.D. I haven't seen you out this way since you and McNelly came all the way out here and arrested me. What brings you to the 'Pass' this time?"

When Legends Lived

That had been in '76, McCain remembered. In those days, as it continued to be, Eagle Pass had been King Fisher's stronghold. Fisher, a notorious gunman-rustler turned rancher, ruled Maverick County with an iron hand. McCain, part of a platoon of Texas Rangers led by their commander, Captain L.H. McNelly, had invaded the stronghold and brought King Fisher out in chains. The only problem, McCain remembered, was that nobody in Maverick County had the guts to swear out a warrant for him. In the end, the Rangers had to let him go.

They didn't give up easily though, the next year McCain found him in Zavala County and arrested him for the previous year's murder of a local farmer. This time, the Rangers were able to get over a dozen indictments, from murder to horse stealing. However, once again prosecuting attorneys suddenly couldn't be found, jury members left town and court paperwork mysteriously turned up missing. Again, all charges were eventually dismissed.

Being extremely fast with a gun, King Fisher boasted he'd killed seven men, "Not counting Niggers, Indians, and Mexicans."

McCain had always regretted that King Fisher had escaped Texas' justice and lamented about it for years.

"Looking for one of your amigos," McCain said. "Bloody Bill Reid."

"Never heard of him," King Fisher said, smiling.

"That's right peculiar, 'cause we happened to run into Cotton Underwood with a posse a couple of days ago. Sheriff Underwood said Reid had spent about a week here with his gang of murdering scum, and that you treated them like royalty the whole time."

McCain was leaning leisurely against the bar, apparently totally at ease. Those around him were not fooled by his demeanor.

Fisher's face turned red. "I can't be expected to know every man-jack that rides through here and stops in for a drink, can I?" he said defensively.

McCain rubbed his chin, "Guess not," he said. "Besides I wouldn't want to have to arrest you again, for harboring a fugitive."

At that, King Fisher threw back his head and laughed. "You tried that twice," he said. "You couldn't make it stick back then, how ya gonna make it stick now? Hell, I'd be acquitted before the sun went down."

"This time it would be different though, Fisher," McCain said softly. "This time there'd be no trial. This time, I'd just take you out and hang you."

"Why, you'd git hung yourself, if you tried that," Fisher stated in disbelief.

"Not necessarily so," said McCain. "I've got the Government's authority to rid Texas of Reid's gang and any of his associates, in any manner I see fit. If fact, the Government is so anxious to clean that bunch up that they've promised me and my deputies immunity from anything we have to do. Consider yourself lucky if I don't start with you."

King Fisher's face was beet-red, now. "Well, this is still my place and I want that Nigger out of it, now," he almost shouted as his face became redder still.

"What ya got against colored folk anyhow, Fisher?" Poe said, who had been standing silently for longer then he usually did — especially during any kind of disagreement or confrontation.

"I was at Missionary Ridge," the big man said. "We went up

against a Black regiment and when we attacked, I saw my best friend take a 'minnie-ball' in the face. I took one myself, through the left shoulder. Still bothers me when the weather turns. Now, I know your Nigger probably didn't have a thing to do with it, but it just made me naturally dislike black faces. So, McCain, take your Nigger, and git."

Tension was thick as McCain's group waited for the explosion they were sure was imminent.

"It might've been mine," a deep voice said softly.

All heads turned toward Moses Penny who, up to that point, had been standing silently at the end of the bar.

"What was that?" said King Fisher.

Looking up, Moses said once more, "It might've been my minnie-ball that got you or your friend at Missionary Ridge. I was there."

King Fisher struggled to maintain control of himself as he sized Penny up, seeing he wasn't armed. "Do you own a Colt, boy?"

"It's out on the horse," Moses replied.

"Can you use it?"

"I've fired it four, maybe five times in about two years," Moses answered.

"You've got five minutes to get it buckled on," said King Fisher. "Then I'm gonna kill you, gun or no gun."

Moses walked out of the saloon without replying.

J.D. McCain eased himself away from the bar, his hand near his pistol, and King Fisher saw the subtle movement from the corner of his eye.

"Now, you're bound to stay out of this, McCain. This is all legal and everything; a fair fight. He'll have a gun and I'll have a gun. All legal," he said again.

"Maybe legal as far as the law goes, but Mr. Penny is no hand with a sidearm," McCain said. "But then, as I recall, you killed a farmer over near Waco. I heard they had to show him how to even cock the gun because he'd never used one before."

"The law said it was a fair fight," said King Fisher. "You're bound to stay out of another man's business, McCain."

"I'll stay out. When it's over, load-up again cause I'll take the next crack at it."

"I'll make it short, McCain," King Fisher snarled. "I've been waiting for this for a long time." He stormed out of the saloon door.

McCain looked concerned for his friend as he left the saloon, followed by Poe and the others. Outside, they saw King Fisher standing beneath the saloon sign that said, King Fisher-Proprietor.

He took a step toward the middle of the street and stopped when he saw Moses Penny standing a hundred yards away. He was holding the Sharps rifle in his huge hand as one might hold a large pistol. As the gunman moved as if to walk towards him, Moses flicked the barrel of the gun up seemingly without effort, and fired. The large slug hit the street a scant two inches in front of King Fisher's foot, kicking dust onto his shiny boots.

"That's close enough," Penny's deep voice boomed.

King Fisher realized he was in a predicament. The Sharps had a definite range advantage from that distance. He was pretty sure he couldn't hit anything in six shots from here, and the Black man had already demonstrated he was an expert with the big rifle.

"This isn't a fair fight," he said. "I asked you if you could use a gun and you lied to me."

When Legends Lived

"I didn't lie, Mist'a Fisher. I haven't fired a pistol in over a year. I use a Sharps," Moses said and smiled. "Not bad with it, either."

"They'll hang you if you shoot a white man. Especially without giving him a fair chance," Fisher told Moses, a trace of sweat beginning to show on his forehead.

Moses looked thoughtfully for a moment, then said, "Maybe you're right, Mist'a Fisher, guess what's fair for you might not seem as fair for me, to some folks."

Slowly, he began to walk toward the gunman. Breathing a sigh of relief, King Fisher watched the big black man walk slowly toward him, silently counting the steps between them. When Moses was no more than twenty-five feet away, King Fisher made a slight movement and the gun he wore at his hip suddenly appeared in his right hand. Fast as it was, Moses Penny's shot rang out a split second before he could fire, and he felt the large slug slam him back on his heels. He dropped to his knees, still holding the Colt in his right hand. Unable to move or speak, he knelt in the dusty street, incapable of even dropping the gun, and watched as the big Black man carefully removed the spent cartridge from the breech of the Sharps. He watched as Moses pushed a fresh round into the breech and slowly raised the barrel until he was looking down its large bore.

King Fisher, one of Texas's most notorious gunmen, knelt in the dust of his own town, unable to ask for mercy or in anyway stop what was about to happen. Moses Penny looked into the pleading eyes of his tormentor and, with a flick of his wrist, tilted the barrel and fired — splintering the sign that bore King Fisher's name, into a thousand pieces.

"Guess I missed killing you for a second time. Once at

Missionary Ridge and now here," Moses remarked. He walked to where Captain McCain was watching with the rest of his companions.

"Captain, I think maybe it's best if I wait for you out by that stream where we watered our horses, just before we got to town," he said.

His captain nodded without speaking, and watched the windows and doorways as Moses mounted up and rode away.

The town doctor labored for hours attempting to save King Fisher's life. He hovered between life and death for three days before finally showing signs of recovery. By that time, McCain's group of Rangers was well on their way back toward the Devil's River.

* * *

Riding by Reid's side at the head of his band, Jenny felt a flush of excitement as she remembered the train robbery a few days before. *My God*, she thought excitedly, *I killed a man! Maybe several!*

Bill had wanted Jenny to finally take part in one of the gang's operations. They'd waited in a small clump of trees near where Reid's men dislodged a rail from the track. Jenny remembered how she could hear the train laboring up the steep mountain slope well before it came into view. When the engineer finally saw the dislodged rail, he unsuccessfully locked the brakes and attempted to stop, but he'd hit the gap and the engine and first two cars overturned. The outlaw band was already rushing toward the train, and Reid's men were aboard almost before the train came to a complete stop. Entering the passenger car, Reid placed Jenny at one end of it and the outlaw named Torres,

When Legends Lived

at the other, telling them to cover him while he moved through the car and collected valuables.

Jenny had been watching a heavily mustached man who didn't seem frightened like the other passengers. She'd stood near the door holding the short-barreled 20-gauge shotgun Bill had given her as a present, when he was finally convinced she would never be able to "hit the inside's of a closed barn" with a pistol. He'd fashioned a pistol grip on it, especially for her small hands.

"Just point it and pull the trigger," he'd instructed.

As she'd watched, the stranger, seemingly unconcerned about her or her shotgun, suddenly pulled a long barreled Webley from a shoulder holster and raised it to point at Reid's back.

Without thinking, Jenny just pointed the shotgun and pulled both triggers. The blasts from both barrels hit the man in the head and, less than ten feet away, it literally exploded, splattering Jenny and those closest to him with blood, brain tissue, and pieces of bone. Wheeling in surprise, Bill immediately began shooting into the car full of people. Jenny remembered with excitement how she'd reloaded again and again, firing her shotgun into the screaming passengers. Bill emptied both of his revolvers, then his hideout gun, and finally reloaded and continued firing, emptying them once again. Details were lost on Jenny now, but she could still hear the people screaming and recall the passenger's attempts to hide behind seats and fallen bodies, as she and Bill slaughtered them in their crossfire.

The carnage complete, she recalled standing in the silent aftermath, smelling the acid smell of powder mixed with the sickly sweet smell of blood, and of hearing the occasional moan beneath the piles of victims. Most of all, she remembered the look of frenzied excitement on Reid's face as he stared at her, standing with the smoking shotgun in her hands, covered with the dead man's blood. She actually thought he was going to take her, right there and then.

Now, almost giggling at the prospect, she remembered she wouldn't have cared much if he had done it to her right then and there in front of all his men.

As it was, he couldn't seem to keep his hands off her, rubbing her buttocks, sending the message to the others that "this is my woman." Crude as he was, Jenny felt a thrill of excitement and a sense of pride for the possessive way he'd treated her, and in what she'd done at the train-wreck. She felt her face redden as she recalled how had Bill attacked her like an animal when they'd finally stopped to make camp that night, and all the things they did together. It'd been the most exciting day of her life — and night. Thinking about it, she almost giggled aloud again.

Afterward, riding at the head of the column with Reid, she was conscious of the way he kept looking back over his shoulder every few minutes. He'd sent Torres and another man, the one with black teeth who kept staring at her, back to watch the trail behind them; but she could see he still wasn't relieved. Reid had told her once that he'd ridden with Bloody Bill Anderson in the war. He said he learned his hit and run tactics from Anderson, and had so admired the man's style that he'd taken the name Bloody Bill when Anderson was killed.

Reid prided himself on his ability to outsmart and evade anyone who might try to catch him. Even the mighty Texas Rangers had little luck in tracking him. But now, there was someone or something, on his trail. He could feel it. He sent out decoys and when they failed to return, set up ambushes which didn't see a thing. Still, Bill always relied on his instincts and was convinced, at least for the moment, that there was someone behind him. They'd changed camps every night for the past two weeks, often in the middle of the night. Still, nothing materialized. Lately, she and Bill would wait until the others made camp for the night, and then move a short distance away. "Just for luck," Bill had told her.

"How would you like to ride down to Laredo, maybe go into Mexico, on to Monterrey?" Reid said to her that night after they'd settled in. "I know some real nice places to visit down in Mexico, Jen."

"You mean quit robbing trains and break up the gang?"

Bill laughed. "No, no. Just take a little vacation. Spend some of that money we been making. We'll split-up into two's and three's, drift on down and meet up someplace down there. Take a little rest, drink some tequila, and when things have cooled off around here, come back to Texas and start all over again," he said.

"Well..." she said hesitantly, "I guess that would be okay. Just as long as it don't get too boring."

"My, my," Bill laughed again, "Ain't you gitting to be the bloodthirsty one? Might ought to change your name to Bloody Jenny," he said as he reached for her.

Melting into his arms, she thought how fortunate she'd been when Bill Reid found her in that school room; it seemed so long ago. She'd never felt for any other man, what she felt for Bill Reid. Jenny loved him more than life — knew she'd gladly give up her own life for this man.

Bill tenderly touched a small curved scar just under her left earlobe, and said, "How did you get that?"

Jenny got a mischievous look in her eyes and holding her

thumb and forefinger about an inch apart, said, "A tiny little horse kicked me."

Then, she covered her mouth with her hand and started giggling. Reid grabbed her by the ribs in both of his big hands and began to tickle her forcefully. Squealing and kicking she begged and pleaded for him to stop.

"I'll tell you the truth!" she gasped. "I'm gonna pee, Bill!"

When he finally did stop, Jenny told him how as a child she'd wandered off from the adults and fell down a flight of stairs, smashing her face into the stone landing at the bottom. "Not nearly so interesting, huh?"

Bill kissed her scar gently and Jenny wrapped her arms tightly around his neck, tears of happiness burning her eyes. She quickly dropped off to sleep and dreamed about a distant lone rider, following them from a long ways away. He looked familiar, but she couldn't make out his features.

* * *

Dixie Thompson watched her brother, Brad, with a touch of resentment as he slept. *How can he sleep in this heat and dust,* she thought?

She was tired of the dust and the bumps and the vast nothingness they'd been traveling through for the past week. She was almost to San Antonio and it would be nice to see her father's sister, Aunt Alice. Aunt Alice was married to Claude Butler, an attorney for the Cattlemen's Association headquartered in San Antonio. She and Dixie's father had been close, so when Sam Thompson established himself in Texas, Alice moved there at the age of sixteen and stayed with Sam for the next two years. It was when she accompanied Sam on the first Cattlemen's

When Legends Lived

Association meeting held in San Antonio, that she'd met the young attorney and married him within a month. That had been almost twenty years ago, and the Butlers were now well established among the San Antonio socialites.

Nate had seen how the loss of her father and Todd and Teresa had affected her, and he was the one that suggested she visit her aunt. Dixie, lonely and withdrawn since the young Rosco Bookbinder departed, jumped at the chance to get away from her beloved Circle-T for a while. Half seriously, she'd asked Brad if he would like to accompany her on the trip and was surprised at his ready acceptance. He hadn't left the ranch since his parents took him to Amarillo when he was eight years old.

She remembered that Brad had been mistreated by the local children and even some of the grownups, based solely on his crippled leg. She knew that Brad was also remembering that trip as she saw the determination on his face as they loaded their wagon and prepared to leave. Now, watching him sleep, she was aware that her younger brother was almost grown and had fate not dealt him such a cruel stroke, his handsome refined features might have placed him in great demand among the young ladies of San Antonio.

Dixie was missing the ranch already and wondered why she'd decided to leave. No, that's not right, she thought. She'd wanted to get away because everything she saw reminded her of a certain young deputy sheriff. Dixie knew he was married and she had no right to think about how it would feel to kiss him, or even do more — as she felt her face grow warm — but she couldn't help it. Rosco had invaded her thoughts ever since she first saw him the morning they brought him in, more dead than alive. Sometimes she found herself fantasizing about him being a widower and returning to the ranch to marry her. At those times, she instantly felt guilty and prayed for forgiveness. Still, she couldn't stop those thoughts nor the dreams that left her shaken and ashamed in the mornings.

Looks like some more praying tonight, she thought glumly.

* * *

Something's not right.

Stump Henry surveyed the high canyon walls, growing increasingly alarmed. He could see the young deputy sensed it also by the way he kept scanning the rocks at the rim above them, as they slowly made their way through the narrow pass. It was a feeling, more than anything else. Like someone staring at you, or the feeling you get when you, all of a sudden, shiver. 'Someone just walked over my grave,' as the old folks would say. Can't wait to get through this draw, he thought, just as he was slammed backwards, out of his saddle. Instinctively, he hit the ground rolling, and three more rounds narrowly missed him that he was sure would've been dead center had he remained when he'd fallen. Huddled behind a rock barely large enough to conceal his body, he examined his wound and ducked as several more slugs ricocheted into the clear afternoon sky.

"Rosco?" he whispered hoarsely.

"Here," from somewhere off to his left.

"You okay?"

"Yeah, but they killed my horse," came the reply. "How about you?"

"Tagged me a mite. Don't know how bad though," Henry said.

"There's one on both sides of the draw. Got us in a crossfire."

"I thought I saw a glint off something as I crawled to this rock. Course I was crawling a mite fast," Stump grimaced with pain as he chuckled softly.

"That makes it kind of dicey. It's at least four, five hours until dark," Rosco said. "It's going to get mighty dry before we can get to my canteen."

"I'm not going to wait until then," Stump said. "I'm gonna go up there and twist that son-of-a-bitch's ears off!"

"You be careful now, Stump," came the whispered reply. "These guys have already shown they can shoot. If we wait for a while without moving, maybe they'll think we're finished and come down to make sure."

Stump coughed, spitting up pinkish blood. "I don't think I can wait, Deputy. I just took a look and they got me pretty good in the belly. I may not last until dark and I don't want to depart without expressing my displeasure to the gentleman that did this to me."

Rosco listened as another muffled cough followed, a short silence…then he said, "How do you want to play it, Stump?"

"I count three and you spray the draw with as many rounds as you can muster. If I make it to the cover of that crack, I can use it to crawl up the side of the wall to that out-cropping of rocks. I should be able to see the whole country from there. How's that for brilliant tactics?" Stump said, chuckling again.

"I don't have a better plan," said the deputy. "start counting."

On the count of three, he raised up with a Colt in each hand and began to pull the triggers as fast as it was possible to do so. Stump reached the crack in the canyon wall without drawing a single shot, just as Rosco ran out of bullets. As he quickly dropped down behind the rock again, a heavy fusillade rained down upon his position, then silence. Inching up and looking at the place Stump had been laying but a moment before, Rosco could see it was empty.

He laid in the hot sun without daring to move for nearly an hour, trying not to think about the canteen of water on his dead horse. As he reached down to pick up a small pebble to suck on, two shots rang out high up on the canyon wall — then silence.

Taking a chance, Rosco cautiously peeked around the rock and caught a glimpse of movement on his side of the draw — near the spot he'd suspected one of the ambushers was hidden. Looks like he decided to come check it out after all, Rosco thought. Convinced the man couldn't see him because of a small rock slide between them, and praying the shots he'd heard was Stump Henry taking care of business and not the other way around, Rosco sprinted to an small concave in the canyon wall, and flattened himself against it. Nothing happened. Placing his guns back in their holsters, he removed his boots and started the fifteen-foot climb to the top, well aware he was exposed to the other rifleman, if Stump had failed to get him.

Can't think about that now, he told himself, as he inched his way toward the top.

After what seemed like many moments, Rosco slipped over the edge and lay for a minute, breathing deeply and quieting his heart. Then, rising noiselessly, he slowly moved across the top of the large flat rock and dropped off the other side, onto another wide ledge. Moving silently in his stocking feet, he slowly inched his way down the sloping ledge until he came to a relatively flat area with a large rock in front of it. The deputy carefully slipped around the rock and saw a figure thirty feet in front of him, crouched behind a boulder with a rifle.

When Legends Lived

As he stepped into the open, Rosco saw the man stiffen and knew he'd heard him. "You can lay it down and live or you can die, right here," the Deputy said. "Makes no difference to me."

The man rolled and fired at the same time, rushing his aim so that his shot went off to Rosco's right and ricocheted off a boulder. Rosco coldly put three bullets into the unknown man who dropped the rifle as he slumped tiredly against a rock. The man groaned softly and Rosco shot him once more.

"Stump? You okay?" he shouted.

From someplace up on the opposite wall, hidden from his view, he heard Henry's faint reply. "I'm pretty puny, mind giving me a hand?"

With his heart in his mouth, Rosco ran down onto the canyon floor, found his boots and slipped them on, then began to hastily climb the other side. He found Henry 200 feet up the side of the wall resting against a fallen tree, a half smoked cigarette dangling from his lips. The front of his shirt had a small pinkish stain on it, and his face looked ashen. Rosco knelt to examine Stump's wound and removing his shirt, saw the bloodless purple, almost insignificant looking hole just below his right chest-bone. Pink bubbles were popping out of the hole. There was no exit wound.

"Guess I'm gonna be a burden to you for a while, son. Can you git me down this hill? I sure could use a drink of water." Stump coughed and pink froth covered his lips.

"We'll get you down, Stump, you're going to be just fine," the Deputy said unconvincingly.

It took him a full thirty minutes to reach the bottom lugging Stump's additional weight. He slipped twice and nearly fell, but the wounded man never complained once. Placing Stump Henry in the shade of a large rock and giving him a small drink of water, Rosco proceeded to make a bed of the blankets available. After receiving a second drink, Stump seemed to sleep as Rosco bandaged his wound and tried to make him comfortable. *If he makes it through the night,* Rosco thought, *I'm heading for Langtry with him in the morning.* Somehow he felt it was his fault, Stump Henry getting shot, for if he hadn't asked for help Stump wouldn't be there now.

The wounded man looked no better at daybreak the following morning and Rosco made hasty preparations to leave. He was brought up short by Stump calling to him softly. He hurried to the wounded man's side and knelt. Stump's face was gray and his eyes looked glassy.

"Son, I'm gonna ask ya for a favor." He coughed softly and fresh blood ran from the corner of his mouth.

Bookbinder nodded Stump continued. "You got something to write on?"

Rosco stood and quickly walked to his saddle-bags where he removed an old wanted poster of the outlaw, Bloody Bill Reid. Hurrying back, he knelt, ready to write.

"This is my last wishes for I fear they killed me, son. First, I want you to take my horse because you're gonna need a good one to git them lowlife sons-of-bitches that done this."

Rosco started to protest, then thought better of it and remained silent.

"Young Billy — Kate Shaw's boy over at the K/D outfit — once admired my Sharps rifle. Boy's got a good eye. Let him shoot it a few times, it's his'n now. See that he gits it. The Colt, too."

Stump Henry's breath was growing more labored as he spoke. Rosco listened to it in silence, until Henry continued. "I got a sister in St. Paul. Lives right on the river. Pretty place." He coughed again. "Got a little savings in Amarillo Cattlemen's Bank. Don't waste it…burying me. Send it all to my sister."

More coughing, but this time much weaker. "Her name's Josie Winters. Short for Josephine. Used to be real pretty. Haven't seen her in twenty years," he said almost whispering. "Got a letter about five years ago, though. She had five kids then. Imagine that. Little Josie with…five kids."

He stopped and Rosco again listened to his shallow breathing for what seemed like a long time. When Stump continued, his voice was fainter and Rosco had to lean closer to hear him.

"Write this down, Deputy: Dear Kate," he paused, his breathing sounded painful now. "I am having a young feller write this for me as I am a bit under the weather. I wanted you to know how much…happiness you brought to my life, just being…near you for these last few years," he rested, breathing deeply, then went on. "I knowed a woman like you couldn't marry someone like me, but I surely had the next best thing…being around you and seeing you every day. I used to pretend Billy and the girls were mine. I don't know if that is love 'cause I don't rightly know if I know what…love is, but I've had a good feeling for you for over twenty years, and just wanted you to know. Tell, Beth and…," His voice was a ragged whisper.

"…the kids I thought about them. Don't fret about me none. I had a good life and thought of you at the end. Your obedient servant, Frederick Stover Henry II."

Rosco could barely hear Stump's breathing by then. He had to lean closer to hear him speak. "Deputy, tell the Captain… these twenty years…have been…a fine ride. Tell him…didn't run out on him… just got careless…maybe too old fer…"

He stopped talking and Rosco waited for a few minutes, then placed his cheek near Stump's nose. Rosco looked down at the ashen face before him, then reaching out, slowly closed his eyes. Stump Henry was dead.

Rosco dug for over two hours in the rocky earth, before he was satisfied with the depth of the grave. Wrapping Stump in his own blanket, the deputy gently placed the old Ranger into the hole and filled most of the hole with rocks to keep out the animals. Mounding up the grave with the remaining dirt, he placed a mound of small rocks over that. Next, he cut a piece of leather from Stump's beat-up saddle bags and wrote on it:

Frederick Stover "Stump" Henry II Texas Ranger
and God fearing man
Killed by outlaws June 24, 1884

Rosco cut leather strips and fastened them onto a crude cross fashioned from two of the larger limbs of a mesquite bush, piling up rocks around the cross to hold it in place. Standing back, he wiped his hands on the legs of his trousers and tried to recite what he remembered of the "Lord's Prayer." When he was finished, Rosco mounted up, gave one final look back at the grave of Stump Henry, then turned and galloped away toward Langtry, Texas. His soul was heavy, and there was vengeance in his heart.

Eighteen

"The law west of the Pacos."
— Judge Roy Bean

RAIN MAKER HAD BEEN watching the band of white men for two days. There were fifteen of them, and a woman. A white woman. He remembered the excited grunts from his men when they first discovered the woman's presence. Soon they would have her, he mused, but first he had to make sure the odds were completely in his favor. Other groups of white men seemed to be chasing the group with the woman and, so far, he'd only watched as the drama unfolded on the trails far below. Rain Maker had twenty warriors, the most he'd been able to recruit in over three years.

Warriors, he thought contemptuously. *There's not five good warriors in the whole bunch.* His grandfather, Quanta Parker, would never have sunk so low as to have used men such as these. But times were hard, Rain Maker reminded himself, and he was lucky to find anyone willing to ride with him against the whites.

Rain Maker had been living in Mexico for five years, and although he couldn't see the invisible line in the dirt separating one people from the other, he knew the intruders could clearly see it, and that they usually wouldn't cross it to chase after him. While there, he'd been careful not to bring any attention to himself or his small band, by the Mexican Government. That way, he was free to raid across the border for the horses and women he needed for trading. Even with the scum that now rode with him, he felt confident he could kill several in the long column snaking slowly through the canyons far below — but he could see they were well armed and he didn't want to lose any of his warriors unless he had no choice. No, better to wait until they split up again and then take one of the small groups. Maybe the one with the woman.

* * *

Since their arrival in the booming cow town, it seemed the past two weeks in San Antonio had been almost one single social event for Dixie and her brother. They'd been in the city for a month and Brad had taken to the life like a duck to water. That was, Dixie knew, in large part due to Hal La'Monte, who'd taken Brad under his wing and even shown her special consideration, as well. Hal had a smooth Eastern accent, was culturally savvy, was always at the right functions and knew all the important people. He seemed suave and debonair to Dixie, who'd never been away from the ranch for any amount of time. Dixie felt her cheeks burn as she thought about Hal, remembering what had happened only two nights before.

Well, why not? she asked herself. *After all, he's charming, extremely handsome and obviously wealthy.* All the eligible — and even some of the ineligible — young ladies seemed to just about throw themselves at him every chance they got. Lately, however, it seemed that Hal only had eyes for Dixie Thompson, and Dixie was, to say the least, flattered. Dixie was one of those rare women who simply didn't know how beautiful she was. Though she knew a lot of the cowboys would hang around forever if her brother Nate would only let them, she figured it was just because she was a girl, and *any* girl might do as well.

When Legends Lived

At first, it had been Hal's hitting it off so well with Brad, that had pleased her so. They always seemed to be together and Dixie could never remember Brad having looked so contented. Every chance Brad got he was singing the praises of his new-found friend. It was Hal this and Hal that, all the time. Then lately, Hal just seemed to find opportunities to be alone with her, as well. Soon, most of the other females took the hint and kept their distance. Two nights ago, things had changed drastically, she remembered, her face burning hot once again. After a dance at her Aunt's home, she'd found herself alone with Hal as they walked through the large manicured garden behind the main quarters. Her escort's deep smooth voice captivated her, as it always did, as he told her of his early life in Washington, and later, the French Quarter of New Orleans.

They'd stopped by the pond and she stooped to pick up a small rock to throw into the water. When she stood up, she was staring directly into Hal's dark eyes. They were nearly touching and Hal reached out to gently brush a strand of hair from her forehead. She couldn't remember going into his arms, if he'd pulled her, or she'd gone willingly. Or, how it was that he was kissing her. Or, for that matter, the abandonment in which she answered his kisses. All she felt was a roaring in her ears, and the fire as it spread throughout her body leaving her weak and nonresistant to his subtle maneuvers.

The world seemed to be spinning, time and space forgotten entirely. Without knowing quite how she got there, she was lying on the grass and Hal's hands were touching her all over; touching her in places where no one had ever touched her before. Fire shot through her with every caress, every touch, every deep kiss. She was smothering. She was lost. Lost. She felt the cool evening breeze on her bare legs and that shouldn't be, for she had worn a long evening gown. She felt the feather softness of Hal's fingers as she uncontrollably lifted herself off the ground to give him better access. She was now completely without a will of her own, floating on rivers of hot lava, swept along in the wetness and heat of passion. All the while, deep, deep kisses. God, she couldn't breathe. She felt Hal hovering over her for just an instant, bracing himself with a hand on each side of her head. She was momentarily terrified for she knew that in just an instant, her life would change forever. Expectantly, she waited for the exquisite doom. There was no turning back, she was ready. Now. Please, *now*!

Then…footsteps…and low voices of someone else on the path. Getting closer, coming their way. She heard Hal swear softly and rising, took hold of her hands, lifting her to her feet. They stood slightly apart, breathing ragged breaths of air to quiet the loud beats of their hearts. Then the voices began to get fainter as, whoever it was, returned toward the main quarters. As the sounds grew faint, Dixie felt Hal's hands on her shoulders gently trying to turn her around to face him. But the time had passed and she firmly told him, no. She remembered how they had returned to the house without saying a word. Dixie had gone inside and didn't see Hal for the rest of the evening; she presumed he probably had departed.

Then just last night, he'd come again. At a point when they were left alone for a short time, he'd tried to talk her into going for a walk in the garden again. She told him what had happened had been a mistake and they should not let it happen again. Hal had been insistent, attempting to kiss her when no one was around. Asking her to be alone with him.

Standing there in the daylight, Dixie was ashamed of what had happened, for nothing like that had ever happened to her before. She knew what men and women did. After all, she'd been raised on a ranch. She just never knew it could be so pleasurable, so filled with magic and fire. She mustn't let herself be left alone with Hal again, she resolved, for even last night when he'd asked so insistently, she was sorely tempted to go for that walk with him again.

Dixie knew what she wanted out of life and a quick roll in the barnyard wasn't part of it. If she held out, Hal would probably ask her to marry him just to complete what they'd started. But, while Dixie found Hal La'Monte exciting and desirable, she was sure she wasn't in love with him. After returning to her room, every time she closed her eyes, she saw Rosco Bookbinder's face before her. *Damn you Rosco*, she thought. *You better hurry. I don't know how long I can hold out. Our heavenly Father who art in Heaven....*

* * *

J.D. McCain, Fishburn, and Poe rounded a bend in the trail and found Moses Penny sitting on his mare, patiently waiting for them as he'd done countless times before. But this time, they could sense something was wrong. As they got closer, they could see that Moses Penny had a sad, painful expression. McCain rode closer and stopped, waiting until Moses was ready to speak.

"It's Mist'a Stump, Capt'n. I found his grave 'bout a mile on up the trail. Looks like that young deputy and him were ambushed — caught in a crossfire."

Penny's voice almost cracked, then finally regaining control, he went on. "The Deputy's horse is up there, dead, and it looks like Stump and him killed the fellers that done Stump. The

Deputy took Stump's horse and went on after them some more," he finished.

"Let's take a look," was all McCain could muster, as he kneed Grasshopper forward.

McCain saw it was pretty much as Moses had described it. *Nice of the young deputy to give Stump a deep resting place,* he thought, observing the site.

Moses Penny, Fish, and Roosevelt Poe discretely decided to leave their captain to the business of inspecting the final resting place of their friend and companion for so many years, and saying the final farewells. As they moved down the trail to conduct a little 'scouting on ahead', they saw McCain walk to the mound of rocks and stare down at the crude cross with its short epitaph.

Alone, he stood without speaking for several moments, then started to say something, paused, and sat down heavily beside the grave. He removed his large hat and sat holding it in his hands, staring up at the top of the canyon wall. After a few minutes, he said softly, "Ah, dammit Stump. Dammit to hell. Why now? We were almost done with it all."

Abruptly he stood and slapped his hat against his leg. "We had some good runs you and me, didn't we? I never asked anything of you that you failed to do. Yeah," he said, nodding his head. "You were dependable." It was the highest compliment Captain J.D. McCain was capable of giving any man.

He continued staring silently down at the small pile of stones until he heard the sound of Poe and Moses returning.

As the two men came riding back from their scouting trip, Poe announced, "Took the fork into Langtry! Hope he don't run crosswise of that whisky-soaked old fool who calls himself a judge."

When Legends Lived

Neither McCain nor Roosevelt Poe were great admirers of the infamous Judge Roy Bean, believing he had little, if any, knowledge of the law and primarily used what he did possess to further his own agenda at every opportunity.

"We should've hung the crazy old billy goat years ago," McCain said, with a dark look. "Well, we can make a few more miles before dark. Let's get mounted up."

* * *

Rosco was glad to get out of Langtry and away from that demented old man who called himself "Judge" Bean. Langtry, Texas, was really a hodgepodge of three tent cities — the communities of Eagle's Nest, Soto City, and Vinegaroon — which were created during the construction of the Southern Pacific Railroad, and still stubbornly lingered. The three townships were situated in a triangle around Judge Bean's saloon, the "Jersey Lilly," named after the English actress Lily Langtry. The Judge was her self-proclaimed, greatest admirer. He presided over all three communities and pompously called himself, "The Law West of the Pacos."

Roy Bean was actually a justice of the peace appointed in 1881. He was officially required to run for the office every two years and at the current time, had lost his last appointment to a new term. That didn't faze the judge, who continued to hold "court" in his saloon, collecting fines for minor and imagined offenses, usually from unsuspecting strangers passing through.

Judge Roy Bean worked under his own set of rules in what he considered his "rightful" jurisdiction and justice, usually to his own profit. One of his typical "rulings" was the time a railroad foreman was accused of killing a Chinese laborer. The "courtroom" — Bean's Jersey Lilly Saloon — was packed with the foreman's friends, a real tough-looking railroad group that visibly made the Bean more than a little nervous. A strained silence filled the courtroom as the charge was read and Judge Bean flipped through his copy of the Texas Criminal Code. At last, he looked up and proclaimed, "There don't seem to be a law against killin' a Chinaman." That was that.

Notwithstanding Bean's insufferable attitude, Rosco thought he'd been able to accomplish several things while he was there. Granted, the Judge had charged him nearly two prices for the sorry mule he loaded down with the supplies he would need for several weeks. Not to mention over-charging for the supplies, as well. However, he'd been able to write a letter to the Amarillo Cattlemen's Bank and another to a woman named Josie, who lived on a river back east. He hoped that crooked old judge would put both letters on the next stage. He had also left a note for Captain McCain, describing the incident leading up to the death of Stump Henry. Judge Bean had charged him a dollar for each letter, him being the post master for Langtry — as well as the sheriff, judge, and mayor. And he had three hired guns to make it stick. Not looking for any trouble, Rosco paid up and left town as quickly as possible, anxious to be back on the trail of Reid and hopefully, his lovely wife Jenny — if she were still alive.

He planned to head toward the area Poe and McCain had described to him, close to the Devil's River. It seemed as good a place as any to start. Poe recommended that once he arrived in the area he start making ever-increasing circles until he 'cut a trail' of a large bunch of shod horses. About three days out of Langtry, Rosco crossed the path of a large bunch of ponies that weren't shod and decided they were probably Comanche or

When Legends Lived

Kiowas, up out of Mexico and looking for trouble. He decided to keep to the high ground and away from trails as much as possible. Just thinking about being in the same area as that group made the hair stand up on the back of his neck.

Several days of winding his way through the foothills found him near the valley where he thought the Devil's River might be. He awoke early from a cold camp, relieved himself and walked to the small stream to get a drink of water, when he saw it. *Damn,* he thought, *it's a wonderment I never saw it when I watered the animals last night.* But there it was, clear as day, right down the middle of the stream he had camped by. He could see the overturned rocks and disturbed debris at the bottom of the shallow stream-bed, as clear as any trail he had ever seen, leading downstream until it disappeared around the next bend. Excited, he hurriedly packed the mule and saddled Stump's horse, mounted and surveyed the campsite. Satisfied it looked the same as when he arrived, he eased the animals into the stream and followed the trail on the bottom of the stream-bed.

Except for the natural sounds of the countryside, he heard nothing. Still, he kept the mule close enough so he could watch its ears, and followed the stream until he could see the river. Two miles down stream, he spotted the exit they made from the water and nudged his horse to follow. Cautious about his progress, he made another cold camp that night and was on his way the next morning as soon as he could see well enough to follow the trail. It was just about full-light when the mule's ears stood straight up and started to flop back and forth. Rosco quickly moved into a clump of scrub-oaks on the side of a steep ridge and strained, listening. He could barely make out the faint sounds of gunfire coming from the other side of the steep ridge.

Dismounting quickly, he tied the animals, took his rifle and the telescope Dixie had given him, and hastily moved up the rugged incline. Reaching the crest, he paused to catch his breath and listen again. One shot rang out, this time surprisingly loud, just below him. He moved to a vantage point by crawling to the lip of a large rock, and using the telescope, peered over to the hollow below.

Indians, a lot of them, he thought. *Looks like Comanches.*

He could also see the bodies of over a dozen people scattered about in the narrow draw. Even from as far away as he was, he could see most of them were mutilated beyond recognition. Those that weren't were being taken care of as he watched. Twice, he heard the screams of unlucky survivors as they were discovered by the Comanches. Rosco felt sick. *Jenny's down there,* he thought, for he was convinced that it was Reid's gang, laying butchered below him.

Rage filled him and he slowly raised his rifle and sighted along its barrel. Catching a slight movement out of the corner of his eye, he momentarily laid the rifle aside and once again, picked up the telescope. Focusing in, the first thing he saw was Jenny. She was a quarter of a mile down the draw from the slaughter area and was leading a saddled horse, keeping her hand over its nose to keep it quiet. A large bearded man followed behind her, also leading a horse. Instantly, Rosco knew it was Bloody Bill Reid.

Jenny, my God! She was beautiful. She looked healthy and clean, not at all as he would've thought. He followed them with the eyeglass until they reached the end of the draw, mounted and quietly walked their horses out of sight.

Rosco ran down the deep slope to where he left the horse and mule, nearly falling twice in his haste. As fast as he dared move, he paralleled the draw to a point where he thought he might pick up their trail, and angled sharply to the right. *Jenny, my darling wife,* he thought, *she's alive! Hang on Jenny, I'm coming!*

* * *

Brad cleaned the gun given to him by Hal La'Monte, for the third time since he'd gone out early in the morning to practice with it. Hal had shown him how to draw and get in a quick accurate shot before most men were aware you were even going to draw.

"Surprise," Hal had told him, "is the best marksmanship you can have."

Hal had also told him about the duels he'd had in New Orleans — and the women, too. That was why he'd had to leave New Orleans, Hal said, and cautioned him not to mention it to his sister. Hal had taken Brad to Mother Rosa's Home for Young Ladies in the old part of San Antonio one night last week. The women there hadn't laughed at his limp, or that he was skinny and pale. Not at all. They'd acted as though they were crazy for him. It had been his first time with a woman and he had gone back twice more on his own since then.

Brad knew he was getting good with the silver plated handgun he now wore everywhere he went. He could see the surprise and respect in Hal's eyes the last time he'd watched him practice with it. He was fast, too. Maybe, even faster than Hal. And, he would get better, because he would practice every day until he was the best. Brad knew men respected anyone who was good with a gun. He knew, because he'd heard them talk of John Wesley Hardin, King Fisher and Clay Allison.

Sparky, the bartender at the Red Wheel Saloon, had told him about the time he saw Roosevelt Poe shoot three cowboys out of the saddle just for riding their horses into the saloon. Sparky had spoken of Poe with respect — and fear.

Hal had taught Brad how to play cards, too. He'd shown him how to easily get the best cards and how to tell what the other players were holding. They'd even worked out a few simple signals and tried them out in low-stakes poker games. Brad didn't know why Hal would want to cheat, for as far as he knew Hal already had lots of money of his own. Hal had said he needed the excitement, and Brad thought he could understand that.

Dixie had been upset last night when he hadn't come home. In fact, lately she seemed upset and jumpy most of the time. Well, she was a stupid little twit and he had his own life to lead. He always remembered to "talk Hal up" in front of her though, and he always remembered his promise to Hal about not telling Dixie the real reason he'd left New Orleans. Brad knew Hal was trying to get next to his sister and suspected Hal had already 'slipped it' to her. He snickered to himself. Serve the little twit right, he thought. He felt the weight of the pistol on his hip and decided to go practice some more.

* * *

Martin Gates arrived in Langtry, Texas, surprised that it was nothing more than a shack of a saloon and a bunch of tents, stuck right out in all the heat and dust, in the middle of nowhere.

"Where is the Court House?" he said to the stage driver, who laughed a deep belly laugh and pointed toward the Jersey Lily saloon.

"You'll find Judge Bean in there."

Martin carried his bag to the front door and strained to see into the dark room.

When Legends Lived

"If you're a'coming in, then come on in," a gravelly voice said.

Cautiously, he inched into the room and blinked his eyes to adjust them. At last, he made out a short, rather portly man with a scraggly growth of beard, standing behind a bar of several rough planks setting on a few barrels for support.

"I'm seeking Judge Roy Bean," Gates said politely.

"I'm Judge Bean," the stout man stated. "Judge, mayor and postmaster, too. What can I do for you?"

Gates could make out the images of several more people in the small room, surprised that there were so many human beings living in such a place as Langtry, Texas. "I'm Martin Gates. I work for one of Chicago's largest newspapers and I'm seeking information on one J.D. McCain, formerly a Captain in the Texas Rangers. He's been appointed special government agent by the President of the United States, and endorsed by the Governor of Texas, to work in the interests of the Southern Pacific Railroad, in the dispatch of this country's enemies; specifically, outlaws and renegades that destroy railroad property and murder its employees. I've been attempting to catch up with him for over six months now to interview him, but I always seem to be a few days behind."

Judge Bean was obviously impressed with the young man's cultured speech. "And you're likely to stay a few days behind him, too. He ain't an easy man to catch up with," he said. "Course, if you did catch up with him, he just might kill you, like as not. I heard he don't much care for newspaper men, Republicans, or the railroad," the Judge said.

Martin laughed deeply at the joke, then stopped abruptly when he realized he was the only one laughing. His face red, he said, "Well, I doubt he'd shoot a man just for asking a few questions."

"Don't bet on it," said a man at the end of the bar wearing a crisscrossed gun-belt and a bandage around his head. "He was in here a few days ago and he wasn't any too hospitable then."

"Did he say where he was going?" the newsman said. "Did he do anything while he was here?" He went on quickly, "I'll pay good money for a factual account of what happened while Captain McCain was in Langtry, and where he might've gone."

The mention of money had an electrifying effect and clearly got everyone's attention. They all inched closer and began to talk at once.

"Hold it, please," Martin said, holding up his hand. "One at a time. I'll get to you all, but please, one at a time."

Martin Gates spent the better part of three hours in the Jersey Lily and left with several pages of notes. After his trained newsman's eye sifted through them later and he extracted the obvious lies and colorful wording, he was able to salvage just about half of them.

According to his information, it appeared that Captain McCain was accompanied by four other men. All of them, except the young railroad man, Packard, had, at one time or other, served with the formidable Texas Rangers, and were well known throughout the region. Especially McCain and "that killer" Poe, whom they all mentioned with a great deal of respect. Additionally, all of them clearly possessed superb skill with a handgun. Martin was amazed that these shootists had practically ruled western Texas as judge, jury, and occasionally, executioner for the better part of a century, yet it seemed virtually no one back east had ever heard of them.

Perusing his notes, Gates was able to decipher a clear picture of what had transpired during McCain's stop in Langtry. During his interview of the motley group in Bean's saloon, he had taken great pains to write down the quotes he was provided, verbatim. It seemed the Rangers had ridden into Langtry in the heat of the day, dirty, tired and clearly in a foul mood over one of their number having been killed along the way. They entered the Jersey Lily and quietly ordered drinks and food. "Shaky" Peterson, had been bar-keeping at the time, for the Judge who hadn't yet slept off his significant intake of spirits from the previous night.

Having culled and arranged his earlier notes to his satisfaction, Gates now read the information he had gathered when Peterson recalled in detail his encounter with Captain McCain. The story fascinated Gates.

"You see a young man stop by here in the past few days, riding a piebald with Montana rigging?" McCain had asked Peterson.

"Don't see nothing, don't hear nothing and don't say nothing," Shaky said, not looking up from his work of shining a stained beer glass.

Apparently McCain was getting just a little tired of lippy bartenders by that time, and gave the man a dark look for a long moment. Then he said, "I'm just gonna ask you this one more time," he said softly. "So think real careful about your answer, 'cause it might be important to you."

Shaky Peterson, who was anything but shaky and standing just over six feet two inches, was a big man for his time and he stood scowling at the smaller man for an instant. Shaky had attended bar in some of the toughest towns in Texas during the past twenty years and had been through his share of brawls and gunfights. He didn't scare easily, but McCain's tone was hard, icy, seem to grip Peterson by his vitals.

"Mister, I said…young feller…roan pony…Montana rig. You see him?" McCain persisted, his cold voice even softer this time.

Peterson stared at the older man for just an instant more, something in the man's eyes making him chose his words this time. He quickly averted his eyes and said, "Sorry, amigo, I guess I just wasn't thinking. Yeah, came through here four days ago, didn't stay more'n a few hours. Seemed in a hurry to git on his way. You folks chasing him?"

McCain ignored his question and instead asked, "Which way did he go?"

"Hell, mister, I don't see every…," Shaky started. Then seeing the clouds beginning to cover the other man's face again, said quickly, "Tom July told me he went northeast toward the Devil's."

McCain slowly scanned the room. "Which one's July?"

Peterson pointed to a lanky individual standing at the end of the bar wearing two crisscrossed gun belts, as though glad to no longer be the object of McCain's attention. July was in charge of Judge Bean's security matters. That meant that he and the other two hired guns who worked with him enforced the Judge's often ridiculous decisions that were handed out in the Langtry court of law. Tom July was also a gunfighter who, with the help of his two cold-eyed assistants, had shot or hung seven men since coming to work for Judge Bean. Shaky Peterson watched with a great deal of interest and hidden glee as McCain started toward the end of the bar.

Leaning against the end of the bar, Tom July coldly watched McCain with a small smile playing at the corner of his mouth, as the old ranger approached him.

"Tom July?"

Without waiting for a reply, McCain continued. "I'm looking

When Legends Lived

for a young man that came through here a few days ago. Maybe headed north to the Devil's area. You see him?"

July slowly eased himself away from the bar and stood upright, his hands a scant inch from his holstered guns. He didn't say anything, only stared at McCain with that tiny smile. In the next instant he was lying on the floor moaning in pain, and McCain was holstering his Walker Colt. A chair leg scraped on the bare floor as someone pushed his chair away from a table.

"I wouldn't," Jake Kellog cautioned softly. His words were quickly followed by the sound of someone sitting back down.

"I 'spect you heard the question the first time I asked it," he said, looking down at Tom July lying on the floor. Then, without looking up, McCain said to Shaky Peterson, "Get me a glass of water."

Shaky immediately did as he was told that time and without comment, handed the glass to McCain, who took it and threw the water on the head of the groaning man. "Stand up. I didn't hit you that hard," he said without sympathy.

At that moment, Roy Bean burst into the room in a fury from a door in the back of the saloon. "Just what the hell is going on in here?" he shouted. "I worked all night and damn well don't appreciate all this noise and commotion first thing in the morning!"

No one pointed out that it was already mid-afternoon.

"Who hurt this man? Shaky, get me my robe and I'll hang the son-of-a-bitch."

Bean continued to run up and down the length of the barroom floor, ranting and raving, until Poe suddenly stepped in front of him and said, "Sit down and shut up, you old windbag, 'fore I rap you on the head, too!"

Bean collapsed into a nearby chair, struck mute by the events at hand. He clearly wasn't used to being treated in that manner, nor being talked to like that.

"I'm Poe and this is Captain McCain, Texas Rangers," Poe told him. "These are our duly appointed law officers. The Captain don't like to waste time and generally don't ask someone a question over 'bout once. After that, he just feels he has to somehow git their attention."

Poe parted his mustache and spit on the floor. "Now, he likely will want to ask some more questions before he is inclined to leave, so I recommend you folks keep that little quirk of his in mind." Poe concluded with a wink he probably intended to look conspiratorial, but only succeeded in looking sinister.

Bean was livid with rage. "July, you and those high priced "deputies" I pay better get your asses moving and shoot these people," Bean said evenly as he pointed a shaking finger around the room. July, who still wore his guns, was now seated in a chair rubbing a large knot on his forehead.

"Judge Bean, I work for you and you pay me well. I don't know about Hank and Charlie, but I don't make enough money to go up against Poe…and I damn sure don't make enough to take on both Poe and J.D. McCain at the same time. If we did, all you'd have are three dead deputies and then they'd likely just end up hanging you, too."

July grinned ruefully, rubbing the tender spot on his head. "Hell, had I knowed who they were, I'd been a tad more cordial."

Martin Gates read and reread his notes three times, with growing excitement. According to the notes, McCain had spent about thirty more minutes getting some straight answers from the patrons of the Jersey Lily. At some point, Rosco's note and letters were referenced and Judge Bean reluctantly gave up the note to Captain McCain. McCain had cautioned him that he would consider it a personal affront if the Judge didn't see to it that Stump Henry's letters were put on the first stage out of Langtry. To his credit, Judge Bean didn't even try to negotiate for additional money. Nor did he attempt to overcharge the Rangers for the supplies they obtained for the trail. In fact, he was quite cowed.

Staring down at his notes for some time, Martin Gates felt keen excitement seeping into his bones at last.

* * *

The trail seemed much fresher than at any time during the past six days. They had long since departed the Devil's River area and had been traveling for several days on a large flat landscape that Rosco determined must be the Edward's Plateau. *Looks like they might be angled toward San Antonio or Laredo,* Rosco thought. *Maybe Reid thinks he's out-run the danger.*

Studying the tracks before him, he estimated they were no more than two-three hours ahead of him. *So near, Jenny. So near.* Spurred on by the fact that he was closer to Jenny than he'd been at any time since the day she'd disappeared, he forced his mount to move faster. He felt a shiver of excitement run through him. He must be very careful from now on, he told himself. The young deputy knew Reid was a very dangerous man and he could take no chances with him.

Topping a rise in the landscape, he instantly held up as a soft whinny floated up from below. Rosco dismounted and covered his horse's nose. He didn't have to worry about the mule answering. That damn mule didn't like anything.

Tying his bandana around his horse's nose, he quietly made

his way to the crest of the hill and using the telescope, surveyed the basin below. At first, he saw only the two horses standing at the entrance of an abandoned mine. Then, he saw Bloody Bill Reid exit the bushes tightening his belt.

He must be holding Jenny inside the mine-shaft, he thought.

He waited, watching as Reid began to unsaddle the horses to make camp for the night. Then, Rosco circled the hill, remaining out of sight and sound range, until he was satisfied he was upwind from Reid's animals. Then, he edged toward the mine entrance.

Rosco reached the edge of the foliage and saw Reid bent over, facing away from him, working on something on the ground. Silently, Rosco moved toward him. When he was about twenty feet away, he saw Reid stiffen as he became aware of the deputy's presence and watched as the outlaw straightened up, still facing away from him.

"You don't need to die," Rosco told him. "I just want what's mine, but I'll kill you if I have to."

Slowly, Reid turned to face him, careful to keep his hands away from his guns. "So, you're the little husband," he said and laughed, relieved to find Rosco's guns still holstered. "Sort of thought it might be you following along back there. Ya should've give up, Deputy, 'cause now I gotta kill you for your trouble. Besides, Jenny don't want to leave me anyway." Reid laughed again and said, "Seems she found a bigger man, if ya know what I mean."

Rosco had been a lawman long enough to know that Reid was just trying to make him angry so he would do something dumb. "Then we're wasting time talking, Reid. Either drop your gunbelt, or use it," he said. "Do it!"

"Now let's not be in such an all-fired hurry to —" Reid began, then in mid-sentence, moved to the side at the same time his hand flashed to his gun in a blur. He was just starting to pull the trigger when the deputy's bullet slammed into his hip. He never even saw Rosco pull his gun.

Rosco, keeping his gun leveled on Reid who watched through slitted eyes, moved toward the wounded man cautiously. At the same instant as he heard the thunderous report of a shotgun, Rosco felt a heavy force hit him between the shoulders, lift him into the air and send him sprawling in the dust, where he lay stunned, helpless to move. Blackness washed over him and he didn't know how long he was out, but finally opening his eyes, found he was still able to see Reid on the ground in front of him. Then a pair of soft rawhide boots moved in front of his eyes and remained there. Above them was the bottom of a fringed skirt and the nozzle of a short-barreled shotgun hanging down.

"You couldn't leave well enough alone, could you?" Jenny screamed at him. "You never could! Well, just look where it got you! Damn you, Rosco Bookbinder, damn you to hell!"

"Jenny," Bill croaked. "Help get me in the saddle. Those Comanche are still around and this deputy probably ain't alone."

Rosco, completely numb and unable to move, watched as his wife helped load the wounded outlaw onto his horse and prepare to leave.

"We gonna leave him alive?" he heard Jenny ask.

"Alive?" Bill made a sound that might have been a short laugh. "Hell, he's dead. He just don't know it! Let's get moving, someone might've heard that shotgun blast," Bill gasped in obvious pain.

Rosco lay with his head resting on the hot ground, watching as the two rode into the tree line, Jenny supporting the wounded

R.C. Morris

Reid in the saddle. With an overpowering sense of sadness, he watched until they left his line of vision and, at last, even the sounds of the horses faded away. Rosco, unable to move, felt a numbing coldness begin to creep through his body and closing his eyes, gratefully let the welcome darkness envelop him.

Nineteen

"White men pray for a long life, but fear old age."
– Chickenfoot

JENNY AND BLOODY BILL REID traveled until Reid was too weak to go on, then Jenny made camp near a rippling stream and nursed him for most of the night. She saw that Rosco's bullet had gone completely through his hip and prayed it hadn't broken anything vital. The next morning Reid seemed much improved but Jenny decided to stay in the covered location for one more day to allow him to gather his strength. As he slept, she constantly observed him, moved to tears by her deep love, and her fear for the outlaw's injury. Finally, she pressed her body against his to protect him from the evening chill, and also slept.

On the morning of the second day, Jenny awoke from a fitful sleep before Reid, and walked to the stream for water to make breakfast. God damned, Rosco Bookbinder to hell! Why did he think he owned her? His meddling might now have cost her the only shot she'd ever had at happiness. She hated her husband for that, and hoped to hell he'd suffered a long time before he died.

On the way back to their small camp, deep in thought about her predicament, she came face-to-face with Rain Maker. Stifling a cry, she turned to flee back the way she had come, only to find several more half-naked Indians between her and the stream. Frantically, she surveyed the surrounding rocks and saw many more, some rubbing their crotches and openly grinning down at her. Despair completely engulfed her as she slumped to her knees with a soft sob. Suddenly, Jenny covered her eyes with shaking hands, and felt impending doom.

The Indians still made no move to touch her. Hearing noises behind her, Jenny jerked her head up and saw several Indians pulling a cursing Bill Reid down the hill. The big man struggled, and in spite of his recent wound, would've been more than a match for any two of the Comanches. As Jenny watched in frozen terror, four of the Indians forced Reid to the ground, roughly binding his hands behind his back. They still hadn't attempted to seize her or tie her up as they had the outlaw. Horrified, she watched as they pulled Reid to his feet and practically carried him, kicking and yelling, to a small crooked tree with limbs close to the ground. Freeing one hand at a time, they first bound his hands and then his feet, so he was left standing in a spread-eagle position, tied to the crooked little tree. Everything had a surreal quality about it, even the comical looking little tree.

"Stay alive, Jenny! Do what you have to, to stay alive! I love you," Bill yelled to her.

In a daze and making small whimpering sounds, Jenny, left alone, sat on the ground and watched as an older Indian removed Reid's boots. A breech-clothed savage gathered twigs and small limbs and placed them around the feet of her lover. He cursed and kicked at the twigs he could reach, but the Indian only tightened Reid's bindings and placed more of the tinder around the bound man's feet. When he was satisfied with his work, the breech-clothed man looked at Rain Maker, and when the leader nodded his head, lit the tinder with one strike of a flint.

"Bill! Oh God, Bill! Please no, no…" Hysteria choked her and she felt very close to the edge of madness.

When Legends Lived

At first, the twigs burned slowly, with almost no smoke. Then as more of the larger branches caught on, the flames leaped higher. It was then that Reid began to scream, and a moaning, half-crazed Jenny covered her ears to shut out his cries.

Old mountain men knew that to be captured by the Indians meant a slow hideous death, and usually kept one bullet for themselves, in case capture was imminent. They knew the Kiowas were masters at the art of skinning their captives, and the Sioux liked to begin with the fingers and toes and hack their prisoners to death a piece at the time. The crafty Apaches smeared honey on their captive's eyes and tied them over a hill occupied by a colony of fire-ants. But when it came to keeping captives alive for unheard of lengths of time while they worked on them with fire or other means of torture, they all agreed the Comanche was the master of torture.

Bloody Bill Reid lived for two days. When the fire would burn too high or too hot, the breech-clothed man would simply remove some of the twigs; when it died out, he would add more twigs. In the end, Reid was begging them to kill him, and at last, bored with the game because he'd lost consciousness and couldn't be revived again, they did just that by disemboweling him — slowly.

Jenny was never tied up. She didn't need to be, for after that first day she was too weak to run even a few steps. All of the warriors had mounted her at least once that first day, some several times. It didn't matter to them that after the first half-dozen or so, she was like a rag doll. Most of the time she remained conscious, she just lay motionless and whimpered. Later, she made no sound at all. Even when she was clearly unconscious, they continued to ravage her. It went on for the entire time it took for Bill Reid to die. Then at last, Rain Maker put a halt to it and they mounted up and rode away — taking their comatose captive with them.

*   *   *

Rosco opened his eyes to find he couldn't move, but was now propped against his saddle and covered with a rough blanket. There was a canteen lying near his hand and a small, smokeless fire blazed a few feet away. He was wondering how he'd gotten here when he heard a light step to his right. Turning his head slightly, he saw an Indian and reached to his hip only to find his guns were missing. As his vision begin to focus, he saw the Indian standing over him, grinning through toothless gums, was just an ancient old man. He was wearing Rosco's two pistols.

"You're alive, huh?" The toothless mouth said, looking sad. "Sorry to see that. Now I suppose I have to give back your pistols."

"Who are you?" Rosco said weakly.

"Before I died many years ago, I was someone else. For my second life, I chose the name Chickenfoot," the old man said.

"That's a silly name," croaked Rosco.

"Yes, it is," Chickenfoot agreed. "That's why I chose it. I figured all the good ones were already taken and nobody else would want this one."

"How long have I been here?"

"Three moons," Chickenfoot replied. "That's Indian talk for three days. You died on the first night I found you. Just quit breathing. I was ready to take your horse and pistols — maybe eat the mule, and leave. I don't like being around dead people too much."

The old man sat there for a moment, as though to think about what he had just said, then continued. "Just as I made that deci-

When Legends Lived

sion, you started breathing again so I waited around some more for you to die. Bad luck you didn't. Now I suppose I'll have to give back the pistols." Then, after another moment, "The glass that sees far, too, I suppose."

Dixie's telescope! "Why, you old thief! What are you doing going through my stuff?" Rosco whispered.

"You were dead! I didn't think you would mind too much," the old Indian explained rationally.

Exhausted from just those few words, Rosco closed his eyes and as he drifted off once more, heard the old man say, "Yes, it's good you sleep now. If you are still alive when you wake up, I'll fix you something to eat."

Rosco's sleep was a restless and disturbed one. He dreamed he saw Jenny standing on the other side of a swollen river, beckoning to him. In her hands, she held a rope. Jumping in, he swam to reach her, but knew at once he couldn't make it to the other side. He could feel the water pulling him down, entering his mouth and throat. Strangling, he called for her to throw him the rope. Jenny only stood there with a soft smile on her face. Her eyes, burning with hate, were the last thing Rosco saw as the river's current pulled him under.

The fever hit in the middle of the night and he woke up Chickenfoot with his delirious cries. In the morning, the old Indian heard no sounds coming from the injured man. After he watered the animals, Chickenfoot leaned close to him to determine if he was still alive and confirmed that the white man was, this time, truly in the other world. He supposed he would have to bury him. White men liked that, though it made little difference in the long run. You still ended up as food for the worms.

Going to the pack mule, Chickenfoot removed a shovel from the canvas and searched the area to find a soft spot to dig a grave. He found a moist area under some trees, and began to dig. It took him almost two hours before he was satisfied with his effort. His labor done, the old Indian sat on the bank of the stream and thought about his recent wealth. He was rich beyond his wildest dreams. He hoped the white man's spirit would not be too angry that he was happy about all his good fortune.

Standing up, he bent backward, stretching his back muscles, then slowly walked back to the campsite. The first thing he heard when he reached it was shallow breathing coming from the white man. At first, Chickenfoot was sure he was mistaken, but upon closer examination found that indeed, the white man had come back to life, yet once again. Standing over the injured man he held the shovel in his hands, looking first at the man on the ground, then at the shovel in his hands. He told himself it would be all the same if he hit the man on his head with the shovel, because the white man would surely die anyway. Then, sighing deeply, he tossed the shovel aside and knelt beside Rosco giving him a drink of the cool water he had retrieved from the brook. In his previous life he would've had no trouble banging the white man on the head to hasten his way down the silver path. But he'd given all that up when he'd bargained with the Great Spirit and was given his second life, and a deal was a deal.

He shook his head sadly — but they were fine pistols.

Toward evening, Rosco opened his eyes and asked for water. Chickenfoot brought him a drink and said, "While you were asleep, you died again." Looking thoughtfully for a moment, he then said with some reproach in his voice, "In all of my years, I only died once before."

The old man straightened and looked down at the injured man. "I will try to keep you alive, but there is little I can do. I think you will die a third death, soon. Then I will bury you," he said, and headed back toward the small fire.

"Take me to a town where I can see a doctor," Rosco croaked weakly.

"What town?" the old man said. "There are no towns near here."

Rosco was silent for so long that Chickenfoot thought he had slipped off to sleep again. Then he whispered, "San Antonio. You could take me there."

"That's a long trip, and I'm not going there."

"What if I pay you?"

The old man thought for a minute. "I have no need for money, what else do you have? Maybe your pistols?" he said hopefully.

"I'll need those pistols, old man. I'll give you the mule, then you won't have to walk anymore," Rosco told him.

Indignantly, the old man straightened up and stated with a bit of ire, "Comanches eat mules, we don't ride mules. We prefer fine horses."

"The horse don't belong to me. Pick something else."

"The glass that sees far. I'll do it for the long glass you carry in your right saddle bag," Chickenfoot stated with finality.

"That don't belong to me either," said the deputy.

"How about the rifle? You have those fine pistols that you are so fond of. You surely don't need the rifle too," the old man pointed out logically.

"The Sharps belonged to another and he gave it away," Rosco said with despair.

The old man stood and looked at him woefully for a long time. Was it possible this white man was even poorer than he was? "Don't you possess anything of your own?" he finally said.

"The mule," said Rosco wearily. "The mule is mine."

Looking thoughtful for a moment, the old man sat staring off into space. "Well, I suppose I could eat the mule. Okay! I'll take you to San Antonio for the mule and you buy me whisky when we get there," Chickenfoot said. "But you have to agree that if you die on the way, I get to keep all your things."

"We got a deal," said Rosco. "You got a right good chance of ending up with the whole caboodle, too."

He awoke to find that Chickenfoot had constructed a travois for him to lie on, which the mule would pull during the long journey. Rosco nearly passed out from the intense pain when the old man helped move him to the travois for the trip.

"It won't be as bad from now on," the old Indian said. "I'll just unhook the travois from the mule and you can sleep on it at night. We won't have to load you anymore that way. I lived on one of these for two months just before my first life was over," Chickenfoot claimed. "It's not easy, but it's not too hard either."

For the next three days they saw no one, as Rosco slipped back and forth between the darkness of death and the light that was life. Several times, he was aware of the old man stopping in clumps of brush or behind large boulders as if hiding from something, or someone. When awake, he heard the constant drone of the old man's voice as he related fantastic stories he swore were true. But mostly, Rosco drifted off and hovered in that never-never land somewhere between consciousness and sleep for long periods at a time.

Once when he awoke, they were camped, and he awoke screaming. His back felt as if it were on fire, and he laid there for a long time with his eyes closed, moaning loudly. When he finally opened his eyes, he was startled to see Chickenfoot squatting beside him, only inches away, peering intently into his face. Rosco screamed again, this time with surprise.

"You appear to be experiencing some pain," the old Indian said.

"No shit! Yes, I'm experiencing 'some pain' you old heathen. Some real goddamn pain!" the deputy nearly cried. There was a putrid smell in the air.

Still not moving, Chickenfoot said, "It does no good to insult me. I have no feelings for your insults because I've been dead once."

Rosco just groaned, feeling weak and completely helpless.

"I'll look at it," Chickenfoot said, as he turned the wounded man over on his side. "Yes, I see what is the matter," he said. "The little pockets are white. Soon your body will start to rot."

He lowered Rosco down on his back and the wounded man again screamed in pain.

"You've got a wonderful bedside manner, damn you. Can you do anything to help?" he groaned.

"I may be able to pick some of the little round bullets out of your back. I saw a black man who visited our village once to do that for our chief. I watched everything he did so I could use it later. I decided not to use it though, because the chief died. So we killed the black man."

"Wonderful," Rosco groaned. "That's great news. Okay, just do it. Anything's better than this."

Chickenfoot made a big show of washing his hands and holding the point of his knife to a small flame of the camp fire, preparing for his operation.

"Will you hurry?" the deputy said impatiently. "I'm probably dying while you're fooling around."

"This is the way doctors act," Chickenfoot stated simply. "I will probably have to charge you more, if you live."

"Don't you think you're violating your hypocritical oath by upping the ante that way?" Rosco said sarcastically.

Chickenfoot stared at him, clearly not understanding. "What is that thing?"

"Oh hell, never mind, just get on with it," Rosco finally said through clinched teeth.

Chickenfoot shoved a piece of rawhide into Rosco's mouth and said, "Bite down on this."

"Whymp?" Rosco mumbled around the gag.

Chickenfoot pondered it for a moment. "I don't know," he said thoughtfully. "But that's what the Black man did."

When he started probing, the pain was almost too unbearable for the wounded man to endure. He tried not to scream by thinking of Jenny; of things they had done together, but to no avail. Finally, he spit out the rawhide gag and tried talking instead.

"How is it...that you speak English, so good?" he asked the old man.

"After I died, I was found by the Catholics. They have their own God and get angry if you don't believe in it, too," Chickenfoot said sincerely. "They are a cruel tribe of people. Their women, the black women, all wear black robes and hit you on the hand with a stick if you do something they don't like. They particularly don't like you to piss in their gardens. I used to do that. Defecate too. But that was before I learned of the white people's custom of saving the turds. The 'black' women hit me on the hands with their stick and took me to a small building that smelled foul. They told me that was where I must go to piss and defecate from now on. I have since learned that it is the custom of all whites to save their droppings in those little houses. I never learned the reason for this though. Do you know the reason?"

Rosco didn't answer, the pain was too great.

Chickenfoot thought about that for a while, then shook his head as if puzzled, and continued. "I didn't like the smell of that place, so one day I went into the garden to defecate instead. It was good to defecate out in the open air again. I dug a hole and covered it so the 'black' women wouldn't find it. Just as I finished, one of the 'black' women came upon me kneeling there. 'Oh, something died? The poor thing, how sad,' she said." Chickenfoot strained to mimic her screechy voice.

"She knelt beside me and insisted I pray over it with her. I stayed there with the 'black' women for one year, but I never understood their customs." Chickenfoot suddenly brightened. "While I was there, I learned to speak good English. Then one day when I was healed, I took all of their biscuits and wine, and ran away. The whites make good whisky and wine."

Even with the intense pain, Rosco could've laughed at the image of this ancient old man stealing the holy wine and crackers and running away.

Laying the knife down, Chickenfoot rubbed his eyes and said, "That is all of the little round bullets I can get. The others are too deep. Maybe you will live a few more days now."

"Thanks for your deep concern," Rosco said dryly. "I certainly hope so, too."

The crude operation eased the pain in Rosco's back, but only for a couple of days. On the third day, the fire was back, only more intense. Rosco continually slipped in and out of consciousness, and was delirious most of the time. Hallucinating, he saw Jenny who kissed him tenderly, then spit upon him, and, as she stood over him, sent blast after blast from her shotgun into his burning flesh. He was visited by Stump Henry, who advised him that death was not too bad after all, and that he should just let go and come with him. He saw the old Indian, Chickenfoot, wearing a hideous mask and paint on his face, dancing around and around in a big circle. Not knowing if he was awake or dreaming, one time he saw Chickenfoot get off his horse, and walk to where some large buzzards were eating a dead animal. Then he stooped down to scoop handfuls of the putrid flesh from the dead animal and put it into a small pouch. In a foggy daze, he watched, fascinated, as the old man returned, knelt beside him and rubbed some of the animal's rotten meat onto his wound.

Much later, Rosco opened his eyes. *I'm still alive!*, he thought. And my back feels a little better, too. Not so much fire in it. He thought he could feel an almost massaging effect in the area of his wound. With his right hand he tenderly reached back as far as he could and touched one of the pockets the buckshot made. He felt something moving. Closing his hand around it, he brought it back in front of his eyes, and screamed. In a second, the old man was beside him

"Are you in pain again?" he said.

"Maggots!" Rosco shouted. "Stinking, goddamn, filthy maggots, eating my flesh! Get them off!"

The old man smiled. "Oh, the white worms. Yes, I put them there," he said modestly. "Two handfuls of them."

"Why?" the deputy screamed. "Why, why?"

Chickenfoot made no move to do as he demanded, just stared at

When Legends Lived

him disapprovingly. "If you continue to make noise like that, some Kiowas will hear you and come and kill us both," he finally said, as if speaking to a child. "Then the white worms can eat us both."

Rosco settled down, biting back his retort. At this, Chickenfoot went on, calmly pointing out to the injured man, in his best bedside manner, "The white worms will only eat the dead meat. That will keep the rest of you from rotting. Maybe it will keep you alive until we reach the white man's town," he continued. "Does your wound feel better than it did a few days ago?"

Rosco had to grudgingly admit that it did, and nodded his head. "Did you learn that from the black doctor, too?"

"No," Chickenfoot said. "It came to me when I had a vision. In my vision, I saw the large black birds with the bald heads, the ones you white people call turkey buzzards. They were eating a dead animal. At first, I thought my vision was telling me to let the birds eat your dead flesh, but, then I saw the white worms and I knew the meaning of the vision."

"Well thank God for that," said Rosco shuddering, as he tried to imagine waking up to find several of those huge vultures pecking away at his flesh.

"Now we must hurry on our way. I have to figure up my fee," Chickenfoot said as he rose, walked back to the horse and agilely climbed into the saddle.

* * *

The small band of Rangers found the butchered remains of Bloody Bill's bunch on the third day after leaving Langtry. Moses Penny saw the vultures first and angled toward them. He came back to report a short time later and McCain's group went in to check it out. Jim Packard was violently sick at what he saw.

"You'd think I'd get used to this sort of thing. I mean, being with you people," he said, looking pale and shaken. "Lord knows I've seen a few things during that time that I never could've imagined back in Chicago."

"No one ever gets used to it," Poe said, as he spit at a small lizard perched on a rock.

"Well, I never see you or Fish or the others get sick," Packard said with reproach.

"It's just that we keep our sickness on the inside," Poe answered. "It's better to let it go like you do. When you get to the point you keep it inside, that's when it starts to become a part of you. You'll never be the same man as you were after that."

"I'll never get used to it," Jim said warily, as he sat down on a rock. He looked as if he were going to be sick again. "I just wish I was out of this god forsaken country and back to civilization."

"Oh, you mean back where those banker fellers and the railroad can legally take a man's home, and his money, and there's nothing you can do but to put a bullet through your own head or jump out of a window?" Poe said pointedly, as he spit at the lizard again.

This time he hit it dead center. He watched with a trace of satisfaction as the lizard scurried away to hide under another rock.

Looking up at Poe, Jim shook his head slowly and laughed quietly. "Touch`e Rosie," was all he said, as he got up, brushed off his pants and climbed back on his horse. "Thanks," and rode off up the trail.

Poe watched him go, chuckling softly to himself and nodding his head once. Then he heaved himself to his feet and went about the business of trying to identify the remains of Bill Reid or the young deputy's long lost wife among the dead. They were back in the saddle within two hours. Once they determined that Bloody Bill and the girl weren't among the remains, McCain decreed that a shallow mass grave be dug and covered with rocks.

"It's the Christian thing to do," he said.

Underway again, it was Moses Penny who first spotted Bill and Jenny's trail and where Rosco had intersected it. Once again, following it to its end, they finally found the mine shaft where Moses was able to read the obscure signs and tell the story of what had happened there.

"Two people shot here, Captain. See that cracked shoe? That's Bloody Bill's horse. The small one belongs to the lady, and I'd know Stump's horse tracks if they was mixed in with a buffalo herd," he said. "Captain, something spooky here. That deputy shot it out with Reid and got the best of him. He must be pure hell on wheels with a six-gun. Then somebody shot him in the back."

Moses looked ill-at-ease, then bravely plunged forward with the telling of his story. "The lady shot Deputy Bookbinder, Captain. Used a scatter-gun. That big blood spot over there? That's where he fell." He pointed again, "There are two empty shotgun shell casings over near the entrance of the mine. The lady's footprints are the only ones leading into, and out of, the mine."

Moses Penny paused, clearly uncomfortable in maligning a white lady. Then he went on, "You can see her footprints in the dust here, small compared to the others." Moses pointed to the ground in front of them. "She walked over to where her husband lay, looked at him and then went to Bill and helped him onto his horse. They rode off together, Captain, that way," he finished, pointing down the trail.

"Aye God!" Poe said, as though to himself, and whistled softly. He stared at Penny in amazement. "If I ever doubted your ability to read sign up to now, I just got over it, Moses. You are a magician, pure and simple."

Moses took the complement without a change in his expression.

"How long ago?" McCain said.

"I'd say 'bout four days. I couldn't read it if there had been any rain," he admitted, looking sideways at Poe.

"Well, damn me if the boy ain't somewhat human," Poe said.

"Looks like someone else came along later and helped Mr. Bookbinder," he said. "It 'pears to have been a Comanche," he continued with a puzzled look on his face. "You can always tell by the wide stitching in the seams on the soles of their moccasins."

"Seems to be more damn people out here in the middle of no-man's land than we last seen in El Paso," McCain said, bewildered.

He walked over to Grasshopper, standing a short distance from the other horses. There, he rested his arms across the saddle, eyes cast toward the ground, obviously deep in thought. Poe had seen him do that several hundred times in the years they had ridden together and knew McCain was just waiting for him to approach him for a conference. Poe walked over and McCain glanced up as he approached.

"Whatcha think?" he said to Poe.

"I'll take Jake and track down Reid and the girl," Poe answered. "Reid's wounded and likely as not, won't have gone far before they had to rest. Soon as we hang him, Jake and me will catch up with the rest of you. Guess it wouldn't be acceptable to hang the filly. Lord knows she probably deserves it though," he said thoughtfully.

"Probably does," McCain agreed. "Let's get to moving then.

When Legends Lived

You should be able to catch up with us pretty soon, 'cause you'll be traveling lighter then we are. If you lose the trail, just remember, we'll be heading pretty much due-east. You'll pick us up on one of your circles."

Poe stared at McCain in consternation, as though annoyed that anyone might suggest he wasn't every bit the tracker Moses Penny was. Not picking up on his partner's agitation, McCain removed his hat and wiped his forehead with the sleeve of his shirt.

"If we go now, maybe we can get to that young man before he dies, or that bunch of Comanches find him."

The two men stood and looked at each other for a moment and McCain finally said to his friend, "You be real cautious out there, partner. Remember the tracks of that war party we crossed paths with a ways back."

Swinging into the saddle, Poe nodded and said, "Mount-up Jake, you and me are going on a little adventure. Take care, Jericho."

Then, they were gone, leaving McCain to stare after them.

At dusk on the second day, a tired Roosevelt Poe and Jake Kellog rejoined McCain's group. They came riding into camp on horses caked with dust and sweat, having obviously been rode long and hard. By the time they'd eaten and prepared for the night, they'd related to the others how they'd found the charred body of Reid, along with signs that indicated the woman had probably been carried off by raiding Comanches.

"More than likely dead by now, then," Fish said, looking at Poe and Kellog, knowingly.

"Either that, or married off to a young buck," Poe said with disgust, spitting between his feet.

"Looks like Bloody Bill got pretty much what he had coming to him," Jake said. "Kind of funny in a way, him ending up like that after all the things he's done."

"I'd say he lasted about two days, from the amount of burn on the body," Poe interjected. "Burnt his feet off right at the ankles, then turned him upside down and slow-cooked his brain. Finally ended up by gutting him, like a hog."

"For God's sake!" cried Jim Packard, leaping to his feet. "Can't we just talk about something else? Can't we, huh?" He stormed away from the fire and plopped down on his blanket, some distance away.

"Boy's a little high-strung, ain't he?" Poe said, arching an eyebrow and squinting at the others.

McCain grunted his agreement and said loudly over his shoulder, "Better get over it young fellow, we got a long ways to go before this is over." Standing, he stretched and went on. "Well, we can't help that now, let's get some sleep and an early start in the morning."

McCain walked to a level spot and commenced to unroll his blanket. "I have a feeling that young deputy is probably dead as well by now." He laid down and was sound asleep in less than a minute.

Young Packard stared at him for awhile, as though resentful he was able to drop off so fast.

* * *

After a cold breakfast the following morning, the lawmen saddled up and headed out before full daylight. It was midmorning when they topped a rise and stopped to survey the level landscape before them. Its table-like flatness was marred only by a deep gully running from their left to right. It ran as far as they could see in either direction. The tracks of the two people they were following entered the draw, but apparently didn't exit on the eastern side. McCain nudged his mount down the steep bank into the bottom of the draw, followed by the others. On the sandy bottom, they once again found the tracks and deep pole marks of the travois, headed down the middle of the gully, almost due south.

The horsemen had been following the trail, now clearly defined in the soft sand, for nearly three hours when Jim Packard heard a freight train, coming directly down the gully toward them. He saw sudden fear in the faces of the other men, and without a word being spoken, they charged their terrorized horses straight up the steep bank on the opposite side of the gully, leading the braying pack animals behind. Jim was a scant step behind, followed by Jake Kellog.

The wall of muddy water was nearly ten feet high and traveling at twenty miles an hour when Jim finally saw it. Then, it was upon them before he could think, hurling him and his horse end over end, down the gully they'd just ridden up. He could faintly hear the screaming of the pack animals and the shouts of the other men over the deafening roar of the water. Then mud and water filled his mouth and eyes, choking and blinding him. Blackness rolled over him at once, and the roar was suddenly gone.

The first thing he was conscious of was someone beating him on the back.

"Come on boy, breath...breath," Jim heard the person say, as he coughed up muddy water, then vomited. "Lord-dy, boy. You do more puke'n than anybody I ever seen."

He recognized the folksy twang to be that of Roosevelt Poe. Water gurgled in his ears and when he had shaken it out, Rosie was still speaking.

"…may have to throw you back into that water just to clean you up."

Jim could now see, and breathe, but with some difficulty. He laid there for a moment and then asked, "Is everybody okay?"

"Well, nice of you to ask, but no. We had a casualty," Poe told him.

His heart hammering, Jim sat upright and stared at Poe. "Who was it?"

Jim could see Poe's lips moving, but the muddy water gurgling in his ears once more, made it impossible to hear what Poe was saying. Then, all at once, he could hear again.

" Polly…Polly," the ranger kept repeating. "Poor old gentle dumb Polly. Kept telling her, she needed to learn how to swim, but no, she tells me, it don't rain enough around here for that."

"P-Polly? Polly who?" Jim Packard said, trying to shake the cobwebs from his head. Then he remembered, the pack mule. The gentle one. He stood on unstable legs and looked with disgust at Poe. "Very funny," he said, sullenly. "Very damn funny." As he stalked off, he heard Poe's distinctive irritating chuckle.

The others were milling around several hundred feet away, taking stock of their injuries and assessing the damage. Just as he reached them, the rain hit. Jim Packard couldn't remember ever seeing it rain as hard. It rained for exactly five minutes, then the sun came out, and it was as hot as ever. Within another five minutes, no one could've guessed that it had rained at all.

"You lost your horse, Mr. Packard, and we lost one of the pack animals with all the supplies it was carrying," McCain confirmed sternly. "You'll have to take turns riding double with the rest of us, until we get to some place to buy you another horse. I told you to stay close. Next time, you'll listen."

Moses came riding up and stepped down. They'd lost the old Indian's trail.

"I don't know how they done it, Captain, but they just disappeared," said Moses Penny.

Captain McCain looked thoughtfully for a moment and then said, "The rain washed out their tracks, most likely. The only thing out that way is San Antonio, but that's one hell of a long ride for an injured man." He looked thoughtful for a moment, then went on. "Well, Scar's trail seems to have petered out anyway, so let's head in that direction, too. We could all use a good meal and a bath. Whatcha say, Roosevelt?"

"I've et' so many damned tortillas and beans that I fart every time I get in or out of the saddle," Poe said. "I could stand a good shot of whisky, too. Sort of help the old digestion. Yes siree!" Poe yipped, spurring his pony. "Let's go to old San Antone!"

Twenty

"All who have died are equal."
– Comanche proverb

SCAR KNEW THEY WERE there before they let themselves be seen. He'd told the three men with him to keep their hands well away from their guns, and not to even act like they wanted to make a run for it. These were tough men. They had to be to stay with Scar, but he could see the fear in the eyes of the two half-breeds traveling with him. Curiously, the other one, the Kiowa, who had more reason to fear his blood enemy, the Comanche than the others, seemed calm and unafraid. At last, the new riders left the cover of the draw to their flank and silently walked their horses toward his camp. Scar didn't look up and acknowledge them until they were only a few feet away, then he rose and spoke in Comanche.

"Rain Maker, my brother. You are far from your usual trails."

Rain Maker eyed the half-breed Apache standing before him, who was calling him brother. His sharp angular face was full of contempt. "All of this land belongs to the Comanche," Rain Maker said. "Why is it that the great Scar now rides with the dog Kiowas?" he said sarcastically, looking at the squatting Indian, who stared back with insolence.

Scar saw that Rain Maker had about twenty warriors with him and there were also four white women tied double onto two horses. Scar knew Rain Maker was returning from a profitable raid where he had taken captives and wouldn't likely try to harm him if he did nothing to provoke the Comanches. Hate him though they may, Comanches hated the white intruders more, and relished the way Scar had killed and mutilated them for over fifteen years without being captured or killed. To them, he surely had big medicine. Scar also knew that Rain Maker was aware that killing the famous Scar would be no simple task, and many people would probably die if he attempted it — Rain Maker, more than likely, being the first.

"He's not my brother." Scar knew very well how to play both sides when necessary. "You may have him if you want him," he said, unconcerned, again looking Rain Maker's bunch over without acknowledging the four white women. "My camp is yours, my brother. Come, join me, I have food…whisky."

Rain Maker dismounted and the rest of his bunch followed his example. Scar noticed one of Rain Maker's braves had to be helped from his horse by two other men. They carried him, doubled over, to a nearby tree and sat him down. The leader saw him looking and said, "One of the women shot the Rabbit and one other of my warriors. The other warrior died and I killed her."

Scar motioned for one of his men to break out the three jugs of sour whisky he'd taken from the farm house after killing its occupants. The Comanche braves whooped loudly as it was handed out. Crowding around, each tried to guzzle more than the last man and soon, most of them were wildly drunk and starting to turn mean. Scar's group didn't drink the whisky, sitting massed together, nervously watching as things unfolded in a manner they preferred not happen.

Neither Rain Maker nor Scar drank any of the whisky. They

sat near the fire cutting chunks off the roasting mule's flank that Scar's men had killed at a raided farm house.

"The Kiowa brought the mule meat and cooked it," Scar told him. "He's a good cook."

Rain Maker continued to eat the mule in silence, ignoring those around him. Elk Walk suddenly stood and staggered to where the women were huddled. Towering over the cowering women for a moment, he stared down at the youngest. She appeared to be about fourteen. He suddenly grabbed her by her flowing hair and began loosening his loincloth.

"Leave the women alone," Rain Maker said. "You've had your taste of them for several days. They must be in shape to trade once we reach Mexico."

Grunting drunkenly, Elk Walk continued as if he hadn't heard and extracted his member from the breechcloth. The young girl was clearly terrified. Excited by her reaction, Scar watched intently.

"That one is for my brother. Leave her alone," Rain Maker said again, not raising his voice.

Clearly intoxicated from the raw sour mash, Elk Walk intent upon his immediate conquest, once again ignored his leader. Quicker than the eye could follow, the Comanche leader flipped his narrow blade underhandedly and it stuck between the shoulders of the hapless Elk Walk who fell to his knees. Moaning, the big man attempted, but failed to reach the blade with either hand. Rain Maker watched with disinterest for a few minutes, then squatted back down by the fire. Reaching for Scar's knife, he sliced off another chunk of the mule meat and stuck it into his mouth. As he silently chewed the stringy meat, he continued to watch Elk Walk struggle to reach the protruding knife handle.

After a few minutes, the warrior sighed loudly, rolled over onto his side and quit breathing. The others whooped and began stripping the body of anything useful, as they swilled from the whisky jugs again.

Scar sat at Rain Maker's side and when he thought it appropriate, opened negotiations. "Do you have something to trade?" he said. "I have four horses I stole from a ranch yesterday, a few scalps, also."

Scar could always get horses. That was easy. What he really wanted and needed, were white women that he could trade south of the border for much needed gold — or if that failed, guns.

"I will take the horses and give you one of the women," Rain Maker said.

"Four horses are worth at least three of that mangy bunch," Scar sneered.

"No. I will give you one," the Comanche replied, arrogantly.

Scar kept his eyes to the ground so Rain Maker couldn't see the fury in them. "Then I must keep the horses, brother. I will be able to trade them in Mexico," he said through clinched teeth.

"Let it be so," Rain Maker said, unconcerned, as he stood up. "I will have the dog Kiowa now."

Without saying a word, he made a motion with his hand and six of the Comanche braves instantly converged on the Kiowa. As sudden as the attack was, the Kiowa wasn't surprised as he shot one of the Comanches through the head with his rifle and then reversed it, smashing in the skull of another brave. As the remaining Comanches quickly joined in, the Kiowa warrior was forced to the ground by their overwhelming force of numbers.

Even then the Kiowa was still dangerous, for he swiftly disemboweled one man and then stuck his knife completely through another brave's arm. At last, the Comanches brought the Kiowa under control. Held down by four of them, instantly two others ripped his trousers from him and in one swipe sliced his genitals from his body, which they stuffed into his mouth, then pinned him to the hard ground with his long pointed knife. Finished, the Comanches jumped back to watch as the Kiowa died. Within a few minutes it was over and Rain Maker mounted his horse, followed by his men.

Scar walked to Rain Maker as he sat astride his mount. "The Kiowa was tough," he told the Comanche. "I have lost a good fighting man and only gained four horses. It has not been a good raid for me. I will trade the horses for one of the women," he conceded.

Turning around, Rain Maker pointed to one of the four white women. A mean-looking Comanche rode up beside her and said something in a deep guttural voice. When she failed to look up or acknowledge him, he knocked her off the horse. She tumbled and lay motionless, while the other women cowed silently in fear.

Scar moved to the huddled form and tapped her lightly with the toe of his boot. Still, she didn't move. Using his foot, Scar turned her over. She lay there unmoving, blankly looking up at the sky.

"This one is used up," he said. "How about that one?" He pointed at the young girl who recoiled in terror of the scar-faced man.

"She's not for trading," Rain Maker said, dismissing her with a slight wave of his hand. "She is for my brother, Grey Wolf, who lost his wife this year."

"Then one of the others," Scar insisted.

"This is the one. Bring the horses," Rain Maker said with finality.

In other words you bastard, take it or leave it, Scar thought. He tensed and looked at the other Comanche warriors. *I could probably take most of them out myself, but it is only horses and I might be able to get something for the woman in Mexico.* He smiled at Rain Maker and, hiding his rage said, "My brother, you have out-traded me again."

Looking over his shoulder, he whistled loudly. "Jimmy-Jumps, bring the horses!" he commanded as the half-breed youngster moved to obey.

With just a slight bit of amusement in his cold eyes, Scar watched Rain Maker and his group of warriors ride away. I will repay you some day…you red devil, he thought. Then Scar's mind turned to his plan. John Eagle, Three Fingers Ned, and Charlie Fenton would be joining him across the border. The loss of the Kiowa was tough. He had been a good fighter and it had taken six Comanches to kill him. Too bad. But, if he sold the white woman for even half of what one usually brought, he would have enough to pick up four, maybe five new men. That would make nine…ten counting him.

It will be enough, he thought.

* * *

Ever since he'd gotten word of Poe's killing his men and releasing the white woman several months before, he'd been seething with rage. Those two old Rangers had been a thorn in his side for over fifteen years. He rubbed an area where one of their slugs still remained, and remembered the circumstances in which he'd received it. Using that Nigger tracker, the two old fools had tracked him all the way to Matamoros and cornered him in a rocky draw. There, they'd killed seven of his men and shot him three times. It was magic that he'd even escaped at all. It had taken months for him to heal, and even at that moment the bullets in his leg and back hurt when the weather changed.

When he discovered it had been Poe who'd rescued the woman, he'd sent John Eagle and Three Fingers Ned to find out why Poe and McCain would waste their time to track his bunch down just to get back one woman. They'd meet him in Mexico with the information. If it was as he suspected — that the woman meant something to one of the two Rangers — maybe he could use the information to finally deal with Poe and McCain once and for all. The thought made Scar smile.

Twenty-One

*"Death wore a black suit and a brace of Colts —
and he was crippled."*

– Citizen, San Antonio, Texas

BRAD THOMPSON WALKED FROM the dank barroom where he'd been playing cards most of the night, into the bright sunlight of a late Texas afternoon. He wore a black broadcloth suit with knee-length coat that was popular for the times. The long coat was pushed back to reveal two ivory-handled Colts he wore low on his hips, tied to each leg.

Yes, sir, he thought, *people were starting to take notice of Brad Thompson these days.* Ever since he backed down that Yankee cardshark last week who'd accused him of cheating. He'd been careful not to kill the man, thanks to Hal's teachings, but of course he couldn't very well have just let it go. He'd badly wanted to shoot the man, but at the last when the shark was blubbering, he thought he could do just as well by letting the others see how he could make other men afraid of him. That's what Hal had taught him. Respect and fear went hand-in-hand. Hal was right. Nobody even seemed to notice his limp anymore.

Even Dixie didn't bother to fuss at him for staying out all night anymore, and she finally even quit ragging him to return to the ranch. She'd recently told him she would be leaving in two days, come if he wanted or stay if he would; she just didn't care anymore. She was leaving anyway.

Brad wondered how much a part Hal had played in her decision to return to the Circle-T. Well, he didn't care what she did. He was getting his at the sporting house, and she and Hal could get theirs anyway they wanted to; he snickered to himself, imagining his sister and Hal La'Mont in a torrid sweaty embrace. Somehow, he couldn't envision it.

Stepping into the shade of the hardware store, he saw two men in front of the doctor's office unstrapping a man from a litter. An old Indian stood nearby, looking on. Whoever the hombre was, Brad was sure he wasn't long for this world. He was covered with blood and looked as limp as a rag. Even from that distance, he had the pallor of death. Fascinated, Brad Thompson walked over, looked at the man's face and recoiled in shock. It was the deputy who'd once recuperated at the Thompson ranch from his wounds. The one Dixie was sweet on.

What a kick! The bastard had been shot again, and was going to die anyway!

Brad laughed to himself and caught the surprised look of the two men. He stopped, then looked them both straight in the eye until they nervously averted theirs. *They know who I am*, he thought, once more feeling the addictive power of having other men fear him. Unflinchingly, he watched them carry the near-lifeless body of Rosco Bookbinder up the steep steps to Doc Milburn's office, then laughing again, turned and strode up the street toward his favorite place.

All of the girls should be awake by this time, he thought.

* * *

Chickenfoot watched as the young man with the look of death about him, walked away. Then he followed the two men carrying the litter up the stairs to the doctor's office. Once inside, Rosco was placed on a large wooden table where the doctor cut his shirt and trousers away, and expertly examined the wounds with the manner of a man who had done so many times. Unnoticed, Chickenfoot walked to the corner and squatted down to wait. Doctor Milburn worked on the wounded man for over an hour. At last, he straightened up and walked to a small table where he poured some water into a granite pan and scrubbed his hands for the fourth time.

Seeing the old chief for the first time, Doc stared at him as he wiped his hands on a towel. "You the one that brought in the deputy?"

"Yes, he died two times," Chickenfoot said. He was still looking in wonderment around the small office at the many tools and potions lining the walls. "If I had all these wonderful medicines I could heal people too."

The doctor was speaking again "...his name?"

"He didn't tell me his name, but I suppose since he died, he can chose any name," Chickenfoot answered.

"Yeah, well you can't stay here. If you want to be here in case he ever wakes up, you can sleep out back in the shed. I'll call you if he does, but I wouldn't count on that happening. He probably won't make it through the night."

Chickenfoot started to walk out and upon reaching the door looked back and said, "With all of these wonderful medicines, if he does die you can bring him back from the dead one more time."

Doc Milburn looked at the empty door for a moment and shook his head.

* * *

Brad went straight to the Sporting House after seeing the

wounded deputy. He spent an hour with a young woman in one of the special rooms upstairs, then decided to return to his own hotel room to change shirts before going back to the saloon to play more poker. Dixie was in his room waiting for him when he arrived.

He gave her a cold look and said, "Who let you in? I may kill the next fool who does that."

Disgusted, Dixie plopped down on the bed. "I let myself in. Are you going to kill me?" When Brad didn't answer her, she went on, "Brad, I don't know why you've changed so much, but please, please leave with me when I go back to the ranch tomorrow. Something bad is going to happen to you if you stay here, I just know it!"

He took a fresh shirt from a rack and put it on. "Then if you feel that way, why don't you stay and look out for me?" he responded with a sneer as he buttoned the shirt.

Dixie looked at her brother as though she'd never seen him before — as if the man in the black suit and two tied-down guns was a complete stranger.

"There is nothing on this earth that would make me change my mind and stay," she said. "Nothing."

Brad admired himself in the mirror and tied his black tie into a perfect knot. He poured a copious amount of hair oil into his hands and rubbed it onto his scalp. Brushing his slick black hair back in the same manner as Hal La'Mont, he looked at his sister out of the corner of his eye.

"Nothing, huh? What if I told you that they just brought that deputy sheriff into town. You know, the one that spent some time at the ranch? Well, he was shot so full of holes he looked like a piece of cheese." Brad laughed nastily. "Didn't look as if he would make it through the day. Probably dead by now," he chuckled again.

Suddenly, Dixie felt as though someone had thrown ice water on her. She sat numbly for a full minute, everything around her having a surreal quality. The world began to spin and she grasped the bedpost to keep from fainting.

"Where is he?" she whispered.

Brad faked surprise and said, "Why do you care? You're leaving."

In a flash, Dixie jumped up and stood in front of him, and he felt the stinging blows as she slapped his face, twice. It sounded like pistol shots.

"Goddamn you Brad, where is he?" she cried, grabbing the front of his starched shirt and shaking him viciously.

Stunned motionless, for his sister had never struck him before, nor had he ever heard her so much as utter a curse word, he stammered, "H...he's at Doc Milburn's o...office."

Instantly, Dixie was out the door, leaving Brad smoldering in his fury. He threw his hair brush at the mirror, cracking it across his image. He was panting, gasping for breath.

If she ever lays a hand on me again, I'll kill her, I swear, I'll kill her, kill her...kill her, he thought over and over.

A violent seizure came over him and he shook for a full two minutes before vomiting into the pan under the bed. Face pale and shirt now soaked with sour smelling sweat, he flopped down on the bed and lay looking at the ceiling. *If anyone ever hits me again, I'll kill them, right there and then.*

* * *

Dixie ran all the way to Doc Milburn's and up the steep flight of stairs. Doc undoubtedly heard her coming up the steps and was watching the door when she rushed in.

"Do you have Rosco Bookbinder in here? Is he injured badly?" she cried, breathlessly.

"So that's his name," said the doctor. "I wondered what he was called." He pointed to a lump on the bed, hidden under a white sheet.

Quickly, she rushed over and knelt by the bed. Tenderly, she pulled the sheet away from the man's face and gasped. It was Rosco all right. No doubt about it, but he was so pale and skinny that he was almost unrecognizable. He looked as if he might already be dead. She placed her hand to his chest and felt a faint beating.

"Oh, he's still alive, alright. I don't know how long he'll stay that way, though," Doc Milburn said. "If he can make it through the night, he might pull through." The doctor rubbed his chin and said, "I suppose you want to stay here tonight too, huh?"

There was only one cot in the room and Dixie suspected it belonged to the doctor. "Please," was all she said, still looking at his patient.

"Well, there's a large chair over by the window. You can use that. I suppose I could get a bed at the rooming house, just for tonight," he said thinking of the Sporting House instead. "If he starts to come around, put a wet cloth on his forehead and I'll be back 'bout daybreak." With that, he departed.

Dixie was still there the next morning and remained for two mornings after that. Sitting in a chair beside Rosco's bed, she awoke on the second morning, to find him quietly staring at her.

"Are you an angel?" he whispered hoarsely.

With a small cry she was beside him, holding him, softly sobbing into his chest. After a moment, she raised her face but he could see the tears still flowing down her face. "That's the second time you've said that to me," she told him, as she gently brushed her hand across his pale cheek.

"How did you find me?" he whispered again.

"Don't try to talk now, darling. Rest first. You're going to be all right. I'm going to stay right here and make sure of that. Go back to sleep, I'll be here when you wake up," she softly kissing him on the lips, and smiling.

Rosco smiled back, then slipped back into a deep, and this time, dreamless sleep.

* * *

The Rangers entered San Antonio just as the day's sun dropped below the horizon. Shades of red, orange, pink and purple splashed in bright swirls and lines across the western sky. Those not accustomed to it would've watched in awe, their hearts quickening at the magnificent sight. But McCain and his bunch had seen it many times before and they were tired. They entered San Saba Street and had barely traveled a hundred yards when Jake pointed out three saloons within the first block. Poe, smacking his lips, was the first one out of the saddle heading up the steps of the nearest establishment. A large sign over the front door proclaimed, "Fanny Porter's Sporting House and Saloon." The others weren't far behind him.

The female bartender saw them coming and started lining up glasses even before they got there.

"What'll ya have, boys?" she said, setting out the whisky bottle.

"That'll do just fine," Jake Kellog said with relish, as he grabbed the whisky and poured three fingers in a tall glass. He passed the bottle down the length of the bar and each man, in-turn, poured his own glass full.

"To Bloody Bill Reid," said Rosie Poe, "may the son-of-a-bitch rot in hell for all the misery he's caused."

The group solemnly emptied their drinks before setting them down. Then, pouring short shots, the men sipped the drinks and pondered their next move.

"Well, I don't know about the rest of you girls, but Mizzes Poe's little boy, Roosevelt, is gonna wash his nasty butt and find the biggest piece of cow this side of Kansas City," Rosie said, grinning widely. "I don't care if I never see another bean as long as I live. What about you, Moses, are you game? Jake, you and Fish? Jericho?" he implored eagerly.

"I think I might tag along behind you, Captain Poe," Penny said politely. "I just might arm wrestle you over the biggest piece of cow this side of Kansas City."

The men laughed.

"I'm in," said Jake.

"Me too," followed Jim.

"You boys start without me. I'll catch up in a while," said McCain. "I want to wire Matt Jennings at Bluebonnet and see how things are going at the ranch."

"Well, don't lay back too long or there won't be a thing left in San Antonio to eat when we git through," Jake told him.

The four men were laughing and talking loudly as they walked out of the saloon. McCain remained alone for a few minutes after they were gone, sipping his drink. Laying a dollar on the bar, he followed them out but turned the other direction. He went directly to the telegraph office to send his wire to the ranch foreman, then started for the single hotel he could see on San Saba Street. Movement caught the corner of his eye and McCain saw the old Indian standing in the alley way talking to himself. Altering his course, he walked up behind the old man.

"Chief, is that you?" he said.

Startled, Chickenfoot turned around and saw McCain.

"You snuck up on me, Hard Eyes McCain," the old man said, using the name the Comanches had given McCain years before. Then sighing deeply, "But that's nothing new, I suppose. The white man has been sneaking up on the Indian for many years now."

"What are you doing in town, Chief? As I recollect, you hate towns," McCain inquired. He leaned against the wall of the building and rolled a smoke. Lighting up, he held the makings out to the old man. Chickenfoot held up his hand, palm out.

"I quit the tobacco when I discovered it was stealing my breath," he said, as he declined the offer. Then after a moment, he continued. "I brought in a wounded man for the healer to treat. Found him over near the Devil's. He died two times before I got him here. He may die again, the healing man says."

Chickenfoot removed his pipe from within his rawhide pouch and lit it up. McCain was not insulted at that, for he knew many Indians considered pipe smoking to be "medicine for the soul" and different than regular "pleasure" smoking. When he was satisfied it was going, Chickenfoot continued.

"A woman shot him. I saw it."

"Yes, I know. His name's Rosco Bookbinder. He's a deputy sheriff over in El Paso. The woman who shot him was his wife," McCain told him.

Puffing contently, the old man nodded knowingly. "Some women are like that. Men have to be careful around them." He puffed a few more times and went on, "My first wife was a cold woman between the robes, but a good provider. When she died, I married a younger woman who was very passionate and experienced with men. Her passion wore me down, and I became weak. I even quit beating her for a time. I think she would've killed me with her great hunger if I hadn't finally stopped mounting her."

Neither man spoke for a time, then Chickenfoot said, "Comanche women like to be beaten, you know. After she stole my strength, she went to find others who'd mount her…and beat her I suppose. I didn't mind too much." The Chief puffed a few more times, apparently deep in thought. "But…she was very angry when I finally stopped pleasuring her. I think she would've shot me if I had left a loaded gun where she could find it." He sat there and thought about it for a minute. "She did stab me once, anyway."

"I suppose when you stop to think about it, Indian and white customs don't appear to be that much different," McCain conceded, trying to maintain a straight face.

"Well, there is that thing about where you defecate," the old man said. "White men also have the notion a person can own the land, too." The old man snorted loudly. "And the thing about how you empty your noses. When I see white men empty their noses, they first take a rag from their pockets, unfold it and empty their noses in it. Then they stare at it for a time, carefully fold it and put it back in their pocket."

He puffed contentedly on his pipe and considered that action for a while as though puzzled by it. Then he knocked the ash from his pipe and asked earnestly, "Why do they save it? What are they going to use it for?"

Having no answer, McCain ignored the old man's question,

finally stating, "Do you need money, Chief?" He tossed his butt down, stepped on it and prepared to leave.

"The deputy…Bookbinder, you said his name is?" The Chief contemplated that for a moment and nodded his head. "Bookbinder — a good name. No need to change it, even if he did die twice. I think there aren't many men who would choose it."

After enlightening McCain with that bit of information, he went on. "That Bookbinder feller is very poor. He possesses nothing of his own. He gave me a mule if I would bring him here to the healer, but the mule died before we got to town. It was a white man's mule and very sick. I was too tired to even eat it. I brought him here anyway." He looked up at McCain. "The Catholic nuns would call that 'a good deed,' I suppose."

"Chief, I owe you for bringing that boy in. Come with me, I've got something for you," McCain said as he walked off. The old Indian sat and looked at the empty alley way for a few moments then, slowly rose to his feet and followed.

A short time later, McCain caught up with Poe and the rest of his men at the hotel restaurant. Lowering himself into a chair, he told them what he'd found out.

"I gave the Spaniard's horse and saddle to the old Indian who brought him in," he said simply. Nobody questioned the decision.

* * *

It took two days before Rosco Bookbinder was well enough for McCain and Poe to see him, and when they finally did get the chance, the young "feisty" Thompson girl had tried to cut them short by saying he needed his rest. Poe told him how they found Reid's burned body and from the sign they found at the scene, it appeared as though the Comanches had surely taken his young wife with them. Like as not, he said, she was dead by now.

Rosco reclined without saying anything for a while, then remarked, "Are you going to try to find out?"

Poe and McCain looked at one another, then Poe sighed deeply and said, "Why not? We just happen to be heading south when we leave here, so I guess we can do a little circling and try to pick up the sign. What say, Jericho?"

"Why not? The railroad might as well get its money's worth."

They heard, right after reaching San Antonio, that Indians or renegades had killed a family of farmers and burned their farm down in the Lower Lipans only a week before. Poe and McCain knew Moses could pick up the trail, even though it was that old.

They talked for a few more minutes under the protective eye of Dixie Thompson, who at last shooed them out, but only after they promised Rosco they'd visit before they left town. As they reached the street Poe glanced at his friend from the corner of his eye.

"Did ya notice that Thompson gal seemed to have more than a passing interest in old Rosco there?" Poe said slyly, and chuckled.

"Now, it ain't none of your business, Roosevelt," his partner scolded. "Don't you start meddling or you'll just have them at each other's throats before it's all over."

Poe stopped walking and acted surprised. "Me? Meddle?" Placing a hand on his chest as though shocked at such an idea, he stood open mouthed for a moment, then said, "Why...what a thing to say to a friend, Jericho. You ought to bite your tongue. I've never meddled in my life!"

Rosie protested his innocence all the way back to the hotel as passers-by glanced at them and smiled in amusement. At last, reaching the steps of the hotel, McCain stopped and stared hard at him. "That man just recently lost his wife and suddenly everybody, you included, is trying to get him another one. If it had been his horse he lost, nobody would offer him another one. People just can't stand to see a man happy."

He started to walk away, then paused. "Don't meddle," he said pointedly and went into the hotel.

Poe stared after him for a few minutes looking perplexed, then shook his head and chuckled to himself. *Aye God. Jericho McCain, a romantic. Who would've dreamed it?* Chuckling again to himself, he followed his longtime partner into the hotel.

Poe and McCain stopped in to see the wounded deputy the following morning and were lucky enough to find Dixie out having breakfast.

"We'll be heading out now," McCain told him. "We'll let you know what we find out. Where will you be?"

"Well, the Doc said I better not even think about trying to travel for a month or so. Then, only by train or stage. So I'll be here at Dixie's aunt's house until then."

Poe smirked at McCain knowingly and raised his right eyebrow at the use of "Dixie's," by Rosco.

"As soon as I can travel, Dixie told me we'll go to the Thompson Circle-T until I'm completely healed. Doc said it may take up to six months for that to happen."

Again, Poe raised his eyebrow at the "Dixie told me," by the young man. Seeing the impatient look on his partner's face, he quickly walked to the only window in the small room and stared down at San Sabe Street, smiling smugly to himself.

R.C. Morris

* * *

It was nearly a week before Doctor Milburn would allow Rosco to even be moved as far as her aunt's home, four blocks away. Even then, he had to be carried on a stretcher with the doctor at his side. By the time they put him in bed at the new location, he was weak and pale, and immediately dropped off to sleep. Dixie was again at his side, wiping his face with cold wet towels and gently kissing his lips after he fell asleep.

"Rest well, my darling," she said. "I'll be here when you awaken. I'll always be here."

As she silently walked to the door to leave, she heard Rosco quietly call for Jenny. She thought, *Jenny's gone, darling, and I'm here to take care of you from now on.*

* * *

It'd been a hard ride to the Nueces River, but once Moses Penny cut the killers trail, McCain was relentless, allowing none of them would rest until they crossed the river. Once on the other side, they made camp and prepared the first hot meal and coffee they'd tasted since leaving San Antonio. Poe groaned and rubbed his back tenderly. Then, reaching into his saddle bags, he removed a small brown bottle and tentatively drank from it. He saw McCain looking at him and winked.

"Laudanum," he explained to McCain. "Doc gave it to me." He took another small swallow and grimaced. "Probably be pissing pure opium in a day or two," he said glumly.

The tireless Moses Penny was already riding when they arose the following morning, scouting several hours ahead of the main party. He entered a narrow ravine, and instantly felt the hair rise on the back of his neck. Quietly, he slipped the heavy Sharps from its case and inched his horse even further into the small gulch. He could smell it. Once a man smells the scent of death, he never forgets it, he thought grimly. He rounded a sharp curve and saw the dead bodies in front of him. He chased the birds and animals away, knowing they wouldn't be there if there were any other humans in the vicinity. Dismounting, he read the "sign" without disturbing the area any more than he necessarily had to. Satisfied, he mounted up and rode hastily back the way he had came.

It was full dark by the time Penny neared his friend's new campsite. Whistling softly to alert the group, he walked his horse to where the other horses were tied. After rubbing down and watering his animal, he returned to the fire, squatted down and gratefully accepted the food and coffee the others had saved for him. It was only after wolfing down several bites of warm beans and beef chunks, and burning his tongue on hot coffee, that he finally told the others about the decomposed bodies he'd found.

"Looked like two groups met there and camped together for a spell. Comanche and renegade, from what I could tell" Moses said, sopping up the last of his beans with a corn tortilla.

He told about the dead Comanche and the dead Kiowa, four riderless horses, and one person being exchanged — most probably female by the look of the footprints. He related how he'd found the footprints of three, or possibly four, other females at the site also. They'd left with the large bunch of Comanches.

"Captain, that smaller bunch might've been Scar. I don't know why I think that, but it was a feeling that just came to me while I was there," Moses said.

The others had been with Moses Penny too long to question the usually reliable "feelings," that came upon him now and then. His story told, Moses refilled his coffee cup, took another plate of food and moved to a location away from the low burning fire.

McCain thought about Moses Penny's tale, then suddenly stood and walked out to where the horses were tied. He leaned against a large tree and rolled a smoke, waiting. After a few minutes, Poe joined him.

"Wha'd ya think, Jericho?" he said. "Go with the odds and follow the large bunch that has the most women, or take in after Scar?"

McCain smoked and thought for a while. "I'd surely love to catch up with that heathen, but I promised that boy that we'd try to get his wife back if we could," he said. "I suppose the smart thing to do would be take the odds and stay with the large group that has the most women." McCain puffed on his cigarette once more, then stepped on it. "You got a vote. What do you think?"

"I agree. Any decision we make is bound to be wrong anyhow, so let's play the odds on this one," Poe said. He started to leave, then turned back. "Ya know, Jericho, you really ought to give up those smokes and stick to a plug of chaw. You can smell the damned things for a mile out here in the wilderness. Besides that, chaw's a lot better for you...classier, too."

"Just how do you suppose that putting a big hunk of some foul smelling brown stuff into your cheek, chewing it up until it's all wet and slimy, then spitting it on the floor, could possibly be classier than simply smoking a cigarette? Your thinking is beyond me, Roosevelt," McCain said, dumbfounded.

"Classier," Rosie winked. "Take it from me."

The others were asleep by the time the two friends returned to the campsite. All three men were snoring loudly.

"Now don't that beat all?" Poe said. "Sounds like a toy shop, don't it?"

"You get some sleep first," said McCain. "I'll take the first watch. You can wake Jake when you get tired."

Poe was snoring too, almost before his head touched his saddle.

As usual, Moses was gone by the time the others awoke the next morning.

"Let's git mounted, girls," Poe said cheerfully. "We'll have a nice cold feast of jerky and biscuits as we ride."

Rolling his bedding, Jake Kellog grumbled, "I been with Moses Penny for ten years and he ain't any where near human. I feel like I didn't even get to sleep yet."

Likewise, Jim Packard was also in a foul mood, aching from the extended ride of the previous three days and lack of proper food. "Won't do any good to kill us getting there if we're too tired to fight once we do arrive," he complained.

"Anybody wants out knows the way back to San Antonio," McCain said shortly from his mount. He swung his horse around to stare coldly at the others. "There won't be any bickering, either. I won't tolerate it."

That ended the complaints for the moment.

Moses had left a clear trail for them to follow and they made good time, but never saw a hint of him for the next three days. Near the end of the third day, they came upon him resting on his mount in the middle of the trail. He wasn't alone. Riding up quickly, McCain's group stopped in a cloud of dust.

"This is Britt Johnson, Captain," Moses said.

"Nigger Britt, is what they call me," said the Black man, holding out his hand across the saddle-horn. "I've heard of you, Captain McCain. You too, Ranger Poe."

McCain took his thin dark hand, then introduced the others. "I've heard of you, too," he said. "That was good work getting those women and children back from the Comanches and Kiowas. Don't know as I would want to try something like that alone."

Recalling the incident, McCain remembered that Johnson's wife, Mary Johnson, had been visiting a neighbor, Elizabeth Fitzpatrick, and her daughter Susan Durgan, at the Fitzpatrick house. The Indians, an unusual mixed bunch of Comanche and Kiowa, swept into the small Elm Creek settlement, where they quickly killed a man named Joe Myers and his boy, out right. As they stormed the Fitzpatrick house, Susan grabbed a gun and ran outside to fight them. Although she fought courageously, she was eventually cut down by the swarming Indians, then stripped and mutilated.

Afterward, they poured into the house, where they captured Mrs. Fitzpatrick, another woman, and six children, among them was three year old Millie Durgan. The story had been that Britt's eldest son had been killed after two of the Indians got into an argument about who'd captured him. They'd simply settled the argument by killing the boy. Then, throwing the rest of the captives over horses, the Indians took them away. In all, the raiders killed eleven people, burned eleven houses and carried off seven women and children, among them, Britt's wife and children. Britt, loaded up with two pistols and a Sharps rifle, had immediately began tracking the Indians, determined to get his family back.

He'd eventually caught up with some of them guarding a herd of horses. Talking "Mex" to them, he found out the Comanches had taken a "white woman" and that the Kiowas had taken several black captives. The band was Penateka Comanches who'd been on the reservation, and it was lucky for Britt that several of them knew him from times past. Once getting on friendly terms with the band of Indians, he'd traveled with them over a month, finding one of the girls, and ransoming her from the Comanches.

In all, this courageous man now before them, had made four trips into the Indian camps to rescue women and children, including his own family. Eventually, he got all of the captives back except one. The Comanches had stubbornly decided to adopt the smallest girl who'd been taken into a Koitsenko family, and couldn't be persuaded to release her.

"What're you doing out here alone again, Mr. Johnson? Good way to get your hair lifted," McCain said, hooking his leg over his saddle horn and commencing to roll a smoke.

"Well, it seems as though the Comanches have been out collecting white women again," Britt said. "A man paid me a heap-o-money to ride out here and see if I could find them…maybe get them back."

McCain offered his makings to the black man and he declined, but when Poe offered his "chaw," Britt accepted gratefully. Poe looked smugly at McCain, who ignored him.

"It looks like they heading straight to Mexico, Cap'n," remarked Moses. "If they do, you want I should follow?"

"Well, we still got a piece to travel 'fore we get there, Mr. Penny, but if they do cross over the river into Mexico, you follow them red devils to hell if you have to. I intend to get those people back if it takes me the next ten years," McCain said, pinching off the fire and tossing the butt to the ground. "You want to tag along with us for a spell, Mister Johnson?"

"Just call me Nigger Britt, everybody does," Johnson said. "And yes, I will ride along with you if you don't mind. I could use the company."

Britt and Moses Penny rode on ahead and Moses earnestly told him, "The Cap'n calls ever'one 'mister,' so you might as well git used to it. He's a man of respect."

Johnson nodded his head.

Twenty-Two

"If there's no honor, there can be no love."
–Rosco Bookbinder

ROSCO HAD BEEN RECOVERING for almost three weeks and could now sit up in bed, even hobble to the window if he used his cane. He still experienced bouts of extreme weakness, but was gradually getting stronger each day. His nightmares about Jenny had all but disappeared, and his every waking thought was now about the lovely and vivacious Dixie Thompson. He'd never known anyone as beautiful as Dixie. His heart begin to pound wildly every time she leaned over to fluff his pillow, or otherwise came close. *At least, everything else seems to be working all right,* he thought and grinned ruefully. He was especially looking forward to her visit today, because she'd told him she would help him outside to sit in the garden. He was waiting with anticipation of that when he heard her familiar footfall. Then she was at the door.

Smiling, she bustled in. "Good morning, Rosco," she said, in a breathy voice that sent him straight to hell for the images it provoked. She hurried to lean over him to fluff his pillow, smelling wonderful. As always, he felt a surge in the core of his being.

"Are you ready to sit outside today?" she said, straightening up.

He could still smell her soapy fragrance and his face was on fire. Swallowing hard and regaining his composure, he was finally able to answer. "I can hardly wait to see what outside looks like. I've been looking at four walls for so long I've forgotten everything else."

There was a small commotion in the hallway and two burley Mexican youths entered carrying a large chair, to which a four-foot pole was attached under each arm. Without fan-fare, they hoisted him into the chair and Dixie covered his legs with a soft quilt. Effortlessly picking him up, the young men carried him down the stairs and into the garden. Dixie walked beside him holding his hand and smiling encouragement. They stopped at a spot beside a small pond, where someone had laid out a blanket and covered it with food for a picnic. It happened to be the very same spot she'd had her close encounter with Hal shortly after coming to San Antonio.

Dixie primly seated herself on the blanket and looked up at him expectantly.

"It's…it's beautiful," he said simply. Then, looking down at her, he said, "And so are you."

They stared into each other's eyes for a long moment, then Dixie colored and smiling, said, "Let's eat, I don't know about you, but I'm starved."

The warmth of the sun, the food, and Dixie, combined to make it the happiest time Rosco could remember in ages. *I have no right to this.* The thought suddenly broke in unwelcome, and he quickly pushed it and any unwanted thoughts of Jenny out of his mind. She'd shot him, hadn't she? She'd made her choice. He deserved some happiness too. But she's your wife, Rosco, a small voice said. *Is not a vow a vow?*

Dixie saw the dark look that crossed his face, and she reached out, grasped his hand, and held it to her cheek. The thoughts were gone in an instant.

That night, as Rosco lay half sleeping, he heard the door to his room open softly and felt, more than heard, someone walk barefooted to the side of his bed. He opened his eyes and in the dark room, faintly made out the form of Dixie standing beside the bed. In the soft moonlight, he could just make out the features of her face as she paused, silently peering through the darkness at him. Then without speaking, she slipped the light robe from her shoulders and let it fall to the floor. Lifting the covers, she slid in beside him and cradled her head on his chest.

"I don't care if it is a sin," she whispered. "I only know that I let you go once and nearly lost you before I ever had a chance to love you."

She kissed the side of his neck gently, then his lips. She looked deeply into his eyes as though searching his very soul. "If all we have is now, I will accept that, but I want you with me forever, Rosco. I've loved you since the first day they brought you to the ranch nearly dead."

He groaned in discomfort as he attempted to put his arms around her and pull her closer.

She kissed him again and whispered in his ear, "Don't worry, I'll help you darling." She carefully positioned herself over him and took the initiative as their enraptured breathing and low cries combined, filling the room much of the night.

Rosco awoke just as the sun came up, to find her already gone. At first, he thought it'd all been a wonderful dream. Except for one thing. He could still smell her faint fragrance on the pillow beside him. A few moments later, the door flew open and Dixie and her aunt marched into the room with his breakfast and hot coffee. Dixie carefully avoided his eyes, with her aunt so close by.

"Dixie tells me you're improving splendidly," the older woman said. "You do look much better this morning. It must be the special care Dixie is providing for you."

Dixie, standing behind, covered her mouth with her hand and almost giggled outright at the look of discomfort on her lover's face. He scowled at her and she mockingly sobered up. Her aunt left the room, giving them both a huge bright smile. As soon as the door closed, Dixie was in his arms, kissing his face over and over again.

"I love you. I love you. I love you," she repeated. At last she stopped and lay her head on Rosco's chest, a small smile on her lips.

"I love you, too, Dixie," he said softly.

She looked up and quietly told him, "Just because of what we did last night and the fact that I tell you 'I love you,' doesn't mean you're obligated to tell me you love me also."

"Listen to me, Dixie. If I've never told the truth before in my life, I'm telling it now. I love you more than anything I've ever known in my life. You're the most important thing in this world to me," he said sincerely. "But I can't marry you. I'm already married, and until I find out what happened to Jenny, I won't be free."

"Then, as I said last night, I'll take what I can get until then," she smiled up at him. "And be warned young deputy, I plan to take a lot."

* * *

Brad Thompson had just received the news he'd been waiting for and was excited at the prospect of getting to shoot someone again so soon after the last one. That one, only three days before, had greatly enhanced his reputation and brought him the respect he'd always sought. He reflected upon the way he'd goaded the cowboy into going for his gun, and then shot him, remembering how some of the men in the bar had come up later to shake his hand and buy him drinks. He'd basked in their admiration for hours and it'd been the greatest feeling in the world. Even better than when he'd watched the cowboy fall bleeding to the floor. He'd heard one man in the room say with wonder, that he'd never even seen Brad's hands move. Brad smiled at the memory.

He'd left the saloon an hour earlier, on his way to get his weekly haircut. On the way out, he'd glanced over at Hal, slumped in his chair, pouring another drink even though it was only ten o'clock in the morning. Hal had been in a dark mood ever since that deputy had been brought back to San Antonio. Brad figured he knew why. Dixie. Yep, it seemed that men just naturally wanted to sniff after his older sister all the time. He supposed if she wasn't his sister, he'd be doing the same. More importantly though, at least for the time being, Hal was spending most of his time drunk and picking fights, and they weren't making any money playing cards. He figured Hal wanted to shoot the deputy real bad, but knew if he did, Dixie wouldn't ever have anything to do with him again.

A few nights after the old Indian had brought Rosco in, he'd offered to kill the deputy himself. After a lot of talking on Brad's part, Hal had reluctantly agreed, but warned Brad the deputy was considered to be fast with a gun himself, over in El Paso.

Brad had seriously asked Hal, "Better than me?"

"I may not have ever seen anyone who's faster than you," Hal told him truthfully. "But you need to wait for a spell. If you do it now, Dixie will figure out that I had a hand in it before too long. Besides, he's in pretty bad shape. You *do* want to give him a fair chance, don't you?"

Brad had smirked. "Don't make no difference to me. He'll still be just as dead when it's over."

The two men had had a good laugh and sauntered to the saloon to play poker. Since then Brad had continued to keep Hal informed on Rosco's progress, as they waited for the day he would finally attempt to leave San Antonio for the Thompson ranch.

Now, excited by the latest news he'd gotten from the old cleaning woman, Brad rushed into the saloon just as Hal opened a new set of playing cards.

"They're getting ready to leave!" he shouted at Hal.

Stopping in mid-shuffle, Hal said, "Who?"

"Dixie and that Bookbinder fellow!" Brad still shouting. "They're packing now to leave on the morning train. One of the Mexicans who works for my aunt told me." He paced back and forth, nervously biting his nails.

"Quit that!" Hal demanded. Then more softly, "It's no problem. You'll just be at the station in the morning when they get there. After all, he's the man that's been dishonoring your sister for the last month by living in the same house with her. You got a right to call him out over it." Hal smiled at Brad.

Immediately stopping his pacing, Brad laughed admiringly. "Hal you're about the smartest man I've ever met." Reaching to his hip, he rubbed the handles of his expensive Colts and smiled. "Protecting the honor of my sister," he said appreciatively. "I like the sound of that. It's like being a hero." He laughed again, but without any feeling.

When Legends Lived

* * *

The 9:40 was due in twenty minutes by the time Dixie and Rosco arrived to check their baggage with the ticket-master. They were both surprised to find Brad waiting for them.

"Brad," she cried happily, "You've decided to come with us, after all."

"Not likely," he said. "I've come to kill this son-of-a-bitch for spoiling you."

Dixie looked at Brad as if he were joking or had lost his mind. "What are you talking about?" she cried. "You just get out of here and leave us alone!"

"You've been poking my sister, deputy, and I'm calling you out. What's the matter?" he said, dropping his hands near the handles of his guns. "You going to let a woman take up your fight?"

Rosco pushed Dixie aside and, balancing himself on the two canes, opened his coat. "I'm not packing, Brad, and I have no intention of fighting Dixie's brother," he said.

"You can use mine," said a soft non-threatening voice.

Dixie turned to find Hal standing behind them, holding his holstered gun out to Bookbinder. Her eyes burned with hatred at the man who had so nearly become her lover only a short time ago.

Rosco, still balancing himself on the canes, smiled. "And who will hold me up while I strap them on?" he said. "You?"

Brad, who'd walked up close to him by this time, stood with his face inches away from Rosco's and sneered, "If you've got any guts you'll fight me, Bookbinder."

A small crowd of train passengers waiting for the nine-forty, had gathered nearby and was now watching the exchange.

"Not today, Brad. Maybe another time," Rosco said evenly.

Quickly, like lightening, Brad's hand flashed out and struck Rosco on the side of the head, nearly toppling the weakened man. Rosco's eyes hotly flashed and he finally turned to Hal La'Monte, holding out his hand.

"Give it to me," he said.

"No!" screamed Dixie. "You'll have to shoot me first. I mean it Rosco. If there is a shoot-out here, I'll stand right in the middle of it."

Rosco looked at her for a moment then said, "Okay, no shoot-out. Not today, I promise."

"You yellow dog!" Brad slapped Rosco in the face once more, then drew back his hand as if to strike Rosco again, this time with his fist.

Dixie swiftly grabbed the gun from the still outstretched hand of Hal La'Monte and stuck it under her brother's chin. "You just go right ahead and do it," she said through her teeth. "Do it, and I'll let this hammer fall."

Brad looked into her eyes and instantly saw how close he was to dying. Backing quickly away he fingered his own, still holstered gun, until La'Monte stepped in front of him and said, "Not today, Brad. There'll be another time."

Brad glared at his sister and the man she was standing with, his face consumed with fury, then turned his back on them and abruptly walked away. In confusion, Hal looked again at Dixie, who stared back at him with hate filled eyes. He started to say something, then he, too, walked away.

The 9:40 was just rolling in and the couple boarded, selecting their compartment. They could hear the other passengers quietly discussing the ordeal as they started to load. Once seated, Rosco said, "Thanks, Dixie. I made you a promise today, but I won't do that again. I won't ever be humbled by any man, again. Not in front of the woman I love — or anybody else."

She placed her head on his shoulder and held tightly onto his arm.

* * *

The Rangers followed the sparse trail as far as Espantosa Lake and stopped for the night. Except for the intentional markings Moses and Nigger Britt were leaving to mark the trail, the rest of them hadn't seen the pair of trackers in over four days. They pitched a cold camp and posted guard on a small knoll two hundred yards from the main camp, that provided a good view of the surrounding countryside. Poe and Jim Packard talked quietly as they lay on their bedrolls.

"Why is Captain McCain being so careful in this area?" Jim said.

Poe shifted his saddle under his head for more comfort. "This has always been dangerous parts, young man," he said. "*Espantosa* means frightful or horrible in Spanish. Robbers used to drop their victims in the lake after killing them. In '76, me and J.D. came through here with a platoon of Rangers. We surprised 'bout thirty horse thieves hiding out near here and we killed seven of them outright. Hanged six more. Took back over two hundred horses, all prime stock."

Poe took out his "plug" and bit off a chew. He offered it to Jim, who hesitated at first, then shrugged and took it, biting off a generous amount. It seemed to please the older man for some reason. The two men lay silently chewing and spitting as the need arose. God, thought Packard, this is some horrible stuff, as he spit again.

"Tomorrow we'll go into Carrizo Springs," Poe told him. "You stay close to me, or one of the others, and watch what we do. Most of the lowlife that come through these parts stop over in Carrizo Springs for a drink and maybe a whore, if there's one available. There ain't a soul in there that's ever going to heaven. It can be a rough place for folks like us, though I 'spect Gullytown is worse."

"Why go in there at all, then?"

Poe looked at him, surprised. "Why if them no-a-counts ever got wind of me and Jericho being this close and not riding in to check it out, it'd be the end of our reputation," he said indignantly.

Jim nodded as though he understood perfectly, although clearly he did not. *These two old fools are going to get me killed after all*, he thought. By the time he was ready to go to sleep, the "chaw" was beginning to taste all right. Reluctantly, Jim spit the tobacco out and closed his eyes. In an instant, he was asleep.

* * *

The following morning began lazily; there seemed to be no hurry to pack up and ride out, in contrast to every other previous morning. In fact, Poe and Fish were still in the blankets when breakfast was being prepared. Poe rose first, cheerfully shook out his boots for centipedes and scorpions, then pulled them on. He arose stiffly and poured a cup of coffee into one of the handy tin cups. Jim asked him why they hadn't hit the trail early, as they had in all the days before.

"'Cause all them lowlife don't git up 'fore noon," he said, blowing over the hot coffee. "We want to be sure that they all seen that we come by and paid 'em a little social call, hee, hee" he winked at Jim, then took a tentative sip of the scalding coffee.

They rode into Carrizo Springs right at noon. The town consisted only of "hide lean-to's," a couple of hodgepodge canvas shacks, and a falling down barn used as a livery stable. The only building that even resembled a permanent structure was the saloon — a dark and dirty place that strongly smelled of stale liquor and urine. Jim was conscious that a dozen pairs of eyes stared at them as they rode up to the only solid structure in the town and dismounted. Fish pulled his rifle and stayed outside to guard the horses, for, as Poe had informed him the night before, more than one fellow had returned only to find his horse long gone in Carrizo Springs. The lawmen walked into a darkened room where they were able to make out about a half-dozen men, sitting around makeshift tables, playing cards and drinking. One, dark-skinned, overweight woman was huddled in a dark corner with a man. Poe and McCain recognized the faces of at least two of them, and knew that at one time, they were wanted by Texas law.

In turn, the people in the dark room, sized up the new comers, noting they were well armed and apparently unafraid. Used to seeing men who dressed and acted like that, the surly bartender set a bottle on the bar and placed four dirty glasses in front of them. Ignoring the glasses, Poe picked up the bottle, wiped off the neck and swigged the foul tasting liquid directly from the bottle.

"Pure panther-piss," he said as he passed it to Jake, who first looked at it dubiously, then shrugged and tipped it up.

"I'm looking for some lowlife trash who stole four white women and headed this way," McCain said, his voice carrying to every darkened corner of the saloon. "I'm Captain J.D. McCain. This is Captain Poe and these men are Texas Rangers. Those of you that know me know I don't spend a lot of time nursing people to answer my questions."

His eyes scanned the room and settled on three men seated at the back of the room. Two looked like half-breeds and the third was a mangy type for sure. At once, Poe and McCain recognized one of them. McCain's gaze finally settled on the man with three fingers.

"Ned, what a surprise seeing you in a dump like this," he said seriously. "The last I heard you had teamed up with Scar and some other renegades, and was murdering women and children out west of here. Too bad you weren't with your half-brother Kiowa Jack and his friends when Poe killed them recently over near Odessa."

"I don't want any trouble McCain. Just a drink. That's all I want," Three Finger Ned retorted, eyes flicking around the room.

Although the three men's attitude and body postures changed slightly, an inexperienced person might've failed to pick it up. The slight tensing of their bodies and the subtle positioning of their hands wasn't lost on any of the Rangers.

Packard noticed that Jake Kellog wasn't looking at the three hard cases McCain was talking to. As he'd done so many times in the past, Kellog was watching everyone else in the room except the three men McCain was addressing. He knew Poe and the Captain could take care of any trouble from that direction. It was his job to make sure neither of them was bushwhacked from the side or rear while they were conducting business. A man stirred near the door and Jake locked his cold eyes on him. The man instantly froze and didn't move again.

"Tell me about the women Scar murdered and raped, Ned," Poe said nastily. "How about the little girl and her parents at the farm over near the mouth of the Nueces last week." He was clearly goading the man now.

When Legends Lived

"I don't know nothing about no murder or rape," Ned retorted.

Poe rubbed his chin as though thinking it over. "Now why do I git the feeling you're peeing on my leg and calling it rain, Ned?"

Nervously, Three Finger Ned looked around the room and said, "I ain't no match for you, Poe. Everyone knows you're hell on wheels with that Walker Colt. I ain't up to it."

"Why, I ain't asking you to draw, Ned. You ain't worth the price of a bullet." Poe spit on the floor. "Git the rope off my horse, Jim. I think this rotten beam will hold all three of 'em. Whad' ya think Jake?" Poe said.

Never taking his eyes off the other patrons in the place, Jake said, "Looks good to me, Rosie, they don't appear too heavy."

Stunned, Jim hadn't yet moved to obey Poe's order.

"Do it now, Jim," Poe said evenly, and Packard slowly moved toward the door to do as he bid. He was only three steps from it when the three renegades made their move. All jumped to their feet at once, and the men's hands streaked for their guns. All, that was, except for Ned, who dove through the window. Poe and McCain each fired once and the two men dropped as though hit with an axe. Poe immediately ran to the window and McCain hurried outside and tore around the building — but Three Finger Ned had already vanished like smoke.

Two other men who'd jumped to their feet when the shooting started, were staring at Jake Kellog who was holding his pistol loosely at his side, and smiling softly back at them. When McCain entered the saloon again, they immediately sat back down and stared at their drinks, as though by doing so they hoped to be ignored during anything else that transpired. It wasn't to be the case, however.

"I give you fair warning. You men have five minutes to hit the road, or pull your hardware. I don't much care which one you choose. After that time, far as I'm concerned you're worm food," McCain stated.

The men looked dumbfounded, as though not believing what they'd heard. Then, suddenly the bartender ripped off a dirty apron, jumped over the bar and ran out the front door. Within seconds, the others literally collided, all attempting to exit at the same time. Within half a minute, the place was deserted and no sounds could be heard except for the clatter of hoofs as the customers fled.

"Burn it," McCain said, and walked out.

Jake kicked over several tables, took one more tentative drink of the foul liquid, made a face, and poured the rest over the tables. He lit it afire and watched the blaze for a few moments, then hurried for the door. "I always knew they made this stuff out of coal oil."

Within minutes, the entire building was ablaze. When the group finally paused to look back from a small rise about a quarter of a mile away, all that remained of the town of Carrizo Springs was black billowing smoke spiraling skyward.

Twenty-Three

THE DAYS ON THE Thompson's Circle-T were hot, lazy and carefree for the two lovers. Rosco spent his mornings doing the exercises Doc Milburn had prescribed, under Dixie's watchful eye. Routinely, he took lunch on the veranda and a nap at midday. In the cool of the evenings, the lovers would pack a picnic basket and take the buggy to their favorite shady spot on a small tributary of the Colorado River. There they spread a blanket in the damp grass, made plans for the future, ate their food while staring into each other's eyes, and made endless love, bathed in the sound of the running stream.

Reflecting back, Rosco honestly thought he'd loved his wife in the days before she ran away with Bill Reid and his bunch. He knew then that whatever it was he'd once felt, couldn't have been love. That was reserved for the way he felt about Dixie Thompson. Being an orphan, he didn't claim to know much about the fine points of "love" anyway, but figured it had to be a mutual thing, shared between two people. He'd never had that with Jenny, had never seen the look in her eyes that he saw in Dixie's. He knew all of that now.

Still, he wasn't free of Jenny. Not as long as he was unsure if she was dead, or alive. The unwanted thoughts kept intruding into the tranquil refuge the Circle-T offered him. He could sometimes see it in Dixie's eyes as well, but neither dared broach the subject and destroy the wonderful turn their lives had taken since they'd rediscovered each other. So day after peaceful day, they soaked up the strength and caring of each other, and basked in the glow that first-time lovers experience, as Rosco slowly healed, and sometimes regressed, in his slow road back from the brink of death.

Rosco had been at the Thompson ranch for over a month when he asked Dixie to accompany him to see Kate Shaw at the K/D Ranch. They planned the trip with the same exuberance that all lovers experience when they were doing and seeing things together for the "first time." Excitement was high on the morning they left for the Shaw ranch, accompanied by three of Thompson's vaqueros for escort. Even though they planned to travel at a slow pace, Dixie prepared him a pallet of straw and blankets in the back of the buckboard, in the eventuality he grew tired along the way. Rosco had difficulty traveling more than four hours a day; therefore, it took twice as long as they'd estimated to reach their destination. Toward the end of the journey, Dixie was becoming increasingly worried about the pallor of Rosco's skin and the weakness he was beginning to exhibit.

* * *

The girls were in the new school built by the neighboring ranchers, who'd pitched in after Kate Shaw donated land for it. The one room school house was located just two miles north of the K/D. They'd been lucky to steal away a full-time, dedicated teacher from a school in Fort Worth, a young widow named Samantha Brooks. She too, had two daughters, seven year old Millie and fifteen year old Hanna. Miss Brooks seemed genuinely concerned about the education of the children in her care, and all the kids loved her. The girls were doing real good in school now and seemed to enjoy it. Billy even went back to school and

When Legends Lived

finished his eighth year, although it probably had more to do with the new teacher's young daughter, Hanna, than any great thirst for education on Billy's part, Kate often thought with amusement.

This particular day, Billy had gone with the rest of the hands to round up spring calves and Kate was finally alone to catch up on some of the small nagging chores she'd been putting off for too long. She was presently working on mending four harnesses and a saddle. That task completed, she was now rubbing them with the can of saddle soap she bought on her last trip into town. The work was hard and sweaty, but she found a certain release in the physical activity, and a chance to escape from the pressures of the past few months.

The ordeal with Beth had been devastating for the entire family and pretty much turned everything up side down for them all. As usual for that time of day, Beth was sleeping. She found it almost impossible to sleep at night because of her recurring nightmares, followed by the awful headaches that came afterward. Kate didn't know which was worse, the dreams when she awoke screaming wildly in the middle of the night, or the headaches that left her crying and drained for days. Poor Beth. She'd made numerous trips into Amarillo and Fort Worth to see doctors, and they'd all wanted her to go to Chicago to see a specialist, but Beth had refused. There seemed to be nothing anyone could do to ease her situation.

Billy felt responsible in some small way, she supposed. Probably because he saw himself as the "man" of the house ever since his father died. He and his Aunt Bethena had always been close, but Kate was completely unprepared for the way he'd assumed responsibility for her welfare since her "tragic event."

That's what the family had chosen to call it, Kate thought sourly.

Almost from the first day Beth returned, Billy had sat by her bedside patiently, just to be there in case she needed anything. When she was better physically and able to sit upright in bed, he would read to her for hours as she remained unresponsive, staring into space at something only she could see. When Beth couldn't sleep at night, or woke up screaming because she'd seen the terrible scar-faced man crawling through her window again, Billy took his old rifle and sat outside her window in full view of his aunt, to show her he was protecting her so she could sleep. Billy now carried the ancient rifle with the cracked stock every place he went and had taken to wearing an old .36 caliber handgun with the missing trigger guard, given to her by her late husband. She didn't even know if it still fired. Kate was proud of her son for the way he'd taken on a man's responsibility of the house, but saddened for the loss of the childhood it had cost him.

One day, about a month earlier, she'd been in search of a cool place to just get away and rode down to the river to enjoy the shade for a while. As she relaxed under a sprawling shade tree, she saw Billy ride up on the other side of the rocky ford. Kate was hidden from his view, and not wanting to disturb his private time either, she remained quite. She was surprised to see Billy take her old pistol out of his saddle bags and strap it on. He walked to the edge of the river where there were hundreds of frogs hopping on the banks, and quick as a flash, he drew the pistol and began to pick the hopping frogs off, one by one. He would run up as many as a dozen straight hits before he would miss one. Then, he would start over and do it again.

Satisfied with his success with the pistol, Billy went to his horse and returned with the old rifle. He began shooting with it, and again, seeming to almost never miss. At last, he mounted up and rode back toward the ranch. Kate sat amazed for a long time. She had no idea that Billy was so driven, nor that he was such a crack shot. Probably influenced by that darn Rosie Poe, she thought, remembering how Poe had taken young Billy down to the river and shot "rocks right out of the air." The whole episode fascinated, yet disturbed her at the same time.

Kate found herself staring at her idle hands holding the leather, and scolding herself, fiercely redoubled her efforts to repair the harness. Within a few minutes, her mind began to wander again, turning to thoughts of Roosevelt Poe and Jericho McCain.

It had been a year since they'd ridden off after that terrible man. She had received only one letter from Rosie and the subsequent telegraph informing her of Stump Henry's untimely death. Of course, Rosie had said Jericho sent his respects, but "You know Jericho, he ain't much for writing," the letter read. Yeah, she knew Jericho…No! She didn't know Jericho. She didn't know him at all. She knew someone from a long time ago, but she didn't know if he was still the young man she remembered.

The last communication had been several months ago, and no further word had come. Kate sighed and laid the harness aside. Picking up a cloth, she wiped the saddle soap from her hands and hung up the unfinished harness. It was time she quit fooling herself, she thought, mildly depressed. She was a grown woman, not some young thing with a school girl crush on a childhood sweetheart. She didn't even know if she loved Jericho McCain anymore. Maybe she just thought she loved him, but he was actually someone else. It's all so confusing.

Then there was Tad Barkley, who owned the ranch adjacent

to her property on the south. Tad was a nice man and a widower with two small boys. He'd visited her three times, and she hadn't discouraged him. He was honest about wanting a mother for his children and that combining the two spreads would be financially wise for the two of them. There was no talk of love. That was just as well, for she didn't love Tad Barkley either. But, maybe it was time to put the pipe-dream about her and Jericho McCain aside, and consider what was best for the children. The girls were growing like weeds and had asked her more than once if she would ever get married again. She believed Billy, now almost seventeen, needed a man around to help take the weight of responsibility off his young shoulders. She was still contemplating those thoughts when she heard the sound of a wagon and several riders outside the barn.

Kate blinked as she walked from the shade of the barn into the brightness of the afternoon sun. Shading her eyes, she made out the three riders and a wagon with a young couple in it.

"Climb down and have some lunch," Kate yelled to the group. "I'll be right up."

Kate hurried toward the house, happy to see strangers, since she seldom saw anyone except for her family and the ranch hands. Removing her floppy hat, she walked up to the wagon and smiled at the young couple. For an instant, Kate was stunned. She'd never seen a prettier woman in her life. The man with her might well have been handsome too, except that he appeared to be in poor health. He was pale and partially leaning against the woman.

"I'm Dixie Thompson from the Circle-T," the pretty woman said. "This is Rosco Bookbinder from El Paso. Please excuse us, but could we put Mr. Bookbinder someplace where he can lie down for a spell? He was recently injured and hasn't fully recovered yet."

"Of course," said Kate. "Have your men bring him into the house," she called over her shoulder, as she led the way.

The vaqueros gently lifted Rosco from the buckboard and carried him into the house behind Kate.

"Place him there," she directed, pointing at a room near the end of the hall.

The Circle-T men placed Rosco on the wide bed and left Dixie alone to care for him. Kate brought cloths and water which Dixie used to gently bathe his forehead.

"I'm sorry," Rosco whispered weakly, closed his eyes, and was instantly asleep.

Kate saw Dixie Thompson as she kissed the man on his forehead and stared down at him with a worried expression.

"Come," she said. "He'll be fine. All he needs is rest." Kate smiled at her and held out her hand to the young woman. "You look like you're ready to drop, yourself. Let me get you something to drink."

Dixie followed her into the ranch's large family kitchen, and looked around, amazed. There was a large stone fireplace in one corner, a long rough-wood table that reached from one end of the room to the other, and a large brick Dutch-oven, built into one wall. She marveled at how neat everything looked.

Kate placed a glass of lemonade in front of her and took a chair, directly across the large table from her. The women hit it off at once and instantly felt comfortable with each other. They talked of Dixie's father and the trip Kate had made so long ago to visit the Thompson ranch. They talked of Rosco's trek across west Texas that resulted in his wounding, and Dixie told of her caring for the wounded man and, blushing, of her love for him. She mentioned that she'd seen Rosie Poe and Captain McCain in San Antonio and, that she'd first met McCain when he brought the news of her father's death to the Thompson ranch. It slowly dawned on Dixie that Kate's subtle questions about Jericho McCain were based upon more than idle curiosity.

Innocently, Dixie said to her, "How long has it been since you've seen Captain McCain, Kate?"

Kate made busy with the pitcher of lemonade, refilling the glasses even though they were not quite half empty. "Oh, I haven't seen Jericho McCain in almost fifteen years," she honestly answered. "I guess I still see him as a young man such as he was back then."

Sensing Kate was fishing for information about the aging lawman, Dixie went on. "He's a quiet man — soft-spoken and polite. Still terribly handsome despite his years," she said, "he appears much younger than I'd have assumed. Also, a very capable one, I hear. He sports a thick flowing mane of almost silver hair and is always well-dressed and gentlemanly. I never heard him utter a curse word, or be harsh toward others."

She noticed that Kate was smiling and leaning forward, with her elbows resting on the top of the table. She went on, telling Kate everything she knew or had heard about McCain's adventures, since he left with Poe and the others. They'd talked for just over two hours when they heard Rosco stirring in the bedroom at the end of the hall. Dixie immediately jumped to her feet and rushed to check on her lover, only to find him sitting on the edge of the bed, looking sheepishly.

"Guess I sort of drifted off," he said embarrassed.

Dixie stood in front of him and pushed a long lock of dark hair from his forehead.

"Shush," she said. "I don't know how you held up on the journey as well as you did." Hearing a slight noise behind them, they turned to see Kate walk into the room.

"I'm Kate Shaw," she said smiling. "I own the place, so if you're not satisfied with the accommodations, I'm the one you complain to."

Rosco tentatively rose to his feet. "A pleasure to finally meet you Mrs. Shaw. I've heard so much about you that I feel as if I already know you."

"Let's move into the kitchen where I can get you some refreshments, Deputy Bookbinder," Kate said.

"Rosco," he said. "Please, just call me Rosco." He followed along behind her, with Dixie providing a steadying arm for support.

After exchanging a few additional pleasantries, Rosco finally said, "Mrs. Shaw, I don't know if you're aware of it, but I was the one with Stump Henry when he was killed." He saw by the surprise on her face that she hadn't known.

"His last thoughts were of you and your children," he went on. "In fact, I have something he sent to you and Billy. That's the reason for our trip here."

He started to rise but Dixie beat him to it and said, "Just set. I'll bring it in." She hurried out.

"She's beautiful, and a very nice person too, Rosco," Kate said with a smile.

"She's the finest woman I've ever known," Rosco replied simply, staring after her.

They heard the sounds of her returning before Kate could even follow up on her remark. Dixie reentered carrying a small brown envelope and a long cylindrical package wrapped in oilcloth. She handed them directly to Rosco. He sat for a moment, staring at the objects in his hand, then looked at Kate.

"I only knew him for a short time, Mrs. Shaw, but he was a fine man. Someone you could trust to ride the river with you," he said simply, and handed her the envelope. "He spoke highly of you, ma'am."

Kate reached for, and took the letter from his hand. "Excuse me," she said, as she rose from her chair and exited the kitchen. She stopped in the hallway, opened the envelope and slowly read the letter as the two young people politely carried on a low conversation in the next room. She read it twice as tears burned her eyes, then folded it neatly and put it into her skirt pocket. Taking a couple minutes more to regain her composure, she headed back into the kitchen, where she again seated herself at the table.

"Thank you, Rosco," Kate said. "That meant a lot to me."

Rosco indicated the package in his lap. "These are Stump's guns. I imagine you read in the letter that he gave them to your son," he said with embarrassment, for suddenly he remembered Stump's letter stated that he had been the author.

Kate just sat for a moment, undecided whether to accept the guns for her son, or to have Rosco take them away when he left. Then sighing deeply, she reached for the package, knowing that she couldn't deny what had been a dying man's wishes — especially a friend like Stump Henry.

"I would like for you both to stay for as long as you can," she told the young couple. "With most of the hands out on roundup, I have room in the bunkhouse for your men, and more than enough room for the two of you, right here. Besides, you need to recover before you start back, Mr. Bookbinder," she told the young man. "The girls will be excited that we have company when they get home from school today, and Billy should be returning in the morning, too."

She escorted the visitors to show them their rooms. Rosco was put in the same room he had occupied earlier and Dixie was given the adjoining bedroom. "In case he falls ill in the middle of the night," Kate told Dixie with a straight face, as she showed Dixie the accommodations. Dixie smiled to herself.

That evening, Dixie and Rosco met Kate's daughters and her sister Bethena. Stump had told Rosco most of the details surrounding Beth's abduction by Scar and his cutthroats; and he had told of the trauma Beth had suffered as a result. Rosco was instantly struck by the beauty of the woman with the sorrowful eyes and the brooding mouth. She was friendly and smiled when necessary, but Rosco had the feeling that she remained miles apart from the gaiety and chatter at the dinner table that evening.

Beth excused herself soon after the meal was over and departed for her room. Dixie, who also knew some of the details of Beth's past, looked at him with sad eyes, and afterward, only picked at her food. That night, just as Rosco was drifting off to sleep with Dixie's head lying on his chest, they heard her scream. Kate had warned them about what they could expect, but they were unprepared for the soft, heart-wrenching sobs that drifted up the hallway to their room. They lasted for a long time.

* * *

Billy Shaw lurched in the saddle and watched Joe Walker cut a calf from the herd, effortlessly tossing a rope over its head. The young animal somersaulted end over end as it hit the end of the rope, and Walker was on it to tie three of its feet together before it came to a complete stop. Young Shaw was almost as good at roping, but Joe Walker was the best all around cowboy most of the ranch hands in the valley had ever seen. There seemed to be nothing Walker couldn't do when it came to riding, roping and general all around ranch work. He could work anywhere, but he remained at the K/D.

The best part, Billy thought, is that Joe has been the K/D foreman for the past fourteen years.

During the past six, he'd been taking half of his pay in livestock, so Billy and his mother both knew it was only a matter of time until Joe would give them notice that he was leaving to start his own spread somewhere else. Kate had already told him that when he was ready, to let her know and she would make him a good price on four sections of grassland with water. Joe seemed in no hurry to leave the K/D and always gave the same answer.

"Maybe in a year or two."

For the past two years, Joe Walker had been working with Billy to show him all he could about "ram-rodding" a spread as large as the Shaw's K/D Ranch. While he was almost always gruff and critical of Billy's progress, secretly he was proud of the youngster's quick grasp of everything he told him about the ranch. He was quick to pass that information onto Kate, if not Billy.

"I don't want the lad to get a case of the big head, Miz Shaw," he would say in his rough Irish brogue. An Irish brogue, in which an occasional Scottish word, or complete phrase, would sometimes suddenly infiltrate.

Kate had once told her son she thought "Joe Walker, an odd name for a man, only a few years removed from the old country," and often remarked on his unique mix of accents. Texas was a place of many such men — men who came to get away from a past they didn't want, or that didn't want them. In Texas, his mother told him, a man's past was his own business. It was the way he lived his life and how he treated his neighbors that mattered. As far as the people around there were concerned, "Irish" Joe Walker, as he was called, was the salt of the earth.

"Ye gonna watch or…or ye gonna work, Mr. Shaw?" Walker was yelling at Billy, out of breath from the just completed, strenuous activity of hog-tying a particularly feisty young calf.

He watched as his young protégé expertly cut a calf, casually tossed a noose over its head and was on it to tie its feet as it hit the ground. It was, the other hands thought, almost a copy of the one they had just seen Irish Joe complete.

"Some time or other, you're gonna miss that cute little toss like ye just made, and that calf is gonna take the hand off at the wrist," Walker criticized.

Billy bore the criticism in silence as he usually did, but as Walker turned away there was a small smile on the older man's lips.

"That's all for today, lads," Walker shouted. "Let's see what Cookie's got for grub tonight."

As the others walked away, Joe fell back with Billy. "Ye done well today, lad," he said in a rare complement. "Now don't forget, your ma wants you home by tomorrow morning."

Billy reddened at Irish Joe's words and said, "Yes, sir, I think I'll get started by dawn though. Anything you want me to see to at the ranch, Mr. Walker?"

"Now, how many times must I tell you, lad? Call me Joe, Irish Joe, or if you must, just plain Walker, but my daddy was 'Mr. Walker,' not me," Joe Walker chided.

"Yes, sir, I'll try to remember," said Billy as he turned to go.

"Billy," Joe said. The boy stopped and looked back. "Billy," he said again, "come and sit with me for a bit."

The older man squatted down where he was and started to roll a smoke. Billy squatted beside his mentor and resting his buttocks on his heels, waited expectantly until Walker was finished. The older man inspected his rolled smoke for any flaws and, satisfied it was perfect, lit up.

He puffed a few draws and finally said, "You'll be seventeen in a month, won't you Billy?" Nodding his head, and not waiting for a reply, he went on. "You be a better man than I was at the age, lad. I didn't know even what a longhorn cow was when I came to this country, and I was twenty-eight then."

Joe blew the smoke in the quiet evening air and watched it until it dissipated. "Your ma didn't know me before I came here and asked for a job, but God bless her heart, she's a saint, she gave me a job and responsibility. She treated me like a man and gave me her trust." Irish Joe appeared to be thinking about what he was about to say, then went on. "I didn't tell another soul what I'm about to tell you lad. But I have me reasons for telling you now."

Billy waited and Joe continued. "I was born in Ireland and lived many years in Scotland and England." He smiled ruefully. "This is why I have such an infernal mix of accents."

He hesitated, looking out over the grassland before them. "I also had other names before I came to work for the K/D," he said. "The one I had in Ireland don't matter, for you won't know it if I tell it. But the people of Ireland know it." He nodded his head, still staring at something Billy couldn't see. "Aye, they know it well, lad," Walker said softly.

He studied the tip of his burning cigarette for a moment, as if unsure how to go on. "I was the most famous highwayman in Ireland, Scotland and the British Isles, for over ten years. Finally, I had to shoot me way out of a bit of a tiff after I robbed a coach just outside Londonary." Again, a long pause. "A baby was killed in the shooting. A little lad of two. My fault? The soldier's fault? Who knows? It sickened me to death, lad, so I stowed away on a boat I thought was going to the Indies. It came to America instead." He laughed shortly. "I jumped ship as soon as I was able and hid out until the ship departed."

Billy was completely caught up in Joe Walker's story and stunned that the man who had treated him as if he were something less than human for the past two years, was now confiding in him some dark secrets about his past. Billy was still unclear as to what the man's possible motive could be. Nonetheless, he hung onto every word Joe Walker spoke.

"I was broke and hungry, but I was determined not to turn to the highway again. I worked in a laundry and earned a few dollars, then staked it all on myself to beat a bare-fisted knuckler named 'Bull' Durham. We fought for thirty-six rounds and I knocked him out in the thirty-seventh. It was a bloody affair lad, but desperation makes a lad hungry," he chuckled dryly. " I couldn't even walk for four days and when I could, I knew I wouldn't make a living fighting the likes of Durham any more." Walker took a last drag off the butt, pinched the end and mashed it into the dirt with his thumb.

He waited so long to continue, that Billy thought the talk was over and nervously wondered if he should just excuse himself and leave.

"I took up the one thing that I was good at," Joe said. "A gun. I worked mainly for big companies like the railroad and anybody else that could pay me well enough. I was what they call, an Enforcer. What I was, lad, was a killer for whoever could pay for it. I called myself 'English Bob.' Hell, I ain't even English," he laughed again. "Me ol' daddy was probably spinning in his grave like a top, me saying I was a Tory, and all."

At the name of "English Bob," Billy stiffened and stopped breathing for several beats. Was old Joe Walker telling him that he was the famous killer, English Bob? He had to be lying, but looking into Joe's eyes, Billy knew the foreman of the K/D, wasn't. English Bob. Old Irish Joe Walker was English Bob. *Holy shit!*

"I won't swear you to secrecy, lad, but I'm a telling you this for a reason and I'd hope you wouldn't use it to end my life here in the valley. I only tell you, because I've a seen you practicing with your mother's pistol — and I suspect that you've got some reason in mind," Joe said. "A reason that involves your Aunt Beth."

Billy stared at him with open mouth.

"You'd be good, lad. In time, and with proper training, you might even become the best shot I've ever seen. What you need though — if what I think you're about to do is correct — is you have to learn speed."

Billy's head was spinning, and the words refused to come.

"Well, dammit boy, do you want a my help, or not?" Joe demanded.

"Yes, sir," Billy gulped.

"Aye, lad," Joe rose to go. "You'll be the best I ever seen if you learn well what I can teach you."

Joe Walker, also known in some distant life as "English Bob," smiled down at the stunned young man and slowly walked away. It was the first time Billy could ever remember, that the foreman had smiled at him.

Twenty-Four

*"As I walked out in the streets of Laredo.
As I walked out in Laredo one day,
I saw a young cowboy all wrapped in white linen.
Wrapped in white linen, as cold as the clay."*

– *"The Streets of Laredo,"* a cowboy's lament

MCCAIN'S BUNCH FINALLY CAUGHT up with Moses Penny on the Mexico border twenty miles west of Laredo. As usual, they found Moses sitting on his horse waiting, but this time, with his new companion, Nigger Britt Johnson.

"Just as I figured Cap'n, they heading across the Rio," he said as if he were continuing a conversation that had already been in progress.

McCain contemplated the news for a moment and replied in the same manner. "We'll need some more supplies if we're to follow them down there, Mr. Penny," he replied. "How do you suppose we should go about this?"

Witnessing this exchange, Jim Parker, once more felt he was on the outside, and out of step, with the four men with whom he'd been so closely associated for the past eight months. *God, he thought, has it really been that long?* He was completely awed as he observed how closely their thought processes intertwined and how quickly the unspoken thoughts of one were immediately acted upon by the others. He felt as if he would never fit in, even if he stayed with them for the next ten years.

Well, Cap'n, Britt here tells me he has a fair idea about where they might be headed. Seems he had to come down here once before, three-four years ago, to find some other people the Comanches carried off. He tells me they have a few favorite places down on the Salado River that he thinks would be a good place to start."

Johnson silently nodded his agreement and Moses continued. "We can check out several of those places while you go into Laredo for supplies, then meet up later with you at Sabinas Hidalgo."

The plan made sense to McCain and Poe, so after "fine-tuning" it a few more minutes, they separated. Penny and Britt Johnson headed south into Mexico, while McCain and the rest rode toward Laredo.

The group arrived in Laredo in the early afternoon the following day. After tying up at the hitching post in front of a sign that read, "*Sheriff, Laredo, TX: Lincoln Tibbs,*" Poe and McCain entered the office while the others waited on their mounts. Seated at a desk facing the door was a neatly dressed, medium-sized man, with a coal black handle-bar mustache. Two matching coal black eyes stared from beneath the brim of a derby hat. As the Rangers entered, he suddenly rose to his feet and stuck out his hand, grinning broadly.

"J.D. McCain and Roosevelt Poe, Aye God! I thought you were dead!" he said.

McCain visibly winced at that statement but grinned and reached out to grasp the offered hand. Then Poe, in his exuberance, grabbed the sheriff's hand and nearly wrenched it from his shoulder socket. It was plain to see these three were old friends who truly liked one another.

"How ya been, Link?" McCain said. "I thought you were

going to retire and settle down with Mabel and the grand kids. What happened?"

"I got two months left, fellows," Tibbs said. "Two months and Mabel and me can move to that cabin we bought over on the Canadian and fish every day. It'll be just like a honeymoon," he laughed. "How long you here for? Ya gotta come by tonight for supper, or Mabel will whack me with that skillet of hers."

"Well, if ya got a few minutes, let's take a walk over to the Red Garter and get something to wet our whistle with," Poe said. "Then, I'll introduce you to the others and me and Jericho will tell you what we're up to."

Never one to turn down a legitimate excuse for a tipple, Lincoln Tibbs smacked his lips. "Follow me gentlemen," he arched his black eyebrows twice and marched out the door, "to the local den of sin."

Poe told Jake Kellog, Fish, and Jim Packard to drop off the horses at the livery and meet them at the saloon. The three old friends were still reliving old times when the other three joined them twenty minutes later.

After the requisite introductions were finished, Jim, still feeling like an outsider, pretty much kept quiet and observed the reunion of the others. Prior to arriving in Laredo, Rosie had brought him up to date on their old friend, Lincoln Tibbs. He'd been a lawman for nearly thirty years, first as the local town sheriff or marshal for more than a dozen tough boomtowns west of the Mississippi; then as a U.S. Marshall, working the badlands of the Oklahoma Territory, and finally as the County Sheriff in Laredo. He'd been in that job for the past seven years and would retire in a few months, despite offers and incentives by the town council to raise his pay, hire him more deputies or elect him mayor, if he'd just stay on. Tibbs' reputation among the citizenry of Laredo was exemplary and almost to a person, they expressed fondness and support for their popular sheriff.

Poe raised his glass and said, "To Link Tibbs, one hell of a lawman for thirty years."

The group shouted, "Hear, hear!" and downed their drinks.

As an embarrassed silence settled on them, Lincoln Tibbs coughed politely and said, "So, tell me, what brings a bunch of hard men like yourselves to my peaceful town? Why are you operating this far south? Last I heard, your area was over around Odessa and El Paso, maybe up in the pan handle area."

McCain told him of the Governor's appointment of the group as government agents, and of having been reconstituted as Texas Rangers. He brought him up to date about their hunt for Scar and Bloody Bill Reid, about the Indian raid where four women had been taken captive, and of burning the outlaw town at Carrizo Springs.

"Well, you boys have been busy. The Springs are out of my jurisdiction and probably needed to be burned years ago anyway, but I want you folks to tell me first before you start to enforce the law around here. I know the personalities involved and I can usually quell things before they git out of hand, where you, being strangers and all, might not be able to do that," Sheriff Tibbs stated.

After receiving their assurances that they would do as he asked if time permitted, they ordered another round of drinks and Tibbs asked a few more questions about the Ranger's current mission, for clarification.

"I live in the white house with all the lilacs in front, right on the edge of town," Tibbs told them. "You rode right past it on your way in. I'll tell Mabel to expect five more for dinner, around six. If you don't show, you git whacked with her skillet."

When Legends Lived

They all laughed and Link Tibbs turned to leave, tossing over his shoulder, "I've got some rounds to make, see you tonight."

"Nice man," said Jim. "How did a congenial fellow like that ever last through thirty years as a lawman and not get killed?"

"Mainly 'cause he's more than a passing hand with a six-gun and he never met a man he was a scared of," said Poe. "If you're ever in a 'tight' and you want someone at your back that you can depend on, Link Tibbs is the man."

"I'll second that," said McCain, and Jake nodded in affirmation, as well.

* * *

The group was mounted and ready to ride out at daybreak the next day. Behind them, they led a well-loaded pack animal with, to Packard's dismay, provisions for living on the trail more than two months. The day before, Jim had sent a telegraph to his father-in-law concerning the progress of the ranger's campaign. He also picked up an "all-points" message from Southern Pacific Headquarters but stuffed it in his pocket, for reading later.

"Lordy, that was some meal last night," Poe said. "I'm still as full as a tick."

Jim conjured up thoughts of just what that meant, and was mildly disgusted.

Several miles out of town, Jake, whose job it was to watch the flanks and rear, told the others that he had a feeling someone was on their tail. Cutting through a fairly substantial growth of scrub oaks, Jake, unnoticed, dropped from the main group. Several minutes passed and then he saw the man he'd noticed earlier in the Red Garter, as he came into view. It's the farmer, he thought. He watched, without sound or movement. Having done nothing to alert the other man, Jake was mildly surprised when he stopped his horse just as he drew even with Jake's position at the side of the trail.

"I'm not hostile," was all he said, confirming to Jake that he'd known someone was waiting. Then, being careful to keep his hands well away from the handles of the two colts Jake could see at his belt, the man who looked like a farmer stated, "Take me to McCain."

The others, waiting just a minute's ride ahead, watched silently as Jake escorted the man to their location. Poe and McCain noticed that Jake hadn't removed the man's hardware and took that as a good sign.

"I'm Captain McCain. You better have a mighty palatable explanation as to why you've been trailing us since we left Laredo, pilgrim."

"I intend to ride with you when you go after the women," the stranger explained.

McCain and the others eyed him carefully and unanimously reached the conclusion that the man was no farmer. "What makes ya think we'll have ya?" McCain said.

"Makes no difference, I'm going, or you can shoot me right here and now," he replied easily.

"Might just do that too," said Poe, parting his mustache to spit.

The man wore bib-overalls, preferred by the farmers of the current day and times, had the rough, scared hands of one who works the earth. But the eyes weren't right, thought Poe. "Who are you, mister?"

"My name is Wes Holden…" the man stopped and sighed

deeply. "No, that's not my name. That's the name I've been using for the past fifteen years that I've been a farmer, over east of San Antonio. A couple of weeks ago my wife was shot and killed by Comanches, and my daughter taken. I followed them to the river but lost their trail. Been around some, but never have been much of a tracker. Mister," he said, staring intently at McCain, "she's only fourteen years old. A baby. You know what they do to white women — and fourteen is a woman to the Comanches."

He hesitated, as if undecided how to continue. "I know I don't look like much to you people," he said. "But I can help. It don't much matter what happens to me once we git her back. She's the important thing."

He took a breath, looked around the faces of the men staring back at him, and continued. "Hell, you might as well know it all. My real name is Wes Tanner. I'm the same Wes Tanner that fought in the Missouri border wars and…yeah, I'm probably wanted by more lawmen than were Jessie and Frank, and the Youngers combined. I'm not gonna sit here and tell ya that I didn't do those things. I did 'em, and more that they don't even know about. You help me git my daughter back from those red devils, and I'll say the same thing to the judge. What do you say?"

McCain looked at the tall man dressed like a farmer, then his eyes slid down to the worn walnut handles of the twin Navy Colts, resting in soft, oiled holsters at his waist. "Don't know of any laws he's broken in Texas, do you Roosevelt?"

"Nary a one," Poe answered.

"You can ride along. If I find things are not as you said, or you have lied to us in any manner, I'll hang you pronto. No talking — just hang you. Understand?" McCain told the man.

Tanner breathed a deep breath and said, "You got a deal, Mister."

* * *

Brad sat in the same chair he'd chosen early that morning and brooded for most of the day. "Gentleman" Brad Thompson, as he was then called around the San Antonio and Uvalde area, had been drinking since he arrived in Laredo two days earlier. He only came to Laredo because he'd heard that King Fisher had put together a big poker game with several wealthy men, but arrived to find it had been canceled at the last minute. It seemed that the notorious King Fisher and his friend, outlaw turned lawman, Ben Thompson, and a couple of other equally no-account fellows, had shot each other to death just two hours before they were to leave San Antonio for Laredo. All of it had put "Gentleman" Brad in a foul mood.

In fact, his mood was so bad, that the laughter and good times of a certain young cowboy and one of the local saloon girls got to be downright unbearable for him. Tossing down his drink, he kicked his chair back and strode to the cowboy balancing the young lady on his knee, whispering in her ear.

Brad kicked the handsome young man's chair and said surly, "I have been annoyed for about long enough by your racket and her squeals. Now shut it up, or leave so I can have some peace and quiet!"

The young cowboy stood and faced the pale stranger dressed in the black suit. "I don't know what your trouble is, mister, but the lady and I are just having a good time. Now if that don't set well with you, maybe you best be the one to leave," he said.

Brad got real calm and stared at the cowboy with eyes that

turned him cold. "I see you're wearing a gun, cowboy. Why don't you make me leave?" he said softly.

The other young man backed up several steps holding his hands straight out to his front. "I ain't no gunfighter. I...I just came in here f...for a drink and to talk with the ladies," he stammered.

"If you don't reach for that piece in a couple more seconds, I'm going to blow you right out of those boots, cowboy. Now, you've been warned fair. Reach!" Brad snarled.

"Hold on!"

The firm voice came from the front of the saloon. Looking around, the two young combatants saw Sheriff Tibbs walking toward them. He approached until he was standing between the two men.

"All right, Randy," he told the cowboy. "You hightail it on back to the Crooked-Y. Tell Mister Pope that I'll be out to see him in a few days."

"Get out of my way, Sheriff. He insulted me and I've called him out," Brad told the sheriff.

"I don't care what happened here, there ain't going to be any gun-play tonight," Tibbs said, and motioned for Randy to leave. Happy to be out of the situation, the young cowboy moved to comply. As he did so, Brad abruptly stepped forward and drew his gun. The sheriff reacted instantly, pushing young Randy out of the line of fire just as Brad pulled his trigger, hitting Link Tibbs in the neck and dropping him instantly. Immediately, Brad turned the gun on the cowboy and shot him through the head.

The others in the room stood by stunned, as Brad, covering the room with his gun, rapidly backed through the door, ran to his horse and galloped away. Behind him, he could hear the angry shouts of the stunned citizens.

R.C. Morris

Lincoln Tibbs, Sheriff of Laredo, gentleman and lawman extraordinaire, took three days to die. As he labored between life and death, the town waited, hoping against hope that he would win this last and most valiant fight of his life. But on the third day, Link Tibbs finally gave up and passed on to the other side. The citizens of Laredo, in a vigilante mood, mounted up the largest posse in the town's history and rode toward San Antonio in search of his killer.

* * *

Scar made the best of his bad trade with Rain Maker by raiding a small pig farm belonging to a poor Mexican family, just before he crossed the border into Mexico. He and his two followers, Joe Bird and Tommie Sees-Far, killed the old man outright because he came at them with a machete. He let Joe and Tommie mount the farmer's fat wife several times and play with her for a while before tying her to a fence-post inside the muddy pigpen. Then they squatted with the couple's two young daughters and the woman for whom he traded the horses to Rain Maker, drank whisky and made them watch, as he carefully slit the taut skin of the fat woman's stomach and let her entrails fall to the ground. The woman, who was near unconsciousness, at first seemed more surprised than hurt, then as the pigs began to root and eat at her entrails, she started to scream. She screamed for almost an hour, at last giving up with a few final gurgling sounds.

The captive white woman sat through it all lifeless, unmoving and staring straight ahead, but Scar had to finally gag the two daughters to keep them quiet. As it was, the youngest girl, about ten years old, continued to whimper for the next two days. The whimpering continued even when he beat her, so he finally quit and just let her be.

Scar left the farm house standing, because he didn't want to alert anyone who might see its smoke. Besides, he didn't know where those damned old Rangers were, and he had a feeling they were still trailing him somewhere. He even sent Tommie Sees-Far back to watch the trail behind them as the group slowly made their way toward Nueva Rosita, but he saw nothing.

Mexican women won't bring a third as much as the white woman will, Scar thought, but he could probably make a little more for those two because they were young and, more than likely, still virgins. He knew some men liked that. Scar knew a place that might give a good price for the entire package. *The white woman might be a problem though,* he thought. She hadn't made a sound since his acquiring her from Rain Maker. *Just sits there and looks out into space. Those Comanche devils must've been after her like a pack of dogs,* Scar mused.

He liked the desolate country they passed through after crossing the Rio Grande River. Low lying mountains, sparse vegetation, hot dry days and cold nights were the norm. He'd been there many times and knew the country better than any man alive. *A man could get lost in this country and never be found,* he thought. *If the old Rangers follow me down here, they won't even get a smell of me.* He considered it lucky that Joe Bird knew this country well also. He'd been raised by the Comanches since he was eight years old, and had spent many days and nights hiding from Mexican *Ruralis* and groups of Texas Rangers raiding into Mexico.

Scar himself, had ridden with Victorio into the Diablo Mountains when the Rangers chased them out of Texas five years earlier. He'd left Victorio and sixty of his warriors upon reaching the Diablos, and hid out there for nearly four years. That was where he was headed now. If he could reach the

Diablos ahead of the old Rangers, they wouldn't find him. Not until he wanted them to. Then he would finally do to them what he'd wanted to do for a long time. Scar awaited that moment with great anticipation.

They stopped just outside Nueva Rosita, a small, dirty town consisting of little more than a couple of whore houses, a pottery maker and some sorry, one-room adobe shacks. Maybe seventy-five people lived there, but Scar didn't take any chances. He waited until dark, then slipped into the back of Jose's, and sent one of the barmaids to fetch the proprietor. A fat man with oily hair and sweat dripping from his face came running back to where Scar waited in the shadows.

Without speaking, Scar made a motion with his head that was meant to show he wanted the fat man to follow him, and retraced his footsteps back past the edge of the town's lights. Leading the puffing man to a small fire, Scar motioned for Joe Bird to bring the females forward, then watched as the half-breed roughly pushed them to the ground, close to the fire.

He knew that in the soft firelight the women would look even better than they would in the brightness of day. Pretending to be unconcerned, he watched as the fat man, rubbing his sweaty hands together, poked and prodded the women in all of their intimate places. The young girl's terror filled eyes followed him as he walked around them and periodically, stopped to run his hand over one of them.

At last, satisfied, he faced the man with the scar. "*Si*," he said, and they began their negotiations.

At the end, both men departed feeling they had bested the other. However, the fat man complained for a few moments longer so as not to appear too happy, for he knew well Scar's unpredictability and his penchant for violence. Jose bent to look at the face of the pretty white woman once more, and when he raised his head again, Scar and his men were gone. It was as though they'd never existed.

Looking nervously around him, Jose hurriedly prodded the females to their feet and started them toward his bar. Jose was smiling to himself as he led them along the crooked path he and Scar had walked, just moments before. He'd give the women to Maria to clean up and prepare for the next night. When he got back safely inside, he would start to spread the word that tomorrow night he would show his customers something different — a beautiful gringo woman for their pleasure. By then, the word would travel throughout the area. He expected a big crowd tomorrow, and smiled. Si, *a very big crowd.*

* * *

Fish leaned back against a small boulder and stared at the millions of stars overhead, wondering if they could see the same stars as far away as Bluebonnet. He'd been allowed to stand first shift of the night guard, because of his cooking duties the following morning. Two hours dragged by as he tried to remain alert, but his mind kept wandering back to the place he'd started to think of as home — Bluebonnet.

In his mind, he couldn't see the baked dirt and the heat as it had been when they rode away. He saw the greenness along the rivers and streams, remembered the trout fishing and the cool evenings. That was how he thought of Bluebonnet in moments such as these. The thoughts were what kept him going when things got so miserable he just didn't feel like he could stand it anymore. Like now. He was filthy, hungry and thirsty, and he would dearly love to see some of those nice smelling ladies in El Paso. Just thinking about it made him smile. He was still smiling when he felt the nick of a sharp knife against the side of his neck.

Stiffening, he rolled his eyes upward to see the face of the person holding the knife. "Dammit, M…Moses, you 'bout m…made me m…mess myself," he said, his Adam's apple jumping uncontrollably. "You sh…shouldn't orda do things l…like that to a man."

"You on guard, Fish?" Moses Penny said. "You better be alert, 'cause there are Indians around here and they'll lift all our hair if you let 'em sneak up on us like this."

"I…I was just thinking 'bout home," Fishburn stammered.

"Yeah? Well, you remember Corporal Stokes, don't you?" Moses asked him. "He was probably thinking about home when they took him, too. I wouldn't want to find you lashed down over an ant hill, with your peeder in your mouth."

Without a sound, Moses moved on down the hill, silently followed by his new black shadow, Britt Johnson. Fish swallowed hard, and looked around nervously as the vivid images of young Stokes came to mind. He felt wide awake as he stroked the trigger of his rifle.

* * *

They'd been camped just outside of Sabinas Hidalgo for two days waiting for Moses and Johnson to show up. McCain and Poe realized the two men were coming long before the others did, and out of habit, moved to the edge of the fire's light. Several seconds later, Moses and Johnson walked silently into camp and stood staring over Packard's shoulder for a minute before making a small noise, nearly scaring him to death. Packard scurried away on his knees before realizing who they were.

"Now *that's* funny," he said. "*That* is extremely damned funny. Maybe the next time, I'll also accidentally shoot myself for your enjoyment."

"Take a place, gents. We have some supper left, there in the skillet. Coffee too," Poe said, chuckling at Packard's discomfort.

Moses and Johnson squatted down by the fire and hungrily wolfed down their food. No one said anything until they were finished. It wouldn't have been polite. Satisfied at last, Moses belched loudly and sighed. Finally, he began his report.

"Found 'em, Cap'n. They in a camp with a big bunch of Comanches. 'Round eighty braves, plus women and children." He took a large swallow of the hot coffee and continued, "Biggest bunch of Indians I've seen since 'seventy-five' all in one place. Be hard to git into the village, though. Right on a river — water on one side and a steep wall on the other. The flat part of the camp is like an island, formed by the water and the cliff."

"Don't you have any good news?" Poe said.

Moses thought for a while and said, "There appears to be three white women and a young girl. They seem to be all right."

Wes Tanner, listening intently, moved closer. "What did the girl look like?" he said hesitantly.

Moses looked at Britt Johnson. "Britt got a better look than I did; what do you say Britt?"

"I'd say she's about fourteen…fifteen, hard to say from where we were. She was dark, black hair, looked almost Comanche the way she was fixed up. Had her dressed in wedding garb, like she was getting married," Britt answered.

Tanner sat back on his heels. "My God. I've got to get her away from them damned heathens."

"How long to get back there, Moses?" McCain said, ignoring Tanner.

"If we start by daylight, we should be there around dark. We can travel fairly fast until we get to the Lampazos, then we'll need to be careful. We'll have to come up on the camp from the high ground, they'd see us coming for a mile otherwise. Britt has a plan for getting into the camp to find out where they are keeping the women."

All eyes were turned on Nigger Britt, who said, "I'll go on alone tonight to a little Mexican village I know, just a little south of here. There, I'll see a man I've dealt with, off and on for a few years now, and pick up some horses and whiskey that I intend to use as trading material. I think the Comanche will let me into the camp to trade."

"Yeah, but will they let you out, again?" Jake said.

Britt smiled faintly. "Well, they always have before. But you know Comanche. They can be unpredictable. When I git there, I'll ride right across the river without even looking up. Hopefully, they'll think I'm alone. Once in the village, I'll mark where they've got the women, by some action, so watch me close. If… when I leave the village, I'll take the women straight to the fork of the Lampazos where it runs into the Salado, on the east side. That's where I'll expect to meet up with you. If you ain't there, I'll wait two hours then try to outrun them to Laredo."

"Sounds like you've done this before, Mr. Johnson. I can't think of any better plan, how about the rest of you?" McCain looked around the circle and saw they were all in general agreement that Britt's plan had a fair chance of succeeding.

Within the hour, Britt Johnson saddled up and rode out again, and the camp settled down for the night. All except for Wes Tanner, who sat awake until dawn.

When Legends Lived

They'd been moving for a full hour when the sun finally came up. All their gear had been tied down so there were no clanging or rubbing sounds coming from their equipment. Each man had been given strips of burlap to tie around his mount's feet when at last, they'd reached the river named Lampazos. As usual, Moses was far ahead of the rest, leaving sign for the main body to follow.

It was late afternoon and the group of men had been in the saddle for six hours straight since the last dismounted break, when they finally saw Moses squatting on his heels, staring out across a shallow river. He stood as they approached and led them back into a stand of small trees just short of the flats.

"We'll head due south from here," he whispered. "The ground starts to rise gradually, then shoots up all at once. We'll take the horses as far as we can ride or lead them, then it's best to leave them with a guard."

McCain acknowledged his remarks and motioned for him to lead out. Jim Packard looked nervously around, as if he expected a hundred Indians to jump out of the bushes onto him. *What the hell am I doing here?* he thought.

Moses was right, the ride wasn't too difficult at first, but in less than a quarter of a mile it turned into laboring work just to get the horses to climb it. At last, Moses held up his hand and pointed at an area beneath some large trees. It was dusk, and in another thirty minutes, he knew they wouldn't be able to see where they were going.

With any luck there won't be any clouds tonight, Moses thought. He knew there was at least a half moon and that would help them get back down to where they tied the horses. The tracker untied the rope attached to his saddle horn, and looped it over his shoulder. Fish was selected to stay with the horses, and acted as though that suited him just fine. The others followed Moses as he set a blistering pace up the steep climb. Aided by the rope he threw down to them, the others had to help one another come up several, almost vertical inclines of twenty feet. At last, Moses put his finger to his lips, and walked crouched down for about another hundred yards. That brought them to a boulder-lined crest. There, following his example, the men crawled to the top and lay on their stomachs. When he was certain all of them were present, he slipped off unnoticed into the shadows.

The camp sprawled across a flat area nearly half a mile below them. Packard was totally unprepared for the size of the encampment. It seemed much larger than the numbers Britt Johnson had given them, but then he remembered Britt had said eighty braves. He hadn't counted the women and children. *Why,* thought Jim, *there must be over three-hundred Indians in that village!*

From where they lay, Jim could see numerous large fires burning, with shadowy figures either sitting, leaping around them. There was a lot of dancing, singing, and an occasional shot fired into the darkened sky. Muffled by the steep canyon walls, the sparse gunfire seemed to be coming from much farther away. It all combined to produce an overall surreal effect. He looked on in amazement for a moment, and was startled when he suddenly felt someone at his side.

"Take a good look at it, son," someone whispered in his ear. "You may never get another chance to see anything like this again." It was Poe, and Jim could see his own excitement reflected in Poe's eyes.

By then, all of the men had settled into their positions and Jim could faintly make them out in the fading light. Poe was lying right beside him, with Wes Tanner a little further to his

When Legends Lived

right. On Jim's immediate left lay McCain, and then Jake Kellog. Moses was nowhere to be seen. *You can bet he's around someplace,* Jim thought. *Probably materialize right out of the night and scare me to death again.* Each of the men had brought their rifles, as well as the Colts they normally carried. Jim had carried his rifle as well, though he sincerely prayed he wouldn't have to shoot another human being that night.

Their timing was nearly perfect, for within thirty minutes they saw Britt Johnson moving through the rapidly failing light on the valley floor, making his way through the water toward the village

That might be the bravest man I've ever known," Wes Tanner said in a low voice.

"The hombre does have *cajones*," Jake agreed.

Britt was leading a herd of about twenty mixed horses. It was apparent the Indians had also seen him, for the sounds of celebration ceased immediately and an eerie silence greeted him as he entered the village. None of the Indians moved as he neared the edge of the light cast by the largest fire in the center of the village. Then a loud whoop went up and the Comanches rushed Britt's horse and pulled him from it. The watching men saw some of the Indians strike Britt but were too far away to determine if they were using their hands, or other objects. In the milling around effect created by the activity they temporarily lost him in the confusion below, then saw him being taken to one of the huts by two men who were holding his arms behind him.

"Guess that's the end of that," Jake whispered.

No one else said anything as the men continued to lie there, waiting and hoping, for a long time.

After what seemed like a century, Britt came out of the hut

followed by a tall Comanche with blue dots painted down his face and chest. He obviously had position and stature in the group.

"That's Rain Maker," Poe said. "If we didn't have those women to git out, I'd dot his eyes for him, right now."

The range was such that Jim Packard doubted even Poe could hit him from where they lay. As they watched, Rain Maker and Britt walked to the center of the camp and sat before the largest of the several fires still burning high. Apparently the chief said something, for Britt's trading whiskey was quickly passed out and there was a collective shout as the celebration began once more.

Jim dozed off for a time, and the next thing he was aware of was Poe, tapping his arm lightly. It appeared that the party was over, for most of the Comanche men lay where they had fallen on the ground, near the fires. The women and children had also disappeared, probably into the tents and lean-to's. Only Britt and Rain Maker were still talking and gesturing with their hands, as several of the sub-chiefs looked on. At last, Rain Maker stood, then Britt and the others stood as well. Rain Maker said something to one of the Comanches, who hurried away to one of the nearby tents and went inside. After a few minutes, he re-emerged, followed by four females, three adults and a girl. All of the men heard Tanner gasp as he recognized his daughter. They watched as more discussion and negotiation went on between Britt and Rain Maker, then the same Indian grabbed the girl by the arm and led her back to the same tent as before.

"No," breathed Tanner, as he watched.

"Easy, son," Poe told him, in a low voice. "You won't do her any good by letting them know we're here."

One of the other sub-chiefs was now leading the remaining

horses away, leaving only Britt's and one other with a saddle on it. Britt helped two of the larger women onto one of the animals and the remaining woman onto his own mount. After a few more words and gestures, he turned his horse around, and leading the other animal, rode slowly out of camp.

Silently, McCain tossed small pebbles to get everyone's attention and made motions for them to withdraw. Following his lead, they moved back from the crest about fifty feet, where they formed a half-circle around him.

"We wait," was all he said.

It was all of fifteen minutes later that Jim suddenly realized they weren't alone and looking up, found Moses Penny standing beside him. "Why am I not surprised?" he asked himself. It was as if he had just materialized in the air.

"It'll be tricky, Cap'n, but I think I might be able to do it. The only thing is, I don't know how spooked that little girl is," he said.

"It's got to be your choice, Mr. Penny. I won't tell you to go," McCain told him.

"I'll go."

"Okay, here's what's going to happen," McCain told the others quietly. "Mr. Penny is going to slip down the wall and try to get into their camp to bring out the girl. We'll stay here and cover him. There is no other place we can do it, even if we move closer to the camp."

McCain, clearly unhappy with the situation, went on. "There is a brush-line just before it clears about a hundred and fifty feet from the tent where Mr. Tanner's daughter is located. Mr. Penny has paced it off and figures our range starts about twenty feet the other side of the brush-line. So, if they can get back to that brush-line, we got a chance of helping him out."

Moses handed McCain his Sharps rifle. "Take care of this for me, Capt'n. You might need the range and besides, I won't be able to climb with both it, and the little girl."

McCain hesitated, then grasped it by the stock. "It'll be here when you get back, Mr. Penny. You take care."

The two friends stared into each other's eyes.

"I'll do it, just before daybreak," the big Negro said quietly. Then, with hardly a sound, Moses Penny was gone.

"That man's a billy-goat," Poe said. "If I'd run up and down this mountain as many times as he has tonight, I'd be ready for burying."

"We'll give him thirty minutes, then we'll move back into our original positions," McCain told the others. "Nobody moves or shoots unless I say so. I mean, nobody."

Nothing else was said until Poe signaled it was time to move back to the crest. Upon reaching their previous positions, they saw that the camp appeared to be sleeping. The fires had burned down, and there was no movement except for an occasional dog. Although the moon cast a good light, none of the men were able to pick up Moses Penny as he moved down the steep wall toward the village.

The moon was still high when they saw Moses break out of the brush-line and run in a crouching position, to the edge of the camp. From there, he stood upright, and as Poe would say later, "strolled in as if taking his girl for a walk in the park," to the tent they saw the girl enter several hours before. Kneeling at the back, he removed the long "frog-sticker" from the top of his boot and cut a small door in the tent. When he was satisfied with its size, he looked around and went inside.

It seemed he was inside for a long time, but Poe and McCain

counting seconds, realized it was only for about a minute. When he re-emerged, he was carrying a kicking and struggling young girl, and they could see Moses had his hand covering her mouth, and was talking into her ear. At last, Moses seemed to have gotten his message through to the girl and she ceased struggling. He walked carefully to the edge of the village and was just starting to cross the open space to the brush-line, when there was a shout from behind them and three figures suddenly rushed toward Moses and the girl.

The men on the crest watched as Moses gutted the first one to reach him, then kicked another's feet from under him and swiftly cut his throat. The third hit Moses high on the shoulder with his war-ax and Moses fell to his knees, just as he pushed his blade into the Comanche's ribs. The little girl stood there through all of it, as though unsure of what to do. Moses then grabbed her by the shoulders and pushed her toward the brush-line, just as several more warriors emerged from between the tents and rushed toward them. The girl then began to run for her life toward the brush-line, and Moses, bellowing loudly, charged the on-coming Indians as his friends watched helplessly from above. They saw him go down, under a mass of screaming Comanches and temporarily lost him from their sight.

The girl was halfway to her goal when about a dozen warriors ran from the tree-line to her right. Running silently, it was clear they would overtake her before she could reach the bushes.

"Hold your fire, they're still too far out of range and you might hit the girl," McCain said, as he leveled the Sharps.

Several more Indians exited the tree-line and were after the girl, as she ran screaming up the hill. The loud blast the Sharps made when McCain pulled the trigger vibrated through the canyons, and without waiting to see if he hit his target, he quickly reloaded and squeezed off another round. Over and over he fired, and a man dropped each time as bodies of Indians littered the ground.

"Oh, to have a few more Sharps right now," Poe moaned to himself.

Three of the Indians were upon the young girl just as she reached Moses's pace mark. The rifles of the hidden men belched smoke just as one of the warriors buried his hatchet between the girl's shoulders as he died. Wes Tanner, who'd long since left his position to meet his daughter, exited the bushes and shot four more Indians so quickly with his revolver, it was hard to count the shots. He quickly ran to his daughter, scooping her up in his arms, and ran back towards the bushes. The men on the ridge continued firing and reloading to fire again, as fast as they could empty their rifles. The slaughter was fast and deadly, and, as if by prearranged signal, suddenly there was nothing more to shoot at. All of the Indians simply vanished.

Jim tried to quiet his trembling hands as he looked down at the bodies heaped on the canyon floor, sick with the feeling he'd been responsible for some of them. One of them moved, then tried to crawl back toward the village. The big Sharps boomed again, and he was slammed to the ground, not to move again. Jim could hear Tanner sucking air into his tortured lungs long before he saw him. Then, he came charging out of the brush, clutching his daughter in his arms. He ran over the crest and lay the girl down gently. Instantly, Poe was at his side with a canteen of water. Jim watched as the two men worked feverishly over the girl and finally heard one faint word, "Daddy...."

Then only the sounds of anguish a father makes when he's just lost his daughter.

When Legends Lived

God dammit! Not after all she had endured. Why God? Why the little girl? Wasn't Moses Penny enough? Jim's mind was in a whirl. He felt disoriented, sick. He laid his head on his arms and wept bitterly.

With no threat looming from below, the others, except for Packard, moved back to where the girl lay and stood silently around the big man, cradling the small girl in his arms. They watched quietly as he held her in his arms, rocking her back and forth, and sobbing the most tortured sounds of grief the tough men had ever heard. Uncomfortable with the sight, they moved back to the crest and sat, staring down in rage at the now silent village. Packard, wiping tears of rage and frustration from his eyes, looked up to find Poe staring at him and quickly averted his eyes.

McCain, let a reasonable amount of time go by, then said, "Roosevelt, try and get him up and moving. We'll take the girl's body down with us. The longer we stay here, the more chance those devils will find our horses, or take in after Mr. Johnson. They got to figure out sooner or later that he was part of this."

Poe and Jim worked with Wes Tanner for thirty more minutes before they were able to convince him they needed to move, and they would take the girl's body with them. Finally, he stood, wiped his eyes, took off his jacket and wrapped it around his daughter. It took less time to walk down the slope than it had taken to climb it, even though it was like ink in the gorge below them. Reaching the bottom, they were challenged by Fish and guided in by his voice, finding their horses saddled and ready.

The men mounted and prepared to ride, except for McCain, who remained looking up at Poe and the others. He and Poe locked eyes for just an instant, in unspoken communication, then Rosie said, "How long do ya reckon you'll be?"

"I don't know. Just wait for me as long as you can at the forks of the river where you meet up with Britt Johnson. If I ain't there by tomorrow night, there won't be any reason to wait any longer," McCain said.

Jim, watching the exchange, silently dismounted and retied his horse to a tree near McCain's horse.

"Just what the hell you think you're doing?" McCain growled.

"You're going after Moses and I'm going with you," he said simply.

"I ain't got time to argue with you boy. Every minute counts, so if I say squat, you just ask how much and what color. You got that?" McCain told him. "If you get in my way, I'll likely cut your throat and leave you behind." He walked back up the rough trail.

Jim stared after him for a few moments. "I think he's starting to warm toward me," he said more to himself than anyone else. Then, he shouldered his rifle and faced up the steep slope.

Poe rode up and quietly spoke to him. "Just do as he says, son. Stay out of his way and don't rile him. He just lost a good friend, and he's grieving considerable."

Then Poe and the others rode away. Wes Tanner brought up the rear, still whispering quietly to the lifeless body of his daughter clutched tightly in his arms. Jim Packard, leaned on his rifle and watched as the group slowly made their way back down the rocky slope, then once more, he shouldered his rifle and followed McCain back up the mountain.

Chapter Twenty-Five

"Vaya con Dios. Go with God."
— Brad Thompson, the outlaw

AFTER KILLING LINK TIBBS and the young cowboy in Laredo, Brad rode all the way to San Antonio without sleeping. He arrived dirty, hungry, and nervously looking over his shoulder every few moments. He immediately sought out Hal to tell him about the shooting and to ask his advice about what he should do. Brad found him playing cards with four other men. Walking up, he said, "Hal, we got to talk, now."

Hal barely looked up at him, then went on playing cards.

Brad nervously watched the door for a few seconds, then said, "Come on, Hal. It's important, we have to talk."

"I'm playing cards right now," Hal said, still not looking at him. "You need a bath, come back later."

Brad's fury consumed him as he reached for the edge of the table and flipped it over, spilling the cards, chips, money and drinks onto the saloon floor. All five men at the table jumped to their feet, enraged. Brad stood back and pushed the tail of his coat behind his gun handles. Seeing that, three of the men slowly raised their hands in front of themselves and backed away.

The other man, a gambler, slowly sized the young man up, then said to him unafraid, "You appear to have problems. I'll find another game." He smiled coldly, turned his back on Brad and Hal La'Mount, and walked away.

Brad could see the fury in Hal's eyes as he stood there waiting for whatever happened next.

"You fool," Hal said through clinched teeth. "You bumbling fool. Killing a sheriff, especially someone like Lincoln Tibbs. It came in on the wire this morning. The Marshall is conveniently out of town today, so you've got about a day's head start on that posse coming up from Laredo."

Brad's face was pale as he righted one of the overturned chairs and sat down heavily on it, facing the back. "What do I do?" he said meekly.

"Do? You run. That's all you can do," Hal told him. "If it was me, I'd head for Gullytown and sit it out for a month or so, then up into the Badlands — the Oklahoma Territory. Maybe on up into the Northwest — Oregon, or even Canada. But run, and run fast. You've got no choice."

"I ain't leaving here. This is where I intended to stay, make a life for myself. No, I ain't leaving," Brad said.

Hal arched an eyebrow. "No? Then as soon as that posse gets here from Laredo, they'll hang you. Like I said, if it were me, I'd run." Hal was smiling broadly.

Rage filled Brad's eyes again. "I should kill you, you bastard," he said evenly. "I thought you were my friend and you're enjoying this mess." He stood up and dropped his hand near his gun handle once again. "Maybe I will kill you. They can't hang me but once."

"Before you do anything else stupid, take a look around, Brad. I bought this place last week. The people in here work for me now."

Brad shifted his eyes to the bar and saw a bartender standing at each end of it, short barreled Greeners laying on the bar in front of them. Both men were staring steadily at him. Across the room, the Faro dealer laid his pistol on the table near his hand. He was also looking at them.

"It probably wouldn't be wise to push this much further, Brad. You might have been useful if you hadn't gone and killed Sheriff Tibbs, but now you're a liability I just can't afford," Hal told him, still smiling. "It's best that you clear out now, because like I said, they're going to hang you."

Brad was smoldering with rage. He still almost drew, knowing he could kill Hal and maybe one or two of the others. But, he thought, I can't get them all. Brad glared his hatred at Hal La'Mount as he backed out of the door.

"It's a small world, Hal. The next time you may not have your employees backing you up." Then he was out the door and gone.

Brad went to his room and packed hastily, found the wad of money under his mattress and departed as quickly as possible. Tired as he was, he rode due west most of the night until the road narrowed to a trail and then the trail disappeared altogether. Finding a concealed area among some large rocks, he was finally able to sleep only fitfully for several hours. Awaking, he rummaged through his belongings for anything he could find to eat. In his haste, he found he'd packed no food at all. *How stupid*, he thought. *I've got to get better at this or I'm going to starve to death before I even get out of Texas.*

Again, he rode west for most of the day, without seeing another living soul. Then, around dusk, he smelled smoke. Guiding his horse into the wind, he finally topped a rise and spotted a small cabin. He was within two hundred yards of the structure when a shot kicked up dirt in front of him.

"That's as far as you go, stranger," said a gruff voice. "Just turn it around and keep on riding. This is private property."

"All I want is food. I'm hungry. I have money and can pay," Brad yelled back.

"I don't want your money, and I ain't got no food to spare," said the gruff voice again. "Like I said, keep moving, I won't warn you again."

Brad considered rushing the place, he was so desperate. But, he knew he wouldn't get within a hundred yards of the shack before he was shot down by the owner of the faceless gruff voice. Reluctantly, he turned his mount and headed back the way he'd come, his stomach grumbling loudly.

Several times over the next two days, he saw groups of men riding in the distance. He always steered clear of them, figuring no one else in their right mind would be out here in that godforsaken country unless they were looking for him, running as he was, or just generally up to no good. Either way, he decided to stay out of sight. Late that afternoon he saw three Indians in the distance moving across a large flat area to his left, and veered farther north, to avoid any possible contact with them. That's when Brad spotted a clump of large trees and rode toward them. He found they concealed a small stream and a fairly large, but shallow, water hole that had been created when someone in the past had dammed up the stream.

Dizzy and lightheaded from hunger, Brad nearly fell off his horse, stumbled to the water hole and collapsed face down in it. His horse walked up beside him and began drinking also. Having drunk his fill, Brad crawled to the base of a large tree near the water and rested his back against it. That was when he noticed the smell of onions. Wild onions. Frantically, he routed in the ground, pulled one and smelled it, then plopped it into his mouth dirt and all, followed by handfuls of others. Brad ate until he was nauseous, then reclined against the tree trunk to consider his options. They were limited he realized.

Stay here and eat onions, maybe shoot the horse and eat him along with the onions, he thought ruefully. In any event, if he remained where he was, the posse would show up sooner or later and hang him from the tree he was sitting under. Or, he could try running some more, in which case he would, in every likelihood, starve anyway once he ran out of onions.

His fine tailored broad-cloth suit was ruined, and a thick layer of west Texas dust coated his face. For the first time since he'd secretly cried when he'd found out his father had been murdered by that creature, Scar, Brad felt like crying again. What a mess he'd made of everything. Trying to be a big man, he'd shot a sheriff who'd never done him any harm, and some young cowboy he didn't even know. He should've gone home with Dixie when she asked. He thought of his sister with a warmth he'd forgotten recently, as he remembered how she'd cared for him all those years after he was injured, even though he treated them all so contemptuously.

Brad wiped his eyes as they suddenly began to sting with tears. If he'd only listened to her pleas and gone with her. But he hadn't. He was now an outlaw. A killer. There was no going back. He would have to start over. That is, if he lived long enough. Brad's eyes closed, and he immediately dozed off.

Jerking awake, he heard a small sound behind him. Swiftly drawing his gun, he rolled at the same time, coming to rest on his belly with his gun aimed at two startled people. Slowly rising to his feet, he kept the gun pointed at the man and woman.

They looked ancient. Behind them stood an equally old gray burro hitched to a makeshift cart. The old man was dressed in the plain white cotton attire many of the Mexican farmers wore. The old woman was dressed in the traditional dark clothing of the local Mexican women, and wore a black 'shawl' around her face. The man held a battered sombrero in his hands, and smiled a toothless grin.

"You got food?" Brad almost shouted.

The old couple chattered softly and continued to smile.

"God-dammit, do you have food? Give it to me, or I'll shoot you both!"

He ran to the cart and started tearing through it, looking for anything he could eat. Discovering a small basket, he quickly ripped it open and saw three tortillas wrapped around some kind of mashed vegetables. Ignoring the old people for an instant, he quickly crammed two of them into his mouth gulping them down, barely chewing. He choked violently, and went into a coughing fit for several minutes. Finally, wiping the tears from his eyes, he saw the old couple still standing there, staring intently at him.

"Take off!" he screamed, waving his gun at them. "Go on! Git, dammit! Git!"

The man gathered the reins of his animal and, with the old woman trailing behind him, slowly led it away, glancing over his shoulder as they left. Watching them go with their meager belongings, Brad's attention turned to the remaining tortilla, which he stuffed into his mouth, thist time taking care to chew it thoroughly.

He became aware that the squeaking of the cart had stopped, and glancing up he saw the old woman and the old man, softly speaking in low tones. Then, the old woman slowly walked back toward him carrying a burlap bag. He pointed the gun at her, but she ignored it and continued coming.

Reaching him at last, she held his eyes for a moment and handed him the sack. He heard her softly say, "*Vaya con Dios.*"

Seemingly without fear, she made her feeble way back to the cart where her husband waited. In a moment, they were gone. Brad opened the sack and looked inside. Fruit. Vegetables. Tortillas and dried meat. A quarter of a sack full. Reaching inside, he pulled out a large carrot and ate it. Then, another. Finally, he huddled beneath the tree again and stared after the old couple for a long time.

Why would they do that? he asked himself. *There's enough food in this bag to feed an old couple like that for a week, and they were poor — this was probably all the food they had, too. Even after I threatened them. For all they knew, I was going to kill them both. Still, they gave me their food.*

Brad contemplated that for a long time, then rose and walked to the edge of the water. Slowly, he pulled one pistol from its holster, stared at it for a moment, then threw it as far as he could out into the water. Pulling the other one, he did the same with it. He watched the ripples the pistols made in the water, then returned to his horse and removed the rifle from its scabbard. He hesitated. *No, a rifle is a tool. At least it could be,* he thought. *A pistol is only for killing.* He'd keep the rifle.

Tying the burlap bag onto his saddle-horn, Brad mounted his horse and again looked toward the direction the old couple had traveled.

"*Vaya con Dios,*" he said softly. "Go with God."

With that, he turned his horse away from Gullytown and headed in a new direction — north.

Chapter Twenty-Six

"BILLY! BILLY, COME QUICK!" Gus Appleton shouted at him from a distance.

Billy Shaw watched Gus as he rode "full-tilt" in his direction. From the looks of Gus's horse, he'd ridden quite a distance. *This had better be important for old Gus to near-kill a good cow-pony over*, Billy fumed, dropping his branding iron back into the fire.

"Billy!" Gus said breathlessly as he reined up beside him in a cloud of dust. "They arrested Joe Walker. They say he killed someone and they're taking him to Fort Worth to hang!"

Billy felt a chill settle over him as he heard the words. It couldn't be true; Joe had been out there for years. How could they do that after all these years? He couldn't let that happen to Joe. "When are they taking him to Fort Worth?"

"Sometime tomorrow. Even got an Army escort. Said he was real dangerous. Can you believe that? Joe Walker, dangerous?" Gus sounded bewildered.

"They've just made a mistake, Gus," Billy told him. "I'll ride to Fort Worth tomorrow, straighten it out, and bring him back with me."

Billy spurred his mount and headed toward the K/D at a gallop. Skidding to a halt in front of the large ranch house, he bounded to the ground and ran into the house, even before the horse fully stopped. Kate heard her son as he hit the front door and ran up the stairs to his room. Following behind him anxiously, she found Billy rolling a change of clothing into his saddle-bags, then picking up Stump Henry's old rifle, turn toward the door.

"Where are you going, Billy D.?" Kate said in a voice that matched her usual state of mind whenever she called him by that title.

Quickly, Billy repeated what Gus Appleton had related to him just a short time before, as he continued preparing for his journey. "…and I've got to get to Odessa before they take him out of there for Fort Worth," Billy concluded.

Kate knew of the closeness that had sprung up between her son and the foreman during the past few months. She didn't know exactly what had transpired between them, but whatever it had been, Billy and Joe had been as close as a father and son ever since. So she judiciously hesitated to tell her son that he couldn't go. Instead, she said, "Billy, do you think it's wise that you ride off alone to Odessa. What if they've already gone? Do you then follow on to Fort Worth?"

"Mom, I intend to go wherever I have to, and to do whatever I have to, to get Joe Walker back to the K/D."

Billy placed his hands on his mother's shoulders, making Kate realize just how much taller Billy was then she, and how much he'd grown and filled out recently. Looking his mother in the eyes, he said, "Joe's a good man and if we don't stand up for good men and take care of our own, then what've we got?"

Kate had no answer, but it was plain young Billy Shaw was no longer a boy. Somehow, over just the past few months, he'd turned into a man. She looked deeply into his eyes, she saw the iron will and determination of his father. Suddenly understanding completely, she wrapped her arms around him and drew him close. "Take care Billy, and come back safely to me and the girls. I love you."

Billy kissed her cheek, smiled briefly, and was gone.

He rode hard and fast, but by the time he reached Odessa, the Army escort had already departed for Fort Worth. Billy stopped briefly at Mr. Henderson's general store, putting some trail supplies on the ranch account, ate a full meal at the hotel restaurant, then headed on for Fort Worth at a gallop. As he rode, he thought of his mother, Aunt Bethena, and his sisters, missing them already. Then his mind shifted to thoughts of old Joe Walker, sitting alone in a cold, lonely jail cell waiting to be hung. Billy thought to himself, That's not going to happen. I won't let it!

As the endless miles droned on between Odessa and Fort Worth, Billy's mind wandered back over the story Walker had shared with him about his past as the famous hired gunfighter, English Bob. He remembered the numerous times he'd taken Stump Henry's Colt out to the river bank and Joe had showed him how to increase his speed and accuracy. Billy could tell by Joe's expression and comments, that he was impressed by his pupil's rapidly improving abilities with the Colt. Billy also knew that only a gunfighter would know all the things that Joe Walker had taught him about shooting.

He remembered the day he'd strapped on the Colt and shown up at the usual spot expecting another lengthy practice session, only to find Joe Walker with two very limber fishing rods over his saddle.

"A lad must learn the art of fly-fishing if he is to be a man," Joe said, rigging up his pole. "Get the other one, lad, and do as I do."

At first, Billy couldn't seem to get the knack of it, hooking everything from trees to roots. But finally, with Joe's help and hours of tiresome casting, Billy finally kept the line in the water. On the second day, he even caught a small fish. Day after day, Billy kept whirling the line around and around his head, flicking it at a spot on the water until he thought his arms would fall off. But he kept trying, because he wanted Joe to think well of him. At some point, he even began to enjoy it.

Over the next few weeks, a session of shooting would automatically be followed by an hour of fly-fishing. Kate, who was the recipient of their catches, never considered their hours together as anything to be concerned about. Billy, gifted with great hand-eye coordination, had become as proficient as his instructor at shooting and only slightly lagged him in fly-fishing by the time Gus brought him the alarming news of Joe's arrest. Now, tears stinging his eyes, Billy rushed toward Fort Worth to save his mentor from the gallows. Joe Walker, was as close to him as his own father had been.

* * *

Kate watched until her son rode out of sight towards Odessa. She sensed someone behind her and knew Beth had come up.

"Where's Billy going?"

Beth was doing much better lately, and Kate knew it was largely due to the way Billy handled the situation. That's why she hesitated to tell her sister the truth about Billy's trip. But at that moment, she remembered how Roosevelt used to say, "Bad news don't git better with age."

Drawing a deep breath, she began telling Bethena the "bad news." All-in-all, Kate thought, Beth took the fact that Billy wouldn't be there to protect her for a while, pretty well. Oh, not that it actually thrilled her, but Kate could see that her sister's attempts to relegate her problems to those of another person who also had problems, was just her way to demonstrate she was doing her part to get better. Still, Kate vowed, every night Billy was gone she would have one of the vaqueros sit on the water tower where Billy always stood guard so Beth could see his silhouette.

* * *

Much farther south, Jim Packard, near a state of exhaustion, held the reins of his horse in his limp hands and slumped in the saddle. He watched as J.D. McCain rapidly climbed the steep ridge next to the trail where they stopped to rest, "to check our back-trail," he'd told Jim.

How did I ever think that old man wouldn't be up for the rigors of this chase? he asked himself for the tenth time. *If I had to climb that hill right now or die, I'd be a dead man. And just look at that old bastard go. He's like a mountain goat. He'll be down here kicking my ass to get mounted in a few minutes and I'll have to tell him to just leave me here,* Jim thought wearily. *I'll stay here and sleep for a little while, then I'll catch up. He'll understand.*

Sure, Packard thought dryly, *you bet he'll understand. In a pig's eye. If I can't go on, he'll probably up and shoot me like he did Moses. What the hell am I doing here, anyway?*

Jim remembered how he'd watched Poe and the others ride off two nights before, taking the body of the little girl with them. He also remembered how he'd climbed back to the top of that wretched mountain once more with McCain to find Moses Penny. Jim Packard had been scared, but he'd also been mad. Angry that Wes Tanner's little girl had to die — angry that he had to kill other men — angry that Moses Penny, whom he'd come to respect as he had few other men, was captured and maybe dead.

When Legends Lived

The previous night when he'd finally gotten back to the top of the mountain, McCain had been lying in the spot they'd vacated earlier, which overlooked the Comanche camp. Packard, breathing hard, had plopped down beside McCain who ignored him and stared intently at the village. It was lighter by then and movement could be seen in the camp below, but it was clear the Comanches were being cautious as they began to stir around. Convinced that whomever had attacked them was long gone by now, Rain Maker could be heard giving orders to his men. A bright glow in the east indicated it would be morning soon, and that worried Jim Packard to no end.

"I don't see Moses down there, do you?" he'd softly said to McCain, more to feel the comfort of another human's voice than for any other reason.

McCain was no comfort. Fixing his hard eyes on the camp below, he remained silent.

They saw a large group of Indians heading toward the area that Rain Maker had used earlier for his council site. Jim jerked with a start. It was Moses! They were carrying him by his arms, dragging his feet in the dust. As his feet hit bumps in the ground, Jim saw them flop around wildly. He felt as if he would be sick.

My God! No, he thought, as gorge rose in his throat. McCain didn't move, and remained silent.

"They broke his legs and feet," Jim whispered hoarsely.

Still, McCain lay stone still. Grabbing his arm, Jim whispered more loudly, "Don't you see what they've done? They busted up his legs!"

"Let go of me," McCain had responded softly, fixing his cold gray eyes on Packard, who dropped his hand from the ranger's knotted arm as if it were suddenly hot. "I see, all right. That's what they usually do when they can't spare anyone to guard a prisoner. It's so their prisoners can't escape until they're ready to deal with 'em."

Watching McCain crawling up the side of the peaked hill to check their back trail, Packard remembered the previous evening, nearly becoming sick again. He'd laid in the darkness beside McCain, watching from afar as the Comanches tied Moses's hands over his head to a large post sunk into the ground, pulling until his feet were a good eighteen inches off the ground. Then a well-muscled Indian in a breech-cloth brought an armful of small twigs and placed them under the soles of Moses's bare feet. He looked expectantly at Rain Maker who stood silently for a minute, and then nodded.

Jim moaned softly, "Do something, Captain. Do *anything.* They're going to burn his feet off like they did Bloody Bill's!"

Jim had watched in horror as the breech-clothed brave tapped his flint once, knelt closer and then blew gently on the spark. Within seconds the twigs began burning and Moses rapidly moved his feet the length of the rope, to escape the heat. The watching men knew the movement would do no good, for the fire started to glow brighter.

Vividly, he recalled how he'd nearly jumped out of his skin as he realized that Moses was staring right at them! *He knows we're there*, he had thought to himself. He had seen Moses silently staring up at them, his eyes seemingly pleading.

In one swift movement, McCain had brought the Sharps to his shoulder and shot his friend through the head.

The report had made Packard nearly jump out of his skin, but the effect on the Indians was worse. Instantly, they'd started running toward the cliff wall where the two men were hiding.

When Legends Lived

The report of the large caliber Sharps boomed regularly, as more and more bodies lay on the valley floor. Jim knew his Winchester wouldn't reach the targets, and could do nothing at that moment but watch as McCain chopped the exposed Indians down.

Many of them had made it to the brush-line, out of McCain's sight — except for Rain Maker, who stood in the middle of the village and stared defiantly up at their position. McCain stared down at the chief and for a moment Jim waited for him to shoot the Indian so they could be gone. He knew the ones who'd made it safely to the brush-line would be climbing frantically up the wall toward them.

McCain had just nodded and suddenly lowered the rifle, stared for a moment longer at Rain Maker, then turned to Jim. "We best be going, boy. That is, 'less you hope to be invited to supper."

Before he'd even finished speaking, Jim had already been leading the way, headed down the steep slope at a dead run. They'd traveled no more than two hundred yards when they heard the Comanches hit their old position at the crest of the ridge. That was when Jim knew they were in real bad trouble and redoubled his efforts and his speed. He fell down the last thirty-five feet of the sloping hill-side, coming to rest at the bottom in an avalanche of dirt and debris. McCain had already reached and untied the horses, mounted, and was holding Jim's reins out to him when Jim got to the horses. Breathless, he barely had time to mount, with the fleeting thought that McCain probably wasn't even human — and probably didn't even know who his parents were — when the ranger put spurs to his horse and raced down the trail.

Jim, rode, doubled over the saddle-horn, his heart pounding wildly, trying to keep McCain in sight. He saw McCain fire from the hip, hitting one warrior in mid-flight as he jumped from the top of a large rock. McCain turned swiftly in the saddle and fired behind them twice more. Jim didn't look to see who his target was, as he tried to maintain as small a target of himself as humanly possible. He certainly wasn't going to fire his gun and draw attention to himself. Feeling caught between McCain's ruthless drive and savage hate of the Comanches, Packard had somehow hung on as they were pursued for the next six hours in a hectic race for survival.

Now, watching his tormentor climb up the small mound where he'd gone to check their back trail, it seemed that McCain's ruthlessness had momentarily won out. But not without a price, for Jim Packard felt as though he couldn't continue to ride for another minute.

Exhausted, he watched as McCain crested the small hill and observed in every direction. When McCain came back down, he'd tell him he would go no further; he just wanted to rest. Then, hearing a shout, he looked to see McCain running down the hill, waving his arms and pointing back the direction they'd just come. He yelled something about Indians, and Packard was already in the saddle by the time McCain reached him. Once more, they spurred their horses into a run. However, they had only been running them for about fifteen minutes, when McCain suddenly brought his animal to a gradual walk. Confused, Jim reined in beside him and saw McCain point to a man waving to them from the tree line. It was Fish.

"There's our bunch," he said.

Jim made as to spur ahead. "We've got to warn them about the Indians coming!"

When Legends Lived

"Ain't no Indians coming," McCain said. "I lost them yesterday morning."

"What do you mean, you lost them *yesterday*? They've been chasing us for two days and they're right behind us now. You said so!" Jim shouted at him.

"Have you seen any Indians since we rode out of the canyon back at the village?"

Jim was stunned, as the realization slowly spread through him. "You mean to tell me there weren't no Indians after us all that time?" His voice had gotten low and dangerous now. "Why did you lie to me, McCain?"

"'Cause, you'd have laid down on me and died, if you'd knowed there wasn't anybody back there. As it was, you damn near did anyway," McCain said, walking his horse toward Fish who was coming to meet them.

Packard was so tired he literally ached all over. "I'd kill you McCain, if I wasn't so damned tired. Maybe after I rest up some," he said wearily. "If I did, the others would probably give me a medal."

"I wouldn't be at all surprised," McCain agreed.

Upon their arrival, Poe and the others built a small but adequate breastwork of wind fall and dead timber, of which there seemed to be plenty in the area. They kept the horses inside of the enclosure for safekeeping and posted a twenty-four hour guard for protection from surprise attacks by the Indians. The three women Britt Johnson rescued sat removed from the others, and whispered sporadically between themselves. They seemed frightened of the other men, with the exception of Britt Johnson.

Soon after the camp's defenses were finished, Wes Tanner had walked to a small grassy area under some big trees and dug a small grave. Then, he returned to his daughter's body and prepared her for burial. The women picked wild flowers along the river bank and made bouquets, while Poe provided a clean blanket and canvas in which to wrap the body. Awaiting McCain and Packard's arrival, the group solemnly began the sad ceremony of burying the little girl.

"I'm sorry, Honey," her father choked as he stood over the tiny grave, scattering a handful of sandy soil over the wrapped object. "I would've liked to take you back and place you beside your mother for resting." He cleared his throat and went on, "I know you'll find each other though, so wait for me, too. I won't be long." He paused for a minute, then said, "I love you as much as any father ever loved his daughter. I'll never forget you."

He coughed once more and walked away, head down, shoulders sloping. With a heaviness of heart not felt for many years, the others watched the grieving man leave, then covered the small grave.

* * *

That evening sitting around the small fire, Jim Packard wrote in his journal and observed those around him. The three women sat huddled off to one side, saying little, except to each other. The youngest, named Sally Brody, was a slender woman of perhaps twenty-five. Britt had told them she had a family somewhere north of Fort Worth. Ever since her rescue she'd had a crooked little smile permanently stamped into her pretty face, like she might burst right out laughing at any moment. A closer look into the woman's beautiful dark eyes, however, revealed a trapped hysteria lying just beneath the surface. Packard wondered if she'd be able to be a mother, or for that matter, a wife, ever again.

When Legends Lived

Ester Abrams, a bookish spinster with sharp chiseled features, was the hardest to read. She seldom looked up, and when she did, it was to cast furtive glances in every direction as if someone, or something, was ready to pounce. She mumbled constantly to herself, or to the other women — or worse, to others not present. Occasionally, she picked up sticks or rocks, and hit herself on the fingers until they bled — always muttering to herself.

Packard suspected she was praying, but each time he drew near, the third woman stood and stared at him with her button-like eyes, as though daring him to advance any closer. She was Obie Zuma, a large black woman, who'd been a warrior princess of the vast Zulu nation, until she'd been sold into slavery at the age of nineteen. Packard had no doubt she could rip his head from his body with little effort, and toss it into the river, absent of any remorse. In fact, Brett Johnson was the only man in camp allowed to approach the women for any reason, then only to provide food or comfort items.

As for the other men, they drank coffee, tossed barbs back and forth and awaited their supper. Jim turned his attention to them and observed quietly. As he understood it, Fish had volunteered to cook throughout the entire expedition because of Poe's devious plan to miss his rotation in the cooking process. Poe had read him a story about a famous French chef, Marie-Antoine Careme, loved and admired by half of Europe for his culinary masterpieces. The story had exceeded Poe's wildest expectations, for it aroused Fish's creative juices and he became particularly intrigued by recipes pictured in the book.

He immediately volunteered to cook for the duration of the chase and soon began surprising them with various exotic dishes which the others now blamed on Poe. Sensing the others' wrath, and fed up with Fish's creative cooking even more than the prospects of having to rejoin his rotation as cook, Poe subtlety attempted to discourage Fish from his gourmet "delights" by bragging about his standard fare of "plain ol' biscuits and bacon." But the damage had been done, and Fishburn seemed determined to be "loved and admired" for his new cooking abilities. If not by "half of Europe," then at least by those present. Lately, Poe and the others had replaced subtlety with outright insults and veiled threats, but with little effect.

That night he had, once again, concocted an artistic, though somewhat suspect presentation, and was apparently quite pleased with himself. He'd proudly announced that supper was being "served" almost twenty minutes earlier, and still the others delayed, drinking coffee, and quietly ignoring the urging of their "chef " to try his latest creation. Finally, with a wide encouraging smile, Fish dished up a large tin plate of the mixture and handed it to Poe, who grimaced and reluctantly accepted the offering. The others held their collective breath as Rosie hesitantly tasted a tentative sample, then smiling broadly at the others, smacked his lips, nodded his head appreciatively, and dug-in.

Starved by then, the others hurriedly filled their plates and also dug in. After a few hurried bites, their smiles turned to frowns and then grimaces as they realized they'd been had. They stared daggers at Poe, who sat smiling, his plate still full to the brim.

"What do ya call this here stuff?" Poe said to Fish, innocently.

Fish beamed at the group. "This is 'Fish' stew. I named it after myself because I made it with the fish I caught earlier," he announced proudly. "It's made with leeks, tortillas…'cause I didn't have any 'taters'…and a delicate wine sauce." He looked smug as he continued, "'Course, I had to use wild onions instead o'leeks and a shot of that sour-mash whisky, instead o'wine, but Antoine Careme said all great chefs had to learn how to substitute when necessary. How do ya like it?"

Jake looked as if he just swallowed a frog. "This stuff would gag a maggot," he said truthfully.

"It may be even worse than that," Britt Johnson followed up bluntly, spitting a mouthful onto the ground.

The three women who apparently had learned to eat almost anything while captives of the Comanches, continued to shovel food mechanically into unsmiling mouths. Wes Tanner, who hadn't eaten much since his daughter's death, sat looking on.

"The ladies seem to like it all right," Fish pointed out defensively.

"Well, when you ain't had nothing but dog and mule for a month, you can eat about anything," Britt told him with a frown.

Packard actually found it to be not too bad. *At least it's not tortillas and beans,* he thought as he ate. He realized the playful insults over Fish's cooking were only the way the men coped with the horrid events of the past few days.

Poe set his full plate on the ground near his foot and leaned back against a tree. "I was just wondering," he said thoughtfully. "Has anyone seen that old pair of 'long-johns' I wore all last winter? I seem to have misplaced them."

Injured beyond belief, Fish filled another plate, all the while looking resentfully at those around the circle, then apparently still deeply hurt, walked away from the fire with the plate of food. As soon as he was out of sight the others chuckled softly, collectively picked up their plates and began to eat with relish.

Fish found Captain McCain seated a short distance from the main group, as was his custom. He handed the plate to McCain who silently accepted it, and watched as his leader began to eat.

Sensing something was on Fish's mind, McCain said, "Sit a spell."

At which Fish sat cross-legged nearby on the ground.

"Everything going well with you, Mr. Fishburn?" he said, continuing to eat.

"It's going well, Captain," Fish answered. "I just miss Bluebonnet some."

Wondering how anyone could be homesick for the burned, dusty patch of land Bluebonnet had turned into since the drought, McCain said, "Well, it's home, I guess."

"The nearest thing to home I ever had," Fish told him. "As soon as it rains again, it'll be just like it was when we first went there. Those bluebonnets were sure pretty, Captain."

McCain, eating, merely grunted, not looking up.

"Captain?" Fish said. McCain grunted again and Fishburn continued. "Do ya suppose it hurt Moses to die that way? I mean, I'd hate to think it caused him a lot of pain."

McCain looked up, continued to chew his food thoughtfully and, looked a little sad. "I think Moses was thankful we was there to help him travel. He had to know it was better that way than what the Comanches planned for him over the next few days."

Fish, who'd never been a deep thinker, mulled over what his leader just told him. After a while, he said, "Moses was a good man, wasn't he, Captain?" He could plainly see the deep sadness in his Captain's eyes, and hear it in his soft words.

"Yes, Fish. He was a good man and a good Ranger. Had he been any other color, he would've worn the star. Maybe some day, folks will be able to look beyond the color of a man's skin and see what's inside."

He sat for a time without talking and Fish quietly stood up, waiting to be dismissed. McCain handed him his nearly empty plate. "That was good food, Mr. Fishburn," he said.

Beaming, Fish strutted back to the fire.

Twenty-Seven

"He who lives more lives than one, must die as many deaths."
—"Irish" Joe Walker

BILLY SHAW ARRIVED IN Fort Worth in early afternoon, and went immediately to the jail. The outer office was empty, but he saw a pair of cold black eyes peering from beneath the brim of a matching black flat-crowned hat, through a small window in another door with heavy iron bars on it.

"I'm Billy Shaw, here to see Joe Walker," he said.

"You probably mean 'English Bob,'" the gray eyes answered.

"His name's Walker. Let me in," Billy said firmly.

"You'll have to give up your Colt before we let you in, young man," he was told.

Billy unhitched his gun-belt and laid it on a table in the outer office. The act was immediately followed by a loud metallic sound as the barred door was unlocked, letting him into the main cell block area. Three deputies armed with pistols and double-barreled shotguns met him.

"He's in the last cell on the right," a tall lanky deputy with a drooping mustache and hard black eyes told him.

Billy walked back to the designated cell and waited for his eyes to adjust to the dark shadows.

"Well lad, tis a fine fix ye find me in," said the familiar brogue, softly. "Ye should'na come, though. T'would be best if ye had'na seen me this way."

"I'm here to get you out, Joe," Billy said. "They've got no right to lock you up like this and threaten to hang you."

"Oh, but they do, lad. They do. In another life, I did things for which a hundred hangings would not make up for. It so happens that for this particular one, I didn't do it though. Ironic, wouldn't you say?"

"When do they plan to do it, Joe?"

"Three days, lad. If it was my choice, it'd be today. I'm not afraid of it you see, but it's the waiting that's the hardest," his mentor said.

"I'm going to Austin to see the Governor. Oran Roberts was a friend of my father's. Dad helped to get him elected Governor, twice. He can pardon you," Billy said.

Joe sat for a time without answering. Then he said, "Aye lad, t'would be nice to get out of this cage once more. But I'm afraid public opinion is against us. The Gov'nor, like as not, with this being an election year and all, will wash his hands of me, and since your father can't help him anymore, wash his hands of you, as well."

Billy stared back, not knowing what to say.

Walker looked at Billy a little sadly. "Don't waste your time, me young friend, you'll only taint your own life by rubbing up against people like me." Joe walked closely up to the bars in front of him, nearer to Billy. "I'm resolved to the fact that the end of this life is upon me. You on the other hand, have a long and productive life ahead. I've no family of me own, but I like to think of the Thompson's as if they were mine." The older man hesitated. "I've no right to say it lad, but I'm as proud of you as if you were my own. You'll be a fine man and a credit to your father's memory."

"I'm leaving now, Joe. I figure I can just make it to the Governor in time for him to send a telegraph back to stay the hanging — if I leave now," Billy said.

"Look at you, lad. You've been in the saddle for a week. You need rest. Don't kill yourself for a lost cause," Walker implored.

"I'm leaving. Is there anything I can get for you, before I go?" Billy said again, determined.

Joe Walker sighed deeply. "You always were a headstrong young stallion, lad. Guess that's what I liked 'bout you from the first. Okay then, go with my blessing. Just remember, if it don't turn out the way you would've hoped, don't blame anyone and don't let it turn you bitter. Accept it as just the way life is and try to make it better, if you can. Promise me, lad?"

"I promise, Joe. But I'm gonna make it there in time, and you're going back to the ranch with me." He was gone before Joe could argue any more.

Joe Walker stood looking at the spot where Billy had stood, for a long time. Then, eyes misty, he walked back to the bunk and lie down on it, folding his arms behind his head. Then he smiled softly.

* * *

Bethena was proud of the fact that she hadn't had one of her awful nightmares in the past two weeks, especially with Billy gone — not one. But it had taken a special effort on her part, and she still hadn't outgrown her fear that the man with the scar across his face would someday be back for her. She was convinced he'd be back. She simply knew it, as sure as she knew the sun came up in the east and set in the west. It was only a matter of time. Beth also knew — in spite of the fact that Kate assured her over and over again that Scar had no further interest in her — that when he did come back, she would kill herself before she let him get his hands on her. Bethena shivered suddenly, picked up her brush and began to slowly stroke it through her hair.

Kate had been so understanding since the abduction, concerning her situation. The whole family had been, but especially, her sister. She felt badly for Kate. Saddled with the children to raise on her own, and now with her 'illness', Kate had little time to lead a life of her own. There was that nice rancher who had come by several times recently, Beth remembered. He clearly had eyes for Kate, but so far, her sister put him off.

It's that damned Jericho McCain, she thought. *First, he took our brother from us, then he took Kate.* Oh sure, he hadn't actually come and carried her away, but he had taken Kate away from her as surely as though he physically had been here. Beth realized she wasn't being entirely fair, but Kate was her sister and she'd stood by and watched as Kate literally wasted her life waiting for that killer, Jericho McCain, to return for her.

Now, Rosie Poe is another matter entirely, Beth thought. She'd harbored a crush on Roosevelt Poe since she was a little girl. She knew that's all it was, just a crush. She still loved Rosie though, as much as any woman could love a brother. That's probably what it was, she thought. Rosie had somehow taken the place of her dead brother. Suddenly, her thoughts shifted to James Packard. Bethena paused halfway through a stroke of brushing her hair, as she remembered the way his dark eyes had devoured her the first time they met. Not only that, but she remembered the way her body had responded to his looks.

Could've had time to get to know one another, and could've

found time to be alone for a while. In her mind, they were on some shady stream bank, lying in the cool grass. Jim was holding her in his arms and kissing her deeply. Bethena felt her body growing warm as her active imagination carried her along in its passion. Except for the tragic event with those outlaws, no man had touched her since she came to live at the ranch, and Bethena missed the intimacy of a man's love. At that moment, in her imagination, she actually felt Jim Packard's hands upon her body and felt his kisses as she responded to the abandonment of her imagined lover's passion.

Bethena moaned softly as she imagined the touch of her phantom lover's skin next to her body and stared into his eyes as she awaited his entry, with heated anticipation. She melted, seeing Jim Packard smile sweetly at her, as he stared down into her face. A hideous scar suddenly formed on his cheek as he took on the swarthy form of an evil man with a jagged scar running the length of his face. Bethena screamed loudly. Hysterically, over and over, she continued to scream. She was unaware of Kate and the girls as they ran into the room attempting to calm her. Then, after almost five minutes of the terrible screams, Beth suddenly stopped as though in a trance, and docilely allowed Kate to lead her to her bed, where she laid staring at that awful place once more, that only she could see.

Kate sent her daughters away to play and remained for a time with her sister. Deeply concerned, she watched as Bethena stared at the wall as though in a deep trance, then, Bethena slept. Kate quietly rose, covered her sister with a sheet and left the room. She'd seemed to be doing so well, especially with Billy was gone. They *all* needed Billy home. Kate missed her son terribly and began to worry because she'd expected him back by then. She would give it a few more days, then maybe ride into Odessa and send out a few telegrams to people she knew to attempt to find out what was going on with Joe Walker's situation.

* * *

They hung Joe Walker the fourth day after Billy Shaw rode out of Fort Worth to see Governor Roberts, but Billy wasn't to learn of it until much later. Upon arriving in Austin, Billy briefly saw the Governor of Texas, his father's old friend, twice, but both times the Governor seemed in a hurry to be someplace else. Becoming desperate, Billy finally barged into the Governor's office during a meeting despite efforts by the staff to discourage him. The Governor was furious.

"Young man, must I inform you that I am the Governor of Texas, and this isn't some roadhouse you can force your way into whenever you feel the urge!" Governor Roberts remanded him indignantly.

"I *know* you're the Governor, that's why I came to you. They're going to hang the K/D's foreman, Joe Walker. He's been with us for more than fifteen years and has surely more than made up for any harm he may have caused before he came to us. You're the only one who can save a man from the gallows. Sir, you knew my father, Duncan Shaw; that's why I came to you for help," Billy said.

"Shaw. Duncan Shaw, yes I believe I did meet him a time or two...owns a ranch out by Odessa doesn't he? But no matter, it's out of my hands now. I can't help you," said Roberts.

Billy was infuriated! "Governor Roberts, you didn't just meet my father a few times, you've known my father for twenty years. You've been to our ranch numerous times, ate at our table! My father pulled strings twice to get you elected to this office. Had it not been for finances provided by the K/D and other ranches like it, you'd still be running a bankrupt little law practice like you were before my father and others put you in this palace!"

The Governor's face turned crimson as the other men in the room stirred uncomfortably. "You get out of here, this instant, young man, or I'll call someone to throw you out. I don't intend to let that murdering English Bob walk a free man. He'll hang as scheduled, and the people of Texas will know their governor will provide them safety from these animals while I am in this office."

Billy glared back hotly at the man, then said softly, "The K/D is still one of the wealthiest spreads in the state, and I'm running the Shaw ranch now. So, don't you expect any more help with your election campaign, Governor. From what I hear, you're going to have trouble gaining enough support to even make a run at it. I can tell you this: The considerable support the K/D now provides to you, will go to whomever can unseat you from this office!" With that, Billy Shaw turned on his heel and departed.

An older, white-bearded man slowly rose to his feet and picked up his cane. After staring at Roberts for a full minute, he finally said, "Being the one responsible for putting you in this office, whenever I see one of your demonstrations of considerable stupidity like the one I have just witnessed, I worry that I made a tremendous mistake."

He walked from the room without looking back. The other four men in the Governor's meeting hastily rose, and avoiding the Governor's eyes, rushed out. Roberts, stared after them, a worried expression forming on his face.

When Legends Lived

* * *

Billy Shaw hurried directly to the telegraph office after leaving the Governor's office, where he sent a wire to Hugh Underwood, a prominent Fort Worth attorney whom his father had used a number of times to conduct legal business for the K/D. The telegram stated:

SEND LATEST ON WALKER SITUATION. STOP.
GOV NO HELP. STOP.
WAITING ANSWER. STOP.
TRY TO STALL EXECUTION. STOP.
BDS

Billy found a small place nearby to eat and returned a short time later to find his reply. It was from Hugh Underwood.

THEY HUNG JOE THIS MORNING. STOP.
GOV PUSHED UP DATE YESTERDAY. STOP.
SORRY BILLY. STOP.
HU

Billy carefully folded the slip of paper and put it in his shirt pocket. He walked out of the telegraph office with the knowledge that Governor Roberts knew Joe Walker had already been hanged, when he went to his office. The calmness of Billy's face betrayed none of the turbulence raging within, as he mounted his horse and somehow found the road back to Fort Worth. He would retrieve Joe Walker's body and take it back to the ranch for burial.

Billy rode for about an hour, looking neither left nor right.

R.C. Morris

The sun had slowly moved half-way across the afternoon sky and he was well away from the city, when he finally dismounted and sat beneath a large tree at the side of the trail, leaving his horse to graze nearby. Feeling helpless and alone, Billy Shaw wrapped his arms around his knees, hugged them to his chest, and placing his head on folded arms, wept bitterly.

Twenty-Eight

AL HAWKINS WATCHED THE lone figure as he made his way on foot across the flat dusty plateau, extending around the five buildings that made up his farm. He leaned against the adobe wall he'd built around the only natural spring within a hundred miles, and studied the stranger as he moved closer. He could make him out pretty well, now. The man carried a Winchester rifle and an old burlap bag that seemed half-filled. Perhaps his only possessions, Hawkins thought. As he got closer, Al observed the stranger was a young man with a noticeable limp, and extremely filthy.

"Looks like you could use a drink of water and some food," Hawkins called out to him.

At first the young man attempted to speak, then merely nodded his head. Al held out a cup of cool water from the fresh bucket he'd drawn when it was clear the stranger was headed his way, which the boy gulped down without stopping.

"Easy does it, boy," he said. "There's plenty, but you don't want to drink it too fast or you're likely to get the trots."

Finding his voice now that he'd had a drink, the young man said, "Thanks, Mister. I sure thought I was finished until I saw your place. Still could've been, if you was someone that didn't like strangers." The young man's face clouded darkly as though something from his past had just flashed through his mind. "That's happened to me, too."

"Well, you won't find that around here, young man. You can

stay for as long as you want, work for your keep, of course, and leave whenever you feel fit to travel again. We ask no questions here at the Farm," Al told him as he led the younger man toward the largest of the buildings. A tall, handsome woman, her hair rolled up into a bun, walked out to meet them. She smiled as she approached and Al waved to her.

"I'm Al Hawkins and this is my wife Sara. What do we call you?" he said.

The young stranger started to answer, hesitated, and then said, "Bart Thomas. From Omaha."

"Well, Bart Thomas from Omaha. It's a long way from Omaha to Oklahoma. Did ya walk all the way?" Sara said, extending her hand as a man might.

"No ma'am. I used to have a horse, but he up and died on me, just outside Lawton. What's the name of this place?" Bart said, taking her cool hand.

"Shawnee. Will you be joining us for supper?" Sara had a deep pleasant voice.

"I surely would be obliged, Mrs. Hawkins, if I can do something to earn it," Bart said.

"There'll be plenty of time for that later. Al, why don't you show Mr. Thomas where he can wash up before supper," she said over her shoulder, as she walked back toward the large house.

"Follow me, Bart," Al told him as they started toward a small building which was close beside what appeared to be a barn.

The young stranger looked around at the extremely neat and clean farm. The crops in the fields and garden didn't have a single weed in them. The fence and the barn — everything, was white-washed. Then he saw the children. There must've been a

When Legends Lived

dozen of them, mostly Indian and Mexican, but a few white children also. They'd been hiding in the barn until they were sure of him.

"What kind of place is this, anyway?" he said in wonder. "An orphanage, or something?"

Al poured some water into a large basin and handed him a thick bar of soap. "Something like that. It didn't start out as such, though. Sara and me wanted children of our own, but something happened. Don't rightly know if it's me or her that can't have 'em, but it don't make no difference now. We took in two babies several years ago and they just seemed to keep coming after that."

Al looked fondly at the children as they walked toward them. "I love every one of 'em. Wish I could afford to keep another dozen or two. Not that it makes any difference. If they come, we'll take 'em in."

"Bart Thomas," was introduced to all the children, ranging in age from two to sixteen years. A little dark-skinned girl about four years old flirted with him behind Al's back. The two eldest boys took him in hand and showed him his sleeping quarters, a small, sparsely furnished room of his own in the back part of the main house. Brad "Bart Thomas" Thompson, finally slept soundly that night. It was the first time in months.

* * *

Scar and Three-Finger Ned remained in the shadows of the scrub-oaks and watched as two of Scar's men crept toward the wood-chopper from two directions. They were nearly close enough now, Scar thought. He watched as Tommie Sees-Far jumped to his feet and rushed the man's back. The wood-chopper must've heard something, for he turned suddenly just as Tommie savagely stuck his knife into his stomach. Mortally wounded as he was, the powerfully-built wood-chopper still managed to bury the blade of his ax between the breastbones of Tommie. Instantly, Joe Smiling Bird, running from the opposite direction pushed his blade deeply between the wood-chopper's broad shoulders. As the big man fell to his knees, he reached behind him and grabbed Joe Bird's leg, pulling him to the ground. Groaning loudly, the wood-chopper rolled onto Joe Bird, wrapped his big hand around the half-breed's throat, locked his fingers and started to die.

Joe's face had already turned blue and he'd ceased struggling when Scar, moving nonchalantly, finally reached them. Scar, stared into his man's pleading eyes for a long moment, then casually raised his pistol and blew out the wood-chopper's brains. Joe Bird rolled away and lay on his back gasping loudly, as he fought to draw air into his tortured lungs.

"Why…didn't you…help…me sooner?" Joe Bird finally got out.

Scar spit at his man, then snarled, "Hell, you think you can handle Poe?" he said. "You two pieces of dog dung couldn't even take this farmer," he snorted contemptuously. "You try to handle either of them old Rangers, and they'll eat you for dinner."

Scar kicked the dead man, turned and moved toward the one-room cabin.

The terrified young woman standing in the middle of the room grasped a tiny baby in her arms. Dark hair framed her pretty face and it was apparent she was numb with fear. Her only movement was as her dark eyes widened and fixed on the scar-faced man when he entered the door. Glancing around the room seemingly without interest, he reached the young woman in two large strides and savagely punched her in the stomach. A scream torn from the woman's throat was abruptly cut short, as the air left her lungs, and reacting naturally, she dropped the baby to the wood floor. Heaving violently, she fell beside the baby, where it kicked and screamed until Three-Finger Ned swooped it up by its feet and walked outside. The young mother heard her baby's screams as she attempted to suck air into her tortured lungs. Trying to regain her feet, she heard a sickening sound as something struck the cabin, and the screams suddenly ceased. Mercifully she fell unconscious.

* * *

Poe and McCain's band headed north back toward Laredo the day after burying the little Tanner girl. Reaching the Rio Grande River, McCain decided to make camp on the Mexican side, and cross the following morning. After another supper of one of Fish's surprises, which looked suspiciously like the one from the previous night and for which he suffered countless insults and threats from the others, Jim Packard sat upon on a rock, opened up his book, and entered the day's activities. Seeing McCain reclining a short distance from the others as usual, Packard stood and walked over.

"Evening, Captain McCain," he said respectfully.

"Mr. Packard," McCain acknowledged, looking up and nodding cordially.

Not having been invited to 'sit', Jim squatted on his heels, as he'd grown accustomed to doing since living around the Rangers. "Something has been bothering me ever since we left the

Comanche camp, Captain. I was wondering if I might ask you a question."

"There's nothing so dumb that someone hasn't probably already asked it. Ask away," McCain said. "But, I might not answer," he conceded, jerking his head toward a space on the ground.

Jim took that as a gesture which meant for him to take a seat, and sat down on a log nearby. He stared at the older man silently for a moment, then said, "You don't think very much of me, do you, Captain?"

McCain, seeming surprised by the question, squinted up at him. "Why, I don't think about you one way or the other," he said. "That your question?"

Jim was caught off guard for an instant, but remained undeterred. "No...no, that's not it. My question is this. When we were on the crest above the Indian's camp the last time, after you had...had shot Moses Penny, you had a chance to kill that Comanche Chief...Rain Maker, I believe you called him? But you didn't do it. Why, after all the hurt he's caused everybody, did you let him live?"

"He was out of range," McCain told him tartly.

"That's just a lot of bull, Captain McCain," Jim said with disgust, knowing he was "skating on thin ice" with such a line of talk to this particular man. "You shot a dozen of his warriors at the same range, so why not him?" he persisted.

McCain turned his granite eyes on Packard, silently observing him as if trying to decide something, then looked away at the horizon. "You wouldn't understand it," he said.

"Try me."

McCain continued to stare straight ahead without speaking

until Jim started to feel uncomfortable. Just as he was about to stand, McCain spoke.

"When me and Poe was with McNally, we chased Victorio into Mexico and killed him and sixty of his braves," he said. "Before that, we hunted down Santana and then Iron Shirt and killed them, too; them, and a lot more of their Comanche brothers."

McCain took the "makings" from his shirt pocket and held them in his hand absent-mindedly, without attempting to roll a cigarette. "Lone Wolf...he was the best of them all. It took us almost two years to catch up with him, but we finally did it. And when we did, we destroyed him and his whole bunch — men, women and kids — everybody." He sighed deeply, seeming moved by his lamenting. "Even killed their livestock and dogs."

McCain paused until Jim thought his explanation was finished, then went on. His voice dropping to almost a whisper. "After each one, I felt like something important in my life had ended. Like it was the end of one kind of life and the start of another." He hesitated, then said, "After we done Lone Wolf, I felt downright sad for the long runs we'd had in them days, almost as if I'd lost an old friend."

He appeared to think about that for a moment, then grunted to himself, as if just realizing that fact for the first time. "Rain Maker, he's the grandson of Quanta Parker...and he's the last of his kind. When he's gone, there'll be no more great war chiefs."

McCain, rolled a smoke from the makings he held in his lap, and lit up. Offering his makings to Jim, he seemed to unaccountably displeased when they were refused and Jim produced some of Poe's chaw instead, biting off a big piece. McCain took a deep puff, studied the tip of his smoke, then continued.

"Did you know there used to be millions of buffalo in this area? Now you can't find nary a one. I hear there're still a few up north in the Black Hills, scattered in a few places — though they're going fast, too."

Jim listened, unsure of where all that was going, yet unwilling to interrupt. McCain smoked in silence for awhile and said, "If you was out riding, been without food for a time and was real hungry, and say you came upon what you knew to be, the last remaining buffalo in the world. What would you do? Would you shoot it for food?"

McCain looked intently at him, waiting. Jim honestly didn't know if he had an answer, and didn't know if McCain even wanted one, so he remained silent. After a time, McCain went on. "That's how it was with Rain Maker. He was the last buffalo left in the world — and I just couldn't shoot him."

Jim silently watched as McCain pushed the cigarette butt into the soft soil and carefully covered it over like a miniature symbolic grave. His eyes suddenly moved away from the tiny grave and locked onto Packard's. "I told ya, you wouldn't understand," he said sadly.

Jim suddenly rose and looking down at the old ranger, stated, "I understand more than you think, Captain McCain. A lot more." Packard then moved back toward the main group, leaving McCain to his thoughts.

* * *

Since Moses Penny's death, McCain had been fighting off the first self-doubts he'd ever encountered — that, and the feeling his life was changing at such a rapid rate that he'd likely wake up tomorrow and find everything in it, different. He also felt as though his own end was drawing near. Not surprisingly, that thought held little fear for him. He'd lived with death for so many years that there was little mystery left about it. But it did make him think of Kate.

Katie. What a waste it's all been. If I hadn't been the kind of man I am, and things were different, maybe we'd have had a chance.

What would happen, he wondered, if he just saddled up and headed back to the K/D? Just chucked it all, and rode away? Asked Kate to marry him and really settle down at something?

Depression rolled over him like a heavy blanket, as he suddenly thought about a dark man with a jagged scar. No, those were all pipe-dreams. They'd never happen, and he was a fool to even think about it. What would happen, was his catching up with that baby killer, Scar — putting a round through his worthless head and hanging him up in a tree for the coyotes to eat. Then — and only then — could he die.

* * *

Looking back over his shoulder at the column of horses splashing across the shallow water of the Rio Grande River, Jim Packard could see little difference in the surrounding countryside. But once back inside the United States, he felt he could get right down on the ground and kiss it. Maybe, just maybe, he'd live through this, after all. The first thing he'd do when he got to Laredo would be to soak in a hot bathtub for two hours. Then have a steak. *Lord yes, a real steak.* According to Poe, they'd crossed the Rio about twenty miles west of Laredo and intended to head east, riding parallel to the border.

Poe had automatically assumed the chore of scouting for the party since losing Moses Penny, and they'd rode scarcely an hour when they saw him hastily returning. He slid his horse to a stop and yelled to McCain, "Buncha hombres headed this way. Maybe a dozen or so. All of 'em are well-armed."

McCain ordered his men to spread out into a small grove of trees beside the trail and pull their rifles. He rode out to the front with Poe, and together they waited for the unknown party of riders to arrive. The two elements spotted one another about the same time, and instantly on guard, the group's leader reined his mount suddenly to a halt. McCain cautiously rode forward to identify them.

Halting about two hundred feet in front of them, he shouted, "McCain, Texas Rangers, here. Who might you be?"

"Douglas Hopper, U.S. Marshall out of Waco," came the reply.

McCain carefully urged his horse forward until he recognized several men in the posse. "Howdy Marshal, what brings you into these parts?" he said.

"We got a telegram from the sheriff over at Del Rio, telling us that they'd some attacks by a bunch of renegades," Hopper relayed to him. "Wiped out three small farms. Two Mexican families and a white family slaughtered — one, just a baby. Carried off three women. Also wiped out a party of five railroad workers sent out to repair a bridge they'd damaged. Most of the dead were face-cut."

"Scar?"

"That's what they think," Hopper said. "Figured he might be headed back this way. Either that, or back into Mexico. Who ya got with you?" He craned his neck to look at the group waiting up the trail.

"We been chasing Rain Maker's bunch. They carried off four women 'bout a month ago. Followed 'em into Mexico and found his camp over on the Lampazos. Got three of the women back. One, the daughter of a man we got with us, died in the attack.

When Legends Lived

A man who calls himself Britt Johnson is with us too; he went into the camp and brought them out. Bravest thing I've ever seen."

"Nigger Britt? I've heard of him. Don't think I'd want to do that for a living."

"Will you be heading back toward Laredo or Waco in the near future, Marshal?" McCain said.

"I figure we were wrong about Scar coming this far east, so we'll be turning back tomorrow morning. Why? Need a favor?" Hopper said.

"I'd be obliged if you'd carry Britt Johnson and the three women back with you when you go. That would save us a trip to Laredo, and we could head on over toward Del Rio and see if we can cut Scar's trail over there," McCain told him.

"Be glad to. You want to camp together tonight and get a start in the morning?"

"Let's do it."

McCain led the group back to where Poe and the others were clustered. Jim Packard received the news about not going to Laredo with something less than grace. In fact, bemoaning this sudden turn of events, he became livid, and threw a small tantrum.

"That simple-minded old man is the meanest son-of-a-bitching-human-being whoever drew a mean-son-of-a-bitching-breath!" he fumed to Fishburn. "He just loves to be dirty and miserable — and he loves others to be dirty and miserable right along with him."

"I don't believe he loves to be dirty and miserable, his ownself," Fish disagreed mildly.

"Ah, but you agree that he loves for us to be dirty and miserable, right?" Jim pushed his point.

"Well, I think he just don't care if we're dirty and miserable, but I don't know as if he particularly likes it," said Fish.

"Ah...what's the use?" Jim said shaking his head disgustedly, and walked away to sulk.

Paying their farewells to Britt Johnson and the women the next morning, Britt shook hands all around and escorted the three women toward Hopper's group without a backward glance. Wes Tanner approached Poe and McCain and remarked he'd be leaving with the marshal as well — if it was all right with Captain McCain. It was plain he was concerned that McCain now knew his true identity, and yet wasn't entirely sure just how he would use that knowledge after now being joined by the U.S. Marshal.

"You take care of yourself, Mr. Holden," McCain said. "I feel sorrow for you — for what happened to your family — but I hope you can put it behind you and start over one more time."

"Thank you and your associates for what you tried to do, Captain. I'm truly indebted to you all for the rest of my life. If you ever need my help, call on me," he turned and mounted his horse.

They saw him wave as the group of horsemen traveled out of sight.

"That boy's got a heap o' troubles in his mind," Poe said, as he swigged from the brown bottle of laudanum that the doctor in San Antonio gave him. McCain could see it was nearly half empty.

McCain grunted, "All right, let's git mounted up."

"Come on girls, put your butts in the leather, we ain't on vacation here!" Poe shouted.

Within ten minutes they were back on the trail, and headed

When Legends Lived

west once more. Jim Packard rode alone at the rear of the short column, and fumed. He found himself riding just behind Poe and McCain, where he could hear their conversation as they talked about the path Scar was most likely to take, long-past runs after various outlaws and Indians, and Kate — the lady whom he'd met twice before.

Eventually their talk turned to the railroad's reward.

"A thousand a piece for breaking up the Reid gang," Poe was saying, "and a few hundred over that for hanging some other gents...and expenses...we got a pretty good nest egg built-up, already, Jericho."

"We haven't finished the job, yet," McCain reminded him. "There's still Scar to deal with."

"I *know* we ain't finished *yet*," Poe said exasperated. "Is that all you ever think about? This chase'n — shoot'n — hang'n business? It's just pitiful the narrow view you have of life, Jericho. What I *meant* was, that'd be another thousand a piece — when we do git him." Having said his piece, Poe chuckled.

McCain, trying not to encourage his talkative partner, rode along silently. Undaunted, Poe continued. "What'd ya gonna do with all that money, Jericho? You know what I'm gonna do with mine? First, I'm gonna visit Paco's. Ain't set my post in months, ya know?" He didn't wait for an answer, but went right on. "Then, I'm gonna buy all the ladies there a fine gift and pass them out when I git back." Poe chuckled to himself again, studying McCain intently from the corner of his eye, as if waiting for an explosion. When there was none, somewhat disappointedly, he continued. "Then I'm gonna buy some of them new 'windmill' thing-a-ma-jigs. Them things that Jim told us about? I'm gonna put them up all over the ranch. Then I'm gonna buy some prime cattle and stock the ranch. What-do-ya-think 'bout them apples, Jericho?" he said. "We'll be gentlemen ranchers, aye God," he said, pleased with his plan.

"You're going to do all that with a thousand dollars?"

"It'll be more than a thousand dollars. I figure all together, we'll have over four thousand after we track down Scar...maybe even five," Poe answered. "That's a piss-pot full o' money, partner, anyway you look at it."

"Oh, I see. You're counting the money I'm going to get, too," McCain said.

"Well sure. We're partners, ain't we?"

"Sometimes I wonder. Seems like you make most of the decisions for us."

"Well, okay, Jericho. Just what is it you want to do with your part of the money?" Poe said, stung by McCain's words.

Thinking for a moment, McCain said, "Probably buy some more horses, build a better bunk house, bank the rest."

"Now, ain't that just dandy? That's what I mean about you having no vision, Jericho." Poe started waving his arms around excitedly. "You heard what Jim Packard said as well as I did. Horses are obsolete. *Ob-so-lete*, Jericho. That means 'old-hat' — out of style. Cattle is where the money's at now. And just imagine Bluebonnet, all green from water being pumped into it by those windmills. Can't ya see that?"

"I can see a bunch of them things sticking up all over our ranch, like tits on a whore," McCain told him dryly.

Poe looked at his partner in total amazement. "Aye God, Jericho, you got a real way with words. Tits on a whore no less. Well, what's wrong with tits on a whore? There's nary a prettier sight."

McCain didn't answer, convinced he'd already said too much, and gotten Poe stirred up.

"Jericho, in all the years I've known you, I've never knowed you to frequent a house of pleasure. When we'd come in from a long run all frisky, and me and the other boys would throw down a few drinks and head for a sporting house, you always seemed to drift off to someplace else. We never seen you there."

Poe bit off a large piece of his tobacco plug and chewed it thoroughly before he continued. "Now, I know it ain't because you don't crave such as much as any of us. Why, I bet that old tally-whacker of your's gits harder than a Montana winter, just like the rest of us — but you got a ramrod up your butt 'bout what's right and wrong, and you ain't about to let anyone know you've got feelings, too."

Poe thought about that for a minute, then continued. "There's just something plain unnatural and dishonest about a man that don't go to the whores when he's got a hankering, at least once in a while. It just don't look right to people. It ain't decent, Jericho…and don't go rolling your eyes at me. You know I'm speaking the dad-burned gospel."

Rosie spit at a rock and hit it dead center. "Let me put it this way," he said. "I know I've heard you say more'n once that you wouldn't trust a man that don't take a drink once in a while. Now ain't that right, Jericho?"

McCain didn't answer so Poe went on anyway. "I know it's right. I heard what I heard," he said. "Well, this ain't much different, is it? I mean, it's practically the same thing, ain't it?"

Still, no reply from McCain, but that usually didn't stop Rosie once he warmed to a subject, and it didn't stop him this time either. "I'll tell you flat out, if it was anybody but you, Jericho,

I wouldn't trust a man that don't get a little poke once in a while."

McCain just rode along, glaring straight ahead, without saying anything.

"Well, say something, dammit!" Poe finally exploded.

"Whether I do it or don't, is my own personal business," McCain said. "It ain't something for public discussion. I was raised to believe that it shows a distinct lack of class to talk about that. But just for your peace of mind, yes. I do. And, I keep it private," McCain finally said. "That should be the end of the subject."

"Well I'll be god damned! Don't that just beat all? He's embarrassed that he's human like the rest of us poor mortals, hee hee," Poe chuckled. "Well, even a watch that don't run, is right twice a day."

Then after a few more chuckles and shaking of his head, said, "…so what do ya think about cattle?"

"I don't like cattle," McCain stated. "They're stupid animals and are only raised by stupid people."

Poe looked like he swallowed a bug. "Yeah, right. Stupid men like Charles Goodnight and John Chisim. Real stupid men that got filthy rich raising cattle and selling them. If they'd been smart, they'd got into horses and made themselves wealthy, like us. Right Jericho?" Poe said sarcastically.

"They didn't have any windmills, though," McCain pointed out to his friend.

"For cat's sake, I know they didn't have any windmills! Windmills just make it easier! Let me explain to you the way it works, Jericho…"

When Legends Lived

* * *

On and on Rosie talked for hours as Jim Packard listened. The subject of Kate and her family, by Poe and McCain, had summoned up thoughts of Bethena. He'd been intrigued by the woman ever since the first time he saw her. If things hadn't unfolded as they had, he might've decided to take Kate up on her offer to stay at the K/D for a while. As he rode, he recalled the hunted look he'd seen in Beth's eyes after he and Poe had returned her to the ranch.

That's one troubled young lady, he thought, wondering how she was now getting along. *Maybe I can get back to the K/D once this is over, before I have to go back to…what? My wife? My job?*

That thought sobered him. Suddenly, Jim thought about the telegram in his pocket. He'd received it from his father-in-law before leaving Laredo, and felt thoroughly depressed. All of a sudden, it seemed he really didn't have anything to go home for, anyway.

His father-in-law's message had advised him that Hattie had decided the marriage was a mistake after-all, and had taken steps to get it annulled. He'd also said if Jim wanted to contest it, he should return right away. Randle assured him, of course, that his daughter's annulment would "have no bearing" on Jim's position with the Southern Pacific Railroad. Jim did a perfect imitation of a J.D. McCain snort, remembering the carefully worded message that made it clear, without actually coming right out and saying it, that Packard should strongly consider staying with his current assignment and see it through to its successful completion, or face certain dismissal.

Well, where does that leave me? he asked himself. *Maybe I will go see Beth when this is over, maybe even stay for a while. That is, if those two crazy old men don't get me killed first.* Jim's thoughts slid back to the young woman with the dazzling smile and terribly sad eyes.

Twenty-Nine

ROSCO BOOKBINDER'S WOUNDS WERE almost completely healed, although he was still considerably weakened from them. He and Dixie, surmising Rosco's wife Jenny had long since been killed by the Indians, finally set a date for their wedding. They agreed April was best, just before spring branding. That way, all the neighbors would be free to come. So, at the end of March, Rosco rode to Odessa for the final fitting of his black suit, he and Dixie had picked out for him to be married in.

He left Dixie in the sewing room, sorting through some white lace material which she intended to use to repair the wedding-gown her grandmother had worn over half a century before. She kissed him sweetly and whispered, "Hurry back, my love. I have a secret to tell you when you return."

She watched as he rode out of sight over the ridge-line, toward Odessa. *Maybe*, she thought, *I should've told him before he left.* But she wanted to surprise him with the news when they were alone tonight. She whispered again, this time to herself, "Yes, hurry home, my love. Hurry home to your wife and your son."

It was a boy, she just knew it, rubbing her slightly swollen stomach while smiling secretly to herself.

* * *

Rosco quietly sipped his beer and thought about the surprise Dixie had promised upon his return. He had no earthly idea what it could be. As his mind wandered, he only half listened to an animated conversation between two whisky drummers leaning against the bar as they bragged about their sexual exploitations. Some words now began to filter through more and more as they registered in his mind.

"...violet eyes prettier than a picture...named Jennifer something or other...slim, but still a handful, if you know what I mean...pretty, dark hair....hot..."

Rosco stunned, stared at the duo for a long moment, then rose and walked to them. "Where did you see the girl?" he broke in, quietly.

The two men glared back, annoyed, but something in Rosco's eyes suggested they shouldn't push it. Instead, the man who had done the talking laughed. "Surely you don't expect me to tell you where I get my best pokes, do you?"

They belly-laughed loudly again. The laughing man never saw Rosco move, but suddenly felt something cold against the side of his head and instinctively knew it was the bore of a large gun.

"Let's try again," Rosco said. "Where did you see the girl?"

* * *

It'd been several weeks since McCain had crossed the border at Del Rio. They were now well inside Mexico and according to McCain, Poe had done a "passable job" of following Scar's trail. He and Poe both agreed Scar was likely headed toward the Los Diablos Mountains.

Wherever in hell that is, Packard thought sourly. *Apparently, nobody else has to agree with that old bastard.*

The weather was rapidly turning colder, and lately he'd been spending a lot of time in the evenings with Jake Kellog, learning to deal 'winning hands' while huddled near the warmth of a small fire. Jake could handle a deck of cards better than anyone Jim Packard had ever known. Later, he'd lie awake and think about a young woman with golden hair and sad eyes, or wonder how the wounded Rosco Bookbinder was progressing, and pray they would overtake Scar before he decided to kill the young deputy's wife.

To top it all off, Jim's stomach was so messed up from Fish's fancy cooking that, when not actually in the saddle, he was squatting behind a bush in agony.

Wouldn't it be just great, he thought, *getting my throat cut by some Indian while taking a dump behind a bush in the middle of Mexico?*

Ahead, Jim could hear Poe telling Fish why he should get rid of his stallion and get a mare instead. As far as he could make out, it all had something to do with the hoofs.

"…mare's hoofs grow back faster, Fish. If a stallion breaks a hoof, you're just stranded for one-two months, until it grows back. Nothing else you can do," Poe said with authority. "Now, you take my mare. If she breaks a hoof, I'll be back on her in a week or so."

"Captain rides a stallion," Fish pointed out to him.

"Yes…well I know the '*Captain*' rides a stallion," Poe said sarcastically. "But, ya don't have to do every little thing the '*Captain*' does. Do you?"

"Everything he does seems to work out for him just fine," Fish said stubbornly.

"Dammit, Fish, we ain't talking about the Captain now, we're talking about you," Poe continued. Vexed by Fish's position on the subject, Poe went on. "If Jericho McCain picked up a road apple, put sugar on it and ate it, would you suddenly develop an uncontrollable passion for horse-turds, too?"

Fish slumped forward in the saddle, contemplating. "I would just ask the Captain why he did it. He may have had a good reason. He usually does."

"A good reason to eat a horse turd?" Poe shouted. "Aye God, Fish, you got to git away from that man 'fore your brain dries up any more than it is." Poe studied Fish until he started to squirm, then inquired with apparent concern, "You git headaches a lot, Fish? Real throbbing, kicking on the barn kind of headaches?"

"I guess I git some from time-to-time," Fish answered.

"I knowed it!" Poe said sincerely. "Your brain is drying up. Sure as God made the horsefly. Probably looks like a dried persimmon already."

Startled, Fish gasped, "I...I didn't know a man's brain c... could dry up," he blurted.

"Sure it can," Poe answered knowledgeably. "What's a brain made up of anyway? Water. Well you jist set a pan o'water out in this sun for a few hours and see what happens. That pan will be bone dry in an hour — jist like your brain is gonna be." Poe spit, saying again, "Yes, sir, bone dry."

He was looking out of the corner of his eye at Fish's jumping Adam's apple. Fish spurred his horse forward, looking back over his shoulder at his tormentor. Poe waited until Fish settled in beside Jake and young Packard, spit and chuckled to himself softly. Then he spurred his mount ahead of the group once more to search for fresh signs of Scar's trail. Several hours later he returned, just as the rest of the group prepared to make camp near a small stream. Riding up to McCain, he said, "Don't know as this is the best place for a camp tonight, Jericho."

"Why? What have you got?" McCain inquired.

"Cut the trail of about twenty to twenty-five shod horses. Might be Ruralis. Don't know any other bunch that would have that large a number of shod horses in one place," Poe said. "There's a place south of here that might be better."

"You lead. I'll get the men up and follow you," McCain told him.

Arriving at the new site, they quickly set up camp and spent the night in a wooded draw that offered some protection from an all-out frontal attack, while leaving a decent path for escape should the need arise. Jake Kellog and Jim Packard occupied their time by dealing each other cards, while Fish looked at the pictures in his recipe book until it was dark. Poe and McCain tried to second guess Scar's route and estimate how long he'd continue to run from them before standing to fight.

"Be real careful you don't ride into an ambush while you're out there scouting," he cautioned Poe. "That red devil would just love to whittle us down and I can't afford to lose anyone."

"Well, I certainly wouldn't want you to lose this 'anyone,' and I just really appreciate your interest in my welfare, Jericho," Poe said sarcastically. "Yes, sir, you're just all warmth and concern for your fellow man, ain't you?"

He stood abruptly, walked to his bedroll, and plopped down, placing his arms behind his head. McCain bewildered, continued staring at him as though he just didn't understand what came over his partner sometimes.

* * *

Packard pulled on a lined plaid coat, blew on his hands, and rubbed them against the morning chill. His mount stamped its

When Legends Lived

foot impatiently and snorted heavy steam through its nostrils, as he tied the bedroll in place. They had just broken camp, when suddenly the thundering hoofs of shod horses approached, closing fast. Startled, Packard watched as the others leaped into their saddles, leaving him temporarily on the ground. Quickly, he swung into his saddle just as mounted men broke from the trees scarcely a hundred yards away.

All were obviously soldiers, for they wore dusty brown uniforms and were heavily armed. They seemed as surprised as the Americans, but soon the officer-in-charge organized them into a ragged scrimmage line. Packard estimated there to be about twenty-five in the group. Once formed, they remained motionless, silently watching the Americans. McCain and his men did the same.

"Ruralis," muttered Poe, spitting with disdain.

The war of wills was lost as a mustached officer shouted, "*Señores! Buenos dias!*"

"*Buenos dias, Cap-i-tan!*" Poe shouted back.

"You're a long ways from home, *amigos*. What brings you to my poor country?" he said, white teeth flashing beneath his dark mustache.

"Horseflesh," Poe answered, without hesitation. "We're down here to buy some of that fine Mexican horseflesh we've heard so much about."

"We have horses for sale, amigo. You come over and I will show you," the Ruralis officer said.

Poe chuckled just loud enough for the man to hear. "I don't think you have anything we would be interested in, *Cap-i-tan*. Those you have all look like pretty sorry specimens to me," he said and spit again.

Fast talking was exchanged among the men in the front rank and the captain. Finally, the Ruralis captain called out, "Do you have tobacco and coffee, amigos?"

"Sure, come on over and git some," answered Poe generously.

The officer laughed loudly and shook his finger back and forth. "I do not theenk so, señor." He laughed again, then said, "And, I do not theenk you are horse buyers, amigos." He suddenly lost his wide smile. "When you Gringos want horses, you steal them in Mexico!" he shouted.

"Looks like he's sized us up and thinks his advantage is big enough for him to start trouble," McCain muttered in a low voice. "Get ready and just follow me and Poe's lead."

"I theenk you and your friends must come with me and we will check on your story, Gringo."

All pretense of civility had now disappeared. "*Por favor*, drop your guns and walk your horses toward me." The officer spoke in a low voice to the men behind him and hands subtly shifted on rifle stocks.

"If we do as he says, we're dead men," Poe said. "Ready, Jericho?"

McCain nodded.

"Now!" Poe shouted, as he and McCain simultaneously spurred their horses straight at the Ruralis. They'd been around long enough to know that at a hundred yards the Ruralis had a definite advantage with their rifles and overwhelming numbers. But up close, they'd have to fight the style that made the Texas Rangers famous. *"Get right in the middle of 'em,"* Captain Jack Hays used to tell them. *"Use your Colts, up close."* That's just what they intended to do, as Poe and McCain quickly knocked five Ruralis out of their saddles before slamming into the Mexican's front lines.

The battle quickly became total confusion as rising dust, gunsmoke, screaming horses and dying men combined into something terrifying and surreal. Jim Packard swiftly shot a soldier from his saddle, then instantly felt something hit him hard, knocking him to the ground. He lay in the dust, partially hidden in the flying debris, holding his horses' reins in one hand and firing upward at obscure images with the other. He knocked another soldier from his saddle, then possibly another. He just couldn't tell. The dust completely filled his eyes and although temporarily blinded, he could still hear men shouting and reports of weapons blasting away in his ears, until finally, all he could hear was a loud ringing. It was terrifying.

McCain, Poe and the others did their share of damage as well, but the Ruralis were seasoned, well-disciplined troops and they fought back hard. Finally, Poe shot the Ruralis Captain through the head, and it was over as quickly as it began. Jim, wiping the muddy dust from his eyes, looked up from his position on the ground to see only the brown backs of the Ruralis's uniforms as they disappeared into the tree line. Only then did he feel the hot pain in his legs. Once again, his eyes filled with mud formed by the thick flying dust, leaving him sightless. Reaching down, he felt his right leg, then his left, and his hand came away, wet and sticky each time. He suddenly felt light-headed and nauseous.

This is not good, thought Packard, just before he passed out.

Poe and McCain quickly surveyed the carnage before them, then Poe examined and quickly dispatched the wounded Mexicans, while McCain attended to his own injured men. He could see Packard on the ground, alive but groaning softly, and Jake desperately clinging to his saddle horn to keep from falling off his horse. He went to Jake first.

"How ya doing, Jake?" he said, as he helped the injured man from his saddle.

"Took one through the arm, Captain. I think it busted the bone," he grunted, as he lowered himself onto a rock. "I'll live, but I won't be slinging a Colt for a while. Take care of Jim. It looks like he took a couple of bad ones."

McCain went to Jim Packard lying in the dirt. He'd been shot through both legs. The right leg looked particularly bad, as a piece of bone protruded from his thigh. Jim moaned softly.

"Easy, son," McCain gently told him. "You took a couple of hits and I gotta move you out of this dirt back into the trees yonder, so I can take a look at it."

Jim blinked, trying to focus, then nodded his head so McCain would know he understood. Although he steeled himself against the pain he knew was coming, he was unprepared for the force in which it hit, and shouted as he was lifted, then carried to the nearby tree-line. He was ashen by the time McCain lay him on a blanket and wiped the dirt from his eyes with a wet cloth.

"You done good out there today, boy. Real good," McCain told him gently. He'd seen the young man in the dirt, holding onto the horse's reins, knocking Ruralis out of their saddles.

Suddenly, Poe stood over Packard and peered down. "Aye God, boy," he said. "Damned if you didn't look just like a real Texas Ranger out there today."

Despite the intense pain, Jim felt a warm glow of pride.

With experience in patching over a hundred gunshot wounds between them, Poe and McCain did a credible job of mending Jake Kellog and Jim Packard while Fish stood watch. They'd seen enough injuries to know that the two men were lost for trail duty. They were tasked with figuring out how to get them to an area so they could recover quickly; and, eventually return to help Poe and McCain continue their present task.

Discussing their options at length, the two partners finally decided on a plan of action. Fish would take Packard, since he was the worst off and needed intensive treatment, to Kate's ranch. Afterward, he'd accompany Jake to the partner's horse ranch where he would look after him until Jake was completely healed. Poe and McCain would continue on Scar's trail and then inform the three men of their location when they were fit to join up again.

After disclosing their plan to the others and getting some resistance from Fish, all finally agreed it was the only course of action open to them. They moved to a safe location and waited while Poe rode ahead to locate another defensible camp-site. They stayed there for two full days before starting back toward the border.

As dawn broke on the third day, they packed, giving Fish both mules, one to pull the litter holding Jim, and the other to carry supplies. McCain and Poe would forage for their food until they could obtain another pack animal. The men shook hands all around, and Jim promised he would soon catch up. As the two groups parted ways, he hoped it wouldn't be the last time he would see them.

Thirty

AFTER LEARNING OF JOE WALKER'S hanging, Billy traveled back to Fort Worth. Upon arrival, he went directly to Hugh Underwood's office. Hugh wasn't in, so he went to see the local undertaker, and found a smallish man in a dark suit filling out paperwork in the back room of the rundown establishment. As Billy knocked lightly, the man reached for a pair of wire-rimmed glasses and putting them on, looked up. Seeing Billy, he smiled.

"Are you the undertaker, sir?" Billy said in a polite but serious tone.

"H.T. Cobbs, at your service young man. How might I be of service to you?" The man spoke in a surprisingly, deep rich voice.

"Could you tell me if Joe Walker has already been buried?" Billy said.

H.T. Cobbs pondered the question as if contemplating a very distasteful subject, then said, "Nope, he ain't." He frowned deeply. "Oh, I got him all ready for burying, but our illustrious mayor got together with a few enterprising fellows and made a deal. Told me to hold up the funeral for a week. Then they had him pickled in alcohol and now have him on display over at City Hall. Charge is ten cents to see him, if that's why you're asking."

Billy stood stunned. Then he felt anger start to burn inside of him. "How much time before he has to be put in the ground?" he said softly.

When Legends Lived

The undertaker heard something in the soft voice that made him sit up straight and answer the boy with a good deal of respect. "Five days, six maybe. Then he'll start to deteriorate quickly. Might last a little longer if he's wrapped in something heavy that keeps the air out," he said respectfully. "Are you family?"

Billy quietly stood for a minute, then almost whispered, "Yes. I'm family." He moved to the small window looking out toward the back of the building. "Will you prepare the body if I bring it back here?"

"Be glad to, son. But you might have a problem getting the body away from the mayor and his partners. Those partners are the Harvey boys, Jack and Morgan Harvey. They might figure they have an investment here and put up an argument," Cobbs said. "They're used to having their way around here, young man. Neither one is apt to buck-up against you, you wearing that Colt and all...but then, they ain't the problem."

Cobbs removed his glasses, lay them on the table in front of him, and rubbed his eyes. "The problem is a young Mexican fellow that handles their disagreements for them. Goes by the name of Chico Terrazas. Just about your age, he is. But he's a killer, make you no mistake about that. He'll give you a chance, such as it is, then if you even get near that pistol handle, he'll shoot you so fast you won't know what happened. He's killed three men since he arrived in Fort Worth. The sheriff won't go near him."

Cobbs fixed Billy with his stare and said, "Let it go, boy. Joe Walker, English Bob, it don't matter what the name was, now. The man's dead and he won't care about what's happening to him. Just let it go," he said again. The older man intensely looked at Billy who failed to respond. He said, "You ain't gonna listen, are you? You're gonna do it anyway."

"I'll be back in thirty minutes. Will you help me prepare him for the journey back to my ranch for burial?"

"Son, if you can get him here, I'll get him ready for you," Cobbs told him. "Just you be careful. That Mexican kid is hell on wheels with a six-gun."

"Thirty minutes," Billy said and walked out.

Cobbs watched him cut diagonally across the street and into the City Hall, and decided to follow. When he arrived, Billy was standing in front of Joe Walker who was propped-up against a large wooden door, his arms and legs tied with rope looped through holes cut through the door to make him stand upright. Over the door a sign read, "ENGLISH BOB – Killer, Gunfighter and Outlaw." A small table sign read, "10 cents." Jake Harvey sat behind the table puffing on a cigar.

"That'll be ten cents there, young feller."

Billy Shaw gave the man a cold stare and said grimly, "I'm putting an end to your little business, Harvey. I'm here to take Joe Walker home for burial, and the way I feel right now, I hope you try to stop me."

Harvey's mouth dropped open, then he smiled and retorted, "Oh, by all means, go right ahead, boy. I'm not going to try and stop you — no, not me. Him," Harvey said, pointing to a slender, dark-skinned youth leaning against a staircase toward the back of the room.

"His name's Chico Terrazas. Maybe you've heard about him."

"I've heard of him," Billy said as he pulled out a folding knife and opened the blade. He stepped in front of Joe Walker's body and cut one of the ropes holding Joe's right ankle.

"I'm sorry, *hombre*. I can't let you do that," came a soft low voice from the back of the room.

When Legends Lived

Billy turned to face the young Mexican. "Is this worth getting killed over, fellow?" he said.

"I don't plan on getting killed today, hombre. Maybe you are the one about to die," Chico said easily.

"There's no reason anybody has to get killed here. Let me show you something first, Chico," Billy told him. "Now don't get nervous, I'm not going to pull on you."

Billy picked up a glass dish from the small table where Jack Harvey rested his cigar, poured the ashes out and turned his body slightly toward the front door, about thirty feet away. Faster than their eyes could follow, Billy threw the ashtray toward the door, and in one smooth motion, drew and busted it in a thousand fragments. It was a move he'd practiced with Joe Walker a thousand times since that afternoon Rosie Poe had shown it to him on the river.

While the echoes bounced through the large chamber, Billy Shaw slipped the big Colt back into its holster and turned to face the young gunfighter. Chico stared at him for an instant, then slowly smiled, and said softly, "*Quien lo haja mejor?*" Then he turned and walked to the back door, closing it softly behind him.

"What the hell did he say?" Harvey demanded.

Billy ignored him and continued to cut the ropes holding Walker to the door.

"Dammit, will somebody tell me what the hell he said?" Harvey shouted again.

Cobbs smirked and said, "He said, Mr. Harvey, '*Quien lo haja mejor,*' which translated, means, 'Who could do better?'"

By then, Billy had Joe's body cut loose from the large door and was carrying him out of the City Hall. At the door, he stopped and looked back. "Don't make the mistake of coming after me. I had nothing against that boy Chico. I do against you."

He walked out.

* * *

Fish, escorted the wounded Jake Kellog and Jim Packard across the border near Eagle Pass. There he sold the horses and mules and bought stage tickets to Langtry, where they caught the train to Abilene, by way of Fort Stockton. It took nearly a month and was a grueling journey for someone even in good health, but it was a life threatening trip for the wounded men, especially someone in the condition of Jim Packard. Although Fish sought the services of a doctor in each town they traveled through, the traveling still took its toll. Arriving in Abilene, he wired a telegram to their foreman, Matt Jennings, to meet him in Odessa with a wagon and two extra saddle horses. Then he wired Kate, telling her of the situation and that he was bringing Jim Packard to her ranch for a while.

Stepping from the coach in Odessa, Matt Jennings was the first person Fish saw.

"You're a sight for sore eyes, Matt," shouted Fishburn, as he disembarked.

As Jennings came close, he grabbed Matt's hand in his huge paw and pumped it vigorously. "It shore is fine to be here; I can't believe I'm home!" he shouted, slapping Matt hard on the back. "It shore is fine to be home," Fish said once more, and Matt looked ready to dodge the ham-like paw again. Matt helped the two wounded men to the wagon, which had a bed for Jim laid-out in the back.

When Legends Lived

"I'm gonna take Jim to the K/D, then I'll return to the ranch as soon as possible. Matt, check the stage every day, in case a message comes in from the Captain. If he finds Scar, I got to be ready to ride out again."

Fish took Jim Packard and Jake Kellog to the doctor's office where the doctor checked their injuries. Once completed, he said, "Both of these men need to be in bed, not out gallivanting all over the country. You do what you want, but if you don't let them rest, they're both going to die."

The doctor pulled Fish aside and told him, "Kate Shaw rode in to meet her son, and bury Joe Walker. They've been at the hotel for over a week waiting for you to show up. She told me to let her know as soon as you got to town, so I sent my assistant to fetch her. They should be here any minute."

They heard running footsteps on the boardwalk, and Kate burst through the doorway.

"Quint, how nice to see you," Kate said breathlessly as she held out her hand.

Fish's face turned red as fire by her use of his first name, as he took her hand and smiled deeply. "Golly, Miss Kate, I just forget ever'time how pretty you are," Fish told her gallantly. His sunburned face became even darker.

Kate smiled sweetly and said, "And how was Roosevelt when last you saw him?" Her mind was on Jericho.

"Oh, he was fine, Miss Kate. Bit of the usual back trouble, but other than that, he was fine." Fish beamed, saying nothing more.

"Well, what about Captain McCain, Quint?" Kate said, impatiently. "Was he fine too?"

"Oh, yes ma'am, Captain McCain was real fine," he nodded his head, still smiling broadly but volunteering nothing further.

Again, she waited, while he just smiled. Finally, Kate became more impatient. "I guess Captain McCain is feeling all right, not wounded or anything? Right, Quint?" she prodded.

"Yes, Miss Kate," Fish answered. "The Captain is just fine," he said again.

Sighing deeply, Kate started to say something else, then just nodded her head and smiled. With that, she walked to the bed where Jim lay and said, "How is Mr. Packard doing, Doctor?"

"Just as I told the others, if he don't get some decent care soon, he's going to die," the doctor answered. "Plain and simple. Just get him to the ranch, and don't let him do a thing for at least two months. Someone who knew how to do it right set the bone, but they must've done it without any kind of pain killer. That'll take a toll on a man's stamina."

"If you can give him something to make him comfortable, we'll get started back to the K/D first thing in the morning," Kate said.

She and Billy loaded Jim and were well underway by daybreak. Despite Billy's attempts to dodge the largest ruts and holes, it nonetheless remained a rough ride as each impact jarred the entire wagon. Nearly half way to the ranch, the pain killer wore off and Jim awoke.

"Dammit, Fish, will you try to miss a hole once in a while. If not, I'll come up there and drive," he weakly called out.

Kate looked over her seat and smiled down at him. "Big Fish is gone. Little Fish is here now."

"Kate — Miss Shaw. Where are we?" he said puzzled.

"Kate, will be fine and we're almost to the K/D," she said. "Don't do a lot of talking. Doc says you'll need to conserve your strength. Try to nap if you can and I'll wake you when we get there."

When Legends Lived

Jim drifted off between sleep and awareness the rest of the journey and didn't complain anymore about the bumps.

Bethena and Kate's two daughters, Tina and Rachel, greeted them, waving wildly as Billy pulled up near the hitching post in front of the ranch house, set the break, and jumped to the ground. With deep concern, Beth ran to help remove Jim from the wagon bed. He was ashen with cracked dry lips, but beads of a cold sweat covered his forehead. Carefully, they carried him to the same room Rosco Bookbinder had used earlier. Jim Packard looked to be in worse shape than Rosco had been.

My God, he's a handsome man, thought Bethena. *Even as seriously injured as he is, he's still the handsomest man I've ever seen.*

With a damp cloth, she gently wet his lips and wiped his brow. Kate left them alone and went to prepare something for them to eat while Bethena continued to place damp cloths on his forehead, staring into his drawn face. Kate smiled as she glanced back over her shoulder. It was the first time she'd seen Beth take an interest in anyone else in months.

* * *

The breeze felt good on Brad Thompson's face as he rested from a hard day of working the fields around the farm. Now known as Bart Thomas, he'd had been at the Hawkins' Children Farm for several months, and felt as though they were more like his family than the home he'd left in Texas. It all seemed like a hundred years ago, but Brad knew he couldn't let down his guard an instant, for if the wrong person recognized him, he would be returned to Laredo and hanged. He liked the way Al and Sara Hawkins always included him in any decisions about running the farm. In fact, everybody, the youngest to the oldest, had a vote. He particularly liked Al's deep booming laugh, coupled with Sara's gentle scolding.

Twice he'd broached the subject of leaving and each time, Al Hawkins had offered some reason why Brad should consider staying longer. Brad sat at the walled-spring where he'd first seen Al, enjoying the cool evening and smelling the poignant aroma of the nearby barn lot. It made him think of a large Texas ranch, many miles and a half a life-time, away. He didn't hear the man approach at first, so intent was he looking out over the neat rows of corn he and the children had planted and now tended. The chest high corn was starting to form ears all ready. Brad was amazed he'd a hand in what the Hawkins' called, "this miracle of life."

"Funny, how things just seem to grow straight and tall when they get the right amount of care and attention, ain't it?" Al said, close behind Brad.

Brad sensed Al was talking more about the children than his crops. Not turning around, Brad answered, honestly. "I've lived around a ranch most of my life and never gave it a thought until now. Guess I was so caught up in feeling sorry for myself that I didn't realize I'm no more than a fly speck in the way things are supposed to turn out."

Al Hawkins laughed his booming laugh. "Well, if you can figure that out at your age, I have great hope for you. I didn't begin to get the drift of it until I was nearly thirty years old."

"How did you hit upon this idea for the 'Children's Farm' instead of doing something else with your lives?" Brad said.

"Well, we've always wanted to raise things and we've always wanted to have children, so we just figured we'd combine the two and raise them all on a farm," Al said and laughed again.

When Legends Lived

They talked about the day's events and plans for the upcoming week, then Al broached the subject of Brad's plans.

"I'd like you to consider staying on and help run the farm. I know you're running from something, son. I've seen the way you watch the skyline, even when you're working the fields. That don't matter to Sara and me, nor to the kids. They love you, and Sara and me have grown to love you, too."

Al let Brad absorb what he said, then went on, as though carefully selecting his words. "You're a good person, Bart. We need you around here and want you to stay with us for as long as you can. No questions now — or when the time comes and you feel you must leave. What do you say, Bart?"

"Brad."

"What?" Al sounded puzzled.

"It's not Bart, it's Brad. Brad Thompson," the young man told him. "My family owns a large ranch down near Odessa. I got some mixed-up ideas in my head and took off down to San Antonio a while back. Took up gambling, women, guns…you probably know the story."

Brad spoke softly and Al leaned forward to hear him. "I killed a sheriff and another man — a young cowboy — down in Laredo. Just so happens, the sheriff was well liked by everyone, from the Governor right down to the people he put in jail." Brad laughed a short bitter laugh, and went on. "If they catch me they're gonna hang me. Probably right on the spot. Can't say as I blame 'em none."

He finished speaking and stared out over the landscape. Then he said, "Now you know everything. You still want me to stay?"

"I haven't heard anything to make me change my opinion of

the person I know," Al told him. "You want to start down in the brushy area we decided to clean out last week?"

It took a moment before Brad realized he was talking about the next morning's work. "Yeah. Yeah. We could turn that whole area into a pumpkin and cucumber garden. Probably sell them real quick to the ranchers around here. What do you think?" Brad said.

Al finally stood, and with a wink and a nod stretched and said good night.

Brad stayed and thought about their conversation, and his mind eventually turned to the others. There was Reba, the eldest, a young Cherokee girl about his own age. He'd considered her plain when he first saw her, but lately he realized just how beautiful she was. Alex was next. He was sixteen and at least part Mexican. "Bumper" a Black youth, and Soto, another Spanish boy, were both fourteen. Charlotte, a pale, thin girl of eleven, hardly spoke, but picked the most beautiful flower arrangements anyone had ever seen.

He couldn't remember the full names of the children, except for Tina, for they were seldom used. At three, Tina was the youngest and the one that had adopted Brad right from the start. With her big dark eyes and happy disposition, she captivated Brad and shadowed his every move. He'd never felt such a sense of belonging as he did on Al and Sara Hawkins' Children's Farm. Brad decided he'd stay for a while.

Thirty-One

AS ROSCO RODE SOUTH with a heavy heart, he'd nearly faltered and turned back twice. But he was well aware of Dixie's stubborn streak and once the fiery Dixie Thompson made up her mind, she wasn't to be persuaded otherwise. Maybe that's one of the things he loved about her so much, her independence and determination.

A lot of good it does me now, he thought. *I've lost the one person in my life that means anything to me. All for a woman who ran off with someone else — and tried to kill me, to boot.*

But Jenny Bookbinder was still his wife and once one made an oath, one lived up to it. *People aren't given any alternatives when they make vows,* he thought unhappily. That's just the way life worked. Rosco knew that even if he could talk Jenny into a divorce, it'd do little to change things between he and Dixie, for she'd made the choice plain — and he'd left anyway. No, his chance with Dixie was gone. He would only be fooling himself to think otherwise.

Rosco never stopped as he rode through San Antonio, and then Laredo. Crossing the border, he continued straight on to Sabinas, which he reached on his twelfth day of traveling. An old man watched him, misty eyes peering suspiciously from under the wide brim of a sombrero, as he dismounted and watered his horse at the village well.

Can't really blame him, Rosco thought, as he pulled a half-bucket of water from the well and poured his hands full of the cool liquid. After all, these folks had little reason to trust anyone from north of the border, especially those arriving on fast horses and wearing two tied down guns. He drank his fill then dumped the rest over his head. Wiping the water from his face, he caught the old man staring at him again.

Rosco smiled and said in Spanish, "It is very hot, Señor."

The old man favored him with a toothless grin and nodded. *Si*, it was indeed hot. Rosco again asked in Spanish if there were any place in the village he could buy a drink of tequila, for he had an awful thirst. The old man told him of two places, the best one being Fat-man Jose's.

Rosco's expression didn't change at the name the whisky drummer had mentioned, back in Odessa. He politely asked directions and flipped the old man a coin. "*Muchas gracias, Señor*," he said, as he walked off leading his horse behind.

He found the place described, halfway up a narrow alley, in a two story building that had the only double-door on the block. Tying his horse loosely at a post, he looked up and down the narrow street, and seeing no one, went inside.

Letting his eyes grow accustomed to the dark, Rosco scanned a long narrow room with several rough tables down the right side. Along the left side of the structure was a rough, splintered wood bar. Only three people were in the room; an obviously intoxicated old man with his head laying on a table, a tough-looking hombre standing at the far end of the bar, and a fat man in a dirty shirt, behind the bar.

Rosco walked to the bar and said in perfect Spanish, "A shot of tequila and beer chaser."

As he pulled a roll of bills from his pocket he felt both men's eyes hungrily fix on it. Rosco lay some of the money, obviously too much for the drink alone, on the bar.

"You have women here?" he smiled at the fat man.

"*Si, Señor*, there are three women that work upstairs," the saloon owner answered hopefully. "Do you want me to send for them?"

"I prefer Gringo women. Do you have them? I heard you sometimes do," Rosco said quietly.

The fat man smiled even more broadly, saying, "Yes, Señor, sometimes I do. If only you could have come two short months ago, I had a beautiful gringo woman all the men wanted. I had her myself, many times. But she was not, how do you say… lively? Yes, lively. She was like a rock. She just lay there, like — nothing. Now I have two young Mexican virgins. You can have them both, very cheap."

"Well, thanks, but I prefer white women and would like to see the Gringo woman. Where did she go?" Rosco said.

The man's evil little eyes studied Rosco, looking at the American with some suspicion, then glanced furtively at the tough-looking man near the end of the bar. The look wasn't lost on Rosco.

"Oh, she just left, Señor. Maybe she went back home?" He threw back his head and laughed deeply, but his pig-like eyes didn't laugh with him.

The gun barrel chipped a tooth as it entered his mouth. From his uncomfortable position, he could see the big Colt's hammer in its full-cocked position and Rosco's grim smile just behind it.

"Let's try it once more, fatty," Rosco said softly. "Just take a wild guess where you think she might've ended up."

Sweat was beading on the bar-owner's face, and he gagged on the metal object in his mouth.

"Tell that greasy looking hombre at the end of the bar to go take a bath or something. If I see him anywhere before I leave town, I'll put a round in his gut, so it'll take a long time for him to die. Then, I'll come back here and kill you. Then, I'll kill both of your families," Rosco told the fat man pleasantly as he removed the gun-barrel from his mouth, just far enough so the man could respond.

Jose spoke rapid-fire at the man, who stared hatefully at Rosco and sulked out the back door.

"Quickly, the name of the place and the man you gave the American woman to," Rosco said harshly.

The sweating proprietor gave him the information as fast and as clearly as he could, for he didn't like what he saw in the young *pistolero's* eyes. He blurted out the place was in Monterrey, a larger city closer to the Gulf. When he'd finished telling all he knew, Rosco slashed him viciously several times across the face with his pistol.

"If I hear of you buying any more women, *any* kind, I'll come back and castrate you," he said. "Then, I'll kill you." He dropped the man to the floor and walked out. The tough-looking man was nowhere to be seen.

* * *

It took several days for Rosco to reach Monterrey. When he finally found the place Jose had described to him, Jenny wasn't there. She had been, the proprietor told him, but she was uncooperative and he'd sold her to someone else — to a man in another town, down the coast.

It became the first of a long list of filthy bars and brothels Rosco searched during the following months in his efforts to find Jenny. Through dozens of dirty little Mexican towns and villages, he unsuccessfully chased rumors and stories of white gringo women, serving the men of various taverns and whorehouses.

At last, a priest gave him some information in one of the many villages he passed through. One of the local men had confided to him during confession of a pretty gringo lady that he had "been with" in a little fishing village recently. A village called San Pablos.

Nearly exhausted by the time he arrived at the village, Rosco knew he wouldn't be up to caring for Jenny and riding back to Texas without rest. Dismounting in front of the first hotel he saw, Rosco rented a dirty little room, pushed a chair under the doorknob, and slept for eight hours straight. He awoke in humid heat, feeling drained but able to now function. After eating a heavy meal of tortillas, beef and beans, he felt ready and went to find the place the priest had told him about.

He finally located it in the filthiest part of the city. The place is a dump, he thought as he entered. A putrid stench overpowered him, but after a few minutes, he got so he could tolerate it to a certain degree. Rosco, asked questions from no one. He simply went from room to room, pausing briefly to look inside, then went on to the next one. There were about a dozen rooms with either one, two, or three women to a room. Usually one or more men were engaged in sexual activity with them, or waiting their turns. Signs in Spanish posted the ridiculously low price charged to buy the services, and the dignity, of another human being. Rosco felt nauseated.

He finally found her in the sixth room he checked. She was lying on a hard bunk-like bed, staring vacantly at the door. She made no sound as the fat man humped and sweated over her. Five other men waited their turn, watching as the pot-bellied man grunted and vigorously thrust his hips. Rosco took three steps and backhanded the man in the face, knocking him to the floor. The others instantly cowered against the far wall, their eyes filled with fear.

Rosco pulled Jenny to her feet with one hand. Finding a tattered cotton dress slung over the bottom of the bunk, he quickly pulled it over her head. Taking her hand, he rapidly led her to the door and out into the blinding sunlight. Rosco lifted the listless woman into the saddle and swung up behind her just as two large men rushed from the doorway. Rosco shrugged slightly and a pistol magically appeared in his hand. Almost comically, the two men skidded to a stop and nearly trampled each other getting back through the small door. Putting spurs to his horse, Rosco rode away, clinging to the limp form of Jenny.

They rode for about an hour, before he stopped to observe her condition. She didn't seem to know him, or even where she was. Finally able to give her a closer look, he could see that she was filthy, her hair matted, and nothing but skin and bones. Fearful of pursuit by the brothel's owner, he put her back onto the horse's back and spurred ahead once more. After several more hours, they came upon a stream. Rosco stopped at the ford and dismounted, gently lifted her to the ground, stripped the torn dirty dress from her, and tossed it aside. Picking her up and carrying her into the water, he set her down in the gentle, waist-deep current and washed her thoroughly. He gently toweled her off with one of his cotton shirts and replaced the dress with a change of his own clothes. With fresh clothes and clean damp hair, she looked like a tiny lost waif.

Rosco cooked for them and fed her by hand, forcing her to eat at least a few bites, even though she often took the food but

When Legends Lived

only held it in her mouth without chewing. At night, she would whimper softly in her sleep, but other than that, made no sound. It took several weeks for them to reach Laredo, and throughout that time Jenny Bookbinder didn't utter a word.

* * *

As he rode away into the morning chill, McCain looked over his shoulder at Poe, seated near the fire. His friend's persistent pain was worrisome to say the least. It just wasn't like him. Jericho could see him bent toward the blaze now, as if he couldn't get close enough to the warmth. Poe had been feeling poorly for about a week, and McCain could clearly see the strain showing in his face.

It's his back, thought McCain.

If they rode for more than a few hours at a time, Poe started to hurt fearsomely again. McCain always thought it had something to do with that time Poe climbed up on the "Widder-Maker," a big stallion they had bought to use as breed stock. He'd thrown Roosevelt, stomped on him and tried to eat him up. Discouraged by his nasty disposition, McCain recalled that they'd finally given the horse to a Kiowa family that lived just outside of Bluebonnet. The very next time they saw the family, the man was riding that nag and it acted as gentle as a lamb.

Now, McCain wasn't so sure the old riding injury was the culprit. It's been going on too long, he told himself.

Earlier that day, he'd told Roosevelt to sit around the camp while he made a few circles trying to cut the trail they'd somehow lost two days ago. The fact that Poe hadn't objected, showed just how badly he was hurting.

Hell, thought McCain, *I ache all over from all this damned riding, too. Getting too old for this shit. Maybe all he needs is a few days rest, and he'll surely get that if I can't pick up their trail today.*

McCain chuckled to himself sourly, thinking suddenly of his prey, that damned Scar. *Got to admit, that heathen is good — as good as any we've ever gone after. Just when you think you're getting close enough to smell him, he up and vanishes like a puff of smoke. Like now.*

As he rode, McCain also wondered how the young railroad man was doing.

That was about as bad a leg wound as any I've seen, he thought. *Looked to me like the bone was busted in at least one of them legs, maybe both. Could be he won't even walk well again — let alone, ride. The young fool should've stayed back east where he came from. At least, he'd still be in one piece now.*

McCain's eyes thoroughly scanned the wide canyon before heading in, and saw nothing had been disturbed — at least, as far as he could see. He had to remind himself though that he was dealing with Scar, and he could be a mite tricky.

God, how I wish Moses Penny was here, he thought. *Taking nothing away from Roosevelt, he's a fair hand at tracking too, but Moses could track a duck across water.*

McCain was still deep in thought when several doves suddenly fluttered noisily to his right. Instantly, years of training took over for McCain as he leaned forward in his saddle, rolling from his horse just as two rounds flew past his head. He came to his feet in a crouched run, quickly sliding into a narrow cut in the rocks at the base of the canyon wall.

He thought he'd seen slight movement just before he heard the rounds go off. Thank God he was riding with Moses Penny's old Sharps rifle across the saddle, for you could never tell when you'll get a shot at fresh game along the trail.

When Legends Lived

Swiftly, he took stock of his position while watching for movement to his front. His back hugged a steep canyon wall that was just concave enough so someone couldn't get above him and fire straight down on him. McCain knew that he had about a dozen rounds for the Sharps and a belt-full for the Walker Colt. Those were the good points. The bad points were he had no food or water and the sun would be up for another five-six hours. It could get pretty uncomfortable around there if they kept him bottled up for too long. Especially when the temperature began to drop as the sun set. Also, he couldn't expect any help.

As he squinted into the unusual warmth of an afternoon winter sun, McCain surmised that while he doubted they would try to rush him before it got dark, there was the possibility that they would do so, since they had the sun to their backs. Poe had told him earlier that based on the tracks he'd been following, there were only five of them, counting Scar. Besides, Scar didn't do things like that. He was a sneaky bastard and would try to kill him without running any more risk than he simply had to.

It could be worse, McCain thought as he settled down and rolled a cigarette. *But it could surely be better, too.*

Just as he settled back and sucked in the acrid smoke, two rounds bounced off the rocks over his head. McCain instinctively ducked his head and chuckled. *Don't know exactly where I am,* he thought. *Either that, or they figure I was nicked by one of their earlier bullets. Trying to get me to move or shoot back. Well, I will...I will. Just show me something to shoot at fellows!*

For over an hour, he scanned the landscape without moving a fraction of an inch.

Then, he saw it. Just a slight thing, but unnatural movement in the windless afternoon. He directed his vision slightly off-center, having found that you could pick up movement better if you didn't stare straight at it. *There. Not much, but definitely something.* The motion was a good fifteen feet closer than the first time. Inch by inch, McCain slowly moved his rifle's barrel to point in the general direction of the latest movement. He made every move in very short, slow motions, so as not to attract attention.

Thirty minutes went by and then a whip-poor-will's call broke the silence. Still, he sat unmoving. An answering whistle farther to his right.

Uh huh. Got you, you sons-of-a-bitches, McCain thought with malice. He shifted his eyes from one position to the other without moving his body at all.

When he'd first seen them, they were two hundred yards, maybe two-fifty away. Then later, he estimated they were about a hundred and fifty, and directly to his front. He figured they'd be making a move in a few more minutes. It worried him some that he didn't see the rest of their bunch.

Well, he thought, *take care of what you can see, and worry about what you can't see later.*

Shifting his eyes from one position to the other, he silently cocked the Sharps, and slowly picked up one of the rounds lying on the rock in front of him. He put the round in his mouth, rim facing out to where he could handily grab and insert it into his rifle without taking his eyes off his front. The old man hunter was ready.

Both stalkers jumped to their feet and rushed him so fast that they were only seventy feet from his position, running silently, when he saw them. In one smooth motion, he raised his rifle and shot the nearest one through the chest, then opening the breech and shoving the wet round he held in his mouth into the chamber, turned it toward the other. When he shot again, the second man was only twenty-five feet away and raising his own rifle. Without waiting to see the results, McCain rolled to the right as soon as he fired, as dozen rounds ricocheted around his old position.

He lay stoically for almost an hour without hearing a sound or seeing any more movement. Then he saw three men running up the sandy sloop of the rise, almost a thousand yards to his front. So that's where they left their horses, he thought. As they reached the top of the sloop, one of them stopped, raised his rifle and fired back at McCain's position. His spent round hit the dirt, over two hundred yards short, to McCain's front. Comfortable he was well out of range, the man laid his rifle on a rock, pulled down his leggings, grabbed his genitals and shook them at McCain, whooping in bravado. Soon, another was beside him doing the same thing.

McCain ran the elevation sights up as far as they would go, stuck his finger in his mouth and held it up, checking for any wind. He aimed at the first man, raised the muzzle another three inches, and fired. At the sound of the report, the men whooped louder and redoubled their vigorous motions. The one who'd started the whole thing suddenly sat down hard on the ground, surprised and holding his stomach with both hands. McCain chuckled softly as he watched the remaining two ambushers lift the injured man by his arms and half drag, half carry him over the rise, looking back with hostility toward his position.

It's your bad luck today, son. 'Cause that just might be the best shot I ever made, he congratulated himself.

After a few more minutes, McCain heard the sound of running

horses behind the rise, that quickly faded out of hearing. Knowing how cagey Scar could be, he still didn't move for another hour, then crawled to each of the two men he'd shot. Both were dead. He ran crouched to a small gully that cut at an angle across the canyon, and quickly put some distance between himself and the open area. With a half a mile distance behind him, he slowed to a walk and thought about his situation.

You're in no small amount of trouble, boy, he told himself, as he walked along. No horse, night coming on, at least a day's travel by foot back to the place he left Poe. He was already getting damned hungry. He'd be more so by the time he got there. *Not to mention, cold*, he thought, thinking about his warm coat and bed-roll as he watched the rapidly setting sun. That is, if those heathen didn't come back first and find him strolling along. *Damn. Damn. Double Damn!*

A noise!

McCain was already crouched behind a large rock, his rifle pointed back the direction he'd just come from, when he finally made out that it was a horse coming up behind him. He aimed at the position he knew the rider would have to pass, and waited. The horse walked into the area McCain had selected for his killing field and stopped. It was Grasshopper.

He edged closer and said gently, "Why you old son-of-a-gun, am I ever glad to see your bony butt."

He put his foot in the stirrup to mount and felt a sharp pain as the stallion gave him an amicable bite on the shoulder. McCain swung himself onto the back of the animal he loved — and hated — more than any other horse he'd ever owned.

"Someday, I'm gonna shoot you as surely as God made little green apples," he said softly, rubbing his shoulder. Then he reached forward and patted the animal's neck, "But, not today, partner."

No, not today.

*   *   *

Three-Finger Ned and Joe Smiling Bird brought Pike into the camp after dark. Scar was seated on his heels, Indian fashion, near the fire, playing cards with the three Mescaleros he'd brought in the day before. The old one had at least a dozen visible scars, obviously from knife and bullet wounds. The two younger ones had fewer scars, but eyes like hard little buttons. *Like a rattler's*, he thought, smiling. They were a mean looking bunch and the other men didn't trust them to be talking Apache with Scar all the time. Scar didn't look up as Pike was carried in and laid on his blanket.

Pike groaned softly and after a while, Scar said indifferently, "What happened to him?"

Three-Finger Ned and Joe Bird glanced at each other and Bird answered, "We ran into some Rangers over near Lagoes Canyon. We fought 'em hard — probably killed three, maybe four — but Pike took one in the guts." He stared down as he continued, "I saw that old ranger McCain, with 'em.."

Scar grunted and said sarcastically, "Just how many is *some Rangers*?"

"Oh, I don't know, Boss. What do you say, Ned?" A sheen of perspiration appeared on Joe Bird's face as he cast a furtive glance at his cohort.

"Half-dozen, for certain," Ned answered, easily. "Next time I'll kill those two old bastards."

"You two mangy dogs? If they come after you, you better

find a hole and pull it in after you. They've killed more of your kind than the two of you have beget. The next time you get a chance at them and miss, I'll give you both to the Mescaleros."

He sneered down at Pike, then spoke rapidly to the Mescaleros. Ned and Joe didn't understand the gibberish and were clearly worried. Scar said something else, then laughed shortly. The Mescaleros didn't laugh. They never laughed. It was another thing that worried Ned and Joe.

"Give me some whisky. My gut hurts," Pike whispered.

Scar contemptuously kicked the wounded man in the side, smiling when he screamed out in severe pain. Scar spoke one word to the Mescaleros and as they silently fell on the wounded man with their knives, he mounted his pony and watched for a moment. Joe and Ned were scared, and backed to their horses. Finally, one of the three stripped the hair from Pike's head, held it high and screamed. The three turned, ran to their horses and jumped on, still yelling bloodcurdling screams. Happy to still be alive, Three-Finger Ned and Joe Smiling Bird followed Scar, but through the flickering fire light, they could see the damage done to Pike. The Mescaleros had scalped him and cut out his tongue. Pike's terrified open eyes told the story. He was still alive.

Thirty-Two

AL HAWKINS WATCHED THE figure of a filthy gaunt man make his way toward him. He was skinny and bearded, and continually glanced over his shoulder — a sight that would've frightened most, but the big friendly man was unalarmed as the dirty stranger drew closer.

"Climb down brother, and have some cool water and grub."

The man nudged his horse closer to the well, took the offered dipper from Al's outstretched hands, and drank the sweet tasting water. Then, without warning, he shot Al Hawkins three times in the chest. Slipping off his horse, the man walked rapidly toward the house and entered, just in time to catch Sara Hawkins as she came from the kitchen to see what the commotion had been.

* * *

Earlier that day, Brad had taken the group of youngsters to the area he and Al had worked so hard to clear the week before. For most of the day they broke the hard rocky ground, then planted vegetables. That morning, Al had stayed back to "mend some harnesses...and such."

Brad suspected he just wanted a little time alone with Sara. He smiled and thought about how much the couple meant to him. The children, too. They were all like family now. Reba. Especially, Reba. He found himself thinking about her frequently, whenever he wasn't with her. He glanced at her now and found her looking at him. She smiled prettily and quickly turned her head, her dark face suddenly flushed.

The children had been excited and happy that morning, as they ran on ahead to chase butterflies and grasshoppers through the tall grass. Brad and Reba walked along together, stealing furtive glances and secret smiles at one another. Alex saw the looks and smiles, and smugly noted them with a maturity of one several times his age.

It was the one thing Brad noticed early on — the maturity of all the kids, from young Tina, right up to and including Alex and Reba. It was a level of maturity only poverty and suffering produced in anyone so young. Brad was the first to admit that, by comparison, his crippled leg was minor when compared to what must've happened to those brave children. He felt a tug on his finger and looked down into Tina's sober little face.

"I gotta go," she said.

"Me too," Brad mocked a whisper to her from behind his hand, causing Reba to smile.

He picked the little girl up and ran to a large bush, gently placing her down and she walked primly alone behind it. She was soon back, smiling brightly, and they ran to catch up with Reba and the others. He realized at that moment he'd never been happier.

Brad glanced up from his task and felt a chill run through his body. He knew something was terribly wrong as soon as he saw the billowing smoke coming from the direction of the farm house.

"Reba — Alex, keep the children together!"

His heart in his mouth, he ran as fast as he could back toward the scattered dwellings. Nearing the tall column of angry black

When Legends Lived

smoke, Brad was filled with a dread he'd only experienced once before — at his father's death. Well before he arrived, he could see the barn was burning, and clearly heard the pitiful screams of the trapped livestock. Brad hit the barn door running, raced inside to hastily open the stall doors to allow the three horses and two mules to run free.

Thick, black smoke choked him and made his eyes water until he couldn't see a foot ahead, but he felt his way along the stalls and slapped the terrorized mules on their rumps to get them started toward the door. They just stood and brayed loudly. The horses seemed to know instinctively the direction of life, as they bolted toward the opening — then the mules followed. The heat was so intense Brad didn't realize he was outside at first, then falling to his knees and coughing, he saw his shirt sleeve smoking and rubbed it out in the dirt. He stumbled to his feet and staggered away from the raging inferno, to the fresh air a distance from the burning barn. His eyes watered and burned from the smoke and it was a few minutes before he could clearly make out his surroundings. The first thing Brad saw was Al, laying as a crumpled doll might, when thoughtlessly dropped by a child.

He uttered a moan and cried, "No!"

Brad ran to the man, gently turned him over, and checked, knowing already that Al Hawkins was dead. He knelt over the man's body for a few moments, fighting back sobs, and finally comprehending what had happened, jerked his head up and stared at the house.

Sara! He ran swiftly inside, where he found her lying on the littered kitchen floor, partially disrobed, vacant eyes staring out the big window Al had installed after she'd insisted he bring it all the way from St. Louis. Brad quickly covered Sara's shame, and wiped his misting eyes with a blackened shirtsleeve. With trembling fingers, he closed the dead woman's eyes and gently brushed a lock of hair from her forehead just as Reba burst through the door, her dark eyes wide and terrified.

"Keep the kids outside, Reba. They don't need to see this," he told her softly.

She looked tearful, then bravely nodded, and went back out the door.

Brad forced himself to move — found some blankets, and used one to cover Sara. As he turned to carry the other out where Al's body lay, he heard loud hoofs enter the courtyard. Panicked the killers were returning, his only thoughts were for the children as he grabbed the pitchfork he'd picked up earlier in the barn. There were four of them. Brad quickly positioned himself between the riders and Reba, who stood in front of the children, protecting them.

A man with a drooping black mustache watched Brad's limping run to the children who were standing in shock. "Easy, boys," the big mustached man said, in a deep voice as he pulled up in front of the other riders. "We're not the enemy, son. I'm Tilghman, U.S. Marshal. What happened here?"

Bewildered, Brad took a deep shuttering breath and said, "I don't know, Marshal. I've been with the others out working in the field all day. We just returned and found the Hawkins' like this."

"Hawkins? That the name of these kids?" Tilghman said.

"That'll do as well as anything, I guess," Brad told him. "This place is called the Children's Farm. Al and Sara Hawkins started it about fifteen years ago as a home for kids that had no place else to go."

"I believe I've heard of them," the Marshal said. "We're trailing a man named Charley Scruggs. Killed an old couple near Wichita Falls last month. Comes from a bad family. Been in trouble since he was fourteen. Rumor is he once killed a man for a dollar, and a woman isn't safe alone with him for more than a minute. Looks like it finally caught up with him this time. Skinny guy...dirty...bad teeth, seen him around here?"

"No, sir. We haven't seen anyone for a month, and that was just a family of poor Indians who Al and Sara fed and gave some blankets to."

"The person that did this, he take anything?" Tilghman said, surveying the outlying area.

"I haven't had the time to look much. Mostly just busted things up, but as far as I can tell, the large coffee can Sara painted is missing. Maybe one of the horses...a little food, too I guess. I really don't know," Brad stated. "You going after him?"

"You can bet on it, boy. What did you say your name was?"

Brad hesitated just slightly. "Thomas...Bart Thomas," he said, volunteering nothing more.

Tilghman looked at him thoughtfully. "Your face looks familiar to me. Ever been down in Texas?"

"No. I'm from Omaha. Up near the Platt."

"Well, we'll git him, Mister...Thomas, right? Bart Thomas... from Omaha." Marshal Tilghman spurred his horse and rode off to the west with his deputies trailing.

Brad frowned as he watched them depart. He'd heard of Tilghman. Everyone knew Bill Tilghman had captured the last of the Daltons in Colorado last spring — that he'd been chasing them almost non-stop for the past several years. Folks said once he got onto you, he never quit looking. Brad wondered, *Was he suspicious of me, or is it just my imagination?*

When he returned to his surroundings, Reba and the children were staring at him, silently waiting for guidance.

I can't let them down, he thought. If I don't help them, they've got nowhere else to go.

Their silent, wide-eyed stares told Brad they were terrified. He knelt in front of them and grasped Tina gently by the shoulders. "Mother Sara and Father Al are in heaven now," he said. "They aren't in pain anymore. They're looking down at us right now watching to see how well we've learned the lessons they taught us."

He pulled Tina's unresponsive body to his chest and hugged her closely. He caught Reba's eye over the child's head and said, "We need some real pretty flowers for the graves, don't you think? Alex, if I can get you, Bumper, and Soto to help me, we'll go up to that ridge Father Al liked so well and dig the best resting places anyone ever had. Is it a deal?"

The boys nodded in silent agreement while Reba herded the smaller children away from the grisly scene. Al had told Brad how he liked to stand on the little ridge to the south of the house, and gaze out over the countryside. He'd said, "You can see for miles from there. That's where I'd like to be buried."

Brad and the three oldest boys took turns digging until the graves reached sufficient depth. Then they placed Al and Sara Hawkins into a wagon, hitched the horses, and pulled them up the little hill.

The smaller children picked nearly a bushel of wild flowers while the older boys built a small fence around the hilltop using wood left from the still smoldering barn. Brad and Reba prepared the bodies for burial by bathing them, and dressing them in their best Sunday clothes. Finally, they summoned the smaller children. Kneeling between the graves, Reba said soft loving prayers and the small children threw wild flowers into the holes. They placed the rest on the mounds after Brad and the boys finished covering them. Reba led the group in singing most of the hymns they'd sang every Sunday after breakfast, and at last they all stood silently, none knowing exactly what to do next.

Brad looked at the pale, frightened faces of the small huddled group and felt renewed resolve, as never before. Tina's dark head rested against him, standing with her little arms wrapped around his leg as she had been much of the day since they'd discovered the bodies. The child's grip was desperate. Brad knew her little world was suddenly filled with tornadoes and he was the only anchor she had left.

Placing his hand on her head, he spoke to the children in a low quiet voice. "The Hawkins treated all of us good," he started. "They taught us that you should help others and be ready to forgive them when they treat you badly. That might be hard for you to understand right about now…I know it is for me. But, they wouldn't want us to hate the person that did this, and they wouldn't want us to stop helping others just because we might get hurt for doing it. I believe what they'd want is for us to carry on with the Children's Farm, caring for, and looking out for each other the way they taught us to."

He paused for them to consider what he'd said, then nodded. "Yes, I think that's what they'd want us to do." Brad met Reba's eyes. "Will you help me?"

"Yes. Yes, I'll be here," she answered, moving closer and resting her head on his chest. The children followed and soon they were clustered together, arms wrapped tightly around each other. They remained that way for a long time, looking out over the view that Al Hawkins had loved so much.

R.C. Morris

* * *

The man's head exploded in a spray of blood, tissue and brains. Quickly, Wes Tanner turned the powerful telescope on the other man, found his startled face in the lens, and gently pressed the trigger. He closely checked both bodies for any signs of life, then slid the rifle with its long tubular device attached to the barrel, into a fine, tooled leather case. He put the case on his horse, mounted and rode away without looking back.

Tanner had returned to the family farm just long enough to put it up for sale. He'd received several offers right away and took the highest bid. Afterward, Tanner rode to San Antonio and sent a wire to a large hunting firm he'd heard of, located in England. Within a few months he got an answer. Tanner remembered well the day it came, for it had changed his life forever.

He'd been sitting in the saloon drinking, a past-time he'd picked up lately, answering the questions of a newspaper man named Martin…something or other…Gates. That was it, Martin Gates, from Chicago, he'd said. Gates wanted to know about his ride with McCain and Poe; the time they went into Mexico and got the women back from the Comanches. That was when his daughter died, too. Tanner quickly shoved the painful thoughts of his daughter's death out of his mind. He could recall that he'd told Gates all he knew about the trip, neither glorifying it, nor detracting from its events. Gates seemed especially interested in the part about McCain shooting his own man…the tracker, Moses Penny.

Thinking back now, Tanner figured it was just as well he'd been nearly drunk and a bit lonely when Gates approached him, or he might've just shot him, then and there. He didn't

When Legends Lived

much care nowadays, anyway. Gates seemed deeply disappointed when he learned McCain had already led his group back toward Eagle Pass, and possibly into Mexico once again.

"I don't suppose I'll ever get to meet up with McCain or Poe. I seem to be chasing my own tail," he'd remarked, as though resigned to the fact.

Martin Gates left Tanner, saying he'd be going back to Chicago on the first available transportation and hoped to see him to talk again.

Not likely, Tanner thought.

As Gates departed, the station clerk had entered and hastily informed him the package from England had arrived, and he was holding it at the station for additional postage. Tanner accompanied the clerk to the station where he paid the outrageous price for the rifle and scope and immediately headed out of town to some quiet place where he could privately try it out.

Although it cost most of the money he'd made by selling his farm, the big-game hunting rifle exceeded his greatest expectations. Tanner fired round after round, smashing every target he set up at incredible distances. Since that day, he figured he'd killed over twenty Comanches, Kiowas and "breeds." He might not rid the world of them all, but he would surely try to make a dent in them, for their taking his life from him. Wes Tanner rode south toward the Mexico border and thought about his lost life and his dead family.

* * *

Even though it was late in the year when Kate and Billy met Jim Packard in Odessa, winter hadn't quite set in yet. The region was funny about its weather. As the old timers liked to say, some years you could have summer all year long, others made you wish you'd started ranching someplace warmer, like Montana, for instance. That particular year had been a little of both, which was unusual in itself. It had started out deceptively mild with warm, summer-like air pushing down through the Colorados giving the illusion of spring.

Then, shortly after they'd arrived at the ranch, it changed, almost over night. It was as if an angry god had decided to punish the region for enjoying the initial mild weather, by sending a savage northerner howling down through the Panhandle all the way to the Mexico border. It was one of the worse blizzards anyone could remember for over twenty years. Those caught out in the open froze to death outright, and many others suffered severe frostbite. Estimates were that over five thousand cattle were destroyed by the cold weather. Having endured the severe drought for the preceding two years, for some it was the last straw. As spring apparently approached for real, some of the same smaller farmers and ranchers that had placed signs on Missouri and Tennessee homes so long ago, reading "Gone to Texas," could now be seen packing up their wagons to move on to other greener pastures.

Jim Packard had been laid up the entire winter and watched most of it pass outside his window, propped-up on pillows from his bed. He'd suffered severely from his wounds and once a specialist was sent by Southern Pacific President, Frank Chase to learn the extent of his injuries. The specialist ended up breaking the bone in his right leg again to reset it, straight. He was lost for days in the fever that followed, coupled with bouts of total exhaustion and weakness.

During the worst fever, he'd frequently think he was with Poe and McCain, in Mexico. He'd carry on long conversations with them, and often as not, curse them as well. When lucid, he often thought about the two old Rangers and found — he missed them. He thought it funny, that when he was with them he considered them to be nothing more than foolish old men, out running around the country like men half their ages. He smiled to himself and admitted he'd surely changed his mind after he'd been with them for a while. Two of the toughest old birds he'd ever seen, that was for sure. Somehow, Jim felt he'd let them down by leaving right in the middle of their operation.

Just the two of them, he thought, *out there in that damnable country alone. How are they going to catch up with that renegade, Scar, and if they do, how will just the two of them fare against his whole gang?*

When he thought about it for too long, Jim became deeply depressed. The only thing that brought him out of it was Beth. She'd been there the first time Jim opened his eyes after arriving at the K/D, and found himself staring into the most beautiful face he'd ever seen. She'd also been there every day since. Jim didn't rightly know how Beth felt about him, but he didn't try to fool himself when it came to her. For the first time in his life, Jim Packard was in love. Pure and simple. When she was with him, Jim felt tongue-tied and awkward. He felt his heart race just at the thought of her.

You've got it bad, my boy, Jim thought. *Nope, didn't learn a thing with Hattie.* But then, the marriage to Hattie had been for all the wrong reasons. With Beth, everything felt right.

As the severe winter finally passed and warm spring weather breezes begin to blow softly across the southern plains, it was evident the drought would continue into yet another disastrous year. The rains usually enjoyed at that time of year hadn't come as hoped for, and stream and river levels remained at all time lows. Most ponds, and even some lakes had now gone completely dry. On the bright side, Jim could start his rehabilitation by moving outside in a rocking chair onto the large wrap-a-round porch. As always, Beth was at his side, caring for him unselfishly.

Jim determined early on that Bethena wasn't much of a talker, but she was intelligent and well traveled, and he soon discovered they had much in common. He told her of the large cities on the east coast where he'd gone to school, and she told him about her visits to California and the Oregon Territory. Once, she'd even been to Paris. She'd picked up a little French. Since Jim had studied it while at Harvard Law School, they spent hours practicing the language between them.

As the weather began to grow warmer, he and Bethena packed a lunch and rode down to the river for the afternoon. They'd sit on a grassy spot on the river bank and she would read to him. It was also there, one cool, spring afternoon, that he kissed her for the first time. Bethena finished reading to him and they watched the busy activity of nature on the shallow stream that had once been a mighty river, and discussed places far away. As Jim shifted his position, he suddenly experienced severe pain in his leg, gasped and clutched it with both hands. She tried to help him, and when they looked up their faces were but a few inches apart. Jim cupped her face between his hands and, kissed her lightly on the lips. It lasted longer than a friendly kiss ought to last, and Bethena responded, at first with warmth and then with fire.

As their passion overwhelmed them, Bethena suddenly froze and moaned, as though in pain. "No…No. *No!*" she screamed as she broke away violently, seemingly horrified by his touch. Then she jumped up and walked rapidly toward the river.

When Legends Lived

Jim, caught off guard by her actions, awkwardly pulled himself to his feet and clambered after her. Just as she reached the water's edge, he caught up and grasped her arm. Eyes wild and frightened, Bethena shook off his hand, withdrew several more steps, and hugged her shivering body as though chilled.

"Beth, Beth," he kept saying softly until she calmed. Jim gave her plenty of room, convinced her behavior was a product of her abduction by Scar. As her breathing returned to normal, Jim slowly reached out, gently covering her hand with his own, and pulled her unresisting, to sit beside him on the ground.

After a lengthy silence, Jim painfully stood and hobbled to the wagon, where he began loading the basket and other items brought with them. Soon, Bethena joined him and began to help. Still, she said nothing. During the short drive back to the ranch, Jim made small talk attempting to draw her out of the shell she'd built up around herself again. His efforts were fruitless as she hugged herself and stared straight ahead until they'd reached the ranch house. Once there, she silently climbed down from the wagon and walked into the house without a backward glance.

Billy Shaw met her on his way out and said, "Afternoon, Aunt Bethena."

She didn't answer him, still staring straight ahead. Billy, puzzled, looked after her for a moment, then walked toward the corral without acknowledging Jim's presence.

The whole thing had been very confusing for Jim. He understood that Beth suffered some psychological and emotional problems as a result of her abduction, but she seemed to enjoy being with him. It was also evident that she enjoyed the kiss they shared — at least, initially. But something had happened, just what, Jim Packard couldn't explain. Then, there was the look Billy gave him as he passed him at the wagon today; a look… almost of hate. Suddenly, Jim felt exhausted. Hobbling to his room, he fell on the bed fully clothed and dropped off into a restless and troubled sleep.

Bethena returned to her room, sat at the mirror and slowly brushed her thick hair. She never consciously pondered it, but every time she became distressed or upset, brushing her hair seemed to help. Somewhere deep in her subconscious mind, was a vague memory of Roosevelt Poe sitting on a rock near a stream, stroking her long golden hair. She didn't know why the images came, and she knew it was probably silly, but somehow, it made her feel safe, secure.

In the protection of her own room, Bethena felt as if she'd made a total fool of herself with Jim Packard. She'd wanted him to kiss her, in fact, she'd almost thrown herself at him, and yet when he finally did, she'd fought to get away. But…I had liked it! she told herself. At least at first. It was only when those awful pictures had flashed in her mind that she'd panicked. She'd seen him again — the man with the hideous scar. But when any man tried to get close, no matter who it was, the pictures of that horrible man always flooded her mind.

Bethena placed her head on her arms and sobbed softly.

*   *   *

It was almost dark when Jim awoke. Except for the faint sounds Kate made preparing the evening meal in the kitchen, the house seemed empty. Outside, he saw no one, but could hear activity by the barn. Using his crutch, he slowly hobbled in that direction until he reached the large barn, rounded the corner and stared toward the corral. Billy Shaw was in the process of breaking a bad-natured pony. Jim halted at the fence and marveled at the grace of animal and man, as one struggled to dominate the other as if in a battle of wills. Jim wondered if he'd ever ride again.

Certainly not for a long time and not like that. He grimaced, as he watched the animal's violent gyrations as it attempted to dislodge the rider from its back. The pony gradually accepted the fact that such contortions wouldn't achieve its goal, and slowly reduced its stiff-legged jumps, accepting its fate.

As the struggle ended, young Billy swung down from the saddle, looked up, and seemed surprised to find Jim's eyes on him. Without acknowledging Jim's presence, he continued the business of unsaddling the animal, then opened the gate to let him run free.

"Aren't you afraid he'll run off to the wild herd and not return?" Jim said to him.

"That's why I let him go. He's free to leave if he wants to."

"Just seems like a lot of work, breaking him to ride and all, then just letting him go," Jim said.

"I didn't *break* him. I don't *break* animals." Billy's voice was cold. "I just showed him there was another kind of life, if he wanted to take it."

Jim watched as the pony ran hard, straight for the distant hills. "That's an interesting way of looking at things."

Billy hung the saddle from the corral fence and closed the gate. "Don't hurt my Aunt Bethena," he said quietly, still not looking at him, "I won't stand for anyone hurting her again."

"Seems to me you might be jumping to conclusions, Billy. I don't intend to hurt Beth. I don't intent to hurt anyone."

"Intentions have nothing to do with it. Whether it's intentional or unintentional, don't matter. I don't want her hurt again, and I'll step in if I have to." He looked up with cold, hard eyes.

Packard leaned on his wooden support and observed Billy with slight amusement. "Are you threatening me, Billy?" Jim smiled softly.

Billy didn't answer, just picked up a small rock near his foot. He flung it in the air, whipped out his Colt in a blur and blew it apart, just as he'd done in Fort Worth to deter a young Mexican gunfighter named Chico. He slipped the pistol back into its holster without batting an eye at Packard. "Just leave her alone," he said.

"What the hell is *that*?" Packard said. "Is that some trick they teach every kid in Texas before he can go to the toilet by himself? Every time I turn around, someone is busting rocks with a pistol for my benefit! Well, let me tell you something kid, you might've frightened me a year or so ago. But since I've been here I've had to kill men and I've been shot, too. So don't try to scare me with some slick circus trick."

The combination of events that day had Jim fuming now. "You ever come after me with that Colt, and I'll take a rifle and pick you off at two hundred yards before you ever get in range," he finished.

Billy's face turned beet red and as he opened his mouth to retort, Kate rounded the corner of the barn and walked toward them.

"What's all the shooting about? Don't you guys know shooting disturbs Beth?"

Billy glared at Jim, then abruptly turned on his heel and walked rapidly away without answering.

"Now what was that all about?" she said.

"Oh, just a little discussion of territorial boundaries," Jim answered. "Nothing to get alarmed about." He hobbled to the fence and draped his arms over the top rung for support, looking out over the dry landscape.

"You look like a man with a lot on his mind, Jim," Kate said.

He glanced at her from the corner of his eye. "Not much gets by you, does it, Kate?" He dropped his head, slowly shaking it. "Everything's so confusing lately."

Kate remained quiet, and after a moment, Jim started telling her about his afternoon picnic with Beth at the river. She let him talk until he finished with his confusing encounter with Billy. When he was done, a heavy silence hung in the air.

"After you and Roosevelt Poe brought her back to us, she suffered from horrific nightmares and depression, Jim. Followed by severe headaches, so bad that sometimes she'd scream for hours. She still has them, only not as frequently or as severe. I think now she just keeps it all inside and suffers alone."

Kate climbed up on the top rung of the fence, and hooked her boots around the second rung. "Billy was very protective of his aunt. He took on the responsibility as man of the house after his father was killed, and I suppose felt some measure of guilt that he'd been unable to prevent his aunt's abduction."

Kate smiled slightly, as she remembered. "It's been well over two years since you and Poe returned Beth to us...it hardly seems that long ago. He was still a small boy, remember? You can see that he's become a man, almost overnight. That's kind of sad in a way, at least it is for me."

Kate had a distant look as she continued, "Billy used to take that old pistol of mine, missing trigger guard and all...I didn't even know it would still shoot," she said. "He'd also take his dad's old hunting rifle, and at night, he'd stand guard on the water tower where he could see Beth's window. More importantly, I believe, was the fact that he knew Beth could also see him there, and realize she was being protected. It was the only way she could sleep without the nightmares."

Jim had suspected some of it, but hadn't really understood Beth's long-term psychological damage. "Kate, I'm in love with her. I want to marry her, have a family, diapers, snotty-nosed kids, you know, the whole thing," Jim confided.

"Everyone's in love with Beth, Jim. That's the story of her life. There've been cowboys who'd ride here from as far away as Amarillo just to see her for five minutes. They never had a chance even back then, and that was before her injuries. Now, I'm afraid no one has a chance. Maybe, not ever again," she said grimly. "I've watched her whenever a man gets within that safe area she's established for herself. First, the eyes change. They become frightened, even wild. She gasps for air and looks as if she'll break into a run…"

She paused, as though searching for the right words. "Well, you've seen it, you know what I mean. Later, she has the nightmares and headaches again." Kate stared into Jim's eyes. "There's been no improvement, Jim. Not in all this time. I've had specialists come all the way from St. Louis to see her. They want her to go back with them, be committed, for 'treatment.' I can't do that, Jim. I've heard about those places. I can't put my sister in one of those."

He could see the pain in Kate's eyes as she discussed her sister's plight.

"So, we live with it every day around here. It hasn't been easy

When Legends Lived

and it's not likely to get any better. All we can do is love and take care of her and pray she gets better. I hope I'm wrong, for both of your sakes, Jim. But I don't think Beth will ever allow a man to come near her again. Do you understand what I'm saying?" She reached out and lay her hand on his arm. "I'm sorry, Jim." Kate slowly walked away, leaving Jim to wrestle with her words.

* * *

Jake Kellogg's injuries healed slowly, mostly due to the rough journey from Mexico back to Bluebonnet. Although his wound seemed to have healed on the outside, he still experienced pain and had little use of his right arm. After several months, he was finally able to lift a Colt, but remained weak and unsteady. Well known for his card-playing abilities, Jake had been offered, and accepted a part-time job dealing cards for Paco. As soon as the "ladies" working at Paco's heard he'd been with Rosie Poe during the past months, he suddenly became a popular man with them. Jake, though a handsome man in his own right, had never been a lady's man, but he found himself enjoying this latest attention.

Jake ran an honest game and it wasn't long before Paco's clientele doubled. Paco, no fool and an astute business man, quickly offered Jake part of the take if he'd agree to stay on, full-time. He declined, saying he had to be ready to ride as soon as the Captain sent word. Paco quickly offered him a partnership if he'd stay and expand the gambling operation, at least, until he heard something from his old captain. Jake agreed, but insisted he'd be leaving if McCain beckoned. It soon became evident that Paco's decision to cut Jake in was a good one. As the business flourished, the new partners hired several more girls and built a small wing onto the back, which housed the expanded gambling operation.

Fish was glad to be back in Bluebonnet, as well. He'd quickly returned to the routine of ranch-life and picked up where he'd left off, helping with the operation. He was pleased to learn that little had changed in his absence. Fish hated change of any kind. He could ride the same mile every day, see the same horses every day, and eat the same kind of grub every day, and even that would've been too unstable for his taste. But Fish worried about the Captain and Rosie Poe; how they were eating and getting along without him. Much as he wanted to stay right there at home, he surely wished they'd let him know where they were, what they were doing, and when he could rejoin them.

Damn, he thought, *I wish they'd just come riding in today so things could be like they used to. Where are they, anyway?*

Thirty-Three

"Modern medicine tends to give pretty strange and newfangled names to some very old diseases."

– Doc Milburn

ROSCO RODE STRAIGHT THROUGH laredo and headed north to San Antonio to see Doc Milburn. If anyone could help Jenny, he'd be the one. After all, he'd patched Rosco up, as near death and as badly injured as he'd been.

Surely he can do something for Jenny, Rosco thought, as he rode north.

The nights began to run together in their sameness as Rosco would camp, make Jenny comfortable, gather firewood, take care of the animals, and cook supper. He'd then attempt to feed her, but she'd only hold the food in her mouth without chewing. He discovered that if he made soup, he could pour some of it down her throat, and at least she got a little of it before she began to choke.

"Hang on, Jenny," he said softly to her. "Just a few more days and there'll be someone that can help you." He hoped that was true.

Rosco often stared at the stranger beside him and tried to find the person he'd once thought he'd spend the rest of his life with. Trying to sort out his feelings toward her, he finally admitted he felt nothing — as if she were but a stranger who just happened to need his help. Still, he was honor bound to do what he could to care for her until she could care for herself. That was the end of his obligation. As for Dixie…well, he tried not to think about her at all. Mostly, he was unsuccessful.

Rosco bought a wagon from a farmer just south of Laredo, and both he and Jenny rode in it with his horse tied behind. Although he didn't anticipate any trouble, he always kept his rifle near his hand in the saddle-boot of the wagon. Several days into the journey, he saw a lone horseman a good mile in the distance. Shifting his weight so his sidearm was more easily assessable, he continued to drive toward the distant rider.

When they neared, Rosco reined up. "Whoa, boy. Howdy Pilgrim! How's the ford over the Nueces? You come that way?"

"Came down from San Antonio. The ford was fine when I came over her, but saw some dark clouds southeast. That's where the rain usually hits first. Better be careful when you start to cross. A flash flood could come up on you fast, and in that wagon you'd be a sitting duck."

Rosco observed the tall man, dressed in dark clothing, and what the ladies might call "ruggedly handsome." His sharp chiseled features added a hawk-like appearance. Rosco thought his eyes looked like glass.

"I'm Rosco Bookbinder, Deputy Sheriff of El Paso. This is my wife, Jenny." He nodded his head in the direction of the woman huddled beside him, hugging herself tightly. She sat silently, unmoving, not acknowledging the man's presence in any way. "We're on our way to see Doc Milburn in San Antonio. My wife's ailing, you see."

"I'm Wes Holden," the stranger said. "I'm a hunter. Headed down toward the border to do a little hunting." He smiled.

That is, his mouth smiled, but Rosco noticed his eyes did not. Rosco eyed the telescope sticking from the leather case attached to his saddle and the two Navy Colts the tall stranger wore tied to his legs. He never doubted for a moment this man was, indeed a "hunter."

I've seen men like you, stranger, he thought silently. *You have the smell of death on you.*

"Well, I hope you have some luck, Mister Holden. I don't recall there being too much game down around the border though," Rosco said. *A bounty-hunter. You've got to be a bounty-hunter, Mister.*

The man leaned slightly forward over his saddle-horn, smiled, and tipped his hat to Jenny. "Good luck on your wife's cure," he said gently. Jenny only stared straight ahead.

Rosco nodded, tapped his horse with his whip, and drove away, glad to be away from this messenger of death. Upon reaching the crest of the next ridge, he turned and looked back toward where he'd left the traveler. Though it was mostly a mile of flat terrain between him and the last ridge, there was no sight of the stranger. Rosco nervously made a mental note to check his back trail frequently during the rest of the journey.

They arrived in San Antonio in the late afternoon. Rosco was exhausted from the long ride into Mexico, and the wagon drive up from Laredo. He felt as though he could sleep for a week.

But, first things first, he told himself. *I've got to get Jenny taken care of, then a hot bath and a decent meal.* He headed for Doc Milburn's office first thing, and found the elderly gentleman bent over a medical book. *Glad to see he's not satisfied with what he knows.*

Milburn glanced up and reached for his wire-rimmed glasses and Rosco could see the startled recognition in the old doctor's face.

"Well, do I know a thing or two? Or what?" Milburn said as though reading Rosco's mind. "Just look at you, fit as a fiddle. To tell you the truth, when that old Indian brought you in here, I wouldn't have given a snowball's chance in hell of saving your tattered butt," he said bluntly. "And when I did, I never thought you'd walk again, let alone ride a horse." He eyed Rosco's appearance with disapproval and continued. "And for some distance too, if my eyes don't lie."

"I've been to Mexico, Doc. My wife was down there. It's a long story, but I'm in bad need of your magic once again."

Rosco gave Milburn only the necessary information he'd need to know in order to treat his wife. It was a sordid enough tale, as it was. He told Doc Milburn about Jenny being "carried off" by Bloody Bill Reid, about how she was "involved" in his being shot in the back, and how that resulted in the old Indian's bringing him to his place for treatment in the first place.

Rosco recounted how Jenny had later been captured by the Comanches when Reid was killed, and eventually sold into slavery in Mexico. He told of how he'd discovered her location from a whisky salesman and rode to get her. "She hasn't made a sound since I got her, Doc. Won't eat, barely sleeps, just stares straight ahead," Rosco finished.

"Well, you look like you need some care yourself, boy. I want you to go get something to eat, take a hot bath, and sleep as long as you possibly can. Leave Jenny here with me. I won't make any promises, but I'll do what I can."

The doctor and Rosco returned to the wagon and carried Jenny to his second story office, placing her into the single-sized bed Rosco had himself lain in at one time. Milburn meticulously examined her, during which he made the low grunting sounds that Rosco remembered so well. He finally turned to Rosco, making a gesture with his hand.

"Go on, git! I can't do my job with you looking over my shoulder. Come back when you don't look like a patient yourself." With that, he turned back toward the woman, ignoring Rosco.

Rosco retreated to the hotel where he rented a room for the week. He climbed wearily up the stairs to his room and, without undressing, fell onto the bed's covers. He didn't move for the next ten hours.

He finally nudged himself awake, but it was only long enough to get undressed and crawl under the covers for another six hours. At last, awake, he yelled from the top of the stairs to the desk-clerk.

"How 'bout some hot water? Lots of it!"

Bathed and dressed in clean clothing, he found a place called "Ruth's Fine Food." Although the place was empty, Rosco selected a chair facing the door out of habit. He ordered steak, eggs, fried potatoes, biscuits, and gravy, and finished it all off with two slices of apple pie and several cups of strong black coffee. As he paid, the attractive young woman who'd served him said, "I don't know how long it's been since you've eaten, but I sure like to see a man enjoy his food."

She made it clear by her eye contact and warm smile, that she wouldn't find his attentions entirely unwelcome. In fact, she seemed down-right disappointed when he failed to act upon her open invitation.

Doc Milburn was just leaving as he arrived. "Oh, there you are," he said. "I'm going to lunch. Come along, we'll talk while we eat."

The thought of eating again made Rosco feel a little sick. "I just had lunch."

"Well, at least have a little pie. I know a widder woman that makes the best pie in Texas," Milburn persisted.

"That wouldn't be Ruth, would it?"

"It sure would! How's about it?"

"Think I'll pass this time, Doc. You go ahead and I'll stay with Jenny and wait. Take your time."

Milburn was obviously disappointed, but grunted and walked out mumbling to himself.

Jenny seemed about the same as when he'd last seen her, propped against two pillow. She appeared to be asleep, but Rosco knew from his previous experiences with her, on the trail, that it might not be the case. She lay unmoving as he sat next to the bed and carried on a one-sided conversation. Rosco didn't know exactly what he was going to do now that he had Jenny back, but it really didn't make much difference.

I've already lost Dixie, he told himself. *Might as well do something for Jenny, as not. Maybe go back to El Paso and try to get my old job as deputy sheriff.*

His thoughts on Dixie, Rosco slipped into a painful, deep depression, sharper than any he'd ever experienced. The pain was more excruciating than the wounds he'd suffered; but at least something good had come out of them — Dixie. His mind wandered back when, in that very room, he lay near death as Dixie cared for him day-after-day. She'd been the first person he'd seen when he opened his eyes, and the only one he'd loved since. Even before that, when he was laid up at her ranch, injured, she'd taken care of him then, too. Seemed like that girl made a career of taking care of him every time he got himself hurt. And just look how he'd repaid her, Rosco reproached himself.

"Oh, hell," he groaned softly, disgusted he was feeling so sorry for himself. *She has got to be better off now*, he thought. What could he ever give her that she didn't already have? Her, part-owner of one of the largest ranches in West Texas, and just look at him, a deputy sheriff. Thirty dollars a month! He'd been fooling himself all along. Suddenly, vivid images of cool grass, a quiet stream and sweet lovemaking invaded his mind again. Abruptly, he stood and forced the images away.

You've got to stop this! You'll drive yourself crazy and who'll take care of Jenny then? Dammit, I had no say in this choice! he told himself for the hundredth time. *A man is bound by his duty, whether he chooses it or not.*

Doc Milburn found him staring out the window when he returned. Rosco's back told him what the young man was feeling, and he shook his head, mildly. *That boy has a heap of troubles on his shoulders*, he thought, as he checked Jenny.

Rosco turned and said, "How was your pie?"

"Mighty tasty, and while I was there, that young widder woman asked if I knowed anyone fitting your description. Said you must have a 'voracious' appetite,'" he said, cocking an eyebrow. "Don't know what she could've meant by that, do you?"

"What did you tell her?"

"The truth! I'm a doctor. I can't afford to be caught lying," Milburn said, still occupied with Jenny.

"Thanks," Rosco said dryly.

"She's sleeping. It's best to give her some quiet. I don't know about you, but I could stand a snort. How 'bout you? Give us a chance to talk. I've made some determinations about your wife's condition."

"Sure," Rosco said. "Might as well. Seems like I'm going to

be here for a while." He picked up his hat and Milburn followed him outside. Neither spoke as they walked toward the saloon, preferring to wait until they'd had a drink before opening any serious discussions.

After downing two drinks quickly, Doc Milburn started it off. "I got some bad news for you, son — if I'm even correct in my diagnosis."

Rosco remained silent and looked at him expectantly.

Milburn had been in the business for over twenty-five years. He'd been required to pass on a lot of bad news to folks during that time, and it still wasn't easy for him. One thing he was sure of though, was that bad news didn't get better if you tried to sugar-coat it. He sighed deeply, and went on.

"Jenny's got something that I can't cure, son," he said solemnly. "In fact, there ain't no cure for it that I know about. At least, not with the medicine we have today." He eyed Rosco seriously, determined not to shirk his responsibility. "Someday, someone, will figure out how to treat it, but for now we're all ignorant."

"What does it do? Will she recover?"

"Eventually, it'll surely take her life — but before that happens, the disease will probably blind her — possibly destroy her sanity."

"What causes it? What's it called?" Rosco sounded stunned at this unexpected news.

"In England, where I came from, folks thought sailors brought it back from the Indies or Africa," Milburn told him. "That's not true, it's been around for centuries. Just never had a name. The doctors there called it the 'Pox.' Here, it's got several medical names you wouldn't even recognize, nor remember."

Doc continued thoughtfully, "Along the coastal areas, they call it…now, don't get riled, boy…they call it 'whore's disease.' That's because folks rightly believe that it's transmitted through intercourse. You know what that means, Rosco?"

His face looked a little blank, so Milburn told him bluntly, "It spreads through sex! One person who's a carrier goes to bed with another person, and that person gets it, too." He hurried on, determined to get it over with. "I don't know how long she's had it, Rosco. Maybe all those months she's been in Mexico, maybe a long time before. Now, the thing is, this disease is funny. You don't necessarily get it every time you go to bed with someone that has it...but you can. Understand?"

Rosco stared blankly. Doc Milburn drained his glass and refilled it from the half-empty bottle on the table. "Are you getting any of this?" he said, gruffly.

Rosco slowly nodded his head, and Milburn sighed.

"You ain't gonna make this easy for me, are you, boy?" He took another healthy swallow, carefully set his glass in its original water ring, and went on, "There are incubation periods, dormant times — things like that. Even the doctors don't completely understand how it works. Anyway, it's not a hundred percent thing, you know?"

He waited for a moment, took another deep breath, then said, "I need to examine you, too, son. Right away!"

A stricken look slowly crossed Rosco's face. "You mean you think I could have it, too?" his mind immediately on Dixie.

"I'm saying that I don't know enough about it to be sure. I just want to be sure that you're all right. Now, when do you want to do it?"

"Now! Right damn now!" Rosco blurted out. He abruptly rose and Doc Milburn looked up at him, startled, then sighed again, stood and followed him out.

* * *

Several hours later, Rosco was sitting on the straight-backed chair in the doctor's office buttoning his shirt, as Milburn was squinting at a medical book in the dim light of a kerosene lamp. Finally, he laid it aside.

"I can't be for certain, but you might've dodged a bullet, son. I don't think you have anything to worry about."

"What about Jenny? Is there anything we can do for her?"

"Make her as comfortable as possible, take care of her the best you can, and above all, treat her like a human being and not some animal that needs to be put to sleep."

"How long?"

"Hard to say. Could be a year. Could be five. Hell, it could even be next month! These things just aren't that predictable, Rosco. Jenny's case is advanced, but I've seen people live for years who are just as bad."

Rosco rose wearily and moved to the window overlooking the street. He stared unseeing down into the street for a while, and then without turning, in a very quiet voice, said, "I don't know where to go, or what to do, Doc."

"You might think about staying around here. That way I could treat Jenny. Besides, if you travel with her in her weakened condition, she may up and die on you. I heard the sheriff has need for another deputy. That's your type of business, ain't it? I could put in a word with the mayor if you'd like."

"Let me think about it, Doc." He paused in the open doorway. "Thanks."

Thirty-Four

MCCAIN RETURNED TO CAMP to find Poe in an unusually good mood and feeling, much better, as he moved around the camp preparing the evening meal without discomfort. He purposely waited until the following morning, to pass on his adventures as they made ready to ride. As McCain tightened the horse's cinch-strap, he suddenly grimaced and discretely rubbed his shoulder, glancing to be sure Poe hadn't seen his gesture.

It did no good, however, for Rosie, never having been one to politely ignore anyone's discomfort, especially his partner, said slyly, "Old Grasshopper took a nip outta you again, did he? Hee, hee."

McCain, lengthened his stirrups and ignored Poe, hoping that would be the end of it. That wasn't to be the case, however.

"You oughta turn that onerous cuss into soap, Jericho. Every time you turn around, he's either trying to kick your head off, eat you up — or some other such foolishness. If I told you once I've told you a thousand times to get a mare. A mare is twice as smart as a stallion. They can last a lot longer on the trail too, and their hoofs grow back faster when they git broke," Poe concluded.

Dumbfounded, McCain suddenly stopped, and slowly turned, to stare at his partner with open mouth. Then, as if he hadn't heard Poe correctly, he gasped, "Their hoofs do what?"

"Just what I said," Poe answered. "Their hoofs grow back faster. I read about it in a book one time."

"Well, I would surely like to have seen that book," McCain said sarcastically. "I'll just bet it was loaded with pictures of hoofs and things like that."

"Now, Jericho, no need for you to go and get nasty. I'm just trying to give you the benefit of my profundity and there you are again, gitting all sarcastical on me. I don't know why I even bother trying to better your lot in life. I surely don't."

McCain snorted and continued saddling his horse. Sliding the bridle over the horse's head, he suddenly jumped back just as Grasshopper lunged, and clicking his teeth loudly. Poe chuckled silently to himself, and McCain shot him a hard look.

Rosie whistled low and said, "Come here, girl."

The sorrel mare he'd ridden for several years whinnied softly and walked over, nuzzling his shoulder. Poe looked righteously at his partner and scratched the horse behind the ears, to the animal's obvious enjoyment. Then, shamelessly showing off as he watched McCain from the corner of his eye, he raised his hand, gripped the reins, and the horse stood in-place and pranced.

McCain snorted again and ignored this display, as he pulled himself into the saddle for another long day's ride.

* * *

Over the next several hours, they back-tracked McCain's trail of the previous day. As they cautiously approached the area where he'd been ambushed, the two split-up and approached from different directions. They located the spot where McCain made his "long shot", and found a trace of blood. Moving carefully over the crest, they found the spot where the ambushers horses had been tied and Poe dismounted to check the signs.

When Legends Lived

Returning, he swung into the saddle and kicked his mount forward, watching the ground as McCain followed, his rifle at the ready, searching the rocks around them.

Poe followed the tracks for two more hours before they discovered the old camp, and Pike's mutilated body. The weather was warmer, and swarms of flies buzzed around the remains. Chasing several vultures off the carcass, Poe examined it.

"Six, seven hours," he said. "Hard to tell after the varmints have been at him for so long."

He scanned the surrounding ground, then pointed to the southwest. "That way. Got some Apaches with them now, too. Can't tell how many — three, maybe four. That makes Three Finger Ned and the other half-breed, the Apaches and our old buddy, Scar. Six...maybe seven of 'em."

"Well, let's get on with it. Sooner we catch up with them and kill 'em, the sooner we get back to the ranch," McCain announced impatiently.

Poe paused with one foot in the stirrup, ready to mount. "Now, I do like optimism out of the people I work with, Jericho," he said without a trace of sarcasm. "Yes, sir, we'll just ride up, and while they sit there and oblige us, we'll shoot each one of those seven killing machines right between the horns, then git our butts on back to the ranch for supper. Nothing to it. Hell, we should be able to accomplish all that by about sundown, if we git started right away. Yes, sir, nothing to it," Poe said with dead seriousness.

McCain just looked at him, sure that he'd missed something, then nodding his head in agreement, spurred his horse in the direction Poe had indicated. Poe gazed after his long-time partner in amusement, slowly shook his head and followed.

By the end of the day, it became evident Poe's back was troubling him once more, so McCain called it a day earlier than he normally would have — claiming he was "plum wore out." McCain cleaned up the supper dishes and watched Poe from the corner of his eyes, as he swigged a deep swallow from his small brown medicine bottle and grimaced as he lay back on his bed-roll. Poe groaned softly.

"Ya know, Jericho? I wouldn't mind traveling, if I could just take that damn Scar with me," he said seriously. "I mean, I would dearly hate to leave this life knowing I'd left something that important undone."

He lay his head down and closed his eyes, and within a minute was snoring softly.

Just what the hell was that supposed to mean? McCain asked himself. *Roosevelt Poe, you get harder and harder to understand every day.*

He went to check on the animals and discreetly gave Grasshopper a wide berth as the stallion rolled his eyes at him. "You heard what Roosevelt said, you damned piece of crow-bait. You just keep on and you're gonna end up as soap on somebody's wash basin," he muttered.

McCain stood guard until well past midnight; long after Poe's turn was scheduled to start, to give his partner as much rest as possible. The next morning, both men were up before daylight, prepared to move once more. About noon, Poe stopped and waited for McCain to come along side.

As he reined-in, Poe spit and said, "Ya notice something, Jericho?"

"Yep. It's the same trail he rode the last time we took in after him," McCain answered.

They both remembered chasing Scar into Mexico, west past

the Diablo's, and finally losing him just south of the Arizona border. It had been one of their most bitter failures.

"That's right. As I recall, we were after him for nine months that time. We chased the cuss nearly to Baja and finally lost him in the mountains to the south of Nogalas. My butt's still numb from that trip," Poe chuckled.

"Maybe we'll get lucky this time. Maybe he'll decide to stop and fight. He's got to know we're back here and this time, we're not going to give up. So, unless he wants to run for the rest of his life, he's got to have it out with us sooner or later," McCain stated.

"Well, it can't be too soon for me. I'm getting too old for this horseshit, Jericho," Poe told his partner with a smile.

McCain grinned as he remembered his own words to Jim Packard earlier. He again observed Poe from the corner of his eye. "Let's give it about two more hours and call it off early for today. We can get a good night's sleep and head out early again tomorrow morning. What say?"

"Sounds good to me," Poe said. "I'm beginning to think I might be in love with my bedroll. Can't wait to see it every night," he chuckled again and spurred on ahead, searching the ground once more.

McCain followed, cradling the Sharps, and scanning the hills around them.

* * *

Brad Thompson stood by the walled-in spring as he'd seen Al Hawkins do countless times, and watched as the distant rider made his way toward the farm. He could hear the comfortable sounds Reba made as she prepared the evening meal for him and the children. Brad smiled to himself as he thought about Reba and her swollen belly. Another baby, Al. Another child for our Children's Farm. I wish you and Sara could be here to see it.

Brad looked differently than before, and it was intentional. He'd gained nearly twenty pounds and had grown a thick, black beard. He'd also let his dark hair grow shoulder-length.

"You look like a mountain-man," Reba had chided him a few days earlier.

He'd reluctantly offered to cut it off, but she'd just laughed and rubbed his face whiskers with both hands.

"No. I like it. You look like a big old bear." Then, she'd gotten serious and kissed him firmly, whispering softly, "My big old bear."

He smiled as he remembered how he'd led her into the room they shared and made love to her until they fell asleep wrapped in one another's arms.

Brad snapped back to the present as he realized the rider was closer now, barely three hundred yards away, and he suddenly recognized who it was. *It's Marshal Tilghman.* Instantly, Brad had very foreboding feelings. He raised his hand but received no return gesture from the lawman. He waited until Tilghman reined-in beside the spring-wall.

"Howdy, Marshal." He reached up and handed Tilghman a granite dipper of cool water, as had become the custom at the Children's Farm. "Lite and have some supper. Reba has it on now," he invited.

Bill Tilghman swung down from the back of the large animal, with an agility that belied the size of the man. "Don't mind if I do. A man can get tired of his own cooking after a time on the trail. But then, you wouldn't know that, would you, Mister…Thomas ain't it? I mean you never been on the trail much, right?"

Brad looked at the Marshal and thought, *so that's it*. Well, he'd known it had to come sooner or later, and Tilghman had seemed a bit suspicions of him the last time he was there.

"Yes, that's right, Marshal. Been a homebody most of my life. Come join us. Supper will be on by this time."

He turned, walking back toward the large farm house. They could smell the aroma of bread baking coming from the kitchen, and Tilghman noticed a new barn where the burned-out one had once stood. Reba saw him as they came through the door and Tilghman didn't miss the worried look she shot at "Bart Thomas."

"Reba, you remember Marshal Tilghman, don't you?" He'll be joining us for supper."

"Of course. How do you do, Marshal?" Reba pulled out a chair and smiled, dazzling him with its brightness. "Please sit here, Marshal Tilghman."

Reba went into the kitchen, returning with heaping platters of hot food, just as they heard children's running feet. The running and pushing stopped just short of the door and the children entered very orderly, each politely speaking to Tilghman. When everyone was seated, they all bowed their heads and Brad gave a short, but sincere thanks for their food.

The conversation was animated as they ate, everybody offering something that had happened to them during the day. Even cute little Tina, who'd found a frog, and claimed she had it in her pocket, 'If anyone would like to take a look at it.'

When Brad assured her that nobody wanted to see her frog while they were eating dinner, she'd pouted, but quickly returned to her bubbly self. Tilghman was amazed at the transformation of the silent, sad little Tina, into the bright child now before him.

Brad saw him looking at her and as though reading his mind, said, "Love, Marshal. That's what love can do."

After dinner, Reba went about getting the children bathed and ready for bed. Brad and Marshal Tilghman relaxed on the large porch, enjoying a smoke and the evening breeze. Tilghman lit up his pipe and leaned against a support on the porch steps. As he puffed for a while, Brad said, "Did you ever catch that fellow that killed the Hawkins?"

"That villain Charley Scruggs? Yep. He was hiding in a gorge just south of here, brewing up some of that coffee he took from your kitchen. Might'a rode right on past him if we hadn't smelled it cooking. Caught him, and took him back to Texas. Hung 'em," Tilghman said, puffing a few more times. "What's the matter," he said, seeing the look on Brad's face. "Don't you think the man should've been hanged for what he done?"

"I don't like to see anyone die like that. I can forgive him and I think Al and Sara would forgive him," Brad told the marshal.

"But we won't ever know what the Hawkins would think, will we?" Tilghman pointed out, "because, they're dead, now, and they can't tell us." He gazed out across the even rows of planted fields. "Mr. Thomas, people have to obey the law of the land. They have to understand that if a life is taken, they must give up their own in return. Civilization will never come to this land until everyone understands the law of the land will not compromise. As long as people understand that before hand, there shouldn't be any question about what to do with a killer. Ain't that the way you see it?"

"I guess that's a point of view, Marshal. But some people do change and they can spend the rest of their lives trying to make up for their misdeeds."

Tilghman smoked for a while, then stated, "A while back, a gunslick down in Texas killed a sheriff and another fellow. Shot them both down in cold blood and ran. A young fellow, 'bout your age. Even had a limp like yours, they say. Funny."

Tilghman knocked the ash from his pipe-bowl. "What do you think should happen to that young killer, Mr. Thomas? Should he be made to pay for his deed?"

Brad hung his head, then spoke so softly that Tilghman was forced to lean forward to hear him. "I think he must pay for it every day of his life, Marshal. You might even be doing him a favor if you did catch him and hang him." Brad looked up and continued, "The bad thing would be if there were others who depend on him in order to live. People whose lives would be destroyed if he wasn't around to take care of them."

The floor creaked and they turned to find Tina standing in the doorway, clutching a doll. As Tilghman watched, she went to Brad and silently climbed into his lap. Snuggling against his ample stomach, she wrapped her little arms around him as far as she could, and was fast asleep in less than a minute.

"You mean, someone like that little girl there?" Tilghman said, pointing his pipe at the sleeping child.

A short time later, Reba came out and found Brad, holding Tina fast in his arms. Tears ran down his cheeks as he stared toward the field, and the back of U.S. Marshall Bill Tilghman, riding away.

Thirty-Five

*"If I owned Hell and Texas,
I'd rent out Texas and live in Hell."*

– General Philip H. Sheridan

SCAR, WATCHING THE THREE Mescaleros gamble for trinkets, heard the clatter of horse's hoofs at the same time the Apaches did, and watched at the point they would emerge from the darkness. He could tell by the sound of it, who the horse belonged to. Scar waited until Bone slid to a halt near the fire, sending dust and dirt flying.

"They're still there, Boss Man, 'bout four hours behind us. Pretty near got my tail shot off trying to get too close. Big caliber. Sounded like it a buffalo gun," he said, breathlessly. "I was careful, too, but those two old birds got duck's eyes. They're damn good. Better than I've seen for a long time," he conceded.

Scar stared at him contemptuously. "If I'd been there, I'd have killed 'em both. All I've got around me are women. Stinking women." Scar spit with distaste. "You get close enough for them to shoot at you, then you come riding in here and tell me you didn't kill either one of them? I ought to kill you myself, Bone."

Bone took the abuse because he knew one small misstep on his part could send Scar into one of his murderous rages.

"Soon, I'll stop and kill them. I won't run from them forever." With that, Scar rose and walked away from the fire.

When Legends Lived

* * *

At the same moment Rosco Bookbinder left the doctor's office, Hal La'Mount was seated in the Buffalo Gals Saloon, dealing black-jack to four other men. He hadn't done badly in this town. He owned the saloon and now the adjacent hotel, and had designs on the livery stable and general store as well. He'd gone about it smart though, right from the first. He'd hired Mick Bishop and Kirby Hope as bartenders — bouncers — and even though they had to bust a few heads once in awhile, they'd more than earned their keep. Both carried double-barreled shotguns and had proven their worth numerous times.

Three months earlier, La'Mount had hired Joe Coffee, too. What he couldn't get away with before, was no problem once he had Coffee on his payroll. Even Sheriff Sweet didn't want any part of the gunman Coffee. No, the sheriff wouldn't bother him anymore. That's not to say that Sweet hadn't been a pretty rough old boy himself during his time, but he'd taken a bullet when he was working as Chief of Security for the salt shipments in El Paso, and was more cautious now, than before. He'd said many times, he just wanted to get his retirement and be alive to spend some of it.

Hell, La'Mount thought, *who can blame him? Sweet will do that too, if he don't push me too hard.* There didn't seem to be much danger of that since he'd hired Coffee.

Coffee had killed seven men that Hal knew of. He'd faced each and every one of them, let them pull and gunned them down. Even La'Mount wouldn't want to go up against him, and La'Mount was more than a fair hand with a pistol himself. He saw Coffee dealing cards at the next table and noted he always sat with his back against a wall, his gun hand empty. One hard customer, Hal told himself, with satisfaction.

Suddenly, Kirby Hope burst through the door and looked quickly around. Spying Hal, he rapidly approached him, and squatted down by the table. "Guess who's in town?" he said breathlessly.

"I ain't got time for games, Kirby," Hal retorted, eyes on his cards.

"You remember that feller you and that Thompson kid ran out of town a year or so ago? Bookman, or something? Well, he's back. And he brought his wife with him," Hope said with a great deal of relish.

Hal stopped dealing and sat motionless, staring at the cards in his hands. His reputation was such that none of the other men at the table complained. "Dixie?" he said. "Dixie is with him?"

"No, no. Not her. Another woman," Hope said hurriedly. "He was married to another woman all the time. And get this, Hal. She was a whore down in Mexico. Can you beat that? A whore." Kirby Hope grinned nastily.

"You lying to me, Kirby?" Hal said coldly.

"Swear to God it's the truth, Boss. I'm not lying. It's all true. One of Doc's cleaning women heard about it through the door. The wife's name is Jenny and she's over at Doc's office right now. She's got some real bad disease, and may even be dying."

Hal La'Mount seethed with rage. Bookbinder had stolen the only woman he ever really wanted and took her away. Hell, maybe he'd just wanted her because he couldn't have her, but that didn't enter into it. She'd belonged to him and that saddle tramp had stolen her.

"Where is he now?"

"Still over at Doc's office. He's staying at the hotel across the street. Can you beat that?"

When Legends Lived

Hal slumped in his chair and contemplated his next move. Then he said, "Coffee!"

Joe Coffee glanced up and La'Mount motioned to him. "Come here, I want to talk business with you. Time to earn your money."

* * *

Depressed, Rosco left Doc Milburn's office and headed back for the hotel. His mind was filled with Dixie, horrible diseases, and the pale face of Jenny lying on Doc Milburn's small bed, surely dying. He wanted to strike out, cry, and scream his confusion and frustration at a god that could be so unmerciful. Never in his young life had he felt such hopeless despair. As he stepped onto the hotel boardwalk, he was stopped in his tracks by a faintly familiar voice.

"I didn't think you had the guts to come back here, Bookbinder. What did you do, dump Dixie for someone else?"

Rosco turned slowly to find the hatred filled eyes of Hal La'Mount.

"You took the only woman I ever cared about, then dumped her!" Hal said, his smooth voice oozing rage. "Now, here you are again, with a wife, and I hear you were married all along."

"Let it go, Hal. You really don't want to push this. Not today," Rosco said wearily.

A short bald-headed man wearing an apron and holding a Greener, moved to his right just outside the saloon door. From the corner of his eye, he saw another man, a gunfighter from the way he wore his hardware, step in front of the hitching rack, also to his right.

Three, he thought. *Old Hal always did like to play with the odds in his favor.*

"Oh, not me. Him!" Hal pointed toward the gunfighter. Coffee rocked on the balls of his feet with a faint smile.

"You don't want to die today, Hal. Let it drop," Rosco told him again wearily.

By then, word had spread about trouble brewing outside the Buffalo Gal's Saloon, and a small crowd had gathered to watch.

"You know…?" Hal started, as he grinned and shook his head in disbelief, "…nah, it just can't be true, but I just heard a nasty rumor about your wife."

"Watch it, Hal. Don't take this any further."

"Hell, I didn't say it, someone else did. I'm just repeating it. You know who told me? He did." Hal pointed at Coffee, still smiling. "It just can't be true." Again he shook his head as if in total disbelief. "Mr. Coffee there told me your wife was a lady of the evening down in Mexico. A whore! I've been to Mexico many times, maybe we even know each other."

"After I kill him," Rosco said softly, "I'm going to kill you." He turned slightly so his side was toward Joe Coffee, and stared at the short man holding the shotgun.

"Kirby!" Coffee said. "I'll handle this."

The bald-headed man lowered the scattergun to his waist and held it pointed away from Rosco. Coffee stared at Rosco's eyes and, with a smile playing at his lips, said, "Whenever you're ready, cowboy."

Witnesses told Sheriff Sweet later, that both men had made their move about the same time. Coffee, maybe even a split second before the other.

"It didn't make no difference," one toothless old man who had seen it all, relaated. "I never seen anything happen so fast in all my life. That Bookbinder feller, I believe that's what you said his name was? It never even looked like he moved. Just sort of shrugged his shoulders a bit and his hardware was in his hand. He shot old Joe Coffee right square between the eyes, then turned and shot La'Mount, just like he'd promised. Hee, hee."

The old man laughed loudly a couple of times, broken up by a fit of coughing and spitting. When he'd recovered sufficiently, he went on with his story to the sheriff. "He kind of held his pistol loosely in his hand, not really pointing it at anything, just sort of waving it in the air, like this." The old man's finger made a whirling motion, obviously enjoying his instant fame. "He motioned with it to Kirby. He told Kirby…he said…" The old man's voice got soft as he squinted his eyes in an imitation of Rosco's facial expressions. "…he said, 'If you drop that scatter-gun and run like a rabbit, I may not shoot you…then again, I might.'" Said, "'You get on the first horse you come to…don't matter whose horse it is, and ride. If I ever see you again, I'll kill you.' Hee, hee. That's what he said. Hee, hee."

The old man coughed a few more times as Sheriff Sweet waited patiently for him to continue. Finally, the witness wiped his mouth on the back of his sleeve and said, "Well, old Kirby took out outta there like someone hit him in the ass with a load o'bird shot. Hee, hee." He had another fit of laughing laced with coughing.

"La'Mount shore had a funny look on his face — like he was real surprised," the old man said. "He just sat there, looking down at the red stain on his pure white shirt, getting bigger and bigger like he couldn't believe it. Died just like that!" He snapped his fingers. He'd wanted to talk longer, but the sheriff had heard enough.

San Antonio Sheriff, T.J. Sweet, hired Rosco on the spot.

* * *

Spring was coming slowly and Rosco had been deputy sheriff for T.J. Sweet for several months. He liked it well enough, and the sheriff, good as his word, never complained about the time Bookbinder spent caring for Jenny. He used the last of his money to rent a small house on the outskirts of San Antonio and moved in his meager belongings the same day. Doc Milburn and Sheriff Sweet helped obtain two small beds and other essential furnishings.

While sparse, Rosco liked it. Particularly the location, for the small white framed house sat two hundred feet from the river, shaded by several large trees. Doc Milburn gave him a rocking chair, and every day he would carry Jenny to the back porch, facing the river, and let her sit a few hours. She never gave any outward sign she was aware of her surroundings, but Doc said it might help.

One day as he just finished lunch, Rosco stepped into the warm afternoon sun and started across the busy street. He'd dodged several wagon teams and riders managing to get to the other side. As he did, he heard a voice call out his name. Looking around, he picked a familiar face out of the crowd.

"Rosco. Rosco Bookbinder, how the hell are you?" Nate Thompson yelled.

Coming up rapidly, he grasped Rosco's hand in a crunching handshake, and bellowed, "Doggone, it's good to see you, Hoss!" He struck Rosco a numbing blow in the middle of his back with a ham-like hand.

Nate, who hadn't been much more than a big youth when Rosco knew him, was now filled out and a huge man. He stood well over six-feet-five inches tall and Rosco guessed he weighed

When Legends Lived

about two-hundred and sixty pounds. None of it looked particularly fat. Nate did most of the talking and finally decided they should have "something to wet the whistle." Their talk finally turned to Nate's family and ultimately — to Dixie.

"Brad got in some bad trouble down in Laredo. Killed the sheriff, under questionable circumstances, and ran off. Haven't heard a breath from him in almost two years now," Nate said. "After you left, Dixie left too."

Rosco's facial expression remained unchanged, but he leaned noticeably forward at the mention of her name. "Oh?" he said, with an apparent lack of interest. "Where did she go?"

"Went back east, Rosco. Just there a short time when she married a feller, name of Decker. Builds boats."

Rosco felt as if he'd been kicked in the stomach. "Married?" he mumbled. "I never heard."

"Yeah, kind of took us by surprise, too. I always thought you and Dixie would end up getting hitched." Seeing the look on Rosco's face, Nate's face reddened. "Sorry, Rosco. I always did have a big mouth."

The two men drank for a while without talking and Rosco ordered more. He raised his in a toast, "To Dixie. All the happiness."

Nate touched his glass and they gulped it down.

Rosco set his glass down and started talking. He told Nate everything that had happened to him, all about Jenny and how he'd left Dixie alone, to do his "duty". He unloaded everything that he'd kept bottled-up inside all those months.

Nate let him talk, and when he was finished, said, "You done what you thought was right, Rosco. A man can't do any more than that."

Late in the evening, they staggered back to Nate's room, and collapsed on the same bed. When Rosco awoke the next morning, the sun was already high and he quickly jumped up and ran all the way back to his house. Juanita, the housekeeper he'd hired to stay with Jenny, was livid. Although he tried to explain, she fired off a string of Spanish at him as she stormed out. Rosco lowered himself into Jenny's rocking chair and held his aching head. He felt sick.

Thirty-Six

JIM PACKARD'S REHABILITATION HAD improved to the point he could climb into a wagon on his own and drive limited distances. He'd had ample time to think about his discussion with Kate, regarding Beth and Billy. Perhaps he'd misjudged Billy and decided to make an effort to get to know him better.

Jim watched as Billy Shaw headed toward the river. For the last month, he'd watched Billy every evening about the same time, as he traveled the familiar route. Picking up his cane, Jim headed toward the corral. One of the hired hands was forking hay into a large stall inside the barn when Jim limped in. The hired-hand harnessed one of the horses to a buggy and in minutes, Jim was following the route he'd seen Billy take.

As Jim approached, he saw Billy's paint grazing in the lush grass between him and the trees which lined the river. He pulled up to the same area and let his animal have his head to also graze. Jim slowly made his way through the brush until he could see the water. A gradual slope in the bank led out to a gravel point that, in effect, narrowed the river. At the point it narrowed, the water picked up speed and depth, causing white-capped rapids. Billy stood knee-deep, whipping his fly-rod repeatedly, into the current.

Jim limped toward him and called out about midway across the gravelly point. Deep in thought, Billy hadn't heard him drive up. He looked up and scowled at Jim's approach, and without acknowledging him, continued to cast.

"Catch anything?" Jim persisted.

"No."

"Looks like a good place over by that jetty," Jim pointed out.

Billy didn't answer. It'd been Joe Walker's favorite fishing hole. At least, it'd been his favorite place to try getting a hook into. He'd never been able to do it, though Billy had seen Joe cast toward it once at the end of every day's fishing adventure. He was convinced a lunker was waiting out there under that fallen tree. Since Joe's death, Billy had lost many rigs trying to get his hook into the confined area. It was as if he wanted to prove old Joe right about the lunker being there. He'd given up on it temporarily, vowing to try again when he became better.

Spying the rod and fishing basket once used by Joe Walker, Jim said, "Mind if I give it a try?"

Without waiting for an answer, he picked up the rod and expertly checked it over. It seemed ready to go. Jim hooked the basket around his waist and eyed the canvas fishing hat on the ground next to it, but catching Billy Shaw's glare, decided against it. He took a deep breath and walked straight out into the swift current. His bum leg, made the going difficult, putting it mildly, he thought glumly. Determined, he inched his way farther out until, about halfway, he suddenly lost his footing and nearly tumbled into the current.

Heart pounding, Jim regained his footing, carefully took a deep breath and blew it out. *I'm a damned fool trying this*, he told himself. He finally approached the point he'd picked out as his casting spot. In graceful motion, Jim whipped his line back-and-forth overhead, until he had sufficient length, then with a delicate flick of his wrist, dropped the hook dead center of the calm jetty. It might've been the best cast he'd ever made.

When Legends Lived

Joe Walker had been right — it was a lunker. An almost unbelievable lunker! He must have been waiting for years for just the right incitement. Jim's rod bent double instantly as the large trout hit the lure, and his line sounded like a fine piano string when it reaches its maximum stretch-point. Mr. Lunker left the water three times in the process of Jim trying to land him. Billy heard it hit too, and threw down his own rod, raced out into the current and yelled encouragement and advice on how to land this fish — the largest one he'd ever seen.

Jim worked the lightweight rig like the expert he was, giving the fish line when he wanted it and taking up the slack when he gave it back. About halfway in from the jetty he shouted, "Billy! Leg's giving out! Take the line, I'm going down!"

Billy trudged through the knee-deep current until he was within an arms length of Packard. As Packard thrust the rod into his hands, and turned toward the shore, he went down. He struggled to regain his footing, taking on mouthfuls of rushing water. He could hear Billy yelling to take his hand, and could see the young man reaching with his outstretched hand. The end of his pole was tipped down and the line appeared to be slack. Jim thrust his head above water and shouted, "Don't worry about me, keep the line taunt! He'll get off!"

Billy just shook his head and kept his hand thrust out. Jim grasped it and was hauled to his feet, sputtering and spitting river water. The line was limp; Jim knew the giant trout was gone. Suddenly, the line shot straight out and Billy whooped and raised the tip of his rod.

"Whoopee!" he shouted. "He's still on!"

Jim slowly made his way back to the bank and sat down, drenched and exhausted, watching as Billy Shaw reeled the huge fish onto the shore. Finally, the colorful fish was lying on the bank, and the two men gaped at it.

"I've never seen a fish like that in my life!" Billy said, staring wide-eyed at Packard. "Have you, Jim?"

The use of his first name wasn't lost on Packard.

"I saw one about this size on the Wallbash River once. Someone else caught it. But, I don't think it was as fat." Jim knelt and examined the large fish. "I believe this is a hen, about ready to lay eggs. That must be why it's so fat."

Excited, he and Billy looked at one other, each unwilling to say what was on their minds. Finally, Jim said, "What do you want to do, Billy? We both caught it, so we both got a vote in it."

Billy looked at the large fish, gasping for air through its gills. "Let's turn it back," he said. "We can catch her again later. That is, if you'll show me how you made that cast." He smiled at Packard.

Packard grinned ruefully. "To tell you the truth, it was mostly luck. But you got a deal, give me a hand so we don't injure her."

They watched the fish as it lay quietly in the water for an instant, then slowly swam toward the middle, flip its tail, and disappear.

"Boy-o-boy, what a fish!" Billy breathed. "Old Joe was right about it being out there. No one will ever believe us, will they, Jim?"

"Probably not, Billy. Why don't we keep this our secret? If we let it out, everybody will be down here trying to catch our fish," Jim said.

He shook the water from his pants leg and squeezed some out of his shirt sleeves. Using his fingers, he combed through his long hair.

"You ready to give it up for today, or do you think there might be another one out there?"

When Legends Lived

Billy took in Jim's sopping clothes. "What about you? You're the one that nearly drowned?" he said pointedly.

Water dripping from Jim's clothing, was making small rivers through the sand, toward the river. Water even spilled over the tops of his boots. They both looked at Jim's wet clothes, boots, and hair, and busted out laughing so hard, they had to sit down on the gravel-bar. After a time, they paused to gasp air back into their lungs, then, glancing at each other from the corners of their eyes, started all over again. Finally, wiping their eyes on the sleeves of their shirts, they ambled to the rods laying on the sand-bar.

On the way out, Billy picked up the canvas hat with Joe Walker's hand-tied flies, that he used to wear when he fished. He held it gently, turning it around and around in his hands. Finally, he handed it to Jim.

"Here. Wear this, so you don't get sunstroke. It used to belong to a friend of mine. A fishing buddy."

Jim placed it on his head, uncannily in the exact tilt Joe Walker had used. He felt some sort of portal had been breached with Billy's offer, but wouldn't know until much later just what it had been. As they fished the rest of the afternoon, Billy would often glance at Jim Packard wearing Joe's old hat and fishing basket, casting in that smooth, graceful, familiar motion and somehow feel the presence of his old mentor and fishing companion. *It felt good.*

* * *

Peeling potatoes, Kate watched them as they returned from the river, aware they'd been down there every day for the past week. They often brought back trout for supper, and lately, there'd been so much that she'd resorted to giving it to her maid, Rita, and her husband, who did repair work around the place. Kate laid down her knife and observed them closer. She would've sworn that there'd been some kind of ill feeling between Jim Packard and her son. Especially, on her son's part, after what she'd witnessed by the corral that day. But as she watched, she saw the two of them laughing and talking like old friends.

Apparently, there was no catch that day, and Kate breathed a sigh of relief. She was getting a little tired of trout. Not catching any fish seemed to have little bearing on their good humor, as she watched Jim slap her son on the back and say something. Billy answered and smiled as the men parted ways.

Well, thought Kate, *will wonders never cease!* Her thoughts moved to Bethena and she frowned. She knew Beth was head-over-heels in love with tall, good-looking Jim Packard. She'd seen her sister looking at him when she didn't know she was being observed, and saw that light shining in her eyes again.

And Jim? He followed Beth around with his sad, puppy dog eyes every time she came into the room. He couldn't keep his eyes off her. Yes, Beth was in love with him, all right, and the man was in love with her sister, but it all seemed so sad. Maybe something more had happened between them than Jim Packard had revealed. She didn't know what, but it had something to do with the headaches and the nightmares returning. She'd heard Beth crying in her room at night, only to find when she went to check, that her sister appeared to be sleeping. Even Billy's return and standing guard on the water tower, didn't seem to help much. At least, not like before. With heavy heart, Kate carried her basket of peeled potatoes inside to start dinner.

Thirty-Seven

"Texas could exist without the United States, but the United States cannot exist without Texas."
– Sam Houston

IT'D BEEN MONTHS SINCE Packard and Kellog were wounded and Fish had taken them back home to Bluebonnet. The two Rangers had been on Scar's trail for almost three years and were somewhere south of Nogales, once more. Three days earlier they'd killed two more of Scar's men. *Soon,* McCain thought. *Soon, Scar would have to stop and make a stand.*

Poe was having a harder time of it, too, and McCain watched him hang onto his saddle horn toward the end of each day. His eyes were glassy and conversation had been almost nonexistent most of the time. That, by itself, would've made McCain wonder, but he'd watched Rosie take a drink from the brown bottle every hour or two, all day long. A few minutes earlier, he'd seen Poe drain it and toss the empty bottle into the brush.

Although there were still another two hours of daylight, McCain pulled up at a level place near a running stream, dismounted and stretched his back. "That's all I can take for today. Let's just make camp here where we got some water."

"Now, don't you go coddling me," Poe retorted crossly. "I can sit a saddle as long as the next man, and just 'cause I got a little o'muscle pull in my back, that don't lessen my abilities. Not in the least."

"I said, *I* was tired," McCain repeated. "I don't care a tinker's damn about your little o'pulled muscle. *I'm* tired. *I* want to rest. Are you gonna gripe about that, too?"

"Well, since you put it that way, my back does feel a mite tender," Poe allowed. "It suits me fine." He dismounted gingerly, attempting to hide any pain.

Especially since he'd just made a "big deal" out of it, thought McCain. *Contrary old goat, probably would've sat right in that saddle and suffered until I fell out of mine from pure exhaustion. Damn, I just don't know what makes Poe so all-fired pigheaded about the simplest things.* McCain was totally unaware that Poe often thought the same thing about him.

McCain set up the camp, gathered firewood and started supper on a low smokeless fire. Poe unsaddled the horses and then collapsed on his blanket, leaning back gingerly against his saddle. When they'd eaten and had finished washing the tin plates, Poe settled back with his chaw and McCain rolled a cigarette. In the comfort of silence that only a long and trusted friendship can bring, Poe spoke quietly.

"I'm dying Jericho."

McCain, unsure that he'd heard his friend correctly, froze and remained quiet.

"It's true. I've known since the time we went to Amarillo. I didn't believe it at first, so I had Doc Milburn examine me in San Antonio, while we were there." Poe paused and watched the crackling fire.

"What did he say it was, Roosevelt?" McCain said in a soft voice. He felt winded, as though someone had just kicked him in the guts. Inside, he was screaming that it wasn't true. *It couldn't be true!* Outwardly, he remained calm.

When Legends Lived

"Milburn said something is eating at me, inside," Poe answered. Milburn had shown Rosie charts and pictures in a medical journal, and told him a lot more, but that would do for right now.

"Can't they just cut it out?" McCain's face remained void of any emotion, but he was still in shock from what he'd just heard.

Poe laughed dryly. "That's what I asked Doc Milburn. He didn't pull any punches, Jericho. Ya gotta hand him that. Doc said...," Poe lowered his voice to imitate the deep voice of Russ Milburn..."He said, 'Roosevelt, I'd have to gut you like a fish.' That's what he told me." Poe chuckled. "Sure paints a pretty picture, don't it Jericho?"

McCain reeled, dizzy, off balance. *This is all wrong! There has to be something they can do.* He and Roosevelt had retired and bought a ranch. They were going to grow old and enjoy it together. God dammit, they'd earned it, and they deserved it. Still outwardly calm, he said, "We'll go to Chicago or someplace where they have specialists who know about these things. We'll take all the time we need and find a cure for you."

Poe sat as though mesmerized by the fire, as he contemplated what J.D. just told him, then said with finality, "Ain't no cure Jericho, and I'm out of time. You gotta get me back to Kate's, while I still have a few reserves to draw on. Doc Milburn told me what to watch for, and maybe I waited a mite too long, you know...hoping. But, hope and time have both run out."

McCain studied his friend, and as usual, Poe was just being matter-of-fact about the whole thing. There wasn't an ounce of self-pity in the man.

Poe gazed deeply into McCain's eyes. "Better get me back to Kate's ranch soon as you can manage, Jericho. While I can still ride. I feel real close to traveling and I don't want to be buried down here, in this hell-hole. Promise me you won't bury me in Mexico, Jericho."

"I ain't gonna bury you in Mexico, Roosevelt. I'm gonna take you back where you can be tended to and healed. Then you and me are gonna track that heathen Scar down and hang him, just like we planned all along. That's the end of it," McCain stated. "We'll get started back first thing in the morning. Get some shut-eye and I'll stand watch."

Poe laid back and was asleep almost immediately. McCain sat quietly by the small fire, gazing at his partner, from time to time. Imagine, him knowing about it all this time and not telling anyone. *Just like that pigheaded old goat to do something like that,* J.D. thought. Unconsciously, he rubbed his smarting eyes. *Must've been in some awful pain and never even mentioned going back home.*

"Jericho McCain, are you so blind and selfish that you couldn't see it, or are you so obsessed with catching Scar that you chose to just ignore it?" It was Kate's voice.

I didn't know, Roosevelt. I honestly didn't know. McCain buried his head in his arms and rocked back and forth.

* * *

They broke camp the next morning; McCain doing most of the work, as Poe seemed weaker than usual. He wanted to discuss his estate and McCain wanted to discuss treatment.

"We'll take you back and get you treated," McCain stated. "There'll be no more discussion about you dying, I won't hear it." What he did hear, was Poe's irritating chuckle.

"I'll make you a deal, Jericho. You humor me and let me plan for the eventuality of my demise, and I'll humor you and talk about treatment once we get to the K/D ranch. Deal?"

He agreed to the uneasy truce as they got under way.

It took eight days to reach Nogales and four more to reach Tucson. At the last, Poe was holding onto his saddle-horn with both hands, dangerously swaying back and forth in the saddle. Upon reaching Tucson, McCain placed Poe in a hotel room and immediately went to find a wagon. Purchasing the smallest one he could find, he took it to the local blacksmith, and explained he wanted the regular seat taken out, and two single seats installed. The one on the right side was to sit upright, but would have a hinge that could drop it into a lying position when needed. This would be done by removing two cotter-pins from the hinged portion of the seat. The seat on the left would remain in the upright position.

"How long?" McCain said.

The big bearded blacksmith rubbed his chin thoughtfully and said, "Four days ought to do it."

"One and a half days ought to do it," McCain shot back. "I got a sick man and I've got to get him back home, fast."

"Tell you what, you give me two extra dollars to hire another person, and I'll do it in two days," said the blacksmith.

"Done," said McCain as he stuck out his hand, "if you shoe these two horses of mine and have them ready at the same time."

The blacksmith grinned and gripped his hand in a bone-crushing squeeze.

As he'd been instructed by Poe, McCain next went to the general store and purchased the items he'd specified. Returning to the hotel, he ordered food for the two of them and instructed the desk clerk to personally ensure it arrived — hot.

He found Poe awake and sitting propped against his pillows. Rosie greeted him cheerfully, although somewhat weakly and J.D. took that as a positive sign.

"You remember to pick up those things I asked you?" Poe said.

"Certainly, I remembered. You think I'm demented or something?" In all the years he'd known Roosevelt Poe, McCain had learned a thing or two about his friend. You had to be firm with him or he got real sarcastic. Satisfied he'd put Poe in his place, he unpacked the few writing items he'd bought.

"Let's see," he said. "Pencils, writing paper, folders, yep, it's all here."

He placed the articles on the bed within Poe's grasp. Poe let them lay, seemingly too tired to reach for them. At last he picked up a pencil and some paper, paused thoughtfully, and then began to write.

McCain, sensing he'd be occupied for a while, went to check on their food. Worried about how Poe had looked when he'd left, McCain didn't want to be gone long. He hurriedly completed his chore, climbed the stairs and silently entered the room. There, he found Rosie, lying with his head on his chest, not moving. With his heart in his mouth, he moved quickly to Poe's side, and swallowing hard, slowly placed the back of his hand near his nose. He sighed with relief as he felt a slight stirring of air.

Damn partner, he said to himself, *lost ten years of my life there.*

He quietly unfolded a well-used military map of the mountainous area between Tucson and West Texas, remembering having been through it about fifteen years before, but that certain details now escaped him.

Sure looks like a long hard trip, he thought ruefully. *Wasn't near that far when I was younger.*

Sitting at the small table, he carefully charted out the most direct route across the mountains to Southwest Texas. McCain

When Legends Lived

shook his head, and mused. A couple more years and the railroad would have the rails laid between Tucson and Las Cruces. *Never thought I'd want to see more of them infernal iron roads crisscrossing the country,* he thought, as he eyed the rugged terrain that lay ahead of them. *But I could sure use one right about now.*

Startled by a loud knock at the door, McCain hastily walked over and jerked it open. The desk-clerk stood with two trays of hot food and a large smile, that froze in place by McCain's glare. The ranger placed his finger over his lips, admonished him to be quiet, and motioned the young man inside. McCain removed the food from one of the trays, along with the pot of strong coffee and silently motioned for the hotel man to take the rest of it back.

As the clerk prepared to depart, a voice floated up from the bed.

"Jericho, would you hand me my Colt, please? If that feller tries to take my food away, I want to shoot him in the leg... maybe just nick him a bit."

The tray clambered as it dropped back to the table and, horrified, the young man ran out the open door. Poe, laying back with his eyes closed, chuckled softly.

"Well, that's just great, Roosevelt! I had to sweet-talk that feller to no end just to get him to agree to bring up food in the first place," J.D. told him. "Now, you've gone and scared his pants off and he may never come back. I'll probably have to worry about the food myself, here- after."

McCain looked away so he hid the small gleam in his own eyes. Poe was still chuckling to himself.

As he ate his supper, McCain discretely watched with pleasure as Rosie shoveled in his food like a starved man. Finished eating,

Poe sighed deeply. "That was so good, it'd make your tongue beat your brains out." He sighed again and pushed the tray away.

McCain retrieved it, and poured both cups full of steaming coffee. They sat in comfortable silence, as they nursed their drinks. Rosie again picked up the pencil and paper discarded earlier and began to write, as McCain observed him from his place at the table.

He don't look all that bad off, McCain thought, *maybe a little tired, is all. When I get him to Odessa, I'll have one of them smart doctors from the east come in and treat him. I don't care if it costs everything we have. If they won't come to us, I'll take Roosevelt to them.* Satisfied he'd made the right choice, McCain lay down on the other bed, and was snoring within minutes.

* * *

After breakfast the following morning, Poe drifted off to sleep again and McCain went to check on the progress of work on the wagon seat. He was pleased to discover that it was nearly done.

"There've been a goodly number of interested citizens watch me make this creation for you, Captain. Some have remarked concerning the fact that I might be 'bout half a bubble off plum," the blacksmith told him and roared with his deep belly-laugh. "But a few have expressed an interest in having one just like it, built for themselves. I might be able sell a few more of 'em, thanks to you."

McCain returned at exactly twelve-noon and picked up the wagon as planned. He drove it to the general store where he purchased supplies and food he'd calculated they'd need to get

When Legends Lived

as far as Lordsburg. Within the hour, he and Poe were in the wagon, headed toward the low snow-capped mountains to the east.

"We can skirt the high-country for a while," McCain told him. "We'll hit the pass north of El Paso and drop down south toward Kate's ranch from there. Going that way, it might be easier to get the wagon through the rough stuff. As it is, I'm not too sure we won't have to leave it somewhere anyway."

McCain's stallion and Poe's sorrel were tied to the back of the wagon. Tucson had long disappeared over the skyline by the time they stopped to rest. As they made camp on the second night, Poe indicated he was ready to discuss what he'd been writing. McCain attempted to hide it, but was alarmed by the rapid deterioration in his friend's health, with just two days on the trail behind them. Poe appeared several pounds lighter, and his eyes seemed to have settled deeper into his skull. He was also suffering from cramps and acute diarrhea. His face might've looked pale and shrunken, but his voice remained strong and firm as he instructed McCain on exactly what he wanted done with his writings.

First, came the letters to Beth, Kate and, surprisingly, Jim Packard. Poe hadn't sealed the envelopes, but McCain didn't look inside. He handed McCain several more sheets, filled with his unsteady writing.

"This is a Will, Jericho. Just in case that treatment of your's don't take," he said with a twinkle in his eyes. "I want you to read over it now, so I can answer any questions while I'm still thinking right."

McCain hesitantly scanned it through once, with misty eyes. He blinked several times, then said, "Getting so I can't hardly see in the light of a fire any more." He made a show of concentrating on the itemized lines before him, then read, "This says, 'from my estate, a present, costing a minimum of ten dollars each, will be bought for each of the ladies employed at Paco's. These gifts will be delivered personally by the executor of my Will, Captain Jericho D. McCain."

McCain lowered the paper and stared at his partner, as if to confirm Poe had already lost his sanity. "Roosevelt, there were three of them gals whoring at Paco's when we left!"

"Four," Poe told him. "There were four ladies working there."

"All right then, four," McCain stated with exasperation. "That's forty dollars. More than a good cow hand makes in a month. Are you sure you know what you're doing?"

"Is it my money or not?" Poe said, with a trace of his famous stubbornness.

"Of course, it's your money, Roosevelt. But forty dollars! For presents. For whores, no less!" Seeing the determination on Poe's face, McCain swallowed hard and meekly said, "Just wanted to check, is all. You do what you want."

"Fine! That's what I want to do," Poe said stubbornly.

McCain had a feeling Roosevelt was smugly laughing inside over forcing him to deliver the presents personally to the women at Paco's.

In fact, Poe was pleased at the prospects, and was certain it would stick in his partner's craw. Might just make dying worth it, especially if old Jericho were to 'bury his post' while he was there. He chuckled softly and McCain shot him a hard look. McCain read item two and looked up.

"It says to give the half-section of land, known as 'the Willows,' and thirty-five head of horses to Fish."

When Legends Lived

The Willows was a strip of decent grazing land with plenty of water when there wasn't a drought. The problem for the ranch, had been it was enclosed on three sides by very difficult terrain, open only to the west. Accordingly, whenever they wanted to rotate stock into the Willows, it had meant a long trip around the southern end through difficult terrain, before reaching a point they could enter.

"I'm not arguing your decision, just curious. Why leave this land and thirty-five head of horses to Fish? He has a job with us for as long as he wants it, and has no one to depend on him," McCain said to his partner.

"That's so he can get married."

Stunned, McCain's mouth dropped open. "Married? Fish don't want to get married. Hell, he don't even know a woman!"

"See, just as I always said," Poe told him. "You got no vision, Jericho. Your life is like a tunnel. There ain't no left or right with you. Only what you can see, straight ahead. You just don't observe what's going on all around you. For cat's sake, why do you suppose Fish made all those trips over to El Paso four times a year, right up to the time we departed on this little adventure?"

"You said it was to see the fancy whores at the new hotel," McCain said, puzzled at what he'd just heard regarding a man he'd thought he knew so well.

Exasperated, Poe said, "I only said that so's not to embarrass the boy. I didn't want to hurt his feelings."

"Since when did you start to worry about anybody's feelings?" McCain said dripping with sarcasm.

Poe cocked his eyebrow at his friend. "Well, I didn't learn my sensitive side from you, that's for sure." He pouted for a moment, then went on. "He's been spark'n a pretty young Mex gal, just outside El Paso. She's 'bout half his age, but he says he loves her. Her father wants twenty-five head of horses as a 'gift', before he'll consent to the wedding."

"Twenty-five head?" McCain whistled softly. "He could get a wife in Mexico for a third of that."

"That ain't the point, Jericho! Fish is in love with this particular girl!" Poe said, sitting up straighter. "I know that love is a concept completely lost on someone of your outlook, but it just so happens it is very real to some of us mortals."

McCain looked at his old friend with no small amount of surprise. "You've been in love? When? With who?"

"Ain't none of your beeswax, Jericho," he said smugly, crossing his arms and looking off into space. "Things like that are best left private." Not budging an inch, he finally glanced up at McCain from the corner of his eye, finding his friend still intently staring at him. Afraid he'd revealed one of his lifelong secrets, Poe abruptly said, "Well, let's get on with it."

"It's Kate, ain't it?" J.D. said softly. "I always wondered why, with your great attraction for the ladies, you never found one and settled down. It's been Kate all along, ain't it?"

Poe didn't answer.

"Damn, Roosevelt, I never even considered that. Maybe you're right. Maybe I've been so concerned about my own direction in life that I don't see what goes on around me."

"Can we get on with this while I'm still alive?" Poe said quietly. "Anyway, Fish has been taking most of his pay in horses for the past year, and has seven pretty good nags. I figure he has to have a few to run even a small spread, so there's the reason for the extry ones."

Not knowing what else to do, McCain read the third item on the paper then quickly looked up at Rosie. "It says I have to take you to Kate's ranch so you can be buried in her family plot. She agree to that?"

"'Course she did. Fer your information, she thinks a great deal of me," Poe retorted smugly. "You, too, though for the life of me, I don't know why."

"What gave you that idea, Roosevelt? I thought she was down on Rangers," McCain offered.

"Beth maybe — not Kate. She loves us both."

"I always thought you and Kate were just friends," McCain said, posed half-way as a question.

"Well, we are just friends. But that wern't my decision. It seems she thinks of me more like family," Poe reflected. "Now will you let it be?" he growled. "We're talking about Fish's future and my Last Will and Testament!"

"Old Quint Fishburn…married. Don't that just beat all?" McCain said in wonderment.

"You'd do a danged sight better if you'd consider it yourself, Jericho," Poe told him.

"Me? With who?" McCain snorted. "Who'd want to marry someone like me?" Poe gazed at him until he suddenly realized what was meant. "Kate?" He said, snorting again. "Have you gone completely off your rocker? Why she'll probably shoot me when I take you back."

"Don't figure she'll do that," Poe stated. "Kate made me promise to bring you with me the very next time I came to visit. That's why I made you give your word to take me back there to be buried. Figured it's the only way I could get you to go back and keep my promise, to boot." Poe chuckled.

"Roosevelt Poe, if I've never told you, you are the most devious and nosey person I've ever known," McCain told him.

Poe crinkled up his eyes, and said, "Thankee kindly, Jericho. Glad you finally noticed. Now, I'm all tuckered out. Do you think we could finish going through this tomorrow night?"

McCain saw that indeed, Poe did look tired. In fact, he appeared exhausted again. Roosevelt Poe had always been the most strong-willed, determined man J.D. McCain had ever known. McCain had seen much larger and stronger men give up and quit, long before Poe even considered it. It tore at his guts to see the tired old man, a shell of the person he'd once been, exhausted simply from a normal day's ride. Within moments, Poe snored gently, as McCain watched his old friend sleep. He suddenly shuddered, as he was filled with a greater fear than he'd ever known.

* * *

Martin Gates had been summoned by his editor, and approached the office with serious misgivings. Entering, he saw his boss, John Kiley, wasn't alone and felt his earlier dread might've been justified.

"Martin, come in. Come in, we've been waiting for you," said an unusually friendly Kiley. Smiles by John Kiley weren't something Martin was accustomed to, and he was instantly on-guard.

"Martin, I want you to meet Frank Chase, President of the Southern Pacific Railroad. Frank, this is Martin Gates. He's the reporter we sent to Texas to cover the railroad's fine handling of the lawlessness issue."

Martin, sizing up the tall, emaciated man, took Frank Chase's outstretched hand and wasn't surprised by his limp handshake.

"I've read some of your drafts, Mr. Gates, and I think with a little reworking, you'll have a fine news series," Chase said. Martin's boss now busily ignored him.

When Legends Lived

Drafts? Reworking? What the hell is going on here, anyway?

Kiley saw Gates's surprise but stalled, walked to his small corner bar, and poured three healthy bourbons, straight-up.

"This calls for a little celebration, don't you think?" he said, passing the two men their drinks.

The two older men raised their glasses and locked their eyes on Martin. Caught by surprise, he spilled some, then suddenly raised his glass too, and drank. "What are we drinking to?"

"Why, to a successful public relations operation, of course! P.R. for the Southern Pacific and good will for our newspaper," Kiley told him. Gates nodded as if he understood, but still felt very confused.

"It's like this, Martin," Chase said. "The story you wrote is pretty good. In fact it's perfect, except for a couple of minor changes. The characters need to be changed a bit." Chase placed his glass down, leaving a large water-ring on the polished wood. "This whole thing was organized and paid for by the Southern Pacific Railroad," he said. "We even sent our representative, Jim Packard, along to accompany McCain and his group."

Chase, took a cheroot from his pocket, bit off the end and spit it into the brass spittoon beside his oversized chair. He leaned back, waiting for John Kiley to light it. Kiley lunged forward with a light, looking somewhat embarrassed.

I see, thought Gates. *So that's the way it is.*

Puffing at his cheroot until satisfied it was going, Chase continued, "The fact is, Mr. Gates, you made those two old Rangers into heroes while our man Packard, and the Railroad, I might add, simply went along for the ride."

"But, that's about the way it was, Mr. Chase. I personally interviewed eye witnesses all along their route and McCain and

Poe actually did all those things I wrote about," Gates maintained. He could see from the corner of his eye that Kiley's face had grown beet red and he glowered at Martin.

Crossing his long legs, Chase studied the end of his smoke. "We — John and I — feel Jim Packard needs to get some of the credit for cleaning up the gangs. The people need to feel the Railroad helped them in their time of need, not those two old killers," he said.

Astounded, Gates said, "You want me to make up things this Jim Packard is supposed to have done, and include it in my story?"

Kiley began to interrupt, but Chase waved him off. "No, no. Not exactly make something up, just change the names around to more favorably reflect the Railroad's participation."

"I see," said Martin, suddenly realizing Chase's intent. "You want me to take things McCain and Poe actually did, lie about it, and say this Packard fellow is the one that really did them. That about it?"

Frank Chase silently smiled at him.

"I won't do it!" Gates said venomously, as he jumped to his feet. "I won't intentionally print something I know isn't the truth!" He turned to leave, but froze as he heard Kiley's raised voice.

"Sit down!" Kiley yelled, and pointed his finger at him. "You walk out that door and you're finished as a newsman. Not only here, but I'll see to it you never write another story for any newspaper!"

Off balance, Gates stared at him incredulously.

"I mean it, Gates!"

Chase stood suddenly and put his arm around Gate's shoulders. "Now, now," he said. "I'm sure we can reach an agreement without resorting to all that. What do you say, Martin? Can't we

When Legends Lived

reach an agreement?" The smile on Frank Chase's lips didn't quite reach his eyes. "Sit down, Martin. Hear Mr. Kiley out. Then if you decide not to, we'll understand." His tone clearly implied that they would not.

Unsteadily, Martin Gates sank heavily into his recently vacated chair.

"I'll just leave you two to work out the details. I'm confident you'll arrive at the right decision," Chase picked up his hat and prepared to leave. "Oh, Mr. Martin, would you mind joining me at my summer home for a few days later this summer? I'll make the arrangements and contact you through Mr. Kiley." With that, Frank Chase put on his hat and left.

As the door closed, John Kiley towered over Gates's chair. His meaty hands on his bulging hips, livid with rage, Kiley glared at Martin. "Now, you listen to me, you two-bit news-bum. You just don't get the Southern Pacific down on you. Not and survive for very long. Frank Chase told you what he wants. Do it! No 'ifs, ands or buts.' Just do it, or you're finished, here and anyplace else you'll ever want to work as a reporter. Do you understand me, Gates?"

Gates swallowed hard, then slowly nodded.

"Good," said John Kiley. "Now, rewrite the piece just the way Mr. Chase wants it and give it back to me. It must be timed perfectly." Kiley returned to his desk. "It seems his man, Packard, was severely wounded by savages and is at some ranch recuperating. Mr. Chase doesn't want the story released until Packard is able to return to Chicago. I understand he'll have to walk with a cane, and will have a very pronounced limp." Kiley smiled. "That'll add a nice touch to our story, don't you think?"

Gates sat numbly, as Kiley started flipping pages on his desk, dismissing him. In shock, he stumbled to the door, as Kiley looked back up. "Oh, and Martin? I want it changed and back to me by tomorrow morning. If it's not, I don't want to see you around here again. Now get out," he growled.

Thirty-Eight

> *"We're like two old bull buffaloes, Chief.*
> *We've been around a long time. Every day, more*
> *of our kind gets killed off, and like the buffalo,*
> *soon there will be none of us left."*
>
> – Captain Jericho McCain

JIM PACKARD AND BETH took a wagon into Odessa early in the morning, while traveling was still pleasant. They held up during the hottest part of the day and the sun was just setting as they arrived in town. A usual round trip took three days, one day to travel each way, and a day to conduct business. Jim and Beth planned to stay for the annual dance and cakewalk held to raise money for the school. This time they would stay for two days and Billy Shaw would ride in later, joining them for the dance.

Bethena had been a virtual prisoner at the ranch for over a year, self imposed to be sure, but a prisoner, nonetheless. She'd eagerly awaited the event for the past several months and during the trip was as lively and bubbly as she'd been before her abduction. Jim was intensely aware of her warmth as he drove the long miles into Odessa and stole sideways glances at her along the way.

She's so beautiful, he thought. *So damned beautiful it hurts to be this close.*

Sitting for long periods, still caused great discomfort in his leg and hip, so they stopped to rest several times during their trip.

As they rode, Beth bombarded him with a steady barrage of stories and antidotes about when she and Kate were children, and things she remembered most about her dead parents. When they dismounted to rest, Jim noticed she'd suddenly become very quiet. Sometimes, he'd feel her eyes on him, or look up and catch her staring at him. Jim desperately wanted to put his arms around her and kiss her. He would've, too, but the memory of that last time still lingered in his mind.

Once, deep in thought, he realized Beth was talking. "I'm sorry. What was that?"

She smiled sweetly. "I said, you look like you're a million miles away."

Jim smiled ruefully, his face reddening, and Bethena laughed outright. She had a rich throaty laugh that Jim found appealing. "It's good to hear you laugh like that, Beth" he said smiling. "I haven't heard it since the first time we met. That time I came with Roosevelt Poe. Remember?"

They both became very still. "You were the most beautiful woman I'd ever seen," he said softly. "I still think so."

Bethena cast her eyes down and said uncomfortably, "Jim... please, don't."

"No, Beth," he said. "I have to say this. I may be leaving soon and you have to know how I feel about you."

Bethena jerked her head up, and he could see her frightened eyes when he mentioned leaving. "Why must you leave? I thought you liked it at the K/D."

Jim sadly said, "I love it here, Beth. I love it because you're here. I could live anyplace and do anything if you were with me."

"Then stay," she said weakly.

When Legends Lived

"Beth, I work for the Southern Pacific. Soon, they'll call me back to duty and I'll have to go. I want you to go with me."

Bethena looked confused and off balance. "You mean leave the K/D? Leave Kate and the girls...and Billy?"

Jim leaned forward, picking up her hand. "Yes, leave. Come with me. I'm asking you to marry me, Beth. I love you. I've always loved you. Please."

Tears formed at the corners of her beautiful eyes. "I need more time, Jim. I'm still sick and I need more time to get over it."

Jim let go of her hand, and pleaded, "You've had time, Beth. If time could do it, you'd be well by now. Come with me and we'll get professional help. I'll help you. Together, we'll beat it, Beth."

As she raised her eyes, he could see the tears, flowing freely now. "Oh, my darling, please understand. I care for you more deeply than I've ever cared for anyone since Howard. I probably even love you. I can't be entirely sure because my...condition is always with me. I know I think about you all the time when you're not with me. I long for you terribly, especially when I'm in bed alone at night." Bethena paused momentarily, then said, "Do you think it brazen of me to say that?"

He moved to take her in his arms but she noticeably stiffened, and quickly stood. "We have to be going." She laughed nervously. "Otherwise, we're going to be out here after dark." She shivered, looking around fearfully, "I don't want to be out here when it gets dark, Jim."

Entering Odessa, Jim drove directly to the hotel and checked them into their rooms. He also registered a room for Billy, because rooms became scarce as more and more people came to town for the festivities. After hot baths and a fresh change of clothes, they met in the hotel dining room. Sitting across from this beautiful lady, sharing dinner with her, Jim felt a stronger commitment toward her than he'd ever felt for anyone.

She felt his stare and locked eyes with him, flashing her radiant smile. Jim swallowed hard, working to control his desire, as Bethena demurely lowered her gaze and picked at her food, smiling secretly to herself. Observers might've quickly assumed they were a young married couple, probably newlyweds on their honeymoon, from their stolen, passionate looks at each other. Jim's face became flushed and he had trouble swallowing his food.

Damn it, James Packard, he thought. Settle down and quit acting like a school boy.

It did little good, as intimate images of Beth continued to cause him substantial discomfort throughout the meal. After dinner, they strolled silently back to their rooms. Jim unlocked her door and handed Beth the key.

"I really enjoyed tonight, Jim," she told him. "More than any for a long time."

She kissed him lightly on the cheek, and was gone. He stared at the closed door for a time, then smiling slightly and went to his room.

The next morning, Jim was up early to check if Billy Shaw had arrived. Reaching his room, he knocked and was greeted by the low muffled sound of someone mumbling. Cracking the door ajar, Jim saw Billy lumped under the covers still half asleep.

"Come on, you want to miss out on all the fun?" he said, grabbing Billy's exposed foot.

Billy raised his head slightly off the pillow, groaned and peered at him through half-closed eyes. Groaning, his head dropped heavily back to the pillow. "Come back in four or five hours," he pleaded, placing the pillow over his head.

When Legends Lived

"Bacon, eggs, biscuits," Jim said, looking intently at the immobile lump. The pillow lifted and Jim could see one of Billy's sleepy eyes peer at him. "Hot coffee, cinnamon rolls — " he continued with malice.

"Okay, okay!" Billy said. "You win. I'm up. Now go away and let me get dressed," he moaned pitifully.

Jim laughed, saying, "I'll go and wake Beth, then we'll meet you downstairs in thirty minutes." With that, he jerked on Billy's big toe once more and departed.

Forty minutes later the three of them were seated in the hotel dining room, the waitress bringing platter after platter of food. Beth laughed her rich laugh.

"My word! Who else did you invite to share breakfast with us? There's enough food here for all our ranch-hands."

"You just watch me," said young Billy, digging in. He helped himself to several eggs and five rashers of thick bacon, then passed it over to Jim, who did the same. Bethena ate a comparatively light meal, watching as the two men in her life destroyed the bounty on their breakfast table. There was scarcely a scrap left when the men pushed away their plates, picked up their coffee cups, and sighed contentedly. Billy, patted his rounded stomach.

"That should just about hold me until about lunch."

Bethena reacted with "mock" shock, and told her nephew, "That should just about hold you until you get back to the ranch." The two men laughed with her, and Jim, finding her eyes, seemed to enjoy her new-found merriment.

The day was filled with excitement of the hustle and bustle that only a town swollen to twice its normal size can create. Food-fairs and handicraft booths abounded. Jim bought Bethena a small turquoise pendant and placed it around her neck. Much to Bethena's amusement, Billy ate voraciously, everything from sausage to apple pie throughout the day.

"You're going to be sick and miss all those pretty girls at the dance and cakewalk tonight," she told him.

"Ha! That'll be the day," Billy mumbled through a mouthfull of sausage and biscuits. "I'm gonna buy me a chocolate pie, and eat it all by myself."

Billy enjoyed telling little anecdotes that Beth enjoyed and they laughed so much she held her aching sides. Back at the hotel in the hotter part of the day, they declared a siesta, and agreed to meet back in the lobby at four o'clock. Jim dropped Beth off at her room, walked next door to his room, stripped to his shorts, and laid down on the bed.

Somewhere between sleep and consciousness, he heard his door quietly open and found Beth at the foot of his bed. Startled, he watched in disbelief as she loosened the straps of her summer dress and let it slowly fall to the floor. She was completely nude beneath it. Jim held his breath, afraid to break the spell, as she slipped in beside him. They lay without moving for a time, staring into each other's eyes. Then Jim placed his lips on hers, and they slowly began the ancient ritual of love. Throughout, Jim was gentle and deliberate, sensing Bethena might bolt if he reacted too strongly. Toward the end, she softly cried out.

Lying there afterwards, Jim brushed a strand of hair from her face as she lay with her eyes closed, tears slowly seeping from beneath her eyelids. He bent and gently kissed each tear as they appeared, until at last her lashes fluttered and opened. She remained still for a moment, then raised her mouth to his once more.

When Legends Lived

It was half-past four when they finally met Billy in the lobby. With fake severity he said, "I'm an important man and I don't usually wait for people this long." He frowned. "Someone's probably already bought up all the chocolate pies."

Placing his hat on he started toward the door, then stopped and glanced back. "Neither one of you look as though you slept a lick. I better get you back so you can get in bed early tonight."

Bethena, darted a look at Jim, reddened, and suddenly burst into uncontrollable laughter.

"If that ain't the laughin'est girl I've ever seen," Billy said to Jim, as they went out.

* * *

McCain squatted on his heels cowboy fashion, smoked, and eyed the swollen stream before him. He couldn't remember having crossed a river there the last time he came through, so it must've been a stream created from flash-floods in the higher-ups which had backed up from the Gila. Still, it was a formidable body of water. The way he figured it, he could set up camp right there on its banks and simply wait for it to recede. That could take days though, even weeks, and Poe might not last that long. Or, he could leave Poe there and try to find another ford. He'd probably get et up by some animal, or scalped by an Indian while I'm gone, he thought. He finally decided he'd wait until the following morning, and if it didn't look any better by then, he'd make a decision.

He walked back up the slope to the camp he'd set up earlier, when he'd first came upon the uncharted river. Damn! The Lord sure was taxing him these days. First Roosevelt's illness, then the daunting task of taking him from south of Nogales clear to Texas. On top of it all, that damned right wagon wheel sounded as though it was getting ready to fall off, and wouldn't that be a fine kettle of fish?

Roosevelt was still sleeping. Fact was, he slept most of the time. Which was just as well because when he was awake, he looked as though he were in considerable pain. Several nights in a row, McCain had heard him cry out in his sleep. With Poe being able to withstand pain far better than most men, that meant he was suffering greatly. He started the evening meal while it was still early, to get it finished before darkness overtook him. He heard Poe grunt loudly, once, and looked over at him. When he didn't move or make any other noises, he went back to preparing the meal.

Jericho McCain was suffering too — maybe not in the same way as his friend was, but with a deeper pain and frustration than he'd ever experienced. He felt helpless concerning Poe's illness and fearful that he wouldn't make it to Kate's ranch before Roosevelt died. He'd long since accepted the fact that Roosevelt Poe was dying; now he just wanted to fulfill all of Poe's remaining wishes. It was the least a man could do for his friend, McCain told himself, though some of Poe's wishes were perplexing indeed.

He remembered one of his recent discussions with Poe about his Last Will and Testament. It'd been a particularly hard day for Poe, and McCain had stopped earlier than usual, using the excuse they needed daylight to read his latest additions. For once, his partner had not objected.

McCain remembered how, on that evening, he'd pointed to a paragraph on the page. "It says here, that after Fish gets his stock, you leave the rest to me."

"That's a fact," Poe had confirmed. "I figured you needed all the aggravation to keep you happy. Some people need love, you need aggravation, Jericho." He had chuckled weakly.

"Well, lord knows I'd be proud to accept them, Roosevelt, but don't you have any living relatives somewhere that would want to have them? I'd consider it my duty to get them to your family, no matter where."

His friend had just closed his eyes for a while, then said quietly, "Just you, Jericho. You're all the family I got."

Now, thinking about his dying partner's words, the memory brought a burning to his eyes and McCain brushed at them with his sleeve. He was suddenly jolted by Poe's voice, whom he thought asleep.

"Hey, you all right, partner?"

"Damn smoke changing directions, that's all," McCain said shortly, peeved that Poe had caught him unaware. "You got an appetite yet?"

"I'm so hungry my belly thinks my throat's been cut. I could probably eat a horseshoe right now, but I ain't too certain I can stomach anymore of that stuff you throw together. It's barely fit for human consumption. Kind o' makes me yearn for some of old Fish's concoctions," he said with a small twinkle in his eyes.

"Well, you certainly don't have to force yourself to eat it if you find it so pitiful," McCain retorted, cut to the quick by Poe's remarks.

"Oh, I find it tolerable most of the time. And like as not, it's all I'll see 'til we get to Kate's ranch."

"I should bury your plate right here and just go off and leave it for all the abuse I take from you these days. Maybe that'd teach you a little gratitude," McCain grumbled.

The following morning, while Poe still slept, McCain prepared to cross the swollen body of water. If anything, it looked swifter and more formidable than the previous day. However, tired of the delays, McCain anchored a rope to a large tree on the camp's side of the river, loaded up both saddle horses, and walked Grasshopper toward the water. The big stallion shied just before entering, but he kept a tight rein and gently spurred the big black on. The full force of the current hit them just as they made midstream, and Grasshopper whinnied in terror, rolling his eyes and swimming frantically for the other shore.

Safely reaching the far bank, McCain walked the horses out and dismounted. He tied the end of the rope he'd anchored on the other side, to a large tree. Then he unsaddled Grasshopper and tied him to a nearby sapling. Begrudgingly, he decided that due to Grasshopper's not being overly fond of the water, he'd accept Poe's certain abuse about the advantages of owning a mare just that one time, and use Poe's sorrel for the rest of the crossing. Switching the saddle over, he mounted and entered the water, reaching the other side without incident.

McCain emptied the wagon, and climbed aboard. He prodded the working animal several hundred yards upstream, then snapped his whip over the horse's head until it reluctantly entered the swollen stream. Half way across, he knew they were in trouble. The horse screamed in terror as the wagon suddenly lurched, tottered, then swept sideways in the swift current. McCain inched up the wagon tongue, removed a long thin knife from his boot, and cut the harness from the terrified animal. He watched it swim free and jumped, just in time to clear the wagon as it overturned and was swept away down river.

Most cowboys didn't swim well, and McCain was no exception.

His mouth instantly filled with muddy water as he was sucked under by the force of the current. He couldn't see as he was swept along, until he felt his hand strike something and instinctively closed around it. It was the rope he had tied across the river on his first trip over.

Small wonder it didn't break when the wagon hit it, he thought. Then, he realized the rope had broken and he was grasping the loose end. He just had time to tighten his grip as he was swept hard into the far bank. He felt the air leave his lungs, but desperately held on for dear life as the current took him under time after time.

Pulling himself up the muddy bank, he sprawled out, sucking the thin mountain air into his tortured lungs. He ached all over, completely exhausted from his exertions. Weary to the bone, he made his way to the sapling where Grasshopper was tied and threw a saddle on him.

Grabbing the horse's ears he stared into his eyes, and said softly, "You and me are going to cross that river again. If you give me one ounce of trouble, I'm gonna make fish-bait out of you. *Comprend?*"

Grasshopper must've instinctively known when to resist and just when to cooperate, because he re-crossed that river twice more without so much as clicking his teeth at McCain, or trying to kick him, even once. It took several more trips to get Poe and all their belongings across, and another hour to find the horse he'd cut loose from the wagon. When he returned leading the wagon horse, the sun was low in the sky and he decided to make camp where they were and leave the following morning. As he poured his partner a cup of the strong black coffee he loved so well, Poe quietly snickered, causing McCain to jerk up his head.

"What?"

Poe just smiled and shook his head, as if he were enjoying a good private joke.

"Well, what?" McCain said again, irritated. "Go on, get it off your chest. You're just about to bust a gut over there. You've had something on your mind ever since we pitched camp, so get it out in the open."

Well, I don't suppose you'd call that a textbook river-crossing. It sure wasn't like anything I would've done," Poe said. "But, since you got everything across without drowning either of us, or my mare, I guess I can't complain."

"No. You wouldn't ever complain, would you? Well, just for your information, that ignorant animal pulling the wagon? The one that very nearly got me drowned? Just so happens, it's a mare." He spit into the fire, "So much for the superiority of your mares."

"Just so happens, it's a gelding, Jericho," Poe corrected, and snickered quietly again. "Used to be a stallion."

McCain stole a glance at the horse, then back at him, as realization slowly sank in. It was all Poe could do to contain himself as McCain rose without comment and walked away, leaving Poe alone with his mirth to chuckle unrestrained.

Underway early the next morning and without a wagon to pull now, McCain decided to use the gelding as a pack animal. He'd found part of the wagon bed floating in a calm jetty several hundred yards down river and had fashioned a travois of it, which he now pulled behind Poe's sorrel. Without the wagon, making good time was even harder, and the water crossing had tired Poe considerably. It seemed he slept a lot more lately, sometimes, dropping off in the middle of a sentence. *Silly old fool,*

When Legends Lived

McCain thought, smiling slightly. *I've seen plenty of his river crossings too, and they didn't go all that smooth, either.*

In the late morning, they dropped over a steep ridge into a small open area. Four men suddenly appeared on horses, to McCain's front. There were three more, to the rear of the main bunch. All were armed with pistols and several had rifles. Bandits! McCain thought, carefully surveying the rocks above him to see if there were any more.

He pulled up and shifted his body so he could reach his holster quickly, then removed Poe's Walker Colt, lying it on the seat next to him. Two of the men held their rifles so they generally pointed in his direction. Otherwise, they made no threatening gestures. He sat without speaking, as they locked wills in a tense standoff. Behind him, he could hear Rosie snoring softly.

"You boys are blocking my path," he finally said.

"Yes, Señor, I know. I am Jorge. Jorge Hernandez. They call me, Poncho. You may also call me Poncho, if you wish," grinned the man in front.

Cain wasn't fooled by it. He recognized the hard calculating eyes that peered from beneath the wide-brimmed hat, having seen the type a hundred times before. The leader of the group was wearing two pistols and crossed bandoleers, but rested his arms on his saddle horn, unconcerned about the old man before him.

"I am sorry to tell you this is a toll road now, Señor. I own it and must charge you to pass. I apologize, but I have a large family and I must make a living. Right, amigo?"

The sun was directly behind the group, glaring in McCain's eyes, and he knew they'd planned it that way. *Professionals.* He'd have to take as many of them out as possible, quick — if he could.

"I'm afraid you're bound to be disappointed, then. I lost all my money in a river crossing this morning — so maybe next time," McCain said. His hand was inches from his gun butt now, and he felt ready.

"You have many fine animals, Señor. We'll let you keep one, and you give the others to me. Then I will let you pass," said "Drooping Mustache."

"'Fraid not, amigo. I've got a sick man here, and I need all the horses I've got to get him to Texas. Now if you'll just move out of the trail, I'll be on my way." He deliberately dropped his hand onto the handle of his gun.

The move wasn't lost on Poncho. "I understand, Señor. You have a good journey and I hope your amigo gets better right away. I will pray for his fast recovery."

He started to turn his horse, then suddenly wheeled and reached for his pistols. McCain shot him first, next, the two men in front, with the rifles. Two of the remaining bandits also tumbled from their saddles, arrow shafts protruding from their bodies.

"*Los Comanches! Comanches!*" one yelled in terror as he spurred his mount and raced away, the remaining bandits close behind.

McCain, hardly breathing, remained very still. He could see nothing moving and fully expected to feel the impact of arrows enter his body at every heartbeat. At first there was nothing but silence, then, like shadows, they moved out of the rocks around him. Sitting on their horses in the straight-backed, noble fashion of the Comanche warrior, they seemed to be almost part of the animals they rode. There were about twenty of them, McCain saw, and knew he and Poe were in serious trouble. He was even more certain of their plight, when a tall bare-chest warrior rode from the rocks and stopped directly in front of him. The warrior rode a spotted pony with war paint on its flanks, and a black handprint over its right eye. The only war paint the tall man wore, was a few blue dots sprinkled on his forehead, down the sides of his face and onto his broad chest. He was a Comanche chief and powerful medicine man. McCain knew him well. *Rain Maker!*

Rain Maker raised his hand, silently pointing in the direction the three surviving bandits had taken. Ten of the warriors whooped and raced after them, the others remained as they were, silently sitting on their horses, staring at McCain and Poe. He wondered if he'd have time to kill both Rain Maker and Poe before the Indians got him. Probably not. He made up his mind to just kill Poe, then try to make them kill him outright. Letting the Comanches take either of them alive was not something to consider.

The leader finally spoke. "Hard-Eyes McCain, we meet again." Rain Maker called him by the Comanche name the "old ones" had given him years before.

McCain had fought the man before him many times in the past and was surprised to discover he spoke almost perfect English. "Yeah, well, I'd just as soon have put it off for a while longer. I have some unfinished business to attend to before I wanted to travel. But, I guess a man can't pick the time and place when he's prepared to cash in, eh Chief?"

Rain Maker nodded his head solemnly. In the distance they could hear sporadic shooting and muffled screams coming from the direction the bandits had taken. It sounded like Rain Maker's warriors had caught up with the fleeing bandits. *Good*, McCain thought to himself. *If it hadn't been for them outlaws occupying my thoughts, I might've smelled these damned Comanche and not be in the fix I've put myself and Roosevelt in.* From the travois behind, he heard Rosie groan then begin to breath deeply again.

"Your friend, Poe?" the Chief said.

"Yeah, that's Poe. He's a little sick. Thought I'd take him back to Texas where he can be healed," McCain told him.

"He's dying," said Rain Maker.

"He's just sick," insisted McCain.

"He's dying," said Rain Maker again. "He has the look. The shadow is around him now."

"Well, I surely hope you're wrong, though I suppose it really don't matter much, from the looks of things. Right, Chief?"

Rain Maker sat atop his painted pony and looked at McCain in silence, for several moments. "There was a time when just the name of Poe would send fear racing through my people's villages," he finally said. "Now...look at him. A sick old man, dying of some white man's disease."

He remained stoic, his lined face unreadable. "You and this man called Poe have killed the Comanche all of my lifetime, Hard-Eyes. For many years, we have sung songs about you and Poe in my village." He continued to stare at McCain.

McCain laughed softly. "Yep, I dare say we have," he said. "We sure killed a lot of Comanches. Probably would've killed more, too, if they hadn't been such danged good fighters." He shook his head slowly back and forth. "And when they weren't ready to fight, we mostly couldn't find hide nor hair of them," he went on. "We'd probably still be fighting big battles like the ones you and me used to have, if the Army hadn't stepped in. They decided the only way to get rid of the Comanche was to kill all the women and children."

For a moment, McCain looked a little saddened by the images those thoughts conjured up. "Guess it worked, but what a price." He shook his head again, "What a price."

When Legends Lived

McCain squinted through the sunshine, as he eyed the Indian chief. "Your people killed a lot of Texans for many years as well, Rain Maker. Before that, your granddaddy, Quanta Parker and his cousin, old Iron Shirt, did a bit of killing, too. Lone Wolf was no laughing matter either, as I recollect. Yes, Chief, I'd say we've both killed our share, on both sides."

The ten warriors he'd sent after the fleeing bandits, returned and silently took their places among the ranks of the others. Fresh scalps dripped from their lances and rifle barrels. Some were smeared with blood. Still, Rain Maker sat as though only he and McCain were present.

"When you came after the white women in Lampazos, the day you shot your black friend, you killed many of my warriors. Yet you didn't kill me. Why did you let me live? I wouldn't have let you live."

McCain chuckled again, and repeated what he'd once said to Jim Packard. "You were just out of my range. Eyes ain't what they used to be."

"No, Hard Eyes. I do not think so. You killed your friend from that range and many of my warriors. Why not me?" he insisted.

McCain thought about it, then softly told the Chief, "We're like two old buffalo bulls, Rain Maker. We've been around a long time. Every day, more of our kind gets killed off and, like the buffalo, soon there will be none of us left either."

McCain pulled his tobacco pouch from his shirt pocket and rolled a cigarette. He lit up, studied the tobacco pouch, then tossed it to Rain Maker, who caught it and made it disappear somewhere within his clothing.

"I figured there'd be someone else come along sometime, who could kill you. I didn't want to be the one to do it, that's all. It just seemed to me it would be the end to a part of the life that I've always known." He puffed on his cigarette, studied it and tossed it to the ground. "Not really all that complicated, is it?"

Rain Maker didn't answer.

McCain looked at the old war chief through weary eyes. "Well, shall we get this little dance over with, Chief? I've come a long ways. Maybe even farther than I'd ever wanted to go." He rubbed his eyes. "Let's get it started. I'm tired" he said almost sadly.

Rain Maker waved his hand and the warriors faded back into the rocks from which they had come.

"You gave me a life once, Hard-Eyes. Now I give you two lives. That means I'm even a better warrior than you. Take your sick friend back to Texas to die. The next time I see you, I will take your hair. It will be something to show my grandchildren. I will tell them 'this is Hard-Eyes's' hair. He was the greatest Comanche killer of them all."

Then, as though they'd never been there at all, the Comanches were gone, leaving McCain to wonder why he and Poe were still alive.

He heard Poe stir behind him, then grumble, "Why ain't we moving? I don't want to die out here, ya know. Be careful of them ledges, too. I seen some back there a piece, and if a feller slid over the edge, he'd fall for four days. Well, quit lollygagg'n! Let's go! For cat's sake, do I have to drive my own death wagon to Texas?"

Thirty-Nine

"There was no cloud in the sky. Not a dove scattered, or a scared squirrel barked. I, myself, Walking Dog, scouted the area and found no one waiting. The nearest cover was easily two rifle shots away, yet none was heard... and that's the way it was the day the great medicine man, Rain Maker died. Surely it was God that struck him down!"

– Walking Dog, Comanche warrior, 1901

AFTER ALL THOSE MONTHS of care, Jenny appeared to be getting better. *Well, maybe not physically better, but certainly better mentally,* Rosco thought. Just in the past month or so, he'd noticed Jenny's eyes follow him sometimes when he walked past, or fed her. Actually, the Mexican woman he'd hired to look after her while he was working, first brought it to his attention. Then he began to watch for it, and sure enough, she was right. At first, he began to notice small things moved from where he'd set them, like her water glass. Then, he intentionally began to set things slightly out of her reach, just to confirm his suspicions.

One of the few times he caught Jenny looking at him, he was stunned to glimpse the raw hatred which emanated from her eyes — for just an instant. Then it was gone, as she resumed the blank stare he'd grown accustomed to over the past two years. Later, he wondered if he'd really seen it at all. But soon, it was all but forgotten as he fell back into his routines of caring for her and of his new job, as the Sheriff of San Antonio.

T.J. Sweet, had finally decided to call it quits and "take up fishing, full time." When he'd submitted Rosco Bookbinder's name to Mayor White as his choice to fill the vacancy, the city council leaped at the chance. He'd been sheriff for six months, rather liking the freedom it gave him, although he wasn't particularly fond of the added responsibilities and paperwork.

Rosco had found her in Mexico, plucked her out of that hell, and had taken care of her ever since. He was also the reason she was there now, unable to live the life she'd wanted with Billy Reid, and now dying of some terrible disease. If he hadn't stubbornly dogged her and Bill across half of Texas, then shot and wounded him, they might've never been caught by the Indians. God, how she wished she'd put her shotgun to Rosco's head that day and finished what she'd started. As it was, she couldn't believe he'd survived both barrels of her shotgun blast in his back. She and Bill had been sure he would lay there and bleed to death, and that he didn't, was the cause of her deep hatred.

In her mind, Jenny could still hear the awful screams of her lover as the Comanches slowly cooked him alive. Forcing her to watch it all, made it even harder to erase from her memory. Then came the forced couplings, over and over again, until at last, her mind had eventually shut down completely. Oh, she still vividly remembered the first dozen or so, the animal grunts and rancid smell of the Indian bucks with sour whisky on their breaths as they took her. Then nothing — just emptiness. Later, she'd retained a limited memory of her time in Mexico, of Fat-Man Jose beating her, of the army of fat, greasy, Mexicans who came to the many whorehouses she'd stayed, to have sex with her. It'd been during those lucid short spans when she'd drowned herself in tequila, and later, opium.

Jenny had been conscious and aware for several months, though she kept it a secret. Long enough to hear the conversations between that old Doctor and Rosco, as they discussed her disease and how of long she had to live. The worse part had been listening to the doctor describe the pain, and subsequent madness she would be subjected to before she died. Yes, thank you Rosco Bookbinder, she thought with contempt. She had him to thank for all of this.

Jenny had discovered some limited movement about a month previously and had hid it from Rosco, and the fat old housekeeper. Oh, she couldn't move very well, but she managed by grabbing onto the furnishings and walls, and hobbled around the room well enough. At first, she searched for a gun with which to kill Rosco, then herself. She soon discovered there was none to be found, and knew from her earlier experiences that Rosco Bookbinder didn't sleep soundly enough to permit anyone to just walk up and shoot him with his own gun. So Jenny fumed. She'd just have to forego that last little pleasure. She certainly wasn't going to sit around this awful place and wait to go mad, though. Her life had ended anyway, the minute Bill Reid died — the only true love of her life.

Jenny closed her eyes and pictured the big wild-looking man with the flowing beard she'd taken as her lover. It now seemed so long ago. That Bill, he sure could make her feel it. When he'd wanted anything, her included, he simply took it. That's what she'd liked about him most, the way he'd been like an animal with her. Jenny almost smiled. Yes, those had been good days, Jenny thought as she pulled herself up from the chair by using the porch railing.

She could hear old, fat Maria in the kitchen, probably cooking the evening meal for her patient, and Rosco. The stupid woman would be occupied long enough, Jenny thought, as she pulled herself along the railing and down the two steps to the level grassy area, lying between her and the water.

Now, the hard part, girl.

Balancing herself, she took short, halting steps, deliberately placing one foot in front of the other, inching toward the swift current of the river. Tiny sweat beads formed on her brow from the exertion. *Over half way now. It looks so cool and peaceful,* she almost whispered. Then she was there!

Unsteadily, she lowered herself to the ground, placing her feet in the running water. It was cool, nudging and swirling around her feet, gently tugging her into its wake. She gazed momentarily at her reflection, as though enraptured. *I'm coming, Bill!* Silently, she slipped down the damp bank, immediately engulfed by the current, and carried quickly away. The last thing she heard was Maria screaming.

* * *

Wes Tanner had been waiting patiently for most of the morning. He'd seen signs all along the swollen stream bed and correctly figured that sooner or later, they'd give up trying to get across and just follow it down stream to find a better fording place. He was on a high piece of ground that had a reasonably level field of fire for a thousand yards. There were several reasons why he'd selected this particular spot. The most important reason was the steep gully which lie between his location and the level area where he intended to kill his prey. He doubted a horse and rider could come close to climbing it. The other reason was, he'd determined they were somewhere between him and the river, and by deducing they obviously wanted to go south, this became their only logical route. It was only a matter of time until they arrived.

When Legends Lived

Tanner had been hunting Comanches for more than a year, and prided himself that he could accurately foretell which trail they'd take to get to a particular point. The trick was to first figure out where they were headed, then it was easy to figure out how they'd go to get there. Comanches, he'd decided early on, were much more arrogant than either the Apache or the Kiowas, and that made them predictable. The Comanche figured he owned this whole damned country, and he'd go anyplace he wanted, wherever and however he damned well pleased. That notion was precisely what gave Tanner his edge. They just couldn't conceive that someone else might be out here, too.

Once Tanner had started "hunting," word spread quickly that someone was killing off the Comanches in Texas. A few citizens thought it was the Rangers, and some figured it was one the other Indian tribes who for many years had to humbly accept the superiority of the mighty Comanche Nation. Tanner had been careful to hide the fact that he was the "Comanche Hunter." One of his covers was hiring on as a hunter for the Army, and lately, by holding several other jobs to include that as deputy sheriff of Pecos.

What almost always raised suspicion was his long rifle with the attached telescope. Lately, he took great pains to dismantle it before returning to town, wrapping it in a large oilcloth he always carried for that purpose. The one time he hadn't, he remembered, was when he came upon that deputy and his sick wife on the road from San Antonio to Laredo. The deputy had seemed to be a suspicious cuss, and at the time, Tanner contemplated circling around and picking them both off before they got to San Antonio. The only reason he hadn't was because that sick wife had somehow reminded Wes of his own lost wife. So, he'd let them live. Maybe that'd been a mistake.

He most likely would head down to El Paso and deal some poker until he saw if there was going to be an uproar over this latest kill. If so, he'd hang around for a few months until things quieted down, then head on down to Langtry, or maybe Eagle Pass. He had plenty of time and there'd always be plenty of Comanches.

Suddenly, he tensed as movement caught his eye in the tree line to his front. He froze, and quietly watched the area for any other movement. Slowly, a lone horseman entered the open area, cautiously peering around. *Comanche!*

Tanner followed him with his eyes, as he walked his horse the entire width of the flat green area and into a grove of trees on the other side. Within minutes he reappeared, tracing the length of the deep gully between Tanner and the tree line he'd initially exited. *Very thorough*, he thought. *The bugger checked everything within rifle range. Don't expect he knows of any rifle that will reach from this hill to that flat area*, Tanner surmised. The lone Comanche finally returned to the tree line and waited. After a few minutes, others came out of the trees to join him.

'Bout twenty of 'em!

He adjusted the long metal tube on the top of his rifle barrel, watching breathlessly as the group's leader passed the first of five aiming stakes he'd paced off for distance, earlier in the day. *Hit the jackpot for sure this time*, he thought, smiling coldly. Looking through the powerful scope he scanned the group, allowing them more time to get well into range. His sight came to rest on a tall warrior at the front of the bunch. He took in the blue dots down his face and chest, and the painted pony with a black handprint covering its right eye. *Something familiar about him*, Wes Tanner thought. *Looks like you might be someone important though*, he thought as he let the cross-hairs settle on the man's broad chest. *So you're first!*

When Legends Lived

The tall warrior passed the third aiming stake and Tanner knew the precise distance to his target. He took a deep breath exhaled. Then he took another and let half of it out. Holding his breath, he gently squeezed the trigger, letting the recoil of the weapon surprise him. *Just like the book said*, he mused.

The heavy round carried the target backward, over the rear of the spotted pony. Several warriors dismounted hurriedly, running to the downed man as he lay in an unmoving heap. *Probably didn't even hear the shot from this range*, Tanner thought. He picked out another target and squeezed off a second round, and watched as it hammered a second man to the ground. Then, he began firing in rapid secession. He shot still another before they realized they were even being fired upon, another as they ran to remount, and two more before they could get out of range. *Six! Not a bad day's work!* His mind drifted back to a vision of a sunny-mannered little girl's face and a pretty wife, too young to know the pain and misery of an untimely death.

Knowing the Comanche, they would be furious at losing their leader and would undoubtedly try to circle around, pinning him against the very river he'd used to trap them. Unhurriedly, he traversed the reverse slope of the ridge, shoved his rifle into the hand-tooled leather case attached to his saddle, mounted the big bay stallion and rode toward the rope he'd tied across the river the previous night. With the aid of the rope he could quickly cross, cut the rope, and be well away before the Indians found a ford to cross the river. He almost wished he could be there waiting for them when they tracked him to this spot. He smiled at the picture of him hiding on the other side, picking them off, one-by-one, as they tried to swim across.

Tanner easily found the rope he'd positioned earlier and

quickly crossed, then cut it and watched as it floated downstream. Scanning the other side, he saw nothing, so he turned his horse south and began to slowly walk it toward El Paso. A bath and a hot meal sounded good right about then. Maybe a little whisky. Hell, he'd earned it.

Forty

*Death? Tarnation...I ain't scared of traveling.
I 'spect it to be just another great adventure."*

– Rosie Poe, as a young man (1860)

BRAD THOMPSON LEANED AGAINST the spring-wall as he had so many times before, and watched as the four horsemen made their way toward him. The farm had been built on the only perceptible rise in the surrounding landscape, and provided a good vantage point to see someone approach from a great distance. Today, as usual, it'd been one of the children who'd first seen the visitors and immediately ran to tell Brad.

Having had many chances to observe various travelers arriving at the Children's Farm, Brad was certain he already knew the visitor's identity. At least one of them. The big figure in the middle sat on one cheek of his butt, letting the other hang over the side like a giant ham hock. Brad knew the reason was to allow quick access to the holstered Colt resting on his hip. The man was U.S. Marshal Bill Tilghman. Brad Thompson wondered if the famous lawman had finally made up his mind to arrest him, and had returned to carry him back to Texas for hanging.

He wasn't particularly worried. He'd long ago resigned himself to the fact that he might someday hang for his past offenses against society, and had made peace within himself. If he was to hang, so be it. He wouldn't resist and he certainly wouldn't fight, although at one time he figured he was probably one of the best guns in the state of Texas. No, he'd seen enough killing, and had done all of it he was ever going to do.

Reflecting back, he was glad he'd told Reba everything about his past. She'd cried and hugged him close. "I don't know what that other man did, but the man I've known since you've been here is full of love and decency. He isn't a killer."

Hearing a small voice behind him, he turned to find his two-year-old daughter coming out the front door. Lesa was his and Reba's eldest child, and at that moment she was trying to find a way to get off the porch steps without falling down, so she could join her father at the spring-wall. She made a determined effort to jump off just as Reba appeared out of nowhere, snatched her up and carried her off, kicking and screaming, into the house. Their baby, who'd been sleeping up to that point, let out a howl, as well. He wondered how they'd all fare if he were taken back to Texas to stand trial for murder.

Alex could help, he thought. Alex had taken on a man's responsibilities ever since the Hawkins' had been killed by that drifter, Scruggs. *I couldn't have made it without Alex and the others*. He had to remember to let them know that — time might be short. Tina, his ever-present little buddy, now joined him at the well, to help him in what had now become a tradition at Children's Farm — serving the cool spring water to every visitor who arrived across the hot flat plains.

"Howdy, Marshal," Brad called as the four approached. He waited until they were close enough, then helped Tina carry the half-filled wooden bucket to the mounted men, where Tina filled the gourd dipper and handed it up to Marshal Tilghman.

"Thanks darlin', I sure needed that," the big man said as he

When Legends Lived

drank deeply. Finished, he handed the dipper back to Tina and she moved to serve the others.

"Climb down and rest a spell, Marshal. Reba will have supper going in a bit, and we always have enough for guests."

Several in the group smiled broadly at Brad's suggestion. Seated to the rear of two of the deputies, were two small children, a boy and a girl, about eight or nine years old.

"Don't mind if I do," said Tilghman. "I brought you a little something and I'd be obliged if you could find it in your heart to do me a favor." Tilghman stretched his back and motioned to the three men and two children to dismount. The children hung back, trying to hide behind one of the horses.

"These two kids lost their parents in an Indian raid up north. Wiped out a whole wagon train of farmers, I hear. Nobody can find any kin folks for them, and nobody particularly wants to take both of them in. You see, they're brother and sister, and we found some family to take the boy, but they won't take the girl. Figured the boy could help out on the farm, I guess," he said.

Tilghman gulped another mouthful of water. "Lordy! That's good! I figured if you could take the girl, we'd drop her off here and take the boy on over to the Bend. How 'bout it, Mr. Thomas?"

"Come on in, and we'll discuss it over supper. Tina, take the children and show them where to wash-up. Come on up to the house when you're finished." Brad walked toward the large house with the adults following.

Tilghman watched as Brad took the baby in his arms, while Reba continued to prepare their food. All of the children, with the exception of the two he'd just brought in, were laughing and enjoying themselves.

The good mood of everyone continued throughout the meal and Tilghman observed the children as they ate their food with good manners and politeness. All except for the brother and sister the Marshal had brought with him. They wolfed down their food as though they hadn't eaten in several days, a fact Tilghman personally knew wasn't true, and behaved as if someone might swipe the food away at any moment. The other children made no comment and seemed to take little notice.

After the meal, all of the men moved out to the front porch to smoke. Brad lit up a pipe, as did Tilghman, the others either selected their chaw or rolled a cigarette. At last, Tilghman spoke. "Have you given it some thought? Seeing as you've added several other mouths to feed since I was here last, I wouldn't blame you none if you turned me down."

"Well, Marshal, I am going to turn you down," Brad said. "But, not in the way you might think. I spoke to Reba briefly about it, and we both think a brother and sister should be together. What I'm saying is, if we can keep them both, we'll accept them."

Tilghman was taken by surprise. "I don't know, Mister Thomas," he said. "The boy was already spoken for by the Higgens family."

"Sounds somewhat like they were making a deal for a hog, don't it Marshal?" Brad said as he puffed on his pipe. "Kids shouldn't be bartered for. You have to take them as they come. These two come as a package, brother and sister. The way I figure it the Higgens either want them, or they don't. If they don't, then we do."

The Marshal smoked thoughtfully and deliberately, then said quietly, "Damned if you ain't right when you put it like that,

When Legends Lived

Thomas. As far as I'm concerned you can have both. You want me to tell them, or do you want to?"

Brad stood, saying, "It's past bed time around here, gentlemen. Alex will be around to show you where you'll be put up for the night. Don't worry about the two kids, Marshal. Reba has been talking to them already. I think this'll go pretty smooth. Good night gentlemen."

The following morning Reba was up early as usual, breakfast was prepared, and she and Brad were waiting when the Marshal and his men entered the kitchen.

"Don't seem to get much sleep around here, do you?" he said to the pair.

"We put in long days, Marshal. The children have been up for an hour already, feeding the livestock," Reba told him.

Tilghman heard a commotion as the dozen or so children arrived all at once. Among them were a freshly scrubbed boy and girl of about ten, who looked surprisingly like the ones he'd brought in yesterday. He noted not only had their appearances improved, but their table manners as well.

After breakfast, Reba packed the group half of an apple pie and several cookies to "ease their travels," and Brad and Tina escorted them as far as the spring-wall.

"Viya con Dias, Marshal Tilghman," he said as the lawmen headed out. "Drop in again."

"You take care of yourself, Thomas," Tilghman said, as he pulled on the reins to turn his mount. He suddenly stopped. "Oh, it might interest you to hear that we caught up with that Brad Thompson feller we were discussing the last time I was here. Trapped him in an old ranch house along with four of his men. Shot it out to the last man. We buried all of 'em over near

Texarkana." He spurred his mount and shouted over his shoulder, "Just thought you'd like to know."

As Tilghman looked back from the small ridge just before hitting the flats, Brad was already walking back toward the farmhouse. Tina stood alone waving her hand. Tilghman raised his in return and smiled, as he watched her quickly scamper to catch up with her father.

* * *

McCain fretted at the delay as he rode parallel to yet another swollen stream, which forced him even farther to the north. He couldn't recall ever seeing as much rain in those mountains as he was experiencing on his present trek. Roosevelt Poe was growing steadily weaker each day they were delayed, and McCain's frustration continued to build at each delay as his sense of urgency increased. He'd vowed, "come hell or high water," he'd get Roosevelt to the K/D before he died, and that was what he intended to do. Well, he didn't know about hell, but there'd surely been enough high water to last him a lifetime. Strangely enough, despite all the rain in the higher-ups, which filled the streams and rivers in the passes and valleys, he and Poe hadn't yet seen rain.

After running first into the bandits and then Rain Maker, McCain became increasingly cautious, slowing them even more. He was puzzled by the Comanche Chief's reasons for letting them go, but after fighting the Comanche, Kiowa and Apache for all those years, he still couldn't understand half of the things they did. For instance, why were he and Poe still alive? For certain, they'd both killed their share of Indians, so it only seemed right that Rain Maker would jump at the chance to

When Legends Lived

hang either one of their heads on his war-lance. *Something to do with medicine I suppose,* he thought. Whatever the reason, he certainly wasn't going to trust his luck again at having some Comanche decide whether he lived or died.

On the nights he was lucid, Poe talked about the things he and J.D. had done and the people they'd known. Sometimes he "fine-tuned" his Last Will and Testament and had McCain read it back to him to be sure it was understood. *Just the way it's intended.*

"You remember the time we chased Sam Bass and his gang up into Colorado?" Poe asked one night. "We never did catch them, but we sure had a time, didn't we?" He winked at McCain, who suspected where this line of talk would lead, and tried to ignore his partner in the hopes he would shut-up or change the subject. That wasn't going to be the case.

"Yes-sir-re-bob! Remember it like it was yesterday. We stopped at that place in one or another of those little mining towns. They called the place…the Happy Lady Saloon," Poe chuckled. "That big German feller 'bout kicked your butt, for real, Jericho, hee, hee. I had to smack him one with the spittoon, 'til you could shake the smoke out of your head and get after him." He chuckled again.

"I gotta admit though, when you finally did get started, you whupped him pretty good." Another soft chuckle, followed by, "Course, the locals didn't much care for you shooting him in the leg, first. Guess they kind'a thought it gave you an unfair advantage or something. Hee, hee."

"I don't fight for sport nor the pleasure it gives some folk, Roosevelt," McCain said shortly. "Besides, I gave him fair warning. Once you tell a fellow one time, he better listen. If he don't, it's on his head."

"Yep, that's always been the Ranger way," Roosevelt admitted, chuckling again. "Tell him once — then just shoot him, aye God. But that's not the reason I brought it up," he said. "I brought it up to talk about little old Squirrel Tooth Alice. You recall her, don't you, Jericho?"

"No," McCain said curtly, looking away.

Poe laughed. "Sure you do! She was the pretty little gal with reddish hair, 'bout the color of a winter fox squirrel? But that ain't the reason they called her 'Squirrel Tooth' Alice. They gave her that name cause she had that pet squirrel she carried on her shoulder all the time. You remember, that's what the fight was all about."

"No. I *don't* remember," McCain insisted.

"What do ya mean…'no I *don't* remember?'" Poe mimicked. "You was in one of them upstairs rooms with her, when that big old buffalo-man came in looking for his 'little Alice.' Purely in love with her too, he was. Or, so he claimed. There you was with only your boots on, when he tossed you out of that room like a whipped puppy. You sailed through the air like one of them circus fellers, and landed naked as a jaybird, smack-dab in the middle of the ballroom below. You've got to remember that, Jericho!"

"All right!"

"*All right*, you remember? Or *all right*, you don't remember?"

"I said I remember some of it, didn't I?" McCain said crossly. "Will you make your point, so we can talk about something important?"

"This is important to me," Rosie said indignantly.

McCain sat and glared at him, and finally, Poe went on. "I always wanted to ask you just two questions about your little tryst, Jericho…"

"Wern't no tryst at all," McCain interrupted. "She wasn't in that room with me. I was all alone."

"...one was, in all the years I've knowed you, you never so much as lifted a finger for any other of the whores we've met along the way. Why Alice? I mean, she was sure a pretty little thing and all, but there've been others just as pretty. Why?"

McCain remained ramrod straight, and continued to stare into the fire. "What's your other question?"

"Oh, I see. You're not going to answer, are you? Just like always, you're gonna puff-up like an old toad, and not answer. Are you?" Poe waited a respectable amount of time, then said, "Well, are you?"

When it became apparent McCain wasn't going to answer, he went on. "Well, my other question is this. Did she have that ugly squirrel sitting on her shoulder all the while you was a poking her? Hee, hee, hee." Poe's face turned crimson from the effort of his laughter.

McCain raised his eyebrow as Poe continued laughing until he was out of breath and suddenly, began coughing. Then McCain said, "Well, I certainly hope you got that out of your gizzard, 'fore it goes and makes you ill. You got any more damn fool questions, or do you want to talk about your will, now?"

Poe coughed painfully a few more times and then spit. When he looked up, McCain said, "While you were sleeping last night, I looked a few of these things over some and I figure we should discuss them a little more. For instance, you say to use the money we get from the railroad to put in at least six of those contraptions Jim Packard told us about...windmills, I believe he called them? Then, if there's any money left, to buy cattle."

"Yep. That's what I said. You don't think I should spend my money as I see fit?"

"I don't have any fault with you burning your money, if that's what you want to do with it. But for Pete's sake Roosevelt... windmills? Cattle? Next, you'll have us planting a garden. Hell, why don't we put in some corn, or some beans, even cabbage?"

Poe rubbed his chin as though seriously considering McCain's suggestion. "No, not cabbage. I hate cabbage."

McCain swore softly, stood, and strode to where the horses were tethered. As McCain made a show of checking the knots in the rope, Grasshopper loudly clicked his teeth at him, and Poe chuckled softly.

* * *

Jim had asked her to marry him soon after their return from Odessa. Ever since the night they'd first made love, Bethena had contemplated his asking. At first she was afraid he would, then as time wore on, afraid that he wouldn't, and she honestly didn't know how she'd answer, if he did. It wasn't that she didn't love him, but Bethena knew she hadn't completely overcome her phobia about Scar's returning to take her away again. Oh, the dreams were coming further apart and she wasn't always watching her bed room window expecting to see him there. But...even though she knew it was silly, deep down inside, Bethena still felt he'd someday be there when she looked.

She scolded herself for the hundredth time. It's over, she told herself. She'd become Mrs. Jim Packard and go east to live for a few years. By the time they returned for good, Scar'd either be dead, or completely forgotten. Besides, Roosevelt and that damned old friend of his, J.D. McCain, had probably already caught up with them and killed the whole gang by now. If anyone could do it, it would be J.D. McCain.

When Legends Lived

He's a man-killer. That's all he knows, Bethena thought. *I guess Rosie is too, but somehow there seems to be a difference between the two. Yes, McCain would kill the scar-faced man this time, and it would be over — finally.* She shivered. *At least I pray so.*

Then brightening, she thought, *I hope Rosie'll be here for the wedding.*

Of all the people she could think of, he was the one most responsible for her being alive today. If he hadn't come to rescue her from those awful men, there'd be no wedding — or any Beth, for that matter.

Thank you, Rosie, she thought, smiling as she hugged herself and spinning around. *Thank you, thank you, thank you!*

They set the wedding date for late June, right after Jim's return from Chicago. That would be just six weeks away. Jim was scheduled to catch the train north in three days and Bethena dreaded his being gone so long. Now that she'd finally found him, he was leaving her alone again. Although she knew it was only for a short time, something about it just felt wrong. Still, she forced herself to think about Jim's trip to confirm they'd planned for all eventualities.

He'd first check in with Frank Chase and demand a position in Dallas, or Fort Worth. Then, he'd ensure all legal entanglements with his ex-wife, Hattie, were settled; and lastly, he'd consolidate all of his property and other assets and have them transferred to wherever the Southern Pacific offered him a position. She prayed it'd either be in one of the eastern Texas cities or in one of the bordering states. That way she'd be close enough to visit Kate and the girls, but still far enough away, hopefully, that her dreams wouldn't come back. And what if the railroad wouldn't offer Jim the position he wanted? Then, he still had his law degree. He could set up a private practice and they'd get by just fine, she told herself.

* * *

Bethena heard Jim and Billy returning from their trip into Odessa and went to meet them. Jim had wired a return answer to Frank Chase and made arrangements for his trip back east. She ran down the curving stairway, out the front door, and onto the large-covered porch that wrapped around the front of the ranch house. Kate had beaten her outside and was already waiting. As Jim and Billy drove up in the wagon, Bethena could see right away something was wrong. Dismounting with his usual difficulty, Jim limped up the steps and kissed her warmly on the forehead. Bethena took both shoulders in her hands and looked deeply into his eyes.

"What's the matter, Jim? Tell me."

Jim led her and Kate inside, removed several newspapers from his satchel, and spread them out on a low table in front of the rock fireplace. "This," he said, pointing at the headlines.

> **RAILROAD MAN CLEANS UP OUTLAW GANGS!**
> Nearly three years ago, Southern Pacific Railroad's V.P., Frank Chase, hatched a plan to rid western Texas, once and for all, of the outlaws and renegades plaguing the citizens. "We'll send in our own man," Chase said. He chose one of their best, Mr. James Packard, and now the rest is history. Starting tomorrow, major newspapers in the country will run a series of stories on Mr. Packard's exploits. Packard returns from his adventure to assume a position of responsibility and importance with S.P. within the next few weeks. Welcome back, Jim, and thanks for a job well done.
> — The Editor

Jim's face was red with embarrassment and rage. "Four eastern papers here!" he bellowed. "And they all say the same damned thing, none of which is true. The whole story is a bunch of lies! The only true statement in any of them, is that I went along."

Dejected, Jim sat on the edge of the couch and placed his head in his hands. "Some hero," he said. "All I managed to do was get myself shot. The real heros are Poe and McCain, and they're not even mentioned."

As the others watched in silence, he slowly shook his head in frustration. "How am I ever going to face those two again? They'll think I'm a real snake-in-the-grass for the railroad. McCain doesn't care for the railroad anyway — and I don't think he's overly fond of me, either. The old bastard will probably shoot me on sight after he hears about this."

"Well, don't be so down on yourself, darling," Bethena admonished. "Jericho McCain don't like much of anything — and hardly anybody — anyway. Besides, Rosie Poe will probably get a kick out of it."

Kate piped in, "She's right, Jim. The worse thing in the world would be for those two to wake up one morning, and find out they've become famous. They'd simply hate it, believe me."

"That's not the point," Jim said. "The point is, the damned railroad used me and now they want to make me a hero for their own benefit. I'm not going to allow it."

"What can you do, Jim?" Bethena said.

"I don't know yet, but I'll think of something before I get there," he answered.

They talked about it a little longer, then Kate, seeing the look Billy gave her, quickly ushered Bethena out of the sitting-room to allow her son some privacy to ease Jim's embarrassment and anger.

After the ladies departed, Billy passed a fine cheroot to a still scowling Jim Packard, and waited until he placed it between his lips. Leaning forward, Billy lit Jim's smoke, then his own. Next, he poured Jim a generous portion of bourbon and one for himself.

"The truth is, Jim, this notoriety thing might not be all bad."

Packard started to interrupt, but Billy held up his hand. "No, wait. Hear me out." He walked to the room's large window and stood with his back to Jim. "A few years ago, the biggest ranch owners in Texas, among which I count the K/D, got together and decided we weren't getting a fair shake. We paid for most of our regional improvements and for running the state, but every time we turned around, we were being hit with more demands for revenue — and even legislation that threatened our very existence."

He faced Jim and sipped his drink, then placed it back on the mahogany bar. "My father and the other big ranchers put together a substantial amount of money to back a governor they felt would handle cattlemen's issues more favorably," he said. "That man was Governor Roberts. During his first term, he did just that. But after being re-elected on our money for a second term, he seemingly forgot those who had placed him into power in the first place. Now he's already working on having his Lt. Governor follow him into office."

Billy took a draw on his cheroot, made a face and crushed it out in an ashtray. "Never did like those things," he said. "Pierce, Goodnight, King and the rest expressed their dissatisfaction at the last Cattlemen's Association meeting, in San Antonio. The consensus was, if we were able to find the right person to run against Roberts, we'd all back him and get him elected. The perfect man would be personable, educated, and above all, not be owned by the Robert's bunch in Austin."

When Legends Lived

Billy looked at Packard, without saying anything more.

"So?" said Jim, dumbfounded.

Billy Shaw smiled at him, saying nothing.

"You're joking!" Jim said, as it finally dawned on him what Shaw was proposing. He jumped up and quickly walked to the large fireplace, spun around, and stared at Billy. "You can't be serious!" he said, laughing out loud, then sobering as he realized he was the only one laughing.

Billy continued to smile at him, silently.

"That's the most ridiculous, hair-brained idea I've ever heard of, Billy Shaw," Packard said. "I don't know anything about being a governor. Hell, I don't know very much about anything."

"You got guts, Jim," Billy answered. "You proved that when you went with McCain and Poe on their run."

"I was *ordered* to go, Billy. I was scared to death the whole time I was out there and I was of absolutely no help to them — probably even hindered them, if the truth were known," Jim contended.

He picked up one of the newspapers, looked at it, snorted and tossed it aside, saying, "The man you read about in those newspapers? Well, that isn't me. So get used to it."

The much younger Billy Shaw wrinkled his brow and observed Packard, in the way a grandfather might look at a naive grandchild. his look was just short of being comical, coming from one so young. But his words rang true.

"Jim...Jim, listen to me," he said. "It doesn't matter whether they're true or not. They're in print now and the world's seen them. This is what sells newspapers and even if you come out and deny it, do you actually believe they'll print what you say?

Whether you like it or not, this is you from now on, so you might as well take advantage of it. Use it, Jim. Run for Governor and change whatever it is you don't like about how things are done by the power mongers."

Packard looked confused, and Billy hurriedly continued, "And if you're worried about what Poe and McCain will think, don't," he told Jim. "Mom was right. Those two would just as soon be tied down over an ant-hill, as become famous. They might even enjoy your discomfort, if what I hear about them is true."

Billy stood and looked down at Jim, who was seated once again on the long couch. "Just think about it, Jim," he said. "That's all I ask. Go back to see Chase, and if you decide to tell him to go fly a kite and are looking for something else to do? Then, I'll go see Charles Goodnight and the others, and see what they say. If they agree, we'll put you and your new bride in the governor's mansion. Damned if we won't!"

Billy smiled once more and walked out, leaving Jim to ponder his proposal.

Forty-One

BONE LED THE WAY back down the mountain. Scar wasn't to be seen, but then, he seldom traveled with the group. Nonetheless, he would usually be there in the evenings — like as not, showing up suddenly enough to make a person mess his pants, thought Bone. That was Scar's way. Bone had killed a lot of men. Women and kids, too. He wasn't afraid of anything that walked, crawled or shit on the face of the earth, but that damn Scar purely unsettled him. You never knew when he'd cut your throat, just to see if you'd bleed. Bone had seen him do it many times.

Three-Finger Ned was a bad one too, but Bone figured he could handle Ned well enough. Likewise for the three Apaches who Scar had let throw in with them. But Scar? He was another kettle of fish — about the deadliest man Bone had ever met. If a man made him mad, he'd kill him. If a man didn't make him mad, he'd kill him, too. In fact, if you ever let your guard down around Scar, like as not you'd end up dead — or worse. *'Cause Scar'd have his "fun" first.* Bone shivered uncontrollably, in spite of himself.

The previous night, Scar had told them of his plan. He'd sent Three-Finger Ned to check out the place of a white woman — one he'd captured once before. Scar reasoned that if Poe considered her important enough that he'd chase them down to rescue her, Scar might be able to use her to trap that stinking old man, and finally kill him. Get rid of that damn McCain, too, once and for all. He planned simply to go to the ranch where she lived and grab her, and use her for bait. If she wasn't there, he'd just grab the other woman or one of the little girls. He'd told them it didn't matter much, for Poe and McCain had some kind of attachment for that family and would come after whoever he took — then Scar could quit running all the time and start having a little fun out of life.

Bone received Scar's promise that if they took one of the little girls, he could have her for a while. *I might get my blanket-ass killed by them old Rangers*, Bone thought. *But if I don't, getting one of the little girls would be worth it.* As he rode, he thought of the blond-haired little girl that awaited him at the K/D Ranch, and smiled.

Since leaving the thin mountain air and entering the flat-lands, Poe seemed to gain more strength and become a bit more talkative. In fact, as he bumped along on the travois, he talked nearly all the time. McCain reaffirmed a fact he'd always known about his old friend — that his skin was thicker than a possum's and you just simply couldn't hurt his feelings by telling him to shut-up for a while. At the best, the words produced a mild chuckle and at the worse, a stinging retort. Either way, you usually felt as though you'd come out on the short-end of the stick in a verbal exchange with Poe.

*   *   *

Poe was talking at the moment. "…and I'm leaving my sorrel mare to you, Jericho," he was saying. "That way, when you finally get fed up with the nasty disposition of that nag of yorn, and leave him someplace for the coyotes, at least you'll have a dependable mount to see you through."

"Yeah, well thanks, but — " McCain started, but Poe ignored him and went on.

When Legends Lived

"No, don't thank me. One other thing I forgot to mention, Jericho. When I'm buried in that family plot of Kate's? I want you to come see me once every year. Make it in the Autumn. I like the weather it then."

"Now, why would you want to make me promise something like that?" McCain said. "You won't be there to see me. You're just doing that so's I'll have to visit Kate every so often. That's right, ain't it? Meddling, just like you always do."

"How do you know I won't be there to see you?" Roosevelt said. "Have you ever heard of anyone coming back and saying, one way or the other?"

McCain rode in silence, fuming. Then, he grumbled with finality, "You're going to make me promise, ain't you?"

"If you want to deny a dying man's last wishes, go right ahead, Jericho. Ain't no skin off my rump. No-sir-ree! Can't say that I'd do it, but you go right ahead."

McCain stared straight ahead. He knew exactly the look Poe had on his face at that moment, even though he didn't look back to see it. "Dammit," McCain said, staring straight ahead.

"I'd just be afraid of restless spirits and such, if I was to deny a dying man, anything," Poe went on. "Course, some folks don't believe in the hereafter, so they don't have to worry about making some poor spirit unhappy — just because they wouldn't honor a dying man's last request."

Poe cocked an eye at McCain's back to see if his words had any affect. "Do you believe in the spirits, Jericho?" he said innocently.

McCain sighed in defeat, and relented. "All right, Roosevelt. If it'll get you off the subject, I'll do it." They rode in silence for a time, then McCain said, "And no, for your information, I don't believe in spirits."

Suddenly, McCain felt a splatter on his forehead, and took off his hat and stared skyward. Within seconds, drops began to fall more rapidly.

"Well, aye God!" said Rosie. "Is that rain, Jericho? Honest to God, rain?"

McCain stopped his horse and sit, letting the rain fall on his upturned face. "Yep, partner," he said almost reverently. "It sure is rain. Appears the drought is over."

Rosie asked McCain to cover him up with his slicker, just to his chin, and as his wish was granted, said, "I want to feel it on my face. Thought I'd die and not feel rain in my face again."

It was only a shower and stopped by the time they made camp that evening. However, the sky remained dark and the air still felt heavy and moist, as though it'd start up again at any minute. The daylight was rapidly fading as McCain fashioned a lean-to from the canvas, and told Poe they were within fifty miles of the K/D Ranch. Both went to sleep that night with lighter hearts than they'd felt in many days.

The rains didn't return during the night, but the next morning heavy black clouds could be seen racing across the sky — at times, blocking out the sun completely. The coolness of the day and the flatness of the terrain, combined to make traveling easier now, and they made good time, rapidly covering the next fifty miles. Sensing they were nearing their final destination, Poe continued to talk McCain's "damned leg off," as they ate up the final miles.

"You know, Jericho? I never thought I'd cash out like this," Poe told him. "I mean, all those scrapes we got into — I always figured I'd get shot out of the saddle down in Old Mexico, or knifed while trying to stop a riot, or something like that. Anything but this. It sure makes you wonder, don't it?"

McCain knew Poe didn't require an answer, so didn't attempt one.

"Still, I can't complain. All the miles we rode, the things we've seen — all the pretty little ladies — adventure, whiskey, and women. Lordy, what more could we have asked for, eh Jericho?"

Suddenly Poe was quiet again and McCain decided let him sleep for a while. *You'll need your strength when we get to the K/D*, he thought. As he recalled, those two sisters dearly loved Roosevelt.

Finally, when within five miles of their destination, McCain announced, "Wake up and get ready for some of Kate's fine cooking. We're almost there, partner."

Poe continued to sleep soundly, and after a few minutes, McCain again spoke his name, still receiving no response. He jerked his horse to a halt, and heart pounding loudly, quickly dismounted to kneel beside Poe.

Tipping back the big Texas hat, he stared at Poe's closed eyes, who still appeared to be sleeping peacefully. Without any apparent self-consciousness, the tough old Ranger reached out a callused brown hand and gently brushed an unruly lock of hair from his friend's eyes. McCain was aware of a loud ringing in his ears and felt as if a large hand had suddenly gripped his heart. The unthinkable had finally happened. Wilson Roosevelt Poe was dead.

McCain abruptly stood, took off his hat, and made several quick circles, beating it angrily against the side of his leg.

"Dammit, Roosevelt. Dammit to hell!"

He stared at the mountains they'd left only a few days before, as if by doing so, Poe would begin speaking once again, and everything would be fine when he turned around again. Fighting the turmoil inside himself, he stood quietly for several moments.

After a while, he turned and knelt beside the travois, slowly rubbing his burning eyes. "Dammit," he whispered again. "Now, look what you've done, Roosevelt."

Unaccustomed tears flooded his eyes, making it difficult to see his friend's face. The last time he'd cried was when he was fifteen and he'd just buried his entire family in Tennessee. The only other family he'd known, lay before him now. McCain wiped his eyes with his shirt sleeve and stared at the calm face before him.

"Damn, Roosevelt," he whispered again. "We were nearly there, too."

Rosie Poe's face was soft and relaxed and all the pain McCain had seen for the past few months was gone. Now, he looked calm, almost peaceful. Kneeling beside his friend, McCain trembled and his heart filled with the sorrow of a great loss. Bowing his head, his long silver hair hid his eyes…and he mourned. From a distance, one would've been unable to hear the soft sounds coming from the kneeling man, nor see the quiet sobs that shook his shoulders.

"What am I going to do now, Roosevelt? How am I ever going to get by without you vexing me all the time?" came the soft whispers. He held Rosie's limp hand in his own, lingering at the form on the litter for a very long time.

After a while, a soft rain began to fall on them.

Forty-Two

*"He was the last of his kind, Kate.
First Hickok, now Poe. There won't
be any more like them."*

– J.D. McCain, Texas Ranger

JIM PACKARD HAD ALREADY departed for the East by the time McCain arrived at the K/D with Roosevelt Poe's remains. Vaqueros had seen him first, riding alone, slowly pulling the covered travois behind, and word spread quickly that bad news was headed their way. Kate, Bethena, Billy and several of the K/D hands were already waiting for him when he topped the rise south of the ranch house. It took nearly twenty minutes from the time they first saw him top the rise, until he rode into the courtyard, but he was barely halfway when Billy Shaw said softly, "That's Rosie's sorrel mare."

His words hung in the air, echoing a terrible prophecy none dared put into words. The group huddled in dread as the lone horseman, slightly slumped forward in the saddle, hat hiding his face, slowly made his way down the dusty road toward them. To those waiting, the scene possessed a sad, lonely quality. Small rivers of dust floated behind the travois's two poles, as the horseman steadily closed the distance between them, towing the object of their worst fears.

Even from a distance, Kate knew the lonely rider was Jericho McCain. *He still looks the same as always*, she thought, remembering how he would slump forward and lean slightly to one side when riding. At last, he was finally before them. The other's faces' a testimony to their foreboding, deferred to Kate as she made her way down the steps toward the horseman. No one made a sound, as if by remaining silent they could forestall the inevitable bad news.

Kate stopped next to the stirrup of the mounted man. "Hello, Jericho." She was stunned by the depth of sadness in the eyes gazing down at her.

McCain touched the brim of his hat. "Kate."

To Kate Shaw, McCain looked as if he bore a great weight on his shoulders. She could tell by his personal appearance, clothing, and the condition of the animals that he'd been continually on the trail for a considerable length of time. Her eyes moved toward the travois. "Is that Roosevelt?"

McCain started to answer, swallowed hard, then looked at the distant horizon, blinking rapidly. He turned back to Kate with pain-filled eyes, and simply nodded.

Kate dreaded to ask, but steeled herself. "Is he..." she couldn't say the word, so finally just muttered, "...all right?"

Once again he hesitated so long that Kate thought he wasn't going to answer, then spoke in a barely audible voice. "Kate, he's...dead." McCain's soft voice cracked slightly.

Behind her, Kate heard Billy swear softly and Bethena scream, "No! No!" starting to sob loudly. Billy held Beth against his chest as she cried into his shirt.

Kate, arms folded, silently stared at the ground. Then, her gaze returned to McCain. "You look as though you're about ready to fall off that horse, Jericho," she said gently. "Get down and come inside. I'll fix you some food while Bill and my men tend to Rosie."

When Legends Lived

McCain stiffly climbed from his horse, and looked around as though confused, disoriented.

This was a Jericho McCain Kate had never seen before — tired, defeated, a shell of the man she'd known all those years. She reached out, gently laying her hand on his arm.

"Come on, J.D.," she said softly.

McCain stared at her as though she were a stranger, then suddenly pulled his arm from her grasp and reached to untie the sorrel's reins.

"I'll take care of Roosevelt," he said curtly, as he led the horse towing the travois toward the corner of the out-building. "He was my friend."

Stunned, Kate stared after him. "He was a friend to all of us!" she shouted angrily at his back as he walked away. "Jericho? Jericho McCain!" she shouted, stamping her foot.

McCain didn't look back. She glared at the spot where he'd disappeared around the house, then turning, walked stiffly back up the steps to the veranda. "Go help him, Billy, and don't let the old fool put you off. No one should have to prepare a friend for burial alone." She paused, then said bitterly, "Not even Jericho McCain!"

As she walked past them to go inside, they could see tears flowing steadily down her face. Bethena wailed and ran after her, while Billy motioned for the two hired hands to follow him. As he rounded the corner, he heard Bethena and his mother crying inside and wished with all his heart he could cry, too.

When Billy returned to the kitchen, he found his mother and aunt silently drinking coffee at the large wooden table. He could tell by their red, swollen eyes that they'd probably been crying since he left.

"Captain Poe has been tended to, Ma," Billy told his mother. "I gave him my dark suit and he looks right proper in it." He spoke as though the deceased were still alive. "Where do you want us to lay him out for viewing?" he moved to the big stove and poured himself a cup of the strong coffee.

Attempting to conceal her red eyes, Kate didn't look up. "Might as well put him in Jim's room; he'll be gone for a spell, I suppose," she said. Bethena sniffed and blew her nose at regular intervals.

Kate suddenly jumped to her feet and went to the cabinet to start preparing the evening meal. "Where's Jericho?" she said, seemingly without interest.

"He was making himself a bed in the barn the last I seen of him," Billy informed her as he hooked a chair with his foot, turned it around, and sat down, resting his arms on the wooden back. Carefully sipping the steaming coffee, he said, "He seems to be taking Captain Poe's passing pretty hard."

Billy and Bethena jerked with surprised at the loud noise the pan made as it struck the far wall. "I'll be damned if that contrary old fool is going to do that in my house!" she cried. "He can join us in here like a civilized person, as long as he remains at this ranch!" The tears started anew as she stormed out of the room.

Wide-eyed, Billy and Bethena silently stared at each other.

Billy finally broke the silence. "I don't recall ever hearing Ma swear before," he remarked quietly, staring into his coffee cup.

Bethena made a sound of disgust. "Well, you'd better get used to it, if J.D. McCain stays around any length of time," she stated bitterly. "I've heard her say a lot worse than that about that man...but usually when he wasn't around. She might've been better off to say it to his face."

"Were they friends, or something?" Billy said, puzzled.

Bethena stared incredulously until Billy's face finally turned red as the realization dawned on him.

"Oh," he said. He paused, thinking about the latest turn of events. "Aunt Beth, are you telling me that my mother and that old man in the barn were...in love...or something?"

Bethena leaned forward. "Billy, listen to me. You may find this hard to believe, but half the men in Texas have been in love with your mother at one time or another. All she had to do was walk into a room and several men would eventually end up asking her to marry them," Bethena told him quietly. "But she never led them on, nor had anything to do with any of them. Do you know why? Because of that 'old man', as you call him."

Bethena rose, and poured another half-cup of the thick black brew. "This stuff's going to kill us all," she said as she sat back down. "Don't sell McCain short, Billy. He was a handsome man in those days. Still is, I guess. And every man he ever met wanted to be just like him. You've heard the stories about him and Poe? They're all true — those and more. The bad as well as the good. He and Rosie cut a wide swath through Texas in those days, Billy — and for that matter, even Poe was in love with Kate."

Bethena stopped for a moment, sipped her coffee, then went on. "But if there were ever two people meant for each other, it was Jericho McCain and your mother," she said, and laughed. "All the men were in love with her, but the only one she could see was J.D. McCain. The only problem was he was too pig-headed to let it happen."

Bethena paused again, staring down at her coffee cup, then said quietly, "I was just a kid in those days. Guess I always blamed Jericho McCain for our brother's death and did everything I could to hinder their relationship." She jerked her head up defiantly. "It probably wasn't warranted, but I don't regret it a bit. He would've just broken her heart if he'd stayed."

With trembling hands, she picked up her cup, gulped a drink, then grimaced and pushed it away. "Even as it was, I've had to watch her cry over that man for the past twenty years. If it'd done any good, I'd have taken a gun and shot him dead myself, but your mother would've never forgiven me."

Billy was shocked at what he was hearing. "He...don't seem to be a bad sort, Aunt Beth. In fact, I kind of like him."

"Now you listen to me, Billy D!" she said angrily. "I've seen too many young men like you follow him off and never came back, and I get sick every time I think about it. You stay away from him or he'll have you under his spell too."

She jumped to her feet. "If you don't listen to me, you'll be taking off with McCain after some outlaw gang or somebody, and the next thing I hear you'll be dead too." She was crying again, her voice becoming more pitched. "And he is too, bad, Billy! He's the devil's own! Rosie Poe was the only good one in the whole lot of them — and now McCain has gotten him killed, too." She ran from the room screaming over her shoulder, "You just stay away from him, Billy! You hear?"

Billy never even had a chance to remind her that McCain had nothing to do with Poe's death.

Kate was livid as she stormed toward the barn. She stopped at the doorway when she saw McCain sitting beside the sheet-draped body of Roosevelt Poe. Instantly, all her anger evaporated when she saw his still form, huddled, appearing almost...frail. Why, he looks like an old man, she thought, and her heart tugged sharply. Kate deliberately rustled her skirts so McCain would

When Legends Lived

hear her as she approached. As he raised his head, she could see the deeply etched sadness in his face.

"Grieving for Rosie won't bring him back, J.D.," she told him gently.

It'd always been easy for McCain to tell when Kate was peeved at him, for she always called him Jericho when she was — and J.D. otherwise.

"I ain't griev'n," he said. "I'm just saying goodbye." He hadn't moved when she first came in, but now he stood, ill at ease, and removed his big hat. McCain had used the time to wash-up and change into clean clothes. His thick white hair fell nearly to his shoulders in long luxurious waves. The pain she saw earlier was now hidden, as his face remained expressionless.

Kate moved closer, then stopped. "How did Rosie die, J.D.?"

At her question, his pain became more evident again. "Those smart doctors would probably call it 'natural causes,' Kate." He made a sound of disgust. "Natural causes. Nothing natural about what happened to Roosevelt. For someone like Roosevelt natural causes would've been going out in a stampede or with a smoking gun in his hand. But, to be ate-up from the inside? Suffering like he did? No, that's just not natural," he said bitterly.

McCain tiredly rubbed his eyes and waited so long to go on that Kate thought he was through speaking. Finally he spoke again, this time in a softer voice. "He didn't tell me, Kate. All those miles we traveled together, he never mentioned a word about it. Must've been in considerable pain, too."

Kate could see the raw agony return with his words.

"He wanted to help me get that damned Scar," he said bitterly. "He just waited so long to tell me how bad off he was, that we almost didn't make it back here like he promised."

McCain dropped onto a hay bail, as though his legs had suddenly grown weak. "We were all the way to Nogales when he finally reached a point where he just couldn't go on. I vowed I'd get him back to your ranch and 'bout got us both killed on the way," he told her, laughing shortly. "Almost drowned us both coming across the mountain streams — ran into Mexican bandidos — then the Comanche medicine man, Rain Maker. Guess we were just meant to get back here, 'cause we sure had everything against us."

McCain had lowered his head and Kate couldn't see his face. He went on in a voice so soft that she had to strain to hear him, "Guess I really made a mess of things, taking off after Scar and his bunch like that. Stubborn — pig-headed! That's what Roosevelt always called me. He said I had a narrow point of view about things and just went through life like I'm charging through a tunnel. I 'spect he was right. Now look at what it cost. Moses and Stump Henry dead."

Kate ached at the unbearable pain reflected in his eyes.

"...Jake and that young Packard boy likely crippled for life — and now Roosevelt..." his voice trailed off again.

"You did what you thought was right, Jericho. It was right. Those animals have to be stopped somehow!" Kate remarked. "I won't stand here and listen while you tear down all you, Poe and the others have done for this state over the past twenty-five years. Without men like you, there wouldn't be a State of Texas."

He hung his head again, as though the talking had tired him. Depression, thought Kate. "Did Rosie have any family that you know of?" Kate said, eager to change the subject. McCain looked up, as though surprised at the question.

He answered her question with one of his own. "Is it true that you promised him he could be buried here in your family plot?"

When Legends Lived

Kate nodded without speaking.

McCain answered her question. "No. Roosevelt had no family that I'm aware of. He once told me his mother came from a well-to-do family back east somewhere. Her maiden name was Roosevelt," he remarked. "Said that's how he come to have that silly handle stuck on him."

McCain thought for a moment, then said, "His daddy came from somewhere up in Missouri or maybe Iowa...I'm not sure. They were farmers, as I recollect. On the way here, he told me I was his only family." McCain spoke with downcast eyes. His voice was soft, but still sounded as though it might crack with emotion.

Then he suddenly looked up, "He never had time to get married or anything like that. It wouldn't have been fair to saddle a woman with the burden of marrying someone in the business we were in anyhow."

"I guess it didn't occur to either of you to ask though, did it?" Kate said harshly. "Someone might not have thought it too much of a burden if you'd bothered asking them how they felt."

McCain stared at her, puzzled. "Are you talking about us, Kate?" he finally said.

Kate looked away, so he couldn't see her face, then she spoke softly. "I might've been at one time. A lot has happened since then, J.D."

"I never had a chance to tell you. I'm sorry about what happened to your brother, Kate. I swear to god, I never knew he was going to enlist."

Kate spun around angrily, fire shooting from her beautiful eyes. "I never blamed you for what happened to Thomas, you jackass!" she said. "You may have blamed yourself, even to the point of cutting yourself off from those who loved you, but I never once held it against you, Jericho McCain." There was that "Jericho" again, and McCain rightly assumed she was upset with him again.

"What about Beth?" he asked. "I imagine she could cut my heart out, given half a chance."

Again Kate's eyes flashed. "Dammit, we're not talking about Bethena! We're talking about you and me," she finally admitted. "That's always been your problem, Jericho McCain. If things weren't neatly organized and nearly perfect, you gave up on them. You were the same way with those who loved you, too."

More composed, Kate said quietly, "I waited, you know. For a long time. But you never even wrote." She laughed shortly. "I might still have been waiting, if you'd only given me a sign."

McCain looked surprised. "I did write, Kate. I wrote half a dozen letters during that first six months," he told her. "Sent them out on the stage run. I must've met every stage for over a year, hoping you'd find it in your heart to at least write and if nothing else, tell me not to send any more letters." He smiled slightly at her. "After that, I just sort of got it through my thick head that you didn't want to be bothered any more."

There was a long silence. "Beth," Kate barely breathed the word. She remembered. Bethena had always insisted she be the one to pick up mail from the Wells Fargo office. She had stated, it "made her feel useful," because Kate was so busy running the store. *Oh, Beth. Beth, why? Couldn't you see how I was hurting?* Kate's face had gone pale.

"I think I see more clearly now," McCain told her, as the realization set in. "Guess we had a bit of help, all along."

Kate wiped a tear from her cheek with the back of her hand.

"Don't say anything to her, J.D., please. You don't know how close to the edge she's been since being abducted by that madman. I think she's turned the corner, but she's still so fragile I'm afraid the least little thing might push her over. Please?"

"You needn't worry, Kate. What's past is past," he said, looking back at Poe's body. "Wishing things never happened won't make it so."

Kate moved to him, took his arm in her hands, and smiled softly when she felt him stiffen. "Don't try to pull away from me again, cowboy," she said, referring to his actions earlier in front of the ranch house. "You're coming with me this time. I'm fixing a nice supper for everyone, then you'll stay in my home tonight — not in the barn like some saddle-tramp. We've plenty of room and that's where I prefer my friends stay when they come to visit."

McCain's eyes held hers for a moment. "Yes, that would be fine, Kate," he said.

With Kate holding tightly to his arm, they started out of the barn. J.D. paused, glancing back at the wrapped body once more. "He was the last of his kind, Kate. First Hickok, now Poe. There won't be any more like them."

Kate squeezed his arm gently. "He'll be fine here, J.D."

Silently, they walked arm-in-arm back to the ranch house.

Kate showed McCain to his room, and while he moved in his meager belongings, she returned to the kitchen to start the evening meal for the second time that day. Billy was still seated at the table as Kate came in and retrieved the pan she'd thrown earlier. He didn't look nor speak to her as she went about her business.

"Something on your mind, Billy D.?" she finally said. She always called him by his middle initial when she was angry with him, or talking serious business.

"What's your relationship with that old Ranger," he said bluntly, not looking up.

Silence followed, as Kate stopped what she was doing and composed herself. Quietly, her softness barely disguising the steel in her voice, she said, "Don't you ever use that tone of voice on me, again, Billy D." She paused. "And don't you judge me. You don't have the right to judge me!"

Billy jerked his head and locked eyes with his mother. His red face glared at her then, confused and flustered he lowered his eyes once again. "You're right, Ma. I'm sorry," he said. "All this just took me by surprise."

Kate placed her hands on his shoulders, then bent close to his ear and kissed him lightly. "Looks like your Aunt Beth has been busy," she said. She pulled up a chair. "Billy, I knew J.D. McCain a long time before I even knew your father," she said. "What we felt doesn't diminish what Duncan and I shared. After all, he gave me you and the girls, and what greater gift could a woman receive from her husband than her children?"

"Did you love him?" Billy said. Not sure whether he meant McCain or his father, Kate took the middle ground.

"I loved Jericho McCain a great deal, Billy. I loved your father, as well. They were both separate and distinct loves of my life, years apart, and as different as night and day in every way. That doesn't detract from the love I had for both of them, though," she told him.

Kate paused, allowing Billy to absorb what she told him. "Your aunt is a very troubled woman, Billy. She's mixed up and sometimes lets her emotions overcome good taste and proper behavior. Don't think badly of her for it, just recognize it and help her get through it by showing her your love," she said.

Billy's eyes were beginning to mist over. "You're the best person I know, Ma. You deserve a little happiness, too. You know I won't be a problem in anything you decide to do." He stood, bent down and kissed his mother on top of her head, then left the room.

Kate lingered, then smiled softly, rose, and went back to her chores.

* * *

Jim Packard checked right into the hotel as soon as he arrived in the city, despite an invitation by his ex-father-in-law to stay with him and Hattie. He'd intimated Hattie was having second thoughts about her decision to have their marriage annulled and might be willing to talk about it, over dinner. One thing Jim was sure of, he certainly didn't want to talk it over — over dinner, or any other time. An hour after his arrival, there was a knock at the door, and Jim opened it to find Thomas Randle. He swung the door wider and stepped back to allow the older man to enter.

"Well, Jim, looks as though living the rough life agrees with you," Randle said, offering his hand. Except for the serious wound he'd received which caused a pronounced limp, Jim looked healthy and tanned. He'd gained at least twenty pounds, none of it fat, and stood straight and confident. Jim shook hands, motioning him toward a comfortable chair near the window.

"Nice room," Randle remarked as he sat down, removed some papers from his satchel, and laid them on the small table in front of him. "Mr. Chase would like you to become familiar with these before our meeting tomorrow morning. Sort of the 'company line,' if you know what I mean, Jim," Randle said.

He winked at Packard in a conspiratorial manner. Jim made no move to pick up the papers.

"There's something we need to discuss first, John," he finally said, using his ex-father-in-law's first name, something he wouldn't have even considered doing prior to his trip to Texas. Its use wasn't lost on Randle, who raised an eyebrow.

"There is a little matter of money the Southern Pacific owes McCain and Poe for their services," Packard stated firmly.

"Yes, yes," Randle said, agitated by Packard's delay. "We'll take care of that first thing after our meeting in the morning."

"I don't think so, Randle," he said, now using the man's last name. "I think you better run on back to Mr. Chase and have him send his lapdog over today — Cranwell, I believe his name was — and bring me a bank draft for the amount I've written on this piece of paper. The draft will be in my name and I'll see that the two men receive it."

"Now see here — " Randle said, suddenly jumping to his feet.

"No, you, see here!" Packard's voice was steady but hard. He also stood, towering over the other man. "I'm no longer the man you used to run around in circles, Randle. Since I've been out west, I've killed men that would make a meal out of you. I find I don't spook as easily as I used to, and I even enjoy a good fight once in a while, too."

Randle glared at Packard, but at last, broke away and cleared his throat. He walked to the window and looked out, his back to Jim Packard. Finally, he turned.

"You're making a bad mistake here, Packard. A real bad mistake," Randle said icily. "Don't try to buck the railroad. If you do, they'll run right over you."

Packard walked over, and silently held the door open. Randle breathed deeply and exhaled. "What is it you want?" he said begrudgingly.

"I just told you, John. Now, take your little papers, put them back inside your little satchel, and drag your little pissant ass out of my room," Packard told him. "If I don't have the bank draft prior to eight o'clock tomorrow morning, you can talk to all the reporters at the meeting for me. I'll be on my way back to Texas."

Huffy and indignant, the railroad's security man hurriedly stuffed the papers back inside his case and quickly left, glaring back at Packard.

Little pissant ass. Jim chuckled, as the door slammed. Sounds like something Roosevelt Poe might say. He chuckled once more, pleased with himself to have used it so naturally.

Within the hour, Chase's "lapdog," Jack Cranwell knocked on his door. With crisp conversation, the red-faced little man provided Jim Packard with the bank draft, indicating where he was to sign the required papers. Within five minutes, he was gone, and Jim headed for the bank, located just up the street. He cashed the draft so the transaction couldn't be stopped, immediately depositing the money into a new account with instructions that it be forwarded to a joint-account at the Cattlemen's Bank in Amarillo, Texas. The names on the account would be Roosevelt Poe and Jericho McCain. Satisfied with his work, Jim went to dinner alone and thought about the meeting the next morning. There will be fireworks for sure, he mused, smiling.

At eight a.m. sharp, Jim arrived at the Southern Pacific headquarters building and passed through a group of reporters who clamored for a comment from him.

"Later, I'll have something for you," was all they could get out of him, as he hurried up the two flights of stairs leading to Chase's office. He knocked and was invited to enter, where he found John Randle, Chase, and a reporter introduced as Martin Gates.

Jim was surprised by the reporter's presence, until Chase explained the part Gates had played in scooping the story by traveling out west and returning with the facts.

Some "facts," Packard thought sourly.

"Before we talk to the other reporters," Chase told the group, "I want to make sure we're all on the same sheet of music."

He outlined the "facts" as he wanted Jim to present them to the newsmen outside. Jim Packard, would be the sole hero, of course, and would have nothing but praise for the way the Southern Pacific handled this operation for the betterment of Texans. Neither McCain or Poe, nor any others involved in tracking down Bloody Bill Reid and Scar were mentioned. Likewise, there were no comments of the dead Stump Henry, killed in an ambush while on the trail of Reid. Moses Penny's name, who had died trying to rescue a little girl from the bloody Comanches, did not appear in the statement, nor did the terrible wounds Jake Kellog suffered, or the sacrifices Fish and the others had made.

Some "facts", Packard thought again.

"...is all over," Frank Chase was saying, "Jim will be elevated to the position of Director of Security for S.P., taking Mr. Randle's place, who will be our new Vice President for the Oklahoma Territory."

Everybody gets paid off, and just what do you get friend? he thought, looking at Martin Gates? Gates met his eyes, blushed, and

When Legends Lived

dropped his head. He averted his eyes from Jim for the rest of the meeting.

Chase stuck out his hand to Packard, and said, "Congratulations, Jim. I know you'll follow in John Randle's footsteps, right into a future V.P. position."

Chase's arm wrapped around his shoulders, as they all exited the building to the loud enjoyment of the large crowd of reporters. Off to the side he could see Hattie, trying to catch his eye. He didn't look at her. Chase waved his arms downward, attempting to quiet the crowd. As the crowd silenced, Chase said, "Gentlemen, I know you've been waiting a long time to hear what Jim Packard has to say." Again, loud applause, and Chase quieted them once more. "The railroad has always stood ready to enhance the living conditions of the people of this great country. No matter what the sacrifice or cost, Southern Pacific is part of the community and will not hesitate to confront lawlessness and injustice." Chase puffed up his chest and smiled broadly. "We have before us an example of our commitment, one of our own brave people, dedicated to preserving law and order. The gallant Jim Packard dragged his damaged and ailing body nearly a thousand miles to tell you of the love and devotion he has for a great organization — the Southern Pacific Railroad."

The crowd again broke into loud applause as Chase and the others backed away, leaving Jim alone, a signal he was to begin. He waited until the clamoring quieted down, politely tipped his hat to the three ladies standing to the side, then acknowledged the large group of reporters.

"Gentlemen," he said, his deep resonant voice carried well. "We live in wondrous times. Standing at the end of one era, we are poised on the threshold of another. This new age will bring many marvelous discoveries such as you and I could never imagine. I, for one, am thankful I'm alive at this particular time in history and given the opportunity to behold them."

No one uttered a sound as a few reporters stopped scribbling and listened intently.

"Likewise, I'm just as thankful I've lived in the times now coming to an end. I'm thankful, for someday I'll be able to tell my grandchildren I was around when legends lived."

Jim heard someone stir behind him and clear his throat, correctly surmising it was Frank Chase.

"Average men they may be, but if judged by their deeds, they would be considered giants among mortals. History, I fear, will not remember them for those deeds, for it is always the rich and powerful who ultimately interpret — and rewrite — history. But remembered or not, they've left their stamp on a vast stretch of wilderness, that without them, might've never become a part of this great country." He paused, then his voice became softer.

"Yes, gentlemen, we truly live in a time of legends. I know — because for the past three years I've been associated with such men. I used to think there wasn't any such thing as a hero," he quietly said. "I believed in power, wealth, and position — that there were only people who took advantage of situations in order to better themselves, or cash in on opportunities — for me, back then, there were people who succeeded and those who failed. How they succeeded was not important."

The crowd hurriedly scribbled into their notebooks.

"During the past three years I've spent in Texas, I've discovered that real heroes are just ordinary men and women who do the things they've always done in order to get certain dirty jobs done. They don't think of themselves as heroes — or legends —

When Legends Lived

nor do they want to be thought of that way. Those people have lived with danger and death every day of their lives. Facing the gun of a killer, riding down a band of savages, or just fighting the land as they wait for their men to return — they don't think it's anything unusual, or heroic, as we might in the eastern part of the country. It's just everyday life for them, and they do it with honor and dignity."

Several of the reporters, had quit scribbling again and were intently gazing up at him. Jim felt an uncomfortable shifting in the group behind him.

"There are a couple of old Texas Rangers who'd probably die of humiliation, or very likely shoot my ears off if they were to find out I did anything to get their names in the newspapers."

The crowd laughed and Jim continued. "I've been offered a very lucrative position with the Southern Pacific to not mention their names in conjunction with my story." That brought a collective gasp from the crowd, and a restless stirring behind him. Jim felt like Caesar must've felt just prior to having a knife shoved between his shoulders.

"If fact, I could make a lot more money, and a lot of people happy right now by just standing up here and taking credit for what they did, than I ever will by telling the truth," he went on. "But, I suppose somebody has to set the record straight, and it looks like that burden falls to me. When you get right down to it, I guess I'm not actually doing this for them, at all. I'm doing it for me. I'm doing it so I can stand to look at the man in the mirror when I shave for the rest of my life."

A loud commotion broke out behind him. Jim ignored it and continued. "I have all the details for anyone who has the guts to go against the railroad and print them. Mr. Gate's story is a real bunch of 'road apples,' as an old friend of mine would call it, but has the names of real witnesses and actual locations. If any one of you wish to do a little traveling to get the truth, you'll find the facts are essentially true. Truthful in everything, except the name of the person getting the credit. Namely, Jim Packard."

Chase moved to step in front of him. Packard showed him his teeth, and said softly, "If you even try that before I'm finished, you're a dead man, Frank."

Chase, suddenly not at all pleased with the spotlight, hurriedly backed away and hid in the group to the rear, as Packard prepared to go on.

Suddenly, a large man in the front rank raised his hand. "Are you trying to tell us the Southern Pacific is lying about this whole episode to cash in on the publicity?" said the grizzled reporter. "What documentation do you have to back it up, Packard?"

"No, I'm not saying the Southern Pacific is doing anything. The S.P. is actually a very good organization, although I concede, I won't be a part of it after today," Jim said. "What I'm saying is that Frank Chase has pressured Martin Gates into rewriting a fine factual account of history, replacing it with garbage to further his own career." The reporters were buzzing loudly now, but realizing Jim Packard had more to say, quickly quieted down.

"As to your question concerning whether I have documentation?" he said. Jim's hand rested on his right breast pocket, where he felt the thickness of his brown leather journal, carried for the last three years, and hundreds of miles.

"I think you'll be surprised," he said, and smiled.

Forty-Three

"Texas is a whore...beautiful and seductive to be sure, but a whore none-the-less. She'll take all you have and when you have nothing more to give, she'll suck the very marrow from your bones. Then on your last day on this earth, when she embraces you for the final time in a cold, damp grave, she'll take what's left of you...and damn her, you'll still love her."
– From Jim Packard's diary

ROOSEVELT POE'S FUNERAL HAD been a hurried affair, but McCain was still surprised so many people showed up with such short notice. A telegram had been sent to Jim Packard, but due to the soaring temperatures, things had to proceed quickly. The miracle of the unofficial west Texas lines of communication proved more effective than even the telegraph at getting the word out. Fish and Jake had shown up with the hands they could spare, all the way from Bluebonnet. After the burial ceremony, the crowd descended on the ranch house, devouring a ton of food and drinks and sharing stories of their mutual friend, Roosevelt Poe. The preacher, who spoke over Poe, cornered Quint Fishburn at the punch bowl after the ceremony. Fishing for compliments concerning the polished remarks he made over the grave, he asked Fish for the third time how he'd enjoyed the services.

"Well, brother Fishburn, you were a good friend of the deceased, weren't you? Did I do him justice with my comments?" the Reverend Pickleman said.

Several K/D riders and Kate and Billy were standing nearby, watching Fish's Adam's apple start to jump, as it always did when he got excited.

"Those were b...b...beaut...pretty words, Par...Par... Reverend P...Pickle...man. Mighty...pretty words," Fish said. "Especially, the ones a...a...bout his being full o' love for ever b...body, and him b...being pious and religious, and all." Fish swallowed, his Adam's apple rolling up and down to the amusement of his audience. "Yes, sir, mighty p...pretty words."

The Adam's apple jumped once more and Fish went on. "They must've been written about somebody else, though, P... Parson P...Pickle...man. 'Cause ever'body that knowed him, knows Rosie Poe wasn't nothing like that man you described. No sir, nary a thing like it. Someone that didn't kn...know b... better, might believe Rosie got into the wrong grave."

He shook his head as he walked away, leaving the Reverend Pickleman smiling sheepishly at those around him.

* * *

Fish, Jake, and McCain prepared to head out the next morning for Bluebonnet, and Kate found McCain alone, as he saddled his horse. She stood nearby until he was forced to look up at her, then smiled, walked over, and hugged him. "Thank you for coming to my home and staying the night, J.D.," she said. "I hope it don't take something like this to get you back again."

Slowly, McCain's arms went around her and he stared deeply into her eyes. "If you want me too, I'll come back in a couple of months, or you can ride down to Bluebonnet and see some of Rosie's windmills. I'll have them up by then." J.D. smiled at her, and she thought he looked ten years younger. Then embarrassed, they stepped away from each other.

"Does that mean you won't be going out after Scar again?" she said, hopefully.

He became very still. "This was my last run, Kate. Scar's probably dead by now anyway, or likely scared off for good. Me and Poe chased that devil all the way to Baja. We ran into the *Ruralis* several times ourselves, so maybe they got him. In any event, my running days are over, Kate. I got a cattle ranch to get started. I hope you can come to see it."

"I'll think on it, J.D." She sounded doubtful.

"I told you, this was my last run — if that's what's on your mind."

"I know you mean that, at least for right now. But people don't change, J.D." She looked pained. "There are two kinds of decent folks in Texas. There are the honest, hard working people, like the Thompsons — me and the girls. We're insulated from much of the bad things that take place around us. Oh, once in a while some get caught up in it like Beth did, but for the most part, we just take advantage of progress, new laws, efforts of those willing to sacrifice to tame the wilderness. We prosper, raise our children, and watch in fascination, and sometimes — horror and disapproval — as others fight to keep us from being overrun."

She seemed determined to finish, so McCain let her talk.

"Then...there is the other kind of person. Just as decent in their own way — but different than the rest of us. They're the ones who fight an awful plague in this land, every day of their lives. They're like the right hand of God, in many respects, smiting evil, without respite — or forgiveness. That's you and Rosie

Poe, J.D. That's Stump, Moses, Jake…even Fish. You're like the wind, you change directions so much. You have no roots, and don't want any. You make terrible sacrifices to your own lives, and at the end, like as not, die alone, crippled and forgotten. Someday, history may honor these people more than we are now able to. It's a sad picture, but true none-the-less."

Her eyes were bright when she looked at him. "I don't want to see you end up like that, J.D. I don't want to be there if it does."

McCain swung into the saddle and sit staring down at her. "We had our day once, Kate. I can change. It can be like that again."

"I'd like to believe that, J.D.. But how can one expect a man who never wore a glove on his right hand for twenty years — to just up and change overnight?"

"I can. Think about it, will you?"

"Count on it, cowboy," she said, smiling this time.

* * *

Returning to Bluebonnet, McCain sent Fish and Matt Jennings to Odessa for the windmill parts. He'd ordered them with Poe's part of the money, which he'd received from Jim Packard as their payment from the railroad. *Windmills*, thought McCain, *tragic — just tragic. I hope you're satisfied, Partner. Still, a promise was a promise.*

"Those damned contraptions," became part of local folklore, and throughout the next year or two, people came from miles around just to see Bluebonnet's windmills. Also, as promised, McCain purchased cattle with the rest of the money and, sent his ranch hands into the rough countryside to catch as many of

When Legends Lived

the wild cows and unbranded calves hiding out there, as could be found. Within months, the Rocking-R was transformed from a horse ranch into a respectable sized cattle ranch. McCain had already been contacted by representatives from the Goodnight, Thompson, and Pierce spreads with an offer to buy his cattle for ten percent under Kansas market price, and he'd readily agreed. That way, he figured he wouldn't have to drive them to market, and that suited him just fine. From everything he'd heard about that part of the country, the railroad and Republicans run everything anyway — and he'd just about had his fill with both.

Thanks largely to the windmills, the range soon turned green and water begin to flow freely in areas where only perceptible amounts were remembered. Every time McCain saw one of the windmills, he had to suppress sharp painful memories of Poe as he'd looked that day on the Mexico border, arguing so adamantly for them. Even the others were clearly affected. Once as his foreman, Matt Jennings, J.D., and Quint Fishburn were branding calves, Fishburn suddenly straightened and pushed his hat back.

"I wonder what old Rosie would have to say about all this?" he suddenly said.

"Say about all of what?" McCain said, slightly irritated, as he looked at the rapidly sinking sun and knew they would have to shake a leg if they were to finish branding that day.

Fish swung his arms in a circle at the surrounding range land and several spinning windmills on the horizon. "Why, all of this, Captain!" he shouted. "The windmills, the way the valley's beginning to look all green now, the cattle, and…well, everything. Even, my being married."

McCain grimaced, placing his hands in the small of his back

as he bent backwards. "Why would he have anything to say about it?" McCain said.

"Well, shucks, Captain." Fish looked a little embarrassed, being put on the spot like this. "You remember how Rosie was. He always had a lot to say about everything, especially living in general." Fish tucked a wayward lock of hair under his wide-brimmed hat and grinned self-consciously. "He was the kind of person that could raise your expectations about life, just by telling you about his. Yep," he said, nodding his head in agreement with himself, "There'll never be another like Roosevelt Poe."

"All I know, is he left a lot of unfinished work for the rest of us," McCain said shortly.

"Well, Captain, we'll all leave a lot unfinished when we go."

* * *

Upon his return to the ranch after Poe's funeral, McCain had been surprised to learn Jake Kellog was the new owner of Paco's old sporting house and saloon. Paco had died several months earlier after being bitten by a rabid bat while cleaning out the old spring behind the establishment. Fish filed him in on the details.

Paco had started going crazy a short time later, slobbering at the mouth and lunging at anyone who got near him. After a while, some of the boys threw a blanket over his head, took him out by the shed, and chained him to a wagon tongue. Jake, had seen it before, and knew the sickness was fatal, so he finally got up the courage to put Paco out of his misery. Early one morning, he took his rifle, went out and shot old Paco. He was buried with full fanfare and more than a hundred people attended the funeral, "counting whores."

When Legends Lived

Jake, owned half-share in the place before Paco's death, and became the full-owner upon Paco's death. Right away, according to Fish, he up and changed the name to the "Texan." Claimed it sounded classier than just "Paco's." Additionally, he built a new card room onto the back, and now had eight working girls. Most of them, "real pretty, too," according to a blushing Fish.

Although it went against his grain, McCain lived up to his promise to Poe and bought presents for all eight of the girls. He delivered them himself, feeling as though Poe was watching over his shoulder just to make sure he did it right. McCain personally handed them out, thinking after each one, "Damn you and your blasted promises, Roosevelt Poe." He would've sworn he could almost hear that irritating chuckle.

At the end of every day, tired and dirty from the day's tasks, McCain sat on his front porch and promised himself that at the end of the particular job they were working on, he'd travel back to the K/D to see Kate.

* * *

Bethena sat on the veranda and watched the sun go down on another day without Jim Packard. *Where are you Jim? I miss you so much.* Each day now seemed to weigh more heavily on her and she had become deeply depressed. Ever since McCain brought Roosevelt home to be buried, the nightmares had returned as well. Frequently, she awoke in the middle of the night, screaming at the sight of the scar-faced man outside her window. Other times, he hovered at the foot of her bed, grinning hideously — reaching for her.

Bethena told herself for the hundredth time she was safe, the scar-faced one wouldn't be coming for her again. But, every evening when the sun set, the cycle of terror began anew. The last several nights had been the worst. Lately, she'd taken to sitting upright against the headboard, hugging her knees, remaining awake as long as she could, until finally exhausted, she drifted off to sleep.

I'd kill myself before I'd let him take me again, Bethena swore. She could never go through something like that again — not ever! Not without losing her mind.

Watching the sun dip below the horizon, Bethena rose trance-like and walked to her room. She sat on the small stool before her dresser, and began to slowly brush her long golden hair. Only this time, the brushing didn't help. Now that Rosie was dead, brushing her hair failed to sooth her, or give her any comfort or peace of mind. She stared at her own haggard expression, then, covering her face with her hands, wept, overwhelmed with despair. Moving to her bed, she fell across it, drew into a fetal position, and finally, lapsed into a disturbed and troubled sleep.

Bethena's eyes snapped open! She could tell it was late — hours had passed since she'd first laid down, because a silver ribbon of moonlight now shown through her bedroom window. There'd been a noise! She was certain of it. A slight noise, by the window. Bethena drew her knees up, until they tucked under her chin. She wouldn't scream and relive the spectacle of the previous three nights. *There! Something had just scraped against the side of the building! The wind, surely. Please let it be the wind!* But, it was a still night, she told herself. The tree outside her window caused shadows to fall across her room, but they didn't move — because there was no wind!

Was Billy on the water tower tonight? Can he see my window? Shivering, Bethena forced herself out of bed, inching herself toward the window. She had to close it or it would drive her crazy the rest of the night. How could she have been so stupid to fall asleep without locking the window to her room as she'd done every night for over three years? She inched closer, until it was almost within arms reach.

Suddenly, a man's bare chest jolted in front of the window! Horrified, Bethena froze, then slowly raising her eyes, forced herself to look at his face. In the bright moonlight his features were clear as she made out the jagged edged tissue which curved from his right eye down his face.

Billy had climbed down from the water tower to get a drink of water from the well before going to bed. Raising the dipper to his lips, his heart stopped at Bethena's bloodcurdling scream. He was moving, even before the scream died away, running toward her bedroom. Rounding the corner of the house, he made out a shadowy figure as it turned away from Bethena's window. The figure disappeared at the corner and in the same heartbeat Billy drew and fired his pistol. The flash blinded him! He paused to blink rapidly, then, holding his pistol high, slowly made his way to the corner — inching around it. The man was gone!

Billy heard running feet behind him. "It is I, Señor Billy," his foreman Juan said, breathing hard as he moved up from behind. His pistol was in his hand, and several more vaqueros quickly joined them, guns drawn.

"Someone was outside Aunt Bethena's bedroom window, Juan. I took a shot at him but he was moving fast and I probably missed him. Spread out and search the area. Every square inch of it — and be careful." Guns at the ready, they spread out and walked through the courtyard. Someone yelled something in Spanish.

"They've found him, Señor Billy!" Juan translated. "It looks as though you did not miss after all." He pointed and they went to him. Lighting a match, Billy looked down at the man he'd shot.

"He's dead. A saddle-tramp, like as not," the foreman speculated.

Gus Appleton joined them, and turned the dead man over. "Anybody ever see this hombre before?" Then he shouted, "Hey Billy, look at this! He only has three fingers on his left hand!"

Suddenly, Billy recalled a story Jim Packard had told him, about Poe and McCain shooting two of Scar's renegades down near Laredo. A third man had jumped through a window and gotten away. That man had three fingers, too. Jim had called the man, Three Finger…something or other — one of Scar's men. His heart suddenly beat wildly, and he spun and ran toward the ranch house, straight to his aunt's room. He pounded on her door, and when she didn't open it, he busted it down, finding her huddled in a corner, knees drawn up under her chin, shivering and whimpering.

Billy ran to her and in spite of her struggles, picked her up and carried her into his mother's room. Kate was there, holding a Winchester rifle. Seeing his mother's alarm, he quickly said, "Take care of her, Ma! I've got to check the girls!"

He took the steps three at a time, until he was outside Tina's door. Breathing deeply to calm his heart, Billy slowly opened it and, remarkably, found his sister sleeping soundly. Quietly closing her door, he ran down the hall to Rachel's room next. Pausing briefly, he listened for any movement inside, then jerked the door open and scanned the room. It was empty! Quickly running to the open window, he looked outside. Nothing!

Billy whirled and raced back down the steps, grabbing a

lantern which hung over the cook-stove as he passed. Outside, upon reaching the area just below the window, he raised the globe and lit the lantern, then knelt to search the flower bed. In the soft dirt, he found moccasin tracks!

Billy pulled his gun and holding the lantern so he could see the tracks, he followed the trail into a small gully nearby. Searching, he found three sets of pony tracks, leading away from the ranch, toward the south. Billy ran back to the house, yelling for the men to saddle up their horses. *Not Rachel too*, he prayed! *Don't let the same thing happen to her that happened to Aunt Beth! Please God, not Rachel, too!*

He raced past her without answering, and disappeared inside. Swiftly, he reappeared, loading shells into a Winchester rifle.

Gus arrived, out of breath, and shouted, "I've got six horses saddled up, ready to ride, Billy!"

"Juan, leave half the men to guard the ranch house, and get the others in the saddle! Who's the best tracker we've got?" Billy said.

"Luis!" the foreman replied instantly. "He was a scout for the Army a few years."

"Get someone to hold the light for him and bring the horses to the gully," Billy directed, pointing at a location nearby. "And tell the men we leave behind that nobody sleeps until we get back."

"Si, Señor," Juan said, as he ran off toward the corral to comply.

They were in the saddle and gone before Kate returned from checking on Bethena, who now lay immobile on Kate's bed.

Hurrying outside, Kate watched from the veranda as the lantern's light slowly bobbed out of sight. "Please Lord, oh please, send my babies back to me, safe and sound!"

The lantern had been gone for sometime, when Kate slowly slid down, to sit on the veranda steps. She remained, watching the last place she'd seen the light, until the morning sun broke over the horizon. Warily, she rose, and went inside.

* * *

Billy and the K/D hands returned two hours after sunrise. Hearing them arrive, Kate hurried to the veranda and watched anxiously as they entered the courtyard. One man was tied over his saddle and another was being supported by two of the riders. She ran to them as Billy stepped down from his mount.

"Who?" Kate said.

Billy said, "Luis was hit bad, and Gus took a round trying to get him back to our position." Billy looked haggard and his voice strained. "They were waiting on us, Ma. Ambushed us! We were just lucky that Luis was good at what he did. He died trying to warn us, otherwise, it could've been a lot worse."

"Did you see Rachel?" Kate said softly.

"No, Ma. But as soon as I get some things packed, we're gonna get after them again," Billy said tiredly.

"No! You can't take these men out there and get them killed, Billy! They're cowboys, not gunfighters! None of you will come back next time. Don't you remember what happened to Nate Thompson when he tried to run down Scar? He left with all his hands and returned with less than half of them."

"What can I do?" Billy said, painfully. "We can't let that madman just take Rachel. I won't do it, not as long as I'm alive!"

"I'll go get McCain," Kate said. "He's chased Scar for the last fifteen years. If anyone can catch up with him, J.D. can."

Billy stormed inside the house with Kate following close behind.

"Fine," he said over his shoulder. "You go get that old man. I'm going after Rachel. I don't need anybody to go with me."

He indiscriminately stuffed items into a burlap bag. Kate went to him, lightly placing her hand on his arm. Billy stopped what he was doing and silently looked down at her.

"I know you have to go. I expect it. You're the man of the house now and it's your place to take care of us. But, just listen to me, first," she said. "You're brave and you shoot like you're the devil's own tool, Billy, but Scar is a master at running and hiding. McCain and Poe had Moses Penny to help them track him down, and to hear them tell it, Moses was the finest tracker who ever lived. Time after time, Scar still got away from them. They were the best Texas had, Billy. The very best! I know, I was there, remember?"

Kate sat heavily in one of the large wooden chairs. "If you find him, it won't be because he's trying to get away. It will be because he wants you to find him. That's the way he is, Billy. He always plans these things in ways to inflict the most hurt he possibly can. Then he simply disappears."

She had Billy's attention now, and hastened on. "Let me get Jericho, Billy. Please! You can go with him, if you want." Her eyes were pleading now. "I just want you to have a chance, so you can come back to me. I love Rachel and my heart will bleed for her until the day I die, son, but, to me...she's already dead. That devil won't let her go."

Tears streamed down Kate's face. "Scar took Beth, a full grown woman who'd been married once, and now look what's become of her. Something like that will kill Rachel, even if we are lucky enough to get her back alive. All I have left now is my other daughter and my son."

Her voice broke, then she went on. "Billy, just let me help you get back safely." Kate was crying openly now.

Billy placed his hand on her bowed head and said quietly, "Go ask McCain, if you think it'll help, Ma. Just remember, he was pretty busted up over Captain Poe's death, so he might decide he's had enough and not even bother. I can't wait and take that chance. The longer I wait, the farther away Rachel will be."

He cupped her chin and forced her head up, gently. "If Captain McCain is as good as you seem to think he is, he won't have any trouble finding my trail and catching up with me before I can reach her," Billy said. "Take someone with you. Scar's out there some place, and I wouldn't want to lose the best Ma a boy ever had."

Kate held her son close for a moment. "He'll come, Billy. If I ask, Jericho will come."

She turned and hurried from the room. Before Billy could get packed and in the saddle, he heard the sound of his mother's horse as it galloped away.

* * *

McCain hadn't seen Kate since returning to Bluebonnet, but told himself it was because he'd been too busy to dwell on it much. But, when he closed his eyes at night, he still could see her face as she'd hugged him goodbye the day he left her ranch. Then, immediately, he'd remember her last words to him and feel a tinge of guilt at his promise to discard his old ways and settle down. His hatred for the man with the scar was still with him, maybe it'd always be. But he had ignored his feelings and stayed at the ranch, working to turn it into a cattle ranch as Poe had wanted.

When Legends Lived

Maybe I'll just ride over there, come midsummer, and spend a day or two, he thought. It would be good to see her, for since Poe died, McCain was discovering just what being "lonesome" meant. But midsummer came and went, as did the other seasons, and suddenly McCain realized it'd been well over a year since he'd left Kate's ranch.

* * *

Fish had graciously accepted the horses Poe had left to him, and married the young Mexican girl who lived near El Paso. McCain and the boys got drunk at the wedding and helped him put up small living quarters on the parcel of land he'd received in Roosevelt's will. Fish immediately moved in with his true love, although everybody thought they made a strange looking couple. Fish was tall and skinny, and most would agree, ugly as a mud fence, while Juanita, on the other hand, was pretty as a picture and hung onto his arm as though he was the greatest prize in the world. Rosie Poe's death-bed prediction proved prophetic, for within six months of their marriage, pretty young Juanita "puffed up like a poison pup." Both were hoping for a boy.

"Hard to figure love," Matt Jennings told McCain one evening after drinking half a bottle of Jake Kellog's best whiskey. McCain had to agree with him, especially in this case.

Fish had asked to continue working for the Rocking-R until he was ready to strike out on his own. McCain readily agreed, partially because he needed the extra help, but mainly because he was reluctant to give up yet another link to the life he'd known for the past thirty years. The arrangement worked out well for all, while maintaining a semblance of the stability McCain sorely needed since Poe's passing.

On the infrequent days when the stage brought them mail, everybody saw the month old newspaper stories about how Jim Packard had saved west Texas from the outlaws, renegades, and such. Those still alive of the original bunch had a good laugh about it, contented their names hadn't also been mentioned. However, Jim's resolute statements to the press finally began to set the story straight. As roving reporters eventually found their way to Bluebonnet to interview McCain, Fish and Jake Kellog, suddenly their good humor vanished. McCain and Fish took to hiding out in the wild-country for weeks at a time, and Jake conveniently changed his name whenever they heard "one of those people" was within fifty miles of Bluebonnet.

It appeared the drought was finally over, too, as a steady rainfall had finally started in late summer and lasted right up to early fall. Old-timers in the area all agreed it'd be an early, and unusually severe winter. McCain reckoned he'd liked the drought just about as well as all the rain they were receiving, though, he was surely proud of that dam he and Moses Penny built on that hot summer day so long ago. Sometimes he'd sit on the front porch of the ranch house and stare at the adobe and rock walls of the dam, picturing the day he and Moses had labored in the unforgiving heat, digging in the hard-packed dirt.

"Do you suppose it's ever going to rain again, Captain?"

McCain jerked awake as he heard the words, looked around, and determined he'd dozed off. Just for a minute, Moses was back with him digging away, and Poe was hanging out in Paco's whorehouse. It had felt good — for a moment. McCain rubbed his eyes and wondered if this was what it was like to finally grow old. Most of the people he'd known were dead, moved away or, godforbid, gone and gotten married, like Fish. Well, one thing growing older did accomplish, was finally make one wake up and accept the fact that the future was sure to be a lonely proposition.

A rider approached from the direction of town, and McCain watched as the splendid looking animal pranced its way around the largest of the puddles left by the short, but copious rainfall. Rain had all but ceased and the rider pulled the bright yellow slicker off, draping it over the saddle horn.

It was Kate! By God, Kate! Heart hammering against his chest, McCain hurried out to greet her.

Forty-Four

"Yep, young man, you just put one end of that gadget in your ear and you can listen to a body's heartbeat. It's a wonderment of modern science, and I 'spect we've gone 'bout as far as we can with medical inventions. It surely is a marvelous time to be alive."

– Doc Milburn

*A*LMOST THERE, THOUGHT DIXIE, looking worriedly at her young son as he gasped deep shuddering breaths. It had been her idea to undertake the grueling trip to visit Aunt Alice, in San Antonio against the doctor's advise. She'd wanted her aunt to see Timothy R. Decker, little "Rocky" as she called him, and there would never be a better time. So, despite her son's respiratory problems, she'd taken the chance and caught the train to San Antonio. She was beginning to believe she'd made a terrible mistake, as she watched Rocky take another shuddering breath.

Maybe when we get there and finally get out of this dust and heat, she thought, *he'll improve.*

Rocky saw her gazing at him, and crawled up into her lap, wrapping his thin arms around her neck. "I love you, Mommy," he said sleepily.

"And I, you," she answered, just as she always did during those exchanges. As always, the phrase made her heart ache as she remembered someone else with whom she'd made that exchange, many times in the distant past. She hadn't thought about Rosco in months. Not until she'd said that phrase again — the one they always used to say it to each other. She let her mind drift, wondering where he was now, if he and his wife...Jenny, wasn't it?... if they'd had any children of their own. *If so*, she thought, *I hope they love their children as much as I love my Rocky.*

She looked down at his sleeping face and wondered how she would ever survive if anything happened to him. He was all she had, and to lose him...well, it would just be more than she could endure.

The conductor walked down the center walkway, letting them know that San Antonio was rapidly coming up. One of the first things she'd do would be to take her son to see the doctor. *I wonder if Doc Milburn is still here*, she thought. She remembered all the nights she and Doctor Milburn had sat and waited for Rosco to die, or get better. He'd told her, "I've done what I can do for him. All we can do now, is wait." And wait they did, she recalled. Waited and prayed. At last, her prayers and Milburn's skills as a doctor finally pulled the injured man through. Dixie felt her eyes sting with salty tears and quickly blinked them back. She hadn't cried for him in over a year, and she wouldn't allow the sight of a familiar town to tear her apart again. She wouldn't!

Dixie wiped her eyes and blew her nose softly, then shook Rocky. "Wake up, sleepy head. We'ree heeeeere," she said.

As usual, Rocky woke up smiling and jumped right up, looking wildly out the windows at the strange sights. The train screeched loudly, as the engineer locked the brakes and brought it to a jerking halt in front of the passenger terminal. Through the dirty window, Dixie could make out her aunt's face in the crowd, as she waved frantically from the depot's platform. Aunt Alice ran to meet them as she and Rocky made their way down the train steps, through the milling people waiting for arivals. Dixie pointed her out to Rocky, and he ran ahead and threw his little arms around Alice's neck, just like he'd known her for years.

The hugs and kisses finally over, Dixie quickly expressed her concerns for Rocky's health, and Alice immediately loaded them into her stylish carriage for the two block trip to Doc Milburn's office. She dropped Dixie and Rocky off at the doctor's office while she caught up on some shopping.

Leading her son by the hand, Dixie made her way up the familiar steps to Doc Milburn's second story office, feeling the familiar stirrings inside. These were the same steps she'd used so many times before when Rosco lay near death for all those days. Despite her resolve to be strong, she felt a little tug at her heart and more than a little sadness at the thought. Just as she remembered, the office door stood ajar as Milburn liked to keep it, primarily because of the little cross-breeze it provided, but that it also let people know he was in.

Reaching the doorway, she peered into the shadows of the cool room, and saw Doc Milburn reading an old medical journal. At her footsteps, he reached for his wire-rimmed glasses. Placing them upon his nose, he peered up at the woman and small boy in his doorway.

"Yes? Can I help you?" he said, rising to his feet. Dropping his jaw, he stared in amazement. "Glories be! Dixie Thompson, as I live and breathe!" He rushed over, taking both of her hands in his old wrinkled ones. "Come in. Come in and have a seat," he said. "Glories be!"

Dixie kissed him lightly on the cheek and looked into his tired old eyes, shocked at how much he'd aged in just the few short years since she'd last seen him. "They're working you to death, Doc. Why didn't you retire like you said you were going to?"

"I was gonna do just that," he said, as they took their seats. "But that young feller who was supposed to come in here and set up his practice got a better offer, and I just couldn't leave these folks without a doctor, could I?"

Milburn looked at Rocky, who was staring intently at the object hanging around his neck. He removed the instrument and inserted the end of it into the boy's ears. Then, he placed the other end near his heart, and watched as the boy's eyes grew wide. Doc laughed as he removed the stethoscope and returned it once more to his own neck.

"I reacted the same as you, the first time I heard a heartbeat through one of these things, young man. I picked this one up just recently on a trip back east. Invented by some foreign feller, I hear tell. It's the newest gadget in medical advances, and it's gonna change the way we do our business from now on. Now, who is this young gentleman, Miss Thompson?" he inquired.

"This is my son, Timothy, Doctor Milburn." She smiled warmly at him. "I call him Rocky. It's Mrs. Decker now, but I still prefer my friends still call me, Dixie. And I consider you among my dearest friends, Doc."

Milburn smiled widely, obviously pleased. "Well, congratulations on both counts, Dixie." he held out his hand and Rocky Decker shook it solemnly. "And pleased to meet you, too, young man."

Dixie got serious and said, "He has a breathing disorder, Doc. All this dust and heat has made it much worse. We'll be here for a couple of weeks. Is there anything you can give him to make it easier?"

Milburn looked into the boy's throat and listened to his chest for a moment, then rose and rummaged through his overloaded cabinet. Satisfied he'd found what he was looking for, he emptied a dark liquid into a small vial. Pouring a small amount into a large spoon, Doc stuck it under Rocky's nose. The boy obediently swallowed the medicine and made a wretched face. Returning to his small desk, the old doctor wrote on a piece of paper with his trembling hand, and gave it to Dixie.

"Follow these instructions. If he don't start to get better almost immediately, bring him back in the morning. Now, how 'bout some lunch? I know where they make the best pie in three counties," he said eyeing Rocky, who suddenly appeared interested. "What do you say, young man?"

Seeing Rocky's large smile and sudden interest, Dixie laughed and agreed. Within minutes, Milburn ran the cardboard hands of the battered old clock an hour ahead, and closed his door. As they walked along, Doc pointed out sights and improvements to the town since she'd left, and laughed at Rocky's excitement of the horses and their riders with the big pistols on their hips. Finally, they made their way across the busy street into the door of a small, but tidy restaurant.

Halfway through their pie, Milburn said, "By the way, have you stopped by the sheriff's office to see Rosco Bookbinder? I know he'd be pleased to see you and Rocky."

He was unprepared for Dixie's stricken expression, and paused with a fork-full of pie halfway to his mouth. Quickly, he began to realize something he'd somehow missed earlier. Thinking back, he remembered two young people as much in love as any two he'd ever known. Something must've happened to change all that, for there she showed up, married, with a son and apparently unaware Bookbinder was even in town.

"Where's your husband, Dixie?" Milburn said softly.

When Legends Lived

Dixie's face reddened and she stared down at her plate, shoving her food around. "Well, he...he's...dead," she said. "He was killed in a boating accident about a year ago. It was right after..." her voice trailed off.

Milburn reached across and placed his hand over her's. "Dixie, let's go over to my office for a while. I've got a story to tell you. One you might not know, but I think it's very important to you and little Rocky."

The trip back to Milburn's office was a much different one than the one over, for neither spoke along the way. Dixie noticed Doc Milburn reset the cardboard clock on his door for yet another hour and closed the door behind them. Now that his stomach was full, Rocky fell onto the small bed Rosco had used so long before, and was instantly sound asleep. Dixie was pleased to see the medicine Doc had given him had worked so fast and he was breathing much easier.

"Have a seat, Dixie," Milburn said, motioning toward the only comfortable chair in the entire office. "I've got something to tell you."

Milburn removed his glasses, laid them on the desk, and rubbed the bridge of his nose. Then, he began. Milburn recalled Rosco's arrival at his door almost dead, and how Dixie had helped save his life. He spoke of the young man's turbulent recovery, and finally, of himself being invited to a "future" wedding. His story shifted to the day Rosco showed up at his office with a near dead woman whom he said was his wife. He went on to tell about why she couldn't be expected to live long.

Dixie tried to interject, but Milburn held up his hand to stop her words. "She ran off with that killer, Bloody Bill Reid...and then tried to kill Rosco. Nearly succeeded, too. Probably would've if it hadn't been for an old Indian, and your constant care, Dixie." He glanced sideways at her and saw small tears forming at the corner of her eyes.

Milburn went on. "Even after I told him the nature of her disease — how she probably got it, and advised him she might remain in a stupor for the rest of her days, he never faltered once. He spooned food into her mouth every day for all those months. He'd pick her up and carry her outside to the porch in good weather, and cover her with a blanket, in bad. He worked long dangerous as a deputy sheriff and paid a woman to stay with her so she wouldn't have to be alone. And through it all, he didn't know if she was even aware of it." He paused, letting his words sink in before continuing.

"Toward the end, I could tell she was becoming more lucid, but I don't suppose anyone knew just how much she'd improved. There were times when I'd visit their place to check on her condition, and notice things. On several occasions, Rosco's back would be turned and she wasn't aware I could see her staring at him. I can truly say, I saw the fires of hell in her eyes. Then, just as quickly, it'd be gone and her trance would return." He rubbed the bridge of his nose again and set his glasses back.

"I don't know if Rosco ever knew about that, but I really don't think it would've made any difference to him. He had to do what he felt was right toward her, and to tell you the truth, I rightly admire him for that. There isn't one man in ten thousand who would've had that sense of responsibility…the kind of gumpson it takes to give up everything important to him to answer his duty that way."

He paused again, then said, "One day while he was at work, somehow Jenny slipped out of her chair on the front porch and

When Legends Lived

made it all the way to the river. It was only a hundred yards away, but it must've seemed like a hundred miles for someone in her condition. Marie, the housekeeper, saw her just as she slipped into the swift current, and screamed at her. Marie said Jenny just turned and looked at her, then was gone in a flash. They found her body about two miles down stream, wedged under a tree. Rosco buried her and pays Marie to keep fresh flowers on the grave."

Milburn rose and walked to the small window facing the main street, his hands clasped behind his back. "I figured me and Rosco had become pretty good friends over the years, so one day when we were having a drink over in the saloon, I kind of pushed the boundaries of that friendship, some. I said, 'Figured you must've loved Jenny an awful lot to have cared for her like you did all that time, Rosco.'"

Milburn turned and looked squarely at her, now. "I could tell right away I'd hit a nerve or something, for his face never changed when he replied. He said, 'Doc, I nearly couldn't stand the sight of her...for what she cost me. If it hadn't been for her, I'd now be married and have children by the woman I really love.' We kind'a dropped it at the time, but later, when leaving the place, he told me, 'Doc, I'm not yet thirty years old, but my life is already over. Someday while I'm out on my rounds, some drunk cowboy will fire off his gun accidentally, or on purpose, and that'll be the end.'" Milburn paused.

"As Rosco started to walk away, he suddenly turned back to me and said, 'You know, Doc, it'll be a relief.' We never discussed it again, Dixie. I didn't know then what he meant by those remarks, but I think I do, now."

Dixie was crying steadily by that time, but still silently. Milburn handed her a fresh handkerchief and she blew into it. "I'm sorry," she said, smiling slightly. "I guess there are some things that still hurt an awful lot. Most of them are my fault."

She carefully folded the handkerchief and handed it back to Milburn. "No more tears. I guess you've figured it out, Doc. There's no husband named Decker and I've never been married. With money, you can buy any kind of papers. I didn't want my son to have to pay for my mistakes, so I invented a father for him after I foolishly forced his real father away." Dixie looked at the sleeping form of her son on the small bed. "He's all that's important, now, Doc. I don't want him to suffer for something I did."

"What about Rosco? Don't you think he deserves to know he has a son? Don't you think you should have some happiness in life, also? Don't jump at the chance to be such an almighty martyr, Dixie!" he said angrily. "Sometimes a person has to make tough decisions when it comes to doing the right thing, or losing something that means the most. Just ask Rosco. But, sometimes, Dixie — sometimes, it takes courage to go after the things most important in life, too." Doc Milburn was direct and didn't spare her.

"You acted like a coward once and by failing to show courage, you risked something that a lot of people never even get a chance at. Even fewer get a second shot. Now all you've got to do is have the courage to not let it get away from you again."

Dixie stood silently for a moment, then softly said, "Tell me about Rosco. What he's done. How he looks. Everything."

* * *

In the city hall of San Antonio, a meeting of about a dozen people was taking place when Dixie, Rocky, and Doc Milburn entered. Rosco Bookbinder, had distinguished himself as the

When Legends Lived

deputy and county sheriff of San Antonio and was being presented papers by District Judge Trent Allen. The judge was in the process of appointing him to the position of U.S. Marshal. Rosco was seated with his back to the door, and didn't see them enter.

"Sheriff Bookbinder, please come forward. Stand there," Judge Allen directed, smiling warmly at Rosco. "Place your left hand on the bible and raise your right. Do you swear to uphold the laws of the Constitution of the United States, protect and serve the people of…"

As the ceremony proceeded, a movement at the rear of the room caught his eye and suddenly, he was staring right at Dixie.

"…please say, 'I do' Rosco," the judge was prompting.

Startled and momentarily confused, Rosco stammered, "I… do," his face suddenly a deep red. He continued to stare toward the back of the room, as the judge pinned a gold star on his shirt, imprinted with the words, United States Deputy Marshal.

Offering his hand, the judge said, "Let me be the first to congratulate you, Marshal Bookbinder. You've earned it!"

Numbly, Rosco shook hands with his well-wishers, staring constantly to the back of the hall. Soon, he was alone in the room with Dixie and the small boy — Milburn having silently taken his leave. Taking a deep breath, he crossed the large chamber and approached them with a strained smile.

Stopping a few feet away, he said quietly, "Hello, Dixie."

"Hello, Rosco," she answered, smiling. "Congratulations on your appointment."

Rosco felt a movement near his leg and looked down to see the boy holding out his small hand. "Con…grat'tions, Mister," he said. Rosco bent and solemnly shook the offered hand, then the boy backed up behind his mother's long skirt.

"Your son?" Rosco said. "How old?"

Dixie hesitated, then answered. "Yes, my son. He'll be four in a few months, though sometimes I feel he's much older." She laughed a small laugh.

She'd studied him covertly as he shook her son's hand, noting that while he'd always been slim, the man standing before her appeared almost gaunt. And there was something different about his eyes, too. A deep sadness. He's suffered, she thought. And not from his wounds. It went deeper than that. Suddenly, she felt an overpowering sense of guilt.

"You must be very proud of him," Rosco was saying. "Anyone would be proud to have a boy like that." He looked down and smiled, and suddenly Dixie could see the young man she'd loved so long ago.

The boy smiled back at him. "You want'a have some pie with us, Mister? My mom and me know where they have real good pie," he said. He yanked on his mother's finger. "Don't we, Mom?"

Not having been around very many men in his young life, it was Dixie's experience that Rocky's demeanor was usually quiet and withdrawn whenever he did have contact with them. She was somewhat surprised by his immediate warming toward Rosco Bookbinder. Maybe not so suprising after all, Dixie thought, as she observed the obvious similarities between man and boy. He simply looks like a small Rosco Bookbinder, she mused, surprised that Rosco couldn't see it as well.

Dixie swallowed hard and forced a strained smile. "Yes, we certainly do, Rocky." Seeing Rosco's expression, she colored slightly.

"Rocky?" Bookbinder said, startled. Then, softer, "Rocky —

that's a fine name for a boy. Someone used to call me that a long time ago."

"Is Rocky your name, too, Mister?" the boy said, in spite of his mother's pulling on his arm. "My mom used to know a man with that name...something like that. She's got a picture of him in that thing on her neck." He pointed to a small gold pendant on his mother's necklace.

Dixie's hand went automatically to the locket as she breathed deeply and glanced around nervously.

"You mean that little gold locket? I once gave a girl one just like it," he said softly. "That couldn't be it though, the shopkeeper said there was only one like it in the whole world."

"Maybe that lady lost it and my mom found it," Rocky offered helpfully.

"Yes," Rosco said. He was staring intently at Dixie. "That must be it. Or, maybe the lady just threw it away."

Dixie bravely steeled herself and finally broke her silence. "No!" she said, raising her chin and returning his look. "No. The lady wouldn't throw it away – not ever! But she might've thrown away something far more precious. I pray it isn't true, however." She hesitated and lowered her eyes. "A good friend told me just a couple of hours ago, that if you feel something is important enough, you have to be brave and fight for it. Now that I'm faced with those prospects, I find my courage has suddenly deserted me." She faltered and turned away from him.

Standing with her head bowed, Dixie felt light hands on her shoulders, and Rosco said gently, "Sometimes, in a scary situation, an angel appears out of nowhere to rescue you. That's happened to me twice."

With a small cry, she wheeled and threw her arms around his

neck, burying her face in his chest, sobbing as though her heart were broken.

Regaining her composure after a few moments, she gripped the front of his shirt with both hands and without looking at him, said, "I'm so sorry. I'm so sorry, for everything."

A large lump in his throat kept him from replying. His heart pounding, he continued to hold her silently until she went on.

"I've ruined everything," she said, more quietly. "Your life… mine…even little Rocky's by denying him the father he should've had."

Rosco stiffened, his mind racing. *The boy was his!* He raised his eyes to the child silently staring back at him. Uncontrollably, Rosco felt his eyes burning as they began to mist.

"If I'd only told you everything that day you left, maybe things would've been different for us all," she concluded, her voice muffled against his shirt. She raised her wet face to look at him.

Rosco looked down at her lovingly and gently brushed a wispy strand of hair from her eyes. Seeing his son's puzzled look, he stepped back, holding her at arms length.

"Come on." He winked broadly at Rocky. "Let's go get some of that famous pie you were talking about!"

Rocky reached for his mother's hand and tried to imitate Rosco's voice. "Let's get some famous pie."

The three of them walked out together, Rocky tightly holding onto his mother's hand. As they reached the boardwalk, he also grasped Rosco's hand, smiling broadly at them both.

Forty-Five

THE LARGEST OF THE three Mescaleros made his way through the twisted contours of the small canyon toward the spot where Scar and the others waited. Scar was comfortable with the notion that Two-Noses could find them, despite precautions they'd taken to hide their trail. He watched as the others shared the last of the half-raw rattlesnake one of the Apaches had partially cooked over the small, smokeless fire. He saw Bone toss several small pebbles at the golden-haired little girl huddling against a rock, her eyes squeezed tightly shut.

She was still wearing the brightly flowered sleeping gown she wore when he snatched her from her bed. It was ripped on one sleeve and smudged, where she'd tried to lie on it during the night for protection from the cold ground. Each time a pebble hit her, the girl whimpered and drew herself into an even tighter ball. Excited by his torment of the child, Bone walked over and squatted near her. The young girl squeezed her eyes tighter, trying to become invisible.

Grinning, Bone slowly moved his hand toward her exposed knee. Shifting just slightly, Scar pulled a broad bladed knife from his boot-top, flipped it to hold it by its blade, then swiftly whipped his arm forward in one blinding motion. The heavy wooden handle struck the unsuspecting Bone just below the right temple, dropping him to his knees. Dazed, he shook his head and blinked, then sprang to his feet, angrily facing Scar, holding his hand scant inches from the pistol he wore in his waistband. Scar, who hadn't moved since throwing the knife, stared at him, expressionless.

"Go ahead, Bone," he said coldly. "It'll save me the trouble you're bound to end up causing me before this is over."

Bone glared hatred at him, then visibly relaxed and rubbed the bloody spot on his head, whinning, "Damn, Scar, that hurt. A lot." He looked at the blood on his hand and then wiped it on the leg of his filthy pants. "You said yourself I could have a taste of this little clam when we got her. That's all I wanted."

"Now, I'm saying to leave her alone until I've taken care of McCain. He may be more likely to try and get her back if she's not damaged goods. White folks don't like women who've been sampled by other men. Ain't you learned anything?" He uttered a Kiowa name, loosely translated meaning "the son of a mother who let a dog father him."

Bone didn't appear to be offended, and continued to whine. "Come on, Scar. That may be another week, at the least. Just let me…" He stopped as he saw the cold expression on Scar's face, then held out both hands, and rapidly backed away. "You're right, Boss. I was out of line. It won't happen again, honest." Bone hastily retreated to a spot where he could sit with his back to a rock, try not to look at his leader, and thank whatever powers that be, he was still alive.

A few minutes later, Two-Noses arrived silently and squatted by Scar. He and Scar spoke in the Apache language for several moments. Bone hated it when they did that! He wondered what deeds they were cooking up, as he tried not to draw Scar's attention back to himself. Then Two-Noses rose and walked over to the fire, where one of the Apaches was gnawing on the last of the snake meat. The larger man grabbed it from his hands, and

When Legends Lived

kicked him away from the fire. Then he took the man's place and finished the piece of meat, licked his fingers, and wiped them on his greasy breech-cloth.

Scar grinned as he watched the encounter. He enjoyed working with the Apaches. They were always predictable — especially, the Mescalero Apache — always mean, always contrary and always vicious. He didn't have to worry about them doing a halfway job on McCain when the time came. He would enjoy watching them work on the old ranger, and he'd let them take as long as they wanted to finish him. Then, he'd let them have the girl as their reward. His grin grew larger and more sinister as he considered it. Yes, it would be interesting to see how Bone reacted to them getting the girl-child. It was time Bone died anyway, for he was stupid and had outlived his usefulness.

Scar muttered three words in Apache, and they rose as one and mounted, the youngest leading Scar's horse to him. Scar strode over and grabbed the girl, swinging her in the air. She screeched sharply as he plopped her into his saddle.

"If you make a move or a sound," he told the terrified little girl matter-of-factly, "I'll cut your nose off with my knife." In one smooth motion, he swung up behind her and kicked his mount in the side.

* * *

Kate had been on the front porch of the ranch house for over an hour explaining the latest tragedy to befall her family, and McCain listened. Only twice did he ask her short questions, but mostly he just listened.

McCain marveled at the strength of the woman who'd been through so much, who'd now lost her daughter and very possibly her son, as well. She never faltered during the telling, and never shed a tear, but he could tell, without a doubt, that her heart was being torn apart. Without being asked, Sabi brought her hot coffee and later, food, which he placed in front of the lady with the sad, beautiful eyes. She drank the coffee, but the food went largely untouched. As she finished, her chin dropped to her chest, and a single tear ran from the corner of her eye, making a track in the dust on her cheek.

McCain rose silently and went inside. When he returned, he wore his Walker Colt and carried a Winchester rifle. Moses Penny's old Sharps rifle was cradled in the crook of his arm. Slung over his shoulder were his sleeping roll and bulging saddle-bags. He'd slipped on his yellow slicker and large hat.

As he stepped out onto the porch, Kate rose and went to him. "Please, don't let him take my kids, J.D. Please."

"You got my word, Kate," McCain said. "It's time I finished the job."

As he started down the steps Kate rushed to him, put her arms around him and placed her lips to his for an instant.

"You come back too, J.D.," she whispered. "We…I…need you."

She stepped back, as he made his way toward the corral to saddle Grasshopper. Within moments, he was headed south, through Bluebonnet. A close observer might've noticed a certain jauntiness in the manner in which he sat his saddle, something that had been missing since the day he brought Poe back to the K/D. J.D. McCain was on the hunt again. He didn't look back.

* * *

Kate rested another day at McCain's ranch before beginning

the rigorous return trip to the K/D. During that time Fish brought his pregnant young wife by for introductions, and Kate was immensely impressed by her intelligence and bearing. Fish lavished praise upon his new bride's cooking abilities and proudly claimed he was already teaching her how to prepare the rich concoctions found in *Gourmet's Fine Foods Cookbook*, given to him by the famous Roosevelt Poe just before his untimely death. Kate nearly burst into laughter when Juanita made an awful face behind Fish's back, at the mention of his gourmet cooking.

Hearing Kate was at the Rocking-R, Jake Kellog also came by to visit with her. Later that evening he, Fish and Sabi held a rather lengthy meeting out by the corral. Early the next morning, Kate awoke to find Jake and Fish saddling their horses, and moments later, watched as they walked out with their guns on, carrying rifles and sleeping rolls. She experienced a sharp pang in her heart, as Fish held his young wife and tenderly kissed her on the cheek, then mounted his horse to ride away. Juanita looked after him, her chin held high, determined not to cry.

For her part, Kate never ceased to marvel at the unquestionable loyalty and devotion these old men had for each other. Jake Kellog, successful business man in his own right, and Quint Fishburn, property owner and recent family man, were willing to risk everything to answer the call of one of their own, in trouble. And little Juanita, bravely watching as her man rode away, perhaps never to see him again. How many times had Kate seen that scene played out? How many times had she personally stood and watched as J.D. and Roosevelt rode off into some dangerous situation? No doubt, the men were brave, but were the women who waited for them any less brave?

Juanita gave her a little smile as she passed Kate going into the ranch house. Inside, she could hear Sabi rattling tin-ware as he cleaned up the breakfast plates. Kate hugged herself as though seeking warmth from the coolness of the damp morning air. *It looks like some clearing to the northwest; maybe the rain is through for now,* she thought. She heard a noise behind her and turned to find Juanita, holding out a cup of steaming coffee for her. Kate smiled her thanks, then seeing the sorrowful look in the young woman's eyes, set her cup on the porch rail and tenderly wrapped her arms around Juanita, who silently wept against her shoulder.

She left the following morning and Matt Jennings escorted her as far as Odessa, where she was met by three of her vaqueros. Kate had plenty of time during the long ride back to think about her and Jericho McCain's relationship, over the past fifteen years. Riding along, she thought, how easy it would be to place blame. He could be such a pigheaded old fool, but was she any less the fool? She could've gone to him instead of waiting for him to come to her all those years. Pride, that's what it'd been. Stupid, vain pride.

Well, where was pride now? she asked herself. Who was the one she turned to when faced with the biggest crisis of her life? And, more importantly, who'd answered her request for help, with no strings attached? As always, it'd been J. D. McCain.

J.D. and Roosevelt, she thought, the two men who loved her. For sure, Duncan had deep feelings for her, as well; he must've had to give her such fine children. But she and Duncan both had known from the start that their marriage would be the sort built on frontier tradition, rather than on the kind of love a woman dreams about. When she looked into Duncan Shaw's eyes, she saw admiration and respect. In itself, that had been good enough for she'd felt the same, and had decided long before their marriage that love need not be the foundation for their union.

Whenever she'd looked into Roosevelt Poe's eyes, she'd seen the same admiration and respect -- but she'd also seen love there. How many times had she wished she could return that love? Now, she realized why she couldn't. It'd always been J.D. If...when he came back this time she would force the issue. She was certain she'd seen the same guarded love in McCain's eyes as she'd seen in Rosie's.

Kate felt the tears burn as she thought of all the wasted years. *Let him come back to me once more, please. Just once more.* This time, she vowed, she'd make it right.

Upon Kate's return home, she found Bethena much the same as when she'd departed; staring fixated at some object on the wall or horizon. Sometimes just a shadow of a smile playing at her lips as she made small brushing motions with an empty hand, as though brushing her hair. Otherwise, it was as if everything except what she staring at, ceased to exist.

Kate's youngest daughter, Tina, spent most of the day with her aunt, reading from her school books and speaking to her, always without response. Kate had seen Bethena's deep depressions many times before and had always been able to work through them, knowing that sooner or later she would "snap out of it" and become lucid once more. Only this time it didn't happen and this time there were no more nightmares — only silence — and vacant staring eyes.

Kate eventually all but settled back into her routine; devoting herself to caring for Beth and sharing time with her youngest daughter, trying to answer the little girl's questions about what had happened to Rachel, and the probable results of it all. She wanted to prepare Tina for the worst, if it should come to pass.

It was late afternoon as Kate finished spooning soup into Beth's slack mouth, wiped her lips and chin, and forced a smiled at her sister. Her heart nearly broke at the sight of Bethena's listlessness.

"There, now wasn't that delicious?" She rose and patted her sister's cheek. "You just sit right here and relax. I'll make up some fresh coffee and be right back."

Bethena's expression didn't change as Kate picked up the soiled eating utensils and departed, glancing worriedly over her shoulder at the despondent woman.

As Kate's footsteps faded away, Bethena slowly turned her empty eyes toward the door, stood and moved to the stool in front of her dresser mirror. She stared at her reflection, then picked up a pair of scissors and slowly, but methodically, began to cut her flowing locks of long golden hair. She never took her eyes off the stranger in the mirror, as she snipped away at her thick mane.

The stranger with short hair and sorrowful eyes looked back at her as she laid the scissors aside. As though receiving silent guidance from some kindred spirit in the looking glass, she reached down and slid open a bottom drawer in the old dresser. Pushing aside soft cotton articles of clothing, she finally found what she was seeking — Kate's old pistol with the missing trigger guard. She carefully laid it on the dresser in front of her. Having found it, she studied the old pistol as though she couldn't remember just what she'd intended to do with it. The stranger in the mirror suddenly smiled at her and she picked it up, slowly raised the small pistol to her temple and firmly pressed the trigger.

Kate, preparing coffee in the kitchen, was the only person to hear the gun's muffled report.

Forty-Six

"I fought the Comanches for over twenty years. Done a spell as marshal of Hayes City, too. Even spent some years as scout for old Zack Taylor against the Mexicans. But you couldn't have paid me enough to go after that heathen, Scar. I wouldn't been up to it, even on my best day."

– Deaf Smith, Texas scout and lawman, 1891

MCCAIN HAD LEFT INSTRUCTIONS with Sabi to get word to Fish and Jake about Kate Thompson's latest woes, and that he'd leave them an easy trail to follow. It never even occurred to him they might not come. If something happened and they lost his trail, he'd meet them in Langtry within the next two weeks, for he was certain, beyond a doubt, that Scar was headed back to his old stomping grounds along the Devil's River. McCain knew that by traveling alone he could travel faster than Scar could with the girl. If he reached the Devil's River before Scar, he stood an even chance of getting to the girl before Scar tired of his game and turned her over to his men.

Almost elated to be back on the trail once more, McCain was tired but alert as he reached a spot just north of the river area he believed Scar would eventually hold up. As he slowly criss-crossed the area, riding in increasing circular patterns, he looked for fresh tracks or any signs of a recent camp site. He surmised that Scar figured if he could cover a lot of ground fast enough, he wouldn't have to worry about anyone being on his trail so soon. After hours of patiently searching, McCain found what he was looking for, dismounted and closely checked out a single set of horse tracks. They were fresh and had been made by a shod pony.

Probably not Scar, he thought, *maybe Billy Shaw.*

Mounting, he followed the fresh tracks as they weaved and twisted through the endless gullies and draws. Catching a glimpse of slight movement in rocks a quarter of a mile to his front, he pulled up and dropped back quickly into a large sandy gully, then took a narrow fork angling off to the right. He resurfaced another three hundred yards to the west, shielded by a large outcropping of boulders. Walking Grasshopper as close as he felt safe, he tied his bandana around the horse's nose to keep him quiet, then on foot, scaled the rock face to look down at the spot where he had first seen the movement. Leaning against a rock looking over the barrel of a rifle was a man with his back toward McCain.

McCain took off his boots and reached inside his shirt, pulled out a battered pair of rawhide moccasins, and slipped them on. Leaving his rifle, he silently worked his way across the rocks until he was just twenty-five feet from the figure.

"If you don't want to be buried right there, let go of the rifle, place your hands on top of your head, and turn around, real slow," he said softly.

The man stiffened as if he were thinking about taking a chance, then as though accepting he'd lose in any encounter, relaxed and did as he was told.

"Billy Shaw! It pains me greatly to see a young feller such as yourself make a complete jackass out of himself. Especially, a child of someone I respect and admire as much as I do your mother," McCain said as he recognized the young man. "If that

When Legends Lived

ain't a good way to get yourself shot full of holes, I never seen one. Now grab your rifle and come on over here — and just be glad I wasn't Scar or some of his friends."

McCain squatted on his heels, observing the young man from under his hat brim, as he walked hang-dogged toward him. *Embarrassed*, he thought, good! *Better to be embarrassed and learn a lesson, than to be dead and beyond embarrassment.*

"Howdy, Captain. What gave me away?" Billy began.

"Just about everything," McCain said sourly. "I won't mince words, Billy D., for there's more at stake here than the thickness of your skin. I'm going after Scar to bring your sister back at the request of your mother. It will be a considerable task, as I've found out over the years of chasing that heathen." He stood and stretched his back muscles.

"She's your sister so I won't deny outright your coming along," McCain told him. "But, if you don't do exactly as I tell you — when I tell you — and how I tell you to do it, I'll put a lump on your head, tie you over your horse, and give it a swat on its rump for home." He could see that young Shaw was furious, as he stammered, then was silent.

"Go on, boy. Get it off your chest right now! This will be the only chance you get," McCain said without any trace of softness.

Billy's face grew even more red as he sputtered, "Damn you, Captain McCain! What makes you think I need any help? I was doing just fine, up to now."

McCain eyed him until the young man started to shift his weight around a little. "When did you lose the trail, Billy?"

"Not that long ago. I was just getting ready to find it again when you started sneaking around," Billy said, hating himself for sounding petulant.

"Billy, you haven't cut that trail in the last four hours. I know because I've been following you. Now, tell me what you know and let's get after that bastard again."

Sullenly, Billy told McCain the trail initially had been clear enough that a blind man could've followed it. Then without warning, it disappeared. He'd been looking for it most of the day.

McCain squatted back down and picked up a small stick. "Come here," he said. Billy squatted beside him as McCain started drawing in the dirt.

"We're here," McCain told him. "If the length of this stick were ten miles long, show me about where you lost the trail, and which direction they were headed when you last saw it."

Billy stuck his finger in the soft sand about three quarters of the length of the stick, then pointed to a spot. "Here," he said. "They were headed south, toward the Devil's. The trail was plain as day, then all of a sudden — gone."

McCain pondered the scene. "Okay! Here's what we're going to do, Billy." He took the stick and started to draw ever-widening circles from the point in the sand that indicated their location. "We'll make circles until we cut the trail. He's headed south and he can hide his trail well enough for a while, but he can't keep doing it forever. It simply takes too much time to do it right. So, if we make these circles, we'll eventually reach the point where he decided speed is more important than hiding."

McCain reached for his tobacco pouch, pouring a generous helping onto a thin paper, licked it, and then inspected it all around. Satisfied, he stuck the cigarette between his lips.

"Something to remember, boy. If we find Scar's trail, it will be because he wants us to find it. That, or he don't care one way or the other if we do find it. Either way, he'll have his reasons," McCain said. He searched his pockets for a match, found one, struck it on the seat of his pants, then stuck the flame to his smoke and drew deeply.

"Now, I'm a fair hand at tracking, but I ain't no match for Scar, Billy," McCain said honestly. He puffed several times and continued. "Moses Penny, maybe. He was the best I ever saw. Poe, ran a close second to Moses — but not me. Besides, I don't see as well as I once did," he stated with some embarrassment. "If Scar wants to hide, we'll have to have the Devil's own luck to find him."

They'd been making circles for several hours when they discovered something had overturned several small rocks on an old game trail. A short distance farther on, the trail reappeared, as if by magic. McCain chuckled softly. "Scar must think he's lost us again. He's quit hiding."

The two men followed the trail until light began to fade, then stopped to make a cold camp for the night. They were back in the saddle early the next morning without breakfast, following the very visible trail until almost midday — then it disappeared once more.

"Probably sent someone back to check his back-trail," McCain said. "He does that sometimes, and if someone's on his trail, he gets sneaky again. He does it to appear as if he don't want to be found, but believe me boy, that ain't the case here. No, old Scar is just playing us along until he can spring his little surprise."

The area where they lost the trail was hard and rocky and provided a riding party a chance to select any one of several trails without being detected. The two men made circles for the next several hours until McCain signaled a stop and dismounted.

"Let's make some coffee and a bite to eat. Won't do that little girl any good if we end up falling out of the saddle."

McCain showed Billy the kind of firewood that would provide a hot smokeless fire, and he gathered it while McCain unsaddled, rubbed down the horses, and then saddled them again for instant use.

Just finishing their food, Billy suddenly straightened and reached for his rifle lying nearby. "Uh oh, Captain, somebody's coming."

McCain continued eating until his plate was about half-empty, then sighed and placed it beside the fire. "I've been watching him for a spell, now."

"Looks like an Indian," Billy said. "I'll take my rifle and get over in those rocks until you see what he's up to."

Billy walked into the rocks while McCain remained seated, waiting for the rider to reappear. Soon the rider emerged through the surrounding rocks. He stopped, startled, then sighed deeply and said, "Hard-eyes McCain. Every time I meet you, you sneak up on me."

"Chickenfoot," McCain acknowledged. "Where you headed?"

Chickenfoot appeared annoyed at being surprised by McCain. "I've been traveling the road between this world and the spirit world. I'm surprised you are able to see me, for I thought I was still a spirit. When I am a spirit, I am invisible to humans."

The old Indian thoughtfully went on. "When I was a child, my great-grandmother — her name was Dream Woman — told me I would die someday and then come back. Because of this, at the end of my second life I would start to become a spirit while still inside this body. She said when that happened, humans would not be able to see me any more." He looked a little saddened. "It doesn't work all the time."

When Legends Lived

The old man hooked his leg over his mount and slid down. McCain was surprised at the limberness of the old Indian. "She also said when that happened, I would have lightening in my hands and I could kill my enemies just by pointing my finger at them." He held his index finger in the air and stared at it as though it were sacred. "She said all I would have to do is think about it, and a bolt of lightening from my finger would strike them dead."

He looked with yearning at what was left of McCain's food, smiling when McCain nodded, then picked up the plate and began to eat with his fingers. "The part about the lightening shooting from my fingers has not happened yet. I suppose that takes longer than learning how to become invisible."

Then he brightened and rambled on. "Just a few days ago, I rode through a whole village of Kickapoos. None of them could see me." He chuckled, shaking his head. "That was very enjoyable," he said, poking food into his mouth.

"Well, you better not let the face-cutter catch you out here riding around on that fine horse I gave you. He just might take it, and that fancy Spanish rig, too."

Chickenfoot wiped grease from his chin, then licked his fingers clean. "I would turn into a spirit and fight him before he could do that, for I've developed a brotherhood with this animal," the old man told him. "I will take this pony with me into the spirit world when I finally go there to live." He finished the food, looked around for more and discovered there was none, then dropped the plate to the ground, having no further use for it.

Licking his fingers again, he said, "I prefer mule or horse because white man's food usually tastes like straw. But this wasn't bad."

I can just imagine, old man, thought McCain, looking at the half-starved old man then his empty plate on the ground.

"I saw the face-cutter yesterday, but he didn't see me," Chickenfoot said. "I was a spirit." He chuckled to himself.

McCain stiffened slightly and leaned forward, paying full attention to what the old man was saying. "Where did you see Scar?" he said softly.

Chickenfoot contemplated his answer. "I may not be ready to leave this world as a spirit yet. Many people have found out they should not talk about Scar, for if they do, soon they will be spirits."

McCain tried to keep the excitement from his voice. "Chickenfoot, I'm after Scar. I mean to kill him this time. He took a little girl — a baby. She was the child of someone I know." He let that sink in for a moment before he continued. "You know what Scar and his bunch are capable of doing to a little girl. Her mother suffers great pain, waiting for her daughter's return. I have brought the girl's brother to help me. Tell me how to find them."

"Is he the boy holding the rifle on me over in the rocks?" the old Indian acted unconcerned.

McCain, almost laughed. *Why, you old son-of-a-gun, he thought. Even at your age, you don't miss much.* Remaining expressionless, he answered, "Yes. He was worried you might be unfriendly." Then, he called out, "Billy? Come on out."

Sheepishly, Billy walked out of the rocks, threw down his rifle and glared at the two of them. Without a word, Chickenfoot rose to his feet with the agility of a man of twenty-five. He stepped to the edge of the rocks thirty feet away, folded his arms and stared out over the vast landscape.

Billy came up behind McCain and whispered harshly, "What

When Legends Lived

the hell we doing here wasting time with that demented old Indian? What could someone like him know, anyway? He's three days older than dirt, for Christ's sake! We need to get back on the trail of that savage, Scar, not sit around here visiting all day!"

McCain cocked his eyebrow. "Oh? Just which direction do you want to take, or did you find the trail over there in those rocks?"

Billy's face turned beet red. "You tell me, McCain! You're the legend around here!"

For a while, McCain didn't answer. "I'll make allowances for the fact that you're all worked up about your sister and all, so let me tell you something before you make a bigger mistake than you have already. You can call me Captain, or Mister McCain, or even J.D. if you want. But you're obliged to sound respectful when you do." He spoke so softly Billy had trouble hearing him. "If you ever use that tone with me again, I'm going to forget you're Kate's boy and put so many lumps on your head, it'll look like you've been gathering honey."

Billy's jaw slacked then he shifted his eyes away from McCain's hard glare.

Pausing, Billy cleared his throat and said, "You're right. I apologize, Captain."

McCain wasn't looking at him now, and Billy turned to see what McCain was observing. The old Indian was slowly headed back toward them. He spoke to McCain, ignoring the young Billy Shaw.

"My people believe that a person's shadow is their other self — the bad self. All that is evil or wrong with a person is in their shadow and when you are weak, your shadow will use every chance to try to overpower you. If it does, evil takes over and you are lost."

McCain didn't move, nor did he interrupt, so Chickenfoot went on. "When I was a young man, like this feller, I was not a good person. Many times my shadow nearly overcame me, but I fought back and as I became older, I found I was not so angry and did not need temptation so much — it became easier to be good."

Billy stirred beside him and McCain shot him a look that quieted him.

"The face-cutter is no longer human. He's been consumed by his other self and is now a spirit. He and the shadow are one. Each time he causes pain or fear, he becomes stronger and grows larger. Soon his shadow will cover this land completely." The old man shook his head sadly, and said, "I told this to the Bookbinder fellow. He didn't believe me either."

"I believe you, go on."

"No one can catch Scar. He is smoke when he wants to be."

"I'll kill him this time, Chief."

Chickenfoot studied McCain for a long time. "Perhaps. Among my people, the name of Hard-eyes McCain is well known. It's said he is a great hunter of men — maybe, the best. I fear even the great Hard-eyes McCain will not be able to kill the face-cutter."

"I'll kill him."

Chickenfoot intently studied his right hand as though trying to understand something. "If only the lightening bolts would come to my hand like Dream Woman told me would happen — then I'd kill him myself."

"Just tell me where you saw him, Chief. He's outgrown his shadow. It's time someone helped him travel."

When Legends Lived

The old Indian gazed at McCain as though trying to reach a conclusion. Finally, he said, "While I was away, I talked it over with the spirits and they lead me to believe that if I let Scar harm the girl, they wouldn't be particularly happy with me." He squatted down and drew an egg-shaped circle in the dust with his finger.

"Just three hours ride from here — not south and not west — there is a canyon shaped like this." He reached down and scraped away one end of the egg and piled a few small stones in the space he'd just made. "At the mouth of the canyon, it is small. There are some large stones in the middle of the canyon opening."

He made an imaginary opening at the other end and drew what appeared to be another smaller canyon, running off the larger one. "The small canyon only goes about a mile, then ends. There is a spring at the end of it, and no way out except the way you entered." He admired his handiwork and nodded.

Billy started to say something, but McCain silenced him with a look.

"Scar has put his horses at the end of the small canyon, near the spring," the old man went on. "When I saw them, they were driving a stake in the ground, here." Chickenfoot speared his finger into the center of the circle, his eyes on McCain's.

Bait! McCain stared at the circle in the dust intently, as though by studying it, he might find some way out of the quandary.

"What does it mean?" Billy said.

"It means that Scar has set up a party and invited us to attend. He's left the door wide open for us," McCain told him.

"Well, that suits me fine," Billy said. "How do we go in?"

"Going in ain't the problem, boy. It's getting out that will be the problem. I figure he's got about five, six men with him. He'll have three placed about here." McCain pointed at the boulders in the canyon's mouth. "And the others, about here," pointing again, deeping inside the canyon. He looked up at Billy expectantly.

"Crossfire," Billy breathed.

Maybe there is hope for the lad, yet, McCain thought. He studied the drawing again, as if trying to solve a difficult puzzle, which indeed he was.

"When I was a young man about his age," the old man motioned toward Billy with his head, "and had many thoughts of a maiden's soft-spot…" Chickenfoot began.

Billy frowned and shot him a stern look.

The old man simply continued as though unaware of Billy's consternation. "…I often went to that area to meet a maiden who had a Comanche name, one that meant, One-who-talks-too-much. I went there because there is a fording place on the western side of the canyon. That was before the Texans came, back when the Iron-shirts were here looking for gold. I met the maiden one day…in the fall, I think."

He thought for a moment, then said, "I would like to tell you that she was beautiful like the flying doves, with eyes a man would trade his spirit for." He shook his head sadly. "She was fat…and smelled like bear grease."

Chickenfoot suddenly smiled. "But she knew what a young boy wanted," he bragged, "and gave freely of it." He smiled broadly at each of them and then sobered when he saw they didn't share his mirth.

Wanting to be helpful, he took on a serious look. "One day while we were copulating like wild mustangs, I heard a noise! So, I crawled to the opening of the small cave and saw twenty-five Iron-shirt soldiers coming out of the mountain. I let them go by, then backtracked them to an opening in the canyon wall."

When Legends Lived

Both McCain and Billy leaned forward, scarcely breathing. "You found another way into that canyon, Chickenfoot?" McCain whispered. When the old man smiled and pointed to a spot on the dirt map, he knew it was true.

McCain quickly outlined a plan and they mounted up and headed due west, Chickenfoot leading. In just over three hours, they saw the Devil's River directly in front of them. Chickenfoot veered left and headed south for another hour. At last, they started up a steep, narrow game trail that rose higher and higher. It was nearly dusk when the old Indian pulled up on a comparatively wide place in the otherwise narrow trail. He pointed toward the rock wall, and McCain was surprised to see a partially hidden slit in the face of the cliff. The old man led his horse through the small opening and the two men followed. Inside, the cavern widened into a large chamber, where they found an ancient fireplace of circled stone and a decayed pile of sticks nearby.

"This is where I brought One-who-talks-too-much. We came here many times. You may still hear her moans echoing in this cave." The old man proudly strutted to the circle of rocks, and began to build a fire with the twigs left over from so long before.

Although McCain didn't feel there was much danger, he and Billy took turns standing guard. *No need to develop any bad habits starting now,* he thought.

Forty-Seven

THE NEXT MORNING AFTER a breakfast of bread and cold beef, much to Chickenfoot's enjoyment, they started out once more. Within an hour, they found the pass the Spaniards had used so many years before. There was just enough room on the ledge to dismount and hobble the horses. Chickenfoot motioned for them not to talk, and to leave the horses behind. Crouching low, they made their way through the narrow cut in the rock to the other side, where the old man motioned for them to stop, silently pointing at the canyon floor below. McCain heard Billy swear softly behind him as they saw the little Shaw girl tied to a stake in the middle of the canyon floor. They observed for over an hour, then McCain motioned them back, withdrawing to where they'd left the horses.

"I saw four of them," McCain said. "I didn't see Scar. Did you?" The others shook their heads silently. "The only reason we saw any of them is because they think we'll come from the other direction — through the mouth of the canyon," McCain told them. "They probably have a man out there watching, who'll give them plenty of warning to get ready for us."

McCain squatted down on his heels and thought for a moment. "That'll be our edge. They won't know we're even in the area yet. Maybe they're napping, this being the hot part of the day. We'll take the horses in through this cut in the rocks. It'll be a tight squeeze, but I think they can make it."

He drew an egg shaped circle in the dust, as Chickenfoot had

When Legends Lived

earlier. "Once on the other side, we'll wait until dark, then sweep in, cut your sister loose, and break for the canyon opening. I'll hold them from the canyon's entrance until you and your sister are well away — then I'll follow."

He saw fear in Billy's eyes. *Good*, he thought, *if he wasn't scared, I'd leave him behind.* He was pleased to also note the youth's obvious determination.

"Well, Billy D., you're about to get what you've been hankering for. Don't think about it too much, you'll do just fine," McCain said as he leaned back against the rocks. "We've got several hours before dark, might as well make yourself as comfortable as you can. Maybe have a little more of those hard biscuits and beef we had left over," he said to Chickenfoot's vast pleasure.

As they ate their meager meal, they rested against the rock face, waiting until the sun went down. "Billy D. Shaw," McCain said thoughtfully. "What's the 'D' stand for? Duncan?" he said off-handedly, as though already sure of the answer.

"Duane," Billy said around a mouthful of food.

McCain straightened and looked at the young man steadily. *Duane*, he thought. *My name! Why would Kate do that? Why would she name her son after someone like me?* He swallowed hard. "Wonder why she called you that."

Still chewing, Billy swallowed hard. "Don't rightly know, Captain. I asked her once and she just said it was the name of someone she admired from a long time ago, who was strong and determined. Guess she wanted me to be the same way." Taking a long drink from his canteen to chase down the dry biscuit, he grinned sheepishly. "She always calls me by my middle initial, when she gets peeved at me." He suddenly sobered, then attacked another biscuit.

Yeah, mused McCain, looking at the young man in an entirely different way. *I know what you mean, boy. She does the same damned thing to me.*

Little more was said as the sun slowly dropped toward the mountain peaks -- the signal that would announce the time had arrived for them to start. McCain thought about Kate and their last two meetings and even the fact that she'd named Billy after him. Maybe after all of it was over he could stop acting like a fool, and if she could tolerate him, spend a little more time with her.

Dammit! Be honest, Jericho McCain, he chastised himself. *You don't mean to "spend a little time" with her, you mean to get into her bed and stay there!* McCain's face reddened, and he furtively glanced in Billy's direction to see if he was observing. He needn't have worried. Billy was snoring softly, lying back against a nearby rock.

Well, why not? Just why the hell not? If she'd have him, that's exactly what he'd do just as soon as this thing with Scar was settled. He surely didn't look forward to going back to live alone on that hard-baked piece of dirt. Without Poe, Fish, Moses, and the others, it seemed more like a tomb each day. And there would be plenty of time for tombs. *Later. Hopefully, much later,* he chuckled to himself.

Apparently his chuckling stirred up Billy and Chickenfoot, who both sat up expectantly. McCain spoke to the old man. "You best get started back down the mountainside, Chief. If we don't make it, Scar will more than likely figure out how we got here, and if that happens you don't want to be anywhere around."

The old chief stretched, paused and gave McCain a puzzled look, as though the old lawman was mad for challenging the invincible Scar. "Good hunting Hard-Eyes. Maybe we will meet as spirits on the other side." He lightly pulled himself into the saddle, and nudged his horse back down the narrow trail.

"Maybe I was wrong about that old man," Billy said, looking after him. "He might not be so crazy after all."

McCain was up, wrapping burlap around Grasshopper's hoofs and tying it with strips of rawhide, as Billy looked on. Grinning, he said, "Wrapping hoofs is an old Indian trick. They can walk the whole tribe right past you without leaving a print, and you'll never hear a thing." Finishing his horse, McCain tied burlap around the feet of Billy's mount as well.

Returning to Grasshopper, McCain narrowly dodged his savage teeth for the third time and soundly slapped the horse's ears. "Behave yourself, you mangy piece of worm-bait" he said softly. "If you let me down tonight you will end up as soap, just as Roosevelt predicted."

Grasshopper rolled his eyes as McCain took a strip of burlap from his saddlebags and walked back in front of him. The large stallion snorted loudly but made no move to take a bite out of his master as the burlap was securely wrapped around his nose, keeping him quiet.

As McCain finished, he tossed a second strip of burlap to Billy. "Wrap your horse's snout, Billy," he said.

After tightening his cinch-strap, he reached into a saddlebag, retrieving the spare Colt he always carried. "You'll need this. Stick it in your waistband so you can get to it fast." He pulled out his own Colt and checked its loads, then, checked Poe's old Walker, which he'd strapped to his other hip.

"If one of us goes down, the other grabs the girl and hightails it," McCain instructed the young man. "No stopping once we're under way, Billy. I gave you that spare Colt to add to your other two, because it will be up to you to keep their heads down while I cut her loose. Move fast and fire often. If you don't do that, we're finished before we start."

They looked at each other deeply, then as an image of Poe flashed through his mind as he said softly, "Let's dance."

Leading their horses, they retraced their steps back through the narrow cut, exiting on the other side. Although the canyon floor appeared black as ink, McCain earlier had memorized the distance between their location and the stake in the center.

"What do we do if she's not tied at the stake when we get there?" Billy whispered.

"She will be," McCain said, as though there were no questioning that fact. He went a short distance, however, stopped and whispered to Billy. "If she's not, I intend to ride right into them. You can do whatever you decide at that point. Whatever it is, I won't fault you." Once again, he started toward the black hole at the bottom of the canyon.

Moving slowly but steadily for nearly two hours, they were almost to the bottom when McCain suddenly halted. He returned to Billy's position, putting his mouth close to the youngster's ear.

"We can climb aboard here. We've only got a short time to work, before that moon pops over the top of the canyon walls."

Billy hadn't even considered the moon, but looking up, he could see McCain was right.

"Get into the saddle and be ready to go when I give the signal," McCain whispered.

Billy grimaced at the loud creaking of leather as they swung into their saddles, and at once, caught McCain's movement as he pulled his Colt from its holster. Placing the reins of the bridle in his mouth the way McCain had shown him, he reached for both of his Colts just as McCain let go with a yell that had signaled ranger's charges since their inception. Billy Shaw's hair stood up on his neck and for just an instant as he wondered what it would sound like to the half-sleeping men who waited. Then without thinking about it, he dug spurs into his horse's flanks and was instantly racing into the openness of the white canyon floor.

Forty-Eight

TO THEIR RIGHT A flash, then another, as both he and McCain returned the fire. Several others flashed and Billy fired toward them, keeping his horse moving as McCain had instructed. McCain was at the stake now, then off his horse, but Billy couldn't see if his sister was tied to it. He continued to fire as fast as he could until his hammer fell on an empty chamber. Shoving the empty pistol into his waistband, he pulled the other one and continued firing without missing a beat. The sound of rounds zipped past, and in spite of the darkness, Billy wondered at the fact he hadn't been hit. McCain was already back in his saddle, racing toward the canyon mouth. Billy couldn't see if he had Rachel, but prayed that he did.

If the gods had been kind to them up to that point, they now seemed to turn their collective backs, for the large lover's moon suddenly popped over the rim, bathing them in its light. Less than fifty feet from the rocks that marked their destination, a shadowy figure stepped out at the canyon entrance, jerked a rifle to his shoulder, and fired. At the same instant, Billy squeezed off his answer and the figure crumpled!

McCain had seen the man with the rifle, but couldn't fire because his arms held tightly to the small girl in front of him. He felt Grasshopper shudder and the big stallion's steady stride falter, as the heavy slug struck. Instantly, McCain and the girl were flying through the air to land heavily on rocky, hard-packed earth!

When Legends Lived

Realizing they were both dead if he hesitated, McCain rebounded as soon as he stopped tumbling, still grasping the girl tightly. Time to check for broken bones later! He swung the girl onto Billy's mount, yelling loudly as he slapped its rump, sending it racing toward the canyon opening. Again, McCain didn't hesitate, firing as he ran toward the shelter of the rocks. Rounds kicked up dirt and dust all around him and something slammed into his back with a numbing force.

Hit, goddamn it! Gotta keep moving, he thought through the loud ringing in his ears. McCain staggered, but miraculously kept his feet, stumbling the last few feet to cover. As he dived over the nearest rocks, a large slug took his leg from under him. He hit heavily and lost his breath; the pain in his leg was almost unbearable as lights flashed behind his eyes.

Dazed and unsure he'd made it to the shelter of the rocks, he heard running feet and searched for his other Colt. The holster was empty!

He grabbed the butt of Poe's pistol and pulled it free just as Billy said, "It's me, don't shoot!" The young man knelt beside him.

"Damn you, boy!" McCain growled. "I told you to keep moving, no matter what!"

Billy didn't answer, as he picked up the lighter man and tossed him over his shoulder, ignoring McCain's grunt of pain. Rapidly, Billy carried him higher up into the rocks, placing him down where he had a good field of fire at the canyon floor. McCain was pleased with that. *That boy'll do okay,* he conceded. Billy left momentarily and when he returned, carried McCain's Winchester. He'd also recovered the lost pistol and carried Moses Penny's Sharps rifle under his arm. Checking the firearms to ensure they were working properly, he loaded each of them and gave them to McCain who automatically rechecked them.

"Leave me a canteen and half of your ammo," McCain instructed. "Then get your sister out of here. They'll be coming shortly, and you've got to get as far away as possible."

Billy didn't argue. They both knew they had only one horse and it would have to carry both him and his sister. McCain was wounded and wouldn't be able to travel far, for it appeared he'd lost a substantial amount of blood. Billy gazed at the old Ranger and said, "I can see why Ma set so much store in you, now, Captain McCain. I never got to know Rosie Poe very well, but I hear he was the same kind of man."

"That he was, son," McCain said and laughed softly. "Now, you lite a shuck out of here before we have company and it gets hard to break away. We'll have time to get acquainted when this is over."

Billy paused briefly, as though he was about to change his mind about leaving, but then said, "Sure. Good luck, Captain." Then he was gone.

Within a few minutes, McCain heard the sound of a galloping horse, headed north.

"Good luck to you, too, son," he said softly.

* * *

McCain flinched as he heard the faint gunshot reports, instinctively ducking as several rounds hit the rocks below him and off to his right at the spot from which Billy had carried him.

"Okay, fellows. Time to pay for your miserable sins!" he mumbled as he reached for the rifle.

They came at him mounted, riding hard, trying to get past him

When Legends Lived

through the opening at the canyon's mouth. McCain knew that in order for Billy and the girl to have a chance, he had to keep all of them bottled up inside the canyon. As soon as they came into view, McCain begin firing into the group. One horse went down, then another. It caused him considerable pain to destroy good horseflesh, but it was the only way he could ensure they wouldn't run the Shaw youngsters to ground. He had to put them all on foot. He coolly shot another horse and swung his sights to the last one, dropping it just as it cleared the canyon and broke into the open.

McCain watched its rider roll as he hit, stumble to his feet and attempt to find cover just as his sights found the center of the man's back. The heavy round slammed the running man to the ground, where he lay without moving. Turning his attention back toward the canyon floor, he saw another injured man crawling toward a stand of rocks, dragging his busted leg behind him.

"Just not your lucky day either, son," he said without sympathy, as he squeezed off another round and watched the man jerk at its impact.

His eyes scanned the entire canyon floor to his front, and could see no other movement. Several horses lay scattered beside his dead mount, as well as the men he'd killed. *Damn*, he thought. *Sure hate to lose old Grasshopper. That was one consequential horse, if there ever was one.*

Except for the caucuses of dead horses and the two men's bodies littering the canyon floor, it was as though nothing had happened. Silence was heavy and nothing moved and forced himself not to doze as the night wore on. Using water from the spare canteen to wet his bandana, he wiped his feverish face, leaned against the rock, and continued to stare onto the silvery canyon floor.

McCain suddenly jerked upright! He'd fallen asleep and he could tell hours had elapsed since he'd killed the horses. McCain shifted his stiff body and watched as the sun came up. *What a sight*, he thought. *One instant dark, the next, full daylight.* He smiled at the presence of several high-flying buzzards that dotted the morning sky.

"Well, howdy Buzzards. You too, Mister Sun, glad I can see another sunrise." *Silly old cuss!* He felt feverish, and gulped deeply from his canteen.

Wide awake and alert now, McCain quickly figured what he was up against. "Scar had five men, all told," he calculated aloud. "Billy killed the one that shot old Grasshopper, that's four. I shot two. That's three left, counting that devil, Scar." Three. With Scar, that would likely be too many. Well, he'd make them pay dearly, and if he was really lucky, he just might get one more chance at the heathen.

"Hmm!" He caught a slight movement in the rocks along the far wall. "Probably thinks he's out of rifle range way over there," McCain muttered. "Well, he never met my daddy." Laying aside the Winchester and picking up the Sharps, he raised the elevated front sights, patiently waiting for another movement in the same area.

There! McCain saw him. *Damn, if it ain't old Scar. Has to be! The face-cutter himself!*

Forty-Nine

EVEN FROM THAT GREAT distance it was hard to mistake someone he'd been chasing for fifteen years. Carefully laying the barrel across the top of the rock, he took a deep breath and let it out. Then another, letting half of it out as he centered his sights on an open space the figure would have to cross if the man continued his current path. *Even if I could hit him from this distance,* thought McCain, *it probably won't kill him outright. Still, it'd be a shot to brag about when I get old.* The thought caused McCain to smile, for he knew there was little likelihood of that happening.

Without warning, the man dashed across the open area and McCain squeezed the trigger. It seemed like an eternity and McCain thought he'd missed, but then the running men was flung against a large rock and slid down, momentarily lost from view. McCain rapidly broke the breach and inserted another round. He brought the heavy rifle to his shoulder just in time to see his target disappear behind the rocks, dragging a busted leg.

McCain chuckled to himself again. "You are one lucky son-of-a-bitch, Scar. But then, you always were."

He saw that his shot had produced mixed blessings, for while Scar was carrying a bullet now, it was also true he'd reached the rocks on McCain's side of the canyon. The old Ranger had no illusion about why he'd been so intent on reaching those rocks. Clearly that would allow the renegade sufficient cover to get closer. In fact, it would allow him to crawl right up to within thirty feet of his position without being seen.

If that don't make the cheese binding, he mused. The pain in his leg was intense and McCain suddenly felt lightheaded, as he again drank from the canteen. *No need to save it, I suppose; dead men don't have much need for water.* Besides, he knew from past wounds that he had to keep from becoming dehydrated, especially in such heat. *I wonder where those other two devils are*, he thought. The worst possible place would be on his side of the canyon, where Scar was also now hiding. *Better if they were still across on the other side.* He sighed. Well, it'd been his experience that given one of two possibilities, the truth is usually the worst one. McCain, accepting the worse case scenario, shifted his body so he'd be in a better position to defend himself in an all-out attack from the new direction.

The wounded Ranger didn't have long to wait, for suddenly, rounds were bouncing off the rocks around him, casting thunderous echoes in the enclosed area of the rocky canyon. Resisting the natural impulse to duck for cover, he leveled his own rifle at the stand of boulders on his right, just as two painted Mescaleros ran at him with surprising speed. His shot hammered one to the ground a scant fifteen feet from his position. The other just seemed to vanish into the rocks and sand. The earlier rounds that had come from a third man concealed in nearby rocks, instantly stopped. *That would be Scar,* thought McCain. No doubt covering for the other man who was now somewhere very near.

Preparing for close-in work, he carefully laid the Winchester aside and slid his Walker Colt from its holster. Holding the muzzle pointing skyward, he closed his eyes and listened intently. After a few seconds, he opened his eyes and lowered the muzzle so it was pointed to his left, just as the second man burst forward. Both fired simultaneously. The man's head exploded as the Walker's slug passed through, and

When Legends Lived

McCain felt the impact of the dead man's shot slam into him. He almost passed out from the red-hot pain jolting through his body, but instinctively knew that if he did, Scar would finish him off. *Wouldn't be in much of a hurry to do it either,* he thought, seeing as how he'd interrupted his planned enjoyment with the little Shaw girl.

Scar opened up again from the rocks to his right, like he had ammo to burn. McCain sat tight and waited, hoping he'd think one of the dead men had already gotten him. But the outlaw hadn't survived all those years because he had been careless, and remained in the rocks, waiting.

"Hey, McCain! You got any water?"

McCain wrapped his bandana around the second wound in his leg. *Better to have one bum leg with two holes, than a hole in both legs, I guess.* Gritting his teeth, he yelled, "Sure do! Several canteens full, as a matter of fact. Was thinking about taking a bath with it in a few more minutes."

"It's a good thing you asked when you did. Come on over and get it. A person never has so little that he can't share." McCain laughed just loudly enough for Scar to hear, hoping to irritate his old enemy into doing something stupid. Small chance of that happening. Scar was the best, and it would take more than tricks and pure luck to get him.

As McCain correctly guessed, Scar didn't take the bait, but remained silent for the next several minutes. "Hey, McCain. I hear your nigger tracker is dead now — that right?"

"Wrong, heathen! He's probably somewhere behind you right now, getting ready to cut your throat," McCain shouted from behind his rock. He listened to see if Scar was moving. Then came the voice again, seemingly from the same location.

"You know what else I heard, McCain? I heard that stinking

old Ranger friend of yours is dead, too. That true?" When McCain didn't answer, Scar went on, taunting, "That's too bad. I wanted to skin him myself."

"You're full of it, heathen! You ran like a rabbit being chased by a fox every time Poe took in after you." McCain's leg severely throbbed. "You know why? 'Cause you were scared of him, plain and simple!" He reached down and loosened the knot just a little, savoring the temporary relief it brought. "He'd have killed you, Scar. He was the best I've ever known, and he'd have killed you if you'd gone up against him."

Again silence. Then, Scar's voice came from the same location. "Maybe — maybe not. He was better than you, McCain, that's for sure."

McCain smiled. *Scar still hadn't moved, that meant he was hit! I wonder how bad*, he thought. "I was good enough to kill five of your men today, heathen," he said and chuckled. "But, you're right about one thing — with Roosevelt Poe and Moses Penny, there was no place you could go that they couldn't find you, given time. Moses could track an ant up a brick wall. Poe wasn't far behind, either."

McCain stopped to listen. Still, there was no sound. "Now, I ain't bad, but I'm not nearly as good as either one of those old boys. That's why I have to make sure I kill you today. I'm just fresh out of trackers." He waited.

A full five minutes went by before Scar yelled from behind his rock. "Last night I let my boys taste that little clam you helped git away from me, McCain. She loved it. Got her all broke in for you now."

McCain gritted his teeth and shook his head to clear it. He knew he was fading fast. *I've got to stay awake, he thought, just long*

When Legends Lived

enough to shoot that bastard's guts out. "You lie more than you used to, and that's a lot! I talked to the girl when I cut her loose last night. She told me you hadn't touched her. And guess what! She wasn't even scared of you — just mad as hell." McCain gave a low nasty laugh. "You've lost your touch, heathen, when you can't even frighten children anymore."

* * *

Several hours went by with no further communication between the adversaries. The fever had taken over McCain's body keeping him disoriented most of the time. As the day's temperature soared higher, his fever rose with it. Once as he floated between consciousness and delirium, he opened his eyes and saw Poe seated on a rock nearby.

"If you ain't just one pitiful sight, Jericho. I knowed the minute my back was turned, you'd get yourself into a mess like this," Poe said. He took a big bite of his chaw, munched on it for a while, spitting at a lizard on a nearby rock. Covered with tobacco juice, the lizard scurried to find safer pastures.

"You and Kate married yet? You're a bigger fool than you act if you don't grab that woman while you got the chance, Jericho. You miss this one, and as far as I'm concerned, it's tough nuts! Had half a mind to do it myself, ya know?" He spit again, standing to go. "One thing ya gotta promise me, Jericho. You'll get that devil, Scar. That's my one regret, that I didn't nail his cajonies to the barn door." He chuckled again and faded away like smoke.

McCain also started fading away, only to be jolted back again.

"Hey, Captain. You think it's ever gonna rain again?"

Moses stood a few feet away, a pick resting on his shoulder.

McCain laughed. "It's already rained, Moses. Hell, you ought to see our dam now. It's so full of water, it's running over the top. Has trout behind it a foot long."

"Damn, Captain. It must be a pretty sight," his trusted old friend seemed to say. "Well, I gotta get back. Just wanted to tell you something about when you're tracking. It's important that you don't look too hard at what you're looking at." He shouldered the pick and walked away. "See ya later, Captain." Suddenly he was gone, leaving McCain feeling very alone.

"Don't go, Moses," McCain whispered deliriously. "Stay and visit a while longer."

A chilling numbness had now entered his body, but he was still lucid enough to know it was just a matter of time until he saw all his friends again. *Cold now, so very cold!* He felt himself slipping into the cold darkness. *What the hell? I had my day.* The numbness was almost complete.

"Hey, Captain. Do ya think it's ever gonna rain again?" Then blackness ended all conjecture.

"Hey, Captain…"

Fifty

"Oh I heard all right, that the old Ranger was supposed to have killed Scar down on the Devil's River around the end of the '80s. But, my sister is married to a half-Apache boy, and he said he seen him in Sonora just last year. Knowed it was him, 'cause of the scar. I 'spect he'll be back."

— Overheard in a Laredo saloon, 1909

WES TANNER WAS ON the west side of the Devil's River, having crossed earlier when he came upon the bluffs along the east side. He'd figured it was better to cross than have to lose time circling around them, later. Tanner had been on the trail for over a week, returning from El Paso, on his way to — where?

Maybe Langtry, then Eagle Pass or Fort Stockton for a while. Who knows? Maybe it's time to head back up north to St. Louis or Kansas City for a while. Let things cool off a bit.

People were beginning to get upset about all the dead Indians suddenly showing up. Most folks figured it was just stirring them up. Besides, he was nearly tuckered out after three years of hunting those damn savages. He could always come back later and pick up where he'd left off. Trying to remain alert despite his weariness, Tanner nudged his horse up the steep incline bordering the river, then suddenly halted.

He never would've heard it if the breeze hadn't been blowing in his direction.

R.C. Morris

* * *

Following McCain's back-trail, Scar smiled as he saw the opening in the rocks. He knew there had to be one, for how else could that old ranger have gotten behind them and surprised him like that. *McCain*, Scar thought bitterly. *It's going to be such a pleasure to kill you someday old man!*

Yes, someday, but not today. Not with a bullet in his leg, and McCain patiently sitting up there in those rocks with a rifle, just waiting for him — maybe even sneaking up on him right now. He respected the Ranger's marksmanship too much to go up against him, one-on-one. The shot across the canyon that had busted his leg, now that was a dandy! Probably not over three or four men alive, could've made that shot. Yeah, McCain was too good to take chances with. He'd started out with five good fighting men that day and McCain had killed them all. Besides, the pain in his leg had set in with a vengeance, and he couldn't seem to stop the bleeding.

He'd head for one of the nearby villages and get patched up. Maybe even send some of them back to finish McCain off. They'd help. Should be easy, too, him being afoot. After all, the families of the Indians Poe and McCain had killed around here had enough good reason to hate him. Maybe McCain would still be up there in those rocks waiting for him to come out of the canyon. If not, there'd be other days.

Using his rifle as a crutch and dragging his busted leg, Scar climbed toward the cut above him. He had to get back to one of the Kiowa villages down near the flats where they would take care of him and hide him. His most pressing problem was if he didn't find a horse soon, he'd likely just bleed to death.

When Legends Lived

Exiting on the other end of the hidden cut through the rocks, Scar saw the Devil's River below, and smiled. *Might just make it after all*, he thought, as he stumbled down the narrow twisting trail toward the valley floor. Then, he heard the soft whinny of a horse.

* * *

Tanner was beginning to think he'd been mistaken about hearing a horse, and considered turning back down the trail. Then, he saw it — nothing much, just a small movement. He kept his eyes on the spot until he'd reached a higher point. Kneeing his mount up the steep incline, he dismounted, pulling his rifle from its scabbard. Edging closer to the drop-off, he rested the rifle on a large flat rock. Peering through the telescope attached to the rifle's long barrel, slowly scanning the far bank of the river. Halfway up the face of the cliff he saw the Indian. Tanner, smiling softly, brought the scope down until it rested on the man's face.

Old, he thought. *I don't think I've ever shot an Indian as old as this one.* He studied the old man and the sleek Spanish-rigged stallion he was riding, as he sat unmoving, staring at the rock wall.

Odd. Something wrong here! Curiously, Tanner scanned the rocks around the old man, slowly, inch by inch, until he found the reason for the old man's actions. Another man in the rocks, there. A man with a large scar on his face, holding a pistol! The man with the scar smiled coldly at the old Indian, gesturing slightly with his pistol.

Why, he's taking the old man's horse!

His scope went back to the old man, who pointed his finger at the hold-up man, obviously saying something. Swiftly, Tanner switched his sights back to the scar-faced one, who was clearly preparing to shoot the older man. Tanner let the crosshairs settle on the scar-faced man's broad chest, slowly took a deep breath and exhaled, squeezing the trigger. The force of the round slammed his target violently against the face of the cliff wall. The surprised man stood frozen for just an instant, stumbled forward, then tumbled over and over down the slope. Disappearing over the abrupt ledge, he fell into the swift churning water, far below.

Tanner brought the scope back to the face of the old man. With the wind blowing directly away from him, the old Indian apparently hadn't even heard the far-off sound of Tanner's rifle shot. He sat, apparently stupefied, staring in amazement at his upraised finger. Pleasantly dumbfounded, he smiled a large toothless smile and rode off down the twisting trail, chanting to himself while holding his finger high in the air — as though he'd just discovered something infinitely wonderful.

"You ain't got much longer anyway," Tanner said to the old man's retreating back. "You don't know how close you come to dying today, old man." Tanner placed the rifle back into its fancy leather scabbard, and slowly made his way back down the bluff.

Epilogue

"I was told that when folks first arrived in the valley, there were those little blue flowers as far as the eye could see. After the drought of the '80s, they went away and never came back. Oh, you can still see them pretty much throughout Texas — except for that valley. It was as if they suddenly figured life was too hard out there, and just decided to move on. They were a lot like the folks that used to live there, in that respect."

– Final entry into Jim Packard's Diary (1929)

A TALL GRAY-HAIRED MAN stood apart from the main crowd, watching as the preacher finished his words over a flag-draped casket, displaying the large Lone Star of the Texas State flag. Flowers were everywhere. In fact, he'd never seen a funeral with so many flowers. He must've known a lot of people, the tall man thought, or more likely, maybe a lot of people knew him. Four military honor guards folded the flag in military fashion, and he watched as the Officer-in-Charge handed it to the woman dressed in black. She smiled graciously as she received it. Her smile hadn't changed much since the first time he saw her.

What a great place to be buried, he thought, *if there ever was such a thing.* Still, if you believed there was something after death, it would be the place to just set back and watch the rest of the world go by. He slowly rotated, taking in the breathtaking view. Poe and Beth were buried just over there, he remembered. *Bethena!* At her memory, he still felt a sharp pang, even after all these years.

Oh Beth, my darling. Why did I go away, and leave you here alone? So long ago, yet like yesterday.

The ceremony was over now, and most of the people were drifting away toward their automobiles parked in the nearby meadow. He saw Kate say a few words to her son Billy and his family, who finally moved away, leaving her to stand alone, by the still open grave. Unwilling to interrupt her last goodbye, the tall man waited quietly until she raised her head and saw him at last. Smiling sweetly, she moved toward him.

"Jim Packard," she said in the same deep, rich voice he remembered so well. He bent for her light kiss on his offered cheek. "Or should I call you Governor Packard? As I live and breathe, it's so good of you to come." She didn't look as though she'd aged a day, yet he knew it had been well over twenty years since last he'd seen her.

"It's been nearly twenty-five years, Jim." She smiled sweetly, demonstrating her uncanny ability to read the minds of those around her. She watched as the last few people walked down the slight grade, disappearing from sight. "So many people came. I didn't even know half of them. Many I'd probably met only once or twice, somewhere, but I guess they knew my husband from some past life."

"Who was that tall distinguished looking gentleman standing to your left? The one with the pretty wife and all the kids?" Packard asked. "He looked vaguely familiar to me."

"That must have been Judge Bookbinder and his family," she answered. "They stayed with me once for a few days when he was recovering from his wounds. He married Sam Thompson's girl and is now a District Judge over by Kingsville. They have twelve children, most of them grown. I always thought she was one of the prettiest women I'd ever seen."

"That may explain all the kids," Packard said, and smiled.

When Legends Lived

Kate returned his smile, but still looked saddened by the day's events. "The man in the wheelchair being pushed by the Spanish lady? That's Quint Fishburn. I'm sure you remember Fish. Poe left him some land over by the Rocking-R, when he died. Quint later bought the entire ranch from J.D."

Jim looked thoughtful for a moment, then said, "What about Jake Kellog? Was he here?"

"Jake's dead," Kate told him. "After Fish bought the Rocking-R, a big combine came in and bought-up most of the valley — even the town of Bluebonnet. They razed the town and ranch and built holding pens for cattle. Now they come in with large trucks and haul them away." She looked at him. "It's really kind of sad, don't you think?"

"It's progress, Kate. You can't fight it," Jim said.

Kate nodded her head sadly. "Anyway, Fish and his wife took the money they received for the sale, and opened a hardware store in Dallas. The last I heard, they have six stores and six kids. and gobs of grandchildren!" She smiled as she made that point. "Jake took his money and moved to Chicago, where he opened up another bar. Fish spoke with a man who knew Jake up there, and he said Jake was running bootleg whisky in from Canada and got into a shootout with the Mounties. Jake was killed. As far as I know, he'd never married."

She moved a few steps away, turned and thoughtfully said, "I don't know the thin man who stood off to himself throughout the service. He reminded me of an undertaker. A nice enough looking man, but something about him kind of gave me the creeps. I think someone said his name was Tanner. Yes, that's it, Wes Tanner. Did you know him?"

Jim remembered, but discretely shook his head. Kate went

on. "He and Judge Bookbinder seemed to know each other. At least they made eye contact several times, although, I don't think they ever spoke."

Kate took Packard's arm, and together, they moved away from the open grave, toward the row of other grave markers.

"Who was the stocky man walking with a cane with all those kids?" Jim said.

Kate tried to recall, then brightened, as she said, "Thomas. He came with Nate Thompson. Nate said his name was Bart Thomas, from Oklahoma. All those cute little kids called him 'Father Bart,' so I guess he's a minister or something."

It was quiet. The sounds of the last motor vehicle had faded away long ago.

"It's so peaceful up here, don't you think?" Kate suddenly said.

Jim looked wistfully back toward the main ranch house. "The K/D has always been one of my favorite places, Kate," Jim told her. "If things had turned out differently, I might've spent the rest of my life here."

"You never married, did you Jim?" Kate said gently. Jim looked back at her with sorrowful eyes, and Kate had her answer.

He swallowed hard, and then smiled, as though painfully. "I never found anybody I wanted after we lost Beth. That's why I left the ranch and didn't come back, Kate. Just too many things here reminded me of her, I guess."

"I could never leave either, and for many of the same reasons." She gazed around. "They're all here, Jim. All the people I love — Bethena, Roosevelt, and my youngest daughter, Tina. She died giving birth to her second child, and is buried over there near that small tree. Her baby's resting next to her. There's a spot for her

When Legends Lived

husband as well, if he ever sobers up long enough to die," she said bitterly.

"Come, walk with me for a spell," she said. "I'm not ready to go back and face all those people just yet."

She took his arm again as they walked between the stones of the well-kept cemetery, pointing out several of the graves. "My first husband, Duncan, rests there." She pointed to one of the larger headstones. "He was the first to be buried here. Now, my second husband is here also. The years have taken a lot from me, Jim, but they've given me an awful lot, as well." She stopped walking, looked up at him, and squeezed his arm affectionately. "I've got good friends, grandchildren, even two great grandchildren," she told him happily. "My son has a wonderful wife and family, and my daughter Rachel married one of the wealthiest men in New Jersey. She's writing a book about her adventure when she was abducted by Scar, as a little girl."

Kate gracefully moved a few steps away, stopped, whirled around and stood smiling. "But do you know the reason I'm not all sad and despondent over the death of my husband? Why I'm not playing the part of a grieving widow? It's because I had thirty years with the man I loved, Jim. Thirty years that I probably should never have had at all. The good things that happened to me during those thirty years more than made up for all the bad years." Her eyes grew slightly misty, as she remembered.

"How did he die, Kate?" Jim said to her gently.

She bent and picked a bright blue flower, of the variety seen growing wild throughout much of Texas. Placing it under her nose, she sniffed. Instead of answering, she said, "Back when J.D. and Rosie bought their ranch at Bluebonnet, these grew wild by the millions; the entire area was completely covered with them. Everywhere you looked for miles and miles, nothing but bluebonnets as far as the eye could see!" She gazed fondly at the blue flower she held in her hand, then closed her eyes, gently rubbing it against her cheek as though to summon some distant memory of a time long past.

"After the drought in the early '80s, they just didn't come back anymore," she said. "Oh, there are still lots of them in other parts of the state — except for that one valley. It's almost as if they figured life was just too rough for them there, and they decided to move on to other parts." She looked sad for an instant then laughed shortly. "Kind of like the people who once lived there and left."

Jim didn't know how to respond, so he remained silent, waiting for her to go on. At last she returned to his original question. "The technical term was, I believe, was massive contusions and abrasions caused from a severe impact to the head. Or, words to that effect."

She took another whiff of the bluebonnet and stuck it in her lapel buttonhole. "In layman's terms, he fell off a bridge and struck his head on the rocks below." Her voice betrayed none of her feelings as she spoke. Jim knew she'd grieve later, in private, as pioneer women had always done. "You recall when they built that wooden bridge over the river about ten years ago?" she asked.

Jim nodded, but remained silent.

"It was that one." Kate moved to a small, unpainted wooden bench and sat down. She patted the bench next to her, and Jim sat beside her. "Actually, it was that stallion he loved so much that caused it," Kate told him. "You remember how he always seemed to pick out the most pigheaded horses for himself? J.D.

said the horse reminded him of another one he'd had once. He'd frequently come in with bruise marks on his shoulder where that darn horse had bitten or kicked him." She laughed softly and placed her hand on his arm.

"Still, it didn't seem to bother J.D. any. He'd always been a fine rider," she said. "He loved to ride. He would've been fine, too, if he'd stuck to riding halfway tame horses."

Kate's thoughts seemed to drift away, as though remembering events long past, then she went on. "It was his missing leg that made it hard to stick to the saddle like he used to," she said. "You remember? It was the one that awful, scar-faced man shot-off when he went to get Rachel back. They had to take it off, right below the knee. I was told Jake Kellog did it with that big old Bowie knife he always carried, after he and Fish found J.D. wounded and near dead." She paused to grimace. "Fish said he nearly passes out even now, just thinking about it. I guess it would affect me that way too, if I'd have been there like those two were."

Kate wrinkled her nose then went on. "That would've stopped most men from ever getting into the saddle again, but not Jericho McCain. I guess that was just one of the reasons I loved him so much." Kate's eyes went soft and misty again, and she paused a minute before continuing.

"Well...I think it was the combination of his bad leg and being unable to ride like he once could, and the fact that his contrary old horse hated to cross that wooden bridge. He'd already thrown J.D. several years ago in that exact same spot, but this time was different. This time, J.D. hit the railing and went over on the rocks below."

Jim could picture the tragic event in his mind.

A few more minutes went by before Kate said softly, "He lived for two days. Unconscious most of the time. He woke up just before he died, though, and do you know what he said, Jim? He looked up at me, his eyes as clear as the first day I ever saw him, and said, 'I love you, Kate. Always have, always will.' Then he just closed his eyes and went to sleep. Those were the last words he ever spoke."

She rubbed her eyes on the back of her sleeve, and Jim handed her a white cotton handkerchief. "You knew him, Jim. Those words were just not in his vocabulary. Even when we got married, he couldn't say them." She favored Packard with another of her brilliant smiles. "It's not that he didn't, Jim," she said. "He showed me that he loved me every day of our lives together. It's just that he couldn't say it. There was something missing inside him that allowed him to express his affection." She suddenly went silent.

Jim now spoke. "I know. It was one of the things I had difficulty understanding about him for a long time, Kate."

"I used to be jealous of Poe," she went on, as if the memory was still painful to her. "I suppose some of J.D.'s other old cronies too — but, especially, Roosevelt Poe. I knew he loved that old man, but I don't think he could ever bring himself to say it." She suddenly brightened again. "But, on the day he died, he looked at me and said, 'I love you, Kate'. Do you know what that means to me?" Kate stood and turned away to compose herself, then turned around and smiled at him, with misty eyes.

She joined him once more on the bench, squeezing his arm affectionately. "It's a good memory, Jim," she said, blinking rapidly.

They sat on the old weathered plank bench without talking for a while, just two old friends, enjoying the company of each other and their surroundings. "He was almost eighty-six, Jim, and rode

When Legends Lived

right up to the day he died," Kate said after a while. "That's a pretty good life, wouldn't you say?" She sniffed quietly.

"It was an excellent life, Kate. There are those who say J.D. McCain was the greatest Texas Ranger of them all — a living legend. He probably led the most exciting, remarkable life of anyone I've ever known. I know he gave me some things to remember. I still have one short leg because of my adventures with Captain Jericho McCain," he laughed deeply. "And you know what? I wouldn't trade my bum leg for all the quiet comfortable lives of everybody I know."

Kate smiled at him then a serious look crossed her face. "When you get right down to it, Jim, it was that old outlaw enemy of J.D.'s that finally killed him," Kate said, sounding a little bitter.

Packard looked puzzled. "I don't understand, Kate. Everyone says the Captain killed Scar in that canyon years ago. Don't you remember the day they found the Captain and brought him back? Fish and Jake said there was a furious gunfight where they discovered the bodies of five of Scar's men, and lots of blood leading up into the rocks. Although his body was never found, there was evidence he'd fallen into the raging Devils River, and drowned. Jake and Fish were sure your husband killed Scar that day," Jim said.

"Oh, I'm sure he did too, Jim. But Scar is the one that shot his leg off, too," she argued. "The leg he couldn't use to grip his horse, and that allowed the stallion to throw him off that bridge." Stoically, she sat there for a moment before going on. "Ironic in a way, isn't it?" The last of the Texas bad men and the last of the legendary lawmen, kill each other off, over thirty years apart. It ought to be a book. Maybe you could even write it, Jim." She laughed, sounding delighted!

Sensing the time had come for them to move on, they both rose, and with Kate holding onto Jim's arm, walked back toward the meadow where Jim's automobile was parked. The grave detail was arriving to cover the grave as they departed. One other automobile remained in the parking area when they arrived, and as Jim helped Kate up into the passenger's seat, a man stepped from behind the other car and walked toward them.

"Governor Packard, sir," the man said, sticking out his hand. "I don't know if you will remember or not, but I met you once, years ago. My name is Martin Gates, Editor of the *Trib*."

Jim eyed the fat bald man standing in front of him and remembered. "As a matter of fact, I do recall you. What do you need?" Jim said shortly, ignoring the hand as he turned, walking to the front of his vehicle.

Undeterred, Gates followed. "I once did a story on Captain McCain and Poe, one that I'm not very proud of. I'd like to do another and make it right. I was hoping you'd help me."

"Afraid not," Jim said, as he cranked his Ford. It kicked right off and, he walked around to the side and climbed up into the automobile. He remained a moment, letting it idle. "Captain McCain always enjoyed his privacy when he was alive," Jim Packard told him. "I don't suppose he would like it none now, if he were to become famous and have a hundred people a day traipsing all over his grave." He gave it gas and moved off.

Kate gazed at him seriously, then smiled gently, squeezing his arm. They didn't look back, but if they had, they would've seen the lone figure of Martin Gates standing in the meadow staring after them.

Afterword

TO REFRESH YOUR MEMORY FROM Ray's first volume of this two-part series, *Gone to Texas*, when turning the page to his biography, About the Author, some might have scratched their heads inquisitively. How did a US Army Special Forces officer with these credentials, and an illustrious and legendary military career spanning twenty-six years, ever decide to write a Western?

Good books often become even richer with an understanding of the back story. There is more to this backstory that you might recall. However, you learned that like many other veterans of the Vietnam War era, the enemy followed Ray home in the form of Agent Orange. He passed away in February 2022.

Whenever Ray and I had brief discussions of family items of importance, the topic of his manuscripts always came up. His imagination with writing genres knew no bounds. I always prompted him to save them, which he heeded, and to inform me where they were located. With his creative juices in gear as a storyteller, he left it up to me to manage the business end of his endeavors; it was a team effort. While rummaging through some papers and boxes, I came across a copy of his first manuscript, a Western. It had only been shared with a few friends. It was *this* manuscript, *When Legends Lived*, albeit never quite finished. He would often tinker with it when insight and imagination tugged at him. He began to write after he retired from the military, almost thirty-eight years ago.

R.C. Morris

As a young man growing up in Missouri, Ray inherited his love of the written word from his father, who was always a voracious reader. Ray recanted he used to watch him sit and read Louis L'Amour, Zane Gray, and Luke Short novels until the wee hours of the morning, wondering what he found so intriguing inside those small cardboard covers. As soon as he learned to read, he began to follow in his footsteps, reading everything he could get his hands on. That interest subsequently led him into a retirement career of writing, and he frequently acknowledged he owed his talent to his father.

When his father passed, Ray wanted those books. They remain on our bookshelf, yellowed, the spines devoid of glue...his treasures. I began to reread Ray's manuscript, the one in the box. It was familiar to me from many years before. He'd always hand off his manuscripts to me to read, and with my red pen in hand, and a keen eye, I might catch a typo or two. His refrain never faltered— "Now don't go changing happy to glad!"

Prompted by his spirit, and nudged with inspiration, I reached out to his publisher who said he *LOVED* Westerns! While he was contemplating this one, I discovered another in his computer manuscript files, same characters, different timeframe.

The craft of storytelling is not always a linear process. Readers have just been introduced to his *first* book, a Western! Surprisingly, it seems he couldn't get those characters out of his head and proceeded to write a prequel to their adventures together. He had yet to weave the two tales together in this epic generational saga, but in his more recent computer files he had marked this one "FINAL." Jerico D. McCain's friendship and adventures with Roosevelt Poe in *Gone to Texas* continued to endure through this one, *When Legends Lived*.

When Legends Lived

Ray lived in a generation that if you were an avid fan of Westerns, you might have experienced some of Elmore Leonard's best novels—*Valdez is Coming, Hombre* and *Last Stand at Sabre River*—and several of his short stories. These, along with *3:10 to Yuma* were made into revered movies. Taking nothing away from Zane Grey, Larry McMurtry (with the classic mini-series *Lonesome Dove*), et al. You might have been hooked on every episode of *Bonanza, Have Gun Will Travel, Wild, Wild West,* and *Gunsmoke*. Much of this might have come from your childhood when eight out of ten of the top shows on TV were Westerns! All exciting fodder to discuss at the kitchen dinner table, that is, when families still ate together at the kitchen dinner table.

Western characters often leave lifelong impressions. Ray named his boat *Blue Duck* after the Indian antagonist in *Lonesome Dove*. He learned how to play music, hunt and fish, that your word is your bond, and to stand up for what you believe. There is a sense of an ingrained moral fiber of the conservative pioneer spirit handed down from ancestors. In Ray's history, some of the early Missouri settlers coming here in the early 1800s brought with them fortitude, courage, toughness and integrity, an extension of their indomitable strength.

Ray's two-volume series is a gritty, period-authentic Western for hardcore Western aficionados. Yes, it's a different time now, but a Western is a Western. It was a different era, a sweaty, tough life; those who made their homes in the West were of sturdy stock. The Wild West was *WILD*, the dastardly foes quite adept at torture; not for the faint of heart of how folks survived and died! There were many villains to loath. The lawmen righted wrongs, justice prevailed. You were always rooting for the good guys even when a bad apple was among them. Those who read

R.C. Morris

Westerns likely relish the violent moments in the "Name of Justice"!

This remarkable tale begins in the Appalachian hills of Tennessee in 1845 when J.D. McCain was a sixteen-year-old youth, yet it spanned eighty-four years through Texas, Colorado, Mexico. Jim Packard's last entry in his diary was 1929. All this history with complex relationships spanning decades, and a cast of both unsavory and common folk characters who required development simply from Ray's perspective, transferred from his mind to his keyboard. He always typed with two fingers.

From Ray's point of view, these Texas Rangers smacked of character, honesty, integrity. Ray knew what made them tick. Perhaps less well known was that Ray's family genetics included some "American Indian blood." In long days past, Indian communities would have gathering places where children and adults listened as the older men and women told stories of life, of life's challenges and the lessons that can be drawn from the edge of life. They knew that it was important to the dying as well as to the living, that lessons are passed on to new generations. Whatever is gleaned from a generation of history through story telling should be passed along to enrich the texture of our lives and of our children's lives.

Ray had this uncanny ability to observe life through relationships and patterns familiar to us—pain, suffering, humility, humor, the content of character, the depth of thoughts, and the serenity of the soul. For this legendary warrior, who had served in Vietnam, in similar roles as he wrote about in his award-winning non-fiction, *The Ether Zone*, the brotherhood and bond with his Vietnam team members persisted throughout the years following the war. Kindred memories had been chiseled into his psyche. Dry humor, like salve for the soul after battle-hardened exploits, were feelings that he easily expressed through Jericho McCain's verbal sparring and good-humored teasing with Roosevelt Poe. The tale honors him and the others who served along with him, all humble legends, and I believe he'd like them to know that.

I'm eternally grateful for the friendship, professionalism, support, and assistance of Hellgate Press, Harley Patrick, and his remarkable creative team, who have shepherded all his books to the public eye over the years.

A sense of nostalgia permeates the soul when reading a good Western, much like looking back at the patchwork quilt of our lives, frayed around the edges. It seems quite astonishing that I have been able to bring this epic two-volume Western of his to life, and there may be others! It has been a labor of love and Ray lives through me.

In Ray's words, he's "traveling!" Thank you for joining him on this journey.

— *Brenda D. Morris*

About the Author

RAYMOND C. MORRIS was born in Jefferson City, Missouri and entered the Army at the fuzzy-cheek age of seventeen. Following basic training, he was assigned to the 101st Airborne Division. With a rank of staff sergeant, in 1963-1964 he attended Officer Candidate School at Fort Benning, Georgia.

In May 1964, as a freshly minted 2LT and the OCS Honor Graduate, his new orders led him to the 6th Special Forces Group. On 2 January 1966, he was assigned as team Executive Officer for the 5th Special Forces Group Operational Detachment (SFOD) 106 at Bato, Vietnam, followed by an assignment in May 1966 with SFOD A-103, Gia Vuc, Vietnam.

In October 1966, he was selected as the Long Range

Reconnaissance Platoon Leader (LRRP) for Mobile Guerilla Force A-100, with operations throughout the A Shau Valley. In 1968, an assignment transferred him to the 46th Special Forces Company in Thailand where he trained Thai Black Panther brigades in reconnaissance tactics and inserted them into Vietnam. In 1970, he'd been detailed under the auspices of CIA operations in northern Thailand, to train Laotian commandos and deploy them into Laos.

In 1968, Ray returned to the U.S. for Ranger School, again distinguished as the Honor Graduate, winning the Darby Award. A new assignment led him back into Southeast Asia, where for two years, from April 1971-April 1973, he was a B-detachment commander with the 1st Special Forces Group (A) in Okinawa. During this time, he was sent to Vietnam twice for temporary assignment with the classified Special Forces FANK Program.

Returning Stateside, he continued his military schooling and went on to hold other key assignments, including Deputy Commander, 6th Region Criminal Investigation Division in San Francisco, CA. In 1983, he was selected to be the Deputy Commanding Officer to reactivate the 1st Special Forces Group (A) at Fort Lewis, Washington. Ray retired from active duty in 1985 after an illustrious military career spanning twenty-six years.

His love for the military has never waned. As a civilian he returned to Fort Lewis, in charge of training the Army's new Stryker Brigades prior to Iraq deployment.

His awards include: Legion of Merit, Meritorious Service Medal, Bronze Star, Vietnam Cross of Gallantry w/silver star and Cross of Gallantry w/bronze star, Army Commendation Medal (2) and numerous service awards. He proudly earned his jump wings, U.S., Thai and Vietnamese Master Parachutist badges, Special Forces and Ranger tabs.

Ray, never one to sit on his duff too long, holds a BA in Criminal Justice from the University of Nebraska, an MBA from City University in Seattle, Washington and a Masters in Justice Administration, Wichita State University.

A lifelong history enthusiast and prolific writer, Ray has used his keen observation of the human condition as the catalyst for expansion of his interests into writing and mainstream fiction. R. C. Morris's 2004 suspense thriller, *Don't Make the Blackbirds Cry*, and psychological thriller, the 2006 *Tender Prey*, are now available as ebooks. In October 2005, commissioned by the Project Delta members to write their story, his love of Special Forces forced him to place pending fiction novels on the back burner to write *The Ether Zone*, published by Hellgate Press.

His recently published 2023 Western, *Gone to Texas*, is the first story in his two-volume series with *When Legends Lived*. His remarkable story-telling voice continues to live on through the publishing of some of his heirloom manuscripts.

When Legends Lived

OTHER BOOKS BY R. C. MORRIS

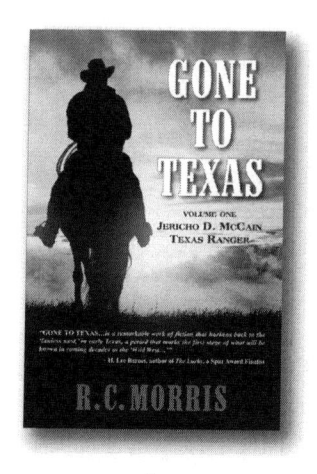

GONE TO TEXAS: The year was 1845. It was Indian summer and deep in the Blue Ridge Mountains the entire McCain family was being buried — except for a lone survivor.

His soft voice was beginning to crack noticeably as he finally addressed the last grave. "I know this is probably the…the…last time… we'll ever be together as a family. I promise you that I will find Taylor and let…him know…about this. I will. You have my word. I love you, Pa." Texas – that's where Taylor said he was going. Texas! The name had a good ring to it. A clean "starting over" kind of sound and that's what Jericho wanted — a clean start.

What the critics are saying:

"*Gone to Texas*…is a remarkable work of fiction that harkens back to the 'lawless West' in early Texas, a period that marks the first stage of what will be known in coming decades as the 'Wild West…'"

– H. Lee Barnes, author of The Lucky, a Spur Award Finalist

ISBN: 978-1-954163-61-4
Paperback 356 pages 6x9 $16.95

Available through most major bookstores,
online at Amazon.com and others, or direct from Hellgate Press.

R.C. Morris

DON'T MAKE THE BLACKBIRDS CRY: Murder, Hatred, Corrupt Politics, the Klan...A Great Thrill Ride! An orphaned and homeless teenager has just broken in and robbed the local store. Hiding in the darkness of an alley, he witness's five young men brutally rape and murder three teenage girls, two black and one white. One perpetrator is the town's star high school quarterback while another is the sheriff's son. When one of the five turns up dead a short time later, he knows he can't come forward!

Morris's debut novel, a gritty mystery of southern culture clash and racial hatred, reminds us that the quest for justice is not always free, and often, when seeking truth or trying to right a wrong, many lives can be affected by dire or unexpected consequences.

What the critics are saying:

"*Don't Make the Blackbirds Cry*, with all of its unexpected twists and turns, makes this first novel by R.C. Morris a difficult book to put down!"
— *Northwest Guardian*

"....truly a page-turner...a fully packed adventure. This author has writing talent and showcases it well in his first debut novel. Terrifying and exciting but most certainly entertaining! ...Well crafted...a must read book."
— *Military Writers Society of America*

Available on Kindle at Amazon.com
or visit Raycmorris.com to read excerpts

TENDER PREY: Fear Grips Seattle! A Deranged Serial Killer is Loose. Have you ever known someone who has been sexually abused? Do you think they'd be conscious of the effects these childhood perversions might have on adult behavior? Do you ever question what could possibly motivate the bizarre acts you learn about your friends and neighbors who appear so normal? Then you'll want to meet Corky!

Detective Frank Murphy and his side-kick, John Henry Drake, get the nod to head up the task force. Who is committing these heinous acts?

What the critics are saying:

"Compelling, tantalizing and filled with complex characters and plot twists…an intelligent treat and great entertainment! It is a terrific read for all mystery lovers. The MWSA gives this book its highest rating of Five Stars."
— *Military Writers Society of America*

Available on Kindle at Amazon.com
or visit Raycmorris.com to read excerpts

R.C. Morris

THE ETHER ZONE: Project Delta and its clandestine special reconnaissance operations proved to be one of the most successful Special Operations units of the Vietnam War, yet few Americans have ever heard of them. This small unit, comprised of less than 100 U.S. Army Special Forces men, amassed a record for bravery second to none. Now, for the first time, the Project Delta "Quiet Professionals" finally share their story.

Highly trained as experts in special reconnaissance techniques and procedures, the covert Project Delta missions were accomplished through recon team insertions into enemy territory. The primary sources of intelligence collection for Project Delta, these tough and tenacious men recount hair-raising adventures.

Enter the world of a highly classified project to learn what makes U.S. Army Special Forces soldiers tick—and learn the legacy of these men of honor, their breathtaking heroics, humility, humor, camaraderie and brotherhood.

ISBN: 978-1-55571-662-2
Paperback   392 pages   6x9 $24.95

Available through most major bookstores,
online at Amazon.com and others, or direct from Hellgate Press.

www.hellgatepress.com

Made in the USA
Middletown, DE
22 September 2023